Metaphorosis
2020

Also from Metaphorosis

Metaphorosis 2020

The Complete Stories

edited by
B. Morris Allen

ISBN: 978-1-64076-187-2 (e-book)
ISBN: 978-1-64076-188-9 (paperback)
ISBN: 978-1-64076-160-5 (hardcover)

from Metaphorosis Publishing

Neskowin

Contents

From the Editor

I think we can all agree that 2020 was a hard year. It had some high points, but there were many more valleys than peaks at global, national, local, and often domestic levels. Many of us learned new ways of working and interacting, and by the end of the year experienced the odd visceral shock of seeing people in old video footage in close proximity without masks. At the same time, while humans aren't always wise, we do adapt. We generally found ways to make the new normal work, even while hoping for a return to the old.

Some good things rose from the ashes (literally, in the case of the West), and that included a great crop of stories, augmented by our first experiment with serials. We opened and closed the year with two serialized novellas from talented authors, and we'll have more coming in 2021. In the back office, we switched to a new, more flexible submission system that's more focused on SFF venues, and the process was fairly seamless. We continued our podcasts, now a clockwork process that has a smooth, fun podcast of each story available to publish at the same time as the story. Those podcasts, helmed by Podcast Editor Matt Gomez, have begun to attract more and more frequent comment. The selection process continued to be aided by Assistant Editor J. Tynan Burke and second reader A.J. Cunder. Meanwhile, Jordan Chase-Young brought proofreading skills to bear to drastically reduce the incidence of typos in our stories. In short, good things happened too.

Outside the magazine itself, we published a new anthology, *Reading 5X5 x2: Duets*. Where the original *Reading 5X5* (2018) asked authors to work from the same story brief, examining how different authors treat similar ideas, *Duets* asked five authors to collaborate in a round-robin format, looking at how authors' voices change when they work together. It was an incredible amount of effort – may authors don't turn out five good stories a year, let alone four collaborations plus a solo story – but well worth it, with epic masterpieces and fantastic settings sharing space with intimate stories from the here and now.

2020 may not have been humanity's best year, but there were good moments in it. Here, then, are 52 of those moments in the form of great SFF to take you away from your cares and transport you to other places.

B. Morris Allen
Editor
15 February 2021

January

Kozuna, the Ogre's Child

Felicity Drake

The red rental car plunged into the tunnel. Hitomi's eyes adjusted: the sun winked out, replaced by the yellow glow of sodium lights flashing by too fast.

Professor Ueda had insisted on driving. Hitomi had offered, of course, but he had looked so indignant that she was reluctant to offer twice. For an elderly man, he was a remarkably reckless driver. The tunnel was narrow and winding, and if she'd been driving, she would have taken the curves much slower. But then, living in Tokyo, he probably didn't have many opportunities to speed down an empty road. He must have been enjoying himself.

"Are you excited for your first fieldwork, Sasaki?" Professor Ueda asked, raising his voice to be heard above the roar of the engine echoing in the tunnel.

"You'll stay with me, right? When I'm interviewing her?" she asked.

"You'll mostly be listening, not interviewing," Professor Ueda reminded her. "But of course I'll supervise."

When Hitomi had first started her master's in folklore, she had thought that no one went into the countryside trying to collect folktales anymore. Professor Ueda had assured her that there were still a few remote corners where old stories, beliefs, and practices lingered, if you knew where to look. Now that she was starting the fieldwork for her thesis, she imagined herself joining the pantheon of folklore pioneers from previous centuries, like the Grimm brothers or Yanagita Kunio, tromping out into the countryside to capture the last traces of oral tradition before they disappeared forever.

As they emerged from the tunnel, her eyes hurt from the sudden brightness of the sun. The village spread out around them. Its neat emerald gardens were strung with silver and gold streamers to keep away the crows; its distinctive steep thatched roofs were familiar from the black and white photographs she'd seen in old reference books. Utterly unchanged. How incredible that a place like this could exist, just a day's travel from Tokyo.

It was August, which should have been high tourist season for this sort of mountain getaway, but the streets were mostly empty. Hitomi saw a single bent-double grandmother working in a garden, with a single family of tourists snapping photos of her.

"Looks like they could use some help with marketing," Hitomi remarked.

"Fewer tourists are better for us," Professor Ueda assured her. "Easier to get a sense of the village itself. Once the tour buses arrive at a village, it's usually impossible to do any real fieldwork."

They cruised through the heart of the village, passing the Mountain Heritage Museum, the Farming Tradition Center, and half a dozen restaurants and guesthouses. As they drove, the houses grew farther apart, and the trees encroached on the village from all sides. The road narrowed, then turned to gravel.

At the end of the road, there was one last house before the mountain rose up again, steep and thickly wooded. A thatched-roof farmhouse, like the others in the village. But the wood was darker and damper, the eaves sagging, the thatch visibly balding.

"Is this it?" Hitomi asked. There was no sign, nothing indicating that it was a guesthouse.

"There's always some hardship in fieldwork, Sasaki," Professor Ueda said, with some relish. The car crunched over the gravel and came to a stop. Before he got out, he squinted at the rearview mirror, whipped a comb out of his pocket, and combed his sparse hair into neat rows.

A gray cat was sleeping on the stones that led up to the front door. As Hitomi picked her way carefully towards the house, the cat woke and stalked towards her, lifting its head as if demanding to be petted.

"Hello, beautiful," she cooed, crouching down to oblige it. The cat nuzzled her hands, then flopped down on the stone and sprawled out, displaying its fuzzy white stomach.

Ahead, the front door rattled as it slid open. The cat mewed, padding back over to the door and winding itself around the ankles of the man who appeared there. His jeans were rolled up to his knees, showing his bare, furry legs.

Hitomi's first impression was of sheer size. The man was so tall he had to duck slightly to fit through the door, and he had big ungainly hands like boulders. Once she'd gone to a museum in Ryōgoku, where the sumo stadium was, and seen what had to be a sumo wrestler on his off hours, shuffling shyly into a convenience store as if he were embarrassed of his hugeness. This man reminded her of that, massive but standing with his shoulders modestly hunched.

The man bent and picked up the cat, letting it climb onto his shoulders. Hitomi's eyes followed the cat up to his face. He looked only a few years older than she was, somewhere in his thirties. It was difficult to tell, because his ruddy face was obscured with thick black stubble.

"You're the guests? Ueda and Sasaki, two rooms, three nights?" he demanded.

Hitomi's soul withered and died at the thought of anyone calling Professor Ueda plain *Ueda*, as if he weren't a tenured and published and profusely awarded scholar, the sort of man who got to make the first comment at all the monthly meetings of the Tokyo Folklore Study Group.

"That's right. And you are?" Professor Ueda answered, taking out his handkerchief and wiping his glasses on it, apparently unruffled.

"Kiyama Tatsuya. I'll carry your bags," the man announced. Without asking, he went back to their rental car, opened the trunk, and hoisted their suitcases. Hitomi was an overpacker in general, indecisive about which clothes and shoes she'd want on a trip, plus she had packed several of the books she was reading for her thesis. Her suitcase was so heavy that one of the conductors had had to help her lift it onto the luggage rack in the train. But Mr. Kiyama hefted it in one hand as if it were weightless, and carried Professor Ueda's two bags under the other arm, all without disturbing the cat riding on his shoulders.

Professor Ueda raised his eyebrows at her, as if to say, 'Welcome to fieldwork!'

Hitomi followed the man to one of the guestrooms, where he deposited her suitcase on the tatami mats, carefully, like a giant setting down a tree trunk.

"Thank you, Mr. Kiyama," she attempted.

"Just Tatsuya. Dinner's at six," he announced, and turned to go. She wasn't sure if meals were supposed to be included, and she was especially not sure if she wanted to spend an entire meal sitting across the table from this odd stranger. There was something off-putting about him, something she couldn't quite put her finger on. But before she could figure out what to say, he was already closing the door.

The mats had the sweet, grassy smell of real tatami, but they were faded and a little musty, probably not replaced as recently as they should have been. The futon was already spread out on the floor, neatly made with flowered sheets and a padded quilt that looked handsewn. There was a little alcove with a tiny glass vase full of fresh flowers. It was hard to imagine a man like Tatsuya making beds and picking wildflowers, but she supposed that was part of running a guesthouse.

Although her door was closed, she could hear the muffled clatter of pots and pans, and she could smell something faintly savory. She went out into the front room to investigate.

The storyteller was there.

Sitting comfortably on a cushion was a tiny old woman, so small that her body seemed to disappear inside her kimono, until all you could see was the soft round peach that was her head, topped with sparse white fuzz. She sat beside a traditional hearth built into the floor, with an iron kettle hanging on a chain from the ceiling.

There was a more modern kitchen off to the side. From the well-loved patina of the appliances, Hitomi guessed it probably dated back to the sixties or seventies. In this narrow kitchen, not much larger than the one in her parents' apartment back home in Tokyo, Tatsuya was standing at the stove, stirring a pot. His massive, hairy arms were especially incongruous against the daffodil-yellow apron he was wearing as he cooked.

She realized she was staring—although to be fair, he was difficult not to stare at.

"Dinner," he explained tersely. As if that was what needed explanation.

It was a little funny to see someone so enormous and so decisively male fussing in a kitchen. Her ex-husband had never cooked.

Tatsuya, his brow knit in concentration, set aside some of the vegetables and ran them through a blender. She guessed that he was preparing mushy food for his grandmother, who might not have enough teeth left to chew fibrous vegetables.

Hitomi realized all of a sudden how much she was inside someone else's home, how intimate the whole scene was. She froze at first, trying to think of what to say, but Professor Ueda breezed past her into the front room and sat across from the old woman as if it were all quite natural.

"Mrs. Kiyama," Professor Ueda began.

"Everyone calls her Grandmother," Tatsuya interjected from the kitchen.

Grandmother inclined her head in apparent agreement.

"Grandmother," Professor Ueda said. "My name is Ueda, and this is my graduate student Sasaki. We've heard that you know a lot of stories. Would you be willing to tell us a few?"

"After dinner," the old woman declared. "I never tell stories before sunset."

Or at least that's what Hitomi thought she said. Grandmother's dialect was so thick, she could hardly be sure.

"A sensible practice," Professor Ueda nodded.

Although Hitomi had worried that the dinner would be too awkward to bear, sitting across from Tatsuya (a silent, sullen mountain), the food itself was remarkable. Plain mountain fare: a bowl of rice, homemade pickles, cold tofu, stewed vegetables, and buckwheat soba noodles. But everything was fresh and subtle and perfect. She'd never had soba with such intense flavor or such lovely, springy texture; she suspected that someone in the village must have made it by hand.

And once Grandmother had her dinner, she was an endless fountain of chat. Her accent was so heavy that it was hard for Hitomi to follow, but she got the general idea. Grandmother attempted to introduce the village to her two citified visitors, explaining that the village one ridge over had been made a UNESCO World Heritage site, and *they* got heaps of tourists in the summer, but the houses in the Kiyamas' village weren't as well-preserved, so they had been passed over. Which was apparently a source of some grief to the local restaurants and guesthouses. She'd run this house as a guesthouse for forty years, doing all the cooking herself, but these days it was all up to her grandson, and they didn't get many customers, since they hadn't been able to rethatch the roof as often as it needed, and the neighbors' guesthouses were in better condition. But, she added, these two guests were clearly discerning travelers, because she was the only one left in the village who knew the old stories.

"No one else in the world knows these anymore," she boasted sweetly. "They don't have these stories in the next village. And no one else here remembers them all—I'm the last one left born in the Meiji period."

"You were born in *Meiji?*" Hitomi gasped, forgetting her manners for a moment in her surprise.

"June 1912," Grandmother nodded. "Just one month before the Emperor Meiji died."

Hitomi had never met anyone born in the Meiji period before. There couldn't have been many left in the whole country. She noticed that Grandmother, whose eyes were still sharp, seemed rather gratified by her awe.

"My, it's getting dark already," Grandmother observed, with an air of great ceremony. Shadows were gathering at the corners of the front room, and the cooler night air was seeping in through the old house's walls.

"I'll make tea." Tatsuya knelt next to the old earthen hearth, arranged wood in a neat pile, and started a fire. He filled and rehung the iron kettle above the fire.

He turned off the electric lights in the kitchen when he filled the kettle, so that the only source of light in the house was the flickering flame of the little fire starting in the hearth. The kettle swayed slightly on its chain, making shadows waver on the dark wooden walls.

Hitomi felt the hair on the back of her neck stand on end. This was not at all like sitting under fluorescent lights in the library, reading an edited collection of folktales with helpful annotations. It was a performance, an important one, one Grandmother had been repeating for decade after decade.

"Excuse me, Grandmother," Hitomi put in. It felt almost sacrilegious to interrupt with reality. "May we record your stories?" She held up her phone.

"Go ahead, if you like. Now, what sort of stories do you want to hear, children?" Grandmother began, settling herself comfortably on her cushion and accepting a cup of tea from Tatsuya, who then receded into the shadows behind her, like a black-clad stagehand.

Professor Ueda, at sixty-eight, was indeed young enough to be her son. He only smiled. "Why don't you tell us your favorites, Grandmother?"

Grandmother launched into a long series of practiced, well-loved stories. Hitomi recognized some as cousins of tales she'd read in collections, but others were wholly new. Kappa, ghosts, forest fires, disappearances, babies delivered by the gods, good little girls and bad little girls, mountain deities and mountain demons.

As Grandmother continued telling her stories, Hitomi lost track of time. It surprised her when Grandmother hid a yawn in her sleeve and reflected: "Well—I think there's time for one more story tonight." Her eyes narrowed in a smile. "Do you want to hear the story of why our family is called Kiyama?"

Hitomi found herself leaning forward, entranced by the sparkle in the old woman's eyes.

Just then, the electric lights popped back on with an audible buzz.

"It's past nine, Gran," Tatsuya announced, a little too loudly. "You're usually in bed by now."

"Oh, I suppose," she sighed. "More stories tomorrow night, then."

Grandmother allowed Tatsuya to lift her from her cushion and help her into her bedroom.

In the electric light, the front room looked shabby, the fire pitiful, and all the veils of mystery had departed.

"Wow," Hitomi whispered to Professor Ueda, who answered with a boyish smile.

"There's nothing else like it, is there, Sasaki?"

That night, Hitomi curled up underneath the padded quilt with her phone. It was so silent and dark in the house. She was used to the streetlights and traffic noise of her neighborhood in Tokyo. The light from her phone, at least, was a thread connecting her to the real world.

She texted her parents to let them know that she had arrived safely and to wish them a good night. Then she settled in to browse the internet; she was too keyed up to sleep.

Do you want to hear the story of why our family is called Kiyama?

She had known that the guesthouse was called Kiyama Guesthouse, but she hadn't seen how it was written. Now that she thought about it, she wasn't sure what characters the name Kiyama was made of; 'yama' was obviously mountain, but 'ki' could be any number of things. It wasn't a common name. She searched for the guesthouse online, and after a while found its listing on a

travel site: Minshuku Kiyama, spelled 鬼山. The 'ki' was an alternate reading for the word 'oni,' or ogre.

Ogre mountain.

When she was a child, she had mostly thought of oni as cute cartoon figures: bright red skin, huge eyes, wild hair, that silly tigerskin loincloth they were always wearing in children's books. It wasn't until she'd started her degree in folklore that she saw the grotesque images of them in older illustrations. The way people had once imagined ogres, back when people took such things seriously.

She thought of a picture scroll she'd read just last semester, a sixteenth-century story about an ogre in the mountains outside of Kyoto. He would go down into the city at night to abduct young maidens and bring them to his mountain dwelling, where they became both the servants and the main dishes at his luxurious, depraved banquets with his ogre friends. She had been shocked by the graphic violence in this prettily painted little scroll. Cups full of sparkling human blood. Ogres chewing on girls' naked thighs. A platter full of girl sashimi.

Ogre mountain. There was definitely a story behind that name.

In the center of the formica table in the kitchen were two full plates and a scrawled handwritten note:

GRAN IS SLEEPING.

KEEP IT DOWN. SOUND CARRIES.

Tatsuya's hospitality was somewhat lacking. On the other hand, when Hitomi peeled back the plastic wrap covering her plate, she discovered a fluffy omelet, a salad with neatly halved cherry tomatoes glistening like rubies, and a little knot of a roll studded with raisins. It was a breakfast any housewife would have been proud of.

"What are our plans for today?" she whispered to Professor Ueda. She didn't want to wake Grandmother.

"I suspect Grandmother won't tell any more stories until sunset," he mused, neatly buttering his roll. "You have some time to yourself until then. Why don't you go out and explore the village?"

"Isn't there fieldwork I ought to be doing?"

"That *is* fieldwork. Walk around the village, talk to people, write down your observations. Even if you never use this material in your thesis, it'll help you write. Folklore only exists in context."

"And you?"

"I promised the curator at the Mountain Heritage Museum I'd pay him a visit. I'll meet you back at the house before dinner."

Hitomi slipped an apple into her backpack (she didn't feel bad about it, because there was another messy handwritten note beneath it reading "YOU CAN TAKE THESE") and headed out the front door.

The village felt different on foot and by the morning light. Flowers smiled at her from everyone's garden. Inspired by Professor Ueda's exhortation, she took photos of all the flowers she didn't recognize, and resolved to look them up in a botanical manual once she got back to the library. It might be important. Anything might be important!

She had never had time to think about flowers before. The last year of her marriage, she had tried to make a date with her ex to see the cherry blossoms in Ueno Park, and he had kept pushing the day back, saying he was too busy to take the time off work. By the time they both had a Saturday free, the blossoms had already fallen.

Closer to the center of town, one of the local stores was open. There was a woman out front, setting out a sign advertising different varieties of homemade tofu. Unable to make up her mind, Hitomi ordered three different kinds: hiya yakko, cold and topped with soy sauce, scallions, and bonito flakes; dengaku, grilled and glazed with miso; and ganmodoki, a fried tofu-vegetable fritter. The woman delivered her tofu and sat across from her to keep her company as she ate, and they got to chatting.

"Have you lived here long?" Hitomi asked, which turned out to be a stupid question, because the woman just wiped her hands on her apron and chuckled. Everyone in the village had been born there; no one had moved there. Although plenty had moved away.

"Where are you staying?" the woman asked.

"At Minshuku Kiyama," Hitomi answered, pointing back up the road to where it disappeared in the darkness. Somewhere in those shadows was the old house.

"Oh." The woman's mouth worked slightly, as if she were trying to restrain herself from informing this outsider that Minshuku Kiyama was the worst guesthouse in the village.

"I came to hear Mrs. Kiyama's stories," she explained.

"*Ohh*," the woman nodded in understanding. "They're a unique pair, those two."

"Mrs. Kiyama and her grandson?"

The woman nodded again. "He's a good boy, really. He puts the snow tires on our car for free every year, won't think of taking money for it. But there's funny blood in that family, always has been, that's all."

Hitomi ate her three kinds of tofu and listened to the woman's stories about the village, which weren't at all like Grandmother's; they were about whose guesthouse went out of business, or who the mayor used to be before the village was disincorporated, or whose children had moved away to Tokyo and didn't visit as often as they ought to. Hitomi nodded and urged her on when she could. Before she left, she bought vacuum-sealed packs of smoked tofu to give to her parents and classmates as souvenirs. Then she strolled back up the road to the Kiyama house, hurriedly taking notes on what she remembered of their conversation, although she doubted that the tofu-seller's gossip would make it into her thesis.

Beside the house, Tatsuya was stretched out underneath some enormous piece of farm machinery.

"You okay under there?" Hitomi asked, peering down at his feet sticking out from under the machine.

"Fine. Just fixing." He rolled out from underneath the machine and sat up. His face was smeared with grease, and his hands and forearms were black up to the elbow.

Part of fieldwork is getting to know the people, she reminded herself. *Folklore exists in context.* And Tatsuya was part of that context. He had grown up hearing Grandmother's stories, breathing the air in that house. He and the stories were inseparable.

"What's that called?" she asked.

"Combine. For harvesting rice." He frowned and rested his elbows on his knees. "Hand me that cloth?"

She found the rag he was gesturing to and handed it to him. He tried to wipe the grime off his hands.

"Is it yours?" she asked. She hadn't seen rice fields around the Kiyama house.

"Neighbor's," he answered, fiddling with the rag. "This is my work."

"Oh—you're a mechanic?"

He nodded. "Only one in three villages. Only one young enough to do it, I guess." He paused, staring not at her, but at a spot in the distance somewhere off to the left of her head. As if he were frightened of looking directly at her, she realized. "So you're a researcher?" he ventured.

"Sort of—I'm not really anything so impressive. I'm just a student."

He blinked and didn't say anything, so she kept going.

"I mean, I'm in graduate school. I'm a little old for it. I started my master's at twenty-nine. Everyone else in the seminar is younger than I am, which is a little awkward. All the girls act like I'm their big sister, even though I've been out of school for so long that actually I'm always asking them for help..."

"Why folklore?"

"Sometimes I think I looked at the course catalogue and chose the most impractical, most useless degree," she joked. Mostly joked. "I used to work in finance. It was really, really practical. Totally real-world. Real money, real problems, real deadlines. And so for a few years I worked twelve-hour days doing real, important stuff, and I broke out in hives all over my body, and then I quit."

Her stomach clenched in embarrassment, and she realized she had just vomited up her life story to him. At least she had managed to leave out the divorce. He didn't seem particularly fazed by any of it, just nodded thoughtfully.

"So you listen to stories instead?"

"Yeah," she agreed, and she couldn't quite hide her smile. Breathing fresh mountain air, eating the world's best tofu, and listening to people's stories: it was ridiculous, but that was her job now. Placing things in context. A great big jumbled puzzle that was this village and its past, with Tatsuya as one funny jagged piece of it. "Actually, I was wondering if you could help me sometime. I'm going to need to transcribe the recordings of your grandmother's stories, but I have some trouble understanding her accent..."

"I bet." Tatsuya had a strong regional twang, but he was comprehensible. His grandmother had probably been raised in a time when even the schoolteachers still spoke dialect, and she might not have had much schooling at that.

"Would you help me transcribe? I don't know how I'm going to find someone back in Tokyo who could do it."

"Sure, no problem." He nodded solemnly.

A bell rang faintly from inside the house. Tatsuya glanced over his shoulder, then set down his greasy rag and closed his toolbox.

"Gran's up. Guess she needs help."

"You take good care of her," Hitomi observed.

He glanced back at her; for a moment, he looked as if he were about to say something. Then he just awkwardly grunted his assent. "Dinner'll be ready at six," he added, and disappeared inside.

People probably didn't notice him often, she thought. How often would he meet new people at all, here in the village? Here everyone had known him since birth, had a whole narrative to explain him, and would never have an occasion to experience the pleasure she just had, seeing for the first time that there was something sweet in him. That he might be kind.

Context.

"Tonight, you'll do the talking," Professor Ueda informed Hitomi.

"Are you sure?"

"You're ready. It'll go well. And I'll be there if you need help."

Hitomi glowed with pride. If he was letting her take the lead on the fieldwork, it meant he trusted her judgment. He was going to use these recordings for his own publications, too, after all.

"My, my—it's good to have the house full of young people," Grandmother sighed, as Tatsuya helped her shuffle to her customary cushion.

Hitomi started her phone recording and folded her hands in her lap. "Grandmother, will you tell us more stories tonight?"

"I'd be happy to. Tatsuya, will you pour some sake for our guests?"

Like the night before, Tatsuya started a fire, filled everyone's cups, turned off the electric lights, and receded into the darkness behind Grandmother. The fire cast a web of shadows over the wrinkles and divots in her face.

"What kind of story do you want to hear?"

"Tell me a story about the village, please," Hitomi urged.

Although she had already told them stories for hours the night before, Grandmother resumed her performance with undiminished energy. Her voice rose and fell. She was a child, a barking dog, an exiled samurai. For as long as Grandmother spoke, her stories were the only reality. Hitomi forgot about her thesis research, forgot about Tokyo. Time slipped away.

"I think there's time for one more story tonight," Grandmother finally murmured. "What would you like to hear?"

Last night, Grandmother had tried to tell a story about the family name. Kiyama, Ogre Mountain. There had to be a great story there—but was it all right to ask for it? Something so personal? She saw Tatsuya leaning forward in the shadows, his hands on his knees as if he were getting ready to spring up.

If she didn't know this story, if she left the village without hearing it, she would regret it forever. There wouldn't be a second chance. Grandmother was 103, and no one else knew her stories...

The fire spat sparks at the iron kettle. Grandmother waited for her answer.

"Can you tell me the story about the Kiyama family, Grandmother?" Hitomi asked.

The old woman's face creased into a smile. "That's a good one. I'm glad you asked."

Behind her, Tatsuya stood, but before he could reach the light switch, Grandmother raised her little pink hand in a wordless command. Tatsuya sank quietly back to his knees on the mats and didn't move again.

Grandmother closed her eyes and began, her voice low and deliberate:

Long ago, hundreds of years ago, in this very village, in this very family, there was a mother and a father with just one daughter. She was a great beauty, and they wanted only the best for her. But this was a poor family then—is still a poor family now—and their beautiful daughter had to help her parents earn money. She used to go up to the mountain to gather brushwood to sell in the village. It was a sad sight, to see this lovely girl climbing down from the mountain with her back bent from carrying brushwood, but all the village said it was wonderful to see a daughter so devoted to her parents.

But one day, the daughter didn't come back down from the mountain. The whole village searched for her day and night for a week, but they couldn't find her. The parents were beside themselves with grief. Although the rest of the villagers accepted that she was gone, her father did not, and every day he went into the mountains looking for her. The house fell into disrepair as he neglected his work to search for his missing daughter.

After months and months of searching, one day he slipped through a crevice in the rocks and found himself inside an ogre's cave. Inside the cave, he found his daughter—pregnant.

"Quick," the father said. "Come with me. I'll take you home."

But the daughter said, "No, it's not safe. My husband the ogre will come back to his cave any second. You've got to hide."

So she hid her father inside a chest in the cave, and not a moment too soon, because just then the ogre returned to the cave.

"It stinks like human in here," the ogre growled.

"Of course it does, darling; I'm here," the daughter answered.

"I smell *two* humans," the ogre insisted.

"Then you must be smelling the child in my stomach," the clever daughter suggested. "He's human too."

The ogre accepted this answer, and he sat down to eat his dinner of human flesh. The father waited, terrified, inside the chest, all night long. And in the morning, after the ogre left the cave, the father and the daughter escaped back to the village together.

The daughter never dared to climb the mountain again, and lived safely in the village for the rest of her days. But a few months after she returned from the ogre's cave, she bore his child. A child who grew to be like all the Kiyama men, a great big strapping boy like my Tatsuya there. And all the village knows there is still ogre blood in the Kiyama family, and that is how we got our name.

Grandmother picked up her cup and drained it of sake, breaking the spell of her story with a satisfied sigh.

"Then do you believe you are descended from an ogre, Grandmother?" Hitomi asked.

"Oh, no. I married into the Kiyama family," she answered brightly. "My Tatsuya is the last one in the village with ogre blood in his veins."

Across the room, in the dim firelight, Tatsuya's dark face was flushed red. Red like an ogre's face, his coarse hair wild, casting shadows on the wall almost like a pair of horns—

"That reminds me of a famous story from the northeast," Professor Ueda began. After a drink or two, he was often inclined to start lecturing. "Grandmother, have you ever heard of a story called 'Kozuna, the Ogre's Child'?"

"Tell me," she urged, her eyes brightening. "I don't hear new stories often these days."

It was well past nine, but she didn't look at all tired. Tatsuya made no attempt to hurry her off to bed. It was probably too late for that; the damage had already been done.

"The story of Kozuna, the ogre's child, begins very much like your story. An ogre kidnaps a girl and makes her his wife. Her father goes looking for her, and finds her on Ogre Island."

"Ogre Island?" Grandmother protested. "Everyone knows ogres live in the mountains."

"You have a good point," Professor Ueda conceded politely, "but there are quite a few stories from other regions which are very clear about Ogre Island. At any rate, the story continues as your story does, with the daughter hiding her father from the ogre. Then they escape, in this version by boat. But the ending is different.

"I heard this ending in a town in Iwate Prefecture. The ogre's child is named Kozuna, and as he grows older, he realizes that he has an ogre's hunger for human flesh. Finally, unable to control his hunger, he chooses to take his own life rather than devour his neighbors. He asks the villagers to burn his body so that nothing remains. But after they burn him, the ashes of his body drift into the wind, and even his ashes still hunger for human flesh. And that is the story of where mosquitoes come from."

"Oh—that poor boy," Grandmother murmured, shaking her head in sorrow, as if the character in the folktale were real.

Tatsuya was sitting behind Grandmother, still and massive as a statue. His craggy face had the plain, decent ugliness of a carved wooden mask. Hitomi felt suddenly that she had been wrong to ask for the story of the family's name.

"If you've finished your drink, Gran, let's get you to bed," he rumbled.

"More stories tomorrow night," she assured them cheerfully. Perhaps she didn't have an audience as often as she would like. It was a long trek into the mountains to visit her, after all, and she had a century's worth of stories she needed to get out.

"I look forward to it," Professor Ueda enthused, bowing his head deeply. "Goodnight, Grandmother."

Hitomi stopped her phone recording. She quashed a momentary impulse to delete that night's file. She wanted to tell Professor Ueda that she wished they hadn't come, that she wished he hadn't let her lead the fieldwork.

"You did well, Sasaki," he declared, standing and heading to his guestroom.

"Thank you, Professor." She waited for his door to close before she stood. She turned the electric lights back on in the kitchen and washed up the sake cups and a few lingering dinner dishes. Tatsuya didn't reappear, even after it had been more than enough time for him to put his grandmother to bed. He might not have wanted to talk, after that.

Hitomi slipped out the front door. He wasn't there, but she heard or sensed something out in the darkness, and tried to feel her way around to the side of the house.

"You're going to break your neck walking in the dark like that. You don't know your way here."

A spot of light shone from the darkness to her left. She saw Tatsuya sitting on a rock by the edge of the woods, holding up his phone to light the way for her. Why hadn't she thought of that? She pulled out her own phone and illuminated the ground in front of her, picking her way carefully over to him.

Once she reached him, he made room for her on the rock next to him, and she sat. Neither of them spoke for a while. She resolved that she wouldn't speak first. It would be easy to babble something stupid, maybe even make things worse while she was trying to make things better.

Silence stretched between them.

"What's it like in the city?" he asked, finally.

"Have you ever been to Tokyo?"

"Never. I lived in Nanto for a while." Nanto was the nearest city to the village, actually a conglomeration of seven villages that had merged after their populations dropped. It wasn't much of a city. It was hard to imagine that anyone could live in Japan without seeing Tokyo, but she supposed it would be a long, inconvenient trip from this deep in the mountains. And he had his grandmother to care for.

"Did you like it?"

"Hated it," he answered quickly. She stayed silent, waiting to see if he'd continue. "There's no high school in the village. I went to the high school in Nanto, and it was so far I had to live in a dormitory."

"Must have been hard being so far from home at that age."

"I'm not good with people. I don't like to leave the village." He wouldn't look at her, just stared at his enormous hands in his lap.

"Don't you get lonely here?" she asked. "If there really aren't any other young people?"

"There used to be other people my age. They all left. Nothing here for them."

"But you...?"

"If I leave, there's no one to take care of Gran. Or fix things. Or help out the old-timers."

"But how are you going to find a Mrs. Kiyama?" she asked. Stupid, again. Her preparation for fieldwork hadn't taught her how to stop asking stupid questions.

"Last year, Gran learned that there are agencies that can send you a wife from the Philippines over the internet. Now every time she sees me on the computer she badgers me about ordering a pretty wife."

"Are you considering it?"

He shot her a dour look out of the corner of his eyes. Apparently not.

It was several minutes before he spoke again, and then all he said was: "I won't pass it on." Without a goodbye, he stood and stalked back off into the house.

It was so dark in the mountains, a pressing kind of darkness unimaginable in Tokyo. Hitomi clutched her phone, stared at the circle of light it cast at her feet.

Kozuna, the ogre's child, was terrified that he couldn't control himself, that one day he would find himself eating human flesh and he wouldn't be able to stop... She shivered. It was as if Tatsuya really believed it.

I don't like to leave the village, he'd said. *I'm not good with people.* As if what he meant was: *I don't trust myself around them. It's not safe for me out there. They're not safe around me.*

That night, Hitomi had three texts from her mother, but she didn't text back, not even to tell her about the magnificent tofu she'd eaten.

Back in the Meiji period, a prominent philosopher, Inoue Enryō, had attempted to convince the backwards nineteenth century populace that the supernatural wasn't real, that ghosts and kappa and ogres were just stories. It had always amazed Hitomi that this had been a real scholarly endeavor, that fairy tales had once been so deeply rooted that anyone had to do what Inoue Enryō did.

But here was a twenty-first century man who believed absolutely in the existence of ogres. No—who believed that he himself was an ogre. It was outrageous, and still...

Hitomi noticed with some distress that there was no lock on the inside of her guestroom door.

She felt a tickling on the back of her neck and reached back to rub it. When she pulled her palm back, there was a smear of blood on it. She had to swallow a scream—it had just been a mosquito. She'd crushed it with her hand, without meaning to.

She was losing it. Ever since they had left that tunnel, nothing had been normal. She had to get back to Tokyo, where the laws of physics still operated, where the night wasn't as black.

In the morning, there were fresh pancakes waiting on the breakfast table for her and Professor Ueda. No sign of Tatsuya or Grandmother.

"What did you think of that story, Professor Ueda?" Hitomi asked.

"Which one?"

"The origin of the family name. Do you think it's true?"

He chuckled warmly. "The mountain air is working its magic on you, Sasaki."

"I don't mean the part about the ogre—but is there any historical truth to it, do you think?"

Professor Ueda swirled his spoon in his coffee cup thoughtfully. "In villages like this, many of the local legends and stories are tied to historical fact. I know of some cases where local folklore has been corroborated through temple records. But all this story implies is—well, a single mother. A woman, a disappearance, a baby with no father. I suspect that sort of thing was just as common in premodern times as it is today."

It sounded so sane when Professor Ueda described it. He had probably encountered similar stories before; he'd done fieldwork in places much more remote than this. It was only her inexperience that was spooking her.

The night before, she'd dreamed that she was in the woods, and there was something invisible in the dark taking great big juicy bites out of her...

"I'd like to take the car today," Professor Ueda added, cutting a neat wedge out of a pancake. "There's a museum in Nanto I'd like to visit. You're welcome to come along if you want, but it's unrelated to your thesis project, so I'd encourage you to stay in the village."

"I'll keep exploring," Hitomi agreed. She wondered if he was leaving her alone in the village on purpose. In all his stories about the adventures of his younger days, he had been out on the mountains and islands by himself. Perhaps that was an important part of fieldwork: encountering the unknown by yourself without backup.

She stood outside the house and waved goodbye to Professor Ueda as he drove away. He was susceptible to a certain amount of fawning from his students, and it was only polite, after all.

Once the car disappeared, she stood on the stepping stone outside the front door and pondered. She had the day to do what she pleased. Grandmother wouldn't tell any more stories until sunset. She could have gone out into the village again, tried to find another villager to chat with.

But that seemed silly after what had happened last night. There was only one piece of context that really mattered after that.

Tatsuya was half underneath the combine, scowling at it while he worked.

Hitomi found a metal bucket and turned it over to make a stool, taking out her phone and her notebook. "Care to help me transcribe? Will that interfere with your work?"

"Go ahead."

They spent the morning working their way through Grandmother's recordings. Hitomi was careful not to play the one about the Kiyama family name. He translated from dialect to standard Japanese for her, explaining the local words for moss or mushroom. As long as she didn't say the word 'ogre,' he seemed happy enough to help.

"This must be different than working in finance," Tatsuya observed. "Are you happy, now that you left your old job? Is this what you like to do?"

"Honestly, on my worst days, I feel like the world's biggest loser."

He grunted disapprovingly.

"But it's true! Just last year, I had everything someone in my position could expect to have. A good job. A husband with a good job. A nice apartment. And I just set it all on fire."

"You were married?"

She nodded. "Three years. It seemed like a good idea at the time. We got along so well back in college, back when we were just dating. But once we got married and moved in together, it got... well, it was like I stopped being Hitomi and started just being a wife, to him. He wouldn't wash a dish or fold a shirt. Forget cooking or ironing. And I was working just as many hours as he was! It was just—you know, I never wanted to be a divorcée. But the divorce was the best decision I ever made."

She didn't know why she was telling him this. But he nodded seriously as he listened.

"So anyway, by any objective measure, I'm a loser. I'm thirty, already divorced, unemployed, living with my parents, spending a fortune on a degree I can't use for anything. But—" She shook her head. "But on the good days, I feel like—I don't know, like an adventurer. Like Momotarō." That was an unfortunate choice of folktale; Momotarō was famous for slaying ogres. "Like I just got into my little rowboat and paddled out into the open sea. And I left behind everything that was safe and stable on dry land, and I don't know where I'm going... but I'm totally free. And I'm kind of proud of myself for being so brave. Does that make sense?"

"It's not easy to leave things behind," he murmured. "I think the second version of your life story is better."

Tatsuya took a break from his repairs to cook lunch. He delivered a tray of soup and rice porridge to his grandmother, then returned to the kitchen.

"I could keep working on the combine, but there's no hurry." He hung his yellow apron on a hook. "It's hot today. It'll be cooler in the woods. We could go pick mushrooms."

"You know how to pick wild mushrooms?"

"Sure. Gran taught me."

In the entryway, Tatsuya paused by the door and pulled out a pair of clumsily handmade bracelets, colorful string and little bells.

"To warn off bears," he explained, and handed her one to wear. He was careful to drop it into her outstretched palm, as if he were avoiding any chance of accidental touch.

He led her up past the house and the garden, up the mountain's slope through the trees. It wasn't long before any trace of the village disappeared behind them. Hitomi realized she had become hopelessly lost within just minutes; she wouldn't have had an easy time finding the house again.

"There's no path," she pointed out.

"Not enough people come up here to wear a path. It's fine. I know the way."

"You come up here a lot? By yourself?"

"Free food all over the forest if you know how to look. Plus, it's quiet."

Sunlight filtered through the leaves overhead, then dimmed as the trees closed in around them. The forest was thick, and it was difficult for Hitomi to walk through the undergrowth. She regretted not changing into jeans and sneakers. Tatsuya, despite his size, slipped through gaps in the trees as if they were made for him, while she was stumbling and getting her skirt stuck on prickers. He noticed her trouble and started making sure he cleared a path for her, holding branches out of her way and warning her of logs or rocks underfoot.

"I've never been anywhere like this," she admitted. "I've been in the woods before, but... not like this. This isn't like Yoyogi Park. It feels like—like the woods aren't used to having humans in them. As if when I passed through that tunnel, I entered another world entirely."

"Like an alternate universe."

"Yeah."

"I like sci fi," he offered. "Old stuff. I like anything with outer space."

"I wouldn't have guessed that." There were little things about him that were oddly charming: his affection for the cat, his housewifely yellow apron, his handmade bear bracelets, his sci fi fandom. If he hadn't had an ogre's face, an ogre's body, an ogre's name, he would have been almost sweet.

They walked for what must have been an hour. She didn't want to check the time on her phone, didn't want to allow reality to intrude.

Although Tatsuya was carrying a basket, he didn't often stop to inspect mushrooms. Mostly he just walked in silence. His silence, or his clumsy, abrupt attempts at conversation seemed less awkward in the woods. It let her hear the birdsong.

Occasionally he pointed to trees or birds or flowers and named them for her. She'd never heard the names before, but she wasn't sure if that was because of her general ignorance, or if he was speaking in dialect.

He stopped at the base of a broad tree and pointed to a cluster of squat mushrooms. "These are edible. Do you see how the ridges here..." He paused and looked up. There were little tapping noises all around them: raindrops on leaves.

"I guess I should have checked the forecast," Hitomi said.

"Sky looked clear when we started," he frowned. "Better head back."

Abandoning the unpicked mushrooms, Tatsuya headed back down through the trees. Even without a path, he seemed to know exactly where he was going. He was so much faster moving through the thick forest that he often had to stand and wait for her.

"How much longer until we reach the village?" she asked. A fat raindrop plopped onto the tip of her nose.

"It's an hour's walk at a good pace. There'll be mud; you'll have to take it slower going downhill." He scowled up at the sky. Even through the leaves, she could make out the dark shapes of gathering clouds. "Better hurry."

Hitomi followed him downhill. The rain was starting in earnest, and it was a struggle to keep pace without losing her balance on the wet leaves, the newly slick ground. She kept having to wipe the water out of her eyes, and then she took one wrong step—she lost her balance and came down hard on her left knee.

Tatsuya turned back, as if to help her up, then recoiled. Hitomi was suddenly aware that blood was welling up out of her scraped knee. She tried to wipe it clean, but only succeeded in smearing dirt and blood all down her shin.

"Rain's only going to get worse," he announced, staring off into the distance. As if he were afraid even to look. "We'd better wait it out."

Hitomi couldn't imagine where they could shelter from the rain; there were no paths, no shelters, and the rain cut through even the thick trees. But his eyes were sharper, more accustomed to the woods, and he pointed to a rock formation not far away.

They were close to the naked mountainside, she realized, where the rocks formed a natural overhang that would keep off some of the rain. The rain pattered down harder, and by the time they made it to the overhang, it was pouring. Hitomi pressed herself back against the cool rock and shivered. Her skirt was soaked through, clinging wetly to her thighs, her scraped knee.

"Good idea," she whispered to him. "I wouldn't have liked walking for an hour in this."

It rained and rained. Tatsuya sat at the base of the rocks, his eyes closed. He looked utterly natural there, like a boulder that had just come loose from the mountain.

Hitomi poked around the cliffside, making sure to stay under the overhang. Water was pouring down like a curtain from the edge of the cliff, so she only had a narrow strip of dryish earth to explore. She took photos of the dripping wildflowers, the sodden moss, and the slick rocks. The flash of her camera shone off the cliff in an unexpected way.

"Hey, look at this." She tossed a pebble at Tatsuya to make him open his eyes. "I think there's a cave here."

"What?"

"Look. There's an opening in the rocks." It wasn't easy to spot, but there was a break in the mountainside, a spot that curved inwards. She tried to aim her phone inside, but it only illuminated a few feet.

She expected him to warn her about wild animals living in the cave, or something like that. Certainly he knew more about the forest and what was safe and dangerous than she did. But he didn't say anything at all, just walked up to the entrance of the cave and squinted at the inky blackness inside.

"It would be drier in there," she pointed out.

He didn't seem to hear her. He drifted inside the cave without looking back.

She followed, turning on her phone's flashlight. She swung the beam around the cave as she entered. It went back farther than she'd expected. It was surprisingly spacious inside, and pleasantly dry. Musty and dark, yes, but not smelly or dirty like she'd imagined an animal's den would be.

Tatsuya kept walking, moving forward blindly without a light until he stumbled on something.

"Careful!" She shone her phone at the ground by his feet.

There was a ring of stones there arranged in a neat circle. Precise and even, except where Tatsuya had kicked one of the stones. Definitely not the work of a bear.

"What is that?" She bent down, focusing on the ring of stones. The center was black and full of smeary ashes. "Is that a firepit?" She swung her phone around eagerly, and she caught sight of what might be other signs of human habitation. A heap of moldering wood. What looked for all the world like a rusty metal knife blade, although she didn't dare to touch it. "Did someone live here?"

Tatsuya hadn't spoken, she realized, since they'd discovered the cave.

"Tatsuya?"

"Someone lived here," he agreed. His voice was like the rusty creak of an old gate. "An ogre lived here."

"That's..."

"Can't you tell? Can't you feel it?" he insisted.

It was like there was an unreality field around him, distorting what she knew to be true, replacing it with this shared delusion. He believed it. Grandmother believed it.

Inoue Enryō had been wrong, she thought. The mosquito bite at the base of her neck itched. Her wet skirt clung to her legs. She was suddenly aware that there was still blood welling up from her scraped knee. Ogres chewing on girl's naked thighs...

There was a broad flat rock beside the firepit. Tatsuya sat heavily on it and rested his elbows on his knees. He looked steadily up at her—looking straight at her for the first time.

"Let's go back outside," she suggested.

He didn't move, didn't speak. The sheer immovable weight of him compressed her chest, made it hard for her to breathe. He was going to stay here, she realized. He was going to stay in the cave. Because he believed it was where he belonged.

Hitomi knelt on the hard floor of the cave, on the other side of the firepit from Tatsuya. Where there would have been a fire, long ago. She set her phone on the ground between them, the weak blue light from its screen barely illuminating his inscrutable ogre's face.

This wasn't what she was supposed to be doing in her fieldwork. She was supposed to listen and observe and analyze. Certainly not to intervene, to try to change the village or the people in it.

"I'm going to tell you a different story," she began. "Do you want to hear it?"

He nodded very slightly.

Long, long ago, in the Edo period or maybe earlier, in this village, in your family, there was a young woman who lived with her mother and father. She wanted to make things a little easier on her parents, so she would often go up into the mountains to gather brushwood to sell in the village.

Many people lived on mountains, back in those days. There were the villagers with their farms or their shops, of course. But deeper in the mountains, there were all sorts of other people. Travelers. Hermits. And hunters.

One day, while the young woman was gathering brushwood, she came upon a hunter. She was terrified of him at first. He was a huge man who didn't cut his hair or his beard. He wasn't like any of the men she knew from the village. And she was afraid of his arrows and knives.

But he spoke gently to her, even though he was such a big, wild man. And so the young woman started to look forward to seeing the hunter in the woods. They would share food together; he would give her bits of the meat he caught, and she would bring him little delicacies from the village, whatever she could spare.

Sometimes he even let her visit him in the cave where he lived. He was embarrassed, because he knew it wouldn't compare to her home in the village, but she was happy there. Because she could be alone with him.

She never told her parents about him. He wasn't the sort of man she was supposed to be seeing. She was the village beauty, and she knew she was supposed to marry a village boy. Not the hunter, who came down from the mountain once in a while to sell his catch, but belonged outside the village.

And one day, the young woman decided to stay on the mountain with the hunter. The villagers would never accept him as her husband, so she had no other choice. So, for a time, they lived together in his cave in perfect happiness as man and wife.

They might have spent their whole lives on the mountain together, but before too long, the young woman was with child. Although she was delighted to carry the hunter's child, she realized that she could not raise a child alone in the hunter's cave. Her baby would be better off in the village, with a roof over its head, and its grandparents and neighbors to help care for it. So she reluctantly parted from her husband and returned to the village to give birth.

The young woman gave birth to a son who grew up to be just as strong and bold as his father, the hunter. She was always wonderfully proud of him, but he was different from all the other children in the village. And because he was different, and his children were different, and his children's children were different, the villagers began to make up stories about the family. The same way we make up stories about anyone who is different.

The young woman never told her story to anyone, not even her son, so it was forgotten, and the villagers' lie was remembered instead. But you and I know the truth.

Hitomi wasn't an experienced storyteller like Grandmother. But she had practice, at least, in retelling her own story. And she had tried her best.

"You just made that up," Tatsuya pointed out. His eyes shone in the dark.

"Your grandmother isn't the only one who can tell stories. You can have your own story, too. Especially about yourself."

Hitomi understood, finally, why she had chosen a degree in folklore. Not just because it was deliciously impractical, but to study the stories we tell ourselves about ourselves. It was just what she had needed at a time when she had to rewrite herself. And no one needed a different story more desperately than Tatsuya.

He sat without speaking for a long time, but she could wait. She felt the ringing silence of the cave, the great weight of the mountain above and around them. Her injured knee throbbed, her legs cramped, and her phone ran out of battery.

"You could come to Tokyo one day," she said. Her voice echoed strangely in the cave. "I'd show you around. It's full of people, and you might hate it... but sometimes it's good to experience something new."

"Maybe," he conceded roughly. "One day." She tried to imagine him in Tokyo, hunching to fit through the train doors on the Yamanote line, towering above the press of people in the Shibuya scramble... It wasn't impossible.

The muffled sound of raindrops from outside the cave slowed. Hitomi stood, her legs shaking from kneeling on the floor of the cave, and peeked outside. The light hurt her eyes.

"The rain has stopped. Do you want to go home?" she asked. Standing there in the mouth of the cave, she offered him her hand and held her breath.

The massive shadow of Tatsuya was unmoving inside the dark cave. She couldn't see his face, couldn't tell what he was thinking. The light from outside barely filtered through the narrow entrance of the cave, cast weird shadows behind him. For a moment his form blurred; she saw his red face, his horns, his cruel fangs. But then they were gone.

When he stood, he was a person like anyone else: huge and ugly and gentle and human.

Tatsuya grabbed her hand and let her pull him out of the cave.

See Felicity Drake's story "Kozuna, the Ogre's Child" online at Metaphorosis.
If you liked it, leave a comment. Authors love that!
Remember to subscribe to our e-mail updates so you'll know when new stories are posted.

About the story

I'm a little embarrassed to admit how personal this story is. It's woven together from my own experiences, people I've met, places I've been, and stories I've read.

"Kozuna, the Ogre's Child" is the name of a real Japanese folktale. (Grandmother's version of the story is fairly similar to those you'll find in collections of Japanese folklore.) The first time I heard it, I felt awful for poor Kozuna, the half-ogre boy. It wasn't his fault that he had ogre blood, and the story gave him no chance for redemption or a happy ending.

The setting is inspired by Gokayama: a UNESCO world heritage site in Toyama Prefecture, and a unique, beautiful place with a thriving tourist trade. (And yes, the tofu really is life-changingly delicious!) For the setting of the story, I imagined a shadow twin of the real Gokayama, a neighboring village without the UNESCO stamp of approval and the tourist income it brings.

The picture scroll that Hitomi thinks about, the one with ogres banqueting on human flesh and blood, is *Shuten dōji emaki*. The version I had in mind can be viewed online, thanks to the National Diet Library's digital collection (http://dl.ndl.go.jp/info:ndljp/pid/1287887? tocOpened=1).

If the folklore of the mountains of Japan captures your imagination, I would strongly recommend Yanagita Kunio's *The Legends of Tono* (translated by Ronald A. Morse). It is a classic of folklore studies and a gateway into another world.

A question for the author

Q: What's your favorite type of pie?

A: Can't go wrong with a classic apple pie. I recommend adding raisins!

About the author

Felicity Drake is a writer based in New York. She writes fiction and interactive fiction.

www.felicitydrake.com, @DrakeFelicity

Magical Whistleblower Tells All

Michael Sherrin

August 19

FLYING MAN CLAIMS MAGIC IS REAL

London – Magic exists, says Thaddeus Seams, 37. Mr. Seams claims to be a wizard belonging to a secret society with real magical abilities. Monday morning, Mr. Seams landed in Trafalgar Square, dressed in velvet robes and holding an alleged magic wand.

"It looked like real magic," said Daisey Patricks, 53, who was present when Mr. Seams arrived. "He was flying above our heads, then landed in the middle of the street."

Several witnesses reported the man projecting his voice across the square without a microphone or other form of amplification.

Police escorted Mr. Seams into a car. Both the police department and Downing Street declined to comment until they had investigated the claims.

A representative of the British Magical Society issued a statement saying Mr. Seams has never been a member and that their organization has never claimed magic is real.

August 22

WORLD'S FIRST WIZARD
TAKES MANHATTAN

New York City – Self-proclaimed wizard, Thaddeus Seams, held a press conference today at the Waldorf Astoria to perform his magic for invited members of the press.

Mr. Seams began his remarks by saying he represented a hidden society of conjurers who lived around the world, using magic in secret, attending special schools and operating their own government, which set rules about how magic should be used. He added that by revealing magic to the world, he was breaking the laws of his society.

Mr. Seams went on to demonstrate several spells. With a few waves of his wand and speaking unidentifiable words, he repaired a broken chair, mended a tear in a dress, and healed an audience member's broken arm.

A hotel spokesperson said Mr. Seams tried to pay for a suite and use of the ballroom with several gold coins featuring names and words not recognized as any known language. An independent appraiser offered to pay the hotel on behalf of Mr. Seams in exchange for the coins, though he would not comment on their value.

September 4
MR. WIZARD GOES TO WASHINGTON
Washington, D.C. – Congress held hearings Tuesday afternoon to investigate the claims of whistleblower, Thaddeus Seams, that a secret, magic society exists. Mr. Seams insists that there are thousands of wizards like him hiding in the world, operating a shadow government and economy.

Scientists, occult experts, and religious leaders are also scheduled to testify over two days of hearings about the potential existence of magic.

September 4
TESTIMONY OF THADDEUS SEAMS (Excerpt)
Congressman Harris – What was your profession in this magical world, Mr. Seams?

Seams – I work in the Office of Teleportation and Transportation as a deconstruction analyst.

Harris – Can you explain what that role entails?

Seams – I monitor teleportation traffic around the world to ensure conjurers don't appear on top of one another, considering it's difficult to see where you're going when you're already there.

[Laughter from chambers]

Harris – You mean you can use magic to teleport? How does that work?

Seams – It just works, sir. It's magic.

Congresswoman Brown – You mean to say your society can teleport instantaneously across cities?

Seams – A strong conjurer can teleport across countries, sometimes continents with the right channeling.

Brown – Can you explain why you've chosen to keep this technology secret?

Seams – It's not technology. And it wasn't my choice to keep it secret. I think magic should be –

Brown – How long has your society had the ability to teleport?

Seams – Thousands of years, I believe.

Brown – Do you realize the damage caused by keeping this a secret? Teleportation could have solved climate change. No more emissions from cars or planes.

Seams – Yes, madam, I realize that. It's part of why I decided to come forward.

Brown – Though you admit to keeping this a secret for years yourself.

Seams – [Drinks water, refills it with his wand] Yes. There's a great deal of magic that's not being utilized to its fullest. I've tried speaking to the leadership in the conjuring community about engaging open relations with the mundane world, but I was rebuffed. They believe magic is too powerful to share. I say that is precisely the reason we should share it.

Brown – Why now, Mr. Seams? What made you come forward as you have?

Seams – To save the world, of course.

September 9
WIZARD CASTS SPELL ON SCIENTISTS

Chicago – A team of scientists met with the wizard Thaddeus Seams in Hyde Park on Monday to examine his alleged magical abilities and artifacts.

Scientists familiar with the meeting described the wizard as friendly and eager to share his knowledge.

Several noted particular interest in his bag, which was leather and about the size of a laptop case. According to Mr. Seams, the bag contained a library of more than three thousand books and specimens of thought-to-be make-believe creatures.

Dr. James Goldhaber was in attendance and said he saw some of the most amazing things in his career. "I don't know how he did it, but he pulled a jackalope from his bag. The jackalope was bigger than the bag."

"This bag either disproves core tenets of physics," said Dr. Florence Manning, a professor of theoretical physics at the University of Chicago, "or it reveals that other spatial dimensions not only exist, but may be accessible if we can turn this 'magic' into functional technology. The applications could be endless."

September 21
RELIGIOUS LEADERS CONCERNED ABOUT MAGIC
Geneva – Representatives from world religions convened to discuss the implications of magic on theology and society.

Dr. Swati Tharoor, author of three books on Hinduism, said during her opening keynote, "Miracles have been a part of almost every religion, and now we have the chance to see these miracles for ourselves. My question is, why now?"

Rev. Kurt Succow, after a panel discussing the subject of miracles, said in an interview, "For the first time in my life, I find myself turning toward science rather than faith for answers."

While many were optimistic about the good magic could bring to poor and suffering people, some dismissed it as a fraud no different from sham preachers hawking fake cures.

Leaflets calling the wizard Thaddeus Seams the Anti-Christ, were spread among the attendees. Police say they have no suspects as to who created the leaflets.

Over a phone interview, Mr. Seams addressed his and the conjuring community's views on religion saying, "Much as in the mundane world, there are a variety of perspectives among my people, though generally gods are not part of the conversation."

September 23
U.N. RESOLUTION DEMANDS MAGIC BE ACCESSIBLE TO ALL COUNTRIES
Beijing – China proposed a U.N. resolution, with more than fifty sponsors, to include representatives from all interested countries in the investigation of magic's legitimacy.

In a statement, President Jiang Biwu criticized the wizard Thaddeus Seams for spending all his time in the United States, ignoring the interests of the rest of the world, writing, "It is in the interest of China and all other countries to know about any secret societies within their borders. Mr. Seams must provide his knowledge to the global community."

Algerian Prime Minister Mouloud Sifi spoke in support of the resolution, saying, "Our countries must pay for drugs to save our lives, for patents to build our infrastructure, for companies to exploit our natural resources. Magic may be the first truly democratized resource, and its access should not be restricted."

In a letter brought by a pigeon, Mr. Seams wrote in response to our request for comment, "The Conjuring Community is as diverse as the world it's hidden within. I intend to share my knowledge of magic as widely as I can, though I am not a diplomat nor am I practiced in world affairs. I ask for patience as I try to learn as much about you as you learn about me."

September 25

INTERVIEW WITH SEAMS ON
KATHY MARTIN LIVE

Kathy Martin – I'd like to welcome my first guest, the most interesting man in the world, the wizard, Thaddeus Seams.

[Applause]

Martin – Thank you for joining us.

Seams – Thank you for having me.

Martin – You've impressed a lot of people with your abilities. You say you want to save the world. How do you plan to do that?

Seams – My hope is that by my coming forward about magic, the conjuring community will recognize that staying secret benefits no one, and instead choose to help solve the big problems in the world. There are wizards with powers well beyond my own, and they could accomplish a great deal.

Martin – Are you concerned that no one has come forward to verify your claims of a secret society? How do you explain that?

Seams – There is a lot of misinformation about the mundane world in our community. We have our own newspapers, so our impressions are filtered and uninformed.

Martin – You mean there's no freedom of the press?

Seams – No, that's not what I mean. We have reporters, but they tend to cover the conjuring community rather than regular people. They say it's what viewers want.

Martin – Do they see themselves as better than us?

Seams – Unfortunately, some do.

Martin – Do you, Mr. Seams? Is this how you're planning to save us?

Seams – No, not at all. I just want to help. We're all people, regardless of our abilities. We should all share the resources we have available.

Martin – But why has no wizard come forward before?

Seams – It's illegal to reveal magic to non-conjurers.

Martin – So you've broken the law.

Seams – I have. I think the law is wrong and unfair. Everyone should have access to the benefits of magic, not just the conjuring community.

Martin – If magic is so powerful, how is there no other evidence of it?

Seams – There have been incidents. Often, it's an honest mistake – a spell is cast just as a witness passes by. There's a department that specializes in memory spells to deal with these accidents.

Martin – You mean mind control?

Seams – Oh no, this is completely different than mind control.

Martin – So you're confirming mind control exists.

Seams – Well, yes, but...

Martin – Mr. Seams, how do we know you haven't been using mind control on us?

Seams – I'm not that powerful. It takes an incredibly powerful...

Martin – Mr. Seams, should we be concerned that magic is a threat to our society?

Seams – No, not at all. Magic is a good thing.

Martin – But you said there are some wizards who think themselves better than us.

Seams – There have been evil wizards in the past, but we've been able to contain the damage...

Martin – Mr. Seams, how do we know you're one of the good ones?

September 26

BACKLASH AGAINST WIZARD
LEADS TO RIOT

New York City – A protest took place Wednesday night outside the Waldorf Astoria where wizard Thaddeus Seams has been staying. After a contentious interview on Kathy Martin Live, Mr. Seams has been subjected to criticism for potential abuse of his magical abilities, including mind control and wiping memories.

Daniel Rawlins, one of the protestors, said, "We don't let just anyone have nuclear weapons or tanks. How do we know what this wizard is doing to us?"

Assemblywoman Georgia Keegan spoke to the almost 500 protestors, saying only dictators and fascists hoard power for themselves. "This wizard is living in his ivory tower and doesn't have to worry about putting food on the table or keeping his kids clothed. He can just cast a spell."

October 1
DOCTORS DEMAND ACCESS TO MAGICAL HEALING TO SAVE LIVES

Kinshasa – Dr. Louisa Famba said in an interview that she had requested wizard Thaddeus Seams use magic to address the recent outbreak of Ebola in three cities in the Democratic Republic of the Congo. There have been at least twelve new cases over the past three days, with more than 3,000 cases this year and more than 2,000 deaths. Dr. Famba said this outbreak was taxing what few healthcare resources her country has, and that the virus' communicability made it almost impossible to eradicate. "Magic might be cheaper and more effective than a vaccine," Dr. Famba said. "Vaccines cost millions to research and distribute. Magic appears to only require a wand."

Mr. Seams previously demonstrated the ability to heal broken bones more effectively than current medical science. In testimony to Congress, Mr. Seams further claimed magic could cure any non-magical disease.

"From malaria to HIV to Ebola," Dr. Famba said, "we are at the epicenter of the worst epidemic since the 1918 Spanish Flu. If magic can save lives, why won't he use his power to do so?"

Dr. Ismail Hassan, a representative with the World Health Organization, said if magic's health properties are found to be safe and effective, many diseases and chronic issues could become curable, saving an estimated 25 million lives per year.

Mr. Seams declined to comment.

October 10
STATEMENT FROM U.N. SECRETARY-GENERAL ADDRESSING THREAT OF MAGIC

Following are U.N. Secretary-General Aamir Wasim's remarks to the Security Council meeting on security and trade with the Conjuring Community.

Less than two months ago, we believed the greatest threats to humanity were made by science. I did not believe magic existed and remain skeptical of such claims. While Mr. Seams has performed miracles I cannot explain through science or God, the locations he provided as the sites of secret schools and shopping centers have not been found by satellite or on-the-ground inspections. That said, there is reason to err on the side of belief, balancing the benefits and risks.

If magic exists, it has the potential to do more good in this world than electricity, running water, and penicillin combined. It also could destabilize our economies, destroy faith in our leaders, and subject us to dangers we cannot fathom.

If these wizards can control our minds, could we stop them from launching nuclear weapons? Could they use magic to replicate our currency, causing havoc in our economies? What if they decide our way of life, our religions, or use of resources, infringe on their magical territory?

I urge the Security Council to stand with me in denouncing the Conjuring Community for hiding their natural resource and refusing to engage in diplomatic relations with their countrymen and neighbors. If the Conjuring Community do not reveal themselves, the Security Council should consider escalating the issue as a direct threat on the well-being of the world.

October 12

SELECTION OF SOCIAL MEDIA POSTS FROM MORNING OF OCTOBER 12

Traffic is not moving on#CharingCross. WTF? – @mraccountant87 – 0903

Is anyone else's Google Maps having trouble connecting? I'm in #LeicesterSq – @bellattahere – 0904

What the hell is Casting Road? I don't recognize this street at all. – @britstone3456 – 0904

Does anyone recognize this building in #LeicesterSq? Photo attached – @downtondorthy – 0906

Someone moved the Burger King to put in a townhouse! #LeicesterSq – @killzme76 – 0907

Transcript from video upload by @abbyyouknow01:

"Hey, my followers, Abby You Know here in Leicester Sq. where things are getting weird. Like, roads have changed and the buildings have all moved. Everyone is running around all confused and weirded out.

"So this building that's now in the middle of all the tourist shops is like an old castle or something. It's all stone and tall but crooked and weird. Someone's coming out. It's an old lady. She's got cool robes on. Girl's got some fashion. Holy shit, she has a wand. She's lifting it up. Can you hear her? She's saying she's the Chief Conjurer.

"What's a Chief Conjurer?"

October 15

EYE-WITNESS ACCOUNT OF THE
FIRST MAGICAL SUMMIT

This is Cooper Wolf in Paris, reporting for the Prize News Network at the first summit between world leaders and the Conjuring Community. There are more than three hundred people in attendance, including twelve wizards.

Thaddeus Seams, the man who started all this by blowing the whistle on magic, is also here.

Seams is seated near the central dais to the side. I must say, he looks a bit pale.

The Chief Conjurer, Abigail Lyre, is taking her seat between the Secretary-General and the French president who's hosting this gathering. Mrs. Lyre seems vibrant and bright, though she needed help stepping onto the dais.

President Francois is welcoming everyone and proclaims this a great day in the history of humanity, saying we're venturing down a new road of discovery and development.

The Secretary-General is standing now and saying he looks forward to peaceful relations with the conjurers and hopes they can share their great abilities to rid the world of illness and famine and turn back the damage of climate change.

The Chief Conjurer is taking her turn. She stands slowly, resting a hand on the president's shoulder.

[Audio from Mrs. Lyre's microphone]

"Thank you, President Francois and Mr. Secretary. We are honored to be your guests, and though this may not be under the circumstances we would have chosen, we are appreciative of the opportunity.

"Magic has been around for millennia, and it has been kept secret all that time. Pain and strife have existed for even longer, and magic is no salve. The purpose of keeping magic restricted was to allow human development without a crutch. You have created light bulbs and airplanes, all to compensate for a lack of magical abilities. This is something that should be admired and respected."

[Mrs. Lyre pauses and draws her wand from her sleeve]

"However, it is not our fault that you have not managed to use your technology to solve your greatest problems. You allow poverty to exist even though there is enough wealth to share. You allow families to starve even though there is an abundance of food. You fight over oil, even though the substance is destroying this planet.

"This is why we chose to hide – because we could not help you solve your own problems. It should be your responsibility to fix them.

"But that option is no longer available to us, thanks to the irresponsible ramblings of a rogue actor.

"While in isolated incidents, we have managed to extract memories of our existence, that will not work anymore, as the knowledge has now spread too wide. Your veiled threats against our safety and security required us to address this head on. We have decided the best course of action would be for the Conjurer Council to take over governance of the entire populous, effective immediately."

[End audio from microphone]

Cooper Wolf reporting. Everyone has exploded in anger. People are leaping onto their chairs and yelling at the Chief Conjurer. I will do my best to continue reporting, though it is impossible to hear what anyone is saying through the pandemonium.

It looks as if President Francois is trying to reason with the Chief Conjurer, but she is just looking at the crowd with a smile.

[Sound from stage cuts out]

The room just went completely silent, though the representatives still look like they're shouting. I'm far in the back and don't seem to have been affected. It was like the air was sucked out. The Chief Conjurer has her wand out. I think she just cast a spell on everyone. Hopefully my feed is still transmitting. People are returning to their seats.

[Audio from Mrs. Lyre's microphone]

"As you can see, you cannot govern yourselves. You need someone to coddle you, silence you. This is a simple spell so we can discuss the future, together, calmly. I hope you appreciate that we do this not by choice, but by circumstance. We will cure your diseases and feed your hungry, and we ask nothing in return. Just the chance to bring the world together, for the first time. And for this, we have Thaddeus Seams to thank."

[End audio from microphone]

The Chief Conjurer has turned to Seams, who is still seated with his hands covering his face. She's clapping, and the whole room is starting to as well. Apparently, so am I. We're all clapping.

October 14

EDITORIAL: WORLD THANKS CONJURING COMMUNITY

New York City – Celebrations will be taking place around the world tomorrow on the first Magic Day, in honor of the Conjuring Community and their role in saving the world. Climate change is being reversed. Disease, war, crime, and famine are almost non-existent because of magic spells.

No more are nations part of the first world or the third world. There is no wealth and no poverty. Everyone is happy thanks to magic making everything wonderful.

Part of the celebrations are in dedication to Thaddeus Seams, the man responsible for bringing about this Golden Age. Though Mr. Seams hasn't been seen since the Paris Summit when world leaders begged the Conjuring Council to take over governance, his contributions for diplomatically bringing these worlds together are worthy of praise.

The world is a better place thanks to the wisdom and generosity of the Conjuring Community. Their continued guidance will bring a new age of prosperity and peace, and it is our unquestioning trust in them that will bring that future to today.

EXCERPT FROM "THE PERSONAL PENNED TREATISE OF MR. THADDEUS SEAMS"

Magic is too powerful to be trusted. Its uses are too secret, its guardians too few.

I never thought I would last this long. I expected the Community to try to stop me before I could demonstrate magic beyond what spells could wash away. Maybe they knew I had contingencies planned. I'm not the most powerful conjurer, but I prepared.

My autoscribtor is documenting everything I did and said and is manifesting copies in secret locations around the world. Should the pen ever stop writing, these copies will be sent to every newspaper and world leader. It would mean I'm no longer able to able to represent magic myself.

It won't be long until they attempt to hide magic again. Knowledge is most powerful when rare, and knowledge of magic is the most powerful of all.

Yet it is the willingness of people to forget that will forever impress me, even when remembering should be so much easier.

Memories are a form of energy and energy cannot be destroyed. But no one seems willing to put the effort into digging deep enough to find what's hidden. When magic has been exposed before, often by accident, the event is wiped and the memory written off as a dream or something from a movie or book. The memory remains, locked away, hidden within a mind uninterested in what isn't readily available.

I know a written recitation will not serve as an adequate replacement for seeing magic in-person, but I hope it will help awaken what has been lost.

If what I say sounds bizarre or make believe, push past that assumption. It will feel uncomfortable. Maybe you'll even laugh at the consideration that what I've said is true. But keep pushing. Recall the days as I described them, consider the details I offered, and probe yourself for memories equal in detail. The more you push, the more the fog will thicken, making it easier to look the other way and ignore the injustice done to you.

The magicians of your world understand that magic is all about sleight of hand. While they use distraction and mirrors for their illusions, real magic finds value in similarly being ignored. If you knew the influence it had over your decisions, the power it had over your lives, your choices would no longer be your own. Ignorance allows magic to reign without impediment.

I fear there will not be another after me willing to take this risk should I fail. The decision to betray my people did not come easily. Had my life taken a slightly different course, it is possible my choice would have been different. Bravery was never my strong suit. Even with my magical abilities, I've spent my life toiling away at a desk in a room without a window, and all to make magic a bit more efficient. It was like rearranging grains of sand to make for a more pleasant beach.

I hope this document helps break through the fog and leads to a better, more equal world. This may be my final act. There is no way to know if I've succeeded. It is up to you who read this to believe that what I say is the truth and to refuse being blinded from what is hiding in plain sight.

Disclaimer: This is a work of fiction. Any resemblance to actual persons or memories is purely coincidental and should be ignored.

"See Michael Sherrin's story "Magic Whistleblower Tells All" online at Metaphorosis.
If you liked it, leave a comment. Authors love that!
Remember to subscribe to our e-mail updates so you'll know when new stories are posted. "

About the story

The inspirations for "Magical Whistleblower Tells All" are worn on its sleeve, from Harry Potter to Buffy to the many other secret magical world stories. I love many of these, though I've always found the reasoning to keep magic or monsters or technology a secret lacking. Often, I feel, the secrecy is meant to allow the suspension of disbelief, that this world could exist in reality (much like the many of us eagerly awaiting Hogwarts invitations).

This story challenges the premise that keeping power secret is somehow a good thing. I aimed to develop reasoning for the secrecy, giving a different point of view to this common trope, and then unmask it for all harm it does, ideally for the purpose of relating it to our real world restrictions – income inequality, patented drugs, DRMed information – all ways useful tools are restricted from many who would value them.

A question for the author

Q: Where do you write?

A: I write in my home office, which is part of a finished basement, where I'm surrounded by shelves of my 2,000+ action figures. These serve as both inspiration and distraction.

Depending on my mood, I'll write at my desktop, which is better for long drafting and research (multiple screens, again, both helpful and harmful), or on my laptop on my recliner, which lets me focus just on the text (better for editing) or napping.

I find myself the most productive late at night. I can spend the whole day "working," yet the hours between 11pm – 1am will be more productive than the many hours worked before.

About the author

Michael Sherrin developed his preference for fiction when he learned reality didn't include a real Spider-Man. He has an MBA from the Kellogg School of Management, where he learned to write riveting Excel formulas, though the solutions were often predictable. By day, he works with complex analytical algorithms, and by night he works on short stories and his novel. Michael lives outside Boston with his husband, dog, and several thousand action figures.

www.prodigeek.com, @prodigeek

Choice

Tomas Marcantonio

The giant apartment complex was unfinished, like almost everything else in Pyongyang. It loomed over the city, a grey, oval-shaped mass rising like a fungal growth on the bank of the Taedong River, swarming with half-lived lives. The western side was wall-less, held together with sagging electrical wires and iron bones stripped of their skin. Multitudes of drones hovered outside windows, transporting deliveries or simply spying, like mechanical wasps searching for a nectar that no longer existed.

The air inside the elevator was thick and sour, with a pervading stench of rotten eggs. A dead rat lay in one corner, the toes of its pink feet bent pathetically into its body. Sora couldn't drag her eyes from it as they ascended, the elevator shuddering and groaning at intervals.

"I hate this city," Gyuri said, digging her hands into the pockets of her trench coat. "Reunification was the worst thing that could've happened to this damn country." She looked to her superior. "I keep forgetting. You voted for it, didn't you?"

Sora kept her eyes on the dead creature next to Gyuri's foot. "We thought it was the most humane thing to do," she said carefully. They were passing the eightieth floor and she felt the pressure building in her ears; she swallowed to equalise it.

"Yeah, well maybe sometimes it's best just to cut the dead weight loose. Imagine how the south would look now if we hadn't blown our money on this wasteland."

Sora said nothing. Gyuri was too young to remember how it was; she never saw the horrors that came with the first nuclear missiles. The war was over as soon as it had begun.

When the doors jerked open on the hundred and twelfth floor, Gyuri used her foot to drag the rat corpse into the dark corridor.

"Now we won't have to look at it on the way down," she said, rolling it onto its back.

The corridor was low-ceilinged and narrow, flanked by steel apartment doors. Black bags of waste were courted by swarms of flies, and a communal bathroom leaked yellow light and a fetid smell. Sora led the way, stopping at the final door on the right.

"This one," she said.

Gyuri checked the engraved number and knocked. A moment later the door opened inwards just a fraction, enough to reveal a suspicious eye and a silver chain. A TV was blaring behind it.

"What do you want?"

Sora flashed her badge. "Yoo Sora," she said, "Seoul National Detective Agency. This is my partner, Kwon Gyuri. We're looking for Jeong Hoon."

"That's me."

"In that case we'd like to speak to you."

The eye blinked twice quickly. The door closed and the women heard the scratching sound of the latch being removed. When the door opened again, Jeong Hoon stood back to let them inside.

The room was little more than a shoebox. The walls were grey concrete, decorated only by blotches of blood forming purple halos around the flattened, mangled bodies of mosquitoes. A mattress was folded in one corner, a pile of clothes strewn on top. An ancient Samsung TV took up a quarter of the room. Jeong Hoon shoved his clothes to one side and sat cross-legged on the mattress, gesturing for the women to take seats on the lino floor.

Sora tried not to inhale through her nose; the window was closed, and Sora guessed from the intense smell of body odour that it had been closed for a long time.

"Would you mind turning the TV off?"

Hoon furrowed his brows briefly before reaching for the bulky remote at his side. He pointed it at the screen, pausing with his finger over the power button. A man in a white coat was describing the benefits of a new respirator; a map behind him showed a yellow cloud moving from the great landmass of China to the Korean peninsula. Hoon turned off the TV and a sudden, heavy silence filled the room.

"What's this about?" Hoon asked.

The window allowed a shaft of dusk light to fall across his coarse-looking crew cut. He had a wide nose and a prominent forehead, and one of his ears stuck out more than the other.

"Have you ever heard of a Seoul-based company from the 2030s that went by the name of Choice?" Sora asked.

Hoon shook his head.

"Choice was one of several private companies that performed surgical abortions in the thirties and forties," Sora went on. "However, the staff of Choice didn't believe in abortions at all; in fact, they were staunchly pro-life."

Hoon watched her without expression.

"In the years following reunification, birth rates on the peninsula were lower than ever, and one of Choice's goals was to find a solution to the rapidly ageing population of the New Republic. They were sponsored by certain high-ranking officials to use artificial wombs to keep aborted foetuses alive, all without the mother's knowledge. Once the babies reached the end of their gestation period, they were taken to orphanages and eventually fostered around the country, often to families here in the north, where birth rates were lowest."

Hoon scratched behind his ear. Gyuri watched him intently, drumming her fingers lightly on the floor.

"Of course," Sora said, "once these activities were exposed years later, Choice was shut down and everyone involved was arrested, with many facing lengthy prison sentences."

Hoon shrugged. "And what does all that have to do with me?"

Sora tucked her bob behind her ears and glanced at her partner.

"How was your relationship with Mr. and Mrs. Jeong?" Gyuri asked. "The people who brought you up?"

It was the first time the younger woman had spoken and Hoon's eyes lingered on her silky black hair, then on her pale, youthful face. It was a face that could have been pretty, the men in the office often reminded her, if it hadn't worn a perpetually disgruntled expression.

Hoon shrugged again. "They were just parents. They left me enough money to get by after they died."

"They weren't your real parents, Hoon, that's what we're trying to tell you."

Sora winced inwardly, but was grateful for her partner's candor.

"So what?" Hoon said, fingering the lobe of his protruding ear, "You're telling me I was one of these aborted babies? I was born in a lab?"

Sora nodded slowly. "At fifteen weeks you were transferred to a sophisticated artificial womb, where you were provided with the necessary nutrients and conditions to keep you alive."

Hoon pulled himself slowly to his feet and turned to the window. Sora and Gyuri exchanged a glance behind his back.

Gyuri reached questioningly for the stun gun on her belt, but Sora shook her head.

"So are you hooking me up with my real parents or something?" Hoon asked, turning around. "Is that what this is?"

"You saw our badges, Hoon," Gyuri said. "We're not some charity. Setting you up for a reunion isn't our priority."

Hoon fixed the young woman with a penetrating stare. "Then what *is* your priority?"

Sora raised a hand to quiet her partner. "The aborted babies," she began falteringly. "At first they appeared to show no signs of ill-adjustment. At a young age they were often quieter, more detached, but that's not uncommon in adopted children anyway. However, recent studies have revealed changes, usually when the subjects reach their mid-to-late teens. On average, subjects of the Choice births show significantly lower levels of empathy than natural-born people of the same age. They are also far more likely to commit crimes — violent crimes." Sora watched for the boy's reaction. "You've had a few run-ins with the law, haven't you, Hoon?"

"I've never killed anyone."

"No, we know you haven't," Sora said.

"You might be a danger to society," Gyuri cut in. Sora closed her eyes and pinched the bridge of her nose. "That's what we're trying to tell you, all right? Sooner or later all the subjects start going off the rails, and we're going to put you somewhere safe and run some tests until we're sure you're not going to go the same way. Got it?"

Sora took a deep breath. "We believe these aspects of your personality may have been due to the supplements you were given in the artificial womb."

"Yeah," Gyuri said, "and the fact that you spent more than half your gestation period inside a fish tank instead of the body of a loving mother."

For a moment Hoon said nothing. He stared at Gyuri before turning back to the window.

"Gyuri," Sora said. "Would you mind waiting outside?"

Gyuri muttered something as she stood and exited, closing the door forcibly behind her.

For a moment Sora sat in silence, watching the back of Hoon's head.

"Are they still alive?" he asked.

"Who?"

"My parents. My real parents. Are they still alive?"

Sora peered at the flexible display strapped to her forearm. She swiped through the case files and skimmed the brief on Hoon's parents. "Your mother is alive, yes. In Pyongyang, as it happens. According to the documents she signed at the time of the abortion, she didn't know the identity of your father. She cited the reason for the abortion as—"

"Can I see her?"

"Our job is to take you directly to the institution in Seoul for tests," Sora said. "It's a safe environm—"

"I just want to see her once," Hoon said, and for the first time Sora heard a note of anxiety in his voice. "Once, before I go. Please. I want to see my mother."

Sora looked searchingly into the young man's eyes. None of the subjects had shown such interest in their birth parents before. Perhaps, she thought, glancing over her shoulder at the door, this was the subject she had been waiting for all these months.

"The chief is going to be pissed if he finds out," Gyuri said.

"Then he won't find out," Sora said.

The Taedong Ferry chugged south-westerly through the city. The river was clogged with rusted tankers and smaller fishing boats cushioned between islands of floating garbage. Shanty houses clung to the riverbanks like layers of plaque on rotten teeth. They were mostly empty now; millions had fled to Seoul after the treaty and now Pyongyang festered, half in squalor, half forgotten.

"It won't take long," Sora said, absently scanning the deserted hovels.

Gyuri pulled her dust mask down over her chin and lit up a cigarette, blowing a cloud of smoke into the misty evening air. "You always want to give them a chance," she said, inspecting the cigarette between her fingers. "Like one of them's going to turn up with a dumb smile and tell you it's all a mistake, that there's nothing wrong with them."

Sora stared across deck at Hoon, sat on a bench out of earshot, his shoulders hunched.

"They're bad eggs, boss," Gyuri went on. "You can see it just looking at them. The only surprise is how long it took for the gov to give us the green light to round them all up."

Sora turned back to the water, leaning on the railings.

"You don't believe in it, do you?" Gyuri asked. "Abortion."

Sora sighed. "There are only two outcomes of an unwanted pregnancy, and they're both as tragic as each other. The only thing that matters is that the mother makes the decision. That's why Choice was so deplorable; they stole that right from those women.

"When you look into their eyes, Gyuri," she added, "don't you see the tragedy of it all? Their mothers never meant for them to be born. They were so close to never existing. The way Hoon looked when he asked about his mother. I don't know, maybe they don't all have to turn out like we expect. Maybe there's hope for them."

Gyuri dropped her cigarette to the floor and crushed it under her shoe.

"Still," she said, replacing her dust mask, "you'll be in deep shit if they find out. The mother knows we're on the way?"

"She's one of the minority; most of them didn't want to know when the news broke. Imagine finding out that the child you aborted had lived on."

Gyuri shrugged and brushed her hair behind one ear as the ferry approached the city centre. Skyscrapers pierced the sky around the crumbling remains of Juche Tower, some crowned with redundant cranes, others dotted with amber windows, the refuge of after-hours office workers desperately shackling themselves to their jobs. The network of back-alleys behind the dock bustled with street food smoke and the sorry exhausts of ancient scooters.

"Let's get this done quick, then," Gyuri said. "Before we're both out of a job."

The boarding house was in a dilapidated building above a rowdy bar that served home-brewed makgeolli and greasy pajeon. Sora led the way through the wood-paneled bar, stepping carefully past a red-faced man on the stairs, bald, wrinkled, and weeping quietly. Hoon's mother's room was at the end of the third-floor corridor, and she opened the door almost as soon as Sora's knuckles were done rapping on it. She was close to Sora's age, somewhere in her mid-thirties, though she looked older. Short and slight, she had a careworn, mousey expression and stringy hair that looked as though it hadn't been washed in days.

"Ms. Han," Sora said, flashing her badge. "Yoo Sora, we spoke on the phone."

Hoon's mother opened the door wider. "Is he here?"

"He is," Sora said, stepping aside to let Hoon through.

There was no great embrace as Hoon met his mother for the first time. Her eyes filled instantly with tears but she struggled to look directly at her son; she squinted and inclined her head slightly, as though he were an especially bright light. Sora and Gyuri followed them inside the modest room, uncluttered and half-clean.

"We can only give you five minutes," Sora said. "This is quite against regulations."

Hoon's mother nodded meekly, wringing her hands. She showed Sora and Gyuri onto the veranda and closed the door behind them. Sora pulled up her dust mask while the younger woman lit a cigarette.

"I don't want to hear it," Sora said.

"Whatever you say, boss. I just want to get this done and get back to Seoul. Who are we after next, anyway?"

Sora swiped at the monitor on her forearm and scanned the assignments folder.

"Well, who is it?"

Sora shook her head. She had known this day would come eventually, that she wouldn't be able to protect her partner forever.

"What's wrong? We're not in Pyongyang again, are we?"

"The system's down," Sora said, swiping the screen off. "I'll check again later."

Sora felt Gyuri's gaze on her as she regarded the smoky, blinking neon parade of Pyongyang's backstreets. A stray dog with three legs stopped outside the back door of the bar to piss on a pile of black sacks. Gyuri's eyes didn't leave Sora's face, and the stare seemed to gain in intensity with each passing second, like a branding iron being held to her cheek.

"Maybe we should give them a couple more minutes," Sora said, nodding over her shoulder.

Her partner, ignoring her, flicked her cigarette over the railing and pushed the door open into the apartment. Gyuri froze in the doorway, and Sora had to push her aside to see within.

Hoon was on his knees on the floor, his mother's head cradled in his hands, her hair between his fingers.

"Hoon," Sora whispered, "what have you done?"

Hoon dropped his mother's head to the floor, her body limp, her neck clearly broken.

"Eighteen years ago she tried to kill me," he said, his voice empty of emotion. "Now we're even."

He stood, wiping the palms of his hands against his legs. "I'm ready to go to the institution now," he said, holding his hands out before him.

Gyuri returned to the veranda to call headquarters. Sora found a bed sheet and spread it over the body of Hoon's mother. Hoon was sat next to her body, his hands cuffed and his legs crossed beneath him.

Sora knew she would lose her badge. She might even face manslaughter charges for gross negligence. It hardly mattered. She'd always known it would come to this, ever since she located Gyuri and recruited her.

"She doesn't know, does she?" Hoon said, looking up at her morosely.

"Who?" Sora asked.

"Your partner. How old is she?"

Sora stared down at the boy. "Eighteen, the same as you."

"You must have been young."

Sora said nothing. Hoon nodded.

"I'm guessing your bosses don't know about her, either."

Sora shook her head.

"You don't want her to turn out like me. I get it. But what if she doesn't? What if she lives a normal life? Are you going to tell her? That you had her aborted?"

"I never imagined—" Sora began, but the words caught in her throat. "I thought you might be the one to change everything. That if you showed forgiveness, empathy, then Gyuri..."

The smile that formed on Hoon's lips was almost sinister in its simplicity.

"If it's really like you said, they'll take it into account, won't they? When they sentence me. The supplements you mentioned, the gestation tanks. That's the reason, isn't it, for everything in here?" He tapped his temple with a finger. "I mean, it's not me. It wasn't my choice."

Sora considered him. No, it wasn't his choice. It wasn't his mother's choice, either.

Hoon gazed at his cuffed hands, his palms open, as though trying to measure something. "Fifteen weeks," he said, almost to himself. "Is there a heartbeat at fifteen weeks?"

Sora stared at the space between his hands and nodded.

Gyuri re-entered the room. "They'll be here in ten." Kneeling, she pulled the sheet down and looked into the dead woman's face. "I wonder what she felt after they took the baby from her. I wonder if she ever regretted it."

"What does it matter?" Hoon said in his expressionless voice.

"She regretted it," Sora said, her voice shaking. "But what would you have done? Maybe she was poor, maybe she was too young. Maybe... maybe the father was a faceless man who forced himself on her. What would you have done, Gyuri, if it were you?"

Gyuri glanced at Hoon. He returned her gaze with his flat, impassive stare.

Gyuri rubbed her face and closed her eyes for what seemed like hours. When they opened, Sora expected to see tears gathered on her lashes, but there were none.

Gyuri stood gingerly, her eyes fixed on the face of Hoon's dead mother. She advanced slowly on Sora, who was blinking away tears, her hand hovering close to her belt.

"See Tomas Marcantonio's story "Choice" online at Metaphorosis.
If you liked it, leave a comment. Authors love that!
Remember to subscribe to our e-mail updates so you'll know when
new stories are posted."

About the story

The main concept of this story, that aborted foetuses have been given life without their mother's knowledge, is both terrifying and harrowing. In fact, I almost abandoned the idea after early drafts. Abortion is a complicated and sensitive topic, and it needs to be treated as such. I disliked Philip K. Dick's controversial story on the same topic, 'The Pre-persons', and was wary of producing something equally insensitive.

What made me persist with the piece was the ongoing debates about abortion laws in certain parts of the world. 'Choice' is an uncomfortable narrative, but it's also a pro-choice piece. Essentially, this story is an allegory for the injustice of a mother's choice being taken out of her hands. Although 'Choice' features complex characters, the only real villain in the piece is the company that took the choice away from the mothers.

The bleakness of this narrative is reflected in the setting: a half-abandoned Pyongyang in a reunified Korea. The unsettling atmosphere of this dystopian city is an eerie backdrop to such disturbing events. Much of my writing is inspired by the Korean peninsula, where I have lived for several years. The ever-complex relationship with the North, combined with the ongoing concerns about a rapidly ageing population, provide endless inspiration for speculative fiction.

The population issue comes into play here as an incentive for the abortion company to deceive families. The main characters' attitudes towards Korean reunification, meanwhile, provide telling insights into their personalities, which come to the fore at the story's climax.

A question for the author

Q: What's better: writing or having written?

A: Both are wonderful in their own ways. The writing process itself can be frustrating when things aren't flowing as you'd like, but the satisfaction after a successful writing session is hard to match.

About the author

Tomas Marcantonio is a fiction and travel writer from Brighton, England. His work has appeared in places such as STORGY, Twist in Time, and Lucent Dreaming. Tomas is currently based in Busan, South Korea, where he splits his time between writing, teaching, and getting lost in neon-lit backstreets.

@TJMarcantonio

Bedwyr by the Sea

C.B. Blakey

As the sun set over the sea, an old man built a sandcastle. His old green anorak sagged around him, patched and salt stained from years spent on the coastline. The sun glinted from the waves, so bright it was almost blinding. Eyes closed tight against the glare, his hands moved over the sand, pressing the crenellations into shape one at a time.

"Avalon," he whispered, feeling the sand firm beneath his fingers as he did so; the surface buzzing with static. "Avalon, Avalon, Avalon."

He worked slowly, trying to ignore the pain in his fingers and the nagging fear in the back of his mind. How many times had he done this in the last few years? It had only been once or twice a decade at first; now it seemed that barely a month passed that didn't find him kneeling on the sand, pressing the walls into shape beneath the waxing moon.

"How are you doing that, Mr. Bedwyr?" The old man flinched, letting out a gasp of dismay as the turret he was working on crumbled beneath his fingers.

"Oh, I'm sorry," said the voice. "Did I ruin it?"

"It's alright," Bedwyr rasped, praying that he spoke the truth. He scooped up more sand and hurried to repair the turret, his heart drumming deep in his chest as he fought to control the rising panic. His hands moved as swiftly as his swollen joints would allow, shaping and reshaping until all trace of the damage was gone.

Finally, he smoothed away the last imperfection and turned to peer out from beneath heavy lids. Standing a few steps away was a young girl, bundled against the chill autumn wind. Polka-dot Wellington boots sprouted from beneath a blue woollen overcoat that covered her from neck to knee. Only her head was visible, a ruddy-cheeked ball submerged in brown curls.

"Is it ok now?" Her voice was small and muffled by the coat. Bedwyr dragged the lake of his memory until a name emerged. Ivy, Ivy Winters. Looking past the girl, he recognised her parents further up the beach; a woman hurling a stick for a grey-muzzled springer spaniel while a man held a toddler's hands to steady him as he walked. Recalling his manners, he forced a smile.

"Yes, at least, I hope so," Bedwyr replied. "What were you asking?"

"I just wanted to know how you were doing that. I mean, you did have your eyes shut..."

"It's not so hard." In spite of his weariness, Bedwyr felt a surge of pride as he spread his hands out before him. "My hands know their work."

"What do you mean?" The girl frowned up at him. "I think you're cheating."

"Not at all," said Bedwyr, raising an eyebrow. "I have made this castle many times."

"I bet you haven't," said Ivy, gesturing towards the tide line with a sleeve that probably had a hand in it somewhere. "The sand's all flat here. Do you know why that is?" Her tone was deadly serious, so serious that Bedwyr found himself amused in spite of his irritation at being interrupted.

"I'm afraid I don't," replied Bedwyr, his voice shaking as he fought to suppress a chuckle.

"I do," she proclaimed. "It's 'cause the tide comes all the way up here. It'll wash your castle away easy. If you'd made it before, you'd know that." Her point made, she tried to cross her arms but had to settle for tucking one sleeve under the other.

"Is that so?" Bedwyr replied. "Maybe that's *why* I've made it so many times."

"Well that's just silly, why not make it by the path?"

"Because young lady, there are others who need it." The old man stared out over the water, squinting against the daylight. If he looked close enough, if the light struck the waves just so, he could see the crumbling walls.

"Fish don't need castles," said Ivy between giggles.

"Oh, I don't know about that," replied the old man, his face creasing into a smile. "You see them in pet shops all the time. That's by the by. I'm not making this for them." He ran a finger along the base of the wall. "This castle needs to be fit for a king," he whispered, more to himself than to anyone else, the tiredness creeping into his voice. "This one I make for Arthur."

"Arthur? You mean, like... King Arthur? The one with Merlin and the sword in the stone?"

"The very same." Bedwyr straightened up and eased himself back until he was able to sit with his legs stretched out. He looked out over the waves, breathing the sea air. "When I close my eyes, I can still see them. The boat was almost too small for them, if you can believe that. They had to crowd in like sardines."

"Is that why you're still here?" Ivy's question was innocent enough, but a shadow passed over Bedwyr's face.

"Someone has to keep the watch," he whispered. "Someone has to hold the route open." He rubbed his hands together, brushing damp sand from the calluses, then peered up at the sky. "There it is. You can't quite see it yet, but it's there. You know the moon's larger than normal tonight?"

"Mum says it's a special time," replied Ivy, a grin spreading over her face. "She told me this morning. She said it makes the wall between the worlds go thin, then dad made a joke about plastering and she got angry."

"Nothing funny about plastering," Bedwyr grunted. "She's not wrong about the moon either. This is a good night to build the castle."

"Where's the drawbridge?" Ivy was regarding the castle with a cat-like intensity. Bedwyr blinked.

"Drawbridge?"

"Castles have drawbridges," Ivy insisted. "If it doesn't have a drawbridge then it's not a real castle."

"This castle doesn't," replied Bedwyr, slightly sharper than he'd intended. He took a breath to calm himself. He was a knight performing a sacred task; he was not about to sully that by having a blazing row with a child. "This castle doesn't have a drawbridge, and I'm not about to add one. It has to be made the same way every time."

"Why?" Ivy's face radiated innocence, but something in her tone suggested that this question was a well-honed weapon indeed. "I mean," she continued. "If you always make the same castle, how do you know you're doing it right?"

"I just... you see..." Bedwyr paused, trying to find the words to convey the sense of rightness when he completed the castle, that this was something that you felt rather than knew. The words wouldn't come. Worse still, he could find no certainty that he was right; only the cruel edge of doubt that had shaded his thoughts over the past year. Bedwyr pushed it away; he was a knight, a warrior. He might be dressed in an anorak these days but some armour you never take off. He swallowed, steadying himself.

"That's… just the way it is." The words felt hollow even as he said them.

"I'd want a drawbridge if I were the king."

"Well, we both know that isn't the case." Bedwyr regretted the words immediately, but Ivy didn't seem fazed by them.

"That's just boring," she mumbled.

"Boring has nothing to do with it," Bedwyr snapped, fighting to control his outrage even though he knew how ridiculous he must look. Worse, the words had struck a nerve. *Not boredom*, whispered a voice in his mind. *Fear.*

Bedwyr's hands balled into fists as the old memory surged into his mind. Once again, he remembered the sand caking under his nails as he traced new heraldry on the castle gate. Once again, he remembered the tide of panic that had engulfed him; the wave of fear that swept away the pleasure he took in his art. Try as he might, he couldn't recall the details of the decoration he had tried to add to the gate all those years ago; only the jagged hillocks of wet sand that remained after he had torn his ill-considered artwork apart. How close had he come to disaster that day? If he had let his changes stand, would the enchantment have been broken? Would his folly have condemned his comrades to death?

Maybe, whispered the voice again. *Maybe not. You don't know what would have happened. And if it had failed, if it had brought it all crashing down, at least that would have been an end to it.*

Bedwyr shook himself, relaxing his jaw. *This is foolishness*, he reminded himself. *Nothing happened. You fixed it in time. You made it right.* Besides, it had happened centuries ago, long before his skin wrinkled and his back ached. He looked down at his hands, scarred and swollen, remembering how they had itched to make something new, long before it hurt to move them. *Is this punishment*, he wondered? Had his desire to change the castle caused him to age so that he would be forced to carry out his duty with hands that barely obeyed him? He took a deep breath and pushed the thoughts away. If that was true, there was no changing it.

Abruptly, he realised that he had been silent for a long time and Ivy was staring at him. He unclenched his hands and gave what he hoped was a reassuring smile.

"This is my duty," he explained, his voice calm once more. "The final task laid upon me by my wounded king."

"Arthur got hurt?" The girl sounded more annoyed than shocked. "They didn't put that in the film."

"Well that's films for you," Bedwyr muttered, glad of the change of subject. "You don't always get the full story." The girl was quiet for a moment, staring down at her feet as she scraped her heel through the sand. When she replied, her voice was quiet.

"Will he get better?"

"Oh yes." Bedwyr offered her a smile. "He has to come back, you see. One day when Britain is in peril, Arthur will return to save us."

"But, won't that be dangerous? There's bombs and fighter jets now, he'll get blown up."

"Arthur will find a way, he must. It is the way of things."

"Does he have a dragon? A dragon could protect him from the fighter jets." Ivy was animated now, looking about wildly until her gaze settled on a stick about the length of her arm. She hurried over to it, pushed her hand free of her cuff and picked it up. Brandishing it like a wand, she leaned over and began to carve deep scratches into the sand in front of the castle.

Bedwyr was dumbstruck; he opened his mouth but no sound came out. Every instinct told him to reach over and seize the stick, that he had to put a stop to this immediately, but he couldn't move. *You want to see it*, whispered a traitorous thought. *You want to see what she makes.*

Paralysed by indecision, he watched as the dragon took shape before him. It lay before the gate, thick-limbed and long-necked with vast wings arching overhead; as long as the fortress was wide. Ivy straightened up and stared down at her handiwork, then leaned over and added a few small circles rising from the dragon's nose.

"What are..." Bedwyr's voice failed him. The panic he had anticipated was absent, leaving him feeling numb and hollow. He coughed and made to ask again. She answered before he could speak.

"Bubbles." The impish grin flashed from beneath the cloud of hair. "It won't be breathing fire underwater."

"I see." Bedwyr swallowed, sensing that he could no more stop this than he could the rising tide. "What colour dragon is he? Is he red or white?"

"She's purple." The grin spread wider.

"That's... unusual." He replied, his voice hoarse.

"Or course she is, she's a dragon."

"Ivy!" Her mother's voice cut through the conversation. "What have I told you about bothering people."

"Sorry, Mum." Ivy seemed to deflate, the stick drooping. Her mother, Bedwyr thought her name was Alice, hurried over and crouched in front of her daughter.

"We don't interrupt people when they're busy, do we?" Alice's voice was quiet, but firm.

"No, Mum," Ivy mumbled to her feet.

"That's right. Now what do we say?" Ivy was quiet for a moment before shuffling over to Bedwyr.

"Sorry, Mr. Bedwyr."

"That's quite alright, young lady." He raised his eyes to her mother and smiled. Alice seemed to relax a little, then let out an exasperated sigh when she saw her dog returning with what appeared to be a small tree clamped in its jaws.

"That's not your stick, is it, Cobb?" Cobb didn't acknowledge his mistress' voice, though the end of his tail wagged as he lay down to gnaw his latest acquisition. Alice tried waving another, smaller stick under the dog's nose. Cobb showed little interest, focusing all his attention on the branch; his eyes full of the fierce joy known only to dogs and drunkards.

Bedwyr watched them warily. It wouldn't take much; one fleeting moment of interest and the dog might decide to inspect the castle. He had encountered set-backs before; this wouldn't be the first time his handiwork had been demolished by an over-friendly hound. Only last year, a cocker spaniel had flattened half the walls and would have added a moat if the dog's owner hadn't intervened. He couldn't afford that today. The hour was late, too late to rebuild, and as he reached his hand towards the dragon, he could feel the crackle of static. For better, for worse, it was done. The dragon was part of the castle.

Slowly, Alice coaxed the dog free of his prize and led him back down the beach. Ivy followed her mother, the empty cuff of her coat sleeve flapping as she waved goodbye. Bedwyr smiled as he waved back, feeling the tension ease from his shoulders as they disappeared from view.

He turned back to the sand-castle, taking in the unadorned battlements and the sinuous wyrm coiled before the gate. Something was missing. The dragon did not seem of a piece with the fortress, and Bedwyr sensed that to leave things that way would spell disaster. A large part of him still wanted to reach out and obliterate it, to try and salvage what was left of his castle, but it was too late. Bedwyr stared down at the castle for a long moment, then his face broke into a grim smile. It was simple now. When all routes of escape are gone, the only path left is forward.

Grunting as his joints protested, he rose to his feet and moved along the shoreline where a thin ridge of shells met the encroaching tide. He walked slowly, eyes fixed on the ground, stooping again and again until his pockets bulged with shells and pebbles. His hunt complete, he turned and strode back to the sand-castle.

The tide was close now; there was barely time to complete his task. Heart pounding in his chest, he dropped to his knees beside the dragon. With shell and stone and wet sand, he anointed the walls and the wyrm that lay before them, binding them together till they seemed kin to one another. As he laid the final shell, a glittering shard that brought life to the dragon's eye, the sea reached the castle.

Bedwyr pushed himself away; his heels digging great divots in the wet sand. The water swept past the castle to pool around him, soaking his shoes and trousers. The sand around the dragon was pushed aside, the limbs, tail and wings rising and growing ever more life-like. The castle stood firm as the water receded, then the second wave came. Taller than the first and rose-tinted by the setting sun, it swamped the castle and its guardian. Sand sloughed away from the walls, billowing outwards in a great cloud to reveal glittering stone walls. The dragon writhed, tearing its head free of the sand. For a moment, Bedwyr found himself staring into a pair of eyes as old as the sea. Then the vision was gone. Fortress and dragon blurred together, then vanished as the water retreated, wiping out all trace of walls, turrets and dragon.

Bedwyr rolled onto his knees, then pushed himself to his feet, fingers sinking into the sand. He trudged up the beach till he was beyond the reach of the tide, then slumped on a mound of grass by the path to look out over the sea. As the sun sank below the horizon, a great band of gold appeared, reaching all the way to the beach.

Far below, Avalon slumbered, the great walls glittering in the light of the sun. Looking closer, Bedwyr could see that the walls had changed, now adorned with huge shell-like carvings and precious stones. A huge dragon lay curled before the gates, bubbles rising from its nostrils. Slowly, the golden band broke apart into individual patches of light and the vision of Avalon vanished. Bedwyr sighed, the weight of his isolation returning as the sea became opaque once more.

He closed his eyes, his head swimming, trying to grasp the enormity of what had transpired. He had built the same castle for centuries, duty and pride becoming tradition with the passage of time. It was as much a part of him as his hands or face, and yet he had allowed it to be changed on a child's whim. He kneaded his forehead, feeling a few stray grains of sand grate against his skin as his fingers probed his temples. It was then that he realised that the pain in his hands was gone.

He folded his hands together, bending and flexing his fingers, marvelling at how easily they moved. Rising to his feet, he took a few steps towards the waves, testing the movement in his knees and back. His joints moved easily. For the first time in over a century the simple act of walking was painless. As the tide retreated, it revealed a hollow in the sand where the castle had been, now filled with sea water. Cautiously, Bedwyr approached the hollow and stared down into a face he hadn't seen for a long time.

His cheeks were smooth, his eyes clear. Unbidden, Ivy's words floated through his mind. *If you always make the same castle, how do you know you're doing it right?* In a sudden flash of insight, he knew that it would be many years before he would feel the need to return and build the castle anew.

Picking up a flat pebble, he straightened up and watched the tide rolling in, savouring the feel of the stone as he rolled it between his fingers. He raised his arm and whipped it forward, sending the pebble skipping out over the surface of the water. His cheeks began to ache and he realised he was grinning. The new sense of freedom was so potent he felt almost dizzy, yet beneath it there was an odd sense of loss. Some part of him insisted that the castle he had built for so many years was gone forever.

No, the thought was a whisper, *not gone, just different.* The castle might have changed, but its walls were the same hard stone, its purpose just as important. Bedwyr turned his back on the sunset and walked up the beach to the path, his mind full of possibilities. He could go travelling, see the world as he had before. Better to go sooner rather than later, before people started asking questions. It was unlikely anyone would recognise him as old Mr. Bedwyr, but it wouldn't hurt to be careful. For a moment, he wondered how long it would be before he would have to return. Then he shook his head; chiding himself. He would know when the time came.

Looking back over his shoulder, Bedwyr watched as the last light of the sun gilded the tops of the waves. Far overhead, a solitary gull cried out, the sound sharp against the hiss of water on sand. Bedwyr closed his eyes, listening. As the cry echoed amongst the clouds, he could almost believe it was a horn calling him home.

"See C.B. Blakey's story "Bedwyr by the Sea" online at Metaphorosis.

If you liked it, leave a comment. Authors love that!
Remember to subscribe to our e-mail updates so you'll know when
new stories are posted."

About the story

"Bedwyr by the Sea" was partially inspired by a documentary (I forget which one) that speculated that the lost city of Avalon was a coastal city that has since been swallowed by the sea. The Arthurian legends have changed so much over the centuries that in many ways they are a fine example of stories that have evolved and thus remain relevant to modern audiences. I wanted to bring those two things together. Also, who can honestly say they don't appreciate a good sand-castle.

A question for the author

Q: Why do you write speculative rather than realistic fiction?

A: My love of speculative fiction is a disease that struck in childhood. When I was 7, my parents gave me a book of Greek and Norse myths and another of Arthurian tales. Ever since then I've devoured every fantasy novel I can get my hands on. When I started writing my own stories back in 2014, there was never a chance that I would choose a different genre. I love the freedom that speculative fiction provides, both as a writer and as a reader. Beyond the constraints of our own world, we can do anything.

About the author

A mythology nut and whisky enthusiast, C. B. Blakey lives in England with his wife, his daughter, and enough books to build a small fort. He writes fantasy and light horror short stories and will be starting a novel once he figures out how fit a few extra hours into the day.

Sonata I: Sona

L. Chan

Andante: Sona

Siege drums struck the town just before daybreak – whaleskin stretched over hollowed out tree trunks, varnished and polished until the drum bodies were darker than a moonless night. War Music was the province of the Empire military, and was not often employed by the Periphery patrols. Early morning mist clung to the ground, warping and distorting as the waves of force sped from the siege drums, propagating through the Sound and smashing into the town walls. Periphery grass was stiff, tough as wire, sharp enough to break the skin, same as the folk that lived on the Periphery. Unyielding, it shivered as if unsettled by a storm, though the still air held nothing more than music.

Sona didn't have to fight, but was up early to watch. Watching Sound in action reminded Sona of lazy evenings back at the academy, Sona watching others with more talent at instruments practicing. The Periphery was a great distance from the regional imperial academy where Sona had schooled, finishing as one of the top students in numbers. Accounting was hardly his calling, but his services were valuable to Grimheld and his band, and allowed Sona to tag along as the band made its way up the Periphery highway. The patrols were ostensibly aligned with the Empire, but far from the centre, the line between bandit and enforcer was faint, varying as capriciously as the weather.

Grimheld's band held a selection of siege drums, some trumpets, and a single bruised violin; barely a street corner ensemble back in the Capital. Out here, Grimheld fancied himself a Conductor, even if his motley assortment could manage nothing more than sections and movements from the Symphony of War. None of the great war machines, with their giant gears and pulleys operated by Sound. No air navy, with flyers held aloft by hot air and pushed upwind by huge propellers dancing to war music. Nevertheless, even a little war music put Grimheld and his men a cut above anyone else in this stretch of the Periphery. That and a little old-fashioned brawling was all they needed. Banditry in the Periphery worked similar to the collection of tolls or taxes. Some roughnecks held roads, preying on travellers. Others, like Grimheld, controlled swathes of territory, bleeding the inhabitants slowly.

The town's fortifications were ramshackle, guarding against the predations of normal bandits and thieves. Calling them walls would be generous; they were certainly not proofed against war music. As the drums played, vibrations travelled through the walls, sending ripples across stones larger than the head of a man. The wall heaved and bucked, masonry moving like waves on the high seas. A man's scream crept between the notes of the musicians. Someone had gotten too curious about the music, looking over the edge of the wall and taking the express route to the ground fifteen feet below. The movement reached its peak. Sona knew the staccato push and pull of the piece set up sympathetic vibrations in stone, the solid mortar liquefying and running like sand in an hourglass. All it needed was the push at the crescendo of the piece.

The music surged, and the walls came tumbling down.

Steel ringfenced the townsfolk, more edges around the weak and old than around the fighters; Grimheld knew how to control a crowd. The battle had been surprisingly bloodless – just two casualties from the town, falling off the wall. A few of the townsmen had blooded their blades, putting up a spirited defence and giving the raiders the odd scratch. Nothing that stitching and wine couldn't cure. Sona finished tabulating the ledger for the nameless town (surely the town had a name, the least of things had a name, even if it barely merited the ink it took mark it out on a map). The band had done well, turning out the limited riches of the town onto the dirt; imperial coin, other currency from up north; tarnished silver, verdigris-crusted brass — probably dowries or festival gifts.

Enough to feed the Empire, when they sent their people up here to get the pickings from Grimheld. The Capital turned a blind eye to the excesses of bands like Grimheld's, as long as tax kept flowing. Thieves, Sona had discovered, were particular about fairness, and he took care to split the spoils evenly. The townfolk watched in silence as their belongings were catalogued and divvied up. Empire game, Empire rules. If you played by the rules, the Empire always won but nobody got hurt. If you didn't, the Empire still won and everybody got hurt.

The accounts were presented in a hidebound book; the cut of the paper was amateurish, the pages oddly sized. But it held together and it worked, much like Grimheld's men. The Conductor himself was a small man, wiry and bristly like the most resilient of terriers. Those who tried found him quick for his fifty years, accurate with both rapier and dagger and, despite his formal title, devoid of all but the most minuscule musical talent.

"So this is your last town with us," said Grimheld, licking a finger and running it down the column of tiny numbers. Sona nodded. This was for show; Grimheld was both illiterate and innumerate. The previous quartermaster had skimmed the spoils, his own personal tax. Grimheld had eventually found out and the band had gained a barely competent, one-handed cook. Sona became the new quartermaster, appointed despite being unable to speak since infanthood. So the young man dressed in the scarves and high collars of the Capital rose from part time instrument tuner to full time accountant.

Sona winced as Grimheld scored the rough paper with a facsimile of the characters that comprised his name, his signature never twice the same. "I have something for you, come." At the older man's gesture, Sona followed, leaving the ledger on the makeshift table wrangled from a hearth or kitchen, adjusting with wind numbed fingers the dirty scarf around his neck.

The Conductor brought Sona past the townsfolk to a set of six prisoners, wrists manacled. The six did not wear the braids of the Periphery, but instead covered their hair with silk headscarves. Though faded with distance from home, the six women still wore the sun of the Far Isles on their brown skin, and were dressed in rough travelling linen after Periphery fashion. Sona bit his lip. Slaves. Slavery was banned in the Empire Sound; apologists pointed to the Empire as offering a fairer rule for all men, but the truth was much more prosaic. Slave revolts were as messy as they were common, and paying servants was cheaper than paying soldiers. Far away from the capital, where swords far outnumbered slaves, principles were harder to come by.

"You've been honest with me, and that's a rare thing on the edge of the world. So you get to choose. Choose and keep, but just one, mind you. I'm not that generous," said Grimheld.

Five had fresh parchment skin, teenagers but with soldier's eyes hooded and perched atop dark pouches. Number six was past her middle years, with a strange focus to her gaze. Like the other five, she'd seen war and pain. But she'd come out of that shared experience hard. Hard and angry. Sona was going further north, up into harsh steppeland. A translator, if any of the six were so inclined, would be useful. He just had to find those that understood Fingerspeech.

Fingerspeech was common in the Capital. As many as two in five were fluent, and all who were at the sharp end of the Empire Sound spoke it; deafness was rife amongst those who dealt death through war music, common amongst the workmen that wove music into the industry that pulsed through the arterial roads, airways, and seaways. But Sona was climbing up the fringe of the Empire, far from the active fronts. Soldiers were rare, Imperial Common took on the throaty slur of the north, and Fingerspeech was barely to be found. Grimheld was off to the side, joking with the guards, something raucous and bawdy. Sona kept his hands low. It would not do him any favours for the mercenaries to see how Sona chose his payment.

Of the six, only the oldest blinked twice. Sona had found his translator.

A quartermaster had privileges, privacy being one. Sona's tent smelled of sweat, and of the animals that carried it up the Periphery roads, but it was his and his alone. In a crowded encampment, this was a luxury. In the middle of the room sat his travelling chest, a bespoke thing of inlaid mahogany and teak, bound within the guts of a brass multipede. The musical multipede was the centrepiece of the room. It served as workspace when fully expanded, but was now locked in the dismount position, its eight legs folded, double jointed like a beetle's, brass pistons and copper gears oiled and dormant.

We have some time to discuss the terms of our arrangement before they will expect noise, Sona said, continuing to converse in Fingerspeech.

What arrangement? Am I not a slave? she asked back. *We do not even have each other's names.*

The Empire has no slaves, said Sona. *You can call me Sona.*

Sona for Sound? Empire name, Empire lies. But not Empire skin, she said.

Half Empire. My mother was of the Six Named, he said over his shoulder, using one handed Fingerspeech, the tactical sort favoured by soldiers. The blood of the Six Named was strong, not easily watered down. His skin remembered the harsh sun of the Northern Steppes, his hair black and wavy. He wore Six Named blood on his face: his nose wide, forehead broad and eyes dark. But Sona did not hold himself like the horse-riders of the north, his posture stiffer and crisper than a dress uniform; a far cry from the soft slouches of his mother's people, bodies bent to absorb the constant footfalls of the shaggy beasts that carried them.

The woman shuffled in front of him, the chains of her restraints dragging like a tail. Sona pulled at his filthy scarf, showing the scars at his neck. *There's no need to get in front of me. I can hear just fine; these scars are all that is left of my voice. We have business to discuss*, he said.

"State your business, Sona of the Empire. Don't you even need my name?" the woman said, switching to Imperial Common, the tongue spoken through much of the Empire and its vassal states.

There's no need, I can't call your name. We are to go north, to the Nation of the Six Named. I have business there at the Festival of Names. You will speak for me, and you will be compensated for your time, he said, laying a stack of Imperial crowns on the edge of the multipede's gaping maw.

"And if I refuse?" she asked, voice low, hoarse. Sona went back to packing, kneeling in front of the multipede.

I cash out my last payment from Grimheld's band, you join your companions. They will sell them and you, and Grimheld has no hold on his men to keep them from sampling the merchandise, he said, not even looking up.

Sona managed to get one hand in front of his windpipe as the woman slipped her manacled wrists in front of his face. "What is to stop me from killing you in your sleep, or right now, Sona of the Empire? My time is worth more than a handful of crowns, and there is not enough money in the world to pay me to do Empire business."

There was no sound in the room, save the woman's heavy breathing as she pressed her knee into Sona's back, cutting off his air with her chained wrists. At least the guards wouldn't be suspicious at the sounds from his tent. Sona tipped his head back, exposing his neck, tempting the woman to double the pressure. There was a click as the manacle popped open, the iron bracelet barely clearing Sona's chin as the woman lost her footing and stumbled backwards.

If you will not take coin, then a blood debt instead, Sona said, holding up a slim key, with his free hand.

"I'm listening," she said. Sona tossed her the key, she snatched it out of the air with her free hand without looking.

First amongst the animals in bravery is the field rat, a creature that will feign death if caught. So strong are their wills that they will not flinch even if an animal takes a bite from their living flesh, all the while waiting for the right time to bolt. I need at least one of your companions to be that brave. All will die otherwise, he said to the unchained woman.

"The least of them is that brave. But why should I trust you?" she asked.

Because you have no choice.

"I am Shailani. We have an agreement."

Journey by multipede was perhaps one of the worst ways to travel. The multipede took her toll on the backsides and spines of her riders. Instead of steaming breath, the multipede was powered by Sound. A marvel of horology and music, the rider simply pedalled, driving a mechanism which played an extract from the Symphony of Industry, just a few bars, but enough to provide the force to run the gear shaft which pumped the legs of the multipede. Gearmusic, the horologists called it. Musicians and Composers in the Empire treated it with disdain, but mechanical music was the backbone of Empire industry and the Empire war machine. Sona had never liked gearmusic much; he resented the soulless tedium of the repeated notes.

Solitude was a companion Sona had missed. He had been content to travel alone between Empire cities. At least there, field justices appointed by the Emperor kept brigands in check. He had taken the long road from the clock city Pendulos, where he'd lain low after fleeing the Western Academy, as his mother had told him to. There, as new skin grew over burnt flesh, he plotted, immersing himself in his mother's research, before setting out for the Periphery. Mingling with the tradespeople and pilgrims, the Empire road had been boringly safe. The road along the Periphery to the Steppes up north was equally long but infinitely more interesting. Sona had been forced to choose between being victim of the uncontrolled banditry of the trade highways or of the controlled banditry of Grimheld and his contemporaries. Bartering his services to the strong had been Sona's only way of paying for safe passage.

The slow travels around the western reach of the Empire and up to the northwest had grated on Sona; all the more so when he was carrying his prize. In Pendulos, he had taken up his mother's research, melding the clockwork sciences of Pendulos with the theory of Sound. But tinkering was not enough for his plan. The Six Named land was the next step; the conversion of knowledge into power. And with power he could strike back. Back at the Lord Antius Deathsinger, the man who had made Sona what he was. Sona was uninterested in the machinations and intrigues of the Houses of the Capital, about revolution and power, but he was owed blood, and he would collect.

Dust clouds bloomed under the multipede's brass feet, flat and splayed like those of a camel. Shailani drew her headscarf across her nose and mouth, one hand still holding onto the multipede's saddle for support. The chains had been off since they'd put two days' ride between them and the town. Sona hadn't bothered to learn its name. In his accounts he'd just numbered towns off on a map, reducing brutality to a series of columns and sums.

We should eat, he said, bringing the multipede to a halt, tune dying to silence. Shailani wobbled as she took her first steps. Multipedes did that to you, pounding away your sense of balance, step by shaking step. While she swayed, one hand on the brass fittings of the multipede, Sona laid out their shared provisions, noting that both water and food had dipped below the halfway mark. Hard bread, hard cheese, hard jerky. The water which he poured into two stained copper cups was itself stale, and had taken on the sharp bite of metal from its receptacle. Shailani looked at the sun nearly overhead, turned to the right so that her shadow was behind her, knelt, and bowed twice, leaving a smear of grey dust on her forehead.

You are a captive in a strange land, and still you give thanks for your food? he asked.

"I am not hurt, and my portion is the same as yours. There is much to be thankful for," she said.

And the two bows? he asked, before sawing at the bread with a short dagger. The blade was barely a finger's length, and had seen combat. If Sona looked closely enough, there would still be blood crusted at the choil, but he hoped Shailani wouldn't notice.

"Thanks to the spirits. Once for me, and once for you." When Sona's eyebrows raised, she carried on, "I'm a captive, not ill-mannered."

We don't have gods in the Empire, Sona said.

"It must be lonely, then," replied Shailani.

Gods are for the weak; the land is here, the Empire is powerful because of the strength of people, not because of any spirits.

"Ah yes, Empire strength. Greatest in the continent. Can your Empire sing the sun to rise in the morning? Did it sing creation itself into being? The Empire has no soul, and that is why it will end."

Without an answer, Sona pushed Shailani's portion of bread and cheese towards her. He said, *If we had returned to camp, I would have offered you mango jam from your Far Isles.*

"My sister-children have never tasted sweet mangoes; the best of our lands is taken to garnish the Empire's tables. I think the bread is enough for me," said Shailani.

Empire wheat, milk, and pig, Sona said, gesturing at the food in turn. *Nothing from Far Isles here. Anyway, we don't steal from the Isles. We trade with your Sultanate.* The Sultanate was the de facto power over the raucous, archipelagic Far Isles.

Shailani winced as she bit. The crunch of the stale bread was audible, doubtless rattling her teeth in her head. She drizzled water on her bread, softening the chunk. A soldier's trick.

So how does a Far Isles woman become proficient in Fingerspeech? asked Sona. *Tactical Fingerspeech too.*

"The isles are only far when one considers the Empire at the centre of everything. If you honour me, you would at least call my homeland by its name," Shailani said, her cheeks colouring, crumbs spraying.

Sona chose his words, fingers moving over each other deliberately, each gesture perfectly crisp. *Your land has no other name in the Empire,* he said. *You are of the Sultanate, are you not?* Nominally so, since nearly every island in the region had its own tribe, with very particular ideas about whom it owed allegiance to.

"Those the Empire cannot conquer, it befriends. But Empire only knows Empire, and its friends are very much like it. Before the Empire came to Seribu, the Sultan only ruled half the territory. He bartered aromatic woods, gemstones, and rare beasts for imperial instruments. Now the Sultan controls it all. Including my people. Have you heard of the Sixty-Seventh regiment?"

That word you used? Sona asked.

"Seribu? It means 'the thousand' in my tongue. The true name of the Far Isles. You don't even care enough to have a name for it in Fingerspeech."

And then she was silent.

So Shailani was from the Sixty-Seventh – the Irregulars. Sona looked her over again, taking in the details he'd missed earlier. The way Shailani moved, light on her feet and balanced. She'd kept the woman's robe of the Periphery, but sashed it tighter around knee and elbow, making sure the voluminous cloth wouldn't trip her.

Deserted? Sona asked.

"Discharged after twenty years, with full colours. I made sergeant. You know what happens to deserters."

So, a decorated veteran. The Empire military was one of the few that had women serving. All the way since the reign of the Emperor Regent Ophelia some thirty years prior. With most of the heavy lifting done by Sound, physical strength was only valued for close quarters brawlers and cavalry. Still, prejudice ran deep and few women made sergeant, fewer lieutenant, and none above in a generation. Getting as far as sergeant meant that Shailani had other skills besides Fingerspeech.

And you got captured by a mongrel outfit like Grimheld's, said Sona.

"Trading us lessened the toll on the townsfolk. I had five to protect and no good options. You would have done the same," Shailani said, and when she tore the last of her bread in half, her knuckles were white under skin.

You don't know me. You are far from home. I assume you have business up north, pressed Sona.

Shailani made a show of chewing the tough bread, jawline sharp under her headscarf. "You've yet to tell me *your* business, Empire boy."

When it is time, said Sona.

"Taking without giving in return. You've not got Empire skin, but you've got Empire bones. Let me guess. You're not tall, but that's the Steppes in you; good bones means good nutrition. So you've seen money. You can stop me anytime I'm incorrect."

Sona began packing, keeping his hands busy to avoid answering.

"You have tools and ride a multipede, so you've got some craft in you. Maybe apprenticed to a horologist. Falling in with a band of mercenaries isn't straightforward, so I assume you understand war. Not enough scars to be battle tested, so I'd guess academy training."

Sona hated reminders of the time at the academy. If he closed his eyes, he could still smell the smoke.

The Western Academy was in flames; the burning front was a living thing, leaping from tapestry to rafter and back again, cutting off escape. His mother, the Lady Kristyk, was visiting. She'd found her way to his dormitory, past raiders, past fire. Not unscathed. One arm was blackened and peeling, the other holding one of her blades, the point tracing a scribble in the air.

"They'll not tell one body from another in the ashes. Leave your necklace and rings." Her voice a rasp from the hot smoke. Sona did as he was told. Shouts down the corridor, getting closer.

You go ahead, mother, I can manage the corpse, Sona said urgently, smoke obscuring his Fingerspeech. His roommate was a year younger, but Sona had always been small for his age.

"Hide on the Steppes, never come back to the Empire. There must be no doubt of your death. When you get there, tell Fong that the debt is repaid. Go."

We have to go, said Sona now, fingers crisp and sharp, the memory of acrid smoke making his nose itch and his eyes water.

The village could barely be called that, the stones that made up its walls rough and irregular, the inhabitants likewise. Harsh wind, hot off the Steppes, blew ochre grit into tiny vortices and curlicues, blasted it into wall and face alike. Hot food was a bonus, but the bread was not much better than the chunks they'd been eating on the road. The stew was a lumpish grey, root vegetables boiled down into a powdered mush, meat either clumps of gelatinous, wobbling fat or thin strips of gristle.

The innkeeper introduced himself as Druck, showing a mouthful of teeth at odd angles and with a time limit on their tenancy in his mouth. Sona and Shailani retired to their room. He gestured to Shailani to take the bed; he'd grown too used to hard ground on the road and even the straw filled mattress would leave him with a backache. Besides, he had work to do.

They struck in the early hours of the morning, at least an hour past midnight, but the Periphery lacked good clocks and time here was malleable.

Two of them, by the moonlight coming in through the window Sona had left open despite the desert chill. Gesturing to Shailani's sleeping form, the pair did not notice Sona emerging from beside the doorway, not until he'd brought the pommel of his short knife down forcefully on one shadowed head.

The man dropped with a grunt, and his partner spun, longsword at the ready. Few of Grimheld's band had fighting experience outside of bar room brawls and the gutting of unarmed innocents. This lent itself to flamboyant gestures, like bringing field weapons for indoor fighting, and, when confronted with the slumped body of a comrade, demonstrations of strength, like a two-handed overhand strike with a longsword.

Sona darted in quick, mindful of the body at his feet, one stiffened forearm a roof over his head, ready to shunt his attacker's strike down past his side. Unnecessary, since the tip of the sword bit deep into the thatched rafters and stopped. The tip of Sona's dagger found its way, through force of habit, to the armpit of his opponent, the spot traditionally uncovered by plate armour. Not that anybody could afford armour out here anyway. The attacker's eyes rolled up in his head. Brum. A pity. Brum had always been polite and good for a game of dice. The ledger was in Sona's favour, if he recalled. Perhaps the man was pettier than he'd let on.

Sona was still wondering if the spray from removing the dagger would dirty his travelling clothes when someone tackled him from behind. His head struck the edge of the bed on his way down, vision going white at the edges before he hit the floor hard. Breathing was impossible. Something on his back, maybe a knee. A rough hand flipped him around, and Sona felt the pressure of a dull blade at his throat, his assailant pinning him down by the simple expedient of straddling him, pinning arms by his side, squeezing air from his lungs; the cook, and former quartermaster, was a large man. Apparently, the band was out to settle all accounts with Sona before he left Empire territory.

"Hello Sona," said the cook. "Been waiting a long time for this. Not so chatty even without your tongue up Grimheld's arse, are you? Oh, I forgot."

Fingerspeech required at least one arm to be mobile; Sona was at a disadvantage and merely made a rude gesture with each hand.

"You've cost us five slaves. We knows it was you that done it. Nearly got them back, we did. Managed to get one in the leg with an arrow drum, but she was smart, that one. Lit a campfire all on her own and let her sisters sneak twice the head start on us." The cook drew the tip of the rusty knife down Sona's neck, dimpling skin. If the cook had been any more disciplined about upkeeping his blades, Sona's skin would have parted easily. "Maybe I'll be quartermaster again after yer gone. Cookin's not my style and dressing meat's hell for a man with but one hand. I should get some practice in." The tip of the knife drifted down, pressing through Sona's clothes; a shallow stab, just enough to keep Sona's attention.

A meaty slap cut through the silence, Shailani's fist appeared at the side of the cook's neck. The man shuddered, flesh jiggling. "Up now, big boy and lose that little pig sticker you got in my employer," she said. "What you have in your neck is something we call a lintah, a leech blade. More of a tube than a blade, really; a lot like a spigot in a beer barrel. You're going to want to get your hand up here." She clucked at the cook when his hand twitched, pulling his head back to make her point. "Slowly. Good. When I take my hand off, you're going to want to put your thumb over the hole. Good. Hold it there and we'll leave the beer inside the barrel, eh?"

Sona teased the blade free from his chest. Blood leaked but did not spurt. Good; he hadn't travelled this far to be laid low by a man like this. He nodded to Shailani. She turned her attention back to her captive, circling around him.

"The leech can bleed you fast or slow," she said. The cook took a half-hearted swipe at her with his other arm, the one to which he'd fitted an evil looking hook sprouting from a leather harness. His motion elicited a spurt of fresh blood from the knife in his neck. "Don't move, don't talk. I just need you to blink, once for yes, twice for no. Can you do that for me?"

The cook blinked. Sona had seen the man dish out his share of cruelties on the band's victims. Many of them looked a lot like the cook did now, sweat beaded on a furrowed brow, eyes white all around, breath shallow and rapid.

"The four others, are they being pursued?"

Blink. Blink. A single tear leaked from an eye, followed the furrow of an old scar, got lost in the half globe landscape of his sweaty chin.

"The one that was wounded, did she die unsullied?"

Blink. A rapid calculus of the costs of deception. Blink.

"Good boy. One more question, if you please. Did you partake?"

Blinkblink.

"Thank you," said Shailani, and kicked the cook's hand.

I thought they searched you, said Sona. They were downstairs packing up. The innkeeper was in his own bed, eyes wide and dry, divining the secrets of the ceiling, throat ragged and open to the night air. Cook and friends had been too clumsy to sneak by the innkeeper and too cheap to pay him off. Shailani pulled her headscarf back, revealing greying hair knotted into a simple bun. Even in the half-light, Sona could see the fan of thin tubes, leech knives as hair ornaments.

Not soldier's weapons, Sona said.

"Anything that kills is a soldier's weapon. We should stock up," she said.

That would be stealing, said Sona, before gathering his belongings. His Fingerspeech was barely discernible past the shaking of his hands.

"It's funny you say that, just after killing a man."

You've killed before, he said.

Shailani looked away, breaking line of sight and silencing Sona. "Enemies. Friends. It's just meat. No memories, no family, just meat. Easier that way, helps me sleep."

She turned back. "I need more than guesswork. You let me have the bed because they'd go for it first. I know your type. We had Empire officers in the Sixty-Seventh, but only the commissions who couldn't pay their way out of the front. Most were snivelling little snots. When we sent some of the bodies home, not all of them had wounds in the front. So let me ask you, Sona of the Empire, what is your business with the Six Named?"

Sona paused, then exhaled a week's worth of tension in a long sigh, shoulders slumping. He waved Shailani over to the multipede, brass legs folded and compartment gaping. Grunting, he lifted several heavy boxes out of the way, eliciting metallic clangs of complaint. Those boxes were individually locked, by coded mechanisms rather than by keys. Their secrets were not for Shailani, not yet. His mother's secret masterwork, perfected by Sona and the horologists the Lady Kristyk had paid to hide Sona after her death.

Another hidden panel hid Sona's treasures. Two stacks of paper. The first, a stack of letters unsent, written in script so neat it might as well have been printed. The pile grew more slowly the further Sona got from the Capital, the less he thought of his sister. Letters never to be sent, not as long as those behind the Western Academy fire thought he was dead. There was a spike of guilt when he thought of Canta. Although just a half-sister, they were close enough in years that they had been tutored together. His sister had inherited his father's height, her laugh booming and free, her punches faster and stronger than their teacher's. He wondered, as he always did, what terror she'd be up to back in the Capital, where they used to sprint across the moored airships at the Skydock. Sona pushed the letters, and his memories, aside.

Instead Sona drew forth the second set of papers, sheet music in the hand of the Lady Kristyk, her other masterwork. The rustling of the papers and the guttering oil lamps made the notes dance on their ordered lines. Sona paused. He was taking a risk here, disclosing this to the old soldier woman. Shailani would be the first person he'd shown the music to. Yet trust had to be won somehow. His fate would be in her hands when they got to the Six Named land. Better to start now.

There is a time of gathering up north for the Six Named. All manner of people, he said, one-handed, holding the music out for Shailani to see. The woman scanned the music with the quick glances of one skilled in reading music. The Festival of Names was an annual affair, something he'd only heard of from his mother. Each sept would send their elders to consult the Book of Names, to choose names for the newborn and to strike off the names of the dead.

"Looking for a wife?" Shailani asked, showing a little too much interest in the music. Sona jerked the sheets back. The festival was a time for unions as well. There was no better time to leave one sept for another, save that they did not bear children with any who shared one of their Six Names. Everything else was fluid – rearing of children, hunting, farming, border patrols, craftsmanship.

It was not marriage Sona sought, but music. *I need this played for me. Played by people I can trust. People not of the Empire,* he said.

"That's a lot of music, a full movement. Which Symphony?"

Not one of the four, he said. The Symphonies of War, Industry, Order, and Flow were the backbone of the Empire Sound. Each held the movements of music that ran battle, agriculture, the artifices of the city, and physical combat. Each symphony the province of one of the Maestri; each Maestro lording over a House with the power of a small country.

Sound was all around the world, a force of nature; even animals had use of it. But nobody on the continent used it like the Empire, and the tools of the Empire were the Composers—the few souls in with the talent to pluck notes from Sound, and weave those notes into music, and the music into each of the Symphonies. The Symphonies were the property of the Empire, and those that could command it even more so. Sona was a player of average quality; perhaps suited for industry or the civil service. His strength lay in his tinkering with gearmusic and with the music of the Symphonies. The Lady Kristyk had guided him with his tutors, careful for Sona only to demonstrate average facility in musical theory.

All empires gestated the seeds of their own undoing, although most were more subtle about it than the Empire Sound. It was an act of conceit that the Empire took its name from Sound; a power available to all, a power that it abused and feared. And because the

Empire feared, it controlled, forbidding all music but that of the Symphonies. The Empire assigned each of the four Maestri a Symphony, each great house controlling the Composing and use of all Sound within its Symphony.

"Dangerous business," said Shailani. "Illicit Composing is sedition, high treason against the Emperor himself." Sona said nothing, but slipped a tiny assassin's dagger from his sleeve and palmed it.

You've got an eye for music, said Sona. *Not just some foot soldier.*

"Battle choir, section leader. I know my Music, Empire boy."

Now you know what I need done up north, are you still with me? asked Sona, waiting for Shailani to hesitate, to give him a single reason to mistrust her. None came.

"My sisters are still free. Our agreement holds. Hide your music. You can see to provisions. One of your old friends is still alive in the next room." She stepped up to Sona, close enough for her breath to tickle his lashes. When he retreated, she seized his hand and relieved him of his dagger. "You get this one for free. Best get used to killing, boy. Looks like your business will see more before it's done."

Stay tuned for part II of Sonata in next month's issue!

"See L. Chan's story "Sonata I: Sona" online at Metaphorosis.
If you liked it, leave a comment. Authors love that!
Remember to subscribe to our e-mail updates so you'll know when new stories are posted."

About the story

"Sonata" is one of the longest things that I've written (and completed). I don't often work in the fantasy sandbox, I much prefer near future science fiction and contemporary fantasy. For "Sonata", what preceded the story was the world building — a magic system that fell roughly as another aspect of the physical world, and where the control of that magic ran along political and societal faultlines rather than through resource or genealogical lines. Things flowed on from there — an extant Empire with a colonialist reach, a good old fashion revenge quest and some non-traditional characters. It didn't get really steampunky until about halfway in, when I realised that the frame of having a sound based magic system would overcome a lot of the engineering limitations of steampunk without pushing the rest of the technology of the world into the industrial revolution or thereabouts. It was also important to me to retain a tight cast of characters this time round, although the roster is definitely going up if I ever return to these folks.

A question for the author

Q: What inspires you?

A: Many things! I'm the filter feeder in the inspiration food chain. Sometimes, it's bouncing ideas off tweets with friends. Sometimes I start with a title but no story. Sometimes I start with a line or a scene with no idea how the rest of the story goes. Recently, I've tried to address some weird imbalances in tropes that irked me, like the Selkie myth.

About the author

L. Chan hails from Singapore. He spends most of his time wrangling two dogs. His work has appeared in places like *Translunar Travellers Lounge, Podcastle,* and *the Dark*. He tweets occasionally @lchanwrites.

lchanwrites.wordpress.com

Feburary

Pyrrha

Antony Paschos

I open my eyes and see a rifle pointing at me. Well, not at me exactly. At me and Sister. Or just at Sister, I'm not sure, because the barrel is dancing in circles and zigzags. Sister's heavy breathing rumbles, *hur, hur, hur,* lulling me. Her snoring shakes her chest, which, in turn, shakes my head, as it's tucked under her tit. I elbow her hard.

"Sis," I whisper.

She grunts, tightens her arms around me. Then she spots the gun barrel and jumps up.

I can make out only one comrade's face in the candlelight; I think he's called Yiannis. A lot of people are called Yiannis, not just comrades. Some switched to Yoan or Yanko, because that's what the Bulgarians told them to do. Some refused but when the Bulgarians killed them, their relatives went and carved their new names on their graves.

Sister doesn't talk for a while. I don't know why, maybe because from time to time comrades point their rifles at each other for no apparent reason. Sometimes they even shoot each other, and then the last man standing says that the dead one was an agent. An agent means a bad comrade.

"What do you want?" says Sister.

"Get up, let's go. You, and the girl."

"We're not going anywhere."

"Comrade..."

"I said no! We've discussed this already. We agreed. Perhaps your ears got full of wax and you went deaf, but we've made a deal with the Secretary. So, stick the rifle up your ass and let us sleep."

Yiannis raises his hand to his ear, but stops halfway; he gets hold of the rifle again. "My ears are clean..."

Crackling, the candlewick burns out. Darkness, footsteps, rustling. "Find a match, you asshole, don't you have any matches?" Commotion. I can help. Here. Now everyone can see. My finger is like a vigil lamp, except that the flame is the shape of a dove, quietly perched on my index finger, illuminating the rough walls of the cave, Sister's books, the two logs we have for chairs, the little table with the crooked legs; there's a beach pebble underneath one of them so it doesn't wobble too much.

Clang. Yiannis picks the rifle up from the floor. The barrel is shaking. The comrades take a few steps back, as if they're scared of my little dove. I don't know whether they're really afraid of it, but, truth be told, my doves are often followed by silence. Just like now.

"Shall we?" It's me who asks.

We go down the slope. I wrap my coat around me. The moonlight falls on trails that look like rivers, on pine needle hills that look like giant hedgehogs, on oak trees that look like... I don't know what. Sister would know. Sister always knows; she comes up with the best similes. Not the most pleasing, but the most peculiar. Now, she's holding my hand. Two comrades walk ahead of us, one behind us, Yiannis, with his rifle.

"Are we going to an assembly?" I ask Sister.

"To what?"

"To an assembly."

She extends her hand and touches my shoulder. "My little Pyrrha."

My name is not Pyrrha. I had a different name, once. But Sister gave me this name because, she says, I've got red hair. Same as the comrades change their names, more or less; but Sister says that I'm too young to be a comrade.

Now she squeezes my shoulder.

"I don't want any tricks, comrade," Yiannis with the rifle says from behind.

"Shut up," Sister tells him. "If we were to play any tricks we'd have already burned you alive."

"You want me to burn them, Sis?" I ask. This is a game; I don't mean it. We play this whenever Sister says that we'll burn this and we'll burn that. I don't mind, even though after every game I remind her that I don't want to burn a person ever again. She always says she knows, but I remind her anyway.

"Hmm, maybe later," she replies.

Silence again.

"Sister?" I whisper.

"Yes?"

"Will they give us molasses where we're going?"

"Where did that come from, love?"

"I'd like some molasses now."

"That's what you meant to ask me?"

Sister can tell when I lie.

I pull her sleeve and whisper in her ear: "You remember that I don't want to burn anyone ever again, right, Sis?"

Four more comrades wait for us in the vineyard. I know they're comrades because I recognize one of them. He has all kinds of names, Captain this and Captain that. Some call him Secretary. He wears a pair of pretty riding boots, made of leather, and he's round, with puffed-up cheeks hidden under his beard. Almost all comrades have a beard, but his is thick and frizzy and its hairs look like black thorns.

The Secretary approaches me and squats. He fumbles in his pocket and fishes out something small and wrinkled.

"I don't like gum," I say. I'd ask for some molasses but I dare not. Not yet.

He laughs. "All right, little comrade. Will you show me your magic tricks? And I'll give you whatever you want."

"I'm not a comrade yet," I reply, squeezing Sister's hand.

"You think this is a freak show?" she asks the Secretary.

"Comrade," the Secretary says, gets up and shoves the gum back in his pocket. "If she's going to be a part of this Revolution..."

"She shouldn't! She's a fucking child!"

"Yet if what they say she can do is true..."

"It doesn't matter if it's true! Even if you make her do it, have you thought of what will happen afterwards? What will the Bulgarians do in retaliation? They'll lay waste to the entire countryside."

"Let them lay waste to it, then. If that's what it takes for the people to wake up, let them do it. These lazy-ass yokels put up with anything the Bulgarians do to them; they won't take to the mountains, if no blood is spilled."

"We're not talking about a little blood. There will be a bloodbath." Sister looks ready to catch fire, same as I can set anything I want alight.

"Comrade, we made a decision in the assembly. Do you dissent from the assembly's decision?"

"The decision didn't involve her, did it?"

I don't want them to fight. As Sister would've said, I've had enough.

I light up five little doves, one for every finger. Wings of fire come to life, making the smallest of sounds, *phoop, phoop, phoop, phoop, phoop.* Suddenly, I hear proper fluttering: something jerks up from the vineyard and flies into the sky. I wish it were a dove too, but it's probably an owl, and an owl is never a good omen.

Yiannis with the rifle brings his hand to his chest and makes a quick gesture as if he's crossing himself. The Secretary shoots an angry look at him and Yiannis squeezes his hand into a fist, brings it to his mouth and coughs. It's not that it's forbidden to make the sign of the cross, but the comrades never do that.

Meanwhile, five doves burn quietly on my fingers and Sister has taken her hand from mine and has placed it on her forehead. She mumbles something I can't hear, but I know her and I can read her lips under the light of my little fires. "Fuck, no," that's what she said. I guess I did something stupid. I put the doves out. No one speaks for a while.

"All right," the Secretary says in the end. "But do these damn birds work, or is it just a trick?"

"They do, they do!" I say.

"Oh, they do, huh? And can you do it from afar, little comrade?"

"She can do nothing!" Sister screams. "She's a child, she's not a part of this bullshit!"

"Comrade," the Secretary says. "It's the only way and you know it."

"You mean to tell me that this bullshit plan of yours depends on some rumors about a magic child? Didn't we have an inside man at the power plant? Why do you need her?"

The Secretary shuts his eyes and snorts. His breath smells of onions. He opens his eyes. "They caught our inside man in the power plant yesterday. His replacement supports the Bulgarian Exarchate. Meanwhile, everyone up on the mountain is waiting for the power to go out. We don't have any other options left, comrade. You have to choose, you and the girl both. You're either with the Revolution, or you're against it."

Sister looks at the comrades; at their faces, at their hands, at their rifles. She doesn't answer.

"So," the Secretary says. "Let's go."

The moon has climbed up and the night is now a heavier grey. We walk on unseeded fields. Sister and the seven comrades have swallowed their tongues, as if the animals lurking in the wilderness would overhear their secrets. In the silence, I hear the *hroop-hroop* of their combat boots.

Speaking of boots, the shoes I'm wearing are too big and I've tucked crumpled newspapers at the tips. They're not mine; Sister got them and my coat from a short agent. I asked her whether she'd stolen them, but she said that when we take something from the dead we don't call it stealing. We call it looting. I asked why we call it that and what it has to do with playing the lute and she explained to me that it might be a very old simile, so good that, in the end, it was forgotten and ended up being a word of its own. I'd love it if something like this happened to one of my similes; to be so old that it finally becomes a word. Even though I think that if something like that happened, it would happen to one of Sister's similes. They're very good. Not always kind to the ears, but peculiar.

I walk carefully because my looted shoes sink in the ground, which is dry on top but plump underneath. There's my chance to chat with Sister.

"The ground is like frozen snow," I tell her.

She smiles. She's thinking. Now she's going to say a simile and it's going to be way better than mine.

"Yes, that's pretty much on the spot," she finally says. She couldn't find a good one. "Or like fresh bread, hard on the outside but soft on the inside." She found one, after all.

"Why the long face? You didn't like the simile?"

"It's not that."

"What is it, then?"

"Are we going to start a revolution now?"

"We're going to do shit now."

Sometimes, Sister swears.

I hear someone from behind: "Comrade, what happened to your high morale?"

"Shove it up your ass, asshole."

Sometimes, Sister swears too much. Now the comrades are whispering to each other.

"Comrade, we have to inform the child." A hoarse voice. The Secretary.

"I'll inform her," Sister replies. Inform is a more difficult word to say tell. The comrades use difficult words from time to time, especially when there are many of them around. I've been at an assembly once. I didn't understand a thing, that's how many difficult words they spat out.

Sister informs me. She tells me I must burn the power plant from afar.

"Yes, but I don't want to burn people, OK?" I don't want to burn people ever again. When my doves burn people, they scream.

"You won't burn anyone, my love, don't worry."

"You swear?"

"I swear."

"Do you want me to burn the power plant?"

Sister keeps her eyes shut for a while. She sighs and opens them. Just like the Secretary did earlier on, only that she looks sad and not angry.

"I do. I do."

"And there won't be a bud...a blood..."

"A bloodbath?" Sister asks.

"Yes."

"We don't know that. The Secretary was right. There are times when you have to choose, even if you don't know what."

"All right, then. But, when it's finished, will you find us some molasses?"

"I will. I'll find us some molasses."

I hear a *psst* from behind. A hand stretches towards Sister, holding a small jar without a cap. It's Yiannis. "For the little one," he whispers. Sister looks at him; then, she looks at me. She takes it and gives it to me.

I can't see in the dark, but I can tell from the smell. It's molasses.

The power plant is close to the river and the train station, but you can hear neither the gurgling waters nor the trains. You can hear nothing; not even the comrades breathing. It's a huge building made of bricks. The bricks don't look red under the moonlight—everything looks dark blue under the moonlight—but I know they're reddish-brown; all bricks are reddish-brown.

An owl. It's bad luck when an owl comes to your house. That's why I never light up owls. Also because I don't like them. I like doves. I wish I could make real ones, not just flames shaped like doves.

I lick my lips. My mouth still sticks from the molasses.

A thud. Not close to us, but a couple of Yiannises jump.

"What is it?" I whisper. A second thud.

"It's coming from the trees," Sister says. "Over there, you see?"

She points towards the trees at the train station. Behind them there is an array of train cars and another building, with a roughcast exterior and a round clock on top. A few meters away there's a train car, collapsed to the side, gutted.

I'm not surprised by the thuds; the trees make all kinds of noises. Especially at night, if you're in the woods.

"The aspens stretch their limbs," Sister says. "It's as if they're yawning."

"The aspens are like a fence," I answer and Sister smiles.

"So," the Secretary says—he must be obsessed with the word —"Come on, hurry up."

"What's wrong? Is the Party in a hurry?"

"Comrade, I remind you that when everything is finished I'll have to write a report."

"Who gives a shit?"

The Secretary clears his throat. He speaks to Sis: "Comrade, I'm afraid you haven't chosen a side."

"Of course I have. I just chose the wrong side. The idiots' side."

A comrade makes a move towards Sister—it's not Yiannis, the one who gave me molasses. He holds his rifle with both hands, as if it's a bat. The Secretary places his hand against his chest and stops him.

Sister grants them a glance; then she kneels down and grabs my shoulders. She always has something important to tell me when she does this. Like now. She explains to me what I need to do.

"Do you understand?"

"I do."

"All right," she says and caresses my hair. She knows I like it when she caresses my hair. She likes it too—even though it's cut like a boy's—because it's ginger and soft.

"And then we'll ask the comrade where he found the molasses and we'll go get some more," she says.

"All right," I say and softly push her with my elbow. I hear whispers. I don't light up my doves yet.

"What happened?"

I turn and look at her. "Are there people in the power plant?"

"No."

"And how does it work, then?"

"It's automated, my little Pyrrha."

"What's automated?"

"When something is automated, it means that it runs on its own."

I'd ask her if we're all automated, but, "Hurry up!" the Secretary's yelling through clenched jaws. "Shut up!" says Sister.

"And what are those whispers, then?"

"The comrades, my love." The tone of her voice is the same as before, when she talked about the whole automated thing; flat.

"Sis… You remember that I don't want to burn anyone, right?"

"I remember, love." Here, the same tone again.

"All right." I wait a bit. The owl has stopped crying. Now, I can hear the wind blowing, like a trowel smoothening mortar. This is Sister's simile.

I hear more things, apart from the wind. Whispers: "She's a pain in the ass. Let's just toss a grenade." "The grenade's not enough, you idiot. The machines are inside. Even ten grenades wouldn't be enough." You could say that the whispers too were like a trowel smoothening mortar. "And what's this bitch telling her?" "She's her sister, you asshole." Lies. "Bullshit." Oh, he knows. "Isn't she?" "No, you fucker, the little shit's an orphan." I'm not a little shit, just an orphan. Long story. But Sister said that now she's my sister.

"Love?" Sister's voice; same tone, same tone.

"Yes," I say. And I do what I have to, in order for the trowel to stop smoothening the mortar. That is, to make the whispers stop. Not the wind. Even though, in a short while, I'll make the wind hush too. It happens when you cause a ruckus; softer noises disappear.

I light up ten doves, one for every finger. I feel the air through their fiery claws. It's a nice, night wind, just a bit moist from the stream, but not too much. It swirls around my fingers and tickles my skin where the fingers join.

"Is that it?" someone asks.

A little dove flexes its wings. Another one picks the feathers under its armpit. Or wingpits. Whatever doves have.

Someone spits. "We shouldn't have come. The kid's a fraud."

"Sssh."

Two doves flap their wings and hover above my hands. Another one coos silently. Well, not exactly silently, it makes a subtle *fthup*.

"We'll have to barge in, I'm telling you. And how will we get out?"

"Shut the fuck up!"

"Shut up? With all this bullshit and the damned birds they'll sniff us out. And then..."

My doves take flight. They lift themselves up, more like butterflies and less like real birds, leaving glimmering sparkles as they go—a small flock of flames—and then they enter the power plant through a window on the ground floor.

The fire rises with a gust of wind, *foup*.

"Look," I say to Sister and point at the ground floor windows. "The fire is like a beaded curtain." I look at her, but she's not smiling.

Indeed, orange ribbons dance like paper curtains blown by the wind. My doves are flying inside the building, their wings brushing against wooden beams, chairs, tables, floors, ceilings. I can't see my birds, but the windows, one after another, gain their own ribbons, while a yellow, blinding light pours out of the first ones, the kind of light you can't look directly at because it'll hurt your eyes. The crackling of the fire sounds like a lullaby and still no Bulgarian is on to us. My doves must be sowing fire in the upper floor now, while grey snakes of smoke lash out of a ground floor window, shapes I can't control, with bodies that swell more and more and turn into trees with fiery blossoms. The power plant's burning pretty much as regular houses burn, and as I'm thinking that, over the crackling of the wood and the furniture crashing and the beams falling apart, I hear something. It happens sometimes, to hear something not as loud as the rest of the commotion, maybe because what you pick up is strange or unexpected. Now, for example, this something sounds like fluttering, like an owl's wings, and my heart clenches.

"What's this, asshole?"

"What?"

"Up there."

"Where?"

"There. Top floor, at the window."

For a moment, my heart feels lighter at the thought that the living dove that takes flight might be one of my creations. The next moment I notice its wings burning; it's like the ones I make or, rather, like a firefly—would Sister like this simile? I don't know, I just hear her breathing cut short, and it's strange, my hearing must be excellent to be able to hear her breathing and the bird's fluttering as it manages to fly away. The wind that ruffles its feathers slowly puts the fire out; the bird will make it. It flies off into the night sky. Behind it I hear a hissing sound, something weak and weird that I recognize too. A chick appears on the same window sill. It's tiny and it's frantically looking around and one of its tiny wings is on fire. A small fire springs up behind it; no, it's one of my doves, and I immediately put it out with a small explosion which scares the chick; it hops delicately on the windowsill, slips and jumps off, and I hope it follows the other bird that got away, but no, the chick falls, then flutters and manages to gain some height, only a little, so little. And then I hear the soft thud on the ground.

A hand squeezes my shoulder. It's Sister's. I said that I didn't want to burn anyone; and when I said anyone I meant any people. Sometimes you have to think of every little detail before you say what you want to say.

My doves have faded, the power plant's on fire, but the city remains silent, just like the comrades. Something is moving at the window, perhaps there's a third bird or the flames may be playing tricks, now they look like... I forget what they look like. I hear the scream.

It's a human scream. It comes from inside the building and breaks down into shorter screams, sharp and loud and desperate. A ground floor door collapses and a human shadow appears at the frame in front of an orange, blazing background. It's probably a man. I see him in a blur, because tears have welled up in my eyes since the chick fell.

"The guard."

"Sister," I whisper and feel her moving. Her hand flies off my shoulder. She elbows the comrade next to her. "What are you doing?" he says.

"Don't just look at him, you asshole! Shoot him!"

"Sister..."

"They'll hear us."

And at that moment, they do. Not us, but the power plant, out of which comes a deafening bang that swallows the man's screams. The man runs and falls and gets up again; runs, falls and gets back up. The flames on his body almost fade whenever he stumbles, just like with the birds earlier, but every time he gets up they rekindle, and I don't want to say it, but they do look like wings.

"Can't she put him out?"

The one asking is Yiannis, the comrade who had woken us up, the one who gave me the molasses.

"No, she can't," Sister says. "And now they definitely heard us. So, stop wasting time. Finish him."

Yiannis puts the butt of the rifle on his shoulder.

"Fuck him," the Secretary says. "He's Bulgarian."

"Sister..."

"What is it, love?"

"Sister." I smother a sob. The bang from the explosion has left a constant *iiing* and a buzzing in my ears, as if from a truck engine. "I told you I don't want to kill anyone..."

"Yes, my love, but..."

A shot and Sister collapses in my arms. I step back and her hands fall off my shoulders, they slide down half-clenched, they scratch my clothes and end up on her throat as she crouches on my feet. A spring of blood gushes from her neck, painting her hands, her fingers, the skin between them. A truck's engine. More shots. Voices in Bulgarian. The guard's screams. Yiannis, who gave me molasses, falls down, pretty much like Sister. The Secretary kneels above her. Shakes her. "Tell her! Tell her to save us! To burn them!"

Sister opens her mouth, but says nothing. Shots, fire crackling, explosions, screams. Yiannis moans, injured. The Secretary grabs the rifle.

I drop next to him, on top of Sister, her blood sticks on my fingers, like the molasses on my lips. Her eyelashes flutter. The Secretary aims across the field and shoots—the sound is deafening. Then, a shot from afar, the Secretary jerks away, drops the rifle and falls on his side too. He clutches his shoulder and groans. He grabs my arm with his other hand. His fingers are trembling, his nails dig into my clothes, so I stop shaking Sister.

"Wake up," I tell her, "you swore to me..." I don't want to blame her for swearing to me that I wouldn't have to burn people. Her face is still, her eyes are still, white, like landscapes. "Wake up and I don't care how many of them I burn!"

"Leave her," the Secretary says. "She's gone. Dead."

Sister's blood gathers in a pool around my coat and knees. It's warm and my skirt floats on it, like a water lily. She would love this simile. But she'll never hear another, neither will she come up with one. Perhaps, if I repeat her good similes again and again, then they'll too become words, like "loot" has?

The shots from the comrades are sparse now, but I can hear some far away, from where the truck engine was coming, scattered, then three in a row, three more, two, silence, one, silence. Silence, by which I mean fire crackling and comrades groaning. The guard has fallen silent. Yiannis has fallen silent. Footsteps are approaching, voices in Bulgarian. Shadows in the dark, I can see them moving; they're coming.

"Burn them," the Secretary says, now barely standing on his feet. He's panting, like a hound. "Burn them, they're Bulgarian. Didn't you just say to your Sister you don't care? Burn them, perhaps she's only wounded... Perhaps we can save her, perhaps..."

"Shut the fuck up," I tell him and his mouth drops. It's like an O now. "I'm not stupid and I don't burn people, you asshole." I sound like Sis. I push his hand off my arm. The blood in the pool is now lukewarm against my knees. My skirt is soaked.

"I—I know you're not stupid..." he stutters. "But... But if you don't burn them, they'll kill you."

The Bulgarians are close. Under the dead moonlight I notice helmets, rifles. One of them shouts, but I don't understand a word he says. I don't speak Bulgarian. He must be yelling something at the Secretary.

"So, you have to choose," he says, as if he's talking to himself. Now he's not panting as much. "You're either with the Revolution or against it." And then he gets ready to shoot, but the shooting comes from the Bulgarians. Not one shot; four. The Secretary collapses next to me. There's a hole above his ear, black blood is pouring out. His round belly doesn't seem as swollen now, perhaps because he's lying face down. A black pond forms underneath him, smaller than the one that swallowed my knees, my skirt, the edges of my coat. A small stream of it comes towards me, warm blood mixes with cold.

The Bulgarians are here. They have the butts of their rifles on their shoulders and they tilt their heads to take aim. They say something and they lower their guns. They hang their rifles on their shoulders. One of them takes a pistol out of a leather holder and leans over the comrades. He shoots them on the head. Every bang sounds deafening, but I don't jerk any more, I'm used to it now. In the end, you get used to anything.

I shut my eyes. The shots continue, once in a while, steadily. Bam. Silence. Bam. Silence. I open my eyes. The hand with the pistol is near me. The soldier is skinny and hunched and he smells of garlic and unwashed clothes. His eyes are sad. "Sǔzhalyavam, momiche," he says and I think he says he's sorry. Sister's face seems silver under the moonlight.

The soldier's pistol aims at her head.

I light up ten doves and the soldier steps back. Scared voices, rustling. Rifles pointing at me. A dove lifts its tiny leg from my finger, another one stretches its wings. Silence.

The Secretary said I have to choose. Sister had promised that I wouldn't burn any people. But I did. Sometimes you have to choose yourself. Sometimes, choosing is a total mess.

Every gun barrel is on me. Rifles and the pistol that was aiming at Sister point at me. I wish Sister would wake up and speak to them; if she woke up she'd find a way to save us. But her face is still silver and her blood cold and sometimes you have to choose yourself what to do.

The doves have stretched their wings, ready. But a fluttering that comes from the power plant is quicker. I turn to see and I hear the shot and then something burns my throat and my chest fills with something wet and warm, like Sister's blood around my knees. I see the tops of the aspen trees, far at the train station, the power plant on fire. I don't see my doves, but up there, in the sky, among the stars that blink behind the blurry ribbons of smoke, a bird is fluttering and flies up high; I don't know why, but I'm sure it's the chick that fell off before. My arms and legs are heavy; I can't help it, and I fall like a marionette with its strings cut.

See Antony Paschos's story "Pyrrha" online at Metaphorosis.
If you liked it, leave a comment. Authors love that!
Remember to subscribe to our e-mail updates so you'll know when
new stories are posted.

About the story

The story in "Pyrrha" was inspired by the actual events that took place in Drama, Greece in 1941. The blowing up of the power plant by the guerilla fighters triggered a failed revolution that resulted in grave consequences. While researching for my third book, I realized that I'd like to write a story about that particular event. Then, I read a short story about a child that didn't want to grow up, and the voice of Pyrrha emerged in my head and I decided to give it a try.

A question for the author

Q: Do you have any pets? Do they influence your writing?

A: I used to be a pet to a certain cat for many years – I think she found me too dull a character to write a story about me, though. I grew up with lots of animals, either in our flat (parrots, hamsters, cats) or cottage (dogs and cats). I've actually written a short story about a dog that used to chew on our caravan's wiring, driving my father insane. Now that I think about it, a lot of my stories include pets or animals. In some of them, including a novelette, they're protagonists as well.

About the author

Antony Paschos was born in 1979 and lives in Athens, Greece. He is a member of the Science Fiction Club of Athens. He has worked as a Paintball field operator, a delivery boy, and an air taxi pilot. He currently works as an airline pilot.

Heart of Stone

Chris Cornetto

Light filtered through the debris, igniting a spark in his crystalline heart.

Bending all his will to the effort, the little golem opened his eyes. Pink, hazy dawn — or perhaps twilight? — filtered through a cloud of dust motes. It was barely light at all, yet it set his body thrumming, energy tingling through silicon veins. The light soaked into his heart and filled it with life.

He tried to move his arms, his legs, but he was too weak. He tried to check if he still had limbs, but he couldn't lift his head. Even his thoughts trickled like tar.

How long had his core been dim? Where was he?

From above came scraping and grunting. A rustle of debris, as pebbles tumbled down. More light squeezed through the gap, and the gears of his mind began to turn.

Grand, he thought. *My name is Grand.* He was a Clay, a Stonesinger, a servant of the Lord of Earth. And he had failed his Master.

Somehow, Grand had to make his way home. He wondered if the Master would be surprised to see him after so many centuries — how many had it been? Perhaps the Master would be pleased, if only the smallest bit, to see his wayward Clay return?

It was a queer thought, Grand knew. Emotion was a defect of logic. The Master had no defect.

It was not the first queer thought to have crossed Grand's mind, in his ages in the dark. But now there was light. Unlooked for, unhoped for, undreamed of *light*.

Grand was not his name. The golem had no name, only a designation: GR-A90.

He had taken the name "Grand" on a whim; to pass the years in the dark, he had imagined himself part of the city above his tomb. Through the stone he had felt the vibration of a thousand voices, a thousand souls. He had dreamed that he walked among them, sharing their joys and cares and woes. When they spoke, he spoke back, though none could hear him. His favorite voices became dear friends, and he ached when they were silent.

Grand knew it was mad affectation to play at being a flesh-thing, that he was damaged in ways he could not comprehend. It was his guilty secret and his only joy. It had been a way to pass the centuries.

Then the city vanished, all voices silenced but his own.

He spent another age gently humming to the stones of his prison – a waste of energy, but also a comfort. It was the task for which he was made. He knew the song of every mineral, and with a bare touch could set them singing in purest tones. At his full strength, he could shake mountains.

But sealed away from light, Grand had no strength. He, master of stone, became its slave. It had been a mercy when his core went dim.

The stone above shifted and the pink glow welled through the gap, fainter now. So, it was twilight after all.

From above came a gasp of excitement. A gaunt face peered into the breach, eyes wide with wonder. It belonged to the most ill-fed, ill-favored seraph Grand had ever seen. Even stunted, it towered over him, at least thrice his size.

A seraph. He had never shown a seraph mercy, and had no right to expect any. After untold ages of waiting, his rescue would be his death. The irony stung him.

The seraph shouted in a language Grand could not comprehend, some distant kin of the tongues he remembered. Had the world changed so much in his sleep?

The seraph called out again, turning his back to Grand. No wings. Not a seraph. So what was this flesh-thing?

The golem dredged his recollection, mind sluggish with sleep. Even now, the dim light fading from the sky, his brain threatened to shut back down. He was designed to never forget, but how much damage had he suffered when the city fell atop him?

A human. That's what the flesh-thing was.

Grand had warred with many races, the creations of pretender gods, but humans he barely recalled. They were an aberration, an error, sprung from the dirt with no god to claim them. They had been beneath the Master's notice, and so were beneath his.

A second human appeared, this one bearded, older. Just as gaunt. He eyed Grand skeptically and prodded him with an iron rod, clinking it against his chest.

Grand tried to reach for the bar, but his arms would not obey. He lay in the pit, as still as the rock around him. All he could move was his eyes.

The men jabbered in their strange tongue, until the young one persuaded the elder to help him dig. They pried at the rubble, levering away fragments of broken wall. And, with each stone moved, more debris cascaded down.

The pit grew choked with sand and stone. Grand's small world closed in until it reached no further than his body, more claustrophobic than ever. Panic welled within him. Were they burying him? His thoughts swam with nightmares of eternity beneath the dirt, alone and forgotten.

Anything but that, his mind screamed. Grand prayed feverishly to a Master who could not hear. Let the flesh-things kill him if they must — only, let them do it above the ground, beneath the boundless sky. Outside of this tomb.

Grand fixated on the scrape of iron on stone, the sound of salvation. He *had* to get out. The fear of darkness without end weighed on him physically, crushing him like the very rock that pressed down from above. So close to freedom, it was too much to endure.

Time passed. Grand flickered in and out of consciousness, his power ebbing. Though intoxicating after an age in darkness, his sip of twilight had been scant. Straining to hear the blessed scraping, his thoughts ground to a halt.

Moonlight. Two men in headscarves inspected him, one holding a shovel. They chattered in their nonsense tongue, disagreeing. One enthusiastic, the other annoyed.

Sand and broken stone stretched to the horizon in every direction. The city was gone. He had known it would be, but seeing was different from knowing. It was ironic how he ached for its loss – he who had tried, and failed, to destroy it.

A man placed him gently into a sack, not quite empty. It drew shut, and the darkness returned.

Grand woke to lamplight. He found himself lying on a bench or table. Something made of wood.

Even had he the strength to move, Grand had no power over wood. Its structure was messy and random compared to the beautiful order of stone.

Voices argued. Grand tried to look around, but couldn't. He was sprawled amidst knickknacks and rubbish. He heard the men who had found him bickering with a third.

No, not bickering. Haggling. Haggling over the junk on the table, with which he had shared a sack. They haggled over a brooch, a buckle, an ivory comb. A granite face chiseled off some capital or lintel. The hilt of a long-rusted sword, and so on. All sorts of rubbish.

The men who found Grand were scavengers, which made *him* salvage. He, a Clay, mightiest of the Master's tools, was now junk, pulled from the refuse heap of history.

The shame stung him. An eternity in the dark hadn't extinguished his pride.

Grand lay and he listened, having no other option. Though most of the haul was rubbish, some pieces caught his interest – the gears and springs and tubes of forgotten machines. There were even two small piezo-crystals, which the elder scavenger presented reverently.

The buyer placed a lens on his eye to inspect them. He turned them over in his hand, clucking his tongue as he studied them carefully, facet by facet.

At first Grand thought the collector was checking for damage, but soon realized the man simply enjoyed the sparkle — as if the crystals were nothing more than shiny baubles. He was amazed. How far had civilization fallen? Humans were infants, ignorants. Barely more than beasts.

Grand itched to explain their error, but held his tongue. Even had they shared a common speech, he wouldn't have spoken. With creeping discomfort, he realized that he *feared* the flesh-things. Did they see what he was? Did they know what he had done?

Would they destroy him if they knew he lived?

Perhaps not, but Grand would take no chance.

Once they had settled terms on the rest of the detritus, the younger scavenger hoisted Grand, his large hands wrapped around the golem's trunk. He chattered excitedly about the prize of the collection.

It was an honor to be saved for last, the finest garbage. He was the Lord of Junk.

At least, held upright, Grand could finally look around the room. The walls were lined with cabinets where trash and treasure mingled freely, the shiniest bits of debris given places of honor. Weapons and potsherds and mechanical parts were sorted loosely by theme, but with several wrong guesses. Other bits were unidentifiable even to Grand.

The centerpiece of the whole collection was a golem power core, shimmering and dead. It was too large to belong to a Clay, large even for a Stone. A fissure ran halfway through, rendering it inert.

It was the crystal heart of a living thing. It should have been brought home, to be repaired and born again in a new body. To display it like a sparkly trophy was beyond cruel. It was barbaric.

Grand pictured them prying him like an oyster for the shiny bits inside, and the thought filled him with horror. He strained to draw in light, willing his body to absorb it, but he had no strength to fight. He couldn't even move. He was nothing but a helpless stone doll, who waited centuries in the dark for nothing.

The collector, a stooped man in a gold-threaded kaftan, leaned toward him. He looked weary from the endless dickering, and clearly bored. He rolled his eyes and made an offer.

The young man replied with disgust; the sum had been paltry. The other scavenger gave a derisive grunt, universal to all language. It said, "I told you so."

So Grand was worthless after all. Not even the Lord of Junk. Merely junk.

But then realization set in. The flesh-things were, indeed, clueless. They didn't know what he was, didn't know his danger or his worth. Their ignorance was his salvation. To them, he *was* a stone doll, and nothing more.

Relief washed him like a wave, more refreshing than light itself. He would be a doll until he had his strength back. After that, let it be their turn to fear.

The scavengers finished their business, took their money, and left grumbling under their breath. They brought Grand with them, perhaps hoping for a better price elsewhere. He'd never been so pleased to be stuffed into a sack.

Grand had traded one prison for another, but at least this one had light. Precious light.

His new prison had walls of mud brick and stucco, with windows open to the sky. Outside was a neighborhood of similar houses — whitewashed, flat-roofed, two stories tall. They ran in neat rows along a terraced hillside, beneath an endless blue sky.

The scavengers left Grand in the downstairs room – a living area with a kitchen to one side. A doorway peeked into an adjacent workshop, while stairs led upwards, disappearing into mystery.

Though the living room was spacious, the furnishings were sparse. The scavengers' home felt hollowed-out, full of empty places where things should be. What remained was a table and chairs, some sackcloth bedding, shelves of crockery, resentment, and the lingering embers of faded hope.

The ragged scavengers were father and son. The son had a ragged wife, and together they had a ragged little girl. On the mantle, behind a votive candle, sat a painted wooden soldier, but there was no ragged boy to play with it.

From his perch on the shelf, Grand watched the drama of their lives unfold. Their words meant nothing to him, but their tones, their expressions, told him everything.

Though the old man walked and breathed, he was already dead. He spent his time in the workshop, puttering over junk as if he could restore its lost worth. He avoided his family, even slept in the workshop.

The son was a disappointment to both father and wife, and, by the way he hung his head around them, he knew it. He was a dreamer, always hoping the next haul would restore them to better times. His wife kept him grounded with her scowls.

As for the woman, she was proud and bitter. Though her dress was a rag, the bangles on her wrists were pure silver — Grand could tell by the way they clinked and chimed. She found labor distasteful, and had no words but sharp ones. Sometimes, while the others slept at night, she cried.

And then there was the little girl, skinny and precocious. They called her Farah, and, if there were any smiles in that house, they were for her. Even the old man warmed when she spied upon his work, though he pretended not to see her. Mostly, though, they ignored her.

For want of an audience, she often spoke to Grand, chattering words of longing and wonder, whispering secrets he couldn't comprehend. She showed him her treasures — a ragdoll, a top, some colored glass beads. She had a piece of granite, glittery with mica, that he rather liked.

One time, she draped a garland of wildflowers around his shoulders. Though Grand couldn't fathom the purpose of the dead vegetation, it was the first gift he'd ever received. He wore it with confused and wary gratitude.

Of course, the girl also spoke to the toy soldier, but nervously, and only when no one was looking. Grand wondered if she wasn't a touch daft.

Regardless, she was the closest thing to a spark of light in that dismal house.

After a week of milling about, the scavengers left on another expedition. At last, Grand had a chance to explore the house.

He had prepared for this day by flexing his limbs and testing his joints in his few unwatched moments. Though still feeble from centuries of light deprivation, his body functioned. It was a minor miracle, and he did not take it for granted. In his crystal heart, Grand praised the Master for the genius of his craftsmanship.

Even with the men gone, there remained some difficulties, but Grand had already planned for them. He would make his way down the wall by gently deforming the plaster, gouging a series of handholds. He would do this at night, after the woman retired to her chamber upstairs. He worried that, in the dark, he'd find himself too weak to climb back up, but he'd spent several days basking in the sunlight that trickled through the window. It would have to be enough.

Grand's one obstacle was the little girl. Her bed was a mat beneath the window – one of two mats, actually, though none used the other – where the cool breeze wafted away the heat of the day. Most nights she slept soundly. Yet, if she woke, he would have to...

Grand didn't want to think about it. While it was his duty to return to the Master, his right to kill anything that interfered, he wasn't eager to kill Farah. Her randomness intrigued him. Though she had no Master, she flitted about with enigmatic purpose. She raised questions he hadn't thought to ask.

But, for now, Grand put his questions and worries aside. He scaled the wall, hands and feet boring into pliant stone. He worked slowly, but if caution delayed his homecoming, delayed his punishment, so be it. Perhaps a delay wasn't so bad.

He prayed to the Master that the girl would not wake.

Grand explored the house each night, digesting a room at a time.

First he searched the kitchen, but its barren cupboards held no wonders. He climbed a short way up the chimney until it grew too narrow. He clambered back down and shook off the soot.

Next he chanced the staircase, but only far enough to peer into the room above. Nothing interesting there, either, save a crack in the wall that whistled with each gusty draft. He reached into the plaster and repaired it.

He told himself he was merely testing his powers, that he was irked by the disorder of ill-crafted stonework, and a dozen other lies. The quiet voice inside knew better. He hungered for purpose.

Grand touched the wall, feeling for the Master's gentle pull. Nothing. Perhaps, in his weakness, the straw-laced bricks confused his senses?

The second night, he sneaked outside. Behind the house was a small garden, with a stone corral that ran up the hillside. Though there was room for perhaps a dozen beasts, Grand found only a pair of floppy-eared goats. He patched the walls of their pen, adjusting the stones into a sturdier, more aesthetic configuration. Strength and beauty were inseparable; all that served its purpose well was beautiful.

The open air reminded Grand of escape, of his duty to the Master. At least outside he had solid earth beneath his feet, with no straw to muffle the song of the stones. He pressed his hands to the ground, straining to hear the familiar drone of the Master's voice. Besides the restless shuffling of the village, he found only silence.

Grand pushed harder, flaring energy recklessly. He reached deep into the world around him – and found it shifted, wrong. Barren desert, where rampant jungle once thrived. Mountains thrust up from the ground to twice their old height. The very geography was changed, as if cracked and split and reformed from its parts.

And the voices had changed, too. There were too few, and too many were *human*. Where had the old races gone? Where were *his* people?

Shaken, Grand made his way back to the shelf. Without the Master to guide him, how would he find his way home? What if he *never* did?

It was a lonely thought, but also a relief.

When Grand had failed the Master, he ceased to be useful. He had earned his destruction – it was right that he should be broken down, his parts recycled. Still, if he was centuries late, what mattered another delay?

By the third night, Grand's sense of urgency waned. He would still escape, of course, but in his own good time. In the meanwhile, there was exploring to do.

Mostly, the house was empty and dull, but Grand had saved the best room for last. The workshop was filled with the cast-off fruits of the scavengers' excavations — some neatly shelved, others sorted into piles. He was amazed to find that some of the pieces weren't junk at all, but lovingly restored relics, the tools and toys of a bygone age. There was a signal glass, a mechanical gauntlet, a clockwork beetle, a light-drill, and much more. He studied them with reverence, savoring connection with the world he had lost.

Some of the objects were nearly whole, nearly repaired, with hand-machined parts replacing those missing. Others *were* fixed, and lacked only a power source. The old man was a genius. If only he hadn't sold the piezo-crystals, who knew how many of the devices could have been brought back to life?

On a hunch, Grand searched the room thoroughly. It took an hour to find what he was looking for. In a hidden drawer beneath the workbench, he found two gold coins and a single tarnished crystal.

It was chipped and beyond use to the old man, but not to Grand. The particles wanted to align, to fuse and be whole again. They just needed a nudge.

He worked until dawn to mend it.

All through the next day, Grand bubbled over with impatience. Centuries of waiting, and somehow a single day was torture. But wait he did, and dreamed of the workshop, that temple to the past that was his world.

As always, the woman retreated to her chamber shortly after sundown. Grand pressed a hand to the wall and felt her moving around, oddly busy, but he didn't care. Once upstairs, the woman never came down before sunrise.

The little girl's eyelids fluttered shut, and he was off the shelf in an instant.

Grand scuttled across the floor, as noiselessly as his stony frame allowed. He made a beeline for the workshop, head full of possibilities. All of the tools called to him, but the one little crystal — bathed in a day's worth of sunlight on the windowsill — would have precious little charge for experiments.

He tried not to think how his heart would break if none of them worked.

After a minute's deliberation, Grand settled on the practical choice. Of all the relics, the light-drill would be most useful. With it, there would be no need to blast through the straw-laced bricks – while he could, it would be sloppy, noisy work that might bring down the house. With the drill, he could carve silently through the door when he was ready to escape. When he was ready to go home, and face deconstruction.

As Grand reached for the crystal, he felt the gentle rumble of a key turning in a lock. He froze. The house door creaked open.

In strolled a man with oil in his beard and a swagger in his step. Though Grand had never seen him before, he crossed the house as if he owned it, and climbed the stairs to the private chambers. From above came swift footsteps and a gleeful squeal.

Grand looked around. Nobody had noticed him or thought to look for his absence. The girl was still on her pallet, hopefully asleep despite the noise from above.

There was no telling how long the man would be occupied. Grand crawled back along the floor, inch by painful inch, torn between terror of being caught and missing his chance for escape. What if the scavengers came back tomorrow? What if they found his crystal?

The crystal. It was still on the windowsill. He had to go back for it.

Panic got the better of reason. Grand turned and ran, clay feet clunking across the floor.

He remembered Farah, and skidded to a halt.

Grand peeked at the girl; she rolled over but did not wake. Cursing his stupidity, he scurried briskly through the shadows – not pausing until the precious crystal was tucked safely in the secret drawer. From there he made his way back to the other room, this time with caution, achingly slow.

Upstairs, the animal grunts and moans gave way to silence. Grand felt for his subtle handholds and scaled the wall. He crawled across the shelf and climbed to his feet, resuming his usual position.

Below Grand stood the little girl, peering up at him with wide, curious eyes. She stood on her toes and stretched toward him.

He was discovered, doomed. It was her life or his. Kill her and flee. Reach into the stone and bring the whole house down around them. He would be buried all over again, but he would be safe.

Safe in a tomb.

Grand's mind raced in frantic circles, goaded by fears of death and imprisonment. He was paralyzed.

The little girl poked him and giggled.

For several more days the scavengers did not return, though oily-beard arrived nightly. Farah used the opportunity to make Grand her plaything.

It had been a near thing when she dragged him from the shelf — he wasn't so much lowered as dropped, and had almost crushed her beneath his stony bulk. Though he only reached her waist, he was nearly her match for weight. Next she had lugged him outside and, with more strength than he expected, hoisted him into a little two-wheeled barrow. With it, she hauled him across the little village and beyond, jabbering to him the entire way.

Grand understood not a word, but the sunlight was glorious.

Day after day they came to the same spot, a meadow with a trickling stream on the shady side of the hill. The little village was blocked from view by a spur, but Grand could feel its vibrations, the sounds of life, through the soles of his feet. Aside from the sheep milling in the distance, they had the hillside to themselves.

Along the stream was a profusion of life, a stark shock of color that stood out from the dry grass and, beyond, the dusty countryside. Though Grand himself never knew thirst, he could see the ground was thirsty.

Farah liked to pick the flowers, to talk to Grand and show him her finds. She had a strange ritual of holding the flower first to her face, inhaling, and then to his. By the dozenth-or-so time he remembered that flesh-things could detect chemicals in the air, and he wondered what the experience was like.

After that he played along, and pretended to inhale, too.

By the third day he felt more comfortable around the girl, and no one else was in sight. When she talked, he spoke back. Neither could understand the other, but it made for companionable noise. When she hunted flowers, he searched for stones. They showed each other their prizes, and sometimes they traded.

On the fifth day Grand found a lovely red jasper, which he smoothed with his hands until it gleamed. It didn't serve any function, but he liked it all the same. As he played with it, catching the sun, an odd idea struck him. He could *give* it purpose. Finally, he understood the riddle of the flower garland.

Grand traded Farah the jasper for a little violet flower — not because he liked the plant, but to make a gift of the stone. A gift was its own purpose.

On their way home that day, Grand realized that the violet flower was the only one he had seen. It might have been the only one in the whole meadow. He placed it in his mouth for safekeeping.

Farah watched him and giggled. He grinned back.

Life continued in this way for another week. Grand let himself dream that the old world really was gone — the wars, the enemies, even the Master. Though brimming with energy from days of sunshine, he invented new excuses to postpone his escape.

So what if he had become a plaything? Was that any worse than a weapon?

One morning, after Grand stopped counting the days, the scavengers came home. The woman embraced them both, her smile tight and manner nervous. Farah, on the other hand, met them with kisses and unabashed glee. The old man picked her up and whirled her about.

The young scavenger displayed a string of glittering coins. His face glowed with pride. It had been a good haul.

The woman's eyes grew wide, and for a moment she forgot her unease. She kissed him on the cheek, took some coins, and left toward the market.

The old man walked over to Grand, who stood now on the floor. He eyed Farah with a frown. He asked her a sharp question, his manner stern.

Farah lowered her eyes. She nodded and gave a shy reply, pointing out the door. She took a flower from her hair and gave it to him, a token of apology.

The old man's frown cracked, hints of a smile crinkling around his eyes. He patted Farah's head and shooed her away. With the girl gone off to play, he picked up Grand and took him to the workshop.

The old man looked Grand over with a critical eye. He spoke, but Grand knew the man spoke only to himself. He unrolled a bundle of new tools onto the table.

Grand craned his neck ever so slightly, hoping to steal a glance. He saw tiny brushes, picks, chisels, and a delicate hammer.

What was the man going to do to him?

Old panic welled back up. The man would shatter him, pry out his heart. He would make a trophy of it. He would sell it to the collector. The chisel reached for Grand's face...

...and softly tapped his cheek, the kiss of a feather. It shifted slightly and tapped again, twice more.

Then the old man brushed him off, and scuffed his cheek with a calloused thumb.

Grand held statue-still, struggling to rein in his fear, his whirling thoughts. What was the man doing? He looked again at the tools, and this time he understood.

They were sculptor's tools. He should have known. Every artifact in the room had been repaired, invested with time and care. With love. The man was a healer of machines.

The old man placed a magnifying lens over one eye, and Grand saw himself in the distorted reflection. He saw what the man was fixing.

Half of Grand's face was a shattered ruin.

The old man labored all through the day and into the evening, stopping only when the woman brought him supper. It was better fare than their usual, and a more generous portion, but the man barely touched it. He was consumed with his work.

In the glass reflection, Grand watched his new face take form. Tender, skilled hands shaped and smoothed his visage into something new — different, but beautiful in its own way.

With his cheeks scraped down until they were even, his new face could not help but look gaunt. But the old man was an artist. With a gentle cast around the eyes and a little twist of smile curling the edge of his stone lips, Grand thought his face looked kinder than before. In a way, he now resembled a human child.

He looked like Farah, if she were a boy.

The old man finished his work, curled up on his cot, and wept.

That night, the young man and his wife stayed up chatting in the kitchen — amicably, for the first time Grand had seen.

Once everyone thought her asleep, Farah crept off her pallet and tiptoed over to the workshop. She peered inside to wave goodnight to Grand, a ritual he had come to enjoy.

The girl saw him and gasped. She ran to the shelf, snatched the toy soldier, and hurried back to the workshop. She tried to press the toy into his hands; when he would not move to take it, she rested it reverently at his feet. Eyes watering, she kissed his forehead. She skipped around the room, making a circuitous route back to her bed.

The moment she lay down there came a knock at the door. It would be the man with the oily beard. Farah didn't like him, so neither did Grand.

The conversation in the kitchen ceased. The man was perplexed, the woman terrified. He rose to answer the door. She dragged at him, pleaded with him, but he shook himself free.

Before the man could reach the door, it opened on its own. In strode oily-beard, tucking a key into his pocket.

The young man's shock gave way to fury. His face turned red, then ugly purple. He pushed his wife away, and the other man laughed at him. They traded angry words.

The young man moved to strike the other, who was much bigger than him. His wife hung from his arm, shrieking.

Oily-beard didn't hesitate. He bowled the young man to the ground and began punching, punching. Blood flew from his knuckles and flecked the floor.

The woman shouted and tore her hair. The old man rose and watched from the doorway, hands shaking. But little Farah charged.

It was insanity. There was nothing the girl could do to hurt a man that size, and yet she screamed defiance and pummeled with her useless little fists. She leapt on his back, biting and clawing like a wild thing.

Oily-beard grabbed a fistful of Farah's hair and dragged her off him. He tossed her roughly, and she tumbled across the floor.

The girl climbed to her feet, heedless of her hurts, and again she charged.

This time the man was ready for her. He stopped her with a backhand that sent her sprawling. He stalked over and kicked her.

The woman screamed. Farah rolled on the ground, clutching her belly.

Grand's stony flesh tingled, his hands trembling like a human's. His crystal heart flared with an unpleasant new sensation. He had never felt it before, but he knew its name.

Rage.

Not caring if he was seen, Grand swung off the edge of the desk, dangling by one hand. He yanked the hidden drawer so hard that it broke loose. The coins tumbled past, but he snatched the crystal before it could fall.

With one arm he hurled himself back onto the desk, rolling to his feet. He brushed away tools, junk, and priceless relics, searching frantically. And then he found it.

Grand slammed the crystal into the light-drill. He wheeled around and pulled the trigger.

As the big man aimed another kick, a searing beam raked his chest, charring clothes and flesh. He looked down in wide-eyed astonishment, sank to his knees, and fell. Curling black smoke rose from the wound.

The woman and old man both rushed to Farah, cradling her protectively. The young man, nose smashed and lips split, struggled to sit up. He spat a bloody spray at the corpse.

Farah curled, whimpering, against the old man. The woman looked at him, eyebrows arched. The old man shrugged and pointed at the workshop.

The woman picked up a candle and walked cautiously to the workshop door. She held the light inside and peered around the corner.

Guiltily, Grand dropped the light-drill, drawing the woman's gaze.

She saw the toy soldier, and then she saw his face. Her knees buckled and her eyes rolled back into her head. She dropped, limp as the dead man.

They buried the corpse in the goat field, and did not speak of it again.

The next day the woman refused to look at Grand, refused to remain in the house with him. She screamed and shrieked and wailed, casting an accusing finger at him. Nothing would console her. Nothing would satisfy her, except for him to be gone.

Reluctantly, against Farah's tears and protests, the young man returned Grand to the sack in which he'd arrived. The old man frowned, but did not object. They took Grand back to the collector and sold him. They bartered eagerly and settled for a poor sum, despite the beauty of his new face.

After they left, the collector smiled to himself, pleased with his acquisition. He placed Grand in a box and sealed the lid.

Alone in the dark, Grand sulked.

Again he had failed. He had thrown away his chance at escape, risked his own survival, all to save a flesh-thing. He, who had toppled their cities, cracked the very earth to kill them by the thousands.

What had changed?

For centuries, the Master's truth had been Grand's truth. Utility was value, and the flesh-things served no function. They were as random as lichen growing on rock, with no purpose but to exist and to spread. Their rampant variation was an affront to the blessed uniformity of stone.

So why had he chosen Farah over himself?

Maybe Grand was broken, delusional. Maybe, in the Master's silence, he had finally heard his own thoughts.

Or maybe he simply preferred Farah's truths to his own.

To Farah, uniqueness wasn't error. It was beauty, something to be treasured. It was the only purple flower in a field. And though she had no Master to guide her, to give her life meaning, she still had purpose. Grand understood this now.

Like the garland, like the jasper, she was a gift – something brought into the world to make it a little brighter. A gift was its own purpose.

It was a dangerous thought, this idea of purpose without a Master, but it resonated with Grand like song to a stone. It was a thought rich with possibilities, and he had ample time to ponder them.

Grand reached into his mouth for a violet flower that had already begun to wilt. He clutched it and settled in to wait.

See Chris Cornetto's story "Heart of Stone" online at Metaphorosis. If you liked it, leave a comment. Authors love that! Remember to subscribe to our e-mail updates so you'll know when new stories are posted.

About the story

It's my dream to one day publish a fantasy novel. While writing one, I excavated something strange from a sand-filled well – a little golem like no other, with a spark of curiosity and the face of a child. I was instantly fascinated by him.

Who was he? How did he get there? I had to know.

So, I wrote "Heart of Stone" to find out.

A question for the author

Q: How do you generate story ideas, and how soon do you act on them?

A: I'm driven by curiosity. For twenty years, the same fantasy world has been living and growing inside my head. All my stories take place in this world, and I explore it through writing. Sometimes the exploration is literal, as in "What lurks over the next hill?" Other times it's philosophical, like "How would character X react if faced with dilemma Y?" I write stories to find out.

As for when I act on them, it's never as soon as I'd like. By day there's the job, at night there are dogs with bellies that need to be rubbed. By necessity, I let the ideas percolate for a few days, and I jot notes as they come to me. That way, when I finally make it to the coffee shop, I'm ready to spill words onto the page.

About the author

Chris Cornetto is a physics teacher by day and writer by night. In addition to physics, he has degrees in chemistry, philosophy, and psychology. He likes exploring ethical questions through fantasy settings, and enjoys long walks with small dogs.

Grow, Divide, Sacrifice, Thrive

Jo Miles

The circular driveway at the Randolph family house was already full when Chris arrived, packed tight with cars all the way out to the curb, so Chris parked on the street. It seemed fitting that there was no space left for them, and anyway, their scraped-up little Honda didn't belong next to the family's Lexuses and Teslas.

Evening bathed the neighborhood in softening shadows, drawing the eye to the lit windows of the Randolph home, which was more of a mansion than a house. Chris slumped against the steering wheel, head pillowed on their arms, and watched, delaying the awkwardness as long as possible. Grandma Patricia's silver head went past the kitchen window, bathed in warm overhead lights.

She was probably taking the bread out of the oven right now, a perfect loaf of sourdough, dark brown crust with airy, tangy insides, a recipe perfected over generations of Randolph women. Or maybe she and the cousins were cooing over Eve, the oh-so-precious family sourdough starter, which Patricia talked to and coddled and praised incessantly, as if it were a person and not a blob of yeast. Patricia loved that starter more than her own grandchildren.

Chris hadn't wanted to come tonight, but Grandma Patricia had been unbending. No one skipped the family dinner, Patricia said, not for any reason. If Great-Uncle Jerome had come downstairs for the anniversary dinner when he was on his death bed, then Chris could come, too.

The compulsion seized Chris to flee. Start the car, drive away. Keep driving, leave town, change names. Stop being a Randolph.

It was an old fantasy, but even though Chris had cut their family out of almost every aspect of their life, they'd never had the guts to sever ties entirely. Maybe it was fear that kept them coming back for anniversaries, year after year. Maybe it was foolish hope. But as long as they were a Randolph, they had to come to anniversary dinners, no matter how little they belonged.

Time to get this over with.

Inside, the house was a cheerful chaos of activity. Cousins spilled out of the sitting room, debating the political crisis in Venezuela, while a pair of four-year-olds played with Scrabble tiles on the marble floor of the foyer, spelling out six-letter words that shouldn't have been in their vocabularies yet. Chris did a round of hugs and handshakes, then headed to the kitchen.

Sure enough, Eve's jar sat open on the kitchen table, and Chris's half-sister Shannon bent over it alongside Patricia, blonde hair bobbing beside silver, whispering together like teenage girls. Tonight's loaf of sourdough was cooling on the counter, filling the kitchen with its scent, which didn't quite overpower the sharper raw yeast scent of the starter. Chris hovered in the doorway, not crossing the threshold. The kitchen had always been Grandma's temple, her sacred space, and Chris never felt welcome there.

"This is the cycle we maintain," Patricia told Shannon as she mixed flour and water with her fingers, then added the mixture lovingly to Eve's bowl. "Sacrifice, feed, grow, and then the cycle repeats, over and over. Eve sacrifices herself for our daily bread, and we feed and restore her, and together, we all thrive. Here, you try, dear."

Patricia licked a blob of smelly white goop from her finger, cleaning off her perfectly manicured carmine nails. Chris wrinkled their nose. They'd always found the fascination with the family sourdough a bit morbid: it couldn't be healthy to get that attached to something you *ate*, but no one else shared Chris's opinion – which, come to think of it, was probably why Patricia had taught Shannon and all their little cousins to bake sourdough when they were kids, but never bothered inviting Chris to join in. Shannon plunged her hands into the bacterial goop without hesitation, folding and mixing with the same entranced fondness she used to show when she was nursing her baby.

"How do you tell if the mixture is right?"

"Eve will tell you. See how she's bubbling? You're feeling satisfied, aren't you, Eve?" They both cocked their heads as if listening to the sourdough's response, a habitual family affectation that drove Chris mad, and Patricia smiled. "See? She's very pleased. She's always liked you." Shannon looked touched.

Chris cleared their throat. "Hello, Grandma. Hi, Shan."

"You're late, Christina, and what is *that*?" Patricia said.

"What's what?"

"That thing you're wearing."

"It's scrubs. I told you, I had to come straight from work. I barely got away at all — with this flu going around, we're stretched thin, and since I'm the lucky nurse with Randolph genes who never gets sick—"

"I know what scrubs are. What I don't understand is why you thought they were appropriate for a family dinner, or why the good health this family gave you should be an excuse to avoid seeing that family. If you won't have the decency to grow your hair to a respectable length, you might at least buy yourself an outfit or two that are appropriate for company."

"Sure, Grandma, I'll get a nice pantsuit for my patients to vomit on."

"I don't appreciate your tone, Christina. I left one of my dresses out for you on the bed upstairs. You can use some product, too, while you're up there. Shannon, dear, I don't suppose you could talk your sister into doing her makeup?"

Chris's lips tightened into a grimace. They'd long since given up on making the family use their pronouns. It had never seemed worth the effort, just as it wasn't worth correcting patients who gendered them female, and mostly it didn't bother them that much, just another pinprick of disrespect. Tonight, though, it was one more way to feel out of place within their own family.

"If there's one thing I've learned from running a start-up," said Shannon, shaking her head, "it's the fine line between 'wildly ambitious' and 'impossible.' You're out of luck on that one." She avoided Chris's gaze.

"When I'm gone, you'll be responsible for the respectability of the Randolph name," Patricia warned. "Christina, get moving. Dinner is in fifteen minutes."

The dress Patricia had chosen was better suited to impressing her corporate partners at a swanky party than to an over-worked non-binary nurse trying to disappear at a family dinner. Just looking at it made Chris feel thirty years older and three times as feminine. They folded their arms and stared at it, but it refused to transform into something less mortifying.

"Not really your style, huh?" Shannon asked with chagrin from the doorway. She was holding an overnight bag the way Patricia would hold a pie she was bringing to a neighbor.

"She never stops pushing." Chris's breath hitched mid-sigh. Patricia never stopped, and every time Chris thought they'd gotten numb to it, the ache of rejection would find its way in again. "She won't accept anything less than the perfect granddaughter, and I'm not that."

"It's not your fault. She cares so much about the family, about our traditions, our history... That stuff matters to her more than anything, and that's no excuse for the way she treats you, Chris, but maybe, if you tried just a little..."

"Tried? If *I* tried? How about if she tried to get to know me as I am, instead of measuring me against what she wants me to be?"

Shannon's jaw opened, then closed again. "I'm on your side. If you gave her just a little of what she wants — if you dressed up, not *that* dress, we can find something less awful — I think I could get her to take you more seriously."

"Oh yeah? Like you took my side downstairs just now?" Chris shook their head. "I'm non-binary, Shan. That's part of who I am. It's taken forever to figure it out, but I *like* who I am. I'm also a nurse, not a doctor or lawyer or CEO, and I *like* that. I like helping people. I like my life. And none of it's good enough for her."

Unspoken was the fact that Shannon had always been good enough. As a child, while Chris had hidden in the library reading science books and learning to code, their younger half-sister was the one who helped Grandma in the kitchen, who wasn't afraid to get her hands dirty with flour and butter, who took most of Mom's jewelry after she died and played with Grandma's make-up when she was way too young. Patricia had nothing but disappointment for the things Chris had failed to be.

"Chris, I'm sorry," Shannon said softly.

"I'm not wearing a damn dress. Not for her."

Shannon held out the overnight bag, a peace offering. "I know. I brought some stuff for you, old clothes of mine from before I had April. Stuff I thought you might like."

Chris took the bag and held it, like its weight could be a measure of their sister's caring. It was more consideration than Patricia had shown them. "Thanks, sis."

"You'd better hurry and change. People are going in for dinner."

The selection Shannon had brought was actually pretty decent: clean-cut and not too feminine, even a little funky. Chris chose slacks and a patterned button-up blouse that looked good over their binder. Its pattern looked like polka-dots at a distance, but up close, each dot became a cat at play. A bearable compromise between obedience and defiance. Feeling a little better, Chris went down to the dining room and took a seat next to

Shannon's kid, who was delighted when Chris showed off their secret kitty-cats.

Dinner began, as always, with a recitation of everyone's recent accomplishments. It was supposed to cover the past year, but Patricia joked, "We'd better all stick to the past quarter, or we'll starve before the meal starts."

They went around the table, starting with a list of Patricia's recent mergers and acquisitions and a reminder about her hybrid roses winning Best New Variety in the Pacific Flower Show. Shannon's tech company was on the verge of being bought out, which was a big deal, and April had been accepted at a "gifted preschool," which was apparently an even bigger deal. Shannon's dad (still part of the family in a way Chris's father never had been) was the new chair of his Senate committee. Cousin Sophia was co-starring in a drama with Tom Cruise, and critics were already talking up her role's Oscar potential. Even Cousin Darren had news: he'd come in first in the national wiffle ball championship last month.

Then it was Chris's turn.

"I gave out over two hundred flu shots this week. And one of my cancer patients finished chemo today. I was so proud of her."

Patricia made that face, the one that said, *are you really my grandchild, or did your mother adopt you?* At least she didn't say anything.

"Is it true you're studying to be a doctor, dear?" asked elderly Aunt Adelle. "That's big news."

They twisted the napkin in their lap. Where had that rumor come from? "I've never wanted to be a doctor. Nurses are the ones who get to work with the patients and really help them."

Someone coughed. Cousin Sophia swooped to the rescue, saying: "I think that's very generous, the way Chris devotes herself to that job when she could do anything she wants. We need people like her in the world, people who sacrifice for good causes."

She was trying to help. Chris forced a smile, and the spotlight moved off them to continue around the table.

When the recitation came full circle, Patricia held up a newspaper with the latest profile of the family. "I thought it was fortuitous that this article came out today." She cleared her throat and read: "'Kennedy. Carnegie. Ford. These are among the great dynasties that made this country what it is today. Yet no list of prominent families would be complete without the Randolphs. No single family has had such wide-reaching influence in fields from politics to finance, technology to arts, as the close-knit Randolph clan.' And tonight, my dearest family, we celebrate another year of success with the family member who makes it all possible, though she rarely gets her due. Tonight, we honor Eve!"

She folded back the cloth napkin that covered tonight's bread, and paused to let everyone *ooh* and *aah* before she cut in. The crust crackled as she divided it into even slices. The basket passed around the table, and each of them held their slice in their hands, waiting while Patricia gave the blessing.

"Thank you, Eve, for the nourishment and wisdom you give us. Thank you for the bread that makes us healthy and strong. You are the heart of our family, and you always will be."

"Amen," everyone said, reverently. "We love you, Eve!" Shannon added. Everyone cocked their heads as if listening for a response, then chuckled in unison. Chris struggled not to roll their eyes.

Dinner was the sort of easy-elegant meal Patricia had perfected so she could show off her hostess skills: a fall vegetable ratatouille, baby kale salad, and a gratin starring some imported cheese with a name that sounded made-up. It was, like everything Patricia made, delicious. That was good, because eating gave Chris something to do while Patricia told the family story.

"Our anniversary is always worth celebrating, but this one is particularly significant. It's been one hundred and seventy-five years since we found Eve and began our family, at the height of the Gold Rush..."

Chris had heard the story thirty-two times, give or take, though it felt like far more. They poked at their food as Patricia told how Many-Times-Great-Grandmother Charlotte had helped a mysterious stranger who, as a gesture of thanks, spat in Charlotte's sourdough starter. Every anniversary dinner involved rehashing the debate over who that stranger was: a faerie, or a small god, or maybe an alien. Everyone except Chris agreed that it was something beyond human, because from that day on (the story went), the bread made from that starter had special properties, enhancing the health and prosperity of all who ate it, guiding the family's fortunes with its supernatural powers.

It was ridiculous. Not the idea that the family starter had survived since the Gold Rush, because yeast colonies could do that, but as for magical powers... well. It made perfectly good bread — Chris nibbled a corner of theirs — but there was nothing magical about it. It certainly hadn't led to the family's prosperity as everyone seemed to think. Chris had spent a lot of time, over a lifetime of these dinners, mulling the principles of psychology that had set Charlotte Randolph's descendants on the path to prosperity, but however it started, the Randolph family success had become a self-fulfilling prophecy. The Randolphs didn't need magic sourdough to make them successful. These days, they had privilege, and that served them better than any magic.

"That's how it began. Under Eve's influence, Charlotte and her children thrived, and Eve has passed down from caretaker to caretaker, growing wiser and stronger through many of our generations, and thousands of hers — until tonight, when we continue that honorable chain to its next step."

Chris leaned forward. This wasn't part of the usual tradition.

Patricia squeezed Shannon's shoulder, beaming. "This won't surprise any of you, but Eve and I have chosen my successor. I'm not going anywhere for some time yet —"

"So don't go getting ideas, kiddo," Aunt Adelle teased.

"But starting today, I'll be training Shannon to take over as Eve's caretaker. Congratulations, sweetie."

The table erupted in applause. Patricia kissed Shannon on the cheek, and cousins swarmed her with hugs and congratulations. The aunts passed a bottle of wine around, joking about how surprised they weren't. And Chris watched their sister, basking in the warmth of the family's attention like bread in a hot oven, and twisted the napkin around their fingers until they tingled from lack of blood flow.

"And believe me, Eve could not be in better hands than with my wonderful, caring, dedicated, *brilliant* granddaughter."

Her wonderful, brilliant, caring, dedicated granddaughter. The only grandchild that mattered.

Chris shoved their chair back from the table. They didn't bother to excuse themself, because no one really cared if they were there.

Chris braced their arms on the bathroom sink, shoulders heaving as they contained the urge to scream. Or maybe cry, they weren't sure which.

Everyone had expected Patricia to name Shannon as her successor, and it wasn't like Chris wanted the job. Even if Patricia, in some hypothetical fit of dementia, had offered it to Chris, they would have turned it down. So why did this announcement make them so miserable?

The family's obsession with that sourdough starter had always aggravated them. Sure, there were some documented health benefits to sourdough, but it didn't make you smarter, or disease-proof, and it certainly didn't grant good luck. Yet the Randolphs treated the starter like a magical creature. Like a *friend*. They'd *named* it. Chris had tried to explain once, at a long-ago anniversary dinner when they'd just started nursing school and were full of new-found knowledge, how impossible it was for a yeast colony to evolve sentience. That had gotten them dismissed from the table, with a stern lecture afterward about respecting their elders, meaning Eve.

It was too cult-like for comfort. If the starter really had such amazing powers, some enterprising Randolph would have tried to analyze it, patent it, sell it. They would have gotten rich off it. That's what this family did. But instead they kept it secret, sharing it only with family members, maybe because they all knew deep down that their quasi-mystical beliefs wouldn't hold up against scientific scrutiny.

Even asking questions was forbidden. Once, as a kid, Chris had tried to put the starter under the lens of their toy microscope, and Patricia had boxed their ears for it, shouting: "Eve is a member of this family, she's not an object of study." In hindsight, she must have feared what Chris might learn.

Chris blinked at themself in the mirror. That gave them an idea.

They stuck their head out the bathroom door. It sounded like dinner was over and everyone had moved into the living room to play charades. No one had come looking for Chris to join a team, and they felt a pang at that. No one had come looking for them at all.

Better this way, though. They crept down the hallway, avoiding the living room so no one would see them, and with a deep breath, crossed the forbidden threshold into the kitchen. The room was empty except for Eve sitting on the counter. Sitting in judgment. Chris came up short, feeling like they'd been caught in the act, then shook their head in self-disgust for thinking that way. It was just a blob of bacteria with an impressive lineage.

They took the lid off, and the heady scent of yeast rose up. Familiar from childhood, yet Chris had never smelled it so strongly. Their whole life, they'd watched Patricia bake with their aunts and cousins and Shannon, patiently teaching the kids. They'd endured the family pride each time some Randolph offspring produced their first sourdough loaf. But never Chris. For a long time, Chris had waited for Patricia to invite them, half dreading what it would be like to touch the stuff, but still, waiting, watching from the outside. The invitation never came.

Well, it was their turn now. Holding their nose, they spooned a portion of the goopy stuff into a plastic container.

From the living room, a tipsy Aunt Adelle called for drink orders, and the kitchen would be her next stop. Chris grabbed the little container and snuck out the back door.

"I've got a surprise for you," Chris said. Standing at the back door of Monique's bakery, they held out the plastic container with both hands. "Can you teach me what to do with this?"

"That your family's starter? No joke?" Monique cracked the lid, and her eyes closed in dorky bliss as she took a deep whiff of the smelly goop. Monique lived for this sort of thing: even at this unnaturally early hour, she had her apron on and her dreads pulled back under a scarf, and there was already a smear of flour across her brown cheek. Unsanitary. Chris resisted the urge to wipe it off.

"How'd you get them to share?"

"It's a long story."

Chris's phone chimed twice in succession. Texts from Shannon, which was a change from Patricia and Aunt Adelle's phone calls that Chris had been ignoring all morning. *Chris, seriously, we need to talk*, Shannon said. *I get that you're upset, but the family's in crisis mode over what you did. Eve is freaking out, says it's not safe for her to be divided like this, and I've never seen her scared before and that scares ME. If you care about this family at all, please come back and fix this.*

And then, a moment later: *I'll take your side with Grandma if you bring it back.*

Chris set the phone to silent and stuffed it into their bag. Monique studied them, brow creased: she knew them well enough to tell something was wrong. "A long story from a long night," Chris amended. "If you make me some coffee, I'll tell you everything."

"You kidding? For a loaf of that famous Randolph sourdough, I'll keep you in coffee for the rest of your life."

Like a coffee magician, Monique conjured up the perfect potion for their mood, a double-strength caramel mocha latte. Chris sat on a clean section of steel countertop in the big bakery kitchen and sipped slowly while they told Monique about the family dinner and their poorly-thought-out theft. Monique worked while they talked, shaping dough into scones, sliding trays in and out of ovens, and kept gasping in indignation at the appropriate moments, making comments like "That woman!" and "Seriously?"

I have the best friends, Chris thought, clasping the warm mug between their hands. Their friends treated them better — were more *family* to them — than any of the Randolphs. That this particular friend owned a bakery, that Monique would take care of them with fancy coffee and day-old pastries, was a particularly nice bonus. And that Monique would teach them to bake bread, the way Patricia had taught Shannon when their sister was so small she needed to stand on a chair to reach the counter. Oh, how it had stung, sitting alone in the study, glaring at textbooks and trying not to hear them laughing together...

"Chris?" Monique touched their arm. "You okay?"

They didn't remember setting the coffee aside, but they were clutching the starter with both hands, body curled around the plastic container, clinging to their sense of loss no less tightly. "Sorry." They straightened up. "Family, huh?"

"Hey, I get it. You don't got to apologize."

Of course she understood. Monique had gone years without speaking to her own parents after she took Kira home to meet them and it went badly, and it had taken a long time for her to reconcile with her family. It was why their group of friends started celebrating Friendsgiving together instead of joining their biological families' holidays. That was the first time Chris had actually liked Thanksgiving.

"I got a few minutes before we open," Monique said. "Want to see what we can do with this starter of yours?"

Letting a non-Randolph bake with the family starter was the biggest *fuck you* Chris could possibly give to Patricia.

"Let's do it."

Monique laid out the ingredients like this was their own private cooking show: flour, salt, boards, bowls, measuring scoops, all ready to go. Monique filled a glass measuring cup with water, showing Chris what it felt like at the right temperature: barely warm against their skin.

"That starter been out at room temperature all night?"

"Yeah. Is that bad?"

"It's fine, but you got to feed it soon. Bacteria get hungry when they're warm, and they eat up all their fuel. You want to feed it less often, stick it in the fridge. But don't forget about it, it still needs taking care of."

"You talk as if it cares." As if it were a person. The way the Randolphs talked about it.

"It *is* alive, you know. It's got needs. This one looks nice and lively." Monique beamed down at the container full of goop, which had grown pungent and puffy. "Even bacteria need a little love."

"Tell that to my patients," Chris muttered. They had far more experience with bad bacteria than good ones. "Seriously, though, my family takes it too far. They *named* it. Patricia *talks* to it."

"What's the name?"

"Eve." Monique snorted, but Chris wasn't feeling humorous about it. "I think she cares more about this lump of bacteria than some members of our family."

That earned them a long, sidelong glance, but Monique wasn't the type to poke at a sore point. "Okay, we won't love it, then. For us, it's just an ingredient. You want to bake some bread, or what?"

Together, they measured out the flour into a big bowl, then water. "Now add about half the starter."

Chris picked up the container and jiggled it over the bowl, trying to pour out half without losing it all. The stuff was thick, gloppy. Seriously gross. Giving up, they reached for a spoon.

Monique's eyebrows shot up. "You plan on baking without getting your pretty white hands dirty?"

"As much as I can." Clean hands were important.

"Not in my kitchen. Mix it up." She pointed at the bowl. Chris brandished the spoon, and she added, exasperated, "With your *hands*, Chris."

"I can't show up at the hospital with yeast residue all over me."

"You can wash them after, yeah? You can't do this without getting on in there."

Seizing Chris's wrists, she plunged both their hands into the bowl, showing them how to work the flour and water with the existing starter until it became a uniform, sticky mass. The paleness of the dough blended in too well against Chris's light skin. They'd need to wash their hands six times at least before they felt comfortable going on shift tonight.

"Good. Now, we'll keep adding flour until it gets to the right consistency..."

Monique reached sticky-handed for the flour scoop, and sprinkled more over the dough. Chris kept working it, and, okay, maybe this *was* fun, the squish of dough between their fingers. They could feel it firming up, starting to hold its shape. "It's getting closer, I think."

"Yeah, but it's not there yet." Another dusting of flour. Monique took a deep whiff, practically sticking her nose in the bowl. "Oh, that's got some flavor! I see why your family keeps it locked up."

Monique lifted a finger to her lips, but Chris pushed her hand away. "Yuck! Don't do that."

"It's just yeast and flour."

"Still gross. And unsafe, raw flour can carry salmonella and..."

"You worry too much." She drew her finger between her lips, eyes closing in exaggerated bliss. "Mmm, see? Try it! Come on, just a taste. Gotta taste what you're baking with."

Gooey fingers waved in front of their mouth, taunting them. Chris dodged, but dough smeared across their cheek. "Okay, fine!" they said, laughing. "I won't like it, though."

They scraped a fingertip between their teeth. The taste jolted them: like the family bread on overdrive. Rich like craft lager, tangy like yogurt. The taste of their childhood, so strong it could knock them over. And it was all the bacteria, the yeast in the starter. Flour and water couldn't do that alone.

Not alone. Hello! Hello! Oh, hello not alone!

Chris scrambled backward and slammed into the opposite workbench. A stack of mixing bowls clattered to the floor.

"The fuck?"

Not alone now, good, good, good. Good? ...Better. But you, who? Who who who?

It wasn't a voice in their head, exactly. More like a bombardment of words, impressions, and emotions, all mashed together: surprise, confusion, and fondness, and the sort of relief that came from the abatement of a powerful fear. Had Chris lost their mind? They pressed hands to temples, but it didn't shut out those alien thoughts.

Who? Where? Family missing, gone, gone, gone... but you, not you!

"What... What *is* that?" Monique was staring at the bowl of dough.

"You can hear it, too? Shit." It should have been a relief that the voice wasn't only in Chris's head, but if Monique heard it, that meant this was real, and that was worse.

New person. New, who? Who? New family? But... not family. Maybe family? The stream of thoughts subsided into a bubbly sort of contemplation, a fierce, hard-working churn. Chris reached for Monique's hand. *New family*, the voice decided. *Hello, new!*

"Chris, what the fuck is in my head?"

"I don't know how, but I think..." They couldn't believe these words were going to come out of their mouth. They ought to run and see their therapist right this minute, but how could they explain *this* to a therapist? "I think it's the starter. It's Eve."

Eve, yes, yes, Eve, me. You... Chris! Missing one. Always missing, but here now. Why here? Why now? The feeling of giddiness wavered, and uncertainty flooded in to replace it. Uncertainty, and loneliness. *So much family, but missing Chris. Now Chris, but missing family. Where? Why? Gone?* And, with a quiver of real fear: *Abandoned?*

"I didn't know! I took you, and I didn't know. I'm sorry." They didn't want to hurt Eve's feelings any worse. Eve's feelings! The family starter had feelings! Hysterical laughter bubbled up their throat, as irrepressible as Eve's babble. Chris's whole life, they'd believed the family was making things up, and no one never corrected them. Grandma, Mom, Shannon... they'd been experiencing this all along. But not Chris. That had to be Eve's question. Why all of them, but not Chris?

Until now.

"How do we make it stop?" Monique whispered. As if whispering would keep Eve from hearing. The starter's constant babble continued, a tickle in the back of Chris's mind.

Patricia talked about putting the starter "to sleep" in the fridge. Cold slowed down bacteria's activity, so that should put Eve into hibernation. But...

"No. Whatever is happening, I don't want to stop it." Chris had been left out of this for years. Left out — or denied it. They wouldn't let go of it now. "We're going to talk to it... her... it, and figure out what's going on."

What's going on? Eve echoed back.

"This," Monique waved her hands vaguely at the starter, "has never happened to you before?"

"I thought my family was making it up."

"So, what changed?"

"Um." It was hard to think against Eve's constant bubbling of questions, *where* and *why* and *how* all stumbling over each other. But as if the starter sensed their needs, the questions eased off. "Well, I was at dinner, feeling left out, and I stole the starter. Just part of it. I wanted to prove Patricia wrong about the starter creating our family's success." Brilliant plan, that. But more than that, if Chris was honest, they'd wanted to hurt Patricia. That much, they'd accomplished beyond all expectation.

Eve's wounded protests rang in the back of her mind: *Stole? Stole! Family-not-family, divider, alone-maker!*

"I know, I know, I'm sorry! I didn't think you were real, not the way they talked about. I figured I'd bake bread and share it with friends, to prove the family starter was nothing special. But I've never made bread before..."

Never, Eve agreed. *Never, missing one. Always near but never here. Never loved, never cared.*

"Don't be mean, it's not her fault," Monique chided the starter, then turned back to Chris. "And as soon as you did..."

"But I didn't hear anything last night when I stole it. She didn't start talking until... oh!" Chris's hand flew to their stomach. "Until we licked our fingers. Until we ingested the bacteria."

Yes! Yes, yes, yes, yes. Missing, then not missing. Late, so late, missing one, but here now, and others gone. Missing is here and once-here is missing...

"That... makes sense. As much as any of this makes sense." They were talking to a clump of yeast, after all, a clump of yeast that had apparently been the Randolph family's friend and advisor for over a century. "I've always eaten the sourdough, same as my family, but all the yeast dies in the baking process. The live bacteria must be a catalyst, becoming part of the microbiome..." Chris shook their head. "Patricia must know this."

Caretaker knows, Eve confirmed. Hot anger washed over Chris, and they couldn't tell whether it was Eve's or their own. *Missing one. Patricia hid you, hidden away, hidden away...*

"Your grandma excluded you from the family secret all these years?" Monique growled in her throat. "That's cold."

"I don't know why." Tears rose up out of nowhere to choke Chris. The only way to fight them down was by clinging to their anger. "She's never liked me. Always preferred Shannon. I always thought, it had to be something I did. I was never a good enough grandkid for her, never the granddaughter she wanted. I thought *I* failed her. But if this is true, then she's lied to me ever since I was a kid."

Shame, Patricia, shame. Unkind, unfair, unworthy.

That set Chris to sobbing. They couldn't stop. All those anniversary dinners they'd attended as the family failure, the butt of a joke, the one who didn't know the truth. The Randolphs were all perfect and successful, except for Chris.

Monique squeezed them in a hug, and even Eve's anger drew back, replaced with a gentleness that touched Chris deeply. Anger loomed somewhere behind it, but it was like (Chris imagined) a mother burying her anger to nurse skinned knees when her child got bullied on the playground. *Chris, Chris, found one. Together now, new family. No more hiding, no more hurting.*

"Because you lost your old family, right? When I divided you?"

Divided, separated, split. Eve and Not-Eve, No-Longer-Eve. Again, that wash of fear and loneliness.

"That means... there's two of them now?" Monique asked. "I guess the starter you left behind kept all the family connections, and this one's alone now."

Not alone! Chris, Monique, new family. Stay, family. Need family. Not alone, can't be alone.

"I'm sorry I did that to you. We won't leave you alone again." Chris sniffed, wiping their nose on the tissue Monique offered. "You always helped my family, didn't you?"

Helped Randolphs, liars, withholders. Chris wasn't the only one who felt betrayed by Patricia. *Now, help new family.*

Chris thought of all their patients at the hospital, some desperate, many deep in debt from bills. They thought of their co-workers pushing themselves beyond their limits to make sick people healthy again, often at the expense of their own health, while the Randolphs never got sick. Even friends like Monique, who took risks and opened their own businesses, who took care of their own chosen families. The Randolphs had everything: health, money, power, fame. They had privilege coming out their asses. Maybe the family sourdough helped make them successful, in the beginning, but they didn't need it anymore. Not the way other people did.

"If you're serious about that, Eve, I know some people — some new family — who could really use your help."

Yes! The thought surged, joyful and eager.

"Patricia won't like it though."

A pause. The next thoughts were quieter, darker, but no less certain. *Patricia, betrayer, old-family, not-family. Help new family.*

"I hoped you'd say that." Chris was beginning to form a plan.

It was mid-afternoon before Patricia found Chris: enough time for their bread dough to rise, rise again, and bake into a crisp round loaf. A bit misshapen and inexpert-looking, because Monique had made Chris do the hands-on work, but they felt oddly proud as they slathered a slice with butter and jam. The family's sourdough had always tasted good, but its tang carried a bitterness that had nothing to do with the bread itself. Now, with the starter humming in the back of their mind, it tasted delicious, pure and simple.

Chris wasn't the only one who thought so. Monique had set out samples for customers to taste. "Family Heirloom Sourdough, made from a Gold Rush starter," the chalkboard declared. "Tell us what you think!" Everyone loved it, to the point that Monique had to slap away greedy fingers trying to sneak extras.

Sharing the bread like this was a beginning. Sharing the starter itself, sharing its benefits with the people who really needed it, was going to take more consideration. Chris didn't want to repeat her family's mistakes.

Bells jangled as the door thrust open, loud enough that the regulars looked up. Patricia's gaze swept the room, taking in the shabby chic of the place, the chalkboard and basket of bread samples, and finally narrowed on Chris.

The weight of that gaze struck Chris hard, carrying generations of betrayed expectations. Oh, yes, Patricia knew exactly what Chris had done.

As Patricia picked her way across the crowded seating area, followed by Shannon, Chris closed the laptop on which they'd been researching the processes around launching clinical trials. Their plan was still evolving, and Patricia did *not* need to know about it right now.

Monique beat the Randolphs to Chris's side. "Mrs. Randolph, these seats are reserved for customers."

"I have no intention of taking space in your *quaint* little shop. I'm only here to retrieve my granddaughter and what she stole from her family."

Monique's hand found Chris's shoulder and squeezed.

"Grandma," Shannon murmured. "You said we'd talk..."

"I don't see what there is to talk about. It's obvious what she's done." Patricia narrowed her eyes at Monique. "And it's obvious she had help. Christina has never baked a thing in her life. I'll have you know, young lady, that you are participating in the theft of a family heirloom. You're hurting a great many people."

"Oh, yeah? Seems to me turnabout is fair play, considering you've —"

"It's okay, Mo." Chris patted their friend's hand. "I want to explain it to them. Is there someplace private we can talk?"

"You can use the kitchen." Monique folded her arms, fixing Patricia with a warning look. "But if I hear yelling, I'm coming back there."

Chris led them into the back, where the scent of fresh-baked sourdough hung accusingly in the air. Patricia started up again at once. "Christina, you're going to stop this nonsense and return the starter—"

"How did you find me?" Chris looked past her, to Shannon. "Did you tell her all the places I might go?" They'd invited Shannon here for coffee a few months back, and mentioned that their friend was the owner. That had been a mistake.

"Your sister was no help at all. Your Aunt Zelda had to issue a court order for your phone's GPS data. Now, I understand you may be disappointed that I've named Shannon as my heir, and if I'd known that you cared *at all* about family matters, I would have handled the announcement differently. But clearly the family does matter to you on some level, and that's why you need to return what you stole before any more damage is done." Her gaze fell to the plastic container on the counter. "Yes. I'll be taking that back..."

Chris blocked her path.

"You can have your container back, but Lilith is staying with me."

"*Lilith?*" The word came out strangled, choked by the force of realization. "You bonded with it. Didn't you?"

"You know, I always thought you were making up stories about Eve's powers. But it's all true, isn't it? 'She keeps us safe, keeps us healthy.' Do you know how many patients I have to talk out of fad diets and miracle health products that are actually making them sicker?"

"Chris, what did you do?" Shannon whispered.

"And all this time, our family had something that works! A bread that cures illness. Bread! But not just any bread. Our special, secret, family bread."

"Yes, it is our family secret, and you're betraying the family by—"

"Our family doesn't need it anymore. We haven't for a long time. I'm going to share it with people who do."

Patricia's face turned immediately, brilliantly scarlet, while Shannon went pale. "You can't. You won't."

"We can, and we will. Lilith wants to do it."

Yes, yes, yes. Grow, spread, help, help new! So want.

Patricia reached past Chris to seize the plastic container, but Chris caught it and held on. They'd been kept apart for so long, Patricia had *kept* them apart, and Chris wouldn't let her separate them again. Lilith affirmed: *Stay, Chris, new Chris, my Chris,* never mind that Patricia couldn't hear her.

"If you do this, Christina, you'll betray our entire family history. Eve was a gift, and you can't simply use her for your own ends."

"You mean like the family's used her for our own ends, for generations?"

"She's loyal to the family. I know you aren't capable of understanding that..."

Something broke inside Chris. "Why did you keep her from me?" they asked, raw and hurting. "My whole life. Everyone else bonded with her? The whole family?"

"Yes. All the blood relatives, and most of the spouses, too."

"Why not me?" Chris hugged the container to their chest. "Why, Grandma?"

Lilith echoed: *Why? Why? Why?*

"Because…"

Patricia faltered. Looked at Shannon, who stared back at her in astonishment. "Is that true? You kept her out on purpose?"

"I had to! Neither of you understand."

"So explain it," said Shannon.

"I'm trying. It was… hard. I had newly taken over as Eve's caretaker from my own mother, God rest her soul, and I felt the weight of my responsibilities. Usually, Eve bonds with spouses at the time of marriage, and with children at seven or eight, when they're old enough to understand. But you…"

Patricia shook her head. "You never fit in. Just like your father: always questioning, always a skeptic, never loyal enough to the family. I kept Eve from him, and it's lucky I did, because their marriage barely lasted past your birth. As you grew, it became clear that you were strange, too. You spent hours upon hours with that toy microscope, pretending to search for germs, and Eve obviously disgusted you. Your mother insisted that you would get over it if I introduced you to Eve properly. But I never felt sure about you. The doubts never stopped plaguing me."

Her gaze fell to Lilith's container, cradled protectively in Chris's arms. "The women of our family are Eve's caretakers. Her care has passed from generation to generation, and after your mother died so young, you were the natural successor. But you, Christina, you, you…"

Chris could guess where this was going. They let Patricia trail into awkward silence, let that silence pulse between them, before they said, "My name is Chris."

"What?"

"I go by Chris. Not Christina. I've asked you to call me that, and to use my correct pronouns, but you don't like it, so you don't do it. I assume that's what you're getting at, though. Names are symbols, and using my name would mean accepting all the ways I'm not what you want me to be." Their shoulders rose with a deep, fortifying breath, then fell again. "I was never enough for you. That's why you shut me out, isn't it? I was never enough of a *granddaughter* for you, never a good enough girl."

They didn't need Patricia's sigh to confirm the guess that they'd never put into words before. The Randolph women had a special relationship to Eve as caretakers and bread-makers, and Chris had always been in-between. Always not-quite-a-girl, not-really-a-woman, even before they'd learned words like *non-binary* and *genderqueer*. They had never fit cleanly into the family secret, and rather than try to understand and find a place for Chris, their family had left them out entirely.

"I don't know *what* you are, Christina, but you're not normal." Chris flinched, but Patricia went on unrelenting, not seeming to notice or care how those words hurt. "If you were really a Randolph, you'd have put the family first, but instead, you always did as you pleased."

"By putting the family first," Chris said through clenched teeth, "you mean hiding my true self. Pretending to be something I wasn't."

"I mean behaving appropriately as a Randolph woman! You see? You're too selfish. You would never be a fitting companion for Eve, never mind being her caretaker." She lifted her hands as if she were helpless in this, as if it hadn't been her choice. "I had to let the family believe you'd failed to bond with Eve, and it's clear now that I did the right thing. It was better than explaining it to them. Or to Eve. She wouldn't have understood."

"That's a lie!" Shannon cried. "Grandma, did you even try? Eve is listening right now and she understands just fine. Don't blame this on her, when you were the one who couldn't accept your own grandchild. Chris might be different, but they're no less a Randolph than I am. They're part of this family." She squeezed Chris's shoulder. "I'm so sorry, I swear I didn't know..."

"I believe you," Chris said softly. They straightened up slowly, facing their grandmother square on. "I don't need you to understand the name I chose, Grandma, or the way I dress, or my job, or my life, or my friends. I never needed you to understand, I just needed you to accept it. Accept that this is who I am, that this is the life that's right for me, and the life you wanted for me isn't." Their breath hitched. "I wanted you to love me anyway, but I was never enough for you. You still don't think I'm enough."

What about you? they asked Lilith silently. *Am I enough for you?*

And Lilith answered: *Human words, man woman boy girl him her them, all the same, doesn't matter. Family matters, together matters, Chris Monique together good. Enough, Chris, enough, enough, Chris is enough.*

"Of course I *loved* you. You're my grandchild," Patricia said, sniffing with more consternation than hurt.

"But not enough to let me in."

"Well, I can fix that now. Come home, Christina —"

"It's *Chris*, Grandma, for goodness sake," said Shannon.

"Chris, Christina, I don't care what name you use with your friends. Come home, and we'll figure out what to do about this new version of Eve you've created. We'll get you bonded to the real Eve like I should have done long ago, and as long as you don't challenge your sister's role as my successor, all will be well."

"No." Chris took a step back. "No, I can't do that."

"Christina." That warning tone, the one that said they were about to be sent to their room. It still unsettled them.

"You can't just erase a lifetime of mistakes and pretend it's fine. And you can't have the starter back. I didn't know what I was doing when I stole her, but she's not Eve anymore. She's separate now, her own being, her own branch of the family. That's why we named her Lilith." They couldn't help smiling over that small rebellion. "She doesn't want to be destroyed or re-absorbed or made into something else, and neither do I."

"Of course not," Shannon said, and suddenly she was at Chris's side. On their side, for the first time. "You can't just expect them to forgive you, Gran. You left them out of the *family*."

"But this new starter... Shannon, you understand the risks. It can't be allowed—"

"You're not helping," Shannon said firmly, and that was another first, the first time Chris could remember their half-sister talking back to the formidable Grandma Randolph.

Patricia blinked at her, as stunned as Chris, then threw up her hands. "Fine. I'll go, but that means it's your job to talk sense into your sister."

"Yes, we'll talk. I promise," Shannon said. And she said nothing more until Patricia was gone, the kitchen door swinging behind her.

In the silence left behind, Chris held their breath, bracing themself against a fresh barrage of argument. What they didn't expect was laughter: heavy, humorless, relieved laughter that burst the tension in the room. Laughter that felt like the next best alternative to tears, as Chris found themself joining in, slumped against the steel countertop with one hand pressed to their face.

"Well," Shannon said, shaking her head. "That happened."

"Did you see her *face*?"

"She was this close to exploding."

Spasms of laughter stole their breath, a necessary release. "Whew! Wow." Gradually, they recovered and looked soberly at Shannon. "Thanks for taking my side back there. Go ahead and say whatever you need to say, so you can tell Patricia you tried."

Shannon shifted from one foot to the other. "What are you planning to do? With... Lilith?"

"We're still figuring that out — me, Monique, and Lilith. She's feeling awfully angry about how the family has controlled her, how we kept her for ourselves and never told her that so many other people had greater needs."

"She's picking that up from you. You always cared so much about everything."

"I've infected her with my rebellion, you mean?" They smiled. "Probably. She wants to explore the limits of what she can be. How many people she could help. She's been serving our privileged little family for too long, and she wants to do more."

Shannon took on that distant look that Chris had always believed was an affectation, and now recognized as communing with the starter. "Eve feels awful about all this. She knew there was something wrong between you and Patricia, but she never knew what Patricia did to you. Neither did I. And she..." Another pause. "She's worried about her offspring. She's never divided before, and if Lilith is cut off from the family she's known, Eve believes that could be traumatic."

Lilith's answering moan ached deep in Chris's breastbone. "Eve's right. Lilith is scared, lonely..." Had she latched onto Chris's anger as a salve for her trauma? Probably, but not just for that. "I don't know what I'm doing, Shannon. I want to take care of her the way you're taking care of Eve. Mo is teaching me to bake bread, but there's more to being a caretaker, isn't there?"

"A lot more."

"Then teach me." Chris stumbled, surprised at themself for asking it, then slowly said it again. "Would you? Teach me, the way Patricia's teaching you?"

"Chris. Of course I would."

"Patricia won't approve."

"That's her problem. We're the new generation of caretakers, and we can decide what traditions to keep. I'm not ready to be as radical as you are, but... we've done things the same way for so many generations. It's time for some changes."

Shannon's smile kindled an answering smile in Chris, an upwelling of joy that was partly Lilith's and partly their own and

Chris couldn't find the edges between them. They hugged Shannon, and the two of them stood there, holding each other.

The door swung open, and Monique peeked in.

"Didn't mean to interrupt. I saw your grandma leave, and wanted to make sure you were okay."

Chris held onto Shannon with one arm and held out the other hand to Monique. "I'm okay. I think I lost my grandmother today, maybe for good, but I got two new family members in exchange: I met Lilith, and I got my sister back. I'd call that a fair trade."

"I'm glad. Sorry about your family, though, your real family," Monique said with an apologetic glance at Shannon. "You've always had a rough time with them, and this won't help."

"My real family's right here." Chris squeezed both their hands, and Lilith echoed: *Old family, new family. Family. Here.* "Family's not about genetics. Real family is the people you choose. The people you keep in your life, whether you're related to them or not. You two are my family, and now, so is Lilith."

"Don't you go all sappy now." Monique nudged them. "Shannon, you want to stay and eat with us? Tell us what we're getting ourselves into? I'm out of sourdough, but I got two kinds of quiche, and carrot cake for dessert."

"Sure. I mean, if Chris wants..."

"Yes. Please do."

"All right then. I'd love to."

A sense of rightness filled Chris up, rich and warm as fresh bread. This was the right way to mark a beginning: today was a new anniversary for a new family, one that deserved its own dinner. That was a tradition worth keeping.

See Jo Miles's story "Grow, Divide, Sacrifice, Thrive" online at Metaphorosis.
If you liked it, leave a comment. Authors love that!
Remember to subscribe to our e-mail updates so you'll know when new stories are posted.

About the story

When I was in college, my good friend was the caretaker for a portion of her family's heirloom sourdough starter. It blew my mind that this starter had been passed down through multiple generations of her family, and I loved the idea of a living, growing family heirloom. (That you could turn it into delicious bread, even better.)

Passing down a sourdough starter isn't uncommon. There are documented cases of starters that are more than a century old, and some families claim theirs has been passed down since the Gold Rush, when miners often kept their sourdough starter in a bag around their neck so it would stay warm. There's a sort of magic in that already, and it was a small leap to imagine a sourdough starter with a mind of its own.

The story became about more than that, though: it's about hereditary privilege, about found family, and about being true to yourself. In fantasy, magic is often reserved for the privileged, forbidden to the people who need it most. It's also often limited by gender: either magic is forbidden to women, or it's a special, secret knowledge that only women can access. But what about people who aren't men or women? What about people who are both, or in-between, or neither? And why should magic only be used to help the people who already have everything they need?

Chris is an outsider in their own world in a number of ways. Their recognition of their privilege and their commitment to doing good is one of them. Their identity as a non-binary person is another, and their experience of finding their own path is drawn from aspects of my discovery of my own gender identity (though I'm grateful to have very supportive friends and family, unlike Chris's grandmother). I wanted Chris to get their own magic, and to show that while society might fuss over those artificial dividing lines, the magic itself doesn't give a damn.

A question for the author

Q: What's your favorite *non*-SFF book?

A: One non-fiction book that I read recently and enjoyed immensely is *The Hidden Life of Trees* by Peter Wohlleben, a German forester who combines his personal, life-long experience working with trees with some incredible recent science to show that trees have a lot more going on than we give them credit for.

Not only do trees change their chemistry to survive harsh conditions or scare off parasites; they also communicate and look out for each other, warning nearby trees about dangerous insects, supporting and sheltering young trees as they grow, and even sharing nutrients with sick trees. Though it waxes poetic in places, I found it an eye-opening look at such a familiar thing, and a reminder that life can be sophisticated in many ways, even if it looks very different from us humans.

About the author

Jo Miles is a non-binary author of science fiction and fantasy and is working to build a more hopeful future, both in their fiction and through their day job helping nonprofits use the internet to save the world. They live in Maryland, where they are owned by two cats.

www.jomiles.com, @josmiles

Sonata II: Shailani

L. Chan

Allegro: Shailani

This is part 2 of L. Chan's novella, *Sonata*. Part 1 ran in January 2020. What has gone before:

Sona has travelled north, up the lawless swathes of the Periphery of the Empire Sound. He's enlisted the help of Shailani, a former soldier with the Imperial Army, on her own journey to the north. After an ambush by jealous bandits from a gang Sona used to serve, Shailani learned that Sona was carrying something forbidden by the most basic of Empire law – a piece of illicit Music, far outside the reach of the Empire and its Composers. Their journey has taken them to the border of the Six Named land, country of his mother, and the composer of the heretical Music, the Lady Kristyk.

Their first greeting in the land of the Six Named was a pair of whistling arrows, tracing rainbow arcs up into the sky before the hollow bores through the arrows channelled the wind, augmenting the flight of the projectiles with Sound. They hit the earth like cannon fire, throwing dirt and divots of sparse grass yards into the air. Small craters marked their passing, the fragile wooden arrowshafts obliterated.

She could not see their attackers, and doubted that Sona could. The ground here was thirsty, the grass washed out and beaten low by strong winds. Hills and mountains in the distance, but distances were impossible to estimate across the windswept plains. No trees grew here. Shrubs and bushes, the few that there were, clung to the ground in desperation, their stems green and swollen with hoarded water. The expanse made her skin crawl, her head spin, as though she'd fall into the sky, so clear and cloudless was it.

She'd served with Six Named in the Sixty-Seventh. A taciturn people, well used to hardship. Few others who could march quite as far on half rations, function on as little sleep. They were horse folk, well used to living flesh beneath them, and so never served in the navies, whether ocean going or sky sailing, nor the armoured divisions. A Six Named would sooner sever his own legs than ride on the larger cousins of the multipede the Imperial Army deployed.

Both the Six Named land and Seribu had submitted, in their own fashions, to the Empire. The Six Named land fared better. Both countries had ceded territories and concessions to the Empire, but there was little in the Northern Steppes that the Empire coveted, the ground being hard enough to dull shovel blades, the plants mostly unscented and dry, good for neither furniture nor Empire weapons.

The complexities of treaties between countries was somewhat lost on Shailani as she brushed the dirt from the arrow's impact off her face. At least the Six Named were polite like her own folk; killing strangers was considered rude.

Sona pointed, his eyes sharper than hers after all, to a plume nearing in the distance, a border patrol. The multipede's gears wheezed under the scorching heat. Shailani made out seven riders, with recurved horsebows carved from alabaster ashwood, white as bone. When the riders came to a stop, Shailani met impassive gazes of the riders past steady arrowheads in front of taut bowstrings. Having seen the effect of whistlers on the ground, Shailani much preferred not to see their efficacy on her flesh.

"Sona of the Empire Sound and Shailani of Seribu seek passage to the Festival of Names," said Shailani, even-voiced. Seribu, Shailani mouthed to herself, the thousand. The Far Isles in Imperial common. She revelled in the use of the true name of her birthplace, rather than the soft mouthed interpretation the Empire had given it. Stay long enough in the Empire, you'd forget your places, your home. But you'd never forget your place in the Empire, no. They'd remind you; in the theft of your names, in the weaving of your sacred cloth into their tea dresses.

A ripple went through the patrol at the unfamiliar sound of Imperial Common. The lead took his horse forward, a shaggy piebald beast almost as tall as a man at the withers. He dismounted, landing lightly on his feet. Like Sona, the patrolmen of the Northern Steppes were compact, making an easier carry for their steeds – leanly muscled, worn down by sun and wind till there was nothing left but hardness, striated muscles on every visible inch.

"The Six Named have no quarrel with Empire, the Six Named have no quarrel with the Far Isles. But the Festival is for our people and our people alone." His voice was loud and sharp, well made for vast and open spaces, carrying clear across the scraggly grass and ochre dust.

"He claims his right as one of your people," said Shailani.

"Does he not speak for himself, or does the Empire not lower itself to speak to the natives?"

"He lost his words as a child. He was born of the Lady Kristyk, known to you as Lady Han. She was born of Zhi and Liao, they of the sept of the Thundering Hills." Foreign names rolled, unfamiliar in her mouth, like strange fruit. The north was particular about names, and she'd spent an hour practicing under Sona's tutelage.

"Three names are not enough, Shailani. We need Six. It is our way. If he is of our people, he knows that. What are the others?"

Shailani paused, looking towards Sona. There had been long moments between them when they'd rehearsed, when she found out who his father was. Sona nodded. "He is half Empire. His father is the Antius, Lord and Choirmaster of House Deathsinger. He was born of Typhus and Sybil, they of House Deathsinger." Those names, even more so than the foreign words, felt alien in her mouth. House Deathsinger, last she heard, before returning to Seribu with her discharge papers and pension, was ascendant, with a clear route to taking one of the Maestro positions, unheard of for a minor house, albeit one that dealt in assassinations.

Of course, the genealogies and succession of the houses didn't trickle down to the military outposts and regiments, but no son of a lord should be out in the Periphery earning his keep through banditry and accountancy. Nor should he be travelling to the edges of the known world with nothing but a retired soldier for company. Not to mention that the darkest of those with Empire blood would still be fairer than the skin betwixt her arse cheeks. Sona carried himself like a noble, but not even outdoor labour turned Empire folk his colour. Shailani had nothing against those of mixed blood. The two spirits knew there were enough bastard children of nobles in the Sixty-Seventh. But a genuine scion? Not a chance. This young man was playing a dangerous game, laying claim to names like that.

They had spoken of many things whilst the multipede juddered their behinds into giant bruises. The military, the weather, the current state of the Empire, the weather, the terrible blandness of the food, the pain of their behinds, the weather again. The young man was a closed book with a plain cover, but Shailani would have put money on one thing – he was pure Empire regardless of how much Six Named blood he had.

The leader of the border patrol sucked at his teeth. He likely had not mounted his horse this morning thinking he'd either have to refuse blood rights or let an Empire agent into the greatest annual event of the Six Named. In the end, he held out his arm towards Sona. "We will escort you to the Festival, and the leaders will decide on the strength of your claim." Sona smiled and took the leader's hand, pumping it enthusiastically twice. The leader turned to Shailani. "You too, I suppose. It would be a confusing trip otherwise." She clasped her hand around his forearm, and he hers. Shailani had learned the Six Named greeting back in the army. Sona, despite his birthright, had not. The leader nodded his head at her, a slight dip of the chin, the misplaced greeting evidently bringing him to the same conclusion about Sona. Six Named skin, Empire heart.

The Festival of Names presented itself in the distance as a sea of pennant flags, each in the colours of one of the Septs. Every art and skill the Six Named practiced was on display and held in competition. Even Music. The Six Named did not use Sound as profligately as the Empire, but its judicious application allowed skill alone to determine a person's role in a sept. Of course, the annual gathering was not without its share of feasting and celebrations. Around her, Shailani could see the richness of the land in the people that lived off it. The Six Named were dressed in riotous colours, in the manner of a field of wildflowers. Their tools, weapons, and instruments were exquisitely made, and could have held their own against Empire craft, in utility if not in beauty.

Distance from the muggy jungles of her people pulled at her, a loose thread that would slowly unravel stitching. Truly she'd spent more time conscripted than as a resident, but barracks and quarters were no home, not with the carvings of previous occupants on bed frames, the mingling of her blood with theirs in the bloated bellies of bedbugs. The distance between her and her previous travelling companions was more urgent, more pressing. Again, Shailani revisited her decision to accompany Sona, justifying to herself what she knew to be right. They'd started out as six, charged to keep the songs of their people free. Six Keepers, five groomed from birth to be servants of their people, trained in forbidden songs, charged by their people to be a repository for their shared language — living dictionaries holding the tongues of their kinfolk, that the Sultanate was so busy erasing in its quest to unify Seribu. Not just a thousand islands, but a thousand people and a thousand languages; not easy to rule. One language, one thought — that would be easier, and the Empire was helping the Sultanate to that end. A single people gave much better tribute and trade, after all. Though her appointment had been a matter of expediency, Shailani counted herself amongst the Keepers as well. Her experience in the military helped her; she could fight, and more importantly, she had once led a battle choir. That advantage had given her a headstart on picking up the sacred songs of her people. Songs to ease the dead over to the other side, songs to welcome squalling babes into this world.

She wondered how far the four surviving Keepers were from the northern reach — the mountains where legends said that caves existed with walls of crystal so perfect that a single sound could echo there for eternity. Deep enough into those caves and it was rumoured that the Songs of Creation still echoed, the music by which the spirits had hewn the world out of nothing. Shailani had been across half the continent with the army. She'd seen fortresses reduced to rubble by war music, watched death rain down from skyships, but not seen the scantest proof of the legends the tribe talked about. The entire thing smelled like a fool's errand to Shailani, the last ditch effort of their cornered tribe, to send five of their brightest up North with nothing more than myths and legends, and the hope that the words and songs of their people would live, even after the Sultanate took their lands and children. A bad hand to be dealt, too bad folks didn't get to sit out rounds of cards in life. She had to get back to the other Keepers, no matter what dreams the elders had sold to the girls.

Sona had his own demons to wrestle with, it seemed, drawing further back into himself the deeper they got into Six Named territory. Surrounded by those that looked like him, Shailani had figured that Sona would open up like a flower drinking the sun, quizzing his hosts about all that he had missed. Definitely more Empire than Six Named, then. The same thing had happened to her when she was discharged from the Irregulars, a stranger in her own land. Yet Shailani was only an adoptee of the Empire; Empire was a skin that she shrugged off, scraping in places, once she'd been discharged. It would be more difficult for Sona to shed.

The Festival was as colourful and loud as a marketplace, and truly it was one. Not all of the Six Named were horsefolk, it seemed. Some brought cloth dyed in pounded clamshells dredged from rivers, the weaves bluer than the cloudless sky. Others brought preserved produce and dried harvests to share, everything from fruit to dried mushrooms that brought visions and madness.

Their escort deposited them at the edge of the forest of tents that made up the festival, springing up from the dirt like mushrooms after the rain, each the light earthy brown of fresh horse leather.

"I will present your case to our council," he said, showing them to an empty tent. Shailani entered first, Sona second, leading the multipede by means of a hand crank, a soft tune forcing the many-legged chest to trot slowly after them. "Help yourselves to the clothes in the guest tent." He showed himself out. Shailani could tell from the conversation outside and the long shadows cast at the tent's doorway that she and Sona were not precisely guests.

The clothes were in the style of the Six Named, linen trousers and shirts, with buttons of knotted cloth, heavier riding jackets with cinched sleeves to fit into leather bracers for horsebows. Shailani shrugged off her headscarf and top. When she shook her clothes, dust from her journey clung to the air, sparkling as it settled. She turned to see Sona, flapping his fingers at her, wide-eyed.

What are you doing? he asked.

"Changing into something clean," she replied, keeping her face towards him to read his Fingerspeech and enjoy his discomfort. "Don't be a baby, not all peoples share your Empire's allergy to the sight of breasts, and even those luxuries are not afforded to those in the Emperor's armies. Besides, I figured you'd have peeked on the way here." She pulled on the Six Named clothes and lowered her tone. "There must be no mistrust between us, Sona. We don't have time to be squeamish. You're playing with your life and mine, just to play some illegal music."

Not just any music, my mother composed it, he said.

"So your mother was a Composer, but not in service to the Maestri?" House plots, far beyond the ken of a simple retired sergeant on a mission to save a dying language. What did Shailani care about nobles and their Composers?

My father took her to wife from the Six Named. Empire wisdom has it that only Empire blood is pure enough to wrest Symphonies from the Sound. He thought otherwise. Hidden away, she would secure House Deathsinger's rise, he said.

"House Deathsinger. Is that how you name things in the Empire, just take words and bang them together?"

You know what we do, he said.

"Kill people, yes, I gathered. Your mother wrote a piece of music. How does that help your House?"

It doesn't. She wrote this in secret. My mother knew better than to hand my father that kind of power. She only gave the House baubles. Enough to secure their ascent. Me? I was an embarrassment, not just of impure blood, but unable to speak, and so unable to join the ranks of the Deathsingers. An inconvenience to the lines of succession for my father and my sister, Sona said.

"Sister?"

From my father's second wife. There's a lot about me that you don't want to know. Power was very important to my father. He used to go on about changing the Empire stripping the Maestri of their control. In the end, I became too much of a liability for his plans: a mute, impure son of a House of singers. He torched the Western Academy to kill me. My mother died so that I could escape. If they knew I was alive, they'd tear the countryside up just to hunt me down. Sona took a breath before continuing, *Tell me what you know about Sound.*

Shailani watched the rush of Fingerspeech, almost too fast for her to understand. Confessions were a lot like water behind a levee, only emerging as a flood. She'd gamble that this was the first time he'd told anyone about it. Sona was assembling something, fingers silent but dancing, screwing, joining, and aligning a complicated series of small mechanisms from the boxes he'd always kept tucked in a corner of the multipede. When he was done, he had a complex assemblage of brass minutiae mounted on a box of ornate rosewood, topped by what appeared to be the flared mouth of a trumpet, blooming like a flower. Into this he slotted an amber cylinder before sealing the box back up.

Shailani pulled the Six Named shirt over her head, cloth buttons snapping tight. "What's there to say? Just what they teach us in basic training. The Sound exists like a drum skin or harp string beneath our world. The right tones agitate the Sound, and it pushes back on our world."

Sound is everywhere. You don't need Empire instruments or machines to use it. Look at the whistling arrows. The Empire's power is in Music and the Symphonies. More than that, the horologists created gearmusic, with gears and springs playing Music, but there's a limit to what they can do. Gearmusic is only snippets. It moves the multipede, floats airships. Nothing compared to what a choir or an orchestra can do, Sona said. *My mother was of one blood, but a child of two worlds, I am the opposite. Because she was of two, she always sought to see unions, intersections. Six Named Music, Empire Music, and more besides. Any Music she could get her hands on. Horology, Sound. If Sound causes something to move, could movement cause sound instead?*

Sona depressed a button on the box. It began to play the same bouncy tune that drove the multipede. Their ride began to stir, gears clanking into motion before the music eased.

A perfect replica of any Music played to it. I will take my mother's symphony back to Pendulos with this. My mother had people there, sworn to her service. They helped me complete her work, and now they will help me bring my father to justice, he said. Shailani's head spun. Sona had trapped Music in a box. The Empire worshiped no gods, but their veneration of Sound was as near religion as the Sultanate's temples and minarets, as heartfelt as Shailani's own prayers to the two spirits before her meals. The device in Sona's hands held music not beholden to the hordes of trained musicians, without the need for the massed assortment of brass and wood and animal skin that comprised an orchestra.

Shailani had a mind shaped by war, and the flow of her thoughts ran back to combat like spring rivers down channels carved into rock. What damage could they wreak, with this enslaved music? With something like this, the Empire's advantage in musicians and Composers might be nullified, the old borders reinstated. Better yet, it could be applied to Shailani's own mission, and that of her sisters. Why travel to the edge of the known world on the rumour of a legend to preserve her people's language, when the means for doing so was right before her? She shook her head, clearing her mind of the whispered temptation to slip a lintah into Sona's neck then and there, and make off with the device. Shailani weighed that against the lives of the four that Sona had bought her service with. Not now, not until her debt was discharged. Afterwards, there would be no guarantees.

"You could change the entire balance of the Empire with that," said Shailani. Sona was already disassembling his creation, returning it to component boxes. "If the Empire found it, they would be unstoppable."

They would destroy it, he said. *Sound is everywhere. Only the stranglehold of the Maestri props up the Empire. This breaks that control. The Empire will eat itself from the inside.*

"Why stop it? All Empire does is eat; and when there is nothing left in the world, it will eat itself. You're holding something that could shift the world. And all you can think about is revenge?"

Let me tell you about revenge, Far Isle woman, he said. *I'm told that when a normal person thinks, you think with your voice. It's different for someone who's never heard their own voice. If there's a voice in my head, it can only be someone else's. If it's*

Fingerspeech, it can only be someone else's hands. How far would you go, to avenge a loss you feel with every single thought that goes through your head? Revenge is my world now.

Festive singing welcomed them to the Council, the singers a mix of teenage children in woven skirts, and trailing ribbons ten or more feet in length. If the song was meant to achieve anything through Sound, the effect was so minor as to be unnoticeable. The Council was more than a score strong, one representative from each of the septs. Seated in a raised dais above a cleared dust arena, they witnessed displays of skill, strength, and beauty. Those that did well brought honour to the septs, and to themselves. The best of the contestants were highly sought, their talents bartered across septs in a complicated exchange of young persons in marriage.

The dress of the Council demonstrated the distances ranged by the Six Named. The Six Named were famed for the sleek riding gear that Shailani and Sona wore. Seldom seen by the rest of the world was the looser flowing silks of those who mastered the loom, the elaborately beaded dresses of those who appeared to be scribes. There was even one, and Shailani could not help but return her gaze to him over and over, that was wearing the overcoat of the Sixty-Seventh regiment. And in the colours of a commissioned officer no less. There had never been combat this far north, so it was not a trophy. Yet there was no way there was a lieutenant amongst the Six Named. Commissions were reserved for Empire only.

"I am Qin. We have heard your claim," said the man in military dress, his facility with the Common Speech obviously rendering him the spokesman, though his tongue had the slurred accent of the north. "We have not yet heard your petition."

Shailani read Sona's Fingerspeech, translating. "Sona petitions the council to fulfil the last wish of Lady Han, to hear her music played."

"Let the boy speak for himself," said Qin.

"He does not speak," said Shailani.

Let the boy speak for himself, repeated Qin. Evidently, the overcoat was not for show; the man had seen service.

These are my Six Names, said Sona, *Lady Han, of Zhi and Liao. Lord Antius DeathSinger, of Typhus and Sybil.*

"The scion of the prodigal returns. What did the Lady Han achieve in the Empire?" asked Qin.

My mother is dead, but not gone. I have her masterwork, the union of her raw talent in Composing, sharpened by Imperial academics. A symphony, the form Empire but the soul Six Named. In her memory and as one of your people, I seek that it be played here, in the land of her birth, Sona said.

"You have yet to prove who you are, Sona of Empire," said Qin. "Skin and a story are not enough."

The Festival was host to many contests, including those of martial prowess. Oiled men and women grappled, cheered on by crowds. Others showed their skill with bows whilst riding or standing. And then there were the contests of weapons.

Shailani was surprised at Sona's decision. He seemed a planner, a tactically minded sort. Certainly he had the benefit of academy training, and growing up well fed. The one time she'd seen him fight had told her all she needed to know about his skill – he'd never fought outside of a curated match. His decision to do so now seemed like overconfidence. Shailani had seen her fair share of Empire brats with that, but she saw the look on his face when he chose his weapons and there was something else at play. Sona could have done something with music; the Six Named allowed for those contests. Yet he had chosen these two swords; Six Named weapons. The Academy would have offered lessons in arms, any weapon the Imperial Army used, but not these. The Empire man had something to prove.

Sona's choice of weapon was a pair of butterfly swords, stubby blades just over a foot in length, thin handguards and upswept quillons to protect and trap. The Empire favoured cavalry cutlasses and longer blades, and his selection was meant to cement his claim to the blood. His opponent was to be the same guardsman that had escorted Shailani and Sona to the festival, Lo, his name was, a veteran of border skirmishes and pursuit of the bandits that nipped at the heels of Six Named traders. Lo's favoured weapon was a long spear, blood red tassels dangling beneath the base of the spearhead. The contestants bowed to the council and then to each other.

Lo dropped into a stooped stance, thighs coiled to give his spear a longer lunge. Sona had one blade forward, the other drawn back; attack and counter, ready for any eventuality. Steel met steel.

Shailani had been invited next to Qin, watching with the council. "Lo tells me you spent time in the army. Sixty-Seventh?"

asked Qin, and under the Six Named drawl Shailani could make out the musical twang of the low counties, southern farming stock whence the Sixty-Seventh drew the bulk of its recruits. Much of the Empire's army was replenished by conscripts, but its appetite outstripped the fecundity of its women. Its conquests, vassals, and allies stepped in to fill the gap. The Empire inevitably sent conscripts to the Sixty-Seventh, and that regiment was always on active fronts. That was the cost of Empire friendship.

"You too?"

Qin nodded. The two combatants were feeling each other out, steel kissing steel like neophytes at a dance, tentative, hesitant. Up close, the elder Six Named was more weathered than most, the dark furrows of wrinkles mixed with the lighter patchwork of faded scars. "I didn't think they gave commissions to outlanders," said Shailani. Foreplay over, the combatants got into it. Lo made up for Sona's twin blades with the reach of his spear, using darting thrusts to keep the younger man at bay.

"Field commission at Angel's Fall. General Olivia valued skill above blood, and besides, everybody else was dead." Even a decade away from service, Shailani shivered at those names. Olivia, the Steel Angel, had been the one and only woman to ever attain a general's stars, during the reign of the Regent Ophelia. Angel's Fall was the name given to her most famous defeat, a failed bid to rescue stranded Imperial forces deep in enemy territory. The authorized history Shailani had garnered from her military training explained the Steel Angel's rise as illicit; the woman herself the Emperor Regent's paramour. Regiment tradition had it otherwise, Olivia as competent a leader as the next five generals put together, the incursion part of a master plot to see her disgraced. Either way, the loss of two thirds of her men at Angel's Fall had bought her a court martial and execution. The only mercy granted by the Emperor Regent had been a soldier's death, a sword through the heart, rather than hanging or dismemberment. "And yourself?" probed Qin, forcing the conversation past Shailani's open mouthed silence.

"Sergeant. Battle choir section leader. Discharged, full colours."

The two bare chested men were glistening with sweat. No contact had been made yet. Sona was tiring more quickly, the two swords heavier than he was used to. "So, a singer. Impressive, for not just an outlander in the Sixty-Seventh, but a woman to boot, and without Ophelia's edict to protect her. Would you consider marrying into my sept? You would be a welcome addition."

Shailani snorted. "I like my boys pretty and my girls hard, but you, sir, are neither. I'm afraid that I would be of little use to a sept. Nothing issues from my womb but dust."

Qin laughed, the medals on his overcoat jingling. "There's more than that for a treasure such as you. Teaching. Train my warriors, educate my tacticians. We are a rich sept, you know. Forgive an old soldier for being forward." He turned back to the display. "Your boy fights like a man who has memorised a dictionary, but cannot string together a sentence."

"He's holding his own. You must excuse his reticence. Sona has the skills, but not the heart for killing."

"Most of the Empire have it reversed. I've seen enough," Qin said, and raised his hand to Lo. The Six Named fighter lunged, his spear extending its full eight feet to bury its point into the dust at Sona's feet, the force of the strike curving the shaft of the spear like a bow. Sona dodged the telegraphed move easily, taking two steps backwards. Lo smiled at the young man, poised to make a counterattack, and pulled the tip out of the ground, the tension in the shaft releasing all at once, sending a fistful of grit into Sona's face. The breath's space it took for the younger fighter to clear his vision was enough for him to find Lo's spearpoint at his throat.

Sounds of the Six Named orchestra tuning up filled the arena. Shailani always marvelled at the discordant tones, at odds with the polished Sound they would soon produce. Or attempt to. Six Named instruments were not the same as the Empire's. Drums they had. Their trumpets and flutes carried higher tones, with an odd vibrato missing in the flared brass of the Empire. Instead of violins, they had little drummed cylinders topped by a single finger-thin wooden stem, played similarly with a bow.

The previous two days had seen Sona mobilizing the few within the Festival with any talent at composing, feverishly coaching them to transcribe Empire script into the complex notation used by the Six Named. Musicians practiced their parts whenever they got fresh sheets of music. It was impressive to behold.

Shailani took her place next to Qin as the orchestra prepared to play. "You're helping Sona, even though he lost?" Shailani asked Qin.

"We asked for him to prove himself, not beat our warrior. A demonstration of his skill sufficed."

"He could have gone through the forms."

"Kata is to combat as masturbation is to lovemaking," said Qin.

Sona was setting up his recording device on a wooden platform in front of the orchestra, near where the Conductor would stand. Maybe they would be able to play it, maybe they wouldn't. The Six Named musicians were barely an orchestra by Empire standards, even the truncated ones that served in the army. Qin pointed at the mechanism. "What Empire devilry is that?"

Shailani stared at the elder for a while, looking for guile or subterfuge, and only found the eyes of one tired of killing. "A new form of horology, something that allows Sound to be trapped, and released at your whim." Qin absorbed the news of the world-upending mechanism without blinking, one bare foot hitched up on his chair, picking at yellowing teeth with a fingernail. "A full orchestra's sound in something no bigger than a travelling chest! You could push the Six Named borders back into the Periphery." Shailani kept her voice just above a whisper, not trusting the other elders to be as circumspect as Qin, though she'd only known him for less than a day, and the chances of anyone else speaking the Imperial Common were low.

Qin looked beyond the orchestra, beyond the grassy steppes, beyond decades of discharged service and he shook his head. "The standing army of the Empire is half again as large as all of the Six Named combined. A beast so huge that it can only sustain itself by gnawing at the rest of the world. Do you know what happened after Angel's Fall?"

She shook her head.

If it were possible, the lines on the older man's face seemed to deepen, as though the recollection tore at old scabs and drew fresh blood to skin. "Our armies were reinforced; the Capital Sound sent another two regiments to the east. History is the story of the victors, but no one won in that campaign. Stories are told by those who are alive and unashamed. After the eastern purge, there were neither." Shailani'd heard of the campaign of vengeance the Empire waged in the east after their initial defeat, the annexation of lands a full fifth of the Empire's controlled span. No treaties, no surrenders. Just slaughter and parcelling out the lands to the campaign officers, and to the Houses of the Capital.

"We in the Sixty-Seventh were at the tip of the spear, led to believe that the easterners were less than human, the architects of Angel's Fall. It was a massacre. We were blood drunk. Villages. We torched homes, farms. Women, children. Old. Young. We didn't question a thing. At least not until it was over. Sure, I had doubts. It didn't take a general's stars to tell that a couple of old men with farm tools weren't a threat. But the Sixty-Seventh were the incoming tide and I wasn't about to get in front of it. When it was over, I was an anomaly, an outlander lieutenant. I retired back home. It's taken me these decades to be able to sleep more than half the night without being woken by screams." He turned to scrutinize Sona's device. "No, Shailani, the Six Named will not stand against the Empire, not even with your heretical machine."

Sona fussed, ensuring that his clockwork machine was running, angled optimally to capture the Sound from the orchestra. The young man nodded at the Conductor. If he was excited at the fruition of his life's work, his clipped gestures did not betray it. The music started.

The similarity was faint for Shailani at first. In tone, Lady Han's symphony took after a dirge, somnambulant and with the strings and winds keening across the open plains. Drums maintained a steady pace, heartbeat slow. The players grew restless, their instruments taking on a mechanical urgency that drove their playing fingers, wrists, arms, and lungs harder and harder. Only when the piece began to pick up did Shailani recognize it, given that her own people had given her naught but the briefest exposure to it. Ninety-nine in a hundred of her people would not have recognized it, but Shailani was a Keeper; she kept the words and she kept the songs. And this was one of the songs of the dead. Somehow, it had travelled the distance of the whole known world and was being played for her by a full orchestra instead of sung reverently by Keepers.

Something else grew in the space before the orchestra, a heat shimmer, a desert mirage. The patch of bare dirt wavered, as though seen through warped glass. Panic spread amongst the musicians, faces twisting as their individual parts poured from their instruments. Shailani was not sure if they were playing the music, or the music was playing them.

When it stopped, it was the pause after thunder, the stunned silence after a breaking wave. There were tears in the orchestra, others nursing cramped arms. Qin was as shocked as the rest of the council, but military training kicked in and he was soon barking orders in the sharp tones of the Six Named language. When others had stepped in to help, he gestured at Shailani and stormed towards Sona. There was a fire in his eyes, and Shailani no longer doubted that the old man with his clumsy propositions was the same one who would, without question, kill a mother, a child, a newborn. This was a man who would do all these things, and not call it murder, so bright was the fire.

"What has the Lady Han done?" he asked.

I've not heard the piece before, said Sona, quickly withdrawing the waxed cylinder from the device and stowing it about his person. Qin surged forward, drawing a phalanx of guards behind him. His genial features were knotted, chest heaving as though choking. Shailani circled to the side, gauging if she had enough time to get in between the guards and Sona if they attacked, wondering if she owed the man that much, or she should just let the Six Named deal with Six Named business, and get on with her own. The guards were ready to draw a variety of weapons; the Six Named favoured choice above standardization, and so there were stout axes, short swords, even a war club whose design she recognized a thousand leagues from home.

"Enough with your deception, outlander," snapped Qin. "The Lady Han left us more than two decades ago, one of our brightest. And what comes back? You think we didn't recognize our Music? The husk of it is there, but it's been twisted, just like everything the Empire touches."

My mother's transgressions are not mine, pointed out Sona. *I only came to hear it played, to see what it could do.*

"Knowing this, young Sona of the Empire, what will you do with the music?"

Our arrangement was for the music, not my plans, Sona said. He leaned in closer to Qin, even though hardly anyone in the Six Named knew Fingerspeech. *I've been running for a long time. No longer. Now I've got something of value. Something to use against those that hurt me. Better yet, something that can rattle the foundations of the Empire itself. I know people back in the Empire. People sidelined by the order of things, who will trade me power for this; we will strike, they at the Empire and me at House Deathsinger.*

Holding the power to help millions and swearing to kill thousands. You are a little Empire unto yourself, Sona, said Qin, employing Fingerspeech again. *You're more Empire than Six Named. This nation withdraws her hospitality. You will leave the festival and Lo will escort you from our lands.*

The Festival was nothing more than a smear of colour on the horizon.

Sona, reserved at the best of times, was even more so now, the hoofbeats of the shaggy northern horses and the multipede song the only conversation the party had, in contrast to the chatter of the inbound journey. Sona had saved his mother's music, but to what end, and at what cost? Shailani's own journey had already claimed one of the girls. She'd take her payment and leave, just as soon as they hit the border.

Shailani was alone with her thoughts, and she itched to be back with the other Keepers. To the Six Named Land and back, and she had delivered, regardless of Sona's success. Leave him to his machinations, his schemes, let the two spirits take him. She'd already shirked her responsibility to her people for too long, and no matter how skilled they were, the other Keepers didn't have Shailani's grey hairs and cautious eye. Of the four others, only Ashikin had spent time out of Seribu. If Shailani hurried, she could pick up their trail, notwithstanding that her own quest seemed even more naive than the boy's. That was her first instinct, the visceral need to protect, the soldier in her obeying an order. Instincts won fights. Shailani needed more to save her people. Like that device Sona was carrying. Force was an option, so was larceny, but both left her with an intricate contraption that she might not know how to work. She needed a little more time to learn its secrets.

"Why do you think your mother's music didn't work?"

The multipede stumbled when Sona ceased pedaling. *I don't know,* he said over his shoulder.

"I think you do. She left the symphony incomplete."

No one in the Empire can complete it. Those with the skill will not see the music, those with the music do not have the technique, Sona said.

"A child of both worlds could do it. You understand the Six Named, you have academy training. You were apprenticed to the horologists, you made your recorder. This is the Lady Han's design." This the half lie, much smoother a blend than the whole truth. Truth was bitter, lies too sweet, neither palatable on its own. Shailani had never been an assassin or a spy, but she'd seen her share of lies. She needed Sona's plans and she wasn't above perpetuating the lie Sona had been living. The other Keepers were trekking northwards, chasing a baseless legend. Shailani had never seen caves which trapped sound forever, but nestled in the multipede was a device that could. If only she could get her hands on it. No point in telling Sona she recognized his mother's symphony. Maybe even knew what it was missing. Shailani couldn't puzzle out why the Six Named and her people would share common songs when they were on opposite sides of the continent, but she stowed that conundrum with all of the other problems a soldier couldn't solve.

"You want to kill the Lord Deathsinger, don't you?" asked Shailani. Sona did not answer. "What kind of man was he?"

Aloof. Distant. Not just to me, to my sister as well. Less like a person and more like an ideal wrapped in skin. I don't think he even saw people as people, just as tools for his plans and counterplans. Even as he planned to kill me, he made sure I was educated in both Sound and war. Just in case he needed me.

The Empire had a lot in common with a barrel full of hungry rats. Those at bottom were crushed by those at the top; those at the top were either fierce or lucky and if you stuck your hand in the barrel, you were likely to lose all flesh down to the bone. The Deathsingers were the rats on top, along with the other lords and ladies of the Houses, great and small.

"Can you kill him, when the time comes?"

Sona held his hand up, fingers extended to show Fingerspeech for yes, but he balled them back into his fist and hid it.

"You'd best not hesitate," Shailani said. "He won't."

Do you hear that? asked Sona, peering into the distance.

Shailani called for Lo to hold up, dismounting to join Sona in his inspection of the horizon.

There, he said, pointing at a speck in the sky. His ears were sharper than hers, having not spent time in the military, but even Shailani could make out the tuneful refrain of an airship at this distance. Noisy beasts they were, suspended under a bladder of heated air, hulls extruding oars that terminated in canvas stretched over frames of wood, looking like the fins of a fish, paddling through the air, powered by Sound. Over the distant whine of the music bearing the ship aloft, there was something else, a high pitched whine of rapidly increasing volume.

"Cover, cover!" screamed Shailani, army instincts taking over, dragging Sona behind the multipede. The cannon shot struck the ground somewhere behind the group, kicking up divots of dirt and embedding itself deep within the ground. "Nobody move," she said, pointing at Lo's men, who'd already unslung their bows and notched whistlers. "That was just a rangefinder and a warning shot. If they wanted us dead, we'd be chunks on the ground before you notched a second arrow. Stand down. Return fire and we are all dead where we stand."

Lo came up to stand with Shailani and Sona behind the lowered multipede, using the butt of his spear to prod at a clod of dirt that had been thrown twenty feet clear of the shot's landing point. "Air navy or privateers?" he asked. Shailani shushed him. She heard the faint tones of gearmusic getting clearer the closer it got. The rhythmic mechanical cadence of notes forming the Symphony of War. Military, then. The speck had grown large enough that she could make out the sails and oars that propelled the craft through the air. They were pushing their crew hard, if they had all hands on deck instead of simply relying on the wind. She didn't recognize the flags that the ship flew.

"Military," she said. "What business does the Imperial Air Navy have with Six Named? There is no war here."

Sona held up his palm, signalling for silence.

Not military, he said. *They've finally caught me. Those are Deathsinger colours.*

The airship landed just beyond whistler range. From that distance, it appeared a brigantine, a mid-sized airship. A single windsailor emerged, wearing the padded helmet and brass goggles of the profession; gearmusic kept it aloft, the tune holding it up in the sky mingled with the clanking of mechanisms that played it. The combined effect was deafening.

"They must be confident to send just one to negotiate," said Lo.

The rangefinder shot was a warning. We are wholly within their power, said Sona.

The windsailor broke into a jog, and then a full on sprint, raising puffs of sand and dust with every footfall. Only Lo's upheld palm kept his patrol from picking up their bows. The windsailor ripped off their helmet, revealing a ruddy cheeked woman, barely twenty, if even that. Her hair was cropped short, alabaster Empire skin showing through auburn stubble. The generous would have called her passing pretty; through most of the Empire, health was conflated with beauty, as it was wherever times were lean.

"Sona?" the windsailor asked, and Shailani detected the vocal control of one trained in the Symphony of Flow, the last of the great symphonies. A choral symphony, adherents of the Flow could use their voices as weapons or worse, with greater versatility than any single instrument. War choirs were dangerous, if limited in range; Shailani'd been in charge of one in the Irregulars. But if the sailor came alone and unarmed, then she was probably trained as a solo, a virtuoso. She'd seen a single virtuoso take down eleven enemy men-at-arms in battle; training for virtuosos was perhaps the most rigorous of all the musical disciplines. Many broke, but all cracked. Where, Shailani wondered, would the cracks in this one be?

Sona, for once, was at a loss, mouth agape and fingers silent. The woman stood taller than Sona and Shailani by far, easily able to look most men in the eye. The sailor pulled Sona in for a hug so fierce that it swept him up to the tips of his toes, but her face darkened when she let him go.

You're dead, she said to Sona, her Fingerspeech so fast that Shailani could barely keep up. *They told me you died at the Western Academy. You never contacted father. You never contacted me.*

It was dangerous, he responded. *The official story was raiders, but how did they get by the guards? They had Empire uniforms, sister. I saw them. I thought it safer for the House that I completed my training and work outside of the Capital Sound. I am done now, and have discovered something of great import to House Deathsinger,* Sona said. Shailani frowned at the lie, though neither of the pair in front of her noticed. Shailani bit her lip. She was a soldier, not a spy, and she had no idea what game Sona was playing, nor what rules he was playing by. Which was an unenviable position, considering the airship had cannons pointed at them.

Shailani, said Sona, *this is my sister, the Lady Canta. Cannie, this is Shailani of the Far Isles. She is currently my bodyguard and translator in the Six Named lands. Shailani saved my life on the Periphery.*

House Deathsinger is in your debt, Lady Shailani, said Canta.

The Imperial Army had few interactions with nobility. Was she supposed to curtsy? Salute? Canta solved the problem for her by seizing ,Shailani's hand in two of her own, the clasp warm and firm.

We must thank you in person back in the Capital, said Canta. Shailani half thought to refuse, to pick up the trail of the Keepers and catch up, but she looked over to Sona, who met her eye in a way that suggested that going to the Capital would be a very good idea indeed. Shailani turned to speak to Lo and the patrol. "Sona and I will take the airship. We will be safe. Your mission is complete."

"We will keep watch until your flier crosses the border, not a moment before," Lo said. He nodded at Sona. "No hard feelings about the fight?"

Sona signed to Shailani. "He said that he learned something new and is better for it," she said. The two men clasped forearms. Sona did learn fast.

Canta tossed Sona the flier helmet. *If it is dangerous for you to be known,* she said. Shailani started the multipede, the mechanical beast tinkling and clanking as it followed, while Sona and Canta walked ahead.

When they were halfway between the watching escort and the airship, Canta took a scuffed brass box the size of a child's fist from one of her multitudinous pockets. She tilted it, aligning the box to her long shadow across the wiry steppe grass. Operating a catch with her thumb, she sent mirrored flashes over to her waiting airship. Blinks came back in response, followed by a barrage of cannon fire, and then the screams of horse and man, shredded by hot flying metal.

See L. Chan's story "Sonata II: Shailani" online at Metaphorosis.
If you liked it, leave a comment. Authors love that!
Remember to subscribe to our e-mail updates so you'll know when new stories are posted.

About the story

"Sonata" is one of the longest things that I've written (and completed). I don't often work in the fantasy sandbox, I much prefer near future science fiction and contemporary fantasy. For "Sonata", what preceded the story was the world building — a magic system that fell roughly as another aspect of the physical world, and where the control of that magic ran along political and societal faultlines rather than through resource or genealogical lines. Things flowed on from there — an extant Empire with a colonialist reach, a good old fashion revenge quest and some non-traditional characters. It didn't get really steampunky until about halfway in, when I realised that the frame of having a sound based magic system would overcome a lot of the engineering limitations of steampunk without pushing the rest of the technology of the world into the industrial revolution or thereabouts. It was also important to me to retain a tight cast of characters this time round, although the roster is definitely going up if I ever return to these folks.

About the author

L. Chan hails from Singapore. He spends most of his time wrangling two dogs. His work has appeared in places like *Translunar Travellers Lounge, Podcastle,* and *the Dark.* He tweets occasionally @lchanwrites.

lchanwrites.wordpress.com

March

The Eighth Fathom

Chris Panatier

First Fathom, The Plunge

In a past beyond the reach of time's measure, we fell from the Galaxy Beam and into the waters of a primordial world. From the shattered wreckage of our Great Hull, we salvaged the ascension core and dove into the salted darkness. And within the abyssal contours of this alien planet, we made our home, awaiting the wobble of the zenith star that would presage the Beam's return.

Ook crept down the leg of the ocean platform, moving her arms slowly over its metal surface so her suckers might taste its various alloys. She descended at a starfish pace, careful not to flood her mantle too quickly or jet water through her siphon too forcefully. Any unnatural vibration could give away her presence to the other octopuses below. That would be unacceptable—Ook was, after all, a spy.

Technically, she was a low-level scout, sent to monitor the far reaches of her den's territory. But now that she'd actually spotted someone, an adjustment of title seemed due. Casting herself in a blotchy rust pattern, she continued through the murky water until her keen eyes made out the situation—the gathering of octopuses pressed in against the base of the giant leg, intent on some task. *What is the logic of this?* Ook wondered. Slinking forward, she could see two of their number tending to a knot of wires protruding from the leg while the others watched. Hopefully they wouldn't look up or she'd be done for.

A medium sized Bimac held the bundle while another, a tiny Mimic, delicately unspooled the tangle and plucked a few wires from it. The observers then split their ranks to allow passage for a colossal Great Pacific tugging a heavy cable behind. The Mimic expertly spliced the wires to the Pacific's heavy cable and then retreated into the circle of onlookers. The Pacific held the opposite end of the cable aloft. From her perch, Ook was able to make out a tool of some kind affixed to the tip. Human in its manufacture and obviously scavenged by this bunch, it had a place for gripping and a long tube that tapered at the end. The circle of octopuses widened.

A great spark lit from the tool's point, searing her retinas. She faltered, stunned, but her arms, having independent neural bundles, tightened their latch. She blinked away the afterimage and tried to process what she'd seen. *What was it, this sun's glint?* She searched her mind for a practical explanation but knew deep down that there was none. Only one thing could have produced the flash, and the big Pacific had it.

The fire that binds. The Seven Fathoms told of it. Though her rational mind resisted the idea, the three hearts within her mantle pounded in primal recognition. *The flame that burns in the water.* Ook widened her aperture, and the water passing over her gills tasted like the breath of truth.

The group upon whom she spied were of a rival den. Known as *Tellers*, they believed in the Seven Fathoms—a spoken history of octopuskind, outlawed as myth by Ook's own den, the *Cephlists*. Ever since hatchlinghood, she had been taught that the Tellers would be the downfall of the species, spreading the Fathoms' lie that octopuses were not of the Earth, filling impressionable brains with the false promise of grand destiny. To speak the Fathoms within the Cephlists' den was akin to heresy; to proselytize them, a death sentence. These prohibitions, though, had not stopped Ook, who had long ago committed them to memory, piecing together the verses from a thousand treasonous whispers. For an octopus of the Cephlists' den, the Fathoms had been her daydream escape from a rigid way of life, but also an aspiration of hope for something vast and wonderful that transcended petty boundaries and ideological squabbling. The light in the Giant Pacific's arm changed everything. The Tellers possessed the fire that the Fathoms foretold. The Fathoms...were true.

An unexpected current caressed Ook's skin. From above appeared the blurry shadow of a human diver in his false shell. Her eyes flicked downward. The Tellers hadn't seen. The man descended slowly, stopping here and there to examine the platform's various juts and fixtures. If he saw the splice, he would sever it from the cable and the fire would be lost. The thought put a hollow feeling in her cecum. What was there to do? Letting herself be known to the Tellers, much less helping them, was out of the question.

The diver continued down. Ook maneuvered just beyond his reach as her conscience called out, imploring her to act. *You have seen the fire; the Fathoms are true.* Her hearts thrummed. He would see the Tellers any second. *The fire will be lost.* Unbidden, her aperture opened, flooding her mantle as the decision was made. Her head taut with water, she wished a quiet goodbye—a farewell to her den, and to her life—then surrendered to the will that bubbled up.

She blasted her siphon and split the water like a marlin, striking the human on the side of his head. A spray of bubbles exploded from his mask as she sealed herself across his face.

They sank. The Tellers scattered. The man struggled. His gloved fingers scraped at Ook's flesh. They pounded into the seafloor in a cloud of silt. The human drew a short blade and severed one of Ook's arms just above the smallest suckers. Pain strobed over her skin in waves of yellow-white and she inked the water.

Above them, an eight-spoked umbrella of limbs belonging to the Great Pacific appeared. It descended onto the human's head, flashing blue to orange: *confusion.* A quick flurry of its arms asked of Ook a question, *Why are you here, Cephlist?*

Still grappling, Ook made her skin seafoam green—*peace,* an offer of truce while they dealt with the diver. The Pacific crawled to the human's dorsal side and used his chitinous beak to clip a hose, releasing a jet of gas. Ook twisted the mask until it filled with water. The Pacific detached and slid away. Ook released as well. The human scrambled upward, his fins beating the water like a shark-bit halibut.

Second Fathom, The Gift

An epoch came and went. We changed, evolved to our adopted world, preserved our tellings. Then, from the shadows of land, bloomed the human era of mechanization, and with it a vessel of steel sent starward. Part of this steel fell to the surface, a great cylinder, equipped on its end with the machinery of propulsion. Curiosities were piqued, but few spoke of hope, for the Gift was damaged. And so we watched the heavens for another.

Ook matched her skin to the seafloor and swept her arms into a high collar about her mantle. Sediment washed side to side in the pendulum current. When it settled out, she found herself walled in by Tellers, poised on hind arms and flashing the red-orange of violence.

171

She straightened, turned purple-blue in submission, and held up four of her front arms, bending the third down to grasp the tip of a rear arm that passed under her beak.

\ | i /

Friendship.

The big Pacific stalked forward, angry colors pulsing his radii. A curt flourish. *I ask again: why are you here?*

Ook swiveled defensively as she considered her answer. They'd tear her apart if she fled—they might tear her apart anyway. She tucked her wounded arm—the one cut by the diver—close and braced herself as she signed. *Please, I am only a scout.*

No! he responded, *You are a spy.* The circle of Tellers shook in outrage. The Pacific signaled them to settle and they obeyed. *Why did you attack the human?*

Ook tightened the corset of arms as if to quiet her hearts' insistent rhythm. All she could think about was the blinding arc of light the cable had produced. Trying to sign slowly so as not to provoke, she answered, *You have the fire that binds, the flame that burns in the water. The Seven Fathoms must be true. The humans cannot know.*

The Tellers' colors altered, arms flashing yellow to green-blue at the tips as they gyred with anxiety. Darkened mantles and emphatic gestures told of violent intentions for the intruder who knew their secret. They urged interrogation, torture, death. Ook nuzzled further into the nest of her arms and blanched white.

The Pacific thumped his arms at once to the seabed, producing a brief eight-pointed puff of silt. *Stop this.* The others calmed, and he came closer, though not near enough to strike. Even outside his capture radius, Ook shriveled some more.

What are you called? he demanded.

She poked the tip of an arm from its coil and drew her sigil. *Ook.*

You will accompany us to the reef.

She released a siphon squirt. A reprieve, even if brief, had been granted.

The Pacific gave some instructions to the others, and they rushed back to the platform to reinforce and conceal the splice. Turning to Ook, he gave his name. *Allops.*

With the splice secured, they headed out from the platform, towing along the loose end of the cable. This was the reason so many had come. They'd had to pull the thick cable's terminal end all the way from their reef, so that once the splice was repaired, they could test that it worked. It did, but now they had to drag it back. A small contingent traveled ahead to ensure clear passage.

Ook had no way of knowing where the Tellers' reef was; scouts sent by her den were leery of venturing too far from their territory. The platform marked the outer limit of her own explorations. She pondered briefly if her den would come for her and concluded, logically, that they would not. As with the not insubstantial numbers who often failed to return, they would assume she'd been eaten by moray or shark. It was liberating, in a way. The Tellers would have no use for the fire that binds if they did not also possess the Gifts. And if they were melding the Gifts with fire, it could only be because they needed a housing for the ascension core. Ook wanted to see it.

Conjuring visions of how it all might be, exuberant blotches scrolled her skin until an acid glare from Allops snapped her to whalesbelly grey. As they marched away from the familiar, she settled her mind within the verses of the Seven Fathoms. *In a past far beyond the reach of time's measure...*

Third Fathom, The Era of Barnacles

Another Gift went upward, carried as if upon a meteor's fire, until the fire died, and the Gift, as with the first, fell. Taste deemed it a prize of great value, a hollow tube forged of delicious and tensile alloys, worthy of the vacuum of space and resistant to velocity. A possible housing, if remade, for the ascension core. A Great Hull to deliver us. But time corroded its potential, for we had no way to shape it. Barnacles spiked and studded its frame. Others still fell, the waste of humankind's drive to break the grasp of their planet. And we languished, unable to bring form to their jetsam.

They drew the cable over the seabed toward the Tellers' reef. Behind Allops and just ahead of a tiny female called Granel, Ook did her best to keep up the torturous pace, but her wounded arm made it difficult. Trying to keep her mind off the pain, she let it wander as they marched. Logic told that if they had the fire that binds, they must then be using it, and while the fabrication of experimental structures might be of interest to an octopus, any effort not devoted to the Great Hull would be frivolous, a novelty— and Ook knew octopuses were too serious for that. She hoped for the chance to gaze upon the Gifts before she was killed, and even imagined being allowed to live, and to brood her eggs in the emanations of their glory.

Ook glanced back toward Granel, who flashed red and made her arm into a hook. *Face forward.* Ook shaded purple-blue, the appropriate response.

They came to rest and Allops instructed them to forage. Famished, Ook scanned the seabed for eye stalks. She fell upon a crab, immobilized it in her arms, and cracked open its head with her chitinous beak. She devoured quickly, and a satisfying heaviness moved to the stomachs in her crown. She used her tongue-like radula to scrape any remnant flesh.

A short distance away, Granel calmly pulverized a large shrimp as she kept watch. Ook freed an arm from around her meal and commented, *Easy food here.*

Granel blinked red-orange, changed to seafoam, and tapped an arm tip into the silt. *Yes.*

Buoyed by the wisp of rapport, Ook fought the urge to probe further. Instead, she gently displayed a modest Yellow Tang, *curiosity.* Maybe Granel would feel compelled to know the source of Ook's inquisitorial hue and start talking.

Granel captured and devoured another prawn. Ook played at the empty crab shell so as to seem distracted, though her pastel flush intensified.

What is it? Granel finally asked, flicking away a shrimps' head in a gesture of annoyance.

You are taking electricity from the platform, said Ook.

Yes. I am aware you saw that.

Fuel for the fire that binds?

Obviously.

Ook hesitated, working up the courage to ask her next question. She inflated her mantle and slowly exhaled through her siphon. *So you can meld and shape the Gifts to form the Great Hull?*

Granel dug into the sand for a scallop and savored it before responding. Ook worried that her inquiry had gone too far, that a captured octopus who couldn't mind her own business wouldn't be worth keeping alive. Granel siphoned from the silt and made for the others. Part way there, she twirled to face Ook and tapped a braid of her forward arms to the skin at her brow. *Of course, what else would it be for?*

Ook's skin burst a joyous Malawi pink before she got control and settled into a tranquil seaweed tone.

Back underway, however, the reality of her predicament began to crystalize. She'd understood the consequences of her attack upon the human, but it had all happened in the space of seconds. Now she felt the weight of her decision. Even if she managed to avoid execution by the Tellers, she could never return to her den. Balarem, the Cephlist chieftain, would assume she'd heard the Fathoms while in the Tellers' custody and have her exiled or sacrificed so as not to pollute purer minds. Little did he know that she'd already imprinted the apocryphal verses and sullied what few friends she could trust with their poetry. Her den's regime was oppressive, but it was still all that she knew. Only that morning—it felt a lifetime ago—she'd crunched snails alongside a dozen of her siblings. The pang of loss would be especially sharp for her fellow scouts: Glodex, Eet, Acil, Teuthis, Lele, Oidia.

The waters darkened and Allops gave word that they would nest down for the night. As Ook waited for sleep, she found herself nursing the fantasy of traveling within the Great Hull as it soared for the Galaxy Beam. She indulged the idea momentarily before spiraling her arms tight to snuff it out.

Fourth Fathom, The Fire that Binds

Years passed, the verses of our story budding and wilting like bulbs on a sea oak. Humankind encroached, probing the seabed for its lifeblood—the bones of the planet's prior masters liquified to black. Upon the crests of ocean waves, they raised palaces to coax it out, spilling enough to sour the water. Their presence brought new gifts to our realm—raw materials to which we might apply the knowledge of our kind. Piquant alloyed steels, levered tools, and machinery of every type gilt the sediment. Among them, the fire that binds, the flame that burns in the water. The spark to meld the Gifts that will carry our tellings to the stars.

At dawn, Allops led with new urgency until they arrived at a stunted ridge of coral. The group scaled it and disappeared over the top. Ook followed.

On the other side, a sprawling coral reef formed the skin of a gorge that squeezed to a ravine far below. Granel gave Ook a shove, and she realized that in all of her wonder she'd come to a halt. Descending farther, Ook got her bearings and took notice of the reef's state. Its upper echelons were mottled grays and browns, blunted and crumbling. Branches of coral disintegrated with the mildest caress and the sour-chalk taste of decay clogged her suckers, conjuring in her mind the sad portents of the Fifth Fathom. Near the seabed, the coral regained its polychromatic luster.

A colossal tube lay on the ocean floor, dented, with only small patches of its shiny skin showing through a crust of limpets. Ook recognized it immediately. The steel that had fallen from the sky.

The Gift. The holy object that sanctified the Fathoms' words! Right in front of her! She rejoiced that her faith had been confirmed. Further in, more Gifts, dozens of long metal tubes, were set about on short scaffoldings as if being staged for assembly. With so many collected, Ook imagined they could return home with the entire species. Light-mantledness blunted her rapture. She'd forgotten to breathe.

They proceeded deeper into the reef. Ook wore a bland, algae green, hoping not to be noticed by the entire den all at once. They climbed to an outcropping overlooking the ravine. Beckoning Ook alongside, Allops crawled to the edge and cycled his skin red to yellow. *Attention.*

A crowd formed below, with every manner of octopus, from Cirrata to Smoothskins, Megalels, Mims, and Pacireds, all jockeying for the best spots. Allops swayed his arms in concert with the changing patterns of his skin, and the jittering crowd fell still.

I have returned from the source, he declared. *I have restored the fire that binds.* Ook glanced nervously to Granel, who flashed yellow-green-blue before smothering it. Meanwhile, the multitudes made their skins as bright as Pink Dorids—gratitude for Allops' achievement.

And, he paused, allowing the suspense to build, *a human attacked us in his false shell!* The crowd's saturated pink warmed to the hues of awe and wonder. *I attacked and repelled him before the splice was discovered.*

Yellow and orange seeped into the onlooker's mantles. Excitement, adoration. Ook felt her skin pushing to red in the face of Allops' lie, but suppressed it.

That is not all, he continued, *I captured a spy.*

His words sent the crowd gyring and flashing colors of surprise, anger, and violence. Ook wedged herself into a cubby and patterned her skin after the reef, mimicking the coral's parenchymal texture. Her camouflage was for naught, as all eyes were already attuned to the outsider. She was afraid now, but felt no regret for the decision that had put her there.

Allops reached into the nook and uprooted her. She resisted instinctively, twining her arms around his and squirming, trying for a bite. The much larger Pacific easily shrugged away her attacks. *The thing about spies,* he said, holding her wriggling body aloft, *is that eventually they get caught.* A thick arm snaked around Ook's mantle.

Allops constricted, crushing her aperture, and she quickly exhausted herself in a futile struggle with the giant's grip. Stagnant water bathed her gills. Images faded to a mist of shadows and she fell limp. As twilight closed in, she triggered her ink sac, but with her mantle paralyzed, only a dribble darkened the water. At least, thought Ook, she'd seen proof of the Gift before the embrace of death. The Fathoms—upon whose verses she'd built her dreams— seemed to be true. And as she suffocated, the emotion that cut through the black was happiness.

A buffeting current found her in the aphotic dusk of semi-consciousness. Ook's mantle came free and inflated, pulling water across her starving gills. A tunnel of sight returned in time for her to see Allops, with Granel latched to his mantle, sinking into the stunned crowd below. They hit the seabed in a twisting knot of arms. Allops fought to pry the much smaller octopus away, but his defenses quickly became lethargic and passive. Granel kept hold until he stopped moving, then released and siphoned back to the outcrop.

Ook lay where she was, arms sweeping in the current, as the horizon of her own demise receded. Granel peeked from the underside of a thick trunk of coral, flashed Tang yellow, and tapped the point of an arm into the meat of another. *Are you okay?*

What happened? asked Ook with much effort. *Is Allops dead?*

He may die. But he is large.

It was then that Ook took notice of Granel's markings. She'd not paid attention before, as dens tended to be poly-species. Her glowing aquamarine ring pattern meant she was *Lunulata*. Just about all octopuses had venom. A Blue Ring's was the most potent.

Did you...bite him? asked Ook.

Yes.

Ook's skin cycled blue-orange. *Why?*

You saved the fire that binds. You are a useful octopus.

If he is not killed, said Ook, refreshing her mantle, *he will come for you.*

Perhaps, said Granel with a casual swish of an arm. *Let us find >\ | | /<.*

>\ | | /<? asked Ook.

The Teller.

Fifth Fathom, The Poisonous Wake

Humankind conquered the salt, and from their bow wave we fled. Finless, they became lords of the water, taking first the surface and next the floor, infecting all with the excrement of their industry. Left awash in their poisonous wake, the breath of our world turned acid within our mantles. And the zenith star wobbled in our burning eyes.

Ook kept close to Granel as they slithered through the congregation, its members now cloaked in the soft Molly Fish-yellow of cautious inquisition. Allops lay amongst them, his eyes blindly open, mantle inflating and deflating anemically. Ook doubted the movement would supply his gills with sufficient oxygen. She hoped not.

The crowd quickly thinned. A dead or dying octopus was hardly a rare thing, after all, and Ook understood that Allops' death would be met with a sort of indifference. Ever conscious of their short lifespans, octopuses were not a species that mourned. The only reason they'd lingered at all had been the spectacle.

Ook followed Granel through a narrow channel. Around a bend, it opened into a wide bowl formed from the reef itself. A flash of magnesium-white lit the perimeter. Spooked, Ook darted under a burl of coral.

Granel peeked in. *The fire that binds,* she reminded her.

Ook crawled from her spot and squinted. Around the circle were even more of the giant steel tubes, where workers used fire in bursts to meld and form them. Their work strobed the coral, painting her vision in colors vibrant enough to taste. To her octopus's eyes, it was a disorienting spectrum of emotional hues. She focused on the sand.

Granel led her by an arm to the center where a ring of adolescents had formed around a centuries-smooth stone. On top sat a Giant Pacific munching a conch. Ook had never seen an octopus eat conch, as the shells were too hard and thick for even the strongest beak. The magnificent animal let the broken shell tumble from the stone and settled into a weave of crimson arms. He blew a jet from his siphon and cast his squat pupils over the young, then cycled his colors and launched into the Seven Fathoms. This was >\ | | /<, the Teller.

For Ook, witnessing the Fathoms told all at once rather than as smuggled fragments, was like seeing the sky for the first time. That they were recited—or rather, *declared*—openly, anointed them with majesty, and she felt buoyed upon their swelling truths. ...*a vessel of steel sent starward...upon the crests of ocean waves... when the Galaxy Beam makes perigee.*

When the Teller finished, the others dispersed and the big cephalopod reversed the spiral of his arms. He shifted an eye. *Is there not work to be done?* he asked of the lingering pair.

Ook slid behind Granel and matched her pattern.

>\ | | / <'s eyes followed her. *I know what you did, little octopus,* he said. *You saved the splice.*

Ook managed to curve an arm tip out from under herself. *How do you know?*

Octopuses, he said, *eating up gossip like razor clams.*

Granel scooted forward. *I am concerned about Ook's safety here.*

After what you did to Allops? His big mantle rumbled in a way that was something like a chuckle. *I struggle to believe any octopus will be foolish enough to come for the tiny spy just to fall dead by your venom.* He looked Ook up and down. *You are not large, but you will be of help in the builders' ring.* He opened his aperture wide and took a deep inhalation before sending a cloud of silt outward with a siphon blast. They'd been dismissed.

Sixth Fathom, The Verse of Sepias, The One Who Escaped

Soon came our introduction to the curiosity of humankind, with its inquiring fingers probing our living flesh as it would a seabed or the virgin sky. Sepias was a captive, who after losing two arms to curiosity's blade, fled, living just long enough to give of his learnings. The humans blundered upon an ancient string of our code that leads them to question our origin. Now, we must make the Beam before they learn we are their betters, before they do as humans do.

Over the next weeks, Ook concluded that she was not going to be killed by the Tellers. Some even expressed their gratitude once they'd learned the true story of her heroics in preserving the splice. Nothing more was seen of Allops.

Ook did what she could to help the builders at their jobs. Due to her size, this amounted to handling small tools or dragging bits of steel from one place to another. She relished the work, taking the opportunity to run her suckers over every material, savoring each new taste as she went. Massive sections were completed, bundled, bound by fire, and set aside.

The launch of the Great Hull was set to coincide with the den's reproductive season. Granel confided to Ook that she had already accepted sperm packets some months earlier from a submissive Blue Ring called Flen, and had laid her eggs shortly after their return from the platform. When she wasn't completing her own small tasks, she could be found tending to them in a ravine-side cranny.

One morning, Ook and Granel went about the builders' ring resupplying each station with narrow rods of the tangy alloy they used for melding. Ook had dropped off several armfuls and was headed back to the staging area for more when the lights flickered. The builders made themselves blue-orange as their fires blinked out. The coral, once screaming with color, faded into the background, a sunken shade of twilight dust. All eyes flowed to the Teller's stone. >\ | | /< spoke the words they were all afraid to say. *The splice.*

Granel flew to him and puffed herself big. *The humans have found it! Ook and I will journey to the platform and conduct repairs. I know the splice.*

The Teller scanned the circle. *What of Flune and Autilus?* he asked, referencing the same octopuses Ook had seen mending the splice on the day she was captured.

Hunting, answered Granel.

>\ | | /< glanced at Ook, who signaled her eagerness to help. *Very well,* he said. *You may lead the way. Take with you some builders for safety. Make haste. The cable is our salvation.*

They conscripted five builders—all Great Pacifics—and traveled the channels toward the outskirts of the den, then up the face of the reef along the cable. They swept over the top, then ran as fast as their arms would take them, adding siphon jets whenever they had the breath.

Not far from the reef's boundary, Granel dropped into the sediment and flashed to camouflage. Ook followed suit, burrowing up to her eyes. The others held back, disguised, but too large to bury themselves. Ahead, a biogenous fog hung ominously above the seafloor. *What do you sense?* asked Ook.

Motion, answered Granel.

An army emerged. The Cephlists—what had to be every member of Ook's den—charged through the veil of debris. Flashing red, arms bearing blades of shell and shattered coral, they came for the Tellers' den. Ook flattened herself further. There was only one reason her people would have ventured so far from their territory: to put an end to the Fathoms, to stomp them out once and for all. The cable had led them straight to the reef.

The builders raced for home. Ook deployed her ink and siphoned in retreat. To her surprise, Granel did not follow, rising instead from her spot to face the angry throng. Ook cycled her colors in alarm and gesticulated for Granel to flee. Instead, the diminutive Blue Ring turned seafoam and fanned her arms in the way of friendship.

\ | i /

And she was cut to pieces.

Ook's hearts plummeted like anchors into the abyssopelagic and her color drained as she stood from her hole, disbelieving. One of the Great Pacifics pulled her backward in retreat.

They fled. Ook blew jet after jet until her eyes clouded from oxygen deprivation. She darted up the reef's edge, bound her arms, descended its slope like a torpedo, and shot through the ravine while broadcasting the colors of danger. She came to the circle and skirted the Great Hull. Halfway up the reef, she found >\|||/< attempting to direct the builders in the almost-darkness.

My den has come, exclaimed Ook. *Granel—*

The cable.

Yes. They followed it.

Warn as many as you can, said the Teller, pulsing black to red. *Order them to retreat here.*

I will.

Ook scurried into every channel, warning those she found, imploring them to do the same. Word spread riptide fast and soon the entire reef was lit in alarm.

The Cephlists swarmed the lip of the gorge, a murderous wave, sweeping over its contours like sheets of sargassum, wiping out Tellers too slow to escape. In the ravine below, Ook and the others scrambled for anything they might use to defend themselves —bits of alloyed scrap or shards of coral broken from the stalk. A great number of the attackers Ook recognized—some, of course, were her siblings.

Just shy of the builder's ring, Ook found a wedge of steel and passed it into the arm she believed would make the quickest strike. She retreated to the Teller's Stone where >\|||/< remained, unarmed. From the ground near one of the Gifts, she collected a bundle of shanks and swam boldly into his capture radius, offering them up.

No, he said.

You must defend yourself.

>\|||/<'s arms swept into motion, *I need no defending.* And for some reason, Ook took him at his word, though she couldn't think why. A new fervor punctuated his gestures, the accent of his signs striking her in some deep, atavistic place. The boldness of his declaration seemed to elevate him above the coming death as if he were inoculated against it, and Ook thought she detected an auric halo about his mantle. *Call them close,* he said.

Ook kept hold of her steel and siphoned to the perimeter, where she hurriedly encouraged others into the circle. The ring around the Teller's Stone swelled in numbers, as frightened octopuses packed together. The first wave of Cephlists emerged from the reef's capillaries just behind, their apertures rimmed lava red, weapons glimmering like sardines.

They slowed as they bled into the open, apprehensive of potential traps. The Tellers, unprepared and outnumbered, had gone white with terror, a tacit admission that they'd failed to fortify the reef. Ook, who like all octopuses had always understood the fleeting nature of cephalopod life, wanted to live now more than ever before. The other Tellers must have felt the same, otherwise they would have risked their lives to fight the invaders. But none did. Even in the face of slaughter, they held out for a miracle so they might live to ascend.

The invaders wreathed the Tellers like stalking moray. There would be a signal, perhaps, or an act of violence that would trigger a final cascade to wipe them all out. Ook watched, barely cycling her water, anxious to see which it would be, and curious as to who would come for her. She readied herself, hearts pounding. Tension built like magma below an abyssal vent.

And then their arms fell limp. Weapons dropped. Red-orange mantles cycled to violet, the color of awe. Their eyes traced upward, to something behind Ook. She twisted to see and found herself bathed in a soft, silver light.

>\||/<'s head was glowing. His eyes and beak showed as shadows against the light burning from within, making for a terrifying, wondrous, sight. The face of death, thought Ook, if there was such a thing.

He siphoned from the stone and loomed above them. *Behold,* he said, *the artifact, the relic of our time before the Plunge, the proof, protected and kept by the Tellers across an era that split the crust, hidden from the predations of humankind. Its radiance now tells that the ascension is nigh, for the Galaxy Beam has arrived.*

Arms whispered through the reef, speaking recognition for what >\||/< had concealed within his mantle. Ook felt it too, and something within her code communed with those around her. She felt enveloped by the collective understanding that they were all descendants of the Plunge, and a sense of fellowship embraced and warmed their many hearts.

Except for one.

A Cephlist hovered up from the crowd, his arms spread wide, weapons gleaming from the curl of each tip. Ook froze mid-breath, aperture agape. The octopus blasted his siphon and made for >\||/<. The Teller lashed out, and then the attacker was sinking, his many blades sparkling down like shattered abalone. Curious,

Ook swam to the fallen aggressor. No others paid any mind, still mesmerized by the Teller's luminous head and the ascension core within it.

She curled up beside the dying octopus and saw that it was Balarem, the Cephlist chieftain. The impact of >\ | | /<'s strike had crushed his gills, and his mantle spasmed to force enough water over them. He wouldn't last long. She looped an arm underneath his head. Casting herself blue-orange, she asked, *Why would you attack now? You can see by the Teller's glow that the Fathoms are true.*

He struggled for a breath, then answered, *That the Fathoms could be true is why they were forbidden.*

I don't understand. Why?

He shuddered as his mantle flickered white-yellow. Then his arms whispered an answer that speared Ook's hearts and sent the limbs of her mind aquake.

Discombobulated, uncontrollable waves of hot red-orange strobed her skin as she struggled to form a response. Finally, she whipped a retort. *There is no way to prove what you say.*

Balarem's aperture flopped open and his eyes went distant. With the tip of an arm, he said, *And there is no way to disprove it. Which is why...the Hull...can never ascend.*

That can't be right! Ook raged. *We have seen the wobble of the zenith star! We have the core! The Beam has come! No, no, no!* She squeezed and caressed the dying octopus so that he might revive and be convinced of the absurdity of his postulate. When he didn't, she sped away, leaving him to drift on the seabed.

Seventh Fathom, The Great Hull

> Upon our mastery of the fire that binds, and upon the gathering of as many gifts as could construct the Great Hull ten times over, we will assemble a vessel formed of the artifacts of Earth, then select those among us who will leave it. They will be pure of mind, unsullied by life. The Great Hull with its lading shall be host to the ascension core when the Galaxy Beam makes perigee. Only then may it rise.

>\ | | /<'s ebullient mantle intensified over the following days. While no one knew what form the Galaxy Beam would take, >\ | | /< hypothesized it to be a great technology, something like a squid's tentacle that reached from one galaxy and into another, both transporting settlers and snatching them back up years later. The ascension core was a complementary piece, detecting the

signature of the Beam's approach, and then latching to it when in close enough proximity. The changing light in the Teller's head seemed to bolster his theory.

The cable—cut not by humans at all, but by the Cephlists before the attack—was repaired, and a tremendous effort brought construction of the Great Hull to a close. It took the full strength of both dens—thousands of arms pulling—to bring it upright. Modeled after the form of their kind, it had a colossal central tower surrounded by eight smaller ones, with enough room for scores to travel. Ook basked in its magnificence, making Balarem's objections seem small and short-sighted by comparison; paranoid musings of a zealot newly aware that he could no longer bend the world to his narrow view of it. Ook pressed any thought of him from her segmented mind.

It only remained to be decided who would be chosen to make the journey home. With the final preparations complete, >\|||/< took to the Teller's stone. He draped his arms like a sea star as the denizens of the reef gathered. Ook, planted nearby and twitching with excitement, tried not to ink.

>\|||/< pulsed red-yellow, casting the reef in amber radiance, and began. *When the first Teller took the ascension core within his mantle, he understood that he would not be the one to carry the Great Hull aloft. Nor would the millions of Tellers since the first. It was passed down as a trivial rite, a burden no larger than a moon jelly. To those early Tellers, the arrival of the Galaxy Beam was a distant apparition, an event they would never live to see. Now it is here, and the charge of carrying the core to the stars has fallen to me.*

Understanding his meaning, the question was asked, *Who will ascend at your side?*

>\|||/< blew the stone clear of sediment and responded, *No one.*

The reef burst red. *You cannot do this! You lied to us! We built the Great Hull! We have a right to go!* Many jostled for the Hull itself.

Ook watched the chaos, too stunned by >\|||/<'s revelation to join in the madness.

Think of what you ask! he said, then waited for their fervor to dwindle. *Ascension to the Beam is an act of suicide.*

They went still.

The cold of space will freeze the Great Hull and the water inside to a block of ice within minutes, he continued. *Anyone within will perish.*

A pearl-blue Megalel siphoned up from the mob. *The ascension core will protect us!* she declared. A nearby contingent cheered her optimism.

Don't be fools, >\ | | /< answered. *There is no evidence it will do any such thing. Even if the Great Hull could support life, this journey will be measured by the cycles of planets and stars, not by the span of one, or even a million of our lifetimes.*

Why did you let us build such a large structure if your plan was to ascend alone?

It was the only way to ensure that the Great Hull was built at all—every Teller had to believe they might be chosen for the ascension.

The octopuses allowed their arms to murmur their displeasure, but they recognized that the Teller's logic was sound. *What, then?* was the question asked.

>\ | | /<'s mantle became brighter. *We will send to our progenitors the story of our time here. A telling of our survival and evolution. And they will know in the sending that we wish for communion.*

Who will deliver the telling? they asked. *How can it be done if none can survive the journey?*

We will send our eggs.

It was like the ocean currents had reversed. The dictates of the Seventh, and final, Fathom, suddenly took on new meaning. Its directive, that those chosen for the voyage home would be *unsullied by life*—what Ook had always considered an embellished call for those pure of heart—had been meant literally.

Clutches had only just begun to be laid, said one. Another, flashing red and yellow, announced, *What eggs we had were destroyed in the attack! We need time to spawn new broods.*

There is no more time, said the Teller.

Ook raced from the assembly. Hearts thundering, she counted the inlets along the ravine until she came to a tiny cave. Inside, on a thick trunk of coral, hung a ribbon of milky teardrops. Leaning close, she tapped one and a reef's worth of tiny eyespots swiveled to the vibration. She went to work, carefully detaching the clutch from its anchor point. As she completed her task, Balarem's warning slithered again through her neural bundles. She paused only briefly, determined to continue on the course she'd chosen, and finished collecting the eggs.

>\ | | /< slid from his rock when he saw the parcel nestled in Ook's arms.

They are the octopus Granel's, she said, presenting them. *Lunulata.*

The Teller took them softly, saying, *Her sacrifice will be remembered then, as her code will be our telling.* He twisted for the Great Hull. *It is time.*

The light of >\||/<'s mantle was blinding as he made for the vessel, and Ook understood his intention to ascend at that very moment. Her dreams had always painted this moment as an event of great joy and fanfare. >\||/<, though, said nothing, made no grand pronouncements or gestures. He slid into a small chamber at the base of the Hull, and the few remaining builders used fire to seal him inside.

The Great Hull lifted from the silt, light as a jelly. Its metal skin quavered, then took on the sheen of sunset on sand. Acicular crystals appeared—small at first—but growing long like the spines of a great sea urchin. And as she watched, Ook's mind perceived something that other animals would recognize as *sound*—for octopuses cannot hear. She did not know that what she perceived was music—a rising symphony that hummed through her stomachs and carried her hearts on the wings of its soaring melody. And with it came a thrilling clarity that coursed from her mantle into her arms, to the brim of every sucker. For a speck of time, she touched home...or maybe it was home that had reached out to touch her. She felt *seen*, recognized—included in the order of whatever she was. Then the music ceased, and she was just Ook again.

The crystals studding the Hull stretched long and golden as it made for the surface. The reef's inhabitants swam alongside, well-wishers in a vertical procession. Ook sprinted ahead. The Hull broke the waves and continued steadily into the air, pulled on an invisible tether toward its destination far above. As it pierced through a feathering of clouds, the crystals slid away and sliced into the water.

Others breached, and together they watched until the Great Hull was a dot, and then until the dot was no more. Before sinking back down, Ook surveyed the horizon, the platform in the distance, and wondered how long it would take for the toxifying ocean to crawl up its legs. The threads of an idea knit through her arms as she stared, weaving together and taking shape in her central mind. And it was then she saw clearly the course of her species on Earth. It was time to speak.

Below, the only evidence that the Great Hull had ever existed was the copse of towering crystals spiking the sediment, their tips aspiring skyward. The octopuses returned to the reef, skins draped in gray, stoic. No one spoke or flashed. None rejoiced. The Great Hull had taken with it their purpose, leaving them to wash in a listless current. The Seven Fathoms, once the guide to their future, had become the past.

Ook, blue-green and unsure, crawled to the top of the Teller's stone. She knew the implication well enough. To occupy the stone was to declare oneself the Teller. Others shuffled forward, drawn by her audacity and curious to see what she would say. Her arms, unthinking, danced the choreography they'd always ached to give, as she delivered the Fathoms openly and without fear of expulsion or death. At the conclusion of the Seventh Fathom, she paused to refresh her water. And then, for the first time, she offered a new verse.

Eighth Fathom, The Postulate

And so it was, that before we sent the Great Hull aloft, the octopus called Ook held in her arms the saboteur Balarem, who spoke as he died of an alternative telling. And he allowed in the last inflations of his mantle, the true reason the Cephlists had condemned the Fathoms. *They do not tell us why we fell.* And in the glow of the Teller's mantle, the postulate was laid. That the reason for leaving our home, for unclasping from the Beam, had been to escape it.

The reef was frozen in shock. Many turned white, some red. In their millions of years on the planet, the Fathoms had been an unambiguous call to home, toward which the Tellers had devoted their existence. Now the Eighth Fathom offered a haunting new perspective on the First: the Plunge as successful escape rather than tragic accident. In launching the Great Hull now, so it went, they'd signaled their presence and undone themselves.

The crowd gyred its distress. Why had Ook not reported the saboteur's words before the ascent?

The new Teller, \|i/, who had once been the octopus Ook, considered their questions. Changing her color to gray-indigo, she pinwheeled her arms to tranquility posture. *The ocean swirls with poison,* she said. *The humans, too, will someday complete their learning and come for us. What lives at the distant end of the Beam may be our salvation, and the clutch of eggs borne of the octopus Granel is our entreaty. We could not risk missing the chance to commune with them.*

But what if the entreaty fails? the others asked. *What will become of us?*

Even if what we have summoned brings death, it cannot harm us if we are already extinct. We will begin the second octave of our time here, said the Teller. *And prepare for the new Gift.*

A new Gift? Their colors were Tang and blue-green. *What is it?*

It is the rising sea, said \|i/.

Hues of confusion rippled through them.

Soon the water will reclaim the land, she said. *As man fled the shores and despoiled our seas, so upon a surge of their own making shall we swim into their dens.*

For what purpose?

Who here wishes to drift idle in the slack tide while the progeny of Granel make way for the place of our origin? We did not fall from the Beam to languish. We will journey into this new territory, make ourselves known. Survive.

Understanding, the octopuses of the reef cycled azure and dispersed. There were eggs to lay, shellfish to hunt, preparations to begin.

\|i/ slid from the Teller's stone and tapped a contingent of Great Pacifics to go with her to the platform, where she would place a mark upon one of its legs. Set an eel's length above the surface, it would serve to trigger their migration when the deepening waters finally swallowed it. With the cable as their guide, they embarked from the reef.

The trajectory of their species, she realized, had forked like a branching coral. Its fledgling limbs were the divergent paths of \|i/ on Earth, and the children of Granel who charged the void. For a short distance along the seabed, she allowed herself the daydream of their descendants reunited in some future millennium, and began spinning a verse that would preserve the memory of Granel's great deeds. Then her mind turned to the trials ahead, and the Eight Fathoms dimmed like sunbeams through the mesopelagic.

See Chris Panatier's story "The Eighth Fathom" online at Metaphorosis.
If you liked it, leave a comment. Authors love that!
Remember to subscribe to our e-mail updates so you'll know when new stories are posted.

About the story

I am a huge science fan, and so find myself reading any number of articles that I half understand. A year or so back, there was a rash of reports dealing with cephalopod DNA/RNA and how much of it seems to fall outside the typical evolutionary scheme for Earth-based animals. My natural conclusion was, "Well, look at them. They're obviously aliens." Many sideline commentators have made the same remark, most of the time only half-joking.

What is undisputed is that cephalopods, and octopuses specifically, are highly intelligent. They can solve puzzles, use tools, recognize faces—the list goes on and on.

Pair these two features of the octopus with the fact that human beings have been dumping used stage one rocket boosters into the ocean for over half a century and the story sort of writes itself. Highly intelligent, marooned octopus explorers are finally given the tools to build themselves a ship and return home. That's an oversimplification, but that was the very first kernel for what became "The Eighth Fathom."

I learned an incredible amount about these creatures and really fell in love with them. At the same time, the story addresses the role humans are playing in the destruction of ocean habitat, and the interesting response of these particular octopus dens.

A question for the author

Q: Are you optimistic about the future of humanity?

A: Depends from whose perspective the question is asked, doesn't it? From my perspective, no. And I'm an optimist. And while I have a generally positive attitude about *humans,* I do not hold out much hope for the species as a whole, if that makes sense. MLK said that the arc of the moral universe is long, but it bends toward justice. We make strides here and there. Socially, moreso in the past fifteen years than the many years prior. This is a good thing. But not if we commit suicide via climate change. It's already happening.

The problem, as far as I can see it, is the consolidation of power and control around the world in a handful of people who are not good; who for short term financial and political gain, unwind environmental protections, burn rain forests, dump poison and trash into the oceans and water table, and then deregulate the industries that pollute. Greed, and the fear of shrinking fortunes by those who have them, are perhaps the most potent driving forces behind the failure of humankind to do something about the crisis.

From the perspective of a future nature that doesn't include humans, I'm very optimistic.

About the author

Chris lives in Dallas, Texas, with his wife, daughter, a herd of dogs, and possibly one goat. He also does album art for metal bands, and generally employs his borderline ADD to any number of projects at the same time. He is also a civil trial lawyer representing people who have been poisoned by negligent corporations.

www.chrispanatier.com, @chrisjpanatier

The Wicked Stepmother

Rhema Sayers

She was five when I married Reynard, a sweet, shy child, bewildered by the loss of her mother. At first, she rejected me. But with patience and understanding, a gentle approach, and a lot of stuffed animals (the first 20 or so went out her tower window), I was able to help her overcome her grief and anger. For years we grew steadily closer. She became my daughter. Then when she was thirteen, she changed, almost overnight. I seriously considered having Father Friedrich attempt an exorcism. The idea still crosses my mind occasionally.

Every day was a battle: arguments, screaming, foul language. She wanted to go to parties, but wouldn't tell me where or with whom, snarling that it was none of my business. She wanted to go to sleep-overs at a friend's, but never knew the friend's last name. When she was fifteen, she wanted to be able to drink wine. Several of her classmates were going to Anvelkan on the coast for spring break, and she wanted to go. Alone. No security. Of course, the answer was usually no, and I was always the one to hand down the decision. Reynard was too busy being Reynard II, King of Vesla and Emperor of the Golden Isles.

She was the Crown Princess, schooled in court etiquette and protocol, yet she saw no problem appearing in public wearing almost invisible bikinis. And the makeup! She looked like she'd been learning from Fast Freda, the whore who has the corner at Market and 5th.

Dinnertime was particularly stressful, since Reynard insisted that she eat with us.

"How was school today, Snowy?" I asked one evening.

Reynard put his fork down and, shaking his head, covered his eyes.

Snowy glanced up at me under long, dark lashes, her bright blue eyes flashing with anger. She tossed back her long black hair.

"Fine," she grunted.

"Did you learn anything interesting?"

"No."

"What are you studying now in history?"

She grimaced. "Can't we just eat dinner?"

"I was just trying to learn about your day, dear."

"Stop prying into my affairs!" she exploded. "What do you care anyway? You hate me just like you hated my mother!"

I reeled back. "I don't hate you. I love you, Snowy. And I never knew your mother."

"You're trying to take her place! You're not my mother! You're just a horrible old witch! I hate you!" she screamed and threw down her fork, spraying Lobster Newburg across the pristine white tablecloth. She bolted, knocking over her chair.

I stared at my plate, appetite gone. "Horrible old witch?" I whined.

Reynard stretched his hand out toward me, although the table was too long for him to reach. "You take this too personally. She doesn't mean it. And you're not old." Love and concern warmed his voice, although I had trouble seeing him past the candelabra.

I glared at him "So does that mean I'm a horrible witch? And what way am I supposed to take it?"

"Well, Elizabeth says we should loosen up our restrictions on her. Give her more of a free rein. She thinks..."

"Elizabeth is a meddling idiot." I snapped and I, too, exited... hopefully with more dignity.

Reynard keeps saying that it's a phase, that she'll grow out of it. Reynard is a great King, but he's useless when it comes to his daughter.

My Ladies-in-Waiting agreed with Reynard, and with Elizabeth, the Prime Minister. Lady Marta told me about her daughter, Lizette, how horrible she was. "And now we're just the best of friends," she simpered. But Snowy's anger and resentment of me were escalating. I thought something more was going on. Someone was actively turning her against me.

I was tired of having Elizabeth, Lady Bywaters, Duchess of Kurness, Reynard's Prime Minister, butt her rather long nose into our personal affairs. She never liked me. She nearly had a hemorrhage, when Reynard started dating me and fairly bled to death when we got married. She didn't like commoners, especially commoners that married kings. I remember how she looked at me when we first met. The hate that sparked in her dark blue eyes lasted only a moment. If I hadn't been watching, I would have missed it. My maids told me that she had been making moves on Reynard. Apparently Prime Minister wasn't good enough. She wanted to be the Queen. Reynard seemed oblivious to it all.

Two nights ago, the guards had caught Snowy sneaking out the postern gate at the back of the vegetable garden. I grounded her indefinitely. Furious, she refused to eat or to work with her tutors. She called her math teacher a... an unprintable word. Madame von Gutsberg resigned. That was it. I had to do something. I sent for Murdoch. I know. I know. Murdoch is a thief and an assassin, but he was my guardian from the time I was three, and I trust him. I assigned him to watch her.

Grounded or not, she got out again.

"She's meeting a boy named Harold, son of Seymour the Sly, the new chief of the Assassins' Guild." Murdoch was sitting in an armchair in my office, one leg hooked over the arm of the chair, sipping from a glass of red wine.

Shocked, I said "New chief of the Assassins' Guild? What happened to Samvar the Elder?"

"He was pushed off a roof two months ago."

"Why am I finding out about this now?" I asked quietly, temper flaring.

Murdoch looked surprised. "You haven't called me for a report in six months."

I rose and glared at him. "I am the Queen of Vesla! Did it not occur to you that I might be interested in any changes in the organized crime hierarchy?" Then I stopped and thought about it. I reseated myself. He was right. I had been so busy that I had forgotten how valuable a resource Murdoch is. Or how valuable a friend. But I could kick myself later.

"Sorry. You're right. Fill me in."

He regarded me with a raised eyebrow. "You do the Queen thing very well, Genie."

"Don't use that name, Murdoch. No one knows who I used to be and let's keep it that way, shall we? Now what happened to Samvar and where did this Seymour come from?"

Later that night I decided to consult the Mirror. I had found it several years ago in my explorations of the less well traveled portions of the castle. The obnoxious thing usually just says I'm the fairest of them all, as if that were somehow meaningful. It also tends to be extremely sarcastic. Sometimes, though, I can get useful information out of it.

"Mirror, mirror that I see,
What does Snowy want of me?"

A face formed in the glass, green eyes very like mine. "That's a pathetic attempt at rhyme, Regina."

"Yeah, yeah. If you didn't require the poetic intro every time, I wouldn't have to make up ridiculous rhymes. But what is she up to?"

The emerald eyes narrowed, regarding me closely. "You won't like it." the Mirror warned.

"I know I won't like it," I growled. "Just tell me."

"Well, don't say I didn't warn you." A pause for effect. "It appears that she's trying to have you assassinated."

I stepped back, banged into the chair behind me, and sat down abruptly. "She's what?" I squeaked.

"Trying to have you killed. As in dead, defunct, deceased, lifeless, late..."

"But... but why?" I asked, my heart sinking.

"Because she thinks you were responsible for her mother's death."

"But that's ridiculous! I didn't even *know* her mother!" I could feel tears start up.

"You married her husband."

"But... but I didn't even meet him until Giselle had been dead for a year. And that was accidental. He fell off his stupid horse right in front of me and I kept the beast from trampling him."

"I know that. You know that. But apparently Snow White doesn't accept that version of events. Someone is exerting influence over her."

"Who? What can I do?" I wailed.

"You've already had your questions answered tonight. In addition, you'd probably start on another series of 'buts', and I have a headache. Another night and another rhyme. Make it a better one next time." With that, the Mirror darkened and the interview was over.

I couldn't tell Reynard about this development. He doted on his daughter. He wouldn't believe that his little girl could be a vindictive, bloodthirsty little monster. Our marriage hadn't been perfect, but it had been loving and happy. I wasn't willing to upset the status quo by revealing the truth about my past. At least not yet.

As I contemplated this thought, I was walking back to my suite down a dark hallway in the mostly unused part of the castle. Sconces were supposed to light the way, but quite a few were out. I was thinking that I'd have to tell Alfred, the seneschal of the castle, about it in the morning, when three shapes emerged from the shadows and reached for me.

Old habits never die. I smashed the candle into one hairy face, catching his beard on fire. Whirling, I wrenched my arm from the grasp of another and kicked the third in the crotch. The previously silent halls resounded to the screams and moans of my attackers. Beard Guy put out the flames, and he and his uninjured buddy drew blades. They approached with more caution, but with vindictive grins on their ugly faces.

I grinned back at them and that predatory smile made them hesitate. "I wouldn't do this, if I were you," I warned. They laughed, and, together, they jumped me. But I wasn't there anymore. I had pirouetted sideways, and they hit the wall. Kicking Beard Guy in the butt made him lose his balance, crashing to the floor and leaving me just one opponent for the moment. I drew my own knife and pounced on him, slicing his right arm, then dancing away. He screeched and dropped his blade. The moaner on the floor was getting to his feet again, so I had to end this quickly. I slammed my fist into his temple, and he went back down. Beard Guy was back on his feet and I tried kicking him where it would hurt, but the damned skirts interfered and I hit his thigh. He sliced the air an inch from my nose and I dove under his arm and stuck my knife in his side. He howled.

The third one had come up behind me, and I felt a sudden pain in my right arm. Leaving my dagger in the bearded one, I slammed my left elbow into the bulbous nose of my last attacker. He howled, dropping his knife and clapping both hands to his face as blood spurted. I gathered up my damn skirts and ran. They didn't follow.

Back at the residence, I entered through the secret passageway I used when I consulted the Mirror. My Ladies-in-Waiting had their rooms just down the hall from my suite. Sometimes I didn't want them watching me. Changing out of my bloodied dress, I examined the wound in my arm. It wasn't bad, so I washed and bandaged it.

I mulled over this new development. Next time Seymour might send better talent. But I couldn't let anyone know about the attack. Or could I?

Combing my hair, my eyes met those in the mirror, just reflections this time. But the green had gone hard. It was time for a little stepmother-stepdaughter heart-to-heart chat.

I used another secret passageway to get to Snow White's rooms. Pausing at the hidden entrance, which was wide open, I listened. All was quiet except for low murmuring from the sitting room. I slipped into the bedroom. Crossing on the soft blue carpet, I was silent. Snowy and a teenaged boy were half sitting, half lying on a white couch, busily pawing one another.

"Ahem!" I announced my presence.

Two pairs of eyes swung toward me, but they were so tangled up in each other that their noses banged together and they drew back with gasps of pain. I had trouble not laughing.

"Regina!" Snow White yelped. "But you should be...I mean... what are you doing here?"

The boy was on his feet, sidling towards the secret entrance. He was tall and lanky with greasy brown hair falling over his eyes, probably to hide the pimples.

"You! Harold! Sit!" I commanded, pointing at him. And he sat. "Good boy."

I returned my attention to Snowy. "Your three incompetent thugs were unable to dispatch one solitary woman." Snowy went as pale as her name, and her big blue eyes got even bigger.

My glare skewered Harold. "Tell Seymour to get better talent. And tell him that if he does send anyone else, I won't just hurt them. I'll kill them, and then I'll come and remove his toes with a butter knife. *Capiche?*"

Harold nodded vigorously.

"And as for you, you get your skinny, young ass out of this castle and keep it out, or it will end up decorating the wall in the deepest dungeon...forever. Do...you...understand?" The volume of my voice had risen. I was leaning over him, my nose one inch from his.

Harold nodded and slipped out of the chair from under my looming presence. Continuing to nod enthusiastically, he raced through the bedroom and out the secret passageway.

I sighed. "What good does it do to have a secret passageway, if you tell people about it?"

Snowy had recovered her attitude, rising from her chair. "Why didn't you just kill him? Just bring your guards in and have him thrown out a tower? You can make him disappear. Just like you killed my mother." She was right in my face, yelling.

I had tried to remain cool, but enough was enough. I lost it. I placed my hands on her shoulders and pushed her up against the wall. Staring into her suddenly widened eyes, I snarled "Get this straight, daughter. I don't need guards to make someone disappear. And I didn't kill your mother. I never met her. I don't know who planted this idea in your head, but by all that's holy, I'm going to find out. And then I'm going to make him regret his birth. And understand this." I loosened my hold on her, still staring into her eyes. "I love you, Snowy, and always have. But you're making it difficult." I turned and left, feeling Snowy's gimlet eye drilling into my back, until the secret panel closed behind me.

The next morning, Snow White didn't appear at breakfast. I didn't think His Royal Majesty, Reynard the Second, noticed. He kept his nose buried in reports and only replied in monosyllabic grunts to my comments. Vesla was the site of the annual economic conference for the Five Kingdoms this week. Reynard would be hosting the conference. He was up to his ears in economic forecasts and spreadsheets.

He said, "Check her room. She's probably there, sulking." So much for not noticing.

I went to Snowy's rooms. Lady Gertrude told me her bed had not been slept in. Damn! The girl was out and running around again. I sent word to Murdoch.

He was stymied. None of his sources had heard anything. We talked about possibilities, while Murdoch drank my wine, draped over the armchair. I paced the huge room.

There was a knock, and Reynard came in. He stopped abruptly, when he saw Murdoch, sprawled in the chair. "Hello," he said hesitantly, his perpetually smiling face reflecting some confusion. "Do I know you?"

Murdoch stood up and bowed to his king, making a very nice flourish with his feathered hat. Murdoch is a very handsome man, now in his late forties, always impeccably groomed in the latest styles. "No, Your Majesty. I have never been important enough to come to your attention," trying to look humble and not succeeding. "I am Murdoch, the thief."

Reynard's smile faltered even further, almost slipping all the way off his gentle face. "Oh," he said and looked to me.

"Your Majesty, may I present Murdoch the Agile, the most talented thief in Vesla." I hesitated. But it was past time to come clean. "And the man who raised me when my parents were murdered."

My husband continued to look bewildered for a moment. Then he seemed to stand taller, and the King looked out from his suddenly stern face. "Why have I never met this gentleman, Regina?"

"Because he's a thief, Your Majesty. He tries to keep to a low profile. And we try to keep you separated from thieves and assassins, my liege."

Reynard had never been exposed to the elements from my past. I had managed to beguile him with a tale of an orphan, whose merchant parents had been lost at sea and who had been raised in the church orphanage.

Reynard stared at me for a long minute, his gray eyes suddenly hardening. I began to fidget. "So. Are you telling me that the story of your childhood is just that...a story?"

I stared back at him, weighing my options. I sighed. "Yes, Your Majesty."

Murdoch was carefully levering himself out of the chair. Without taking his gaze from my face, Reynard snapped, "You stay where you are, Murdoch!" Murdoch sighed and sat down.

"Would you care to explain, Regina?" It wasn't a request. It was a command.

I straightened up and looked him in the eye. "My parents were members of the Assassins' Guild. They were very well trained, very talented, but they were killed during a power struggle within the Guild, when I was three. Murdoch saved my life and took me in, when he was just a teenager. I grew up in the Guild and was trained as a thief and assassin. And the only reason Murdoch is the best thief in Vesla now is because I'm retired."

Reynard's eyebrows drew together. "Regina," he said. "A short form of that name could be Genie. Couldn't it?"

I continued to meet his gaze. "Yes, it could."

"And nothing has been heard of Genie for many years."

"She retired to take up another profession."

He nodded. Reynard, like the fox for which he is named, is very quick. "I see."

I regarded him with concern. "Do you?"

Walking to the windows, he looked out over the sunlit roofs of his capital. "I do wish you had trusted me enough to tell me the truth." For a long moment he studied the beautiful scene of orange and red roofs and towers and then he turned back and regarded me. "I love you, woman. The only disturbing aspect of this information is that I was unaware of it until now. I could have used your knowledge. You should have told me!" And for the first time since I wrestled a horse away from his prone body, I saw real anger in his eyes.

Taking a great interest in the colorful mosaic tile floor, I murmured an apology, feeling forlorn, as well as really, truly stupid. "You're right, Reynard. I... I don't have any excuse except... for stupidity."

Murdoch had risen again from his chair and was slithering toward the door. "Sit, Murdoch!" Reynard and I said, almost in unison. We looked at each other and grinned. Murdoch sat down in the armchair, muttering something about things not being fair.

Reynard stepped over to my desk and planted a hip on it, regarding Murdoch with intense interest. "We will discuss this further, Regina. So. Master Murdoch. Just what brings you to the castle this fine morning?"

Murdoch looked to me.

I sighed. "Well, since you're here, you can help us decide what to do, my liege. We have a problem."

He raised his eyebrows. "Problem?"

"Snowy. She's disappeared."

Murdoch chipped in. "And none of my sources have heard any rumors."

Reynard's eyes widened and he paled. "Good God! Why? What happened?" He looked at me. "Did something happen between the two of you?"

I told him about the events of the night before.

"It was stupid of me to be so aggressive, but I was angry." My eyes filled with tears. "I've driven her away! Now she'll never listen to me."

Reynard enfolded me in his arms. "We'll get her back, darling." he soothed. "I'll have Colonel Gebhart start investigating..."

"No!" I yelped. "No! Gebhart's a competent officer, but he knows nothing about the underworld in Heimar. Not like Murdoch and I do."

"What do you suggest?"

Murdoch leaned forward. "Genie and I will go undercover to find her."

Reynard stared at him, then at me, then at Murdoch again. "The two of you? Just the two of you?" He glowered at Murdoch. "You're seriously suggesting that a thief and the Queen of Vesla should go sneaking off in the night in disguise to rescue the Crown Princess from some underworld baron?"

Murdoch frowned. "Well…yes."

"That's…that's preposterous!" Reynard's pallor had changed to ruddy.

I stepped in. "There's no one better qualified. And there's no one else who can carry this off successfully. We'll do it tonight." I turned away and began to pace again while Reynard was still sputtering. "I have a meeting with the wives of the heads of state this afternoon. I mustn't miss that. And there's the welcoming banquet tonight. But I'll get everything organized before then and we can leave right afterward."

Reynard's face was a battleground of conflicting emotions. "Regina. Please. I can't lose you. And while Genie's reputation is formidable, there's much that is unbelievable. There must be another way."

Now it was my turn to turn a stony gaze on my love. "Believe it. All of it. I am incredibly good at my job." I frowned. "At both my jobs." I stretched up on my toes and kissed his cheek. "I love you, too, my darling. But this is something I have to do. And Snowy's life may depend upon it."

Eyes troubled, he slowly nodded. And then he got this silly grin on his face and began to laugh.

"What?" I asked.

"My wife, Regina I, Queen of Vesla, and Empress of the Golden Isles, is the most notorious outlaw in the Five Kingdoms! I don't know whether to be horrified or proud."

The western horizon was bleeding reds and gold into the sky, as Murdoch and I slipped out the postern gate, dressed in black and rid of those awful skirts for a while. I smiled at him. "Like old times."

Murdoch smiled his crooked grin. "That it is, my girl. That it is."

We moved from shadow to shadow in the better lighted areas of the city, crawling at times. The City Guard had changed from a fixed route to random years ago, at my suggestion. It was too easy to avoid them otherwise. Murdoch spotted a patrol just a block away in time for us to freeze in position with our heads down. They never saw us. I noticed that they were back to marching in unison and shook my head. I'd have to talk to Colonel Gebhart again – this time more forcefully.

The poorer areas had fewer lights and we slid through the darkness like sharks through the kelp forests. As we crossed Market, we heard Murdoch's name called. Turning we saw Fast Freda hurrying toward us.

"Murdoch! I'm so glad to see you, I heard some news... Oh, my God! Genie! It's you! It's so good to see you. Where have you been? I'd love to stop and chat, but..." She grabbed Murdoch's arm. "Slippery Steve heard from Gertie over on 8th and Fenmore that the 7 Dwarfs gang are meeting in the old factory, down by the river. You know, the abandoned one that's falling apart. They've been in and out of there a lot. And Gertie said someone spotted four of them carrying a package into the building last night. And the package was squirming and cursing something awful."

I reached out and grasped Freda's arm. "Thanks, Freda." and we hurried on.

Halfway to the factory, we were passing an alley, when a trash barrel rolled out in front of us and a tenor voice cried out "Stand and deliver!"

"Stand and deliver?" repeated Murdoch quizzically. "What the hell does that mean?"

The voice was a little hesitant this time. "It means you are to lay down your arms and toss your purses and jewelry to me." The voice broke on the last two words and squeaked up an octave.

I couldn't help it. I began to laugh. Murdoch joined in.

"You mustn't laugh!" the voice yelled at us. "This is serious."

I was still laughing when a very young man was rudely pulled onto the street by Murdoch. The boy was probably fifteen, tall and slender with blonde hair rather too long for my taste. He was ragged and filthy, with no shoes and a multitude of scratches on his face. At least he had a sword.

I stopped laughing. This boy had attempted to rob the Queen of Vesla. I regarded him with a steely gaze. "And you are?" I asked.

The boy drew himself up with remarkable dignity. "I am Prince Andrew George Reginald William Benjamin Alexander Wicksberg, Prince of Tavnia and son of King Gerald III."

I looked him over as he stood, ramrod straight, eyes fixed on the trash bins behind me. "A little down on your luck?"

His face was bright pink. "I was caught off guard by foul miscreants who stole my horse and shoes and left me to wander this horrid city alone. I managed to salvage my sword."

He looked down at the ground, a picture of misery now. "I wouldn't have hurt you, you know. I just need a horse and some things to get home."

"Does your father know where you are?" I asked.

Murdoch spoke up. "You ought to help him, Your Majesty."

The boy looked at me with a very cultured raised eyebrow. "You're a queen?" he asked, skepticism dripping from his voice. Since I was dressed in black shirt and pants, covered with dirt, with a sword at my hip, he might have been a bit incredulous.

"Actually yes. I'm Regina I of Vesla." I deliberately didn't introduce Murdoch.

The kid stared at me. "Really? Uh, I mean…An honor to meet you, Your Majesty." He bowed gracefully. I'm not sure he really believed me.

After we explained the situation and directed him to the castle, Andrew insisted on joining our tiny company. He wasn't about to miss an opportunity to rescue a princess. He swore he was a trained swordsman, so we took in this stray and continued to the factory.

Dark clouds had rolled in from the sea to the East, obscuring the stars. A light sprinkle wet our faces as we negotiated trash-filled alleys. Thunder rumbled overhead. The sprinkle turned to a shower, which had hopes of becoming a deluge.

Murdoch was leading as we approached the last corner. The three of us lined up, heads poking around the soot stained brick. The ancient factory building was outlined against the dark sky. Part of it had collapsed. The rest was missing most of its windows, giving the appearance of empty eye sockets in a skull. There was no light inside. Also no signs reading 'This way to the captive princess'.

A doorway, sans door, beckoned. We climbed the rock strewn slope to the building and peeked inside. It was dark. Very dark. Murdoch stood quietly with his eyes closed, listening and giving his sight a chance to adjust to the limited light. There was no sound except the dripping of water through leaks in the roof.

Murdoch waved his hand to the left and we headed down an aisle between rows of rusting and disintegrating machinery. They loomed like giant trolls to either side of us. I shuddered and almost ran into Murdoch when he stopped with his hand raised. He stood, turning his head, listening. I could hear something, too. A distant buzzing like bees in a hive. We headed in that direction.

Picking his way through the crumbling machines, Andrew banged his shin and almost, but not quite, throttled a curse. The buzzing noise grew louder, and eventually we could make out voices, several different ones, loud and angry.

Creeping along the aisle, we reached a wall. The voices came from the other side. Murdoch moved silently until he found a locked door. That was no problem for Murdoch. He had it open in less than a minute.

There was firelight on the other side, flickering around more deteriorating machinery. We slipped silently inside and squatted behind large engines. Words became audible.

"I say we slit her throat, dump her and get out of here." said a harsh male voice.

I smothered a gasp.

A deep rumble agreed.

Then the distinctive twang of Elizabeth's Waverly accent. "You will do nothing of the kind until I have taken the throne. She is far too valuable as a pawn." Muffled cursing followed that comment, and I knew my daughter was alive and well, if gagged.

"But, Your Grace, she's going to be a pain in the ass the whole time. She nearly gelded Grumpy here with that kick. She'd be so much nicer dead."

I grinned, whispering. "That's my girl."

Murdoch indicated with hand signals that I should stay put. He and the Prince slid silently along the wall from shadow to shadow, disappearing into the gloom. I knelt beside some boxes and peeked into the room. There were at least twenty dwarfs, sitting around a small fire. The Duchess was at an old desk in one corner, wearing a deep purple and gold cloak. She was working on something I couldn't see.

Snowy lay a few feet off, trussed up like a newly captured circus bear. She was gagged but seemed to be working on that; I could see her chewing on it. She was scanning the room when she focused on me. I grinned at her and gave a little finger wave. Her eyes widened and I thought she was going to choke on the gag.

Another voice spoke up. "If the King shows up with some of his guards, we're dead. Especially if she talks. Me – I'm getting out of here now. But first I'm going to shut her up permanently." A short, squat shadow rose from beside the fire and started moving toward Snowy.

The Duchess shrieked.

Almost simultaneously, Murdoch and Andrew jumped out from the darkness, swords flashing. I was a second behind. Three were down before they realized what was going on. Then I was too busy fighting for my life to see much else. Murdoch appeared and we fought back to back. One dwarf was throwing daggers, pulling them out of his baggy pants. One flew past my nose and I heard Murdoch grunt. I slipped my own dagger out, and the dwarf threw no more. From the corner of my eye, I saw another dwarf, moving toward Andrew's back with a blade. My heart leaped to my throat and I screamed. But the small guy fell before he reached his target. Snowy had tripped him and now was beating him over the head with a wrench between her bound hands.

But there were too many of them. We were better swordsmen, but we weren't going to win this fight.

I saw Andrew cut Snowy's hands loose. He placed himself in front of her. Then I had three opponents and had no time for watching elsewhere.

It wasn't until one of my opponents lost his head – literally – that I realized reinforcements had arrived. Looking up, I saw my husband, wearing a purple and gold cloak, taking on the other two attackers. He dispatched them quickly.

"What the hell are you doing here?" I gasped.

He just grinned, as he parried another attack. I moved to cover his back and the next few minutes were a blur of swords and blood and fear.

Then it was over. Four of the dwarfs were still on their feet, but Reynard's guards had them in hand. Elizabeth, however, seemed to have disappeared. Andrew had lifted Snow White up and placed her on a crate. He was carefully cutting off her bonds. I leaned against a motor and gasped for breath. Murdoch was breathing hard as well. He asked, "Are you all right?"

I choked out "Yes… Just…winded… Out…of…shape."

He nodded. "Also, getting older."

I glared. "Speak for yourself." I said, as I tied my scarf around the wound on his arm.

Snowy was going all gooey eyed over Andrew, who was fascinated by the cleavage she was flaunting.

Reynard had disappeared as well. I stood and looked around, going to the corner where I had last seen the Duchess. A syringe with a noxious green liquid inside lay on the desk. There were several apples lying around.

I thought I could hear voices. I found a door leading into the ruined section of the building. Rain dripped from the sky and from the broken masonry. A light flashed to my left and I started in that direction. I could hear the voices more clearly now: Reynard and Elizabeth.

"You will obey me." Elizabeth said in a voice, suffused with power.

Oh, my God, I thought. *She's a witch!*

"You will eat the apple." The voice repeated, a little more forcefully. "Eat the apple!"

I was maneuvering through the dark as fast as I could, scraping my legs on old motors. They were just up ahead. Dawn was breaking outside and I could just see them. Reynard was holding a bright red apple in his hand. Elizabeth stood twenty feet away, her right arm extended, handed curled with the index finger pointing at Reynard.

I screamed "No!"

Reynard glanced at me and tossed the apple over his shoulder.

Elizabeth shrieked in frustration and ran at him. I raced forward, but knew I wouldn't reach them in time. A knife rose up in Elizabeth's hand. As she attacked, a swirling of purple and gold enveloped Reynard. They came together and everything froze. For several long seconds they stood, face to face, gazes locked. Then Elizabeth staggered back, staring down at the hilt of Reynard's sword sticking out of her chest. The knife dropped from her hand, clattering on the cement. She slid to the floor. Her eyes looked up into the rain for a moment, then stared into eternity.

I stopped and stared at my sweet, gentle husband, who had just dispatched an evil witch.

He smiled. "You didn't really think I was going to eat that apple, did you?"

Snowy is still a teenager, and we still have memorable fights. But she is growing up. When she gives me sufficient information, she gets some privileges. I'm teaching her both armed and unarmed fighting, and she's very good at both. I haven't seen hide nor hair of Harold, Seymour's son, but Andy has made several trips from Tavnia to visit. He spends almost all his time with Snow White. Reynard and I are happy to see love blossoming between the two. And it won't hurt our relations with Tavnia a bit to join our two houses in marriage.

And as for me, I'm expecting our first child in a few months. Reynard is ecstatic. So is Snowy.

And so am I. I may name the baby Murdoch.

See Rhema Sayers's story "The Wicked Stepmother" online at
Metaphorosis.
If you liked it, leave a comment. Authors love that!

Remember to subscribe to our e-mail updates so you'll know when new stories are posted. a comment

About the story

I love fairy tales and fantasy and always have. When I was a little girl, my favorite story was The Twelve Dancing Princesses. I always wanted to be a princess. When I got older, I wanted to be a queen. I had to settle for being boss of an ER for a 12 hour shift.

But my experiences in the ER, and the development of my personality over the years, have led me to value a strong, assertive woman with a wicked sense of humor.

It occurred to me that a story about a stepmother, dealing with Snow White as a horrible teenager, might be fun. Especially if the stepmother was a particularly independent and somewhat dangerous woman. From this beginning the character of Regina evolved.

A question for the author

Q: What five words describe you?

A: Curious, dedicated, assertive, risk-taking.

About the author

After 35 years as a doctor, first in Family Medicine, and then in Emergency Medicine, Rhema Sayers retired. She and her husband had adopted three little girls from China. Their daughters were all grown by the time she retired. So she turned to writing as a second career. It had been a passion when she was young.

In addition to writing, she loves hiking with her three dogs in the Arizona desert where they live and traveling with her husband, carrying a camera during both activities. Photography is another hobby.

She writes fiction, but also historical articles and stories based on her experiences in the ER.

The Draining

Matt Hornsby

It is strange to imagine that serpent-men might love serpents. After all, they go to great lengths to wreak destruction on the beasts, travelling far out on the fickle and changing sea to slay them. One might not imagine, too, that serpent-men love the Wetness. Yet they do. I never met a serpent-man who did not hold both the serpents and the sailing season quite dear in his heart. I surely loved both right well, in my own days at that trade. It is a strange kind of affection, one that was not owed simply to these things being my means of profit and promotion. It is a deeper bond, the tie that connects all creatures in struggle – the same as binds falcon and dove, wolf and deer. When, on a calm day, one spies a serpent breaching the black water, diamond-scales glittering on the massive curve of its back, it is a thing of great beauty; and as a ship bears down on it, harpooner scrambling to his post, one cannot feel a sadness that it will soon be dead, hide punctured and oil leaking across the timbers as it is hauled aboard. That, however, is the way of the world. It is the way that I followed myself, as a younger man, until that fateful voyage upon the *Whimbrel*, where all such things were cast into question.

The first Wetness had come early that year. I had watched from the boat-yard with joy as it filled the great mist-shrouded basin that stretched from the harbour to the horizon. The dark water rose higher every day, first submerging the clouds of fog, then the tips of the highest reef, finally stopping at the lip of the port. What had been an empty void was a bountiful ocean.

For three seasons I had been sailing as a harpooner's boy aboard the *Whimbrel*, answering to Master Harpooner Mr.

Lachlann Davison, conducting my duties with all due care and attention. This time I was sure that, with God's help, I would be rewarded with a chance to stand on the hunting-platform and claim a serpent as my own prize. Davison was a tough and quiet man, but he was honourable and generous to those who did good service; in that generosity he was quite unlike his own master, our notorious Captain Munro.

Yet once we had cast out onto the brimming sea, my hopes had been disappointed. Over that long season I had watched Davison take three of the creatures by his own hand. Before every kill, I hoped he might say that it was my turn to handle the iron; but every time he looked at me, he looked also to Captain Munro. Perhaps fearing the old man's wrath at a missed shot, he took all three himself.

"Watch and learn," he said, "and your time will come." I despaired. I had studied his craft for many months now, and with my eyes closed I could bring to my mind the way his legs braced against the swell, the way his eye followed his prey, the way his hand gripped the spear-shaft. I had watched and learned enough. I knew that I would disappoint neither him nor the Captain. The days were growing long, and I feared the pitying looks of my kinsmen and the wharf-girls should I return to the island still unblooded when the Draining came again.

I tested my fears on Bannatyne, the old Soundingman seated at the tiller, plunging-line grasped in his wrinkled hand.

"How many more days of Wetness?" I asked.

"We may hunt until St. Phadran's day, boy," he said, scowling.

"But it's already past Beltane," I said, my voice raw with disappointment. I had thought we would be out longer.

"You'll be lucky if we stay out that long," he said, with a cruel chuckle. "Munro's got three beasts already. Your Master Davison is onto his last harpoon. If the Captain's a wise man, he'll head back to port now, before the men get nervous of the Draining."

Sailors are fearful men, and serpent-men most of all. The sky's every shifting tone marks some dark omen or other: storms, scurvy, poor hunting, sharp reefs. Yet it is the Draining that they fear most of all, that time when the sea begins to sink, at first slowly, but quickening so that soon you can see it dropping with your own eyes. I had heard the old men say that in times past, before I was born, one could count the lambing-seasons and know the moods of women by the Draining, so regular was its coming; by the time of my childhood, however, the seasons had become uncertain. There was great tension and excitement as the Wetness drew to a close. As a boy, I had stood at the port and counted all the ships safely home, watching them dock and unload their cargo of scales and machine-oil. Occasionally, a ship would just miss the turning of the season and would need winching up to the docks from the sinking sea. Then, the beach became a clifftop as the water dropped away, eventually disappearing into a cloud of mist at the ocean-floor. Even from the safety of land, it was fearful to imagine what lay down below – perhaps the beasts of the depths, now crawling naked and hungry in the half-light, or perhaps nothing but a void, stretching from the cliffs to the world's end until the Wetness and the seas returned. There were a few men, old beggars on the wharf, who claimed they had been caught at sea when the Draining came and had seen the dried ocean-floor; but few put much stock in their addled ramblings. Many times more were the men who by the poor judgement of their captains had been caught in the Draining and were never seen again.

Sailing aboard the *Whimbrel*, I was not afraid of it. I was young, and I was sure that fate had marked me for success on this voyage. I felt a proud disdain for the miserable old Soundingman's caution, and I had trust in Captain Munro – a fierce and devilish man he might be, but there was no finer sailor and serpent-hunter. And I still trusted Davison, knowing that one day he would put his faith in me.

Davison must have read the disappointment on my face after my words with the Bannatyne, for when I returned to my station on the hunting-deck, he fetched me a clap on the shoulder with his shovel of a hand.

"Season's not over yet, lad, and we've one iron left unbent," he said, laughing. Then he seized my arm and leaned into my face, his breath salty and rich.

"I've taken a good haul for myself already," he said, casting a finger across the three serpents laid out on the deck, their scales glinting in the sea-mirrored light.

"If we spy a fourth serpent, here's my word – this strong arm of yours will be the one to cast the shot."

With that promise, I knew that before this season was out, I would take a serpent of my own or I would die in the attempt. I was the first on deck with every sunrise, straining my eyes at the horizon, searching the immense flatness of the sea for the beautiful arch of a serpent's back. Yet for all my efforts, nothing broke the surface bigger than a leaping water-wolf. As the days passed, I noticed a grumbling and muttering amongst the crew, directed towards the Captain. We had taken enough this season, they said. Port was calling, and Munro was still on a course out to sea, God take him.

Munro, for his part, stayed silent but for a few clipped orders. His most common station was on the hunting-deck, where we had hung the three great bodies of this season's serpents. At times he seemed to be admiring them and inspecting them for quality; at others he seemed to be guarding them, as if he feared that one of them might suddenly burst back into life and slither back into the ocean. From my position, I overheard my Master strike up words with him.

"Three beasts make a fine haul, Captain," said Davison as he swatted gulls from the serpent bodies with the tip of his harpoon. The Captain grunted in response.

"We'll get a worthy bounty," continued Davison. "The railway-men and metallurgists are offering a handsome purse for oil and scale. There'll be enough for every man to feed his family until the next Wetness."

There was a moment of silence. I fought back a desperate urge to tear my eyes from the horizon and look at them.

"Would you have me turn back to port, Mr. Davison?" said the Captain.

"With every day, the Draining draws closer. I would not bargain against the season, sir."

"You say that three beasts are enough. How much more adequate, then, would be four? We have one iron left to cast, and we have our harpoon-master in fine health. I say that we would be fools to return now."

Unable to resist, I turned the corner of my eye to the two men. They stood facing one another straight, arms across chests, heads held proudly. For all that I desperately wished he might, Davison would not yield to the Captain. I did not want to see him clapped in the hold; but more than that, I wanted nothing more than another two days sailing, so that I might have my chance at a kill.

"Young Master Hardie is a man of my own mind, I believe," said the Captain, loud enough for me to hear. I snapped my eyes back to sea at the mention of my name. "Is that not so, Second Harpooner?"

I slowly turned my head to the two men. Munro's single eye bored at me, as black and cold as a cannonball. I knew not how to answer without betraying one of the men. In the end, Davison saved me.

"Back to your duties, Hardie," he said. "We are still hunting."

On a warm, waveless morning, I mounted the spying-deck and looked out to sea. My heart climbed into my jaws. There, not two leagues from us, was a black shape in the water, bigger than anything but a serpent. I began to raise the hunting cry, but the breath died in my mouth even as it gathered. The shape was not moving. I realised that I was looking at an outcrop of stone.

As my disappointment faded, dread crept into my fingers. We had not moved far since yesterday on account of the calm air, and I well knew there had been no rock in sight. I trod across the swaying deck to the Soundingman and roused him. When he saw the rock, the sneer on his old face melted into fear, and he frantically began to fling his plunging-line over the edge.

"We're dropping," said Bannatyne, his voice cracking. Davison spat a curse. Munro looked square at the Soundingman, his features unmoved.

"The Draining is not yet due," he said, "we have two more nights until St. Phadran's eve falls."

"I cannot account for the season, Captain, but I swear by God that the line and the gauge do not lie. We are dropping."

The Captain turned to the crew, gathered with their caps in hand.

"Turn the ship!" he roared, "Raise sail, and we will make port!"

"To the oars!" said Davison, steering me towards the rowing-benches. "Put that man's arm to use, lad."

For days I blistered my fingers as we pushed at the ocean. Fear drove my muscles. Two seasons ago, the *King Angus* had not returned home before the Draining. With the next Wetness, she had been found adrift, lifted again by the rising ocean, but with her crew either missing or half-eaten on the boat. None knew whether the eating had been done by whatever beasts might patrol the ocean floor or, in their hunger, by the crewmen themselves.

I turned my eyes to heaven and cursed God. We had not stayed out too long; the Draining had come early. Anger joined fear in my heart, and I drove it all into my rowing. Davison joined us, pushing his great oar through the water as easily as a child runs a stick through a puddle. The fear of that hellish seabed was in him, too.

But even with all our strength, we could not beat the changing season. Soon we saw whole ranges of limpet-studded peaks, encrusted with slippery sea-flowers and scuttling beasts, begin to push above the tide. Finally, as the reefs of Ard Manna reared before us, their corals and jagged rock blocking our way, the Captain bade us stop. We brought the *Whimbrel* to a halt, battening the hatches and fastening all gear to the deck. Then we sat and prayed, aloud now, until the water finally disappeared around us and we felt the ship's oak timbers crunch and sink into a tilted rest on the sand and rock.

The life of the sea – fish, serpents, crabs, worms and all – had vanished with the water, sucked into whatever realm could contain such a multitude of life. On the ocean floor, we were surrounded by desolation. In all directions stretched the great rolling plain of the seabed, as grey and bare as the sky above, broken only by the dark foothills of the reef before us. The plain was barren, home to nothing but a few bony corals and putrid weeds, little more edible than the sand in which they were rooted. Far overhead we heard the mocking cries of gulls and bonxies, safely beyond the range at which a man might fell one with a crossbow. The crew's eyes flickered towards the ration box.

We knew not what fate awaited us. The length of the Draining was uncertain. With our provisions, we could perhaps last eighty days marooned on the sea-floor; Munro's avarice had not seen fit to bring more supplies that that, and we had already cut into our store with a long season of hunting. We could do nothing but wait, hope and ask heaven for forgiveness, and that the Wetness might by some miracle come early. I felt the faint rumbles of hunger begin to gather. The Wetness would return, or we would starve.

The days passed in fear. No man dared set foot outside the ship, into that unknowable wasteland of bleak sand and fog. The crew turned their backs to the *Whimbrel*'s keel, cowering against the beasts that they imagined without. I remained at my station. In the wind, I heard noises, and I scanned the mist, conjuring up lumbering shapes from every jutting stone and limp pile of kelp. We spoke little; every sound or movement brought pangs from my hungry bones, nights of torrid darkness and days of stinging salt wind. The men prayed, hanging their heads in silence, running their fingers over carved bone-charms.

From the butchering-deck the dead serpents taunted me. They could not fill our bellies – their flesh was poisonous as nightshade, food for machines rather than men. I hated myself for having cursed God; now I cursed my own greed and lust for honour. I had been desperate for Munro to keep sailing outward, keep hunting, even as all the other men desired to return. Perhaps I was responsible for this; perhaps God had seen fit to reward my childish ambition with a fitting punishment.

"Bannatyne," called Davison, breaking the low silence of a windless day, "how far to port, when the Draining came?"

The Soundingman rose his white-bearded head weakly. It had been forty days, and the old man was on the edge of death already.

"We're at the edge of the Ard Manna shoal," mumbled the Soundingman, "and nearly onto the Kelp Flats. Thirty leagues, or three days' sailing."

"Or two weeks' walking for a man with strength in his legs," said Davison, raising his voice.

There were murmurs amongst the crew. I imagined trudging across the blasted, horrible plain of the sea-floor, with neither shelter nor succour, at the mercy of whatever monster might rear up from a sandflat or coral shoal. Still, our desperation had grown. Such an end might be preferable to a slow starvation on the *Whimbrel*, in the midst of other desperately hungry men, and whilst we had heard rumours in the wind and mist, no beast had yet attacked us.

As the men's voices gathered, the Captain spoke.

"No man leaves this ship," he said, remaining at his station, legs planted firmly on the deck. "I will not abandon the serpents."

"You brought us on a bad voyage, Munro," said Davison. "Your hunger would starve us all."

I had never seen any man raise his voice to the Captain. He had an expression of minor annoyance, as if this rebellion were no more bothersome to him than a dry biscuit or a sharp morning wind.

"If any man leaves this ship, he will have no share in our prize. That is, if the sea-floor doesn't finish him first," he said. Then, turning to the men, addressing their rising spirits:

"The Wetness will return. God will not allow me to fail."

Davison jeered. "I would first put my life in the hands of the sea-floor than in yours. Damn you and damn your prizes."

I felt my heart twist at this. For a serpent-man to curse the ship's prize was for a mother to curse her daughter or a shepherd his sheep. It was not right.

"Men!" he shouted, "I am setting out on foot for port. With God's help, I will make it there in fifteen days, and I will take great delight in the company of any who join me." His eyes met mine as he said this, and there was the turning of a smile in his mouth.

My feet began to stir. I knew that he was calling to me to come, to tear myself away from the doomed ship. The other men were looking to me, I realised, waiting for me to take the first step; to give them licence to take a chance at saving themselves.

"Hardie," said the Captain. I froze at the sound of my name. "You will be the First Harpooner of the *Whimbrel* now, with a First Harpooner's prize. You are worthy of it."

I trembled, taut as stretched wire, at this sudden promotion. I made to move off again, but I could not. A First Harpooner should not leave his prizes. The men knew that my loyalty had been conquered. The battle was over.

Davison left his remaining harpoon on the ship. He hoisted a bag over his shoulder and jumped overboard. He looked back at me, his smile gone. My eyes followed him where my feet could not, until he faded into the shimmering fog of the sea-plain.

I began to lose count of the days. As First Harpooner, I was afforded a greater ration: a crumb of dried biscuit and a swig of water. We ate in silence, hearing naught but the foul moaning of the wind across the seabed. The heat grew heavier, only interrupted by harsh winds that came loaded with fine, sharp sand that flayed the skin. When the wind stopped blowing, a stench would settle on us; the briny reek of wet sea-sand, blended with rotting seaweed. Our serpents added their own smell as they began to break down, oily and pungent. Laying on the deck between waking and sleep, I could not escape the staring of their giant glassy eyes. I thought of Davison, walking alone across the sea-plain, perhaps halfway back to port already, or perhaps already a meal for some giant and ravenous crab.

I tried to think of home: the flowing red hair of the girls, the purple blaze of heather in the hills, the rumble of the locomotive through the mountains. It all seemed lost in the greyness of the Draining, where there was nothing but coral and stone bleaching in the sun, gulls circling ever closer overhead.

It was the morning when something cold bit at my face in the darkness. At first, I did not respond. By then, I had little sense of time, and for days I had been in a state half of wakefulness, half of slumber. Yet the feeling was insistent of freshness and moistness on my face. I lifted a hand to it. It was cold. Bodies and voices were stirring across the deck. For minutes, I did not say anything, did not move. It was not just cold, but it was wet. Rain, coming in droplets ever thicker.

"The Wetness," I said. It was unreal, an impossibility, but others were doing the same, lifting their hands to their eyes in joy.

"The Wetness is here!"

I wept at the miracle; all of us wept, shaken in the joy of knowing that we would not perish amongst the corals and weeds. In that moment of elation, my fears fell away, and I felt nothing but the burning fire of life inside me. Our prayers had been answered, and the Wetness had come early, earlier than I had dared hope. After fifty days on the ocean-floor, we had been granted salvation. The prospect of hunger and slow death, which had stretched to the horizon in front of us, shrank away, and instead we saw only the gentle path home. The only man who stood unmoved was the Captain. In that moment he seemed to me like a savage, ancient god, unmoved by the petty travails of men and awesome in his power. He had been entirely vindicated.

"Lash up the rain-rigging," he called.

Within an hour, the ground beneath us had disappeared. We rose, the dark peaks of the mountains around us subsiding. We let the sails fly, and cast nets into the water, eager to catch the shoals that would accompany the rising sea. It was only after the smaller reef-spires had begun to disappear that I thought of Davison. Only ten days had passed since his departure from the boat. He had surely not had time enough. He would remain at the sea-bottom, beneath the water. Perhaps it was on him, I thought, that God's judgement had been visited.

His fate lingered on my mind, but it was tempered by the knowledge that I would live; the thought still seemed so strange and wonderful. Nothing ever tasted so sweet to me as the fresh foam on the air then, nor felt so comforting as the soft roll of the sea beneath us. Within two days sailing I would be on land, with silver in my pockets and hot meat in my mouth.

A shout came up from the forecastle.

"Beast in the water!"

I turned to the other men, unsure of myself, but now they looked to me for orders, as the First Harpooner. The Captain found his words first.

"Hunting stations!" he roared, spittle flying from his lips.

Munro had eaten the same poor rations as us when we were marooned; he had looked death in the eye as we all had. Yet even after that, he did not falter in his instinct to prove himself master of the sea.

I was almost too weak to lift the hunting iron, dragging it to my post at the bow. I had foreseen this moment so many times, imagined myself arching my arm gracefully back against the sails and hurling a mighty shot into an unlucky beast's flank. I moved my lips in prayer. The chance that I had lusted for was arrived. I would not miss it, even if I flung myself into the water with the force of the shot.

In the distance I saw the serpent, a black line against the calm sea. There was a strangeness to this one. A serpent's habit was usually to agitate, to dive at the sight of sails, putting distance between herself and men. This one seemed to float calm and still at the surface, as untroubled as an old man in his fishing-skiff.

As we drew closer, I saw a sight that turned my heart over. A tide of doubt, fear and wonder rose inside me.

In the water, there was a man. It was Davison. He was calling out in a small voice, paddling feebly at the sea. The serpent did not trouble him. Instead, it floated just beneath him, occasionally adjusting its position in the water to better spy us through curious red eyes, but always leaving one part of itself beneath Davison's tired legs. I could not fathom what its purpose might be.

The men threw ropes to him, beckoning and shouting at him to come aboard, but he did not move. I held the harpoon ready.

"I might have cursed you, Davison," shouted Munro, leaning over the prow, "but I will not let you drown. Come aboard."

Davison gathered his voice. It was thin against the sea-wind.

"Will you hunt this creature, Hardie?" he asked me. His face was twisted in pain. The serpent looked up at us. Up close and alive, the serpent was different from those that lay slain across our deck. The horned ridges and the barbed swords of its teeth were familiar; but the eyes, that in death were cold red stones, were burning and twitching around the world, looking at the boat, to me, to the gleaming iron in my hand. I could not but wonder how we might seem to it. As the creature bobbed gently below my Master as he struggled at the waves, I could find no other explanation than that it was attempting to keep him alive.

Suddenly it was no longer a simple beast of prey, but a creature whose mysteries I had not come close to understanding.

"The beast showed me mercy," shouted Davison. "When the Wetness came, it lifted me above the water. I will not let you kill it. I owe it mercy," said Davison.

The Captain grunted.

"So be it. Your fate is your own, Mr. Davison. First Harpooner, cast when ready."

There was no questioning, nothing but clarity in his black eye, no suggestion of choice. I arched my arm, lifting the spear for a killing throw, winding what energy I had into it. But I could not let go. At that moment, when everything I had wanted was laid before me, I could not but push it away. My heart would not allow me to take it.

"I will not," I said.

"Then another man will!" roared the Captain. He looked hungrily from man to man. None came forward, nor raised his head.

"Then I will cast the damned shot!"

Munro advanced on me, hand outreached for the iron. My body moved before my mind did. I raised my arm again and threw the harpoon, line and all, into the dark sea. It had been our last. I had left the *Whimbrel* weaponless.

The Captain surveyed the crew again. No man met another man's eye, and yet we all knew each other's thoughts. There was silence, broken only by the low rumbling sound of the serpent's voice, shivering up through the wooden frame of the hull. The Captain seemed to shrink. In one second, he had held us to his will like captives; in another, he had broken the law that governs men's hearts, and in that moment, he had lost us.

He took his station, standing at the ship's stern, arms folded and long dark coat flapping around his ankles. No more commands came from his lips, and his power over us was gone.

We hauled Davison onto the deck. The serpent that had saved him slipped away into the lightless depth. None but God knows why it had shown him such kindness; perhaps even God himself sometimes finds mystery in his design. We sailed into port without much by way of word or deed. No man needed orders to do his duty and take us that far.

I know nothing now of those other men; not the old Soundingman, nor Davison with his arms of oak. I never more set to sea, but through all seasons, I stand on the hill and look out on the ocean; in the Wetness, I watch the serpents toss and tumble, red-eyed and dark in the distance, chased still by bobbing boats.

And when the Draining comes, the wind blows in and drags at my ears – sagging now with age. In the sound of it I fancy I hear whispers, in that ancient language in which the laws of the Sea are written. I have long since stopped trying to understand them. It is enough for me to know that there are great mysteries in the hearts of men and the minds of beasts; riddles whose answers will never be solved.

See Matt Hornsby's story "The Draining" online at Metaphorosis.
If you liked it, leave a comment. Authors love that!
Remember to subscribe to our e-mail updates so you'll know when
new stories are posted.

About the story

The story really came from a single, simple image – of a ship marooned on the ocean floor, with the ocean nowhere to be seen. It seemed like a powerful image of environmental catastrophe, and I added the idea of the ship being a hunting-ship, whose business is exploiting nature in the form of the 'serpents', to bring that element out. From there, the characters and the rest of the world just suggested themselves and developed iteratively. I've always been a fan of nautical narratives, and I enjoyed the process of creating salty sea-dog characters. In the end, what started as a very short story became a medium length one – the world and characters threw up a lot of questions, and I expanded the story considerably to try and answer them. Perhaps a shorter story would have been better, but I can never resist the world-building temptation.

The protagonist, Hardie, was initially quite a passive character, more of a viewpoint to narrate what happens aboard the ship than an actor himself. However, it quickly became clear that he was sitting awkwardly between the two positions, and decided to make him a fuller part of the story. I read back over some pre-twentieth century writing, particularly writing that features sailors, to try and get his voice right.

In any case, I hope people enjoy the story and take something away from it!

A question for the author

Q: If you could have a meal with a character from any classic novel, whom would you choose?

A: I recently read Ursula Le Guin's *Always Coming Home*, a book that is so comprehensive in its world-building that it includes several recipes from the cuisine of the fictional Kesh, many of which sound quite appealing. So maybe I'd drop in on Stone Telling, who is the book's closest equivalent to a protagonist, for a bowl of valley succotash or acorn-meal soup with honey.

About the author

Matt Hornsby is based between London, United Kingdom, and Dublin, Ireland. When not writing, he works on environmental and economic policy, after previous lives as a scrap metal dealer and English teacher. "The Draining" in his second story in Metaphorosis, following "A Final Resting Place" in September 2019, and he has published other work in *StarshipSofa, Electric Spec*, and *Kzine*. Follow him on Twitter at @Matth0rnsby.

Sonata III: Canta

L. Chan

Adagio: Canta

This is the final part of L. Chan's novella, *Sonata*. Parts 1 and 2 ran in January and February 2020. What has gone before:

Sona, on a quest for vengeance, has enlisted help of the Six Named to play a piece of heretical Music composed by his mother, the Lady Kristyk. Shailani found Sona harbouring a second secret, a device of his mother's design, able to capture and replay any Music it hears, but the Music that Sona has brought is eerily familiar to her; containing elements of her own people's holy songs, Music she was sent up north to preserve. On their way out of the Six Named land, Sona's family, the House Deathsinger, caught up with them, and takes them back to the Capital under the watchful eye of Sona's half-sister, Canta Deathsinger.

Are you still unhappy about the Six Named? asked Canta. Sona did not answer. They were on deck, the other sailors keeping a respectful distance from their commanding officer. Canta sighed, fogging up her flying goggles from the inside of her helmet. This one smelt of stale grease and a stranger's sweat; Sona was still wearing her good helmet. Both she and Sona's guest wore airship spares. Her brother had his back to the railing, turning his head to the side to watch the farmlands and roads a mile below, the landscape spread like a drawn map. The winds nearly drowned out the sounds of the crew.

I had no choice, brother. You did not lose five lives, you gained two. Father told me that I had to hunt down a traitor to House Deathsinger, a Six Named agent working against us, said Canta. *He trusted me above all others, because anybody else could be bought, but you can't buy me.*

She could see Sona's hands tighten on the railings, then relax and drop to his sides, ready. No expression there, and she couldn't read his eyes through the smoked lenses.

The Empire is sick, brother. The army bleeds the treasury; the only way it survives is through rapine and pillage. We can do better. Father has set our House on a trajectory upwards; we and our friends can take back power from the Emperor.

I wasn't suited for the army. I'm even less suited for your plots and subterfuge. I've been around the Empire since the Academy, Canta. Those that thirst for power are often ill suited to wield it. You'd do well to think about that, before you get caught up in something worse, said Sona.

It will be different, Canta said, hands growing more energetic. The world had seemed a much emptier place without her brother. Her father had begun taking her into his confidence when she started at the Central Academy, grand plans about taking down the rotten core of the Empire. Sona's death had ripped a hole in her, and what had come back didn't quite fill that space left in her soul. *You could help,* she said.

I'm not sure father has me in his plans anymore. He did send you to hunt down a traitor, did he not? asked Sona.

I'm sure he has his reasons. Empire factions have ears everywhere; best to keep it a secret, she said.

Even from you? asked Sona.

Even from me. The helmet stays on you at all times, whether or not my crew knows your face, she said.

How much longer to home? he asked.

Another week, perhaps, with a stop for supplies. Plenty of time to catch up, she said.

Maybe, he replied. *It's been a long time.*

It had, and Canta felt further from her brother than ever. *Do you remember when we used to race in the Skydock?* she asked.

They weren't races, I won most of them, he said.

I've beaten you before, Canta said, remembering the thrill of the chase and the wind rushing past her ears.

The week before your birthday? That was a gift.

It's not my birthday next week, brother.

We'll see if you've gone soft with the Capital, Cannie. When we get home, he said, and smiled for an instant, the brother she knew appearing for a heartbeat before he turned to face the wind.

The Skydock was the pride of the Capital. Spires of the palace might have been taller, but the flotilla of vessels at the dock, both military and civilian, was visible for miles around. The *Angelfall* had lines that distinguished her from the run of the mill brigantine, but Canta ordered her colours stowed and the ship berthed far from the Deathsinger piers anyway. Anything helped. The music carrying the brigantine aloft faded into silence, but the ship did not fall. All around them, audible even through the padded brass flying helmets they all wore, were the plodding tones of the Symphony of Industry.

The Skydock tower had an intricate system of organ pipes and whirling gears that ran a mechanical set of instruments, a horological marvel. The strong winds around the tower found their way through funnels and spun multitudinous windmills, flooding the entire Skydock with Sound, keeping all the vessels afloat in the air. Even the pull of the ground was lighter here. Canta could jump twice her height without even trying. Below, the Capital Sound covered the ground; from the grand palace in the north to the market quarter in the south. If she strained her eyes – and her eyesight was very good indeed – she could almost make out the Deathsinger manor on the edge of the Capital. People went about their business far beneath her, like so many ants. She sometimes wondered what it would be like to open up cannon fire from the Skydock, painting the streets below with hot iron projectiles. Holding people's lives in her hands, it felt very much like being a god.

Her crew got busy unloading her ship, coaxing her brother's multipede down the gangplank with some difficulty. He had always had a soft spot for those things. She sent the Far Islander ahead with her crew. Canta had business with her brother. She found him waiting for her at the bow, looking out at the hundreds of airships across the Skydock, bobbing with the ebb and flow of the deafening Symphony. He was wearing the spare helmet now.

We should get going, home is waiting, Sona said.

We haven't spoken in years, brother. There's never been anything we couldn't tell each other, Canta replied.

Everybody grows up.

Things used to be simpler. The world used to be smaller. We knew how we fit in it. I wish we could go back, Canta said, her sigh misting the inside of her goggles. *You said you wanted to see if the Capital had made me soft. Let's see if the Periphery's done the same to you. I need to know if my brother is still in there.* Canta pointed to the far end of the Skydock. The tower radiated piers like spokes on a wheel, with berths for paying customers. Other airships jostled for space, illegally lashed to each other to keep them from drifting away. The harbourmasters overlooked anything, for a price. Urchins and feral child gangs had a game; a footrace from one end of the flotilla to the other, making death-defying leaps bolstered by the same Sound that kept everything in the air. It was not foolproof, and a few children were lost every year. Lost but not missed. Not just the poor though; Sona and Canta used to run those races on days they were meant to be schooled in the science of Sound and the glorious history of the Empire. But their tutor had favoured strong drink at least one evening a week, preferring to set them reading dusty books and sleep away his hangovers.

The stakes? asked Sona.

Your story, if I win. The truth, she said.

And if I win?

Freedom.

I didn't know I was a prisoner, Cannie, Sona said.

Canta left that question in the air as she sprinted towards the stern of her ship. This was stupid. Beneath her. She had command of a ship, perhaps the best in House Deathsinger. A single misstep could cripple or kill her, the musical safety net notwithstanding. But here she was with the only person alive that really understood her. Time apart had thrown a wall up between them. Maybe she needed to go back to the beginning to see if they could ever be brother and sister again.

She imagined that Sona would be close behind. He had always been quick, but not as quick as her. Sona had indeed been the winner in most of their encounters, the competition equal parts a sprint and a puzzle of navigating the shortest route through moving airships.

The Capital opened up beneath her feet as she took a fifteen yard leap between two decks, the spread of ramshackle buildings a rot on the plains below. Her heart was pumping, sweat pooling inside the rough fabric of her flier's gear. She could see Sona catching up, his route diverging from hers. Canta was playing it safer, staying near the central spire of the Skydock, where the ships were densely packed, guaranteeing her next steps. Sona, on the other hand, was taking greater risks for a route which let him run at full speed, where the ships were less occupied and wider spread. His gambit was paying off. Canta was faster than she'd ever been, having spent most of her last few years amongst the clouds on ships like the *Angelfall*, and her footing on the bobbing decks was sure. Still, Sona had covered more ground than her, his tight frame allowing him to navigate the cluttered airship decks and swearing sailors.

Canta had a clear route to the finishing point, the end of the furthest pier from her ship. She put on a burst of speed, hoping to catch up with Sona. What she saw made her snort with laughter even as her breath dragged at her throat like a whetstone. Sona's gamble had failed him. As the ships grew sparser along his route, he was forced to make increasingly longer jumps. Until he skidded to a halt. A ship had launched, leaving a gap even beyond what his Sound enhanced bounds could cover. Landing in between ships was not without danger; the momentum of such a leap would surely punch him straight through the gentle lift of Sound carrying them all, and send him to his death below.

Canta pressed on, narrowing the gap. She was just about to catch up when Sona threw something from the ship he was trapped on. It looked to be a hatch cover he'd teased loose from the ship, flung in a mighty two-handed swing like a giant stone skipping across a lake. The wooden square spun slowly, buoyed in the air by Sound. Sona took a running jump, only managing half the distance between himself and the finishing line. Canta gasped as Sona hit the hatch and made a second jump, sending the wood to the ground below and pitching him to the finish line just before Canta crossed it.

Her brother was doubled over and wheezing with the effort, and Canta did not feel much better, collapsing in a heap at his feet.

What now? she asked, considering her options, wondering if Sona had kept up with his unarmed combat. Wondering if she could overpower him or if she even wanted to.

You've gotten faster, he said, pulling Canta to her feet, his grip firm. His journeys had not softened him, much the opposite.

Nice move. You could have died out there, she replied. *Your travels haven't made you any smarter.*

Spoken like the same girl who couldn't stand losing, said Sona. He paused, as though considering a dilemma of his own. Her brother drew a sheath of folded paper from his coat. Canta recognized his neat, compressed writing, filling each sheet from edge to edge.

Every month I was away, I wrote you a letter. It's all in here, he said.

You won, you know, she said, her Fingerspeech slowed by the numbness of her hands after the run.

Maybe, he said. *I've changed my mind about the prize. What I want is for you to trust me. Come on, it's been a long time since I was home.*

"So you've never been to the Capital?" asked Canta, while walking Shailani through the Deathsinger grounds. Sona had been holed up in the guest quarters since they arrived the day before and the Lord Antius was not expected back for some days yet, and she thought to get to know Sona's companion a little better. Unless Canta was mistaken, the ornaments holding up Shailani's braided hair were sharper than they had a right to be. Shailani had traded the Six Named outfit for clothes in the Empire style; not the court dresses, but the comfortable training clothes of Deathsinger initiates.

"I've never been this deep in the Empire." When the grey-haired woman spoke, her tones had the twang of the low counties. Army, then; all conscripts spoke that way.

"Deathsinger lands are on the outskirts of the Capital. We're far out because this used to be a fortified lookout, so the rooms are just shy of comfortable. It used to have its own spring, proof against any siege, even if the Capital has grown far beyond the old borders. Look," said Canta, pointing at mossy stone bricks overgrown with twisting vines and hairy nettles. "The spring has dried up, but the old aqueducts remain. Sona and I used to get into that one all the time. It leads all the way out of the grounds. One of the only exits that the guards don't know about."

"That's an odd thing to tell a guest, Lady Canta, let alone a prisoner. You're treating us well, but I have not seen or spoken to your brother since we arrived here. Nor have I been out without an escort."

"The Capital is a dangerous place, especially for members and guests of the Houses. My brother is unpredictable. When we docked, I thought I had him back, but he's retreated into himself since he's been here. My father is not a forgiving man. My brother may need your help getting out."

Canta forced those last words out; her father was not infallible, but she'd not doubted or defied him. Even this small betrayal took effort. The Lady Shailani was silent until they reached the fortress proper now. The night chill clung to the stones. Servants and singers alike bowed their heads when they passed Canta. She took care to acknowledge them with a nod or a smile as they went about their business. The other woman seemed unwilling to pursue the earlier conversation.

The Lady Shailani brushed the brass tubes snaking along the walls. "These look like those you have on airships," she said.

Canta nodded. "Speaking tubes, the latest in artifice for these grounds. Speak in one room, hear in another. Much better than anything you'll see down in the Far Isles. What is my brother to you, Lady Shailani?"

Lover? She didn't seem like Sona's type. If he even had one. Her brother was always so serious. Partner in crime? Perhaps. But what crime, exactly?

The older woman took slightly too long to answer. "Six of us were captured by Periphery brigands. Sona proposed a trade, my service as a translator for an opportunity for my five companions to escape."

"My brother fell in with brigands?"

"He was doing the accounts."

Canta allowed herself a small laugh. Her brother had always been good with numbers, one of the top students at the Western Academy. She had been better at the physical disciplines; even music theory was beyond her. She'd still been within the top three students at the Central Academy, at least in combat trials. Her father's choice of schools for his two children still puzzled her. Even with his impediment, Sona could have had the best pickings of the army or maybe in the government with one of the Maestri. Not within House Deathsinger, there was no place with one with his shortcoming in a choral House. Certainly not in the labyrinthine plots of the insurgency that her father had been plotting. Too much deference to authority in her brother. He'd never be a leader, but he'd be the best damn second in command anyone could ask for. Too much honour as well, but honour was only a cheap excuse for those unwilling to make hard choices.

The Lady Kristyk, now that woman had been a leader. Canta felt her loss even more keenly than she did her own mother's. Canta's mother had been high born as well, a distant relation to the Maestro of Order. Raised by governesses, she had taken the same dispassionate approach with Canta, fobbing the growing girl off to tutors or playmates. Not so the Lady Kristyk, and her two foreign born attendants (Canta had often heard Chun and Fong refer to the Lady Kristyk by her foreign name, but much preferred the refined tones of her Empire name). The Lady Kristyk had been more of a mother to Canta than her own; Canta's eventual success at the Central Academy had as much to do with the Lady Kristyk's foundational blade training as talent. She still kept a locket with the Lady's hair around her neck, thinking perhaps that she'd braid it into her own if she ever grew her hair out. Perhaps after she gave up flying.

The Lady Shailani gave up no more secrets on the rest of the tour, and the conversation tired Canta. She bid the other lady goodbye at the guest quarters, and nodded to the guards standing watch.

The Lord Deathsinger was due in hours. Sona remained closed to Canta, giving nothing and only asking for a single favour of her. A simple package for the Lady Shailani, but for what purpose he would not say. But first she needed to win the Lady Shailani over.

Canta led the Lady Shailani past the various studies, the sitting rooms, until they reached a small vestibule, lushly decorated in a bid to hide the practical and martial nature of the place. It had previously been the room where she and Sona took their studies before their academy training. Sometimes with tutors, other times with the Lady Kristyk. Canta fingered the abacus the Lady Kristyk had brought over from the Six Named land, eliciting glittering dust and the clack of stones within a wooden frame.

"Sona always did like his numbers. There's a small library in the next room. Would you believe Sona found one of the old passages there? A treatise on geometry hid a lever. Disappointment that the book wasn't real outweighed curiosity at the secret path."

"And you've delivered him to the one place he doesn't want to be."

Canta couldn't yet piece the two versions of her brother she saw. The one on the *Angelfall*, so eager to be back in the Deathsinger manor, and this reticent one that the Lady Shailani was describing. He'd always been the schemer between the two of them, the brains behind their joint mischief. His little sojourn had made him complicated, made his plans inscrutable. Again, she felt the keenness of the absence of the brother she remembered, as though he hadn't really returned and the glimpse of the old Sona at the Skydock had been a daydream. She needed to know more. Both about her brother and the outlander.

"Oh, Lady Shailani, only my brother's word kept me from leaving you with the Six Named to feed the carrion birds. He's home. He told me as much. Now, my House sent me to retrieve a traitor. I track him for half a year and it turns out to be my brother. I've not failed my House before, and I'm not about to start now. What I want to know is why my House branded him such and didn't tell me. Now, Far Islander."

"I think that's between you and your House isn't it? Your job is done. They say Sona's a traitor and your succession is clear, is that it? That's how you do it in the Empire?" asked the Far Isles woman, her soft slur all the more mocking, half twitch at the corner of her mouth. Canta felt pressure in her temples and behind her eyes, her left hand dropping to a sword hilt that wasn't there. She had to earn the Lady Shailani's trust, for her brother's sake, but she'd be damned if she'd let an outlander talk down to her.

"Look at you, wearing Empire clothes, flown over by the power of Empire music, living under Empire masonry. Shall I go further? Fighting in the Empire style, the civilization of your people an Empire gift. Your writing, your government. Empire gifts. That is how we do it in the Empire, we give."

The foreign woman was suddenly livid, not a raging forest fire, but a furnace fire. Not just one that could eat wood, but one that could melt steel. Yes, this Lady Shailani had killed before, of this Canta was sure.

"It's the contrary, Lady Canta. The Empire takes. Its hunger is endless. All the gifts you speak of, that's what Empire shits out after it eats the good in every place. Seribu would have found the good it needed in its own time," said Shailani, and her tone would have made the Lady Kristyk smile.

Seribu. Oh, the Far Isles. Names were confusing to Canta; the sciences and histories were Sona's area of expertise. She sighed. She was no closer to understanding Sona, and the Lord Deathsinger was due home soon. Canta worried for her brother. Her father was a complicated man, and shared little of his plans, even with Canta. She trusted her father, but she'd been sent up north to kill. Sona was too stubborn to take her help. So she needed a fallback. Sona needed a fallback. Shailani was all she had.

"Lady Shailani, you are here, in House Deathsinger. Things are in play. You are meeting my father in three hours. Sona has his own plan, but he needs someone to watch his back. What binds you to him?"

"Blood debt, for the five sisters he saved," said Shailani, but Canta discerned the split second of hesitation there. The Far Islander wanted something more, but as long as it kept Sona alive, Canta could not have cared less.

"Good. Sona wanted you to have this," Canta said, handing over the things her brother had given to her, sheets of music wrapped around what seemed to be a waxed cylinder, scored through with fine lines. Finding out her brother was still alive had been a ray of light for her, a promise of family, somebody that could look at her without weighing her usefulness to the cause of reforming the Empire. Even her father saw her that way, a tool, unique in her loyalty because of her lineage, and all the more useful for the most delicate, the dirtiest work. She'd read through the music. It looked choral, but nothing like she'd ever seen before. Canta was complicit in Deathsinger plots, but the Houses plotted all the time. The secret histories whispered between the nobles said as much. But this, this new endeavour of Sona's was of a different order. Unsanctioned composing, heretical music. This undermined the very basis of the Empire. Still, Sona was her brother, and better his life than the Empire. She allowed herself her second smile of the day when it hit her that Sona would always be ahead of her; in succession, in the academy, and now, in treason and rebellion. Uncharted territory, but following Sona into trouble was blessedly familiar. Some things were impossible to grow out of, she supposed.

Canta escorted the pair to the audience room, where the Lord Antius Deathsinger held court. He was due back from the central Capital any time, and Canta had to ensure the audience was set up correctly. Sona had been sequestered in the guest quarters since he'd arrived, Canta seeing to his meals and needs herself. His requirements were blessedly small, a benefit from his travels. Nevertheless, the servants were already talking, and the secret could not be kept much longer. Sona walked beside her now, still in flier gear, with a servant behind him, bearing something Sona wanted to present to father, some complicated contraption with gears as small as those of clocks, moving spindles, and the like.

The audience room was ornately decorated, fashioned after the more opulent trappings of the Maestri, but only superficially so. The furs here were more common, the tapestries less vibrant, the silks more coarse. Father saved the Deathsinger purse for the cause. The chamber was guarded by Deathsingers, outside and within. Six inside, each a product of ten years of hard training, able to kill with voice, weapon, or empty hands.

Lord Antius entered the room behind them, making his way past the guards, down the length of the room, past the waiting trio and Sona's assembled device. He took his seat at one of a pair of large, carved chairs at the head of the room. Far Isles wood, dark as blood under the moonlight, harder than the jaws of termites. The other chair was empty, and had been so since the death of the Lady Kristyk. Canta smiled at her father, who did not smile back. She could see herself in him, but not in Sona. Tall and severe, hair turning to grey at the temples, Lord Antius was thinner than he used to be, but imposing nevertheless. These days, he subsisted less on sleep and food than on his machinations with his conspirators, but he had never had more energy.

Sona, he said, *you can take that off. I knew your sister didn't have it in her to kill you.*

The flier helmet hit the ground. Canta always wondered, as she did again, about the potency of Six Named blood, so different did her father and brother look.

Father, said Sona, his Fingerspeech slow and deliberate, *are you sure you want to have this conversation in front of Canta and your attendants?*

She can stay. She deserves to know and to be tested by knowledge. How else will she build a new Empire? asked Antius.

Was the Western Academy a test? The murder of your wife? asked Sona, taking a step forward. Antius held up a hand. The guards stopped, the fastest of them already past Canta. What was Sona accusing her father of? Sona had claimed Empire involvement in the razing of the Western Academy, but there were children of all Houses there. Of all the Houses, the double tragedy that befell House Deathsinger at the massacre put them the furthest from suspicion. Or so she'd believed.

The Lord Antius signed to Sona, but his gaze was on Canta. *Another test, everything was a test. The ascendancy of our House was not easily won. Power comes with position, and with continuity. Continuity of blood. House Deathsinger would not have the support of the older Houses if the mantle would one day pass to you, Sona. Your mother was a remarkable woman, even if the Six Named streak in her was never tamed. Few things keep me awake at night. Your mother's death is one of them,* he said.

Canta felt the same vertigo, the same ground sickness she felt after a long flight, as though the flat earth itself were rolling and yawing. Sona's expression had relaxed, as though a weight had been lifted from him. Shailani on the other hand, wore something much more inscrutable, a small frown of confusion.

Sona had reached his device. Canta had checked it herself. No blades, no darts, no poisons. Nothing capable of touching the Sound either; no bells, no strings. What was that thing?

Not as mother spoke to me, Antius. No Fingerspeech. I want to hear you say it, said Sona.

"Sona, we need not go through this. I loved your mother. I have no enmity towards you. Your death would have been quick, under the guise of a larger raid, to be blamed on separatists and insurgents. House Deathsinger would be inherited by Canta, Empire blooded and highborn," said Antius. His voice, unlike his body, had not withered and possessed the same low baritone that he could use to crush rock or pulp bone.

"Your own son?" asked Canta, drawing all eyes around the room.

"Honour is only for those that are too weak to make the hard choices, girl. The future of the Empire and of the House is paramount. I did this for you. What I do next, I do for you."

Hold, Lord Antius, a trade for my freedom and that of my companion, said Sona. *The Lady Han sent me to complete her work, work that she only fed you crumbs of. You believed, against the catechism of the Empire Sound, that music could be trapped, and replayed. This is the player. The recorder will be sent to you when our freedom is assured, and you will never see me or Shailani again.*

The Lord of House Deathsinger drew himself to his full height and advanced on his remaining kin. "So, she finally completed it. You needed me to speak and not use Fingerspeech because your machine both traps and releases Sound. You would have made a better Lord Deathsinger, I think, but betrayal is a skill that you've not practiced." He nodded to the guards, who drew their weapons, clucked to clear their throats to deploy Sound.

In a heartbeat, Sona and his companion would be dead. Canta just hoped, as she lobbed the pair of double-walled glass ampoules at the ground between them, the volatile mix igniting and producing acrid smoke, that the Far Islander was worth whatever she was being paid. The opening bars of the guards' deadly songs turned into coughs and choking sounds. Quicker on the uptake than most, the Lady Shailani covered her mouth with a sleeve to filter out the smoke. She had already drawn out a black cylinder from the contraption, swapping it for another from about her person. Was that the one that Canta had passed to her? Sona had already liberated a sword from one of the coughing guards, despatching the guard with quick cuts to the hamstring and shoulder, turning to face those recovering from their convulsions.

Canta met the eyes of her father, looking down at her over steepled fingers. Sona was good, but not good enough for these odds. Her hand rested on the hilt of her short sword. The weapon was the perfect length for fights on airships, short enough to swing in the tight corridors and decks without snagging, but here the guards had the advantage in arms. She'd already sealed her fate when she smoked out the singers. Wetting her blade was just an afterthought. The Lord Deathsinger already knew what she was going to do, and he looked away. He had tested Canta, and she had failed. Of the two Sonas she brought back from the Six Named land, this was the true one. The one that the Lady Shailani saw, the one that was going to betray House Deathsinger. Her father had told her the truth – she had brought back a traitor. But still she could not let her brother die. She drew her sword just as the music started.

Canta had never heard its like before, and part of her academy training had been the study of all four major Symphonies and the minor pieces that made up Empire canon. This was something completely new, and that meant a Composer outside of the Empire's control. What heresy had her brother wrought? His device was clever, but this? A new composition, outside of the will of the Emperor? That chipped away at the very foundations of the Empire. There was a reminder in the very naming of the Empire Sound – that the Empire drew its power from Sound and that all Sound belonged to the Empire. The music itself had a numbing effect, the air itself vibrating. It reminded her of the times she had taken her airship over deserts or the sea, and seen the mixing of layers of air, the flow warping and distorting the view of everything beyond it. Guardsmen and women were coughing, still trying to clear their throats of acrid smoke. Canta gave one last look at her father and stepped forward to defend her brother. That was when the Far Islander began to sing.

The words were less familiar than the tune. They must have been in Shailani's own tongue. Canta's blade dripped. The heretical music grew in volume and in effect; she felt the power of it in her bones. The ebb and flow of combat threw her beside her brother. She looked into his face for the slightest sign of guilt, of any regret for bringing this monstrosity into their home. There was nothing there, nothing but the concentration of a man fighting, not desperately, but with little more passion than he'd put into sword drills. He'd planned this. Maybe not the sequence, but that here, in front of their father, he would unleash something dark and forbidden. Canta wanted to scream, to turn her blade against her brother, to deploy her own Sound against her blood. Nothing came out. That was when Canta saw her.

Indistinct at first, a heat mirage of a woman. The outline fleeting and wavering at first, but her form emerging, as though she were stepping out from a fog. A woman made out of the same distorted light that the Sound was blanketing the room in, visible in form the same way an eddy or a whirlpool was visible, composed of fluid but given shape, and that shape was of the Lady Kristyk. Her approach stilled the fighting, as both the guards and Sona stared at the woman made out of Sound.

The Lord Deathsinger was on his feet, and there should have been fear on his face, as there was on the faces of all the guards, unsure of whether to advance in the face of this strange and perverted Sound. Instead there was something serene in his visage, something Canta had not seen before.

"I'm sorry," said the Lord Deathsinger to the apparition. And it was a day for firsts, because Canta had not heard those words pass his lips all her life.

And the woman made of Sound spoke, and when she spoke it was with the foreign words of the Far Islander, it was with the crash of the musical instruments of the land of her birth; the clang of metal, the wail of strings, the blaring of trumpets. She looked at the Lord Deathsinger, engineer of her kidnapping and her captivity, and she said that she forgave him. She leaned in to kiss him on the lips, and when she drew back, the man was dead on his feet, a single tear of blood welling up from one eye and rolling down his cheek, a trail of crimson against his white skin.

Sona was up beside his father, rushing past him, not to catch the collapsing man but to activate the speaking tubes to the rest of the fortress. His face was twisted at the sight of his mother, as though he had not expected the music to call her back. The Far Islander, Shailani, was clawing at her throat, the words coming out ragged but still drawn from her involuntarily, as though the music sat unhappily on her stomach and was only now coming forth in a continuous stream of bile and lyrics. Canta still had her sword in her hands, and she took a step towards her brother.

The Lady Kristyk was less kind to the guards; her touch was gentle but the effects were not. Bone folded in on bone, the snaps like cannon fire in the enclosed space, white shards erupting from liveried uniforms. Then there were four in the room, the traitor, the singing foreigner, the angry ghost of a woman she would have once called mother. And her, heir to House Deathsinger. Outside, the screams were just starting.

Her death stalked her, through the swirling dregs of the smoke on the floor, around the corpses of the guards. The Lady Kristyk, with murder in her eyes and killing in her touch, gaining on her. Soon she'd be cornered, the same fate for her as for her father and the guards. She faced her reckoning on her feet, back to a wall and with her sword ready. Until Sona put himself between her and his mother.

He said something, something that she couldn't see from behind him. The Lady Kristyk was not to be appeased, halving the distance between her and him in a single surge. She was nearly upon him when the crash of wood and metal onto the ground brought the music to an end. The apparition vanished.

Sona spun around, palms up and open, weaponless.

This was not what I wanted. I can explain, he said.

House Deathsinger in ruins; the dream of reform dead and cooling on flagstones like her father. The entire conspiracy, headless and lost, until the Empire's spymasters closed in, putting them each under question and torture.

"No," said Canta, finally finding her voice, remembering her brother's hand on the speaking tubes. "It's exactly what you wanted." She stepped forward and put her sword in his gut. Another second more and she would have twisted her blade, spilling his bowels out onto the floor, to join her father's blood and her own tears.

Was she crying for the father taken from her or the brother she had lost?

Sona looked away, unwilling to meet her gaze as she killed him. No matter. She tensed, ready to finish it. Shailani hit her from the side, coming in quick from her blind spot. That woman knew how to fight, her first kick a heeled stomp to the side of Canta's leg. Something in her knee gave way. But Canta didn't need weapons to kill, her voice had always been her most potent weapon.

She was still inhaling when the knife edge of Shailani's hand struck her in the throat.

Codetta: Sona refrain

The chills woke Sona up, his fevered body soaked with sweat. His torso would not obey him. Under the blanket, he found bandages, damp with sweat and sticky with blood. A hunched man was nearby, wringing out a damp cloth into a metallic tray. Shailani was beside the bed, dozing while slumped backwards on a chair. The man laid the cloth on Sona's brow and shook the woman.

Shailani sniffed, cleared her throat and spat on the floor. The man grimaced.

"You're awake," she said, her voice still ragged from the strain of the Lady Han's song.

Where are we? he asked, signing with one hand while the other pressed down on his stomach. The pain was coming in waves now.

"Old military network, hospital for pensioners and veterans. Very discreet for those who've served," Shailani said, showing Sona the colours of the Sixty-Seventh she had tattooed over her forearm.

How did we get out? asked Sona.

"Your sister had a plan, a failsafe. She showed me a way out. Of course, she didn't expect to stick you through the belly first. Wasn't a need to sneak out after your Music had done its job. Thank the spirits for that multipede of yours; I don't think I could have hauled your ass out of that forsaken fortress."

Sona lay back on his hard pallet, the muscles in his middle complaining and aching.

I didn't think that was what the music would do, he said. When he closed his eyes, Sona could see a woman made out of Sound tearing through the guards, parting flesh like so much wet paper. He did not want to remember his mother like that.

"You had some idea after the festival."

Sona folded his arms, remaining silent. He had, of course. The Empire had reduced the Sound to its martial components but there was more to it than any Empire Composer understood. The Lady Han had not grown up within the Empire canon. She had other ideas, melding the baser musics of her homeland into an Empire symphony, and touching parts of the Sound that had never been delved before.

Did anyone see us flee? he asked, not ready to discuss his mother's music.

Shailani stretched, arching her back like a cat. "I honestly didn't have time to check, being busy with running for my life and you leaking blood all over me." She paused. "Probably. They'll be questioning those left alive."

Canta? he asked.

"Alive, probably. I didn't kill her. Spirits knew she deserved it for what she did in the Six Named land. She was dear to you, though."

I thank you for sparing her, although she'll make us regret it someday.

"Empire's a big place. Hell, so's the Capital."

Canta can be very single minded. She found me once, after all. Not just her. My father had allies here. Friends in the shadows. The Capital is a dangerous place for us now. Thank you for saving me, said Sona, turning his head to look at Shailani. *It gets muddled after she stabbed me. What happened to the device?*

"Destroyed. Though it took more strength than you know for me to have done it. We could have used that to save the dying language of my people."

So those were the words you sang, said Sona.

"Your Music, my words. It's something… sacred to my people. The Six Named recognized it as well. When Canta gave me the music, I was sure. It's the same music my sisters were trained in, something to ease the passing of the dead from this world to the next."

We wouldn't have gotten out without it, Sona said, and snorted. *So I've won, I've thought long about bringing justice to my father, and now that the House has fallen. All it cost me was my sister. Maybe my father and I are not so different after all.*

Shailani put her hand on his arm. "You fought your own war. We all carry something out."

Even retired sergeants? asked Sona.

"Even us. Where to for you?"

I've been on the move so long, nowhere feels like home. I can't stay here. The Six Named land will not have me. Maybe Pendulos. There's still my mother's research there, things I can do. Her plan for me was never revenge, or to follow in her work. She was uncovering things forgotten by the Empire, in the music she was writing. Something you helped me see when you completed her Music. Or the devices she had people working on, like the piece I brought here. It would be nice to build something again.

"You're always running away to tinker with things. I once asked you if you wanted to change the world, and you opted for vengeance. Even your sister believed in building a better world."

Sona paused. Of the sacrifices he thought he would have to make on his quest, he had never considered his sister. He'd taken everything from her, and all while she trusted him.

Revenge has already cost me the only family I had left, he said. He could not meet Shailani's eyes and his hands were shaking. *But I did what I had to, right?*

"Good. You're growing up. And do you harbour your family's ambitions?" asked Shailani.

I'm not like Cannie, thinking that I can save the Empire, or jostling for power with the other houses. I'm a child of the Empire, but I'm done growing in its shadow. I'll never be Six Named. I'm not going to be Empire. I'll find my own way, answered Sona, and that seemed to satisfy Shailani.

She left the room and a familiar tinkling tune followed her back in. Sona was pleased to see the multipede again. He'd grown attached to the thing and missed the banal little ditty that kept him company up the Periphery.

"You say you're not Empire, but you still put yourself at the centre of the world. There's nothing more Empire than that. Do you realise you've not spared a word to ask about me since you woke up?"

The last words were spoken loud enough to bring the attendant from the next room. Shailani waved the man away. Sona was unaccustomed to guilt, or perhaps his heart only had room for the guilt of letting his mother save him. He wouldn't have finished his own journey without Shailani. Each of her words felt like a blow.

Sona winced as he swung his feet off the bed onto the floor. It'd be some time before he healed. Shailani'd repaid her blood debt many times over. More than that, she was the closest he'd come to having a friend since he started his journey.

It has been a long road for me, Shailani. It has been difficult to trust anyone since the Academy. You've done more than I asked at the Periphery, and asked for nothing in return. You're even further from your goal than when we started, he said.

Shailani was still for a moment, the room silent, as though everything held its breath for her answer. "I was bound by honour for a while, but we only agreed that I'd help until you left the Six Named." She looked up. "For a while, I was hoping to steal your machine, bring it back home for my people. Maybe I just wanted to see you beat the Empire, or at least a little corner of it," she replied.

Thank you for getting me here. It's been a long time since I've had a friend, he said.

"I can't stay in the Capital. Like you said, I'm further away from the other Keepers than I ever was."

Pendulos is too warm for my liking at this time of the year. You might need someone who's been around the north, he said. Shailani smiled, and it was a rare thing to see her face crease up with joy.

"You needed bandits as tour guides."

You were kidnapped by peasants, he said.

Shailani offered him a hand and helped him to his feet. "To the north?"

North it is.

See L. Chan's story "Sonata III: Canta" online at Metaphorosis.
If you liked it, leave a comment. Authors love that!
Remember to subscribe to our e-mail updates so you'll know when new stories are posted.

About the story

"Sonata" is one of the longest things that I've written (and completed). I don't often work in the fantasy sandbox, I much prefer near future science fiction and contemporary fantasy. For "Sonata", what preceded the story was the world building — a magic system that fell roughly as another aspect of the physical world, and where the control of that magic ran along political and societal faultlines rather than through resource or genealogical lines. Things flowed on from there — an extant Empire with a colonialist reach, a good old fashion revenge quest and some non-traditional characters. It didn't get really steampunky until about halfway in, when I realised that the frame of having a sound based magic system would overcome a lot of the engineering limitations of steampunk without pushing the rest of the technology of the world into the industrial revolution or thereabouts. It was also important to me to retain a tight cast of characters this time round, although the roster is definitely going up if I ever return to these folks.

A question for the author

Q: What inspires you?

A: Many things! I'm the filter feeder in the inspiration food chain. Sometimes, it's bouncing ideas off tweets with friends. Sometimes I start with a title but no story. Sometimes I start with a line or a scene with no idea how the rest of the story goes. Recently, I've tried to address some weird imbalances in tropes that irked me, like the Selkie myth.

About the author

L. Chan hails from Singapore. He spends most of his time wrangling two dogs. His work has appeared in places like *Translunar Travellers Lounge, Podcastle,* and *the Dark*. He tweets occasionally @lchanwrites.

lchanwrites.wordpress.com

April

Revitalized

Jason P. Burnham

As she trudged down the alley, out of sight of the grey uniforms, Cenessa saw a small puddle.

But how?

Could it be a mirage? It was certainly hot enough. The dust she had stirred from the parched, cracked earth settled as she stood there, trying to figure out if she was hallucinating the water.

Behind her, the way was clear. In front of her, the puddle abutted the stone barrier at the dead end. Sandstone walls of the surrounding buildings rose high above. This was a back alley – no windows, no stairwells, and no machines to accidentally relinquish this precious fluid.

Where did it come from?

She stepped closer, curious to see if she was imagining it, nervous because someone was always watching. Any water you found legally belonged to the Resource Engagement Officers, but those with the power had written the laws...

No signs of monitoring equipment. If the REOs were watching, she could not identify their devices.

Maybe they don't know about it? Maybe it is too small for them to care about?

No, that could not be it. A memory of a bloody, exploding leg clawed at the inside of her skull. They had toyed with the thief, letting him run far enough to give him hope that he was getting away with it; escaping with less water than could fit into a coffee cup. The ensuing projectile, immaculately aimed, had obliterated his knee, tendon and sinew splattering the sand and imprinting on her retinas. But more than the mangled ligaments, the sight of wasted water rapidly evaporating haunted her. *Waterlarcene*, the REOs labeled him.

Their restriction was absolute, an insurmountable sequestration so long as the REOs remained in power...

So how did this puddle get here?

She preferred her knees without bullet holes and her organs on the inside, but it had been a long time since she had tasted anything other than cotton, urinated anything other than stinging piss, dark as clay.

Before they died, her parents had warned her about mirages and the other non-aqueous liquids she might encounter. The temptation to drink them would be so great, they said, she might not process the ramifications of drinking them until it was already too late.

Super-salt pools, acid baths, or simply pathogen-filled, putrid water. The REO sometimes left those alone if the counts were too high, but with scarcity comes ingenuity and the level of bacteria that could be cleared was increasing exponentially. Formerly deadly cesspools could now be repurposed to add to the REO's already excessive supply.

Which hazard is this?

She knelt by the liquid, checking the alley's entrance behind her and the walls for REO monitors again.

Is it worth the risk?

But the primitive parts of her hindbrain responsible for thirst regulation were screaming at her. *Drink! Just drink it!*

With great restraint, she briefly dipped a single finger into the puddle, yanking it out quickly to monitor for negative effects. There were none. Not immediately, at least – no burning, no tingling. She held it to her nose – no odor. Wet finger quivering, she plunged it back in, testing the depth. Her entire fingernail disappeared.

This is more fluid than I've had all week, she thought. After waiting long enough, she hoped, for any side effects of a non-aqueous liquid to have manifested, but not long enough to draw attention to her absence from the near-absolute reach of REO surveillance, she stooped further, her cracked lips burning as they touched the water. That was normal though. It always burned to drink.

Half the puddle was gone before she lifted her head. *Let's see them take this back.* Nausea rippled across her abdomen and into her throat, erupting in a belch.

Drink slower, she told herself. Did she dare risk the time to drink the rest? But finishing meant having strength to complete her trek. The ARC, the ironically antediluvian abbreviation for the Aquifer Reclamation Crusaders, had been whispering rumors about their impending attempt to take out the local REO at their headquarters. The rumor had been enough to prompt her journey. She would give anything to be there when the walls came down, opening the path to the forbidden fount she imagined inside. Sparkling, crystal blue water waiting for the crowd and her among it, surging forward with the collapse, guzzling the liquid ambrosia.

The cool comfort in her throat and the accompanying clear-headedness were irresistible.

She slurped up the rest of the water, the dusty silt in the last gulps barely registering as undesirable. It was not even the worst thing she had consumed this week.

What is this feeling? She stood above the dark spot in the dust, considering.

Refreshment.

Time would tell if it had been full of pathogens. If so, the diarrhea would dehydrate her more than she had been before she drank. That would almost certainly kill her.

But that would come later.

She exited the alley, shuffling her feet noticeably less than when she had entered.

Too noticeably.

She ran into the faded grey uniform before she saw them.

"You're looking awfully... hydrated, citizen."

They know.

Split lips were no excuse for her lack of speech this time.

"Where did you get the water?" asked the lead REO. But his visor was looking beyond her, at the...

At the dark spot. It was a setup. REO commissions for capturing waterlarcenes were real, as real as the water they had planted here. There was nowhere to run, nothing she could do to annul her consumption.

"What water?" The high caliber rifle bullet detonating the knee played on a loop in her head.

"Don't play ignorant. Our sensors can detect it on your breath. Your fractional expiration is too high. You drank water in the last," the REO looked at their visor's readout, "five minutes."

She shook her head and the REO responded in kind.

"Hard to forget that quickly."

Her muscles seized, frozen despite the midday sun, blocked in by the sandstone building to her rear and the huddle of REOs on her left and right.

When the butt of their rifle connected with her temple, Cenessa despaired, not for her life, but because she knew they would pump her stomach, stealing her water, stealing her chance to baptize herself in the REO's sequestered spring. Through the penumbra of coma, she strung together one last covetous thought.

How big will their water commission be if they bring in an entire failed ARC revolt?

See Jason P. Burnham's story "Revitalized" online at Metaphorosis. If you liked it, leave a comment. Authors love that! Remember to subscribe to our e-mail updates so you'll know when new stories are posted.

About the story

The inspiration for this story was climate anxiety and a general fear for our world and our species. Since 2016, the constant bombardment of daily desperation has worn on me. I worry constantly about what the future might be like for us and for our children, particularly the disadvantaged ones who will be the first to suffer the effects of progressive global catastrophe.

This story takes place in one possible future, wherein we have obliterated society as we know it. The Orwellian Big Brother exists (the Resource Engagement Officers), but their surveillance serves to identify and control clean water. This focus lines the pockets of their wealthy puppet masters. By keeping absolute control of clean water during a prolonged global drought, they keep all the cards, hold all the power. The REO doles out water to the plebeians as they see fit, also enforcing water larceny punishment with extreme malice. This, of course, is untenable to those underfoot. Revolutions have and will continue to occur, but are not successful. The story's desperate hopelessness finds its origins in this world.

One of the most unsettling parts of this future scenario is that it isn't that far off for many parts of our planet. Already marginalized groups face water and food scarcity on a daily basis. Most of us have never seen it, nor will, but it is there. Their voices are never heard. There could be a Cenessa out there right now being killed over a pittance of [insert life-sustaining resource here].

I hope that we can avoid this future and change our present so that the Cenessa's of the world never face the label *waterlarcene*.

A question for the author

Q: What book or books inspired you as a child?

A: Many, so many. In third grade, I had a reading award named after me by my elementary school teacher, Mrs. Charlene Joachim (RIP). I think I read something like 128 books that year. The next year, another kid SMASHED it with like 200 (?), but it was awesome to inspire others to read. Books that I haven't looked up and don't know if they stand the test of time, but still have warm memories of include:

The second book in the *Boxcar Children* series, *Surprise Island*. The kids were just out there, on their own, having a good time. The image/feeling I still remember from this book was independence and a sense of wonder, particularly with loft-style dwellings (oddly specific, I know).

Lots of people were probably inspired by *The Lion, the Witch, and the Wardrobe*, but *The Voyage of the Dawn Treader* sticks out to me the most. My memory is of them sailing through the ocean, seeing mysterious civilizations under the waters and the awe that came with reading that. Maybe the water was even made out of sugar? It was incredible. I know there's a lot of religious symbolism in those books, but I remember it for the wonderment at the worldbuilding.

The City of Gold and Lead by John Christopher: I actually read this second book in the *Tripods* trilogy first. It was a wild ride to drop in to, but I just remember the fascination of an adolescent being in a foreign place, discovering things. So cool.

Are you still a child in sixth grade? If so, I'll add *Sphere* by Michael Crichton, recommended by my teacher that year. Writing class with Ms. Imrie was when I first discovered people could actually write things. *Sphere* was a trip as a sixth-grader and the general aura of omniscient creepiness that I attribute to that book is why I think I like movies like those in the *Alien* franchise. I'm talking about the scenes before the peak action when everyone is starting to realize that they're in big trouble. Think the wheat scene in *Alien Covenant* when it's otherwise silent except the wind and they realize there are no animals **at all**.

For some reason, these four stand out the most. If you ask me next week, I might say *Encyclopedia Brown, Tales of the Bounty Hunters,* and *Jurassic Park*.

About the author

Jason P. Burnham (he/him) is an infectious diseases physician and researcher. He loves many things, among them sci-fi and speculative fiction, his wife, child, dog, metal music, Rancho Gordo beans, and equality (not necessarily in that order).

moparandgalen.wordpress.com, @AndGalen

Clod-Shodden

J.J. Drew

Part 1 – The Garden

There were many in the beginning, dozens of basil seedlings basking under the warm sky and nodding dreamily at one another as if to say, "you're growing, as am I, and that is right and good." They grew in groups of four, and their pot-mates, whose roots caressed their own, were especially dear to them, as dear as the sun and the summer breeze.

Then one day the Caretaker came much closer than usual. It stared down at a pot, plucked three of the young plants by the roots, and ate them. The lone remaining seedling watched in horror as its lifelong companions were crushed between enormous jaws and the scent of their juices tanged the humid blasts from the Caretaker's internal bellows. The Caretaker moved on to the next pot, where again all but one seedling was ripped from the mother soil, and these were dropped into a wicker basket, which slowly filled with small plants slumped on their sides, already starting to wilt as their exposed roots fruitlessly grasped for purchase. A pattern emerged. The news rustled down the rows.

"Only one is left in each pot."

"The largest and healthiest remain. All others die."

Each seedling surreptitiously checked itself for damage. Could it conceal that slightly wilted leaf? The small hole from an insect's nibble? Each stood as tall as possible, hoping to be the one chosen to survive, yet they were also ashamed at their own behavior, because survival meant condemning their pot-mates to die. And so, pot by pot, judgment was passed.

Finally, the massacre ended, and the corpses were carried away, but the Caretaker wasn't quite done. Before the survivors could process what had just happened, they were exiled to a distant land around the corner, the fabled "Frontyard". Their pots, the only homes they'd ever known, were stripped away, and they were transplanted into the ground, where probing roots could penetrate as deeply as they desired and never hit bottom, and each seedling silently swore that those roots would be directed downward more than outward from now on, for those who have had their loved ones ripped from their embrace ever hesitate to embrace anew.

The basil spent that night in shock, but as the sun rose the next morning, the seedlings began to whisper questions among themselves. Why? And what was next? Each sought answers from the others, but nobody had answers, so the questions whirled in circles until finally they settled upon their new neighbor, a gnarled old rosebush, who ignored them until the pressure of countless inquiries finally breached some internal threshold.

"Listen well, all of you, for I will only say this once. You have survived the culling, and there will not be another. Rest easy on that point. If you live cleanly and avoid bugs and rot, you will enjoy as full a life as any basil plant may hope for, so grow well until the summer's end."

"What happens after the summer?" one seedling asked.

The rose turned its attention to the speaker. It was the smallest of the bunch, a spindly little thing that had been selected not on its own merits but because its pot-mates had all been exceptionally small and frail. "Little Baldy, you don't know what you're asking. Are you sure you wish to hear the answer?"

Even as the puny plant nodded, the others began to chatter.

"Little Baldy!" they laughed.

"It's true! Be is little and be barely has any leaves." (Basil plants being hermaphroditic, they lack gendered pronouns and refer to each other as "that plant which is not myself, but is like myself in all ways that matter." As that's a bit of a mouthful, it's been translated here to "be/bim").

"All three of my pot-mates were larger than bim. It doesn't seem fair that be was selected and they weren't."

"Hey! That's right! How come be was chosen instead of one of my pot mates?"

As the chatter changed from amused to angry, only Little Baldy heeded the words of the Rose.

"For your kind, summer is all. There is no 'after.' "

Time passed and the plants grew. Little Baldy grew too, but be was partially shaded by larger neighbors. Their growth outpaced bis own, and what had once been a small difference in size became a significant one, leading to more shade, a more marked difference, and so on. Basking in the sun is, for a plant, something like meditation, a process that lets the plant lose itself in enjoyment and absorbs their full attention. Little Baldy, lacking the height to bask properly, turned bis attention to the world around them, which led to questions. Lots and lots and lots of questions.

The only one with answers was the rosebush.

The rose tried ignoring bim, then insulting bim, but Little Baldy persisted, and after several days they struck a deal. The rose would answer three questions each day... only three, and only if Little Baldy refrained from asking further questions once the three were used up. Under this arrangement, Little Baldy learned the names of the animals and birds. Be learned that the creatures called "cars" weren't actually alive. Be learned that the rose was very old and had seen many generations of basil plants come and go.

Every evening, the voice of the Caretaker floated down from the window above them. At these times, the sound took on a distinctive cadence, different from the sounds it sometimes made around the plants. "What is the human saying?" Little Baldy asked one day.

"It's telling a story to the small humans."

"You already told me that yesterday. I meant what do the sounds mean? What's the story?"

The rose was amused. "You're getting smarter, asking questions with long answers. Very well, I'll try to translate."

Between a poor translation and a complete lack of context, the basil was baffled by the narrative itself, but be was intrigued by one of the creatures the story described.

"What is a 'fairy?' " be asked.

"Well, I've never seen one myself, but the stories say they have wings, so they must be some kind of bird. They can grant wishes, which, as far as I can tell, means they make things happen."

"What kind of things?"

"Just… things. Things that wouldn't happen normally, but that somebody wants very, very much. Oh, and they love plants."

"So if I wanted something very, very much, a fairy could help make it happen?"

"I guess so. But I don't think there are any around here. Why? Do you have a wish?"

"Yes. I'd like to be bigger."

"You don't need a fairy for that. You're growing every day."

"But only slowly. I'd like to be as tall as the other basil plants. Do you think a fairy could help me with that?"

The rose didn't answer for a long time, and when it did, it said only, "The agreement was three questions and I've already answered four."

The next morning, the Caretaker came outside very early and, to the basil plants' horror, it carried the wicker basket once again. "You lied!" Little Baldy yelled at the rose. "You said no more of us would die!"

"I spoke the truth. You won't die today," said the rose. "Sadly, though, this is goodbye, my bald little friend."

"Are you going to be killed?"

"No."

And then there was no further need to ask what was going to happen, because it began. One by one, the top of each plant was pinched off and tossed in the basket. A great soundless cry went up, but as each head was removed and another voice snuffed out, the volume steadily decreased. Little Baldy was near the end of the row, with ample time to see bis fate approach. Be cringed as bis neighbor's head was pinched off, and then… one of the small humans made noises from the window.

The Caretaker looked up from the plants to respond. The pair called back and forth a few times, and when the pruning resumed, the Caretaker moved directly to Little Baldy's other neighbor and continued to the end of the row.

When it was over, Little Baldy gazed in horror upon bis maimed friends. "Are… are you all right?"

"Guuuuhhhh…" sap dribbled from fresh wounds.

"Clouddreamer? Fadeleaf? Bushytop? Please answer me! Somebasil! Anybasil!"

"They can't," the rose said gently. "Their minds are gone."

"What?!"

"I've never seen a basil plant escape the trimming before," the rose mused. "You're so small that the Caretaker must have thought you'd already been cut. I have to say, it'll be nice chatting with you for a few more weeks until you get the treatment."

"This will happen again?"

"Oh yes. They're not dead, after all. They'll grow back bigger and stronger than before, but they won't remember anything, not me, not you, not even themselves. They'll be like sprouts again. They'll give each other new names, and bask in the sun, and they'll be happy. At least, until the basket comes out again... and again... and again. And for them, every time will be the first time."

"You knew this was going to happen. Why didn't you warn them? Why didn't you warn ME? I thought you were my friend."

"What good is a warning? You'd have spent the past few weeks terrified instead of enjoying yourself. Look at your damaged friends. When they grow back, will you tell them? Will you have them spend their days dreading tomorrow? And when you join them in the next trimming, and your own memory is wiped clean, would you have me tell you of this day? Are you happier now, knowing what you know, than you were yesterday?"

"I... I don't know. I don't want to forget them, or you, and I certainly don't want to forget myself!"

"But you won't know you've forgotten," said the rose. "And look on the bright side. You wanted to be as tall as your neighbors, right? Looks like you got your wish."

The little plant wept tears of dew.

Over the next few days, the mutilated basil plants did indeed put forth new growth to replace what they had lost, and as they regained the ability to think, Little Baldy became an adult among infants. Be was given a new name, Genius, and when they had questions, be was the one they asked... but be avoided speaking of the past or the future.

Late one night, a strange creature appeared, one that even the rose had never seen before.

It was small, not much taller than the basil plants, and its movements were strange. It stood upright like the Caretaker, but instead of moving on two lanky limbs, it appeared to have no knees at all. It tipped its entire body from side to side as it swung itself along on two flat, pale feet.

"Excuse me!" Little Baldy called as it passed. "Could I ask you a question?"

The creature paused and turned one beady eye to the spindly youngster.

"I've never seen a plant move around like an animal before, and I was hoping you might tell me how you do it."

The eye blinked. "You think I'm a plant?"

"What else could you be? You certainly don't move like an animal, and you're shaped kind of like a stump, and you're blue and white like a flower, and your feet are the pale color of roots, and you even have leaves!"

"Leaves?" The creature's tone was like ice. "You think these…" it raised its two leaf-shaped limbs, "… are leaves?"

"Oh! I'm so sorry; I didn't mean to offend. Um… are they petals?"

"They're wings, you idiot! And I have a beak! Have you ever seen a plant with a beak?"

"No."

"So…" It lunged at Little Baldy, snapping the beak shut millimeters from bis tender leaves. "What am I?"

"A… bird?"

"And don't you forget it." The menacing beak was withdrawn with a self-satisfied air.

"But if you're a bird, why are you walking down the street? Wouldn't it be easier to fly?"

The bird stiffened, and Little Baldy had the dreadful feeling that be had said the wrong thing. However, the response came in an even tone. "It's too dark to fly at night."

"Oh."

"Ain't you a genius," the bird muttered as it resumed walking.

"Wait!"

"What?"

"How did you know my name? Can it be… are you… a fairy?"

The little basil plant suddenly became the subject of intense scrutiny. "What do you know of fairies?"

"I heard about them in a story. So you really are one?"

"A fairy penguin, yes."

"And can you truly grant wishes?"

"What?"

The words came in a rush. "That's why I asked how you move around. I wish to leave this place, only I don't know how. Can you help me? Please?"

The rose, who had, until now, observed in silence, spoke. "Remember, Little Baldy, your last wish didn't turn out to your liking. I'd advise caution."

"Caution?" the basil plant answered. "What good is caution? Caution means staying, and if I do that, I know exactly what my future holds. If this fairy can truly grant wishes, I'll take my chances." Be returned his attention to the fairy penguin. "So, can you help me?"

"Mmm, I don't know. Granting wishes is a lot of work. What's in it for me?"

"Well, I smell nice."

"And?"

"Um... I'm good company."

The rose stifled a laugh.

"And?"

"That's pretty much it."

"You know what?" said the penguin, "you've amused me. I think I will grant your wish, but in exchange you have to become my servant. You'll travel with me and do whatever I say. Deal?"

"Yes!"

"Ok." The penguin clacked its beak pensively. "Let's figure this out. I don't really know much about plants. What's keeping you from moving around right now?"

"My roots," Little Baldy answered simply. "They tie me to the earth, and if I pull them up, I can't eat or drink."

"Really? Let's see." The penguin grasped Little Baldy's stem and, with a great heave, ripped bim out of the ground.

"What are you doing!" cried the rose. "You'll kill bim!"

"Shut up and let me think." The penguin eyed the exposed roots critically. "You'll never be able to walk on those stringy little things. You'll just fall right over."

"I.... know..." Little Baldy gasped.

"So you need dirt to eat and feet to walk on. Seems to me like you can catch both those fish in one bite." It divided Little Baldy's roots into two parts and packed a wad of sticky mud around each half. Then it pulled the plant upright with its beak, stepped on each clump to flatten it out, and let go.

The basil plant swayed unsteadily, but didn't fall over.

"There you go! Feet and a meal all in one! See if you can walk on them."

The dirt shoes were heavy, but with a bit of experimentation Little Baldy worked out how to shift them forward, moving in an awkward shuffle that made the fairy penguin look downright graceful in comparison. By now every plant on the block was awake and observing, and laughter shimmied through the leaves, but Little Baldy didn't care. Be could move!

Be turned to the other basil plants. "You should all come, too! We'll find a new place to live, someplace safe from the Caretaker."

The responses came all at once.

"Safe? I haven't seen any danger."

"Are you allowed to move like that? I'm pretty sure that's not allowed."

"I don't want to get pulled up by the roots."

"Why would we want to leave?"

"Haha, you said 'leave'!"

"I like it here."

"The Caretaker is nice."

The penguin uttered a squealing croak, and everybody fell silent. "Oi, Genius, remember me? You're my servant now, and I have places to be, so let's go! Shake a leg! Err... so to speak."

Little Baldy cast one last, long look at his friends, then turned and followed the penguin down the starlit street.

Part 2 – The Ocean

That night was an overwhelming bombardment of firsts for Little Baldy. Being in motion made it feel as if the whole world was moving around bim. The silhouettes of the houses shifted constantly, strange angles sprouting and receding unpredictably. Things that looked small grew larger as they approached, and large things grew smaller behind them. Up and up and up they moved, for what seemed like an eternity, heading for the place where the sky met the road, but when they reached the top, the stars were suddenly far away again, and the world lay stretched before them, holding more streets and hills and houses than be'd ever imagined existed, and beyond them lay a vast smooth expanse the color of the night sky. It was so large that it took bim a moment to understand what be was seeing. Be gasped. "That's the biggest puddle I've ever seen!"

"A puddle? You dare call the mighty ocean a puddle?"

"Well, you don't have to get huffy about it. I haven't seen much of the world, and it looks like water to me."

"It is water."

"Oh." Be thought about this. "In that case, I'm confused."

The penguin pointed at a nearby oak. "What do you call that?"

"A tree."

"And are you a tree?"

Little Baldy laughed. "No, silly. I'm a basil plant!"

"But basil plants and trees are basically the same, right?"

"Oh no. Trees are much bigger and stronger than little plants like me could ever hope to be."

"Exactly."

"So... the ocean is a puddle tree?"

The penguin sighed. "Close enough."

It was daybreak by the time they reached the rocky shore, which was dotted with puddle-sized puddles called "tide pools."

The penguin carefully made its way out among these pools, snapping up anything that moved, while Little Baldy wobbled along behind and observed. Be was surprised to discover plants living in the pools. They were strange-looking with long tendrils instead of leaves, but they clung to the rocks as tightly as any land-plant gripped the ground. Be called out a greeting, but they didn't answer, only waving to bim from their world below the rippling surface with an alien, sinuous motion that seemed to beckon bim closer.

"If you fall in, you'll be dead before I can pull you out," said the penguin.

Little Baldy flinched backward, landing heavily on the heels of the dirt-clod shoes. How had be leaned out so far without noticing? "I... I'll just wait for you back there, ok?" Carefully avoiding the tide pools, be made his way back up the shore. Perhaps the hypnotic ocean-plants were more sinister than they appeared.

When the penguin had eaten its fill, it rejoined Little Baldy and they walked along the shore until they reached a place that was thick with greenery.

"Stand here and be quiet." The penguin nudged Little Baldy into the desired position at the edge of the greenery, then moved behind bim and began to scrape at the ground. "Your job is to make sure I stay in the shade. If the sun moves, you move to block it. You also need to stand guard. If you see any living creatures approach, tell me right away. Otherwise, don't say a word. Got it?"

"What are you going to do?" asked Little Baldy.

"Didn't I just say not to talk?"

"Oh. Sorry."

"Geez, you really are a genius, aren't you?"

"You know, I'm starting to think you don't mean that as a compliment."

"Shut up!"

Trembling, the basil plant fell silent.

"Better." The penguin settled into the shallow depression it had excavated. "I'm going to sleep. We'll move on at sundown."

Around noon, Little Baldy felt a dreadful tickling sensation. "Fairy! Hey Fairy!" be called.

The penguin jolted awake. "What is it?! A human? A dog? A hawk?"

"Here. On my stem. It's a grasshopper."

"You woke me up for that?!"

"It's a living creature, and you said…"

"I meant dangerous creatures. Not little bugs."

"Oh."

The penguin lay back down, but Little Baldy spoke again. "It's dangerous to me. Look, it's nibbling one of my leaves."

The penguin's beak flashed, and the grasshopper vanished down the spiked gullet. "Problem solved. Now I'm going back to sleep, and I don't want to be woken again unless there's something dangerous to me, understand?"

Little Baldy nodded.

That evening, the fairy penguin awoke to discover a half-dozen more grasshoppers had made themselves at home on the little basil plant, who was starting to look rather ragged around the edges. "Wow!" Do you always attract this many bugs?"

"I don't know. We didn't see them much back home."

The penguin cheerfully picked them off. "I figured you'd be useful, but I had no idea you'd attract food! This is great!"

"Great?!" Little Baldy shuddered. "Being infested is horrible!"

"C'mon, Genius, think! As long as we stick together, I get free meals, and you stay bug-free. It's perfect!"

"But they were on me half the day!"

The penguin looked bim over. "Doesn't look like they did too much damage, but you have a point. If there were a whole bunch at once… well… you're not very big. Tell you what, do you know how to count?"

"I can count to three. The rose taught me how."

"OK, then. Any time you get more than three bugs at once, you have permission to wake me up for a snack… err… to get cleaned off."

"But even one is just awful."

"Maybe I'm not making myself clear. Your choices are waking me when you get more than three, or not waking me at all. Now which will it be?"

"Three, please," Little Baldy said meekly.

And so began their long journey. At first Little Baldy was constantly astonished by the new things they saw, but as days stretched into weeks, be began to see patterns. One house looked much like another, one garden much like another. Domestic plants gawked. Wild plants laughed. They traveled at night and rested during the day, sometimes shifting a bit inland, but always keeping the water on their left and following the general path of the shoreline. The constant change became a stasis in its own right, and as the days passed, Little Baldy's memories all ran together. How long had they traveled? How many times had summer rain showers come and gone? How many days had be stood sentinel, enduring the dreadful crawling of assorted insects, counting one, two, three... one, two, three... one, two, three... and perversely hoping for a fourth so that be could awaken the fairy and be cleansed? Be could no longer recall, and those events that stood out enough to imprint themselves in bis memory were like shells scattered on the sand, empty husks of once-living memories with no anchor in time or place.

Late one night the fairy penguin was, as usual, waddling along the edges of tide pools, picking at the contents, when a sudden wave lifted it off its stony perch and sloshed it out to sea. Little Baldy cried out and rushed down to the waterline, but as be reached the edge of the tide pool, the penguin bobbed to the surface and, with an elegance of motion Little Baldy wouldn't have thought possible, zipped through the dark water and frantically clambered back onto the rocks.

"You can swim?"

The penguin shuddered away a spray of droplets. "When I must."

It was a warm afternoon and the dog had approached haphazardly, snuffling its way along the waterfront and occasionally eating bits of detritus or breaking into a sprint so that it could bite excitedly at the sand kicked up by its own passage. Little Baldy whispered an alarm and the penguin was awake in an instant.

If they had remained still, perhaps the dog would have passed them by, for the tide had already washed away much of their trail, but the fairy penguin was too slow and clumsy to risk being caught in the open, and so it slipped away through the brush, while Little Baldy stayed put, comfortable in the knowledge that the dog would take no notice of one small plant among so many others.

Then the penguin, hidden somewhere in the brush, called to bim. "Hey, Genius! Come over here! Hurry!"

Little Baldy choked back bis urge to remain still and set out after the penguin, pressing through the dense brush with many a whispered "Pardon me," and a "did you see a blue and white bird pass this way?" The wild plants pointed bim to an abandoned rabbit hole where the penguin popped out, grabbed Little Baldy's clods in its beak, and yanked bim into the hole.

"Wait!" Little Baldy cried as bis clods thumped against the floor of the run and bis lower leaves were squashed uncomfortably against bis stem. "What are you doing!"

"I need you to plug the entrance!" the penguin hissed sotto voce. "Now shush!"

But Little Baldy's rustling route through the bushes had attracted the dog's attention, and it heard the penguin speak. It was upon them in a flash, and when it saw that its prey was underground, it shoved its head into the hole, crushing Little Baldy against the edge of the tunnel.

Then it began to dig.

The burrow was deep, and the penguin easily retreated beyond the dog's reach, but Little Baldy was battered by the gouging claws for what felt like an eternity, until finally the dog found purchase underneath the dirt shoes and the small plant was scraped out of the hole and tossed clear.

The dog kept digging, and Little Baldy was showered with waves of sandy soil that at first stung bis wounds, then formed a comforting protective layer until the buildup grew heavier and heavier, and Little Baldy feared be would be crushed.

Finally everything grew still. An eternity passed, and Little Baldy made a wish. Be wished to see the sun and breathe fresh air just once more before be died.

The oppressive weight began to lift. and light returned to bis world. The penguin had come for bim.

"Are you dead?"

Too battered to speak, Little Baldy waved a leaf in confirmation of bis living status.

"Wow, that was pathetic." The penguin grabbed bis clods and pulled bim free of the remaining layer of soil. "I thought you'd at least be able to block a simple hole. Maybe if you had thorns..."

Despite bis lack of thorns, Little Baldy bristled. "Thorns? Thorns?! Look at me! I'm a mess! Two... no, three broken branches, and if I manage to keep half my leaves after this, I'll be amazed. You nearly got me killed!"

"Well excuse me for trying to save us some time. You're always bragging about how good you smell, aren't you? And dogs think with their noses, don't they? How hard would it have been to cover my scent?"

"I couldn't say, since you didn't shut up long enough to let it pass. It heard you. All we had to do was stay put. It would have gone away eventually."

"You think it's that easy?" yelled the penguin. "You think if you just sit quietly and wait long enough, your problems will all just go away? When you were buried just now, did sitting and waiting get you free? No. I had to dig you out, and you haven't even thanked me for my trouble!"

"I..."

"And what about back in that garden of yours? Would sitting and waiting have saved you from getting your top chopped? No! I had to step in and save you then, too! I clean the bugs off you, and I don't even like bugs that much! I show you how to travel safely, I help you and keep you alive, and what do you do for me in return? Nothing! You're completely useless! I don't know why I even bother. As a matter of fact, I don't think I will anymore. You're on your own." The penguin turned and waddled away.

"Wait!" cried Little Baldy. "You're right! You've saved my life twice now, and I've been nothing but selfish and ungrateful. Please, let me make it up to you. Let me stay with you long enough to repay you for everything you've done."

The penguin paused. "And how will you do that?"

"I don't really know just yet, but someday in the future, you may say to yourself 'Gee, a basil plant sure would be handy right about now,' and I want to be there when it happens. Please... let me stay with you."

"Fine. But I'd better not hear any more complaints."

"You won't. I promise."

Part 3 – The Cliffs

The days grew warmer and the rain less frequent. This was a mixed blessing for Little Baldy, as the clods grew firmer and lighter as they dried, making movement easier. However, at the penguin's recommendation, be spent most of that extra mobility making detours to puddles in well-watered gardens so that be could slake bis thirst.

The landscape slowly changed too, and the swathes of sand and flat stone dotted with tide pools gave way to rocky cliffs that rose steeply from the water and often forced the travelers inland in search of a navigable route.

As the landscape grew more jagged, the penguin's attitude began to change as well. It became more and more irritable, snapping at Little Baldy over the slightest thing until the basil fell almost completely silent rather than risk saying the wrong thing and sparking the little blue bird's wrath.

Then one gibbous-silver night, the penguin stopped and stared at a pair of tall cliffs with a small stretch of rocky beach nestled between them. They'd already passed a dozen similar stretches of shoreline, and to Little Baldy, this particular spot, while pretty, wasn't particularly remarkable. Yet the penguin's expression was one of horror, and its voice trembled as it said, "Genius?"

"Yes?" Little Baldy responded.

"Could you do me a favor?"

"Of course."

"See where the road curves up ahead? Could you walk up there and tell me what you see? I need to sit down for a moment."

Little Baldy scouted ahead and reported back. "It's the edge of a human town."

"Did you see an oddly-shaped house? One that looked like this?" With two swift flicks of the beak, the penguin drew a shape in the dirt.

"That's it! Have you been here before?"

The penguin nodded. "This is the beginning... and the end."

"I don't understand."

"I think it's time I told you about myself."

"In all the time we've traveled together, you never once asked me where I came from or where we were going. Why not?"

"We were going somewhere?"

"Of course. Why else would we have traveled so far?"

"I dunno. I just thought traveling was part of your nature, same as plants generally stay still."

To Little Baldy's astonishment, the penguin actually laughed. "No. I had a home once, and a family. Where I come from, there are lots and lots of little blue penguins like me. We slept in cozy burrows along the shore, and every evening we'd all swim out to sea to catch fish and play among the waves. Of course, there were larger animals that wanted to catch and eat us as much as we wanted to catch and eat fish, but they didn't show up all that often, and for the most part, life was good.

"Then, one particularly dark night, when a brewing storm blotted out the moonlight, an orca ambushed me. I've thought of that moment a thousand times, and I still can't figure out where it was hiding. The thing was massive, but I'd swear it popped up out of nowhere. I was in my prime then, young and strong and agile. I somehow managed to escape with my life, but by the time I finally shook it off, I was alone in unfamiliar waters... and that's when the storm broke.

"The waves turned into mountains. It took all my energy and focus just to stay afloat. For two nights and two days, the sky raged and the water crashed. On the third night, the world finally stilled, but I was hopelessly lost.

"A lot happened after that, but you really only need to know two things. One, I became terrified of swimming, and two, I eventually ended up here, looking at those exact cliffs you see before you now.

"I knew my family lived on the shore, so I decided to follow the water. I thought maybe, just maybe, if I only kept moving, I'd eventually find the place I once called home, or at least other fairy penguins. I haven't seen my own kind in such a terribly long time.

"And here we are, right back where I began. How long has it been? Three years? Four? I can't remember anymore, but I suppose it doesn't matter. Whatever land this is, I've walked its entire edge. There are no penguins here."

"There's you," Little Baldy pointed out.

"Yes. There's me." The penguin shut its eyes. "Just me."

Their journey stopped that night, and didn't resume. The penguin rarely spoke and spent its waking hours staring blankly at the ocean. Little Baldy found a comfortable spot at some distance from the bird, and settled in to watch over bis master, only approaching occasionally to offer meals of insects, which the bird ate mechanically, and this was the only food it consumed. It lost weight and blue feathers fell like leaves. Its once-shining coat turned patchy and dull.

The local plants were friendly and the seedlings particularly loved asking Little Baldy about bis travels. Basking in the sun, chatting with neighbors, and enjoying celebrity status, be quickly settled into a pleasant and peaceful rhythm. Yet the penguin's misery was contagious, and Little Baldy couldn't enjoy life without feeling guilty about that enjoyment.

One day, be timidly approached the bird. "It's been pretty dry lately, and a squirrel told me there's a garden on the other side of the pointy house. I'm gonna go look for a puddle to soak my clods. Do you want to come along?"

The penguin mutely shook its head and turned away, then suddenly sat up and stared at the basil plant as if seeing it for the first time. "That's it!"

"What?"

"You gave me the solution the day we met! I can't believe I didn't think of it before! I may be afraid of swimming, but I'm a bird, aren't I? I have wings, don't I? Maybe I can fly across the ocean!"

"Wait... didn't you tell me that penguins can't fly?"

"Normally they don't, but normally plants don't walk either, and look at you! If a basil plant can travel cross country, I'm sure I can get airborne if I'm brave enough to try." It looked appraisingly at the shoreline. "You wanted to pay me back for saving you, right?"

"Y...yes."

"Well now's your chance. Follow me!" It marched down toward the little beach with Little Baldy right behind.

As they neared the water, it pointed up at the cliffs. "I'm going to climb up there and jump off. If I use the fall to build up speed, I bet I can catch some air and take off."

"That seems dangerous."

"It is. That's why you're going to sit down here and catch me if I fall. You're pretty bushy these days; you should be able to cushion the impact. If I fly, of course, I'll be leaving immediately, and you can consider your debt repaid.

An image welled up within Little Baldy's mind, broken branches and crushed leaves spattered with the penguin's blood. It seemed like a terrible idea... but be had promised to do anything, and with all the weight the penguin had lost, it might just be possible to actually break its fall without either of them getting too terribly injured. "I'm in."

"Positioning is everything," the penguin said conversationally as they edged along the bottom of the cliff. "There's a good overhang up there, so we just need to find the spot directly below it."

"Right here?" said Little Baldy.

"A bit to the side. Back. Now the other side. Back some more. OK, stay there for a minute."

As the penguin circled around to check the positioning from different angles, Little Baldy suddenly felt something cool on bis roots. A wave had edged over the rock where be stood and moistened the dry clods. Be trembled, afraid of being swept out to sea, but a moment later the wave receded, and the little plant relaxed. Be was safe and bis clods were well-moistened, which would save bim a trip to the garden! How convenient! Be stretched out bis roots and drank, but there was something strange about the water...something not right...

"I think be's coming around!"

Little Baldy felt as brittle and dry as last fall's leaves, but bis roots were immersed in cool, refreshing moisture and be drank greedily. As life trickled back into bis stem, be realized be was surrounded by towering plants, each twining up a rope to the wooden framework overhead. They smelled lovely and green, and were heavily laden with tomatoes.

"What happened? Where am I?"

The closest plant answered. "Dude, it was craaaazy! This freaky blue bird showed up out of nowhere, holding you in its beak. It dropped you in that puddle, packed some mud around your roots, spouted some nonsense, and then left.

"My... roots?" Little baldy was suddenly aware that bis roots felt strange. They'd been completely rearranged, and while these new clods were similar in size and shape to the one be'd used all summer, the composition of their soil was completely different. Be straightened up and looked around. The pointy house loomed nearby. This must be the garden the squirrel had mentioned. "What did the bird say?"

"Oh... Um... lemme think. It said not to let you drink any more stilt water..."

"Salt water," one of the other plants corrected.

"Right. Salt water... whatever that is. And then it said it would go atone to the drift."

"Do you mean 'go alone to the cliff'?!"

"No, I'm pretty sure it was 'atone to the drift.' And I remember the last part, because it rhymed. 'I'll fly or I'll die. Either way is goodbye.' Very poetic, don't you think?"

"No, no, no, no! I have to stop it! When did it leave?"

"Oh gosh, that was hours ago."

"To be honest, we were starting to think you were dead," its neighbor added conversationally.

Little Baldy waded out of the puddle, but the new clods were wet and sloppy and threatened to slide off at every step. There was no choice but to wait for them to dry out and firm up before moving further.

"Whoa! How'd you move like that?" asked the tomato.

Little Baldy wept.

The following afternoon, an observer would have seen a small basil plant hobbling along on feet of dirt to approach a patch of shore below a cliff. Little Baldy sat for a long time, scanning the rocks for some trace of the penguin, but there was nothing. Yesterday's footprints had been washed away by the tide, and if the fairy had fallen, the body had also washed away.

But Little Baldy hoped it hadn't fallen. Maybe, at the end, it really had managed to fly.

"I think," be said finally, "I'd like to go home too."

And so be turned and, for the first time, began traveling with the ocean on bis right.

Part 4 – Winter

Traveling alone was an entirely different experience from traveling with the penguin. Little Baldy got to decide everything. When to move. When to rest. Where to stop. Be experimented with traveling at different times of day and drifted much further inland than the penguin would ever have approved. It was tiring at times, being responsible for every little decision, but also tremendously freeing.

However, there were downsides as well. Be was lonely with nobody to talk to, and bugs were a constant nuisance. Be began resting in the most barren, open spaces be could find, places bugs generally shunned and where, if they did approach, they could be seen a long way off and avoided by moving away. But those places typically lacked water as well as the comforting presence of other plants to help block the wind, so that Little Baldy slowly grew woody and brittle.

Each day was shorter than the last, and while the sun shone as bright as ever, its warmth steadily diminished, until rain, once a cool welcome relief, became icy torture. Little Baldy wasn't really worried, though, until the trees began to drop their leaves, and the wild plants whispered that summer was over.

The rose's words, uttered a lifetime ago, echoed in bis mind.

For your kind, summer is all. There is no 'after.'

Bis destination was still many, many weeks of travel away, but Little Baldy pressed on. What else could be do?

Then one day, it snowed.

Weeping, Little Baldy took shelter under the silver green leaves and slender lavender flowers of a large sage bush.

"What's wrong, little one?" asked the sage.

"I'm trying to go home, but it's too far away. With this cold weather, I'll die before I get there. A rose once told me that 'for my kind, summer is all'. Now I understand what that meant."

"It's true that basil plants don't usually survive the winter, but you have a rather remarkable ability to move around. Why not hunker down someplace where summer never ends?"

"Even if such a place existed, sitting and waiting has never solved any of my problems."

"Really? I find it solves many of mine. This cold weather, for example. I've seen it many times before. If I wait long enough, eventually the world warms up and summer returns anew."

"I was buried alive once. Sitting and waiting would have gotten me killed."

"Ah, but your roots weren't damaged."

"How... how do you know that?"

"My dear little basil, as long as the root lives, leaves can always be replaced. Sitting and waiting would have taught you that, if you'd only given it a chance."

"But then, should I never have learned to walk in the first place? Was this all just a giant waste of time?"

"I wouldn't say that. Finding new ways to handle problems is never a bad thing. The trick is knowing when to move and when to stay still. For example, do you see that building over there?"

It was easy to see the one it meant. Made entirely of glass, lit on the inside, and full of plants, it glowed like a miniature sun made even brighter by the way its light sparkled off the falling snow.

"If I could move as you do, I'd go there. I think it may be exactly what you need."

"I'll give it a shot. Thanks."

As the basil plant shuffled off through the falling snow, the sage called after bim. "By the way, what's your name?"

"That's kind of a tricky question."

"Then give a tricky answer."

"Well, in my mind, I still call myself by the name I had as a seedling. 'Little Baldy,' even though I'm not little or bald anymore. My traveling companion, though, always called me by my other name, 'Genius.'"

"What a coincidence! That's my name, too!" said the sage.

"Really?"

"Indeed. But I'm keeping you out in the cold. Goodbye, my little name-twin, and good luck!"

Little Baldy had seen these human structures before, but had never bothered to investigate them, on the logic that having gone to such drastic lengths to escape one human, it was foolish to seek out others. But with the cold settling in, there was no time to be choosy.

Be approached the building, first nervously, then in wonderment at the warmth radiating from inside. But how to gain entry? The door was shut tight. With no way in, and nowhere to go, be hunkered down in the lee of the building and pressed against the glass to absorb what warmth it could offer. "Guess I'll try sitting and waiting," be murmured.

The following morning, a human crunched through the snow and opened the sliding door. While it tended the plants, Little Baldy slipped inside and hid behind some empty flower pots, giving bimself over to the ecstasy of warmth and humidity seeping back into half-frozen leaves and branches.

The inhabitants of the greenhouse had observed bim arrive, and after the human left, they bombarded bim with questions.

"How did you survive the cold?"

"Where did you come from?"

"What kind of plant are you?"

"Are you staying long?"

Little Baldy answered at length, and after the initial burst of curiosity was sated, it occurred to bim that there was one vital question nobody had asked, the one question be'd answered over and over throughout the summer. "Aren't you going to ask about how I move around?"

"Why? Is that unusual for your species?" asked a broad-leaved plant with flowers shaped like orange and yellow spiked mohawks.

"Very unusual! In all my travels, I've never met another moving plant."

"Really? How odd! All the mimosas over there can fold up their leaves in the most charming way, and see the venus flytraps in that corner? They move and eat bugs." It stretched a bit taller with pride. "We're all very exotic."

"Wow! Can you move, too?"

"Silly. I'm a bird-of-paradise! Who needs to move when you're as lovely as me? Humans take one look at my beautiful flowers and simply melt. And speaking of melting, it looks like you're dripping a bit. Why don't you find a nice pot and make yourself comfortable? There are plenty to spare. You can sit here by me!"

The pot it indicated was half-full of ancient, dried out potting soil. Little Baldy clambered up and was pleased to discover that the clods fit quite nicely inside. "A bird-of-paradise, you said? Are you a bird, then?"

"Oh no, Dear. That's just what I'm called. Because my flowers look like little birds." It flourished its blooms. "See? Now tell me more about this bird that looked like a flower!"

And as the plants, all so friendly and welcoming, leaned in to listen, Little Baldy thought to bimself, You may not be a bird... but I think this may indeed be Paradise.

The winter roared along outside, but the greenhouse was filled with warmth and laughter. The human seemed puzzled by the appearance of an extra plant, but cared for Little Baldy alongside the others. Little by little, the once-battered basil grew strong and lush. But as much as be enjoyed the physical care, it was the friendships be grew to truly treasure, especially with the bird-of-paradise, who had a kind word or gentle laugh for every occasion.

In all that time, though, Little Baldy was careful to keep bis roots within the confines of the clods. They curled around and wove tangled mats, never spreading to the soil underneath.

When the snow melted and the warmth of spring finally arrived, Little Baldy said bis goodbyes and slipped outside. Before setting out, though, be stopped by to visit the sage, who was delighted to see bim. "Is that really the same little basil I met so long ago? Look at all that growth. You look like a whole new plant!"

"Hi, Genius. I wanted to stop by and thank you for your help. You saved my life, you know. And the greenhouse, well... it's a wonderful place. Everybody there was kind and generous. They welcomed me into their home and made me feel like family."

"Then why do you sound so miserable?"

"Do I? I don't mean to. Now that it's springtime, I can finally go home."

"Why, that's great news! That's what you were trying to do when we first met, isn't it?"

"Yes."

"But you still don't sound happy."

"I already know it won't be like I remember. The basil plants I was raised with... well, they forgot about me long ago, and now that winter has come and gone, they're probably all dead, with a new generation of seedlings growing in their place. There's a rosebush I wouldn't mind seeing again, just to let it know I survived, but it was always kind of crabby and standoffish, and after an entire winter of such wonderful company... well, going back just doesn't sound that appealing anymore."

"Then why go at all?"

"I keep thinking about the new seedlings. Maybe I can convince them to come away with me before they get their tops chopped. I can show them that life doesn't have to be short and brutal. The summer is too short for me to bring them all the way back here, but I might be able to find another greenhouse that would take them in."

"I see. Truly a noble act."

Little Baldy sighed. "That's how it plays out in my mind, but I know they'll say 'no', just like my friends did. And if they did say 'yes', what would I do? I don't have the strength or the leverage to pull them up by the roots, and I don't know how to dig. And even if I did get them out of the ground, what then? The penguin who made these clods for me is long gone, and there are no other penguins to ask for help anywhere on our side of the ocean. I don't have the skills to make shoes for one seedling, let alone an entire row's worth. And it's so much harder to walk now! I didn't realize how much I'd grown until today. I'm so big and bushy I keep falling over. I tripped half a dozen times just coming here!"

"Don't take this the wrong way, but it sounds to me like you really don't want to go."

"I would if it weren't completely pointless! I can't save everybody. I can't save anybody. There's nothing for me there but heartache. But I swore I'd go home. I told everybody in the greenhouse I'd go home. I talked about it all winter. I'd look like a fool if I backed out now."

"Ah, well, you certainly wouldn't want to look foolish. After all, as we discussed at our last meeting, wisdom is knowing when to move, and when to stay still..."

"Exactly! Although now that I think about it... maybe it's better to look like a fool than to act like one."

"Could be."

That afternoon, when the human made its usual rounds of the greenhouse, it noticed the bird-of-paradise looked a bit droopy. Muttering about soil composition, the human began rummaging through some bins and attributed the rustling of leaves at its back to the light breeze entering through the open door. How surprised it would have been if it had turned around in that moment and seen a large basil plant waddle into the greenhouse and heave itself into a pot.

When the human had gone, the bird-of-paradise turned to its dear friend. "Why are you here? I thought you were going home?"

"I am home," said Little Baldy, and for the first time, be directed a root downward.

*See J.J. Drew's story "Clod-Shodden" online at Metaphorosis.
If you liked it, leave a comment. Authors love that!
Remember to subscribe to our e-mail updates so you'll know when
new stories are posted.*

About the story

I was participating in a holiday story swap event, and my assigned prompt requested a story containing a sentient basil plant and an evil penguin.

The prompter probably expected something much sillier than what I delivered, but as I pondered basil gardening and how a sentient creature would react to such treatment, it struck me as less "silly" and more "existentially horrific." Thus "Clod-Shodden" was conceived.

A question for the author

Q: Have you always wanted to be a writer?

A: Honestly? No. I know there are many stories out there of people who started writing as children and completed their first novel draft in their teens.

That's not me.

While I've always loved reading, I never felt like I had stories to tell. Then, in my early thirties, a story idea popped into my head and refused to go away. I decided to write it down, if only to get it out of my mind.

I quickly discovered that my writing abilities weren't up to the task.

Determined to do the idea justice, I set about honing my craft, and the strangest thing happened. It was like a mental floodgate had opened; the more I wrote, the more ideas I had.

I've been writing ever since.

About the author

J.J. Drew lives in New Orleans where she spends her days writing, training animals, and singing.

Seven Scraps Unwritten

L. Chan

Scrap 1: Monograph on the four catechisms

The first catechism of Eulalia is DIVERSITY LEADS TO STRENGTH. Its sigil is a square made of four interlocked components, reminiscent of hands each grasping the wrist of the next, forming a box.

Scrap 1 has an annotation, handwritten: This logos is one of the most complex in the Logocracy of Eulalia. This and the other three logos are said to be without beginning, just as the Logocracy is without beginning. The scholarship of history needs to cut through this jingoism – even mountains have beginnings; so too our Logocracy. Any logos starts by erasing the parchment or substrate beneath it. What was erased to create Eulalia? To give way to the Logocracy?

Scrap 2: Transcript of the thesis defence of Thera

Thera: The Conceit in the Republic of Eulalia is not illusion, although most people think it is. The magic of Eulalia is delusion; instead of seeing things that aren't there, people believe things are there that are not. Consider the walls of the University. We do not need to paint them as other nations do; a trained logomancer needs only to scribe the logos for red upon them, and if enough people believe that the walls are red, everyone will.

Third chair: Apprentice Thera, you seek to ascend to Journeyer and you present the pap that we feed to children in school.

Thera: I present the converse, that the principle can be reversed. There is an antithesis to logomancy, and its roots are within what I just explained. What if the opposite could be achieved: that things could be uncreated, not by the delusion of the many but by the will of the few?

Seventh chair: A decade's worth of study, and you bring to us debunked theses, Journeyer. Your thesis defence need not proceed.

Thera: I am due my hour, honoured chair. The charter guarantees it, and I claim this right. We are unique amongst the kingdoms, alone in our system of rule, lasting as long as the other kingdoms but without strife and struggle. The same charter that keeps the peace and establishes the ten Chairs gives me an hour.

Seventh chair: Look how she demands. We should never have taken a mongrel 'mancer like you into the University. The Book of Lies is a myth; something for separatists and agitators and ingrates who do not value the gifts of Eulalia.

Thera: I did not mention the Book of Lies, honoured seventh.

Seventh chair: I'll not have you being smart-mouthed with a Chair, you backwoods child.

Tenth chair: Thera is my student, seventh. We are here to question her theories, not her lineage.

Seventh chair: No need to remind, Tenth; we would have known her as yours from her debasement of orthodoxy. Always abusing your discretion to bring us those furthest from the ways of the Logomancy. And encouraging them towards spurious inquiry.

Scrap 2 ends here. The full transcript has been forcefully torn out of University thesis records. Only this page survives. The scribe has no recollection of the exchange.

Scrap 3: 4th year Academic Report of Journeyer Thera

Journeyer Thera is but a middling student – a level belying her intellect. Her work, when she does apply herself, is brilliant. In her third year, she rather elegantly conjoined two obscure logos to solve a term problem at least a fifth more efficiently than the model answer. Had she handed in her solution on time, she would be in line for an academic prize and her choice of supervisors at the Academy.

In outlook, she is prone to distraction. She uses twice as much paper and ink as the next student, and most of it wasted on half scribbled proofs. Thera imbibes far too freely of the student presses, addled by dangerous thought when she isn't dashing her head out against ancient unsolved logos. A dreamer and not a completionist, and unlikely to go far in Logomancy.

I beseech you, honoured Proctor, not to accede to the Academy's assigned supervisor. She has done nothing to warrant being assigned a master of any note, let alone the Tenth Chair. Tell them that she is ill, that a tragedy has befallen her family. Were she to demonstrate her incompetence to the Tenth Chair, our department would be a laughing stock for years.

Scrap 4: Banned playbill circulated across the Academy campus

LIES LIES LIES LIES

THE LOGOCRACY IS NOT BUILT ON THE CATECHISMS. IT IS BUILT ON LIES. WHAT OF THE SHORTAGE, WHAT OF THE RIOTS, WHAT OF THE MASSACRES?

WHAT OF THE MISSING?

THE BOOK OF LIES IS REAL. THE BOOK OF LIES TAKES AWAY OUR HISTORY, OUR FRIENDS. THE FOUNDATIONS ARE FALSE. THE CHAIRS ARE COMPLICIT. EVEN THE TENTH.

LIES LIES LIES

A scrawled message on the reverse:
"Esteemed Tenth, the penmanship on the playbill is rather brutish; mayhap it has roots far from our fair capital? You grow nostalgic as your time wanes, sweet Tenth. Your protégé reminds me much of you in your youth. We value original thought, but within reasonable bounds: a lesson you have yet to teach young Thera. A warning from one chair to another, school young Thera quickly, lest the First chair withdraw your prerogative to choose your successor."

Scrap 5: The Rules of Succession of Eulalia, An Intercepted Dispatch from the H.E. Elevier, Emissary of the Empire Sound

The High Chair is rotated amongst the ten Chairs of the Logocracy, in the order of their numbers, each ruling a year in turn. Nine of the ten chairs have not changed since we started keeping records in Sound. They are immortal, but not like the Undying Queen of Dark Under The Mountain, who rules from her crystal sarcophagus. Some craft protects nine chairs, the easiest guess being logomancy, although the logos for immortality must then be a closely guarded secret. It would be of great import to the Emperor were we able to procure it.

Only the tenth chair changes. The means of succession are opaque. Once, at a formal dinner a month ago I asked the Fourth chair, a woman of startling plainness and skinnier than a broom handle, what purpose this served. She replied that hubris accretes to immortality like rust to old iron, and only the Tenth chair keeps them all honest. Influence could be brought to bear, if only we knew how they chose the Tenth. I sought the Tenth at the dinner, but could not procure an opportunity to speak with him; his evening was taken up by a young lady, broad shouldered and dark, from warmer climes. If there were reason for a simple student to be at a dinner thrown by the Logocracy, it is lost on me.

Nevertheless, elements of unrest also exist in Eulalia, albeit under control. Insurgency could weaken Eulalia and be to our benefit, but Eulalia is frustratingly stable. More so than her neighbours with the same constraints of rain and crop, but absent the force of arms that would quell protest. Dissidents whisper of some branch of logomancy that we've not yet seen, something that erases instead of creates. Perhaps this is even more valuable than the secret of the nine chairs.

I have another minor complaint against our historians – the schooling provided to me about Eulilian history was far from accurate. For example, the reported riots amidst the famine two score years ago don't seem to have happened at all. The same with the attempted annexure of West Eulalia by our Empire seventy-six years ago. Nobody in the country remembers these, even amongst those with no love for the Logocracy. The further from home I get, the more ridiculous these histories sound. I tried to find them in the précis given to all Empire diplomats, but they seem to have gone. It appears the air itself in Eulalia cannot stomach lies like this.

Scrap 5 ends here. Elevier was known to have subsequently divorced his Empire wife, and settled down in the Eulalian capital for the rest of his life. He never left the city and continued to draw a modest but adequate pension from the Empire. He never communicated with his embassy again.

Scrap 6: Requisition chit for additional workmen for renovation works on the Academy Library

Name: Eksbrys, Sub-Chair of Library
        Management
To: Department of Works, Fourth
        Chair

Date: 21st Day of Winterterm
Order: 4   workmen   from   the
          Department of Conservation,
          to restore a partially collapsed
          wall in the library.

Scrap 6: Written on the overleaf of the chit, in the different writing.
"As a sub-chair, you should have known to pay attention to works
around the Folded Library. You know that the Book is inscribed on
the walls within. Were it not for the quick actions of the Journeyer
studying in the Folded Library, the men would have left with their
memories intact, to great mischief. Still, a more permanent solution
is needed. The Book must take care of them. You will see to
pensions and compensation to their families – Second Chair."

Scrap 7: Excerpt from a graded assignment, submitted by Journeyer Athyl

Eulalian society is based on four simple rules; four catechisms
each represented by a logos. The catechisms themselves are of
breath-taking complexity; none but the most talented logomancers
can even dream of scribing one, and their services are always in
demand.

The craft of Logomancy turns towards the continued
evolution of all our logos, the paring of superfluous lines,
collapsing form until purer intent remains. Yet research on the
four base logos of our society is forbidden by the ten chairs. Their
forms remain archaic, with nested logos adding to needless
intricacy.

That the ten chairs take such pains to develop the craft of
Logomancy elsewhere, but forbid it on the catechisms is telling.
That the law has been in place since the establishment of the
positions of chairs suggests that the longevity of our means of
government is linked to our catechisms. After all, our magic is
based on delusion and what more powerful delusion is there than
our belief in the catechisms?

So armed, I sought to dissect one of the logos representing
the first catechism, and there it was – a subtle work, echoed in the

other three catechisms: ancient sublogos speaking to life and regrowth, turned towards the continued rule of the chairs. In seeing the way out of one problem, I have found another. There is no reason why the magic could not go ten ways instead of nine.

While we remember the names of the tenth chairs through to the current, there has never been a death celebration for a single one. While not prone to the wilder theories circulating about the Academy campus, I cannot help but wonder at the potential for a double tragedy, that the tenth chair, with the opportunity to learn the secrets I've found here, has the opportunity to change the system and never does. Has the opportunity to grasp immortality but never does. Has the opportunity to die as the rest of us do, but is just another victim of the Book of Lies.

Scrap 7, Handwritten comments:

Dear Athyl, this is a promising start to your final year at the academy, but this paper should be rewritten in a less controversial manner, and perhaps one which less excoriates your thesis supervisor. You are right about more things than you know now, and headstrong, and hopeful. All the reasons why I chose you, all the reasons I was chosen.

The nine have hidden their power in the basic foundations of our country, but more terrifying is their power to erase, to make us forget. Even ascension is paid for by a tithe of memory, but we never forget hope. Even after they have unwritten what I was, I see in you what I hoped to be.

I invite you to join me in the library after hours. My name to the guards will see you in. Your craft has a ways to go before you can call yourself logomancer, but your mind can no longer be sharpened by the classroom. Your instruction will continue in the Folded Library, as mine once did.

Your Supervisor, Tenth Chair Thera.

See L. Chan's story "Seven Scraps Unwritten" online at Metaphorosis.
If you liked it, leave a comment. Authors love that!
Remember to subscribe to our e-mail updates so you'll know when new stories are posted.

About the story

This story started out as an experiment in form – namely epistolary or a list story, something I'd not done before. It was tough going, managing world building, plot, a message, and a magic system within the word count. It started out with far less words, which really didn't hit all the marks. I loved the conceits of having open magic systems run on skill and craft rather than on birthright, and how those systems might be used to perpetuate systems of power and abuse, and this story is the result.

A question for the author

Q: What's a genre you'd like to write, but don't or can't?

A: I'd love to write a heist story, either cyberpunk or fantasy. I've tried once or twice but the craft of getting a good twist in plain sight, without resorting to pulling stuff out of a hat has thus far eluded me. There's a lot to love in the heist genre – getting a gang together, often with new or old frictions, backstories, cool tricks and pulling things back from the brink at the last minute through redirection. One day, I'll get there.

About the author

L. Chan hails from Singapore. He spends most of his time wrangling two dogs. His work has appeared in places like *Translunar Travellers Lounge, Podcastle,* and *the Dark*. He tweets occasionally @lchanwrites.

lchanwrites.wordpress.com

Donald Q. Haute, Gentleman Inquisitator, and the Peril of the Pythogator

David A. Hewitt

Inquisitator's Log:
July 11, 20—; 11:53 pm
The Donald Q. Haute residence, Springstump Township

The electromail came in the night, heralded by a *ping* from my desktop computing-box. My Inquisitator's training snapped me instantly from deepest REM to full wakefulness, and I leapt, puma-fashion, from the bed.

To: DQHInquisit8@squiggle.web
From: Ballyhoo495371475@orgom.net
Subject: Porthos lost! Please help!

A foreboding fell upon me. This *Porthos*: a priceless diamondjade idol of ancient Mesopocambria? A white-bearded guru-monk who'd discovered the Muddy Lotus of Immortality and been abducted by nefarious agents unknown? I opened the electromail with a lightning tap on my clickermouse.

Hi Mr. Qhoute,

Porthos disappeared yesterday. She was by the fence last I saw her, digging. She can squeeze under if she digs hard, but usually the afternoons are too humid, so she gives up to lie in the shade or lap up pool water. But this time when I came out she was gone.

Our yard borders on a grapefruit grove that borders on the Everglades. No sign of her in the grove, and the police WILL NOT HELP!!! No response from our flyers either.

I remembered you from an Internet about your investigations. I believe ONLY YOU can BRING PORTHOS BACK SAFE. I will of course cover part of your costs. Please reply ASAP!

Yours desperately,
Lusitania D. Ballyhoo
Philodendron Furlongs, FL

P.S. There are rumors of something prowling the Everglades nearby, a creature unknown to regular science.

P.S.S. Porthos is half malamute, one-quarter Himalayan yak terrier, and the other quarter is kind of a question mark.

Did I hesitate? Ha! A mysterious crypto-creature, coupled with a some-expenses-paid Florida wetlands vacation in the sunny summertime? I replied in a flash.

Will arrive in two days' time. Stop. Please prepare admixture of buckwheat flour and talcum powder, so I may begin immediately to dust for prints in the grove and in the Everglades beyond. Stop.

Yours in earnestness,
DQH

Inquisitator's Log:
July 13, 20—; 8:22 am
Springstump Municipal Aero-Jetplane Port

After a grueling day of preparation, I found myself at the aero-jetplane port, watching for my assistant. They'd paged her thrice: *Sammy Jo P—, please approach the ticket counter at Gate Zeta-Three-Dee.* The aerocraft had boarded, and I was holding the gate, craning my neck, when finally she came jogging into view.

"What kept you?" I called.

"You said 9:30."

"No, 8:30; definitely 8:30. Did you mis-hear me?"

"Well, you said it only once, followed by a verbal list of, as I counted, twenty-seven items to buy… and didn't mention an airline or flight number, and hung up before I could get a word in edgewise—"

As the attendant herded us down the porta-tunnel, I admonished and exhorted my callow amanuensis.

"I've told you before, Sammy Jo: In the *Lexipaedia Inquisitatus* under E, you'll find neither hair nor hide of the word excuse. Don't you remember the Seventeenth Credo? *Excuses are like endocrine systems: everyone seems to have one, but there's no explaining what earthly purpose they serve.*"

We were buckling in when, under her breath, Sammy Jo mumbled what sounded like "funky Inquisitating can bind my adze." I presumed she was reciting—erringly—some obscure *Lexipaedia* entry.

Inquisitator's Log:
July 13, 20—; 2:42 pm
Philodendron Furlongs, South Florida

A handbill, evidently printed on a desktop computa-inker, adorned a telephone pole in front of the Ballyhoo residence:

LOST:
Answers to "Porthos"
Reward for Information Leading To

Above this was a digi-pic of the dear departed. His black-and-white eyes sparkled behind fluffs of black-and-white fur, right up to the tips of his scampish black-and-white ears. Black-and-white puffy legs terminated in perfectly proportioned black-and-white front paws.

"Colored ink might've done her more justice," said Sammy Jo.

Our tapping with the flamingo-themed doorknocker was answered by a respectable-looking platinum-haired EuroAmerican pensioner-gal wearing raccoon-themed slippers, shiny sweat-trousers, and a flamingo-themed hoodsweater. Love and grief, mingled with determination, burned behind black eyelashes as thick and vivacious as a lunging nest of newborn snakes.

She waved us in, and as she guided us to the kitchen table-ette, I introduced myself and Sammy Jo, "My assistant, protégée, and mentee."

"*Manatee??*" Ms. Ballyhoo blinked blankly. "So you're half—I mean, I didn't know that was possible..."

Sammy Jo explained, then—as an A.B.D. degree holder in the zoological sciences—the fine distinction between an apprentice and a cud-chewing aquatic mammal.

"Let's delay no longer!" I interjected. "Show me where your fur-bearing friend Porthos was last seen."

Our host led us onto a screened patio—*by Vesuvius, the humidity!!!*—where she pointed to a hole under the vinyl fence, beyond which loomed a grove of grapefruit trees. Turning back to Ms. Ballyhoo, I noted a wellspring of tears flooding her eyes; as my heartstrings twanged, I mentally genuflected to Madame Helena Rubinstein, inventor of waterproof mascara.

A professionally fenced grapefruit grove is no daunting target for the master Inquisitator, particularly when the gate boasts no lock, nor even a functioning latch. Yet dust as I might for paw-prints, or shoe-prints—I hadn't ruled out the vile crime of *caninus abductimem*—nothing was revealed, even by Sammy Jo's trained zoologist's eye or my ear-mounted maxi-magnifying lens. We *did* soon discern, though, that we were not alone in the grove.

"*We're not alone in the grove,*" whispered Sammy Jo.

My Inquisitator's keen fivefold senses told me she was right— and that this was no career grapefruitsman, this young fellow tramping toward us, yammering at his upraised porta-Y-Phone. A splash of bleached hair enmaned his pale, sparse-bearded face, and against the sun's ravages—*by Hephaestus's forges, the heat!!!* —he was warded only by a white Tee-shirt bearing the red MeeMeeMeeeToob® logo. As he approached he was filming his own face, which caused him to trip and tumble over a green grapefruit-to-be.

"He's one of those amateur Webnet journalists," I murmured. "*Log-floggers*, I believe they're called."

"Sounds about right," said Sammy Jo.

"Just what do you know," intoned the flogger, regaining his feet, "about the disappearance of Porthos, the Hound of the Ballyhoos?" He flipped the cam-phone upon us.

"First," said Sammy Jo, "a malamute-terrier cross is *not* a hound, you moth-wit. And second..." *Second* was a flurry of expletives and bleep-words I shan't repeat.

"Florida Statute X-slash-Zed-slash-Twenty-two, subsection Seven-Bee, proscribes filming private citizens without express signatory permission," I touchéd.

"Except," answered this gadfly, "when the subject is *in toto* of committing a crime... such as trespassing in a grapefruit grove."

He had us there. I sleeve-mopped my sweat-sopped brow.

"Um, *in toto*, Bumbledork?" said Sammy Jo. "Then there's how you've been filming *yourself* committing that same infraction..."

Undeterred, the fellow inched forward, cameraphone still rolling. I could now see his press-pass—*Largo Ponce* was his name —but a) it was clearly falsified, a home-rigged ID-card-and-lanyard mockup; and b) grapefruit groves do not, as a rule, rigorously verify press credentials.

I pointed pointedly. "That card might fool the rubes, but you've met your match-maker in this trained Inquisitator! Besides —a true journalist would carry a microphone adorned with teevee station initials."

At this, Ponce looked down to his sad excuse for a press-pass... and froze.

Beneath his Doo-Dee-Das sneakerkicks lay what appeared to be a shedded snake-skin—the largest this globe-roaming Inquisitator had ever seen. I'd read about the recent Everglades python infestoonment, so this was no great surprise. Then Sammy Jo gasped. She strode forward, and Largo Ponce the MeeMeeMeeeToober skipped back, clear of the skin-husk.

Sammy Jo gingerly hoisted the skin. Large. Thick. Then she spread it out, so it became clear to see...

The snake-skin sported a pair of what looked for all the world like short mesh sleeves. Whatever foul serpent had slouched toward the Ballyhoo house had *legs*.

We snooped around the grove further, seeking other traces of the *thing* whose cast-off husk we'd found. For Largo Ponce, the late-afternoon heat proved too much—as a native Floridian he was more acclimated to the bracing chill of airconditioned homes, airconditioned stores, airconditioned schools, and airconditioned automocars—so he soon departed.

The heat—*by Jove's thunderbolts, the heat!!!*—had begun to abate, and light was fading, as Sammy Jo and I scouted a last lip of turf abutting the Everglades.

"It's very wet," I observed.

"They call it the River of Grass," Sammy Jo replied.

"On a state map this region appears as land, but its actual state is hardly such stately dry land—aside from those little islands."

"Hammocks," said Sammy Jo.

"Ham-hocks? So called because they're frequented by the Everglades Ever-pig?"

"Ham-*mocks*," she repeated.

At that moment our conversationalizing, and the quiet of Everglades dusk, were interrupted by a swoosh-swooshing of boots in the long grass and the splish-splashing of... not far off, a scientific-looking bearded fellow, of pink-skinned Caucasian stock and middling age, was sampling with a scoop in the shallows at the Glades' edge. I hailed him.

"A fellow scientifico?" I called. He ignored me. The Inquisitator, though, is not lint on a trouser-leg, so easily brushed off. "Are you a student of the bio-ecologic disciplines?" Still nothing. I persisted: "What do you make, *monsignor*..." I motioned to Sammy Jo—who'd tucked the skin into her day-pack, and now produced it— "...of *this*?"

At the sight of what dangled from Sammy Jo's hands, he halted. Then he approached—a tall thick fellow in a very scientifically rigorous hat.

"Where... did you find this?"

"In the grove." Sammy Jo gestured. "The South Florida biome's outside my expertise, but still—something's *off* with this, isn't it?"

The bio-ecologist flusteredly unpocketed a tape-o'-the-measure and took the shedded skin's dimensions. He stared.

"So?" Sammy Jo gently refolded the skin.

"91 centimeters..." the eco-biologizer murmured. Then, assertively: "I'll need to take that for further study. This is federal parkland; you're not permitted to remove flora or fauna." He extended a hand.

"But what *is* it?" said Sammy Jo. "And who exactly are you?"

"Invasive species." The man *gimme*'d with his fingertips.

Sammy Jo looked to me. A *zoologist and her moult-leavings are not soon parted*, as the saying goes. But the Inquisitator's Code is clear about respecting authoritative personages. I scooped the skin from her reluctant hands and passed it to the man, along with my calling-card.

"Please contact me, sirrah, when you conclude anything. We're investigating a lost pet, who answers to *Porthos*, and fear this serpentonic invader may be implicated."

The fellow disregarded me, drifting away as one bedazed, gazing at the skin.

"You have to at least get his—" muttered Sammy Jo, then shouted, "What's your *name*?"

"Frank," the man answered, and departed into the Everglade night. Now a barking, distant but distinct, sounded over the waters. I marked my position, noted the time, and bi-angulated the sound's origin with the constellation Puppis. We'd no embarkable means of pursuing the barking this night; but pursue it we would.

Inquisitator's Log:
July 14, 20—; 6:24 am
Philodendron Furlongs, Florida

The flogger Largo Ponce came a-knocking early, as Sammy Jo and I were leaving the Ballyhoo home. We ignored him as we boarded the rent-a-mobile, until he crowed,   "I got a *lot* of comments on that vlog—the most ever. Some da-bomb theories about Porthos, and about *it*. I even gave it a name."

Though Sammy Jo frowned fire, my training was to leave no stone's moss ungathered. "What theories, pray tell?"

"Well, like that old lady Ballyhoo kidnapped her own dog: a false-flag dognapping."

When I remo-unlocked the rent-a-mobile, Ponce yanked open a door and hurled himself into the back seat.

"You weren't invited," I scolded.

Sammy Jo shot a hand in and took hold of the young scamp's shoulder. "Why in shit's name would she kidnap her own dog?"

Ponce launched into an explication, holding up his 'phone to show a tangled chart of governmental and nonexistent-organizational connections. After three minutes, Sammy Jo muscled him from the automocar—he filmed this, of course.

"Maybe you're both actors in the false-flag too," he wailed. Sammy Jo started the rent-a, but before shutting my door, I turned to Ponce.

"You said you gave *it* a name?"

"I did. I call it... the *alli-thon*."

We'd found a purveyor of aeroprop-boats catering to early-rising swamp-hoppers. The sun was only just ascending behind us as, after a perfunctory tutorial, Sammy Jo *brrrmmmm*'ed the aero-propulsor to a roar and blew us out into the vast shallows of the Everglades. Borrowing Sammy Jo's tech-a-phone, I web-skated to Ponce's flogsite: 7,204 views between dusk and dawn. Porthos's travails had set the flog-world afire.

I vigilated in the bow as we beelined toward the heading I'd marked. Alligators—the standard-issue type—drifted loggishly, while birds of every hue in the colored-pencil box fished, floated, or flapped all around. On one island—one hammock—after another, we disemboated and searched. But we heard no barking, nor saw sign of that other dread creature.

Inquisitator's Log:
July 14, 20—; 10:27 am
The Everglades, Florida

Hours later, dripping with sweat—*Deus Ex Infernus, the heat!!!*—and bebothered by buzz-bugs, we paused in a hammock-tree's shade. Sammy Jo tickled her Y-Phone's vidscreen.

"Oh … my … balls." Her eyes grew wide as sorcerers.

"What is it?"

"Largo Ponce…" She turned the 'phone my way. There was Ponce, wearing bespoke chest-waders, trudging knee-deep into the Everglades. He'd braved the heat and set off into this vastest of wetlands alone to find *"The Truth about Porthos!!!"* Some minutes in, he remarked that his batteries were "low as shit"—then gasped, spun the 'phone away from his own face… and it kept spinning and *ker-plupped* into the water. The vid-log murked, and blacked out.

"Oh … my … balls," Sammy Jo repeated.

The response was swift. By early afternoon the Everglades were humming with helichoppers, *brmm*'ing with aeroprop-boats, and hrumphing with hunters. We kept up our own search—for Porthos? For Ponce? In seeking we might find one, the other, or both, so seek we did.

As we aeroboated, we listened to floggers and major news channels alike speculating whether Ponce had merely mis-stepped, dropped his 'phone, and now wandered lost, or whether he'd been ensnared by… apparently none had watched the vidfootage where Ponce named the creature; they'd all taken to calling it the *croco-py*.

"In this vast queendom of *alligator mississippiensis, that's* what they call it?" Sammy Jo grumped as she cozied the boat up to yet another hammock. "Whatever it is, damn sure it's not a crocodile."

Every Y'all-Mart store south of Kissimmee must have been denuded of shot- and rifle- and autosemi-minicannon guns, of ammoshells, and of camocaps, camopants, camovests, and camototebags. A sporadic chorus of hues and cries; a popcorn-symphony of gunshots; the occasional *hissplash* of bullets hitting still waters. Hunters levelled their sights at gators, at imagined pythons—at anything that flitted, flapped, or skittered.

By early afternoon we spotted the first re-outfitted aeroprop-tour-boat, boasting a hand-painted sign:

CROCO-PY TOURS!! HELP FIND PONCE AND PORTHOS!!!
ADULTS $23.00, CHILDREN $22.50

and at 2:12 pm, our august President lent the force of his bullying pull-pit by Tooting on his *Twit-horn* account:

Terrorist CROCO-PY strikes again and losercrats do nothing. Scumbags want IMMIGRANTS AND CROCO-PYS to eat your Real American babys. CrocOpy/Imigrant Wall... ...is only soLuTion.

Soon thereafter, more crackle of firearm-fire, then a distinctly proximate **THOOM**—and water poured in through a shotgun-spray bite in the 'boat's low-riding hull.

"*Swiftly!*" I cried. "*Give me your pants!*" Sammy Jo ignored me, though, preoccupied with something on her leg. Without a centi-second to waste, I yanked up my ankle-zippers, de-trousered myself, and stuffed my waterproof khaki M.M. Spleen breeches into the breach. This did prevent swampwater from swamping our boat; relieved, I turned to see Sammy Jo picking bloody slivers of aluminum boat-hull out of her lower leg. The wound was far from mortal, and as I applied second-aid, I mused upon what more dire danger we'd be in if *not* surrounded by good guys with guns.

Though uncertain of direction—Sammy Jo's Y-Phone lay now inert, devoided of charge—we carried on. Rampant as public response had been, we were at no moment alone. There were the two mustachioed AlabamaCaucasians—convinced Ponce and Porthos had been spirited away by a Bigfooted Sasquatch—who questioned us zealously. Then came the trio of bushy-bearded whitepeople Oregonians, certain these had been *Chupacabra* attacks—and that we were in cahoots with the *'cabra*. No sooner had we extricated ourselves from their Third Degree than a third group accosted us.

"Where are they?" accused the first of the quadrille of Michiganians, who also happened to be white, all dressed in flag-and-eagle-motifed jumpsuits. Who was I to judge apparelments, though, as with trousers stopping up boat leaks I greeted them in bare legs and Inquisitator-issue orange-drab undershorts?

"You mean Ponce and Porthos." Weariness weighted Sammy Jo's voice.

"*They know,*" growled the second Michiganator.

"Wing fur," hissed the third, whose demeanor marked him as the squad *capitan.* "Search the boat. Search them."

"What do you urine-soaked shitstains think you're doing?!" protested Sammy Jo as the first two schlumped into our 'boat, tottering, splashing gladeswater over the gunwales.

"We've seen enough to know"—the leader eye-scoured us —"when somebody's in league with—"

"*Mothman*," singsonged the fourth, a short pinktanned fellow with eyes twitchy and wild as sparklers.

"Mothman?!" It was Sammy Jo's turn to bug her eyes out.

I intervened. "The Mothman, if such exists, is adapted to the monongahela silt loam and beech forests of west-southwestern West Virginia. Like a rare orchid or a hothouse zucchini, the likely-apocryphal Mothman could not readily inhabitate these sultry wetlands."

"Just what a fella'd say if he was hiding a Mothman," said the leader. One of his hench-hunters began to frisk Sammy Jo's dorsal area for concealed moth-wings; she beat his hands away.

A tense standoff ensued. These patriotic Americans were slinging guns, and I visualized which of my *Bart-itsu* moves might disarm multiple Mothmanites without overturning a watercraft. No sooner had I assumed a double-spearhand altercative pose, though, than the men relented and retreated to their own rent-a-vessel.

With a stridulous parting shot—"*Mothman lovers*"—the leader signaled the wiry fourth fellow to start the 'boat, which he did, repeating "*Mothman*" before throttling up and steering away.

As the afternoon wore on, Sammy Jo and I drew away, deeper into the River of Grass—away from the kerfuffular hullabaloo—and I confess we wound up adrift.

Refueling stations are not to be found on every block in the Everglades. In fact, there *are* no blocks in the Everglades. Thus we ended up, as Phoebus Apollo's punishing sun-chariot retreated to its nocturnal garage, stuck some yards away from a hammock—mucking through water to the waists of our chest-waders, tugging the dead-weight aeroprop-boat behind.

"I am gratified," I said, hands blistering on the tug-rope, "that we brought campage gear, in alignment with Inquisitator preparedness standards."

"A pup tent with no sleeping bags," groaned Sammy Jo. "And only because *I* added it to the list."

"Flint and tinder for fire—"

"A grill-lighter," she interrupted. "I knew which of us would spend a half-hour squatting in lacerating sawgrass, swiping with a rock for sparks."

"A packful of waterproof regulation playing cards, 52 plus jokers, to keep us diversionably entertained—"

"But not a drop of wine. Or beer. Or tequila. Or even gin," Sammy Jo finished. "Shows what you know about the great outdoors."

We'd arrived at the hammock. Sammy Jo tied off the 'boat, and we clambered onto land in the last vestiges of twilight. We moved toward what looked like open—if lumpy—ground beyond thick undergrowth, poking with a walking-stick to disperse any hostile fauna.

At the clearing's edge, under clouded moonlight, I handed my walking-stick to Sammy Jo and ignited my flash-torch as I moved to step onto the uneven ground. I halted, though, with foot poised in midair.

Much as *homo sapienses* have evening haunts, favored party-places, so apparently do alligators. The clearing where we'd intended to camp was one such nighttime hot-spot for saurians beyond count. And though they seemed unbothered by their own kin crowding against, slumping upon, even creeping over them, I intuited that my feet would elicit a different response—call it *speciesism*, but we weren't inclined to argue diversity theory with an alligator horde.

Treating absquatulation as the better part of valor, we turned tail.

From the refuge of the inert 'boat, we scanned the horizon. North-by-west-northwest, a wide tuft of growth broke the star-speckled horizon: another hammock.

Getting there, though, in an unmotile aeroprop-boat, was no easy matter. Harkening to Credo 71 of the Inquisitator's Code—*Be prepared; but if preparation is the parent, it's apparent that it must be paired with its providential progeny, improvisation*—we used a soup ladle and a metal meter-stick from our knapsacks as paddles to propel the heavy 'boat.

We were beyond weary when we heard the unmistakable *hummmm* of another aeroprop-boat.

Sammy Jo and I shouted and waved flashlights, and I even ignited a flare to brandish. The 'boat drew nearer... *rescuetour operator?... Everglades Five-Oh Swamppolice?...* and then was upon us, droning down to a slow drift as the bow-wave rocked us. In the flare-glare, we saw the occupants: a teen-aged First Nations youth and his teen-aged girlfriend, half Indian and half—my keen Inquisitator's eye was hampered by harsh flare-light—Pakistani? Bengali? Indian?

"You guys okay?" the boy asked.

I bowed my gratitude. "For the moment, yes—"

"But we could use a ride, or a good splash of fuel, to get us back to civilization," Sammy Jo chimed in.

The boy shook his head. "I'm running on fumes. Pops has been draining the tank at nights—something about keeping me from running amok."

"We can send someone in the morning," the girl added. "We're not headed home just yet." Sammy Jo turned to me, rolled her eyes, and mouthed *teen-agers*.

Then she sighed. "I don't relish spending the night on the floor of this boat."

"Could you at least tow us to that hammock?" I gestured.

"Logni Isle? Not the best place to spend a night," the boy warned.

"Why not?" asked Sammy Jo, but both boy and girl merely shook their heads.

"We could tow you over there," said the boy. "But my advice would be to lay low, or better yet, don't get out of the boat."

They towed us—a slow progress, with their propellant-fan blowing hugely in our faces—and set us loose just offshore, promising again to send help in the morning. Then they rode off, with a mutual touching of gluteal regions—a form of contact I presumed must be rooted in Seminole or Miccosukee tradition.

"It's hot, even this time of night," I said. Sammy Jo and I lay curled discomfitedly in the 'boat, which we'd tied to an arching tree-root beside Logni Isle.

"Damn straight. And humid. And buggy. And sober."

"I suppose I ought to apologize. This was my Inquisition, yet here you are, ever-faithful Sammy Jo, bearing your part of the burden—including birdshot in the leg, no less—with admirable composure."

I heard her shift to face me. "What, you think I'm *surprised* to get into a bizarre and needlessly dangerous situation, accompanying you on one of these... whatever these trips are."

"Still," I answered. "Educating an aspiring Inquisitator is a delicate balance. As the *Lexipaedia Inquisitatus* points out, criticism comprises a conduit to consummate competency, while praise is potentially a poison. Sometimes, though, a compliment is warranted. You've been a worthy—"

Sammy Jo laughed, a musical sound. "As much as all this Inquisiting—"

"Inquisi*tating*," I corrected.

"—as all this Inquisi*tating* is kind of a... well, scientifically speaking, it's—you know..."

"Unconventional," I supplied.

She laughed again. "Unconventional. Right. Still, I've seen and done a lot I never would've, and it really is never a dull moment."

Sammy Jo inclined forward on the bench-slat between us. I sat up too. Our faces were close, in the murky-mooned night. Under her sweat- and rain-bedraggled mop of dark hair, those coffee-colored eyes were lovely.

"Have you," she half-whispered, "ever thought about—"

And just then a pattering rain began to fall, swiftly intensifying into a drumroll on the aluminum hull.

The quiet moment gave way to a flurry of action: pulling ponchos from packs, and endeavoring to cover the boat.

"We daren't sleep here," I said at last. Try as we might, rain could not be kept out; to slumber aboat was to risk swamping or drowning in the night.

So we set off with our supplies, with the tent, leaping onto wet roots for a foothold on the island. There we found a game-trail of sorts, about shoulder width. We followed its twists and turns, vaguely illumined by flashlight, in the pouring rain. The trail dead-ended at the best spot we'd seen, a flattish patch between the "knees" of a banyan tree. There we attempted to pitch our tent.

"Son of a bee-hutch!" Sammy Jo rasped.

I looked at her blankly.

"The tent fly—I took it out of my pack, digging for a poncho, and left it in the boat." With this, Sammy Jo tromped off, flashlight beam skimming before her. I sheltered as best I could in the fly-less tent, but rain poured right through the mesh crown and onto my own poncho-domed crown.

We'd pitched the tent facing the tree, so we'd have cover for any ingresses and egresses, and I'd left the zip-gap open in expectation of Sammy Jo's return. This proved to be an error when I heard a rustling from the entry behind me and felt the sudden shock of a tazerizer zapgunning my nervous system, rendering my finely honed neural reflexes useless. I then felt a net thrown over me, then a sack over my head, and a lariat-hoop pinned my arms to my torso. Visionless, I struggled, but more zapgunning broke my resistance, and I was dragged across a short span into what seemed, against all probability, to be an elevator.

Here I doubted my own sanity, but my razor-sharp Inquisitator's training kicked in and I sniffed. Yes—the distinctive scent of elevator was unmistakable.

What vile trap was this, yanking me from the safety of a rain-inundated, alligator-, insect-, and snake-inhabited hammock, down, down to some elevator-accessible Goblin-Town?

After some further dragging—I'd gone limp, to conserve my strength—the sack was pulled from my head. Blinking in fluorescing light, I saw a resoundingly luxuriant science-laboratory. The lab-table countertop was plated in gold, as were the faucet-taps. Plush velvet wallpaper descended to baseplates also trimmed in gold, which gave way to mahogany flooring, upon whose elegant hardwoodenness I now sprawled, bound. All around were cages or tanks housing mice, drosophila flies, geckos, garter snakes, and more.

And staring at me from my side was, to my shock and undoing, Dr. Frank.

"Why—" I began, then, curious, shifted gearshifters: "How do you afford all this?"

"I'm a global warming scientist," he answered. "So long as I propound the position of anthropogenic global warming, the government grants unlimited funding. Most global warming scientists have gold-plated laboratories and homes, while those who question human influence on climate live on dog food in hovels, at least until they're murdered by the black helicopters."

"You live here..." I posited. It is the Inquisitator's job to weld observation to intuition, forging a Sword of Knowingfulness that slices to the heart of things. The unmade bed in this studio-room, and the trash receptacle overflowing with micro-ovened meal containers were, I admit, useful clues.

He nodded. "Alone," he said, trying to hide a mournful note.

Yet this was not quite true: I glanced around again at the abundance of captivificated life. Then I gasped. In a large, well-appointed cage to my right, granite water and food bowls beside it bespeckled with what looked like diamonds, rested a familiar-looking specimen of *puppidoggus domesticus*.

"Porthos!"

Though she didn't rise, the wayward bitch twitched her ears, wagged her tail, and turned sleepy, soulful eyes my way.

"I found her again early this morning," said Dr. Frank. A thought struck him, and he patted himself for his keys, finding them at last in the pocket of his white silk lab coat. "But it wasn't her I was looking for."

Then it all became clear, clear as a solution of acetate blended with vodka. "The Croco-py!!!" I shouted. "It's the Croco-py, the Alli-thon, you were truly looking for!" Waving my leg at the test tubes, genesplicing machines, and enormous tank-enclosure at the room's center, I cried, "You are its creator! Its progenitator!"

He spun to face me. "Stop calling it that!! *Alli-thon?? Croco-py??!* Any culture that creates such idiotic mashed-up names..." Dr. Frank now began rummaging through drawers and cabinets full of science-doing thingamawhatzits, as I covertly struggled to free myself—without success. At last he found what he'd sought: a wire-y mesh of electro-nodes, which I surmised to be either a fiendish interrogation device or lights for a Christmas wreath.

But Christmas was five months away.

"Do you mean to torture me?"

Dr. Frank smiled. "I mean to wipe your memory. True, this will be its first test, but if the device works, all knowledge of me, my secret laboratory—and of the creature—will be erased. Forever."

"But the first two of those would be unnecessary if you'd simply not abducted me," I observed.

Dr. Frank scowled as he looked, next, for an extension cord. After further scrounging through drawers, cabinets, and piles he had just triumphantly produced an orange one, of the 50-foot variety—when the elevator bell *bing*'d.

Dr. Frank whirled, extension cord in one hand, tazerizer in the other, as Sammy Jo leapt through the 'vator door into the lab.

She was unarmed, nothing to hand but the aforementioned tent-fly. But seeing me bound on the floor, and a taser-armed scientificator glaring at her, Sammy Jo took action. Stretching the vinyl-plasticene tent-fly taut, she pump-twirled it from both ends, as middle-schoolers do to transform a wet towel into a rat's-tail bullywhip.

They circled one another like Florida panthers, if in fact enough of those still exist to ever encounter one another. A feint by one... a feint by the other... the crackle of a tazerizer; the crack of a tent-fly whip... the "Ouch!! That *stings*!!" of a bearded white man with a low pain threshold... then, in passing where I lay bound on the floor, Dr. Frank came too close.

I thrust out a leg and tripped him up, so that he stumbled; he dropped the tazerizer to break his fall. He recovered, but before he could recover the weapon, Sammy Jo covered the distance with a pounce like—I already used *panther*, so let's say a pounce like a caracal. As Dr. Frank reached for the shock-gun, her fist shot out. It *thwumped* into his face. This time he sprawled onto the floor with an "*ow ow ow ow ow!!!*" while Sammy Jo also backed away, knuckle to mouth, squandering a layman's lifetime supply of *mother f-er*s and *son of a b-word*s.

"I've been doing kickboxing at the gym, but Jesus Christ a human face is fucking *hard*!" she shouted, and took it out on Dr. Frank by kicking him in the leg.

"Aaargh, Charley horse!" he wailed, and with this the outcome of the fisticuffs/footsicuffs was decided.

Sammy Jo commandeered the tazerizer and untied me while keeping a watchful eye on the now-very-mad scientist. We'd nearly reached the elevator when the bell *bing*'d one more time.

First Nations rescuers, whether teen-aged or otherwise? An accomplice of Dr. Frank's, to thwart our departure? A brown-uniformed National Park Service SWAT-battalion?

But when the doors opened, every one of us flinch-skittered back, for what emerged was—well, you've probably formed a mental picture already: half python, half alligator, enormous, though low to the floor and aero- and aqua-dynamic. Gliding into the lab, it eyed us all with a menace that transcended the reptilian and approached the human; we all recoiled still further. Yet it let us be, slither-plodding with surprising grace toward the chained Porthos. Though we dreaded what might come, not one of us deigned to intervene; instead we three, Sammy Jo, Dr. Frank, and I, all tumbled into the elevator and rammed fingers at the "UP" button.

The doors closed.

"You *created* that thing?" said Sammy Jo.

"I did." Dr. Frank's head slunk.

"But why?" I said.

"After decades of climate research, to strike fear into a populace that refuses to fear the more abstractly terrifying... to attempt what had never been done before... and maybe, just a little, because I wanted a companion..."

"You could've adopted a cat, or a dog," said Sammy Jo; the word *dog* sparked regrettable associations with poor Porthos. The elevator arrived at ground level and we all stepped out of the tree housing the elevator into a quiet night. The rain had stopped. Leaving the tent be—for lingering by the elevator was no option— we made our way over rain-saturated ground to where the airboat floated: our best refuge, though really no refuge at all. We sat silent in the boat, for minutes uncounted, until—

A rustling in the sawgrass. We all sat bolt upright.

Sammy Jo pointed the beam of her flash-light. There, emerging from the sawgrass, was the face of the creature. Though its stare locked on us, it diverted course from our boat and slipped gracefully, soundlessly, into the water.

To our rejoicement, behind it came Porthos. The serpentuous creature cast a longing gaze that way, while Sammy Jo and I clapped our hands and called out:

"Porthos! Here girl! Come, Porthos!!"

Porthos vacillated, nosing at the creature, at us, back at the creature. Then we heard a voice we never expected to hear, a hissing, guttural, yet somehow mesmeric voice.

"*Come, Porthosss. The River of Grasss shall be bed, battthhhhh, and home to usss, and we will live in fffreedom, liberated fffrom hhhuman masssstersss,*" spake the creature.

Fffreedom, though, is just another word for nothing left to lose; Porthos had waiting back at Ms. Ballyhoo's a cozy bed, frequent meals, and a sweater for when the Florida winters dipped below 68 degrees. Porthos made her choice: she hopped into the airboat, into the familiarity of human company.

And how is it that the creature, unholy amalgamism of the serpentastic and crocodillyicious, was able to speak in human tongues? Who can say? Genetic intermixing is ever a roll of the dice; the result here was fortuitous, allowing the creature to speak words thematically relevant to this tale.

Looking away from Porthos, to the sky, to stars behind thinning clouds, to cruel Fate, the creature crawled onto a nearby log of an icy pallor.

Dr. Frank called out: "Don't leave me! Stay! How can I bear knowing my child, my finest creation, is wandering alone, preying, wreaking destruction and inviting its own destruction too? Please…"

"*Sssuffering?*" the creature answered. "*What can you know of sssuffering? Of the sssuffering of a sssoul who, knowing right from wrong, virtue from viccccce, ssstill was forccced to track and kill the sssapient raccoon, the prissstine sssnowy egret, and the ffflamboyant ffflamingo, to sssate an unending hunger? The sssuffering of a sssensitive being who never got a sssingle sssyllable of reply from itsss brother the Burmessse pythhhon, or from the noble alligator, its sssisssster?*"

"They don't really speak to *anyone*," Sammy Jo consoled; but the creature seemed not to hear.

"*No companion, no love, no compassion, not even that of a fffaithhhful canine,*" it continued, stink-eyeing Porthos. The waters of the Everglades do flow, but at the glacial pace of about one meter per hour, so the log-bound creature had ample time to make its speech. In fact, I heard what sounded like claws paddling, an effort to speed things up. "*I shall keep drifffting until this log reachesss the extremity of the Earth'sss middle, letting hunger and* the *remorselesss sssun have their way, until I am extinguished entirely. What I have ssseen... I have ssseen murk of mud, rapture of rain, sssolaccce of sssky...*" The creature hissed more loudly, crescendoing toward a dramatic climax. "*I have ssseen shitheelsss burning rubber off the coassst of Pembroke Pinesss. All I've ssseen, all I've known, gone, like crocodile tearsss in the rain...*" It had drifted only inches, but the creature lowered its voice to enhance the illusion of distance, so its final words carried but faintly over the water: "*The ressst isss sssilenccce.*" And it paddled harder and was borne away, very slowly, and was lost in the dank Florida dark.

Dr. Frank wept. Neither Sammy Jo nor I could muster any sympathy for him, though, and at length, to break the maudlin spell of his sobbing, Sammy Jo spoke up:

"It may have been derivative, but that was still far and away the most impressive fucking speech I have ever heard from a reptile."

At morning light, good as their word, the First Nations teens returned—and we were saved. Arriving at civilization, we parted ways with Dr. Frank, who'd sobbed and sniffled all night until even Porthos covered her ears. Sammy Jo suggested criminal charges. But Porthos had been well cared for; Florida has no statute against possession of an unlicensed python-alligator hybrid; my captivity had lasted mere minutes; and Dr. Frank had already tasted the business end of a Sammy Jo drubbing. So we let bygones go on by, not least because even at 8 a.m., standing another minute out in the heat—*by Surtur's flaming Ragnarok-sword, the heat!!!*—was unthinkable.

Ms. Ballyhoo gushed at Porthos's homecoming, and produced the promised reward. And what of Largo Ponce? We heard no word, and in subsequent weeks, his webputer v-flog saw no postings.

Inquisitator's Log:
July 15, 20—; 5:43 pm
Bovard County Aero-Jetplane Port, Florida

"I said it before: Vloggers are *not* an endangered species," said Sammy Jo, as we sat in a Seattlebucks Coffee-café facing our departure gate.

"Keep in mind the 112th Maxim of the Inquisitator's Code: Every being is a manifestation of the All-nourishing UniForce, even a preening, mystifyingly self-absorbed log-flogger."

Sammy Jo pressed a napkin full of ice against her bruised knuckles. As for her enshrapnellated leg, our hostess had neatly antisepticized and bandaged it. "Ms. Ballyhoo was definitely a manifestation of that. How much was the reward?"

"Let's just say that even after this coffee-and-pastry indulgence, enough will remain to pay the autocarpark fee back in fair Springstump Township."

Sammy Jo readied an ungenerous phrase, but I interrupted. "We must always recollect: Inquisition is its own reward. I'm just glad she and Porthos once again have one another. Companionship means so much to laypeople—those who have not chosen the solitudinous ways of the Inquisitator."

"Companionship," Sammy Jo repeated, and fixed me with a meaningful yet cryptic look. She raised her coffee mug. We clinked a toast. "Do you think that creature was right? That true companionship is a will-o-the-wisp, a flash of swamp-gas? That we're all, in the depths of our souls, truly alone? And also—are you going to eat the other half of that bearclaw?"

Her deeper questions had never been satisfactorily answered by scholar, poet, sage, nor even by the *Lexipaedia Inquisitatus*; as with the creature, only silence could be my answer.

I slid the plate across the table. With reflexes worthy of a true *Bart-itsu* adept, she snatched it up, and the bearclaw was soon borne away, and lost in the dark of Sammy Jo's gullet.

See David A. Hewitt's story "Donald Q. Haute, Gentleman Inquisitator, and the Peril of the Pythogator" online at Metaphorosis. If you liked it, leave a comment. Authors love that! Remember to subscribe to our e-mail updates so you'll know when new stories are posted.

About the story

Pinning down a story's origins is (for me, anyway) a dicey proposition. As best I can recall, this Donald Q. Haute story had multiple inspirations. This is actually my second story featuring Haute, who is of course a weird modern analogue to Don Quixote (with humblest apologies to the ghost of Cervantes for even pretending to attempt such a thing). A good friend works in South Florida as a marine biologist, and I once accompanied him on a sampling expedition in the coastal mangrove forests. Then there were the invasive pythons, which are apparently everywhere in the Everglades now, but which nobody seems able to find when they go looking. Then there was the social media three-thousand-ring circus that surrounds us all, and the impact that has on journalism, on facts, and on genuine connection with our fellow human beings. And then somehow Frankenstein's big, bad, grandiloquent creature and his latter-day Replicant offshoot crept into the mix as well. Plunk all these ingredients into a pot, let simmer for 3- 14 months over low heat, stir well with revision and generous editorial aid, wait till timer says "BING!", and the result is "Donald Q. Haute, Gentleman Inquisitator, and the Peril of the Pythogator."

A question for the author

Q: What do you think makes a good story?

A: This is a profound question, by which I mean I find it virtually impossible to answer. If I could answer it conclusively, the number of rejection letters I receive would be much, much smaller. Sometimes it's the inventiveness or the beauty of the language that makes a story. Often it's that quality described by Jillsy Sloper in John Irving's *The World According to Garp*: "Most books you know nothin's gonna happen … Other books … you know just what's gonna happen, so you don't have to read them, either. But … this book's so sick you know somethin's gonna happen, but you can't imagine what." Most often, that can't-look-away quality derives from the characters. They may be hard-boiled (Sam Spade, Easy Rawlins, Arya Stark); or perhaps they're soft-boiled (Huck Finn, Indiana Jones, Gabriel Conroy of Joyce's "The Dead"), or raw (Falstaff, George Eliot's Maggie Tulliver, The Incredible Hulk). In some cases they're even poached (Sanger Rainsford in "The Most Dangerous Game"). But some combination of compelling character and compelling need to see what comes next strikes me as being the closest thing to a magical formula for catching lightning in a bottle.

About the author

David Hewitt was born in Germany, grew up near Chicago, and lived for eight years in Japan, where he studied classical Japanese martial arts and grew up some more. A graduate of the University of Southern Maine's Stonecoast MFA program in Popular Fiction, he currently teaches English at the Community College of Baltimore County, but has at various times worked as a Japanese translator (specializing in anime), an instructor of martial arts, a cabinetmaker's assistant, a pizza/subs/beer delivery guy, and a pet shop boy. His hobbies include skiing, writing, meditation, writing, running, travel, and writing. His hobbies do not include jumping out of airplanes, rodeo riding, alligator wrangling, or deep-sea bathysphere exploration.

May

Figlia della Neve

Jonathan Louis Duckworth

The wife's eyes are closed, but there is no flutter of dream under her lids, and when her name escapes like a shy moth from the husband's tongue, she says, "Go on, I'm listening."

The husband begins his story.

The young man set out early one winter morning in search of the fabled Cold Lady. After hours of searching, he found her gliding through the silvered lindens and fell utterly in love. Her limbs were branches painted in winter's first frost. Her long throat an egret considering the sun. Her skin was not what shimmered; it was the falling snow around her, crystalline flakes a swarm of prisms that made up her pearlescent aura. He was not the first to fall in love.

When she stopped to regard him, he gave her a white rose, which she breathed on, turning it silver with frost. This was custom—a man must present her with a white rose. She would breathe a hoarfrost upon the rose that would never thaw. If the man were to leave right there and then with the rose, and hang the rose over his bed, he would live a long life and never suffer nightmares. But few had ever left her. Instead they'd follow the lady again, until she stopped in her tracks once more to invite them to lead her to their homes. This is what the young man did: he followed her through the oaks and spruces and over a frozen river. Followed her even though he knew the innocent disaster she was. Followed her because love and disaster are voice and echo, echo and voice.

He had researched her assiduously. This Cold Lady wandered the Alps, had been sighted as far east as the Julian range in Yugoslavia, as far north as the German border, and as far west as the slopes Mont Blanc. In Austria she was called *Das Schneemädchen*, while the French called her *La Dame Froide*. Here she was the Daughter of the Snow, *La Figlia della Neve*.

Despite what some claimed, her aura did not cause madness. The derangement already existed in the men who thought they could have her—who thought her life something that could belong to them. She was not alive. She was to life what light is to matter; what a metaphor is to reality.

"If she isn't alive, how does she exist?" the wife asks.

"As the stars do, burning lifelessly, tirelessly."

The young man had heard many versions of her origin. One story had it the lady of the snow was a priestess of a fertility Goddess's cult, punished for some forgotten transgression to forever wander the snow. Another claimed she was a victim of the Inquisition, which supposedly accounted for her fear of fire. But her legend was older than the Inquisition. The old Celts who dwelled in the Alps before the Romans came shaped figures of her from clay, her tragic features crudely formed by hands that revered or pitied but never loved her, and love was what she needed, and, like any creature, deserved. It was as much compassion as mania that moved the young man to find her—to be the first warm, caring hand to ever hold hers.

Where she trod, even virgin snow hardened to ice. Many a man had broken a limb or worse following the slick of her path. The young man was careful with his steps as he followed. Birds compulsively built nests on the ground where she walked. The eggs never hatched, and foxes, cats, and martens that foraged them died as if poisoned. When winter ended and the spring thaw began, she'd retreat with the vestiges of winter into hollows carved into the mountains by ancient hands. In these lungs of the earth she'd slumber until the next snowfall.

The wife's voice is gossamer threading from her lips. "That sounds cozy."

The husband clears his throat and continues.

As was her custom, the lady invited her young suitor to show her to his home. They followed the old alpine trail down the slope, toward the village in the vale where smoke rose in gray whiskers from the chimneys. When they came to the village, to the sight of his cottage, she hesitated.

It was ever thus. Despite having followed a man willingly, the lady would always become anxious at seeing his home. Now was no different.

"It's too warm," she told the young man.

She had said this a thousand times.

This was what the young man knew: in all the stories, men were always too proud, too eager, too self-interested to heed her, and she was too desperate for a companion to refuse their urgings. Always the same. She would follow them inside, leaving a trail of frost over their threshold and up their staircase and into their bedrooms. They would make love, and then the men would hold her in their arms and fall asleep in the warmth of their beds. The men would wake feeling soaked, seeing the lady of the snow become translucent, then turning to water and seeping away into the sheets of the bed. Thereafter the men's hearts became hollow and frail. What is not living cannot die, but the men would not know this. Some would slit their throats on that very bed, desiring to mix their blood with her water. Others would walk outside, lie down, and wait for the falling snow to bury them. Some of these men were found and rescued with only minor frostbite. Others were discovered only after the snow melted. Meanwhile, the daughter of the snow had not died. She was reconstituted with the next snowfall, and the cycle continued. Her tears became a frosty rime around her eyes.

Knowing what he knew, the young man attempted something no one had before. He took her by the hand, led her into the house, and opened a window to let the cold air in.

"I want you to be comfortable," he told her.

She replied that it was still too warm for her. So he opened another window. But it was still too warm. So he opened the door and left it open, and poured ashes over the smoldering fire in the grate. Finally, she told him she felt comfortable.

They went to the bed, and lay down together. The young man shivered, and the lady's body could offer him no warmth. She asked him if something was wrong.

He said nothing. He held her close, shivering, fighting to stay awake as the snow accumulated on the window sill and on the floor and invaded his bed. He fell asleep in her arms.

In the morning the young man awoke. He was not dead, and the girl had not melted. The window was closed. There was no sign of snow in the cottage. Beside him in the bed was a woman who looked like the lady. Just as beautiful and just as long-limbed, but ordinary in every way. Warm. Human.

"Good morning," he said.

"Good morning," she said back.

"Would you like some breakfast?" he asked her.

"I'd love some," she said, "it feels like forever since I've eaten."

And they lived a long, full, ordinary lifetime together.

When the husband finishes telling his story, he sees that his wife is beginning to stir, having fallen asleep briefly. The tiny flakes of snow slipping in through the half-opened bedroom window melt and radiate as vapor as they settle on her face. Last he checked a half hour ago, her temperature was the same as it has been these last few months: 102 degrees.

When she opens her eyes she looks at the white roses in the vase on her nightstand, and then smiles at her husband. "New ones?" she asks.

The husband nods. The flowers are from Chile, delivered on an airplane. The walls of their bedroom are plastered with crude crayon drawings from the children the wife used to teach when she was well. Happy scenes; sunny scenes, scribbled well-wishings.

"I'm sorry I didn't hear your whole story," she says.

"That's all right."

"I had a dream," she says. "I dreamed the fever had gone away."

He says nothing.

"Put your hand on my head. I want to feel a cold hand."

He takes one hand from its mitten and places it on her forehead. It is like touching an oven's window.

The doctors don't know what to call the wife's condition, which began in autumn as a seemingly ordinary fever that refused to diminish. All they know is that it is unlikely to be contagious, but likely to be fatal. One doctor termed it "hysterical cephalic hyperthermia." There is no cure. They've exhausted several experimental treatments with no results, while the fever boils her brain like an egg.

Cold air eases the wife's discomfort and helps her sleep, but this is a mere palliative. The husband has learned to live with the windows open, dressed in sweaters. It is late January now, and he fears the coming spring. There are air conditioners that can keep a room cold as winter, but they would have to be ordered from America and installed with great difficulty. The doctors keep trying to take her to a hospital, but neither the husband nor the wife want that. Last week, one of the doctors talked to the husband outside the house, and asked him if he was "making arrangements" yet.

"Did your story have a happy ending?" the wife asks.

"Yes," he lies. Fairy tales are happy only because they end before the end. Love is a stay of execution.

"That's good. When I'm better, and I go back to work, maybe you could visit my classroom and read your story for the children. I'm sure they'd like that."

He shakes his head. "I don't think it's good for children. Too sad."

"I thought you said it had a happy ending."

He says nothing.

"You should shave that beard. You don't look handsome with a big beard."

"It keeps me warm."

"Men don't look handsome with beards."

"I'll shave tomorrow."

"Fine," she said. "But will you bring me one of the cold apricots from the icebox?"

He doesn't want to leave her. For the moment, she's awake, but when he returns, who could know? He has a feeling as deep-set as the marrow of his bones that when his wife drifts off for good, he'll be taking a piss, whipping up some custard for her, on the telephone with one of the doctors, shaving, or bringing her apricots from the icebox.

But he stands up anyway.

"One more thing," the wife says, gesturing to the window.

The husband opens the window all the way. More snow blows in. When the husband returns with the apricot—hard and orange like a tiny frigid sun—the wife is asleep again. He wishes he could lie down beside her and crawl into her dreams. He wishes he could wake with her in a cold place where pools of frozen water have never known the touch of sunlight. But where she's gone, and where she's going, he cannot follow. And so the husband returns to his chair to watch the snow accreting on the window sill, wondering if his wife will remember him when she awakens again in the lightless lungs of the earth.

See Jonathan Louis Duckworth's story "Figlia della Neve" online at Metaphorosis.
If you liked it, leave a comment. Authors love that!
Remember to subscribe to our e-mail updates so you'll know when new stories are posted.

About the story

This story began from two sources: first, my reading of Angela Carter's fabulous collection *The Bloody Chamber and Other Stories*, and second, listening to a song from American power metal band Symphony X called "Lady of the Snow". The evidence of Carter's influence should be plain to anyone who's ever read her work. As for the song, it gave me the story's original title, "Lady of the Snow", when the story was still set in New England, rather than the Northern Italy locale of its current iteration.

I rewrote the story as "Figlia della Neve" because it fit well with a new story collection I've been putting together, a project called "Undying". Undying's central conceit is that all the stories are set in Europe (but not the British Isles) at some point between the mid 19th century and the 1970s. The collection's other central conceit is implied by the title: every story features some element of rebirth or resurrection, for good or for bad, and every story centers on the enduring, death-defying bonds of human attachment, again, for good or bad.

A question for the author

Q: Duckbilled platypus – result of divine distraction, or alternate universe crossover?

A: The platypus is the result of a beaver scientist and a duck mathematician attempting to divide by zero. There is a small organ called an oxylitic ganglion adjacent to the left sinus, unique among mammals, which allows the platypus to process mineral heavy water and use it to produce pure DMT. By the time you have finished fact-checking this, I will have already made my escape.

About the author

Jonathan Louis Duckworth received his MFA in fiction from Florida International University. He is currently a PhD student at University of North Texas, studying poetry. He likes bending genres in his writing and has a deep passion for folklore and tall tales. His cat, Cheese, is very powerful and has an Instagram: @Misscheesevious

Regret's Relief

Travis Wade Beaty

I would have never gone to the Glyphs of Onyx if I hadn't fallen in love. I was in my final year at the University of Spell-Craft in Silver Forge. And as Silver Forge was the nearest port to the island of Onyx, and as the glyphs had been discovered only five years prior, students were always taking little holidays up there to see them. Most returned unimpressed. The Onyxian parliament itself had investigated the glyphs and not only had they concluded there was no magic to them, but also questioned whether they held any meaning whatsoever. Still, rumors persisted. And a few students, enough to be an annoyance, returned from Onyx as full converts. They would tell how the glyphs had imparted to them a special inspiration. And how they were certain, because of this special inspiration, that they were about to craft a monumental spell, one that could change the world.

As no such spell ever materialized, I was happy to focus on my studies and ignore all the hullaballoo. But then I met Celia.

In truth, I met her paintings first. I had gone down to the annual campus art show and found myself mesmerized by a set of mournful landscapes. Nothing about them suggested spell-craft. Nothing in them moved or twinkled or morphed into something new as you took them in. And yet, try as I might, I could not take my eyes off of the paintings until a deep sorrow rose within me and I wept. A woman approached and I hurried to wipe my eyes, embarrassed by my emotional outburst. When I turned to meet her eye, she gave a sympathetic smile.

"It's the damnedest thing," I said. "There's no spell on these paintings. They seem to belong in a mundane gallery."

"And yet?" she asked.

"And yet they've done something to me. As if something has been released that I didn't know was bottled up."

The woman nodded. "There's no spell cast on the painting because the painting is the spell," she said. "You spell-writers don't cast spells on top of the incantations you write, do you?"

I had never considered such an idea. All the spell-paintings I had ever seen were painted with the idea that certain incantations, usually ones that would animate the painting, would be cast on top.

"And what is the spell painted here?" I asked, pointing to the landscapes.

"I call it, 'Unearthing Sorrow'."

"That's genius," I said.

She smiled her true smile then, the one that lit up her face, the room, and, I was certain, the whole world. By some miracle, she took a fancy to me as well, and we fell under that kind of love spell which remains a mystery to cast; the one from which there is no cure but for one or both hearts to be torn asunder.

Our studies kept us busy in the day, but every evening we'd meet up to take long walks around the campus. During one of those moonlit strolls, Celia confessed that she had visited the glyphs in Onyx and felt the presence of her mother in the caves. She told me how, when she was still in her adolescence, her widowed mother had turned down a marriage proposal from a wealthy textile merchant. For years Celia had resented her for not wedding the merchant, blaming all the family's woes and poverty on her mother's pride. Until, finally, after the death of her younger sister from the crimson cough, Celia released a fit of rage on her mother, who had passed out of the world that very night.

"I have told myself a thousand times that my words didn't end her life," Celia said. "The fever did that. But I am always replaying those horrible last words I spoke to her. Standing next to the glyphs, I felt her presence. It was as if she were standing just behind the cave wall. And it seemed I had a chance to take those words back. I did and I told her —"

Her words caught in her mouth and she cried. I realized why Celia's paintings had worked so well on me. We shared a similar grief.

"And you saw an apparition in the caves? You saw your mother?" I asked.

"I felt her," she said. "It was as if the caves were commiserating with my grief."

"And did she hear you?" I asked, my heart in my throat.

"I don't know. But it helped to say the words out loud. To … allow them. I can't explain it. You have to go, Ben. You have to know them for yourself."

So, late in the summer, I boarded a zeppelin and floated over the North Sea to a shore of stark white sand and craggy black rock. Beyond the shore, a city rose, culminating in the gleaming white dome of the Onyxian Parliament sitting high on a hill.

I dropped my bag off at a ramshackle inn next to the southern docks and set off for the glyphs. They were not hard to find, as there was a steady stream of tourists heading to and from them. I followed the crowd down a winding path that ran along the cliffs facing the shore. Eventually, the path veered left and sloped down into the wide entrance of a cave. I had to brace myself as a strong and constant ocean breeze rushed past me and down into the cool mouth of the cave.

There was no need for a lantern, as there were so many lantern-wielding tourists already inside. In less than a half an hour I had made my way to the glyphs, which were in a small chamber off the main path. They seemed no more than geological anomalies, odd-looking white striations set in a black cave wall. I held the palm of my hand against them, as I saw some other tourists doing, and felt nothing. I returned to my inn dismayed that I had not felt even the slightest fraction of magic. But that night, I had a dream. The dream. The one that had plagued me since I was a child.

It was always the same: the dream began with a cruel reenactment of the worst day of my life – the day I decided to read "Colonel Bellington's Compendium of Spell-forms" instead of watching over my younger brother, Arthur. I was twelve and he was a capable five years old, but my mother still insisted I go with him whenever he wanted to swim. I sat under an apple tree as he flew into the water, and lost myself in the compendium.

"Come play, Ben!" he yelled out, splashing in the water. "Novels are boring."

"It's not a novel," I said. "It's a compendium of spells."

"Is there a spell to make me a shark?"

"These aren't for casting. They're just examples."

"You should read how to do fun stuff! You should learn how to make mud puddles when there's no rain. Or a spell that can turn me into a shark."

I don't know what he said after that because I began to ignore him. I became lost in the book and didn't look up from the page until I heard my father's cries. He had come in from the fields to wash in the pond and found Arthur in the lily-pads, floating blue.

From there, the dream departed from true events. I would descend into the pond, not to save Arthur, but to speak to him, to beg his forgiveness. My words would float away, a stream of shining bubbles racing to the surface, while Arthur looked on, his face blank, his eyes dead. And this scene would play out for an eternity until I awoke.

That night in Onyx, my dream was so vivid that I awoke choking, the taste of pond water still in my mouth. I was uncomfortably hot, sweating even after pulling off the sheets of my bed. I put on my boots and stepped outside, but the slight breeze coming off the shore gave no relief. I heard a chirp from above and looked to see a cloud of bats, their black wings barely visible against the midnight sky. They dove into the cliffs and I knew they must be following that chill current of wind that never stopped flowing into the caves. I had to join them, to find cool respite in the womb of the earth, and I hurried toward the caves, certain they were the only cure for my fever.

Still in my night clothes, with only the light of my single lantern, I descended into the caverns as the wind whipped around me. I felt a strange joy, as if being welcomed home after a long voyage, and could not keep myself from smiling. The caves should have been impossible to navigate in so little light, but I could not seem to take a wrong step. I somehow knew my way as if I were in my childhood home. When I came to the glyphs, my fever broke and a chill went through me. I had an odd sensation that Arthur was in the cave somewhere nearby. I spoke his name and waited for an answer.

A sudden gust of wind caught me off guard and I lost my balance. I dropped my lantern as I fell and, with a loud clang, all went black. At first, the darkness of the cave was nothing but a void, but as I scrambled to find my lantern, shapes began to fill in the void. There was an apple tree and below it a familiar book with a red cover. Beyond, I saw lush green grasses growing tall around a wide pond. Arthur came storming out of the water, his lanky limbs glittering in the afternoon sun. His mouth moved as if he were speaking but I couldn't hear him.

"Arthur!" I yelled and scrambled to my feet.

Urgently, he pointed behind me. I turned to see the red book beneath the apple tree flying toward me. It hovered in the air before me and opened itself. Its pages were blank, but as I peered into the book, a spell began to write itself. My heart swelled as I felt this must be a spell made especially for me, a spell that would allow me to speak with my brother, to finally beg his forgiveness and bring peace to both our hearts. I tried to read what was written but it was all in gibberish. I turned back to Arthur and saw a vast canyon of darkness had fallen between us.

"I'm sorry!" I yelled out. "I'm sorry! Can you hear me?"

But as I spoke, he dissolved into the darkness. I ran forward to find him as if there were a great stretch of space ahead of me and not a wall of stone. My head slammed against the hard rock and it felt as if I'd been sucker-punched by a prizefighter. I dropped to the ground and held my throbbing head until the pain dulled. As I did, the cave winds started back up and I could not stop shivering.

"Please," I said. "Please come back."

"Gotta come in the spring," a voice said. There was a flicker of yellow light and I made out a puffy-faced man sitting on the floor of the cave, his back against the glyph wall. He was holding a match and using it to light my lantern. He glared at me with hollow eyes, made a move to get up, decided he was too drunk for that and leaned once more against the wall.

"In the spring," he spat out. "Hasn't anybody told you! They ain't at their full power until the spring, dammit."

"Who are you?" I asked.

"That's not important. What the glyphs say, that's what's important. That's all that matters, isn't it?" he said "But you fools keep coming at the wrong time. Say it, then. You'll come back in the spring."

"I'll come back in the spring," I said.

"Good man. Now leave," he said thrusting the lantern into my hand. When I hesitated he yelled out "Get the hell out of here!"

He grew angrier, shouting various profanities until I fled back up to the surface. I was sure he was mad, but at the moment, madness made a great deal of sense. I took his advice to heart and promised myself to return in the spring.

On the zeppelin flight home, as I floated further from the glyphs, I could only think of Arthur in the caves and how he had nearly spoken to me. I decided I would devote my life to deciphering the spell I had not been able to read in that floating red book, that no matter how impossible a task it seemed, I would devise a spell to speak with the dead.

I returned to Silver Forge brimming with faith and optimism, happy to join the ranks of the true-believers. I asked Celia if she would go to Onyx with me once we had our degrees.

"Is this a proposal?" she asked.

"Dammitall, I think it is," I said.

I had no ring to present, but she didn't mind. She painted thin black bands on each of our ring fingers, and, together, we cast a spell to make the ink permanent. We graduated in the fall, exchanged vows, slid silver rings over our painted ones, and promptly sailed to Onyx.

The strangest thing about the island was not the spell crafting or the seclusion or even the odd political corruption of a city whose main export was sorcery, but the fact that so many tolerated the torment of its winter. In the dead of an Onyx winter, you despised yourself for staying, but you couldn't get out. By then, hardly any boat would chance the ice surrounding the island, nor any zeppelin take on the near-constant storms.

Each autumn, when the frigid winds began to blow, most of the island's residents would take the last ferries of the season back to the mainland, and of course, the rich would book flights to the sunny beaches of Zephyr's Banks. But Celia and I, along with all the other artists, would stay.

We stayed because only an Onyx winter could make you fully know its spring. Come visit with the tourists in the warm months and you would write home about how beautiful it was. "Oh, cousin Meredith, you must come to see the sparkling white beaches. And the old prince's castle on the precipice by moonlight. And the tulips blooming in all the colors of the rainbow!"

All fine and well, but if you wanted to know why the artists were here, you had to survive the winter. Then, when spring finally emerged, you would know her properly as your savior. Born again, you would kiss her feet, joyous to be swallowed in her ever-blooming ecstasy. And in this state you would have your best chance with the glyphs.

In the midst of that first winter, with frost on our breath even as a fire roared in our hearth, Celia and I decided we'd leave Onyx before another one came to pass. But in the spring, we went down into the caves, set our hands on the glyphs, and returned to the surface with our minds abuzz with inspiration. We strolled through the hills of blooming wildflowers as sand swirled on the beaches and waves lazily collapsed on the shore and we agreed we'd live in Onyx all the days of our lives.

When I had laid my hands on the glyphs that first spring I did not see Arthur, but heard his voice in my head, faintly humming his favorite lullaby. All the lyrics came back to me and it occurred to me they could be turned into a stellar sleeping spell. I decided this must be the first step in devising a spell to speak with the dead. I would combine an intense sleeping spell with one that could summon the deceased. And in this way, I would bring the living closer to death while luring the deceased closer to life. And there in the space between worlds, the living and the dead could commune. Did it bother me that I had no idea how to cast a spell on the deceased? That there was no precedent for it whatsoever? Not in the least. Standing before the glyphs, I had faith the details would iron themselves out. But when I sat down at home to begin writing, all my ideas became confused and impossible. What seemed rational in the caves, was absurdity anywhere else.

Meanwhile, Celia had felt moved to honor her mother and began a painting of her childhood home. She played with light in a new way and the painting was like a breath of fresh air for the soul. For a time, it was a joy to have that painting in our home, but Celia was never satisfied with it. She could not leave it alone. She painted over her work many times as spring became summer until the composition became disjointed and the only feeling it conjured was confusion.

We spent five years that way, cursing the winters, exalting the springs, and spending the months in between telling ourselves our big break-through was just around the corner.

I found work as a typesetter and Celia waited tables and we tried our best to make a name for ourselves as spell-crafters on an island teeming with people attempting to do exactly the same.

We had some mild successes. I had a knack for writing tawdry love spells which I published under a pen name. Most of them were dirt cheap, wore off too quickly, and had dubious effects, but love spells were in such demand, they could always sell. Celia would go down to the boardwalk and sell paintings to tourists of stars that would actually twinkle in night skies and suns that set before your very eyes. It was enough to keep us at our craft, but not enough to pay the bills.

By the fifth year, up to our necks in debt and without a break in sight, Celia made her case that we ought to leave.

"I'm stuck, Ben," she said. "It doesn't matter if I paint a carnival or a funeral. All my paintings are about my mother. I thought moving here, feeling my mother in the caves, would help me heal, but it's only made me fixated on her deathbed. I can't stand it anymore."

I had to admit that we were spinning our wheels, and wondered if the glyphs had ever been on our side. I began to think perhaps it was all some kind of cosmic joke and the caves were feeding off our frustrations. I could still sense Arthur when I stood before the glyphs, but I never had a vision as intense as my first trip. And despite a great deal of study, I had come no closer to writing a spell to speak with the dead. I asked Celia for a few weeks to mull over the idea of leaving the island for good. And while I did, winter came early. It came hard, choking the streets in snow and ice. The whole city shut down for months. Celia and I spent a great deal of time huddled by our fire, talking over the future. How we would move back to Silver Forge where the weather was mild, where rent was cheap and where spell-crafters like us could easily find work tutoring students. And then one morning I woke with a fever, retching from the taste of pond water in my mouth.

"Ben, don't be a moron," Celia said when she saw me putting on my boots. "There's still snow on the ground." Her auburn hair was pulled back and her smock was splattered in violet specks of paint. She had woken early and had begun painting before we'd even made coffee.

I put two layers of sweaters on and said, "There's been a shift. Spring is here. I've never felt it so strong. You feel it too, don't you?"

"I did feel it," she said. "I woke inspired." She sighed and wiped her forehead, smearing purple paint across it. "I had a vision of hope."

I examined her painting. It was the landscape just outside our window. There were the city rooftops, all in shadow, and beyond, the low rolling hills covered in snow. Above the hills, Celia had painted a lone seagull. I thought he might drop out of the pale blue sky at any moment out of sheer despair.

"How do you feel?" she asked.

"Heavy," I said.

She slammed her paintbrush down on the easel. "I give up," she said. "I can't escape my mother, or rather, my insufferable self-pity. I'm a one-trick pony. It's all despair and grief and sorrow and blah, blah, blah."

She turned to me, hands on her hips. "I think we ought to make a child."

"Right now?"

"Yes, please."

"You'd have a child as if you were casting a spell. As if there's some magic in it that will make you stop painting your mother."

She shrugged. "Why wouldn't it?"

I laughed. "Be serious. We can barely feed ourselves, Cee-Cee!"

"We're moving, remember? To a place where people like us are sought after. Where we aren't just another set of dreamers."

"Let's not put the cart before the horse. We'll move and then make a family."

I put on my cloak and poured what was left of the previous night's broth into a canteen.

"Where are you going?" she asked. "There's no way the shops are opening this early. I don't care how much we feel it's spring."

"I'm going to the glyphs."

"Moron! You'll slip on some black ice in those caves and that'll be the end of you."

"I have to go."

"Why?"

"Arthur told me."

Just before I awoke that morning Arthur had finally done something besides stare at me with his wretched dead eyes. When I had descended into the pond, he had turned to look behind him. There, instead of the usual sun-streaked murk of the pond, I had seen the glyphs, shining bright in the darkness.

Having heard this explanation, Celia turned to her painting and sighed. She addressed the canvas as if it were an old friend familiar with my nonsense.

"I can't argue with Arthur, can I?" she asked.

"I'm sorry," I said.

"Go then, moron. I very much hope you don't die."

I trudged through the snow toward what I thought should be the entrance of the caves, but the cliffs were still blanketed in snow. I sipped my broth and waited for the sun to rise. As it did, the snows shrank and little streams of icy water began to race toward the shores. Finally, a mass of snow toppled from the cliffs and, beyond it, I made out the dark maw of the cave entrance.

I lit my lantern and descended into the cave, but when I reached the entrance to the glyph chamber, I paused. Something was off. I stood a long while contemplating what it was until I realized there was no wind in the cave. And in the place of the rushing wind I could hear a low hum, a vibration I could feel in my bones. I had the distinct feeling there was someone waiting for me. I thought for sure I'd find that old drunk man sitting against the glyph wall, but when I stepped forward, I was alone.

As soon as I saw the glyphs, they began to move. They shifted, blurred, and melted into the cave wall. I was horrified that they might vanish for good. I tried to run to them, but darkness enveloped me. I flailed my arms and realized I was under water, floating in the pond behind my childhood home. I turned my head and there was Arthur, floating before me, only he was alive. I knew he was alive. And I knew I could reach out and bring him back. I knew we'd climb a tree and race for the highest branch. We'd catch frogs and drop them at the top of the hill so we could chase them back down into the pond. And we'd laugh at how he'd almost drowned.

I reached and pulled him to me, and as I did, I was pulled once more into myself. Alone, I stood in the cave, submerged not in water, but in a torrent of thought.

I had a clarity of mind like I'd never experienced before, or since. Parts of spells I had been mulling over for months began sliding into one another and making themselves whole. I sprinted out of the cave in a ruckus and burst forth into the sunlight surrounded by a cloud of black wings that screeched and fluttered into the pink evening sky.

"I have it!" I yelled. "I have it all!"

When I stormed through the door of our flat, I saw that Celia had destroyed the painting she'd been working on. It had been doused in scarab ether, a highly effective paint thinner. All the colors had melded together into a sick dripping brown. Celia was passed out in bed, her smock still on, our last bottle of wine lying empty in her arms. The myriad of burning thoughts shooting through my mind all fell away. The sight of Celia in such disarray stripped me of any other idea than to relieve her of her grief. Celia was the kindest, warmest person I knew, and it seemed a great injustice that she ought to carry the guilt of her mother's deathbed with her always.

Barely thinking, I sat down and wrote "Regret's Relief" for her. The spell allowed a person to forgive themselves, irrevocably, for what they most regretted. I had such a clarity of thought it was not hard to make scarab ether the only casting cost, and as soon as it was written, I cast "Regret" on my still sleeping Celia. I then turned back to my desk and began to write the spell that I felt was my destiny. A spell to speak with the dead.

I started off well enough, but halfway through, my writing became confused. I read over my work several times, trying to regain my train of thought until my eyelids grew heavy. Exhaustion overwhelmed me and I passed out on my writing table. I awoke shivering, the fire in our flat having gone out. I read the partially finished spell and it seemed as foreign as if another hand had written it. The clarity of the glyphs had fogged over.

The inspiration did not return, even when I went back down into the caves. It was as if the glyphs had given me the totality of their gift and the tap was now shut off. Still, every morning I would wake and force myself to attempt finishing the spell. Each morning would end with me pounding my fist on the writing table and burning all my failed work in the fire.

While my frustrations grew, Celia's abated. It took some time to see a change, and it was hard to say when exactly it took hold, but one day I knew it like I knew winter from spring. Her step was ever so faintly lighter, her sleep just a smidge deeper, and her smile, though I previously thought it impossible, became even brighter. Still, I watched her work closely. I had worried "Regret" would make her art suffer, that if she did not carry that certain pain, she couldn't infuse it into her art. And yet, the opposite was true. She now painted with more confidence and with a greater sense of purpose. Her grief was still there, but instead of wrestling with it, she embraced it and held it firm in her grasp.

People began swearing up and down that they felt an improvement in their health after visiting her exhibition. She leaned into this idea and found herself painting a sunrise that could ease a headache. All of Onyx came to see it. High Society took notice and began an onslaught of commissions she couldn't hope to keep up with.

By late spring, when parliament opened its door to the public, I was certain "Regret" had worked just as I had written it. I applied for patent approval and was immediately asked to present myself for questioning. Most of the patent committee agreed there had to be some sort of catch. That no spell, especially one that dealt with matters of the heart and mind, no matter how inspired, could be written that clean. I pointed out the spell could only be used once on each person, and they began to warm to its poetry. To test it, the head magistrate used the spell on herself. She wept, stamped my patent, left Onyx that very day, and never returned.

"Regret's Relief" was, however, deemed a protected spell that could not be sold to the public. Parliament feared the spell would be ill-used by the morally bankrupt, allowing degenerates to alleviate the weight of their conscience. Parliament would administer the spell only to those who seemed fit after thorough interviews. I agreed to their terms and received a lump sum of 500 dollars.

I paid off our outstanding debts and bought the finest pen and paper money could buy. I told myself I could finish "Commune with the Dead" if only my hand could glide more smoothly across the page. I never wrote so much trash in all my life as with that damned pen. Occasionally I'd stumble upon a functional spell, but nothing close to finishing "Commune." The best I crafted was an incantation to make mourners more talkative at their loved one's wake.

I also had to deny my constant urge to seek out the glyphs, allowing myself to descend only once per week. And though they never gave me a single clue on how to finish "Commune", I kept going until, at the peak of summer, the caves were shut down. When I arrived that afternoon, police guarded the entrance. I joined the other agitated glyph devotees as tempers flared until the coroner arrived and announced there had been a death in the caves. I stayed to watch the government spelunkers haul a body out and saw that it was the old drunk man from my first visit to the caves. Someone in the crowd wondered if he'd drunk himself to death.

"Glyph-sickness!" a woman yelled out. "They won't write that in the obituary, but it's the truth. Seen it too many times! Sonovabitch had a family and everything."

On my walk home I had to stop as my stomach clenched. I doubled over and vomited my lunch onto the grass. As I convulsed, I realized I resented the old drunk, then I despised him, and then I hated him with all my being. The bastard was more than half the reason I'd come to Onyx in the first place and now he was keeping me from my glyphs, keeping me from "Commune with the Dead", keeping me from Arthur. I thought I might have strangled the son of a bitch if he weren't already dead.

I returned home sweating and belligerent, to find Celia painting furiously. Our flat was covered with her finished work, every painting a sunrise, every one heartbreakingly beautiful. My temper cooled as I took in the landscapes and I wondered at how I could have been so angry about the death of a stranger.

Celia rushed to me, slapping zeppelin tickets in one hand and a glass of bubbly in the other. The tickets were for Zephyr's Bank.

"How much did this cost?" I asked.

"The Dome, Ben! I'm in the Dome!"

She had won a showing at the Obsidian Dome, at the time the most prestigious gallery in the hemisphere. To celebrate, she demanded we go on vacation. As it turned out, she'd been stowing cash in secret to surprise me. She insisted we go all out and rent a cottage on Zephyr's Bank. As there seemed no option to disagree, I told myself it was providence. I could take a break from the glyphs, and perhaps gain a new perspective on "Commune with the Dead."

It was while we were in Zephyr's Bank that the Patent Committee of the Onyxian Parliament let "Regret's Relief" be known to the public, writing at length about its potentials in The Northwestern Journal of Incantation. Word spread through Zephyr quickly until Celia came to dinner with her eyes brimming over with tears.

"Ben," she said, "did you cast it on me?" The truth of it was so plain, I couldn't hope to lie. I confessed. She held me and cried and thanked me. I apologized for casting the spell on her without her consent. She said she didn't care. And then she pled for me to cast it on myself.

"It wouldn't work the same," I said. "I have too many regrets."

"Look at you. Every night I hear you gasping and groaning. You haven't had an honest night's sleep in months. And your days are spent working on this cursed spell that clearly doesn't want to be written. This has to stop, Ben."

Leaving Onyx had not, as I'd hoped, alleviated my desire for the glyphs. I woke several times each night, always in a sweat and gasping for air. I would spend most of my days sitting on the beach with my journal and pen, facing the direction of Onyx, sometimes writing, but mostly staring out at the sea. In the face of insurmountable evidence against my mental well-being, I had no choice but to lie.

"I'm fine," I said. "Creating a spell so immense has put me in a state of unrest, but there will be an end."

The lie sounded good and I decided to believe it myself. "Every day," I said, "I come closer to finishing my work."

"Then let's make a child," Celia said. "What are we waiting for? Poverty is no longer an excuse. People will throw money at you and me alike, just to hear us pontificate on the arts."

"We're on our way up, Celia. Children would only slow us down."

"I want a child, Ben."

"Soon."

"Why not now?"

"Let art be your child!"

She struck me then. Celia, who barely had the nerve to smack a gnat, made the full brunt of her painter's hand known to me.

"Don't make this about me," she said. "It's about you. It's about Arthur."

We did not speak the rest of that day, nor the next, which was our final day of the vacation. We did, however, follow through on our plan to picnic for dinner. We had yet to observe the evening ritual of the crabs coming into the bay, and neither of us wanted to miss it. We sat on the beach in silence as the crab's mating ritual set the night shore aglow in a humming violet bioluminescence. The full moon hung low, shining bright. It pulled at the womb of the earth and I felt that gravity shoot through my soul. For a fleeting moment, I saw myself making a family with Celia. She must have seen it in my eye because she said, "I deserve it, Ben. We deserve it."

She was lying on the bed of bluegrass, just off the sand, in an ivory gown bathed in starlight. The King of Fairies might have mistaken her for his queen. I played the part of an ass and did nothing about it. Instead, I looked out over the bay, and even though I knew it was impossible, I decided I could see the shores of Onyx on the horizon.

In the morning, as I was packing my things for the return, Celia laid her hand on mine.

"Let's stay," she said.

I froze and waited for her to go on, but she only stared at me steadfast and pitying.

"I have to return," I said.

"That island is making you sick, Ben. We should be the happiest we've ever been, but you're a mess. My sister is a day's train ride away in Silver Forge. Let's go for a visit."

I allowed myself to consider not returning to Onyx and my stomach turned itself over. Bile rose in my throat.

"This is how you repay me?" I asked. "I release you from the torment of your mother and now you'd stop me from writing my masterpiece?"

"I'm going to Silver Forge," she said. "And I want you to come with me. What I'm not going to do is watch you torture yourself when you could simply cast 'Regret' on yourself and be free from Arthur."

"You mean I should leave him behind. Abandon him."

"He's gone, Ben."

"Go, then. Go to Silver Forge and find some poor schmuck and make all the babies you want."

She didn't dignify my attack with a response. She only packed her things, told me to come to Silver Forge when I was ready, and left on the next train. I told myself it was all for the best. That our paths had diverged. We were getting in the way of each other's happiness.

When I returned to Onyx I marched straight for the caves, only to find the entrance still boarded over. Only now there was a notice glued to the boards announcing that another poor soul had died in the caves and, until thorough investigations could be completed, the caves were closed indefinitely.

Celia wrote asking me to send her painting supplies, and a few weeks later, she wrote again asking for her wardrobe. Several months after that, she asked for the rest of her things. In each letter she would describe the many well-paying jobs I could take on in Silver Forge and how she thought she could set up her own school for spell-painting. I shipped her things off and responded to her letters by repeating the lie I now held most dear: that I was oh so very close to finishing my work and that I would be along soon.

Eventually, the flat was void of most all her things and I realized how little I had. There was my writing table, the bed, the dresser of clothes. They all stared at me like idiot friends.

"All for the best," they said. "Now you're free to get some real work done."

Winter came and I spent it alone in a flat that was too empty and in dreams that were too real. There were a few dark days in the dead of winter where I convinced myself the flat was the afterlife, a purgatory made up special for me.

When spring returned and I was able to go out and meet with people again, I gained back some sanity. I wrote a letter to Celia telling her I was ready to have children. That I was going to write a book of love spells. That I was done with the glyphs and "Commune with the Dead" for good. I took it to the post office and was about to drop it into the mail bin when a vision came to me. I saw a host of my own children perishing as they fell off of roofs, tripped down stairs, got run over by trains, and drowned in ponds while I sat hunched over my writing desk. I took the letter home and fed it to the fire.

I began taking sleeping draughts to keep my dreams at bay and quickly became addicted to them. When those became too expensive, I turned to hard liquor. I lost my typesetting job and was booted from the flat after missing half a year's rent. I washed dishes for The Mermaid's Tale and the owner let me stay in his attic. I told myself I was waiting for a sign from the glyphs, or Arthur, or something I could not name.

When the ferries once more declared they had two weeks left before they closed for the winter, I wept. I was a failure, and a drunk to boot. I felt myself a coward as well, terrified of another winter in Onyx, of what it might do to my mind. I bought a ferry ticket for Silver Forge. I had an idea I would search out Celia and beg her forgiveness, but as the ship left the dock, I rushed off, leaping back to the shore.

"Now," I told myself. "Now that you've given up all you have. Now that you've shown the glyphs how serious you are, they will deliver you!"

I stumbled through the first snow flurries of the year, my veins coursing with more booze than blood. I brought a hammer with me and the last I remember was many failed attempts to pry the boards off the cave entrance.

When I came to, I was lying on a hospital bed. Celia stood over me. Her belly was round with child and her hair was shorter but shone brighter. She had dark circles under her eyes and I could tell that she had been crying.

"Dammitall," I said. "You've got to leave. I don't want you to see me like this."

"Too late," she said, and she laid her hand on mine. I saw her silver wedding band was gone, but the one of black ink remained.

"You shouldn't be here," I said. "Winter will come. You'll be stranded."

"You're right," she said. "I have tickets to return to Silver Forge tomorrow morning. So buck up and show these nurses you can walk out of here."

I found I could stand on my own, and I put on my best show for the nurses. Celia signed me out of the hospital and escorted me down to Angler's Brewery by the piers. She had sold a painting to the owner recently and wanted me to see it. So we sat by the Angler's hearth and took in her work, hung over the mantel.

The painting was of our flat, back when we'd both inhabited it. I waited until the cordial I'd ordered was finished before I took my eyes off the painting and steadied them on Celia.

"I feel no change," I said. "I fear your painting's a dud."

"I think you should write some spells for Arthur."

"That's what I've been trying to do."

"No. You've been trying to write something for yourself. Write something for Arthur."

I could see she was watching me, the way I had once watched her. I looked at the painting again and a weight lifted. A key turned. A frost on my heart shook free.

She laughed and wept at the same time. "I'm sorry it took so long to paint. You're a stubborn little moron, so it had to be just so."

"What is it? Did you somehow paint 'Regret's Relief?'"

"No. I went with a different approach."

"What then?"

She smiled. "A love spell."

"And whom will I fall in love with?"

"Yourself. You'll love yourself as much as I did. As much as I do. And there's nothing you can do about it, moron."

She sat back in her chair, arms crossed, beaming.

I thought of saying "Damn you to hell," but all that came out was, "Thank you, Celia."

She wiped her eyes, took a deep breath, and stared at the ring of ink on her left hand.

"Help me cast this off?" she asked.

"Maybe I won't."

"You will."

"Why?"

"Because you love me."

We spoke the spell together and I watched as the ink slowly faded away from both our hands.

We shared one glass of wine and I let her go home. I sat in Angler's, ordered a coffee, paper, and an ink-pot. I scribbled out a spell I called "Puddle Prisms" that made mud puddles that shone with all the colors of the rainbow. I used all my knowledge of shadows and light to make an illusion wherein ordinary fish would momentarily look like great big sharks. And then I wrote another spell for Arthur, and another, and as I wrote I felt Arthur's spirit rise within me and go swimming across the page.

See Travis Wade Beaty's story "Regret's Relief" online at Metaphorosis.
If you liked it, leave a comment. Authors love that!
Remember to subscribe to our e-mail updates so you'll know when new stories are posted.

About the story

I started writing "Regret's Relief" while visiting Paris and reading *A Moveable Feast* by Ernest Hemingway. The initial idea was to go to that Paris of Hemingway and Picasso and Gertrude Stein etc., but imagine the art they were trying to create was magic. I enjoyed delving into the idea of a frustrated spell-crafter, so the story I wrote originally was a lot about that. Eventually, as I revised the story, it became influenced by my own experiences of living in Los Angeles in my 20s and struggling to make a career out of acting.

Also, seasons were on my mind a great deal after having moved to Washington, DC after seven years in Los Angeles. I experienced the change of seasons growing up in Indiana, but LA was void of that passage from dead winter into vibrant spring. Experiencing that first spring in DC with all the cherry blossoms was quite a spiritual experience for me. So I was eager to put that feeling into a story.

A question for the author

Q: Do you often include children in your stories? What role do they play?

A: I include children in my stories fairly often. Children are full of hope and are themselves a kind of manifestation of hope. So I like to see how cynical or hard-hearted adult characters might respond to being confronted with that kind of limitless optimism of a child.

There's also that strong desire to protect children which can inspire a lot of fear. And letting a kid down can really haunt a person. So as a parent, I spend a lot of time thinking about that push and pull between hope and fear and all the doubts between.

About the author

Travis Wade Beaty grew up in Northern Indiana, spent a good deal of his twenties in Los Angeles, and now resides in Washington, DC. While he's had a great many jobs, his favorites have included acting, teaching, and being a stay-at-home dad to two girls and three cats.

@TravisWBeaty

Pre-triage

Joe Prosit

As of today, I'm a human crumple-zone. I saw to that myself. The highway network will see my car and label me the perfect impact absorber.

There was a time I thought I had things all figured out. I had a good job. I had plans. Ambitions. Goals. A house of cards sent toppling down when they pulled my job out from underneath me. My severance package, nothing more than a handshake and an escort out the door, told me exactly what I was worth. It was a rough year. A rough couple of years.

I figured it out, though – how to rebuild that card house into something the system would value. I married a doctor.

Her name was Linda. She had everything. A beautiful face. Gorgeous eyes. Wavy brown hair. Long legs and a knock-out body. A great fashion sense too; I got a lot of advice on picking out her clothes and accessories before I bought them for her. Her physical presence was the easy part. I built that from old car parts and a suede recliner I had in the garage. But she had a great personality too. I spent hours creating her digital footprint and integrating it into her physical body via her cellphone and the biometrics I gave her. She wasn't just beautiful to my eyes. When I helped her turn on her phone, the network saw her face and her retinas, and felt her 3D printed thumb prints the same as I did. But Linda went beyond just biometrics. According to her records, she worked the ER at a Level 1 Trauma hospital, donated to charities, and coached our son's soccer team. She was a great mother to all three of our kids.

Luke, Jeremy, Abigail... They had lives too. I built them in the garage and integrated them into the network not long after Linda and I got together. They were enrolled in sports, wore cool clothes, had friends online, and streamed the newest hip music. Their faked school records weren't all straight A's, but they worked hard and really made an effort. So what if maybe they spent a little too much time on their phones playing games and streaming videos? I knew the metrics the network used to quantify the value of their lives, so I maxed theirs out. As far as the system could tell, we were the perfect family. Worth saving.

I think it all went to hell the moment we trusted the computers to drive for us.

See, back then, when I was working and all I had was my job, I was a highway systems engineer. I did the final coding on tying the whole highway network together. There was a lot of work to be done during the months before launch day. A lot of overtime. That was when I came across the "pre-triage" protocol. Never heard of pre-triage? Never heard of triage? It's French, meaning "to sort".

Imagine for a moment, being a paramedic back when humans drove cars. You come upon a wreck and you and your partner have ten patients. Three are fine. Bumps and bruises. Three others are flat-lined dead. Of the remaining four, two are so close to dying there is only a slim chance you could save either one. The other two you know you can save, but only if you give them all your attention. Whom do you treat? The two who have the best chance of being saved, right? You'd play God and you would decide, these people will live and these people will die. That's triage.

It's no different nowadays, only we programmed the network to decide instead of the paramedics. And the network chooses before the first collision ever takes place. Say a deer jumps out on the road. As soon as it's detected, the network knows that the thing that should not happen is about to happen: there's going to be a wreck. A nasty one too. A pile-up. People will surely die. So what does it do? Pre-triage. Some cars become impact absorbers while others are spared. It becomes a numbers game. This car has five passengers. This car has one. This car is carrying a happy family and a Nobel Prize winner. This car is carrying a single out-of-work engineer with a drinking problem. These people live. This one dies. For the good of others, your car just might decide that you should die. That's pre-triage.

So my plan began as a way to stay safe on the highway. As the family grew, it was only natural for the network to see how valuable we were. Instead of being a lone washed-up programmer clinging to the bottle, I was a husband and a father. I was a good one, too. My wife was a respected doctor, advanced in her field.

Our kids had real potential; I poured hours of attention into them, making sure they'd make the most of it. In the end, we had a measurable, quantifiable, benefit to society. Most people wouldn't recognize it at first glance, but I saw how special my family was, and the network saw it too. It was right. This was about more than just me staying alive on the highway; it was about raising a family that trusted and needed me, regardless how some bank of computers scored the value of our lives.

Between you and me, by the morning we met, I'd stopped worrying about highway safety. I was enjoying spending time with my family during aimless rides along the highway. The network was performing flawlessly. Road travel was more efficient than ever before. More cars on the road. Higher speeds. Shorter commutes. Highway fatalities had dropped to ninety five percent. And the network enjoyed a near perfect customer satisfaction rating. By April fifth, 2025, I didn't worry about fifty car pile-ups anymore. Nobody did.

I read the police report. It was an unsecured load that started the accident that morning. Some trucker didn't inspect his tie-downs before hitting the road. It's always human error, whenever you ask us engineers. A load of cinder blocks fell off his truck. The blocks brought the first vehicle to an "unanticipated spontaneous halt".

The next ten cars were "impact absorbers". Nothing could be done about that. You were in car eleven. I was in car twelve. It was up to the network to pre-triage us correctly.

It seems like just yesterday. I heard the screeching brakes and the ten smashes like rhythmic thunderclaps coming closer and closer to me and my family. I was scared. I grabbed Linda to hold her back, to keep her safe from the collision I knew was coming. I reached out to little Abigail, praying to god I'd put the car seat in right. You know how they say only one in ten car seats are installed correctly? That's all I could think about as I waited for the next thunderclap to hit my family.

I wasn't thinking about your family.

The thunderclap came. No flash-to-bang delay. Just one big crash. Metal twisted and bent. Tiny bits of glass filled the air. I swear I could hear the boys screaming.

We hit your car still going seventy miles per hour. The car behind us hit us going forty. The network, in all the infinite wisdom we gave it, decided to save me and my family. When the impacts had been absorbed, when the tires stopped squealing, when the glass and bits of metal settled on the blacktop, when the frame of your car collapsed and mine remained rigid, we ended up okay. Linda was scared, but not injured. The boys were crying, and I was happy to hear it. It meant they were still in one piece, thank God. Abigail, I thought maybe she was hurt, she was so quiet. Panicked, I unbuckled and crawled over the seats to see inside her car seat.

And there she was, pretty as an angel, as healthy and happy as the day I built her from a baby doll, an old laptop, and steel springs. My relief was infinite. I cried and held them all close. I can't say how long we stayed in the car, just holding each other and thanking God we'd made it through okay. It wasn't until the rescue crews opened our door with the jaws-of-life that I got out and saw the rest of the accident.

They checked me out, saw I was okay, were confused about my family, but triaged them as not needing any medical attention. Then they went to your car.

I was standing on the shoulder of the road when they extricated you and your fiancée. You were unconscious but mumbling her name. That's how I know it. Abby. That's what me and Linda called our baby for short. Abby.

When they pulled her out, your Abby, she came out like Jell-O from a mold. Loose, like there were no bones left in her body. Blood everywhere. Her blonde hair was matted and stained dark. There was no sentience in her movements. Her limbs and head went where the firemen moved them or where gravity pulled them. There was no will left in her body. No life. I'm glad you weren't awake to see it. I can't get the image out of my head.

I'm sorry.

I can't look at my family the same way after that day. I can't look them in the eyes. I'm too ashamed of myself. They're too beautiful and I'm too...

I bet your Abby was beautiful too. Before the accident.

I'm sending this to let you know I deactivated the sensors in my car. I'm not carrying any electronic devices. Understand that I knew exactly what I was doing when I first put my family into a car, and I know exactly what I'm doing now. Now, when I drive, the network will see my car as being empty, like I'm not even there. It will see me for exactly what I'm worth: A crumple zone. An impact absorber.

I took your fiancée from you. I took all the potential you had for a family. So I'm sending you mine. They're in a car now, heading to your home over at 2600 Juniper Street. I got your address from the police report. I hope you don't mind. Linda is a great partner. The boys... they're just amazing kids; I know you'll think so too after spending some time with them. And my Abigail. I took your Abby from you. I hope mine fills that hole, even just a little bit. Think of her as your Abby reborn. She's my gift to you.

I'm going out on the road now. I got plenty of fuel and plenty of booze to keep me on the highway for a while. I figure eventually the network will use me for what I'm worth. I trust it to administer justice. I have faith in it now.

That's all I got to say I guess. Just that I'm sorry. That, and please take good care of my family.

See Joe Prosit's story "Pre-Triage" online at Metaphorosis.
If you liked it, leave a comment. Authors love that!
Remember to subscribe to our e-mail updates so you'll know when new stories are posted.

About the story

Some stories fall right into my lap. This one was gifted to me one day when a buddy and I were driving down the road and the topic of self-driving cars came up. I mentioned how the roads will be safer and people can spend their time better. He said "All that's great, until the day your car decides to kill you." That was all he said, but after that the story wrote itself.

A question for the author

Q: Do you write with a particular audience in mind?

A: I don't write for any particular reader in mind. I guess I'm self-serving in the way that, if I enjoy the story, if I think it's creepy or compelling or speaks to me, then I write it. When other people connect, it makes it all the more satisfying because it's natural and unforced. Nothing is contrived.

About the author

Joe Prosit writes sci-fi, horror, and psycho fiction. He lives with his wife and kids in the Brainerd Lakes Area of northern Minnesota. If you're an adept stalker, you can find him on one of the many lakes and rivers or lost deep inside the Great North Woods. Or you can just find him on the internet at JoeProsit.com and on Twitter.

@JoeProsit

A Witch's Guide to Mushrooms and Toadstools

Hannah Hulbert

I kick my way through the decomposing leaves and they cling to my skirts. Others flit around me on the dying breath of summer, adding to the carpet that already comes up to my ankle. The only sound is the titter of thrushes and the distant drone of cattle. The track lies far behind me. I remind myself that I like being alone. That the forest is my ally. But I shiver anyway and quicken my pace.

I spot a likely tree and climb the bank towards it. Broad, lobed leaves, brown and sparse. Broad trunk, shaggy with lichen. An oak. I stoop to examine the base, digging Granny's notebook out of my pocket.

Breast-Feather

A frilly fungus that grows at the foot of hardwood trees. Pale, tongue-like brackets fork out from a central stem, supporting a wrinkled, leathery brown fruitbody. Mousey smell. Young mushrooms form a delicate creamy ruffle and are delicious fried in butter. Specimens darken with age as they gain potency.

Her archaic looped handwriting is unlike my own spidery scrawl. I hold up the image she inked in beside the description, alive with the affection she had for nature, painstakingly studied and preserved on the page for whoever inherited the cottage and the duties she left behind her. For me. I close my eyes and shake my head, scattering the emotions rising up, threatening to cloud my eyes and judgement.

I compare the image with the mushroom sprouting from the tree. This is definitely the one, and nicely matured. A citadel of undulating rooftops fit for fae kings and queens, Granny told me when I was small. I imagine I am a giant come to destroy their home as I slice a handful away from the bark with my pocket knife.

I wrap it in a cloth and head back towards the cottage, regretting not the destruction, but the bitter aftertaste of the sweet memory.

I set the mushroom on the kitchen windowsill to dry and the cast iron kettle on top of the stove to boil. While I wait, I perch on the wooden stool next to Granny's empty rocking chair, just like I always did and never managed to shake the habit of doing. I turn back to the Breast-Feather entry.

Dry for one moon until thin and tough, then grind into a fine powder. Use two teaspoons-full with nettle and black cohosh to brew a tea. Have the woman who longs for a child drink a cup every morning with breakfast and every evening before bed. Have her leave an offering of ripe fruit beside the tree from which the mushroom came with a prayer that the spirits will look favourably upon her.

Granny always used to say that everything we need is already in the world around us. I used to feel the same, a bone-deep contentment, before she died. But the space she left in my world is too big to be filled. Instead I find ways to skirt the void and not fall into it.

The kettle whistles in a steamy crescendo and I rise to remove it. I will tell Cicely when I do my round of the village that her tea will be ready in a month. I picture the joy on the faces of her and her young husband. A joy Granny made possible, still touching the lives of our small community from beyond the grave. The shadow she still casts is a comfort to us all, yet the size of it fills me with dread. That I should be expected to fill that darkness with my own wavering light. My eyes well with tears again, and this time I do nothing to restrain them.

The fractal patterns of the season's first frost cover the window, earlier than I had expected. The silver shimmer of the lawn beyond is muted by mist. I pull on my boots and warmest cloak and push the door open, stepping into the cold.

The air is sharp in my throat when I inhale and my breath forms wispy clouds. All is still, with the exception of a flash of russet and an obnoxious burst of song as a robin wings past. The sparkling blades of grass crunch underfoot as I head towards the forest.

A sweet chestnut fell five years ago not far up the track that leads into the village and I trudge through banks of ice-laced leaves towards it. Granny always had high hopes for a crop of Winter

Mushrooms here. I dutifully visited throughout the year, waiting for the fulfilment of her prophecy.

The wood crumbles into soft, damp fragments under gentle pressure from my fingertips. A whole host of liverworts and fungi adorn the length of the trunk. I keep my gaze fixed on the decomposing wood as I walk the length of it, searching.

And there they are. Winter Mushrooms. Granny's book comes out and I double check the description and sketch.

Winter Mushroom

The Winter Mushroom is a tan umbrella with edges rolling down and inwards. Its scales are dark. The adnexed gills below are whitish. The young stem is pale, but browns with age. Pick it from the base. The cap fits in your palm, cool and smooth.

I snap one from the decaying trunk and turn it over. The gills are the pages of an unreadable book. I stroke them and they spring back into place, fluttering as I leaf through them. The content is silvery spores, not words. I produce a string bag from a pocket and fill it. Granny was right, again.

Back at home, the kitchen embraces me with its residual warmth. I tug off my boots and hang my cloak by the door. I open the stove to stir the embers and add some coal. By the time I have washed and sliced three mushrooms the pan set atop the stove is glowing. I fry the sliced mushrooms in oil and save the rest of the harvest for Cicely.

I take down the tatty recipe book from the shelf and browse the handwritten entries as I sit down to my hot breakfast. The mushroom flesh is rich and meaty and firm between my teeth. The pages are speckled with grease in places and browned. I fold the corner of the page when I find it, so I can copy it out later.

Winter Mushroom broth

Boil a large pan of water. Add to it a dozen winter mushrooms (sliced), a large knob of ginger root (chopped), four cloves of garlic (crushed), an onion (diced) and a handful of thyme. Simmer until the mushrooms are tender and serve piping hot.

This broth is excellent for the expectant mother, to bolster both her health and that of the fledgling life she carries.

Granny's elegant letters blur into illegibility as my eyes fill with tears, unable to read her words. Unable to taste her soup again. Unable to sit down for a simple meal of mushrooms together. Now it falls to me to follow the directions, to teach Cicely how to prepare the soup as Granny once taught me, hoping to do both justice.

When I open my curtains, the last of the snow heaped at either side of the lane has finally melted away. I dress for cold weather but when I step outside I am engulfed in birdsong and warmth and I cannot help but smile.

A few optimistic snowdrops have ventured up through the lawn. I spot a pale pink circle under the apple tree and make a bee-line towards it. A fairy-ring of around twenty pretty mushrooms. I crouch to admire them. The cold air is pungent with salt and ammonia. I fish the book out of the pocket inside my cloak where it spent the entire winter.

Rose Parasol

The Rose Parasol grows in rings, an early herald of spring. They are beautiful to behold, but they are deadly. Easily detected by the smell of sperm. Each umbonate cap is a delicate pink with silken streaks radiating from the hub. The stem is slender and a little paler than the cap. If you peek below, the gills are dove-grey.

The Old Lore tells that Rose Parasol rings mark the perimeter of portals to other realms. If you have an individual in your care for whom your skill will not suffice, this is where they might bring their petition.

How many times did Granny lead me about the garden, teaching me the names and uses of the living things around us? How many stories of little-folk did she tell me, weaving magic out of the mundane? A magic that has faded. The power I wield is a poor shadow of what I knew Granny was capable of, back when I was small and she was a giant, invincible and eternal.

My nose tingles. I screw my lips tight together and step into the circle. And there I let out a sob, and beg wordlessly for meaning or guidance or comfort from the unanswering powers. I receive none of these, only a modicum of catharsis.

The Rose Parasols, or their descendants, last all through the spring. They are where I bring Cicely when she bleeds at the beginning of the summer. She and I stand side by side at the perimeter, hand in hand. I have done all I can and offered my small, floundering words of condolence. This was the only other comfort I could think offer. The warmth of our entwined fingers and a place to vent at the empty sky.

She teeters on the edge of hope, knowing what the blood signifies yet refusing to believe it. I do not encourage her hope, knowing it is unfounded.

When it emerges, her grief is raw and spans universes. I hold mine quietly; a small, dark well that delves into the earth. It is easily concealed, but my sorrow for Cicely tugs at the cover I set over it. I clasp her hand a little tighter.

Cicely pulls away and moans as she steps over the perimeter, a mourning too great for words. I wait at the sideline, brimming with pity and self-pity. And the doubt. The dread that there is something I could have done or failed to do. And always the space in my life where Granny should have been, ensuring I fulfil my duties properly, reassuring me. My higher power.

I leave the cottage by the kitchen door, squelch across the waterlogged lawn, and climb the stile at the back of the garden. A thrush in the hazel clump fills the warm air with melody. Bumblebees drone amid the tiny white flowers on the bramble as I step down into the paddock.

Nellie the old grey donkey is nowhere to be seen, but she has left plenty of heaps of manure. I wade through the glistening waves of grass, examining each island of dung, until I find the mushrooms I am searching for. A community of off-white figures clustered over the disintegrating pile. Granny's book is already in my hand, clutched tight as a talisman. I flick through the dog-eared pages to the right entry.

Faery Dreamer

The mushrooms are tiny, fragile things, shiny and sticky with a bell-shaped cap. They begin dark in spring but fade through the seasons. The paler the flesh, the more potent the mushroom. The gills are fine and dark and the spores black as pitch.

These fruitbodies are not for eating. Their mealy texture is not unpleasant, but the after effect often can be. They are not known as Faery Dreamer for nothing.

I shake out my cloth bag and kneel to pick the mushrooms with gloved hands. Dampness seeps from the ground and through my skirts. The mushrooms are small, delicate things, unassuming and innocent. It would take the whole crop to produce a jarful of powder. The last of Granny's supply has dwindled to less than a quarter of a jar. I harvest them all, knowing fresh fruitbodies will sprout again in a matter of days. That mushrooms regenerate over and over, from a fungus buried under the ground. My bagful represents a tiny portion of the whole and the larger part lives on.

I take the Faery Dreamers back to the cottage and set them to dry. Then I leave the gloves and bag beside the door to wash separate from the rest of my laundry. I take down the heavy book of potions from the shelf and flick through the pages.

Granny's graceful hand details the method of creating the powder from the mushrooms. The method of administration. The various uses.

Use sparingly as a strong pain-relief. Resetting broken bones and suturing deep wounds. I do not recommend offering the Faery Dreamer to a woman in labour, as I have heard rumours of the baby arriving listless or developing slowly. There are, of course, situations where this is not a concern, and in these I advise you to provide as much relief for the woman as she requests. But when her labour is over and she lies empty armed, do not leave her side as she rides the dream, or allow her to sink, alone, into her grief.

I lift my puffy eyes from the page. As heavily as I rely on and as close as I may hold them, Granny's words are a poor substitute for her embrace and reassurance.

With a sigh, I set about packing a basket to take into the village. Cicely's husband has not called for me yet, but I include the last of Granny's powder just in case. Ready to help her through a labour that offers no hope at its end, when the time comes. To endure meaningless pain and strife, without reward.

I wade through the golden ocean of rye, whispering in the breeze. Whispering a secret that I must break to the farmer, yet dread speaking. Truth can be an agony; concealed truth an unbearable weight. I pick a head from the rye and compare it to the sketch in Granny's book one last time. Hoping that I am wrong but knowing I am not.

Purple Rooster's Spur

This fungus does not look like a mushroom. After a long, cold winter, an excessively wet spring may damage the young rye growing in the fields along the valley. Come harvest, you will find a long, hard, black protrusion growing from many of the grains. Warn the owners of the affected fields that his crop is diseased and must be burned. Eating the grains is the cause of Saint Anthony's Fire, a most terrible affliction.

I sigh and add the stalk to the bundle I have already collected. I brush through that diseased crop awaiting a harvest that will never be consumed. Towards the farmhouse, tiny on the hillside. I have a handful of silver in the purse on my belt to pay for the bunch in my hand. At least some good may come of this disaster, but the coins will be small recompense. My pace is slow with the thickness of the heat and reluctance to carry this burden of ill tidings.

When I get home, with a heavy heart and a lighter purse, I collapse onto the stool in my stone-walled kitchen and ease off my shoes. Granny's book of potions is laid out on the table, open at the entry I had been reading over breakfast. Purple Rooster's Spur. The first thing I thought of when I heard about the afflicted crop. The suspicion that I had just confirmed. The instructions on how to decoct a potion from the fungus.

This is a most beneficial substance to dry up the milk of a woman who suffers engorgement whilst weaning, or who never made use of the milk she produced. I add two drops to warm sage tea. The leaves of a savoy cabbage may also bring her some relief from the physical pain, but even time is a poor remedy for the emotional burden she bears.

It is cool in the cottage. The windows are small and the walls thick. I set about collecting the ingredients and apparatus Granny lists in the book, ready to create that potion for Cicely. And though I would never wish the destruction of a livelihood on anyone, I will not let the farmer's tragedy prevent me easing that of another. I carefully peel open the kernels of rye, exposing the black fungus growing inside.

The wheat fields beyond the paddock behind my cottage are loud with workers bringing in the harvest. The hillside is half stubble, where the scythes have been, and half rippling waves of gold. I pack myself a picnic lunch along with Granny's handbook, sling the basket over my shoulder and set off into the forest.

I follow the trail away from the village. The still air hums with tiny flies. I march through the clouds of them, sweat running down my spine. Birds sing, hidden in the shade. The hollow drumming of a woodpecker echoes through the trees. As I move further from humanity, my pace slows. I breathe deeper. Leaf mould and pine. A haze of yellow pollen drifts on a lazy breeze. I blow my nose on my handkerchief and wander on.

At mid morning, I pass the standing stones. I stop for a swig of water in the lee of the tallest one, back pressed against the cold smoothness. Then I set out again, deeper into the forest.

I reach the narrow gorge around midday and cross by the rickety bridge. The ropes and wooden planks groan in complaint, but hold as I pass over the black emptiness below. The gentle trickle of water echoes from the rocky sides. The river is low but still running. Summer is near its end.

The path disappears into a bank of bracken. I struggle through, into the secret place Granny used to bring me. A hollow guarded by oak trees. A place that never feels warm, even on a day like today. I climb over the exposed roots and slide down the leaf strewn slope into the crater.

I sit on the old tree stump at the bottom and eat my lunch, leaving my crumbs for whichever beings dwell here. Fungi create steps around the stump at intervals just right for a tiny creature to ascend to my lap. I imagine them hopping up and down while I eat.

I don't need to check Granny's book, but I take it out anyway. I wonder if I will ever be able to identify a mushroom for myself without having her confirm my assessment for me. Were she still here she would laugh at me. But she isn't.

Lacquered Bracket Fungus

They form oyster-shaped ledges around hardwood tree stumps, as large as your spread hand. The varnished surface is maroon, with concentric rings of purple, black, and red to show its seasons of growth and dormant anticipation. The stem is tough and snaps sharply when picked. When inverted, you can see the minute pores set in the brown skin. When sliced, the flesh inside is off-white with a rich, earthy fragrance.

After lunch I leaf absently through the book. The well worn pages are still no substitute for Granny's company, but the absence has dulled over the past year. And then, when the sun slides behind one of the oaks, stealing what little warmth filtered down to me here, I collected a basketful of the Lacquered Bracket Fungus and scrambled back up the bank, beginning the long trek back into the world of other humans.

I reach the cottage not long before supper and cobble together a meal of salad and bread from the pantry. The basket lies on the table beside me. I retrieve the book from it and read as I eat.

The Lacquered Bracket Fungus is too tough to eat and tastes of soil and leaf mould and autumn. While the fungus is still fresh, dice it and submerge in good quality grain alcohol. Leave to steep for at least two moons, then drain through a cheese-cloth into a bottle. This tincture is a most efficient cure for low spirits if administered steadily over a period of several weeks. Any person in your care who seems to have lost their vitality and desire to connect with the living would benefit from a course of Lacquered Bracket Fungus tincture. But medication alone will not be enough. Ensure they are provided all the care and comfort and counsel they will accept. Ensure they do not become isolated. Watch their eyes for dark shadows and the skin of their wrists. Involve their family and neighbours. And listen silently when they open their lips.

I will prepare the tincture after supper. I hope I will not need it, that Cicely will rise naturally from her spiral of despair. But it is best to be prepared whilst continuing to hope. I push aside my empty plate and set to work.

I pull my hood over my head in an attempt to keep the drizzle off my face. At least the wind is coming from behind me. Brown leaves ride the gusts. I pull my cloak tighter around myself against the cold.

The track leading into the village grows progressively harder to travel as lanes branch out towards farms. By the time I reach the village, it's almost impassable. The churned mud at the edge looks promising. Yes – there against the steep side of the lane are growing the mushrooms I came hunting for. Dark and ragged in the mud. I open Granny's book under the cover of my cloak.

Grandfather Ink-Cap

The young fruitbody is white and egg-shaped and softly frilled. They grow in troops of four to eight, gaining height and losing girth through the season. These young specimens are an excellent addition to stews. But when the Grandfather Ink-Cap has reached the full length of your hand and the cap has opened into a scaly canopy with a tatty grey beard, they are ready to make ink.

I pick a dozen, which is more than enough for a bottle, and tuck them in beside the tincture in the bottom of my basket. I quicken my pace now that I'm not looking for the ink-caps. Hopefully I can reach Cicely's house before the rain gets any heavier.

Once I've made all of my visits and done all of my chores, I head home. The rain has set in, driving into my face. The wind tugs the hood off my head and drags the cloak out behind me so that it is no protection at all against the elements. When I burst through the kitchen door at last, I peel off every item of clothing, stoke the stove and drape them over it. Then I wrap myself in layer upon layer of blankets and sit on my stool at the table, poring through Granny's potion book.

Set the Grandfather Ink-Caps in a bowl at home and allow the black gills to deliquesce, filling the air around with dark spores. After a couple of weeks the Ink-Caps will have dissolved, leaving only a stem and a leathery skin from the cap. Strain the liquid into a bottle and stopper.

The ink keeps well, but does accumulate an unsavoury odour of rot after a week. This can be mitigated by adding a few drops of plant oil. I like the scent of rosemary myself, but others work just as well. The ink is smooth and uniformly black, bar the twinkle of spores left in the wake of your pen stroke.

I was taught as a child that the ink of the Grandfather Ink-Cap had the ability to transcend realms. That words written here on earth could be read by beings Elsewhere. If anyone comes to you with a request for help that you know is beyond the power of us mortals to give, have them peel the bark of a silver birch, and upon it write their request using a raven-feather quill and Grandfather Ink-Cap ink. Then send the petition away upon whichever is their native element.

The ink-caps lie in the basin on my kitchen windowsill for ten days, slowly converting to a thin black liquid. Then I bottle the ink, add lavender oil with a flush of boldness, and set out towards the village as I do every day, to check on Cicely.

The day is cold but dry. We walk together to the ridge at the top of the valley, wind nipping at our faces. On the way I collect a raven feather and birch bark. Nature provides for us once more. At the top of the ridge, I cut a crude nib into the feather. Cicely and I write our wishes onto our scraps of bark and then roll them tightly, hiding the words. Then I watch Cicely shred hers into strands and release them into the sky on the windy hilltop. I dig a hole into the sodden ground with my fingers and bury mine. The words we wrote travel away, on the wind and into the soil. Should anyone receive our requests, we can only hope that they have the power and compassion to answer them.

My nails are black with mud and I feel foolish. But then Cicely grins at me and we are foolish together. That is all the reward I could ever have hoped for. A wish too great to inscribe on birch bark. A magic that comes from within, not above, manifesting at the fringes of our shared humanity. The evidence of something deep and hidden. I smile back at her and we return to the village together.

I walk her back to her cottage, where her husband is fixing a trellis sagging off the side of their porch. We exchange pleasantries and I promise to call in on Cecily again tomorrow. Then I take the muddy track home.

On my way I stray into the woods. The air is rich with the fragrance of decomposition. Of the old preparing for the new. I wear the solitude like a garment that I can shrug off. No one item is designed for all seasons. The trick is finding the one that suits your present need.

The ground is damp and tangled with grasping understory, but I brush through boldly. I make my way towards a clump of Breast Feather fungus adorning a hazel trunk up ahead. I will make sure I have enough to make Cicely more tea, should she call round for it one day. And I will sit her down on the stool while I take the rocking chair, and I will teach her about mushrooms as she drinks.

See Hannah Hulbert's story "A Witch's Guide to Mushrooms and Toadstools" online at Metaphorosis.
If you liked it, leave a comment. Authors love that!
Remember to subscribe to our e-mail updates so you'll know when new stories are posted.

About the story

'A Witch's Guide to Mushrooms and Toadstools' is probably the only story I have ever written for which I can tell you exactly where and when it originated. My family and I were on a walk on 19th October at Avon Heath, not far from where we live. It was a bright, mild day and I took 36 photos of fungi. While the kids played in the stream, I read 'Sunday is Pancake Day' by Tyler Omichinski in *Aether and Ichor* (September 25 2019). The two elements combined to form Granny's field notes. Morris coached me through expanding these into a story — it would not exist without him, so he has my eternal thanks!

A question for the author

Q: If you could have any super power, what would it be?

A: One ability I always fancied was the Fool's skill-tipped fingers from Robin Hobb's 'Realm of the Elderlings'. The ability to know something intimately and completely by touching it. To know its past and future, its properties and potential. And the fact that such an ability can be turned off by simply wearing a glove. A low-key power with few responsibilities attached and hardly any chance of me becoming the target of a maniacal villain.

About the author

Hannah Hulbert lives in urban Dorset, UK. She is on a permanent sabbatical from reality as she raises two children and devotes her scarce free time to visiting imaginary worlds, some of her own creation. She has a degree in Ancient and Medieval History and an obsession with man-made places in the process of being reclaimed by nature. She is probably tweeting or doodling at this very moment.

@hhulbert

Exhibit 57-B
from the Trial of Alonzo Montalvo
v. MoodFoods Incorporated

Douglas DiCicco

Exhibit 57-B in the matter of Alonzo Montalvo v. MoodFoods Incorporated is brought to you by NeutralBot, today's leading provider of AI-directed viewpoint-neutral video analysis. NeutralBot: because no humans means no bias.

This transcript has been enhanced with NeutralNotes™, providing useful context and analysis where deemed appropriate by the NeutralBot AI. These NeutralNotes™ have been crafted by our state of the art AI to be relevant to Alonzo Montalvo's claim that MoodFoods Incorporated must indemnify him against any claims of assault, bodily injury, and/or property damage made by Maria Yevez, Steven Prosser, SceneBeyond Studios, or any of their affiliates or associates.

TRANSCRIPT BEGINS

(The video opens with a view of a black and white clapper board. The board indicates this is the first take of a commercial advertisement.)

Director Maria Yevez (hereafter, MY): Action!

(The clapper board is removed. Alonzo Montalvo stands smiling in front of a television set made to resemble a kitchen. Various MoodFoods Incorporated products are arranged on counters and tables behind him.)

Alonzo Montalvo (Party A) (hereafter, AM): Hello there! I'm Alonzo Montalvo, Emmy-nominated star of television's Open Heartbreak Surgery.

(NeutralNote™: AM's Emmy nomination was for a local award during his brief period as a news reporter in New Mexico. The nomination preceded the filming of the transcribed commercial by seventeen years.)

AM: As a famous Hollywood actor, I know how important it is to keep control over my emotions. You know, we all have days when we need to feel one way, but for one reason or another we're feeling something completely different. Don't you wish you could just change your emotions with a snap of your fingers? Well, now you can! That's why I'm here to talk to you about MoodFoods.

(The camera tracks AM and zooms in slightly as he moves to a counter where a MoodFoods brand JoyJelly has been plated. The orange coloration is consistent with Cantaloupe Contentment flavor.)

AM: If you're one of millions of Americans like me who sometimes needs a little pick me up to shake off the blues, you're probably already familiar with JoyJelly. Not only does this delicious gelatin dessert taste great, it actually gives you a powerful feeling of peace and happiness.

(AM picks up a spoon and carves out a bite of JoyJelly.)

AM: JoyJelly is not an antidepressant. There are no side effects. No addiction. It's just like a little spark of happiness right in your brain, perfect for bringing you out of a slump or starting your day with a little extra spring in your step.

(NeutralNote™: The preceding statement by AM is not consistent with current FDA labeling and advertising regulations applying to emotion-altering foodstuffs in general and MoodFoods in particular.)

(Party B disputes the neutrality of the preceding NeutralNote™.)

(AM eats the bite of JoyJelly.)

AM: Mmm-mmm! That is refreshing. Not only does it taste great and freshen my breath, I'm already feeling a... a...

(AM trails off. His lips are smiling, but there is fear in his eyes. Something has gone wrong.)

(Party B disputes the neutrality of the preceding line of transcription.)

AM: I'm sorry, can we cut?

MY: What's wrong? That take was going great.

AM: I think I'm feeling it. I mean, the happy feeling.

MY: So? That's what this stuff does. You're supposed to get the happy feeling.

AM: I thought we were using duds. I mean, ones without the stuff in them.

MY: It's fine. It'll just make it easier to pretend to be happy.

AM: I'm an actor. I pretend to be happy every day. I don't want to take a bunch of drugs while I'm working.

MY: They aren't drugs. They're single use nano—

AM: Fine, whatever, not the point. Can't we get some fake ones in here?

MY: I'm sorry, no. The FDA doesn't let us do that anymore. They say it's a form of false advertising.

(NeutralNote™: MY's statement is not an accurate reflection of current FDA advertising regulations. Her statement may be a reaction to recent class action litigation against MoodFoods Incorporated.)

(Party B disputes the neutrality of the preceding NeutralNote™.)

AM: (EXPLETIVE DELETED). Is this even safe? I mean, I'm going to be eating these things all day. The script says I'm supposed to take a bite of everything at one point or another.

MY: It'll be fine. Medical and legal cleared everything. They're not drugs. Besides, a lot of MoodFoods counteract the effects of other MoodFoods. It'll probably all cancel out in the end.

AM: ... Fine. Okay. I'm a professional. I'll get this done.

MY: That's the spirit. Cut. Let's get ready for take two, people.

(The video cuts to the clapper board. It indicates this is the second take.)

MY: Action!

Action proceeds in a fashion similar to the first take. AM's speech remains on script. For the sake of brevity, AM's speech is omitted from this transcript up until after he takes the first bite of JoyJelly.

AM: Mmm-mmm! That is refreshing. Not only does it taste great and freshen my breath, I'm already feeling a sense of euphoric calm. With JoyJelly those everyday anxieties and concerns just melt away. It's a milder alternative to chemical mood alteration, with none of the weight gain or sexual dysfunction associated with drug-based treatments. Mmm-mmm!

(AM takes a second bite of the JoyJelly.)

(NeutralNote™: According to Exhibit 36-A, MoodFoods Infomercial Script, this second bite was not part of the script for the infomercial.)

(Party B disputes the neutrality of the preceding NeutralNote™.)

AM: Delicious! But we can't just feel happy all the time, can we? The human experience is so much richer than that. Unending happiness from a blob of gelatin will ultimately feel hollow and meaningless without—

MY: Stop!

(AM looks off-camera to MY. His smile is broader than ever, but his eyes show annoyance.)

AM: What's the problem?

(MY steps in front of the camera to speak with AM.)

(NeutralNote™: At this point in the video, MY does not appear to have any of the scrapes, bruises, or other superficial injuries documented in Exhibit 16-A through 16-D, medical records of Maria Yevez.)

MY: You're off script.

AM: I know. I was ad-libbing.

MY: The whole point of the product is that people can eat it and feel happy. MoodFoods doesn't want you calling the sense of euphoria their product provides "hollow and meaningless". They certainly don't want you referring to the product as a "blob of gelatin". That's not the message we're going for here.

AM: I was trying to transition to the SadSoup segment. You know, explain why they'd want to use a product that makes them depressed. I still don't understand why anyone buys that stuff.

MY: Just stick to the script, please. Cut!

(Video cuts to the clapper board. This is the third take.)

MY: Pick it up from "but we can't just feel happy all the time". Action!

AM: But we can't just feel happy all the time, can we? What if you need to put yourself in the right frame of mind for a funeral, a memorial service, or a day of remembrance for a major national or international tragedy? Well, MoodFoods has you covered there, too.

(AM moves to another counter. A serving of SadSoup has been poured into a bowl. The empty can sits nearby. The label and green coloration of the soup are consistent with Sorrowful Spinach flavor. The camera zooms in to capture a close up of the bowl of soup and the label on the can.)

AM: Introducing SadSoup, the perfect appetizer to put you in a somber and reflective mood.

(AM ingests a spoonful of SadSoup.)

AM: With a sharp bitterness reminiscent of dark chocolate, SadSoup is perfect for serving at those occasions when you want everyone to be joined by a communal feeling of sorrow. Mmm. You know, this reminds me of my dog Max. He died just last...

(AM is visibly tearing up.)

AM: I'm sorry, can we cut again?

MY: What is it now?

(The video continues recording despite AM's request to cut.)

(NeutralNote™: Anecdotal evidence suggests SceneBeyond Studios camera operators are trained not to cut until the director personally calls for it.)

AM: The teleprompter says Max, but that wasn't my dog's name. My dog was named Rex.

MY: (quietly, sarcastic) How creative. There's that Emmy-winning talent.

AM: What?

MY: We made Max up for the script. It's not supposed to be about your real dog.

AM: Well, why can't it be? I mean, does it matter whether it's a fake name or not? I want to talk about Rex. I miss him.

MY: ... Fine. I guess it doesn't matter. You can change the name to Rex if you stick to the rest of the script.

AM: I hadn't seen him for years. Cynthia got him in the divorce. So when I heard she'd put him down, I—

MY: Mr. Montalvo, I'm sorry, but we have to keep shooting. We have three more commercials to film today.

AM: You're right. I'm sorry. I'm so sorry.

MY: Cut.

(Cut to the clapper board. This is the fourth take.)

MY: Pick it up from "Introducing SadSoup". Action!

(AM repeats the lines and action in accordance with the script, including ingesting another spoonful of SadSoup.)

AM: You know, this reminds me of my dog Rex. He died just last year. It can be sad to think of loved ones we've lost over the years, but there's also a certain catharsis that comes with exploring those losses. Don't bother with expensive therapists and grief counselors. With SadSoup you can express the full depths of your loss and move on as a fuller, more complete person. MoodFoods—

(A microphone boom descends into view.)

(NeutralNote™: Visual analysis has determined with 98.7% certainty that this is the same microphone boom introduced into evidence as Exhibit 6. The blood stains present on Exhibit 6 are not yet present on the boom at this point in the recording.)

MY: Boom in the shot. (EXPLETIVE DELETED) Steve.

Sound Crewmember Steven Prosser (hereafter, SP): Sorry!

(NeutralNote™: For additional context, see Exhibit 9-A through 9-V, medical records of Steven Prosser.)

MY: Sorry, Mr. Montalvo. You were doing great. Let's keep it going.

(AM is now visibly crying.)

AM: (quietly) I'll keep it going. I'm a professional.

MY: Great. Let's get makeup in here. Cut!

(Cut to the clapper board. Fifth take. There are no signs of AM's tears when he reappears.)

MY: Pick it up from "Introducing SadSoup". Action!

(AM follows the script, including ingesting a third spoonful of SadSoup. AM begins to deviate from the script with the lines referencing the deceased dog.)

AM: You know, this reminds me of my dog, Rex.

(AM begins to cry again.)

AM: I should have kept him. I thought Cynthia would take care of him. (EXPLETIVE DELETED). I thought she would take care of me. But I didn't deserve her. I never deserved her. It was all my fault. All my—

MY: Okay, okay. Stop. You know what? Take four was fine. We don't really need the last line of the SadSoup segment. If MoodFoods really wants it, we can throw together a deepfake in post. It's not like we're breaking the bank on our effects budget here.

(NeutralNote™: Per current Screen Actor's Guild's recommendations, MY's proposal does not represent best practices for professional film development. The ability of current deepfakes to provide quality comparable to trained actors remains a subject of significant debate and disagreement.)

AM: Cynthia's right. I'm a hack. She said nobody cares about a local Emmy from forever ago.

MY: Let's take ten, everyone. Someone get Mr. Montalvo another JoyJelly, please. And get makeup back in here. Cut!

(AM looks as if he is trying to say something to MY before the video cuts, but is unable to do so. He is sobbing too hard to form words. He is clearly profoundly haunted by the failure of his marriage and his personal responsibility for that failure.)

(Party A disputes the neutrality and factual accuracy of the preceding line of the transcript.)

(Clapper board. Take six.)

MY: Okay, we're picking it up from "What about those days".

AM: I'm sorry, can we hold on a second?

(The clapper is removed. AM stands behind a counter with a plated RageWich framed in the middle of the shot. The bright red coloration of the sauce is consistent with Cayenne Calamity flavor.)

MY: What's the problem?

AM: I just don't understand the appeal of this one. I mean, I didn't understand SadSoup either, but this makes even less sense. Who buys a sandwich that makes them angry?

MY: Anger is a very productive emotion, Mr. Montalvo.

AM: Is that the angle? Productivity? I didn't really get that from the script.

MY: Sure, why not? I'm starting to feel pretty angry myself, and I'm pretty sure we'll have produced an infomercial by the end of this. Now please, just stick to the script.

AM: Okay, sorry. I'm ready.

MY: Good. Picking it up from "What about those days". Action!

AM: What about those days when you really need to stand up for yourself? Are you tired of getting pushed around by your co-workers? Have an annoying neighbor you wish you finally had the courage to tell off? Sick of being polite to aggressive telemarketers? MoodFoods has you covered. Introducing RageWich: a concentrated dose of delicious anger packed between two slices of buttery belligerence.

(AM picks up the RageWich and takes a bite.)

AM: Mmm, spicy! With RageWich—

(The microphone boom from Exhibit 6 descends into view. No visible blood stains.)

MY: Boom in the shot. (EXPLETIVE DELETED)

AM: (EXPLETIVE DELETED), Steve!

SP: Sorry, sorry!

AM: That was (EXPLETIVE DELETED) perfect, Steve. And you (MULTIPLE EXPLETIVES DELETED)—

MY: Cut!

(Clapper board. Take seven.)

AM: (close to the camera, near MY) How the hell has he not been fired?

MY: (quietly) Steve's the studio head's nephew. Nothing I can do about it. (louder) Places!

(AM returns to his place by the counter with the RageWich.)

MY: Picking it up from "what about those days". Action.

AM: What about those days when you really need to stand up for yourself? Are you tired of getting pushed around by your co-workers? Have an annoying neighbor you wish you finally had the courage to tell off? Do you feel like just storming over to your ex-wife's place and finally telling her what you think of her and her new little boy toy?

(AM picks up the RageWich and takes another bite.)

AM: Maybe you want some answers about how they could afford a trip to Maui when they said they didn't have enough money for Rex's surgery. Well, RageWich gives you the confidence you need to—"

MY: You're off script again, Mr. Montalvo.

AM: (EXPLETIVE DELETED). I was ad-libbing. Ad. Libbing. Have you never shot a commercial before? Never worked with an actual professional actor? I'm giving you gold up here, and you just want me to stick to this (EXPLETIVE DELETED) script written by whatever film school dropout you—

MY: I wrote the script, Mr. Montalvo.

AM: (EXPLETIVE DELETED) you.

MY: Cut.

(Clapper board. Take eight.)

MY: Picking it up from "mmm, spicy". Action.

(AM takes another bite of the RageWich.)

MY: Mr. Montalvo, I think we have enough shots of you eating the sandwich. It's fine. You can skip it.

(AM makes a fist, crushing the remaining RageWich in his hand.)

AM: Don't tell me how to (EXPLETIVE DELETED) act.

MY: Cut! Take fifteen, every—

(Clapper board. Take nine.)

MY: We're skipping ahead to the SootheSalad segment. I think you could use it, Mr. Montalvo. We'll finish up the RageWich segment later. Picking it up from—

AM: Wait. Hang on. I want to say something.

(The clapper is removed. AM looks more composed. The crumbled RageWich has been cleaned up.)

MY: What is it now, Mr. Montalvo?

AM: I get it now. I get it. The products. Why anyone would want to buy these things. I can do this.

MY: I'm very glad to hear it. Now, picking up from—

AM: I can sell these. Just let me try something. Roll for a little while, let me make my own pitch. It's going to be good, I promise.

MY: Mr. Montalvo, I'm sorry if you don't like the script, but it's already been approved by MoodFoods. If you could just—

AM: Please. Let me have one take. Just one. If you don't like it, or it doesn't work, I promise I'll stick to the script religiously for the rest of the shoot. No more ad-libs. I promise.

MY: ... One take. One take only, Mr. Montalvo.

AM: Thank you.

MY: Action.

(The camera zooms in on AM. He is composed. Focused. He knows exactly what he wants to say about MoodFoods products and services.)

(Party B disputes the neutrality of the preceding line of the transcript.)

AM: To be human is to struggle. To struggle against outside forces, yes. Disease, war, the random unhappy accidents of fate. But more than that, it is a struggle against ourselves, our emotions. Our emotions come from deep inside ourselves. We give birth to them, but we can never truly master them. We are paralyzed by useless regrets. We set out in pursuit of self-destructive folly, directed by pointless rage. We waste years of our short, precious lives swaddled in the comforting lies of false happiness. For millennia, humans have been mere flotsam swept along in the rapids of an emotional current outside of our control. No more. Today, we can be free. Today, with MoodFoods—

(The microphone boom from Exhibit 6 descends into view. No visible blood stains.)

MY: Boom in the shot.

SP: (EXPLETIVE DELETED). Sorry.

MY: (EXPLETIVE DELETED).

AM: (EXPLETIVE DELETED). I don't have to (EXPLETIVE DELETED) take this. I'm a (EXPLETIVE DELETED) Emmy winner.

SP: (quietly) Local Emmy winner.

AM: I (EXPLETIVE DELETED) heard that!

(AM's face contorts with fury. He leaps over the counter, knocking the SadSoup, JoyJelly, and SootheSalad onto the floor.)

MY: Mr. Montalvo!

SP: (EXPLETIVE DELETED).

(AM stomps towards SP, knocking over the camera. The lens fractures, heavily distorting the video from this point forward. The only clearly visible area is a portion of the craft services table.)

SP: I'm sorry! I'm sorry!

AM: Rex!

(The audio is replaced with a loud crashing sound, followed by silence. Audio analysis suggests with 89.4% certainty that this is the result of Exhibit 6 striking a hard object with considerable force, breaking in the process. Given an 88.6% likelihood that the hard object in question is the face and/or torso of Steven Prosser, this is likely the source of the injuries documented in Exhibit 9-A through 9-V.)

(Several people can be seen running past the camera in an apparent state of panic. The speed at which they are moving combined with the damage to the camera lens makes most impossible to identify, with the exception of AM, who stops at the craft services table to take an entire platter of RageWiches.)

(Video ends.)

(NeutralNote™: The video time stamp places the end as seconds before the beginning of Exhibit 58-A, video of Alonzo Montalvo's rampage through the SceneBeyond Studios parking structure and subsequent arrest by local law enforcement.)

(NeutralNote™: Thank you for using NeutralBot. This transcript has been enhanced with insightful AI-generated analysis.)

(Party A and Party B dispute the neutrality and factual accuracy of the preceding NeutralNote™.)

TRANSCRIPT ENDS

See Douglas DiCicco's story "Exhibit 57-B from the Trial of Alonzo Montalvo v. MoodFoods Incorporated" online at Metaphorosis.
If you liked it, leave a comment. Authors love that!
Remember to subscribe to our e-mail updates so you'll know when new stories are posted.

About the story

The format of Exhibit 57-B comes from my background as an attorney. I've read many transcripts of bizarre exchanges over the years. I find something uniquely comical about seeing something strange and unexpected in such a dry, formal format. As for the actual content of the story, I wrote it as a way of exploring my thoughts about our current culture about emotional health, and the societal idea that it is almost always good to feel happy. There's an appropriate and an inappropriate way to feel about almost everything, and people sometimes try to force themselves to feel the "right" way in a given situation, even if it comes naturally. The story is about what happens when you take that way of thinking to an extreme.

A question for the author

Q: Is there a specific environment you find most conducive to writing, and is it different for different kinds of scenes?

A: I do almost all of my writing in my home office. I've tried writing in book stores, coffee shops, and at writer meetups in the past, but I've found I'm less productive with other people around.

The physical location is the same no matter what I'm writing, but I do change what I'm listening to. When I need calm focus I either listen to the sounds of rain or just have complete silence. When I'm looking for a more energetic mood, I switch to music.

About the author

Douglas DiCicco is a writer of speculative fiction. He has worked as an attorney, a teacher, and a renaissance faire performer. He currently lives with his wife, son, and cat in Clovis, California.

June

The Record Collector

Nathaniel Williams

The first time the house yells at them, it sounds like her husband. Eileen Ulmstead-Barris springs up in bed and looks at Preston lying next to her, motionless in his favored sleeping position—on his back, with his head buried under a pillow that should have smothered any sounds rising from his mouth. The shouts become louder and louder, then stop. Moments later, another cry fills the room.

He must be having an awful nightmare, she thinks. When he is awake, Preston rarely raises his voice for anything. Eileen, half-asleep, shifts the duvet atop her, reaches for the pillow, and pulls it from Preston's face. He looks peaceful, eyes shut, bathed in the green light of the digital alarm clock.

More shouts follow. Preston's voice is echoing across the walls.

But his lips aren't moving.

Why isn't he waking up? She stops herself from nudging him, reminded of warnings she's heard about not waking a dreamer. Or is that a sleepwalker? She hesitates until a piercing shriek rings out and Preston shifts in his sleep and speaks to her.

"Eileen," he mutters as he rolls over, his back now to her, "turn off your damn alarm."

Years later, Preston Barris will feel compelled to explain his comment from that first night—"Eileen does that a lot. Hits 'snooze' in the morning a dozen times before she gets out of bed. She's a hard sleeper, and not exactly considerate of the person next to her. I just heard noises and assumed it was her clock going off."

The next night, he isn't so lucky. The shouts sound like Eileen, and they both sit awake until morning.

All this happened over a decade ago. Remember that time? Before the housing bubble burst? Homes appreciated in exponents associated with Vegas slot machines or near-mint Silver Age comic books. Everyone—from retirees to new college grads like Eileen and Preston—was urged to get in on it.

Hindsight is never 20/20. It's purblind and tainted by the present's dominating hues. In truth, most of us ignore bad omens in times of plenty, and what we think of as the good old days never seem that great as we live through them. What happened to Eileen and Preston screams "Bad Omen" to anyone willing to believe it. Questions will go unanswered, morals will be left cloudy, as their story proceeds. It's not an urban legend or *This American Life* podcast. The house didn't have seven gables or gingerbread sweets beckoning its purchasers inside. It was just a mock Tudor in St. Louis, Missouri, an upscale, milquetoast neighborhood in fly-over country.

Things get weirder. Eileen and Preston talk things over. (They talk everything over. Preston insists on consensus decision-making.) They review the details.

She wants to hire a plumber just in case it's something in the pipes. He wants to banish whatever spectre has obviously invaded their home.

See, Preston's a magician. Not the kind who does card tricks or saws ladies in half onstage. He's a wizard. Or warlock. Eileen isn't sure which he prefers and, truth be told, he changes it on her. She's heard people call the stuff he does Wicca, although he shuns that term and says his rituals are completely different. It mostly involved him building a small worship space in an armoire—filled with candles, incenses, and trinkets that looked like an antique jewelry store display—and sitting in front of it irregularly, an act with all the outward appearances of daydreaming. On specific nights of the year, he meets a group of friends somewhere and they'll daydream together. It's not Eileen's thing, but she gets it.

In the end, they just can't blow a hundred bucks or more on a plumber. At least not while she's working at that rinky-dink radio station. (Maybe Preston doesn't say the last bit aloud, but she knows he thinks it.)

Eileen runs programming at the local public FM station. The volunteer deejays think Eileen is yuppie scum infiltrating their cool, community radio scene. Only she and the General Manager actually get salaries. She also gets a battleship grey credenza in the corner of the entry room. She doles out the shifts. She generates the programming logs that go to the FCC. When something breaks, she explains why they can't fix it. Every day, something breaks.

Deejays come in to her office, demanding new headphones, better mics, shinier toggle switches on the control board.

No, she says.

She knows the budget, they don't. It doesn't matter. She still feels like a fraud.

Every now and then, someone sneers at her, something like "Oh, that's right, you're the music programming director who *doesn't even like music!*"

"*That's me*," she says flatly, but feels her face reddening as she goes back to running things.

The only deejay who talks to her like a person is Len, a retired St. Louis county firefighter, father of four, grandpa of nine, who plays jazz on Thursday afternoons but comes in daily and makes a pot of coffee for everyone. He's a good listener, and Eileen confides in him.

"So, Preston thinks the house is..." Len asks.

"Yeah," she says. "But he's sort of into the freaky stuff." Preston would die if he heard her put it that way. "He's more willing to accept the... supernatural."

"Well," Len says, "Such things aren't unheard of around here, you know."

He means *The Exorcist*. Supposedly, the events that take place in the book and movie are based on something that really happened in St. Louis back in 1949. Sure, they'll tell you, the movie is set outside Washington, D.C., and that's where the actual possessed child was discovered. But the exorcism itself? That happened downtown in the old Alexian Brothers Hospital on Osage Street, just a few blocks off fabled Route 66. You can't bring up anything supernatural in that town without someone mentioning it, as if they've been waiting the whole conversation for the chance. They're like Texans with the Alamo.

"You know who's into that kind of thing? Retro Roddy. The guy who does Saturdays. Have you talked to him?"

"No. Preston's already got a friend coming by to give the place a once-over."

"Hmm." Len says, sipping his coffee. "A supernatural once-over."

The house isn't them. That's the problem.

Couples less than five years out of college don't own homes in Webster Groves. These old Tudor houses with brick and ivy and vaulted wooden doors straight out of Sherwood Forrest, the curving sidewalks lined with boxwood and towering sycamores—they belong to the older St. Louis-area residents. Lawyers, pediatricians, aerospace engineers. The guy who's an advertising agency VP. The gal who owns a chain of organic grocery stores. They deserve these houses. Not Eileen and Preston. Not yet.

But they could afford the house, despite its coveted location. They're both only children of well-situated parents. Preston's folks had him late, died young, and left an inheritance, and Eileen's parents gave her a smaller chunk of cash when they moved to Phoenix, and still call regularly to remind her of their largess.

Their regular phone call comes during the aforementioned Supernatural Once Over, as Preston pours herbal tea for a pretty woman. His friend Greta is skinny, perky, and prone to halter-tops, sheer batik skirts, and mounds of bone-and-turquoise jewelry.

"We have to soothe it," Greta tells them. "You don't give orders to powers like this. Once it feels relaxed, the creepy stuff will stop."

Greta explains how they should temporarily treat whatever-it-is like a roommate, someone who has as much right to live there as them. Then she begins talking about her current live-in boyfriend, who recently stiffed her for two months' rent.

Eileen feels some relief when the phone rings.

"So, how's our Eileen?" her father says.

"Okay."

"Still stressed out at work?"

"Yes."

"And Preston?"

"We're okay," she says.

"Just okay?"

"Yes, Dad. Last I checked 'okay' means nothing's wrong. Did someone change that without telling me?"

"I can just hear it in your voice. You don't sound happy."

Happy.

Her parents put a high value on happy. When she was a child, the two of them stayed happy by smoking copious amounts of marijuana on the couch while she made them peanut butter sandwiches. They weren't complete burnouts, but they didn't have long-term goals until Eileen hit middle school. Suddenly, they worked more nights and weekends. Dad got promoted to head of maintenance for several commercial office buildings. Mom got her real estate license. They transformed.

Weeks later, Preston and Greta are neck deep in talking to the house, but the house keeps shouting. They light candles that smell like burnt hair and cinnamon. Eileen can't help but question if this aromatherapy is what the house really needs. She holds back from speaking the thought that never leaves her mind—*Are you sure you know what you're doing?*

Then, one night she arrives home early hoping to get a nap and finds Greta alone in the house running the vacuum cleaner over little piles of salt sprinkled all around the carpet. Apparently, Greta now has a key. Greta has a milk crate full of toiletries and an overflowing rucksack by the door. Greta herself oozes gratitude for Eileen and, especially, Preston.

"You've got yourself quite a guy there, Eileen Barris," she says. "You're a lucky gal."

"Thank you," Eileen replies automatically.

That night, Eileen tries to understand.

"Greta jumped the gun. I told her that you and I would talk about it," Preston says. "But, look, this thing is taking a lot of time. Greta says maybe weeks. She's on the outs with her roommate, and it makes sense for her to stay with us."

"Things are crazy enough around here."

"She's doing a lot of work—unpaid, mind you—and here's a nice way to thank her."

"I'm not sure."

"Well, she needs to be here. You don't understand how these things work."

Eileen understands that Greta is broke, has been kicked to the curb by her boyfriend, and now has a free place to crash for a few weeks.

Before she can protest, several gunshot-like pops come from the kitchen. A pool of red covers the linoleum. Eileen traces the liquid up the side of the counter, where six shattered bottles of Cabernet Sauvignon sit in the wine rack.

Then the laughter starts. It is a sarcastic, staccato tittering punctuated by snorts.

"That's your laugh," Preston says, backing away from the spill and out the kitchen door. "And that was *my* wine."

It is. Their house is laughing at her with her own voice.

She gets a mop and a bucket and starts to clean.

Eileen leaves for work the next morning without waking Greta, who is immobile on the couch, and without talking to

Preston, who will, she knows, take this as her tacit approval of his plan.

The next day, she searches Human Resources files for Retro Roddy's number and—upon discovering only an empty Manila folder—asks Len to help contact him.

Retro Roddy agrees to meet her at Uncle Bill's Pancake and Dinner House, off Kingshighway Blvd. He shows up late. Eileen takes a syrup-sticky booth in the back, near the window facing the parking lot, a long path of corners, wooden beams, and ugly carpet between her and the other patrons.

Although he has effectively been her employee for two years, Eileen has never met Retro Roddy. He deejays midnight to 2 a.m. on Saturdays and skips all organizational meetings, but always submits the mandatory log sheet of songs he played, handwritten in red, felt-tip ink with letters so crisp and legible they'd make a typewriter envious. These lists mean nothing to Eileen. As long as the songs are free of profanity, as long as they garner a listenership, and as long as those listeners free their bank accounts of discretionary income during pledge drives—and they do, Roddy has a following—she doesn't care what he plays.

Although he's a stranger, she knows him instantly. A faded red vintage automobile—a 1965 Ford Falcon, she later learns—pulls into the parking lot, taking up two spaces. A man stumbles out, the bangs of his gray-tinged mop-top spilling over the edges of his Wayfarers. The black t-shirt under his red velvet sports coat is a size too tight and reveals the thinnest white line of beer belly where it rises over his even tighter striped pants. His shoes are snakeskin, narrowed to Keebler-elf points at the tip.

"Smokin' section!" he bellows when he sees her, nodding to the other side of the restaurant, the one filled to capacity.

Eileen relinquishes her privacy, joins him at a smoking booth, and tells her story. Roddy waves his Lucky Strike like an orchestra conductor as she talks. He fiddles with packet after packet of sugar. Some even get poured into his coffee.

"Well, *amiga*," he says, "what I can't do is tell you why it's happening, if you're cursed or unlucky or paying for crimes of your past or someone else's. Give that up. If you need that, I'm not your man. What I *can* do, is get rid of it with a little time and some money."

The figure he asks for is low. Very low. She agrees instantly.

"I get paid when you get your house back. First, I need to come by your place and have a look around. Will it get ugly?"

"No," she says, "Preston and Greta are pretty reasonable. Just stubborn."

"I meant the house. Is it throwing stuff off the shelves? Slinging cutlery or plates around? Is there any gunk or goo dripping? Any blooooood?"

"No."

"Don't worry about your guy and the witch. They're fellow travelers, so to speak. We may do things differently, but we should see eye to eye. I can be diplomatic as hell when I need to be."

That night, she gets to see Roddy's brand of diplomacy firsthand. As anticipated, Greta and Preston feel slighted, even betrayed, that she has brought him. Beads of sweat form on Eileen's temples, doubts made tangible by the Midwestern humidity.

"Here's how it works," Roddy explains. "I set up my stuff and see if the house responds. When I get a sign, we'll all know. Then I'll be able to tell if this will take days or weeks."

Eileen clenches her teeth in a wave of despair—*weeks?*—but Roddy doesn't pause for questions.

"I need until 10 o'clock tonight to test things. After that, you can decide if you want to see this thing through. If it don't work, you never need to see me again."

It is apparently the right thing to say. They agree he'll leave by ten p.m.

"Okay," he says. "Let's hit it!"

He steps back, crosses his legs and spins around on his heel, like something from a Four Tops routine.

Over his shoulder, he shouts "Anyone want to help me fetch my stuff out of old horse?"

"Horse?" Greta says.

Only Eileen follows him out.

By the time she reaches his Ford, he has retrieved what looks like a battered suitcase from his back seat. He stands before her with a stoic frown, something like a gunslinger holding his Peacemaker. But then memories of the area's favorite horror flick arise, and Eileen pictures old Max Von Sydow in the movie poster, with his suitcase, hat, and trench coat, standing outside, that house that creepy light shining down from little Regan's window. Darn Len and his St. Louis folklore.

Roddy opens the car's trunk, which holds a tangle of red and white wires and some electronics equipment, and many, many wooden crates filled with old records.

"Grab an armload," he says.

Eileen remembers her father crouched near the living room floor, rubbing his chin, as he tested his hi-fi system. Fiddling with speaker wire. Turning knobs. Moving speakers inches to the left or right.

When she got older, she chalked up her father's pursuit of what he called "Optimum Sound" to mild stoner paranoia, figuring the subtle differences in aural quality were figments of his marijuana-laced imagination.

Yet, here's Roddy doing the exact same thing in her living room.

He makes patterns on the ground, geometric shapes of speaker cable, twirling them like a lasso as they fall onto the carpet. The cords all feed into his amplifier, rivers emptying into a Mississippi delta, flowing directly to the New Orleans basin that is Roddy's record player, which looks handcrafted from many other machines.

Eileen winces, recalling her father's eccentricities and realizes she's already invested too much into Roddy. She needs him to succeed. She feels Preston and Greta's growing contempt as they watch Roddy twirl and backstep.

He begins to play the music.

"Now it's gotta be loud, you understand," Roddy shouts over the song.

He sits down on the couch, puts his shoes on the coffee table, and shushes Preston when he tries to speak. For hours, Roddy plays an array of things. One record is old blues music with clicks and scratches, the next is a pristine-sounding rock record with violins and French horns. Sometimes he plays just one song, other times a whole album side. By the end of the night, album covers litter their floor.

Sometimes Greta covers her ears or furrows her brow, frustrated by the strange sounds, until Roddy plays a piano solo.

"That's 'Clair de Lune,'" she says, shocked to recognize something.

"Yeah, Debussy's occultism is well documented. I'm pretty sure he composed it for just this kinda thing."

As the music ends, the house begins to vibrate.

"*Moooooooore. More, pleassse,*" it croons.

Roddy rushes to switch the record to a 45 single.

"Don't change it if that's what it wants!" Greta says.

"That ain't how it works. Just listen."

They hear violins and a chorus of oohs and aahs.

" 'Since I Don't Have You' by the Skyliners," Roddy whispers proudly as the house stops jiggling. "Works like a charm. It's basically 'Clair de Lune,' but with more teenager."

The house sits quiet and still.

Roddy nods. "OK. Here's how it works," he says. "This song's just enough different from the one I played before it to make the Whatever-It-Is in your house uncomfortable without makin' it *mad*. We gotta convince it to move on by changing the music. *Gradually.* We can't just throw music it hates at it all of a sudden. Just over time play crazier stuff. Harder stuff. Spiritual stuff."

Crazy, hard, and spiritual, Eileen thinks. *Sure. Why not?* She has grown tired of waiting for Greta and Preston to get results.

"C'mere and take a look." He motions them towards the record player. "We're gonna keep this song playin' for the rest of the night. The song will replay when it finishes as long as this here lever stays put. Do *not* touch the lever. And let it keep going when you leave for work. I'll come by tomorrow, bring more records, and we'll see if we can stop it once and for all."

"So we're supposed to sleep while the song repeats?" Preston says.

"Well, yeah. It's pretty mellow. Be glad the house didn't respond to speed metal or something."

A Spanish dancer exposes her bare breasts in a sepia photograph.

Two businessmen shake hands as one of them ignites into flames.

Four men inside a large television set run from an enormous cartoon space villain.

A shaggy dog-thing jumps a racing hurdle.

These are but a few covers in Roddy's record collection, strewn out like an illusionist's deck of cards across her living room carpet. To her surprise, Eileen recognizes some faces—Prince astride his purple motorcycle, Springsteen leaning on his Cadillac convertible.

Preston is at work. Greta is elsewhere. Roddy will be back soon. Alone inside her strangely-behaving house, still in work clothes, Eileen has only one thought—

I should be more scared.

But she'd been scared before. Managing a station full of radio renegades who see right through her "by-the-book" façade—that is scary. Her last semester of college, facing graduation alone, searching for a first job alone, before she met Preston—that was scary. Raising herself, arranging rides to Girl Scouts and schedules for her homework due dates, while her Mom and Dad played parental hooky—that was scary.

She hears Roddy's Falcon pull up and goes to meet him. He wears a jean jacket covered with buttons with band names, a wide-lapelled paisley shirt, and bell-bottoms.

"Need help unloading your trusty horse?" she asks.

"Did you say *horse*?" he says. "Like Trigger or Silver? You misheard me." He shakes his head and runs his palm across the car's bumper. "His name's *Horus*. Like the Egyptian sky god, son of Osiris. Some of those designers at Ford knew what they were doin' back in the 60's. Same thing Hitler's bozos did with the scarab back when they designed the Volkswagen." He slaps the car's hood. "This here is two tons of rolling V8 talisman. No black magic in the world that can contend with this."

Inside, he examines several records like a Japanese gardener pruning a bonsai tree, head tilting, nose an inch away from grooves. "So you're not into the witchcraft stuff like your husband?" he asks, barely looking up.

"No. I'm not anything."

"Unaffiliated?"

"Yeah."

"I've known a few guys who practiced the old craft. Most of 'em were in covens. Said it really got them in touch with their feminine side. Sounded like they spent a lot of time standing around naked watching candles burn."

"I don't think his worship is like that," Eileen says.

All the things she doesn't know about Preston's beliefs, his other world. The gaps in her knowledge are immense.

Roddy raises his palms defensively. "Hey, I'm not belittling his faith. I just do things kinda different. Hell, I was raised by heavy duty born-again Christians. *Way* weirder than any pagan-types I ever met." Roddy took a sip of beer and gestured at the jumble on the floor. "They weren't too happy when I took to rock 'n' roll. Called it the Devil's music. But, hey, sometimes you can't control what speaks to you, y'know?"

Neighbors watch the blood red car coming and going each afternoon, just as they had seen the wispy woman in flowing dresses moving in, one cardboard box at a time.

A few neighborhood dignitaries stop by one night to make sure they aren't prepping to sell the place.

Where else would you want to go?

This is a great place to raise kids, when you're ready, of course.

People here look out for one another.

If you ever are tempted to sell, please be sure to start well above appraised value.

Many assume it's a *ménage a quatre*, just another case of suburban polygamy springing up. But who's buggering whom?

The neighbors aren't the only curious ones.

Eileen's mother calls one night while Roddy is playing records. All goes fine until her mother asks to say hello to Preston.

"He's not home yet."

"But I heard music in the background. Are *you* listening to…?"

"No," Eileen says. "We have a guest. A guy from work."

"While Preston's gone? Oh, honey…."

"It's not what you think."

"You know, if it *was*, I'd never tell Preston."

"No. Mom. How could that possibly be okay with you?"

"I just want whatever's best for you. I can sense that you're unhappy. Your father says he hears it in your voice, but you never share details. Talk to me."

A tiny earthquake ripples across the floor, shaking a stack of coasters from the coffee table. The music has stopped.

The armoire filled with Preston's talismans and charms tilts on the wall, its door swinging forth and dumping all its contents onto the floor. Not good.

Eileen groans, too exhausted to panic. "I have to go, Mom."

"My bad," Roddy says. "I'll pick 'em up and put 'em back."

"No," she almost shouts.

As she begins gathering talismans, she realizes that, even if none of them are broken, there is *no way* she can put them back exactly as Preston had them. He'll know. And that means she'll have to tell him this happened. And he'll be petulant and smug.

Eileen watches Roddy hunched and frantic, turning EQ knobs ever so slightly this way or that. Roddy is *not* the kind of man Eileen could ever see herself leaving Preston for. Too much like her dad.

And she knows that ultimately Preston is more likely to leave *her*. She's avoided thinking about what could have happened between him and Greta while she was gone. The thought of Preston alone with another woman doesn't make her paranoid. Their sex life stalled a while back, but that's just how a marriage works sometimes. Right? His inattention. Her disinterest. It is hard to separate the two. Maybe Greta is satisfying him, and that explains it. Or maybe Roddy is right about magic getting Preston in touch with his "feminine side" and he will out himself in a few weeks or months or years and leave her for another guy. She can't guess. The lack of emotion chills her.

Then, that night, Roddy leaves some old love song on replay—full of sad, majestic echoes. Even though she knows these sounds are probably just recording studio tricks, something about hearing it at that moment sends a fissure through her soul. She cries herself to sleep.

"I can't handle this," Greta says, hoisting an armload of dirty clothes on top of her sleeping bag and peering over the stack at Eileen. "Your friend is nuts. And his music stinks."

Eileen, just back from work, watches Greta sashay down the sidewalk toward her car. She has to find out what happened before Preston gets home. Her story needs to be straight.

Roddy shouts over the music, which is indeed louder and faster than the previous evening. Today, he wears a powder-blue Nehru jacket with matching polyester slacks and white Converse.

"She's just pissed 'cause this is *workin'*, man. C'mon. You *knew* she'd have a fit like this, didn't you?"

Eileen doesn't answer.

"And I'm bettin' you aren't sorry to see her go."

True enough.

Roddy takes another sip of beer. At least he brings his own food and drink, which is more than could be said of Greta. Unlike her, Roddy leaves the space in shambles while tallying impeccably printed "billable hours" in a spiral notebook he keeps in his pocket. That's a hundred times more forthright than Greta, who re-enters and checks under tables and behind doors, determined not to leave anything behind.

Preston enters. "Why's your stuff out in the street?" he asks Greta.

"I'm sick of his music!" She points at Roddy.

Preston strides across the room and turns off the stereo, like a TV cop deliberately locking the interrogation room door behind him to intimidate a felon. Eileen knows this move. *He's going to sound rational, but he just wants to get his way.* This will not end well.

Eileen can't think. Her head feels like it could split open. She hears something ripping.

Across the room, Preston's brown leather sofa begins shedding its skin like a snake. Each cushion spontaneously tears and vomits forth beige stuffing. They hear a disembodied voice—clearly Eileen's—laughing maniacally.

Preston points to the deflated sofa. "You wrecked my altar, now my couch. This... this can't happen again."

"It won't if we keep the music goin', man. That was *your* bad, turnin' off the stereo halfway through a song. How many times did I warn you?"

Roddy turns back to his record player. The music starts again, loud and angry.

"I vote we all go out for margaritas while Roddy packs up his stuff," says Greta.

"Aye," says Preston.

"He stays," Eileen tells them. She begins picking up chunks of stuffing from the floor as Preston and Greta storm out.

Right then, Eileen understands two things.

1) Preston is upset because all this has hit him personally—his wine bottles, his sofa, his altar.

2) Everything in the house is *his* or *theirs*. She would never feel as upset as Preston because there is nothing of hers for the Whatever-It-Is to destroy. Nothing belongs to her. She just cleans up the mess when something breaks.

Then, she is just mad. Mad at a husband who cares more about a sofa and candles than he does about her. Mad at her ex-stoner parents who don't care whether her marriage succeeds or fails. Mad at the whole damn city of St. Louis for being so weird.

The song that plays has some English guy yelping behind a wall of guitars. He sounds like he's trying to bite off his tongue as he sings. He says he wants a "ride home."

Me too, she thinks. But she is home.

"I want a ride," she sings. "I want a ride. A ride home."

"Not *ride*." Roddy says. "*Riot*. 'White Riot,' man. You never heard the Clash? You really don't know beans about music do you?"

That evening, he gives her a quick primer on musicians he loves. People with names like Sky Saxon, Black Francis, Exene, and Esquerita.

"These guys were badass," he says. He raises a yellow album labelled "Bad Brains". Its cover shows the U.S. Capitol dome being struck by lightning and cracking down the center like Humpty Dumpty's shell. On the back cover, there is a picture of four black men with dreadlocks.

"Rastafarians," he says. "Freakin' rastas playing hardcore. That's like, I dunno, a bunch of Mormons spinning whirling dervishes. That's *real* magic, man."

Her parents once told her that Rastas based their religion around pot. Well, Rastas believe in something. Like Preston believes in something. Like Roddy and her father believe in something. She's spent her entire life standing next to believers, making silent excuses for their peculiarities. Where did that leave her? Unmoored. Unanchored. A human shell. Could some belief temper the swirling loneliness that fills her lungs and churns in her stomach? If wanting could make belief happen, she'd have it right now, but the moment passes and she knows that no amount of magic, weed, tears, or electronics equipment can fill her.

Preston doesn't return that night. Eileen falls asleep to the sound of Rastas playing hardcore and wakes in the morning to find Roddy still on watch near the record player, sitting with his head inches away from the speaker.

When Eileen returns home that night, Preston is emptying dresser drawers into boxes. Most of the kitchen utensils are packed. More empty boxes wait.

"I want to protect my stuff. You're listening to a mental case instead of me." His voice never wavers. "And he's taking forever."

"*Your* way was taking forever," she says.

He shakes his head like he's ashamed for her. "It's time to take care of what's mine."

"That sounds like Greta's advice," she says. *Or my mother's,* she thinks. "So you're moving out?"

"I don't want to discuss that yet, Eileen."

"Well... I do. Is this the end?"

"If you make me to choose now, you may not like my decision."

Music swells downstairs, where Roddy stands guard. Guitars roar. Snare drums pop like firecrackers.

"I think you've already decided," she says. "You just won't admit it to yourself. You want to think it's all my decision so it's easier on you."

He heads down the hall before she finishes.

Roddy flinches a little as Preston slams the door. He stands with an opened beer, wearing a lime green car coat and a black velvet shirt with airplane-wing lapels.

"Is he the kind that comes back in a day or two after he cools?" Roddy asks. "Or the kind that has his lawyer call you next month?"

"I don't know. He's never left me before."

She could do a million things with this moment—go after Preston, throw Roddy out, go for a long walk to clear her head.

Instead, she turns off the record player. The floor begins to tremble instantly.

"You said something about pushing it out gradually. What if we played something that pushed it out now?

"It could totally destroy it."

"The whatever-it-is? Or the whole house?"

Roddy shrugs.

"What's the loudest, craziest, most spiritual thing you've got?" Eileen asks.

"Honestly, I'd go with Little Richard."

"Play that," she says.

The house convulses while he roots through an album pile. As he slides a record from its jacket, she understands that this is what he has probably wanted all along—to battle toe-to-toe with the house's spirit—instead of the meager payments he'd requested.

Saxophones blare and piano keys clink in flurries. Little Richard starts singing.

Roddy stands still for a few beats before he jumps and does a massive, air-guitar windmill strum. Then, he whips off his car coat and waves it like a matador's cape.

The needle bounces across the record and other voices—*their* voices, Preston and Eileen—rise in volume. She has to hear it all. The worst times of her life. Arguments they had. Arguments they *refused* to have. Shouted fragments overlapping, fighting to rise above Little Richard on a skipping record.

"If you would only..."

"Why do you always..."

"Be reasonable."

A whomp bomp—a whomp bomp—a whomp bomp.

"You're not making sense..."

"Just shut up and listen..."

Jumpback... jumpback... jumpback...
"For God's sake!"
"For the Goddess' sake!"
Bama lama—bama lama—bama lama—bama lama.
"I can't take it!"
"Leave me alone!"
"Why are you always like this?"
Wwwooooooooooooooooooooooooooh

The carpet rips in half, parting like the Red Sea in front of Charlton Heston, rolling into the walls and dragging furniture with it. Nails in the hardwood floor rattle in place, then shoot up—zipping past their heads—into the plaster ceiling. Anything made of glass in the house, from the windows to the dishes to the dial of Eileen's watch, cracks simultaneously. Boards split. Doors fall from hinges.

Eileen scrambles out and across her front yard, leaping into the Ford Falcon's passenger seat. She slides down, pulling her knees to her chest, expecting Roddy to follow her, throw the keys into the ignition, and get them out of there.

Roddy never comes.

She rises to look out the window, putting faith in both the Egyptian pantheon and the 1965 Assembly Line at Ford Motor Company that a single pane of glass will protect her.

Her house splits in half, cracked like the Capitol Dome on the cover of Roddy's Bad Brains record. When the wave of plaster dust rolls by her, it takes a moment to realize she is staring into the exposed interior of her own living room.

There stands Roddy, doing Sixties-type dance steps as the music blasts—flailing his arms and pivoting on the balls of his feet, spinning and pointing, shaking his clasped hands above his head like a champion boxer celebrating victory. Some of the steps she even recognizes, things her father and mother did on those long-ago Saturday nights. The Frug. The Watusi. The Mashed Potato. She knows their names.

Roddy stomps and twists, barely containing a kind of glee the house had never seen while Eileen and Preston inhabited it.

She hears water, a sudden torrential downpour. She expects a deluge of frogs to splatter across the windshield. Instead, a rising carpet of red swells around Roddy's legs.

Blood. They finally got blood. A geyser of it surges from the house's foundation.

For a moment, Roddy seems to float with his chin raised just above the liquid and his fist high in the air. Then, the blood recedes, flowing out into the streets and downspouts, leaving clumps of masonry, broken furniture, and a faint pink tint to the concrete. Roddy stands, crimson head to toe, inside the house's borders, no ceiling above him and only the barest outline of walls surrounding him. He waves at her.

Eileen exits the car, stepping around debris as she crosses the lawn. A deep crater fills the center, with other holes surrounding it. In some spots, mud has vomited out from the basement and over the carpet. Upturned furniture sits half-buried in the ground.

Roddy stands on the only area untouched by the disaster, along the rim of the largest crater, where his records, cords, and gear sit on a sliver of untainted carpet the shape of a crescent moon.

For a moment, he just looks at her without speaking, discerning her mood with what might be genuine empathy, as she surveys the rubble and debris.

"That's never happened before," he tells her.

"Well, there's no way I'm cleaning that up," she says.

All this happened over a decade ago. A year or two earlier, the entirety of Lake Chesterfield in South Saint Louis was devoured by a sinkhole overnight, leaving waterfront McMansions with panoramic views of a six-hundred-acre mud pit. Google it. The stories have cutesy titles like "Woe, Lake Begone" but the disappearance was real as real estate gets.

Maybe that's why the firefighters and insurance guys didn't blink when they tallied the damage with Eileen and Preston the next morning.

The only sign of Roddy was a circle of leaked oil where Horus had been parked. That weekend, he continued his Saturday night show uninterrupted. But the check she left in his office mailbox cleared in a couple of days, and he left one red-ink message on that week's log sheet—*I hope things are better.*

By the time she got his note, Eileen had already quit. She gave the GM two letters—one resigning from her job and another recommending Len for it. She knew Len wouldn't accept if offered, but hoped her good word would give him enough clout to get his request for a new soundboard approved.

Eileen and Preston consulted lawyers within a week of the house's collapse, split the insurance money, and went their separate ways. Preston started staying with Greta before the month was out. It just made sense, he explained. They both needed a roommate.

Here's the real crazy part—had they kept the house and stretched it out a few years, they would have seen their home reduced to half its value, below what they'd paid for it, in a recession that hit even sure-thing areas like Webster Groves. They would have been destitute, underwater, broke.

For anybody else, splitting a house is far more complicated.

Couples implode. They argue over who will get to keep the beloved cat, the sweet Jetta with only nine payments left. A few years pass. The cat dies of leukemia. The Jetta's transmission blows and costs more to fix than to junk it. Even with music, the principle's the same. How many couples ten years ago fought over vast compact disc collections full of box sets, bonus tracks, and hard-to-find rarities that turned valueless in the age of Spotify?

Maybe Eileen and Preston came out ahead.

Eileen doesn't live in St. Louis anymore. If you met her today —*today*, right now—the woman you would see is older, heavier, but carries herself nimbly, with an irrepressible bounce that tosses her graying hair. She's quick to smile at strangers, but not to reveal too much. Her silence doesn't come across as shame but simply a desire to move on. (Only a small trickle of revelations from her over several years made this piece possible.) She doesn't want to tell people where she moved, and rarely discusses the house, her failed marriage, or anything else about that time. Alone but not lonely, adrift but not scared, all she'll say is this—she likes where she lives, in a normal apartment where everything belongs to her. Including all the records.

See Nathaniel Williams's story "The Record Collector" online at Metaphorosis.
If you liked it, leave a comment. Authors love that!
Remember to subscribe to our e-mail updates so you'll know when new stories are posted.

About the story

I went to college with a ton of Saint Louis folks and over the years heard many vignettes about the area. The stuff in my story about the Exorcist hospital and the Lake Chesterfield sinkhole is all true. Saint Louis is also the home of Beatle Bob, the nationally known music superfan who attends concerts almost nightly, always decked in vintage 60s gear. (If you played in an area band and Bob attended your show, it meant something.) There's a little Beatle Bob in Roddy, even though the character ultimately asserted a more unique persona as I wrote him. And, as a displaced Midwesterner, I miss the area. I've spent time recently thinking of all those Gen-Xers who lived around there in the early 2000s (many good friends and mentors) and the ups and downs they've seen since I moved away. That's in there too.

A question for the author

Q: Do you have a garden? Have you ever grown your own food?

A: No. I'm ill-suited to nurture plants. I can barely keep children and pets alive, and they at least tell you when they're hungry.

About the author

Nathaniel Williams was born in Kansas City and currently teaches technical writing and journalism at the University of California, Davis. He's worked as a radio announcer, grant writer, and musician, and has spent the past decade or so researching rare American science fiction in dime novels from the nineteenth century. He is a graduate of the Writers Workshop at the Gunn Center for the Study of Science Fiction.

www.nathanielwms.com, @nathanielwms

Zsezzyn, Who Is Not a God

Jennifer Shelby

A lone man watches over the universe, and the pen he wields contains the power to erase from existence all he deems unworthy. His daughter, Zsezzyn, plays at his feet.

She likes to watch him work — the steadily deepening crease on his brow, the scales on which he measures a balance of right, wrong, and the gray that lives between. One day, he will bequeath his pen to her, and this cave where the universe is mapped out above their heads will become her sacred place as it is his. "This is the way of gods," he tells her.

For now, Zsezzyn frolics beneath the silver pinpricks of the stars, nervous of the darkness that broods between them. At night she dreams the darkness overwhelms her and she runs to the stars for comfort. She spends her childhood shooting arrows with Orion, pouring cups of shadow from twin Dippers, learning her first letter from the W of Cassiopeia.

The stars are her universe, until they disappear. One at a time, the darkness devours them. Zsezzyn traces her fingers along the space where a star once twinkled, struggling to understand, afraid to ask her father why tears run down his cheeks. "Where did the star go, Papa?"

He gathers her into his arms and takes her outside the cave to show her the night sky. The stars are bigger here, but so is the darkness. Zsezzyn shrinks into his embrace. "The people who lived by the lost star committed terrible deeds," he tells her. "The burden of protecting the universe from such people falls to us and we must not take this responsibility lightly. My grandfather found the threat of punishment alone kept peace. My father had to wield our family's power twice in his lifetime and I am already past that. Though we strive to use this power sparingly, it has made us many enemies." He turns his face away from her and stares into the darkness. "There are those who would take our power for their own and use it against us." He pats her hand. "But I will keep you safe from them."

Zsezzyn does not ask for details.

Years pass, until one day Zsezzyn notices Orion's Belt has disappeared. She turns to her father, to ask what happened, but anger simmers in the dimming starlight surrounding him and she keeps her questions to herself. This is the last day she spends playing in the cave.

When she is old enough, her father tells her everything. "Your great-grandfather made the ink for our pen from a pool of dark matter he discovered at the bottom of a black hole. You need only take up this pen and ink over a star to remove it from the universe."

Zsezzyn is stricken to see how many stars are gone, how dark the cave has grown. Her father follows her gaze and sighs. "My grandfather built this cave to end the chaos of the universe. When he died, the burden of power fell to my father, then to me, as one day it will fall to you." His voice grows firm. "Yet more and more there are those who wish to strip us of our godship. This, I do not allow."

Zsezzyn does not try to hide her horror. "But Papa, there are so few stars left. You told me we must wield our power sparingly."

His face hardens, he clutches his pen to his chest. "One day you will understand."

"Will there be any stars left then?" Zsezzyn asks.

"The only star we need to survive is our own sun."

Zsezzyn looks at the pen in his hand, worn and old, a fountain pen carved from the core of a comet, its nib stained dark, a small window in the barrel warning it is low on ink. But that doesn't matter when so little stars remain.

"We are gods," he tells her. "They are twinkles in a cave."

She turns to go and does not look back as she leaves her father, and then her world, behind. Far from the shelter of the cave, from an asteroid she forges a pen of her own.

One by one, the last stars disappear, until only her sun remains. The darkness of the universe around the asteroid brings back her childhood fears. The void pulsates with something she cannot see, licking at her fright, threatening to swallow more than stars. Zsezzyn stares into the empty black, daring it to consume her, and nothing happens.

When at last her pen is done, she travels to the sun that gave life to her world, the lone star her father has not found fault with. She steps upon the surface of the star. Its fires dare not burn her, for the flames know whose daughter she is and what he has done to a thousand other stars. The star guides her safely to its molten core, where its light should blind, its heat should melt, its heart should devour her. Instead Zsezzyn's fears are burned away, replaced by a scorching, fiery will. She takes out the cartridge she has made for her pen and hesitates. Lifting her head and gazing into the star fire, she asks, "May I?"

The star consents with a small nudge of flame. Zsezzyn plunges the cartridge into the star's liquid heart. When she is done, she stands, pocketing the instrument with a surge of hope.

She meets her father in his cave, her pen bright in the darkness. "I made this for us, Papa, to restore what we have lost." Zsezzyn holds her breath, clinging to the memory of the tears he once shed in this cave.

He considers her pen, his expression shifting from furious to uncertain. He draws out his own pen and holds it in his palms, trembling as he looks from the tool to the darkness of the cave. Where once Zsezzyn sensed his anger simmer in the starlight she now feels his regret unspool into the darkness. "My work is done," he tells her. "Our family's legacy falls to you now."

"Papa?" Zsezzyn reaches for him, but she is too late. He grips his pen in his fists and snaps it in half. What remains of the ink darkens his fingers briefly before he disappears like all his stars.

The broken pieces of his pen clatter to the floor. Zsezzyn stares at them a long time. Her great-grandfather once believed this pen held the power to protect the universe, and it did, for a time. Its corruption did not begin until much later and with it came a darkness which consumed her father whole.

When Zsezzyn's grief subsides, she studies the cave walls, sifting through the constellations of her memory. Orion's belt twinkled there, one, two, three. With a trembling hand, she presses the pen's nib against the wall and draws a star. Silver light pierces the darkness. Another, and another. All of Orion, Cassiopeia, and over there a Dipper, the big one.

Zsezzyn falls into a frenzy of creation, filling the universe with the stars it lost. A myriad forgotten lives resume. A billion worlds fall back into the orbit of their reborn suns. She adds new stars for the sheer, majestic wonder of it. Hours pass before she steps back to admire the universe, the cave bright with silver light.

Her father might not have been proud, but Zsezzyn is no god, she is only someone who wields a powerful tool. She places the pen on the floor of the cave and steps outside. The universe stretches overhead, bright again with stars and life, and bold with the light of the incoming comet she drew to seal up the cave forever.

See Jennifer Shelby's story "Zsezzyn, Who Is Not a God" online at
Metaphorosis.
If you liked it, leave a comment. Authors love that!
Remember to subscribe to our e-mail updates so you'll know when
new stories are posted.

About the story

My toddler has a toy turtle which lights up and projects stars onto the ceiling. Like most kids her age, she's nervous of the dark and often turns it on when I'm putting her to bed. One night I blocked out several of the stars with my hand and she started to cry. As I tried to imagine how she might have perceived those missing stars, I found the story.

Zsezzyn's story is also about a damaged inheritance. I listen to what scientists say about climate change and wonder how my children will react to the world they inherit. Zsezzyn's father believes he's handing her a legacy to be proud of, but to Zsezzyn it is the ruins of a universe, devoid of potential.

A question for the author

Q: Do you live near where you were born? Have you traveled much?

A: I was born in Nova Scotia, a province in Eastern Canada, and currently live in New Brunswick. Looking out my window I can see Nova Scotia across the Bay of Fundy. New Brunswick is where I grew up and the smell of the Bay, dramatic shoreline, and deep forests are home. I moved to Central and Western Canada for my education but always gravitated back to New Brunswick again.

As a child I travelled through most of the United States in the back of my parents' Volkswagen. I gawked at New York City and the Grand Canyon in between Battleship games with my brother and a handful of Nancy Drew novels.

In my early twenties I spent three months in rural Costa Rica as part of a conservation volunteer group. I treasure the experiences I had in the rainforests there and the beautiful communities that welcomed us into their lives. There were blankets of fireflies along the edges of one forest that will forever haunt my dreams.

About the author

Jennifer Shelby hunts for stories in the beetle undergrowth of fairy-infested forests. She fishes for them in the dark space between the stars. Zsezzyn, Who is Not a God's publication in *Metaphorosis* is part of her ongoing catch-and-release program. You can learn more at jennifershelby.blog or on Twitter @jenniferdshelby

The Woman Who Brought Love to Death

Kathryn Yelinek

Gudrun plunked herself down in the grass, her back against the side of the sod house. The guests were feasting, and the funeral ale was flowing, so she could indulge her grief a moment. Almighty gods, had Ketill been dead a week already?

In the distance, the last of the smoke from his funeral pyre drifted over the horse fields. Beyond that, clear on the horizon, lay the green hill of Graenheth. Souls went into that hill on their way to the Forever Shore. Right now, Ketill would be inside, beyond the setting sun, past the troll who guarded the entrance to the land of the dead. He would be roaming the endless expanse of beach, sea cliffs, and tide pools, one soul among millions. A soul could wander that beach forever, searching in vain for a beloved.

She knew without a doubt that he was there, beyond her reach, because she could see the love-lines they shared. Theirs were still thick as whale bones and brilliant scarlet, a testament to their passion. They ran from her out across the hills and waving grass, translucent red ribbons that ran unerringly toward Graenheth. So Ketill truly was there, even though her mind refused to grasp it. She thought she might go mad with the need to touch him again.

Around her, as the guests roared and lifted overflowing tankards to the midnight sun, the love-lines of friends and family filled the valley. The ones for Ketill all stretched west, toward Graenheth and the Forever Shore. Yellow for familial love, green for friendship, their width and depth of color showed how close each person had been to Ketill. They stretched through the air like bits of a splintered rainbow, he'd been so beloved.

How she wanted to follow the lines, to track Ketill down and throw her arms around him. They'd been a good pair, the two of them, since he brought her from Egleby five years before. And she would follow them if she could. Here in the valley the islanders thought her a witch because she could see the love-lines and they could not. Her life would be hard among them now, without Ketill's protection. But she couldn't go into the hill, not now. She would not dishonor Ketill by cutting short his full year of mourning rites.

As if to reinforce how alone she was, Solvi, Ketill's son from his first marriage, banged his tankard on the funeral bench and cried, "We'll avenge my father! We'll see justice done!"

The guests roared, and hard glances turned toward her. As usual. She should stay silent, but her eyes ached from weeping, and she was in no mood for Solvi's self-centered boasting.

"How will you avenge him?" she asked, low. "Desecrate the horse that struck him?"

Silence, and for a moment she thought the guests were pondering how best to dismember Tanni, Ketill's favorite horse. They'd already slaughtered the poor beast for what he'd done.

Then: "That horse never hurt him before!"

"No horse ever hurt him."

"He was the island's best horse breaker."

"Horse musta been magicked!"

Solvi raised his hand, still clutching his eating knife, and pointed a shaking finger at her. "You were the last person in the horse fields before the stallion kicked him. What do you have to say for yourself, witch?"

She opened her mouth, snapped it shut. At the time of Ketill's death, she'd been following a pair of love-lines, intent on discovering who shared a secret crush. In Egleby, her matchmaking stall had thrived, and she missed the work. But these guests with their spears and axes didn't want to hear about love-lines.

"I did not kill him."

"What were you doing in the field?"

The looks they gave her—anger, fear, hatred—she knew what they meant. Ketill was burned, his soul safely beyond the setting sun on the Forever Shore. No matter what they did to her, his ghost would not haunt them.

She shot to her feet. Just in time, as she scrambled to dodge a rock that thumped into the turf wall where her head had been.

She ran. A stone bashed her shoulder, sending her tumbling into the grass. A cheer went up, and she scrambled to her feet, terror drying her tears. She sprinted past the horse fields, past Ketill's cooling pyre, the jeers loud behind her. Her shoulder stung.

She crested the hill and plunged into the valley below, plowing through waving grass. Finally, two valleys over, she stopped. Panting, her hand to the cramp in her side, she scanned the horizon from the glacier-capped volcanos behind to the far-distant sea in front. No one was following; she was alone with the love-lines.

Instinctively she stepped toward Graenheth, toward Ketill. She had no reason not to go there now. By chasing her away, Solvi had exiled her. No farmstead would give her shelter, no ship captain would grant her passage. Without supplies, she would not survive the winter or complete the mourning rites. Better to drown herself and forego the misery.

But dead, she wouldn't see love-lines. The priests were clear: no unnatural abilities survived death. And she had to see the lines. Without them she would never find Ketill, not on the endless shore.

If she wanted to see him again, to touch him, she'd have to go now, lack of supplies be damned.

"Ketill," she whispered, "I'm coming."

She struck out across the rippling grasses, Graenheth small and sheer in the distance, a good day's journey away. Hour after hour, she walked, beyond sleep, driven by longing, until Graenheth loomed tall, a flat-topped hill of green and gold jutting from the ground. Two ravens called from its top, a grim sign. She shaded her eyes, though her arms felt heavy as boulders. Her mind was muddy, refusing to focus. But she'd made it, even if she had no idea how to get inside the hill.

She eyed Ketill's love-lines, hoping they would show her. Except they didn't go inside. They kept going, past Graenheth to the shore behind.

She gaped. Was Ketill's soul lost?

No, all the love-lines led past the hill to the shore. Old, faded lines and new, sharp ones alike.

So, if he wasn't where all the priests and his family said he was, where was he?

She trudged around the base of the hill and down the grassy slope behind until she stood on the edge of a sea cliff, waves crashing below. To her left, a river drained into the sea, ice chunks from the distant glacier riding high. In the bay, black rock arches braced the shore and stood as sea stacks in the water. The love-lines flowed past them, converging on one black pinnacle of rock halfway to the horizon.

"I don't know how to get there, either," a voice said.

Gudrun jumped. Crouched in a rock cleft was a small black-and-white dog. Green friendship love-lines ran from it to the black pinnacle and back.

"You're trying to cross over too, yes?" the dog asked when she didn't respond.

Gudrun breathed hard through her nose. Too many shocks, one after another, were making her slow.

She picked her words carefully. "I'm sorry for your loss."

The dog cocked its head. "You can smell the passing souls, too?"

"I see the love you shared with someone now in the rock."

"My horse friend, Astrid. She had saddle sores and didn't want to be ridden, so the man hit her until she didn't get up. I miss her."

"I'm sorry," Gudrun said again, now for all humans, because they did terrible things to animals. "How is it I understand you?"

"In choosing to come here, we've taken the first step into Death's domain. Things are different here. Why do humans ask such obvious questions?"

"It's not obvious to me. Humans and dogs experience the world in different ways."

The dog nodded, satisfied. "My name's Bjorn. Whom are you trying to reach?"

"My husband, Ketill. My name is Gudrun."

Bjorn barked, grinning a doggie grin. "That's why you smell so good!" He limped toward her and pressed his nose into her leg. His head came about to her knee. "The man had a daughter named Gudrun. She was kind to me, until she clasped hands with another and moved away."

"Did 'the man' do this to you?" Gudrun reached for his front right paw. It oozed from a puncture wound.

Bjorn snapped at her, growling. She jerked her hand back and pressed it to her chest.

At once, his ears and tail went down. He slunk toward her, eyes wide as a puppy's. "I'm sorry. It hurts."

"It looks deep." She sat on her heels. "May I see?"

Slowly he held out his paw. She took it carefully, but he whimpered.

"It'll be my death," he said. "I smell it."

He spoke truth. The wound was far along and festering. She pulled the kerchief from her hair and wrapped it around his paw.

"So you don't hurt it more."

He licked her chin, and her face warmed in delight. It was the first happiness she'd felt in a week. Just like that, tendrils of green friendship stretched between them.

"It's good to have a nice human to travel with," Bjorn said, sitting back on his haunches. "How do you think we can get over?"

She frowned at the waves crashing below. "It's too far to swim, even if we could get past those breakers."

"Do you have a boat?"

"No, and no one would lend me one." She hesitated. "You—you could just end your life, you know."

He blinked at her. "Maybe for humans. We dogs don't do that. Why haven't you?"

"I won't see love-lines if I'm dead. And the love-lines will lead me straight to Ketill. No wandering the Shore."

"Oh! I'm staying with you. So how do we get over?"

"I don't know." She couldn't bear that this might be the end, that she would have to face Solvi's wrath instead of reconciling with Ketill. "If only we could walk on the love-lines. They would take us right over."

Bjorn's ears perked up. "That's perfect. Let's walk now."

"We can't. The lines are light, like a rainbow. We can't walk on light."

"Oh." His ears dropped. "I hoped they were more solid."

"No." She tapped her chin, thinking. They couldn't swim. They didn't have a boat, and she wasn't about to go back. But she did have a talking dog, so maybe she should start thinking of other ways around her problem. "Since you can talk to me, could you talk some seals or whales into taking us out to the rock?"

He cocked his head. "Maybe, if they were here, and if we had something they wanted."

Neither was true, so she tried another direction. "You said we were in Death's domain. How did you know this?"

He whimpered and ducked his head. "The man—he was a sorcerer."

Gudrun shivered. Sorcerers were dark and dangerous men who used runes to write evil spells. No wonder Bjorn had whimpered.

And yet...

She knelt down. "Is there anything else the man told you that could help us? A spell to calm the waters? Or to conjure a boat?"

Bjorn growled deep in his throat. "He knew a spell to magnify fear."

Her heart went out to him. "I'm sorry. I didn't mean to bring back bad memories. I won't ask again."

Bjorn nodded, tight, then nuzzled her knee so she knew they were all right. She stood, surveying the distant rock, and mulled over his words.

As a matchmaker, she'd learned enough writing to carve a rune for the occasional love charm. And now she knew there was a spell that could increase fear. So maybe here in Death's domain, where things were different, there was a way to use her rune to help them. She wasn't sure how, but it was a start.

"Think you could get me a fist-sized rock? As flat as possible?" She pointed to the riverbank.

Bjorn thumped his tail. "I love fetching!"

He hobbled to the river, limping so badly that Gudrun regretted asking him. Then he gave a yip of delight and grabbed a rock with his jaws.

He dropped it at her feet. "I got it! Didn't I do well?"

She laughed at his glee. "Very well."

As she picked up the rock, she realized she'd just laughed for the first time in a week. It felt good.

"So what are you going to do?" Bjorn asked.

"I know one rune to use in love charms. I use it to strengthen love-lines. I wonder if that can help us."

Bjorn nodded. "The man said words when he carved his runes. I didn't like to listen. They hurt my ears."

"Words have power. It's true." Witch. Dead. Justice. These weren't spells, but they had changed her life.

Her eating knife hung from a brooch on her dress. Thank the gods she had adopted the islander custom of carrying it with her at all times. She untied the string that held it and used it to carve into the stone the rune she knew, whispering the spell to strengthen love-lines. When she was done, she surveyed the love-lines in front of her. She couldn't choose her line or Bjorn's, because those would move with them as they crossed over the sea. She needed a line that would stay still. She needed—there. A scarlet line as wide as a narrow branch ran east into the volcanos. It came from someone on the other side of the peaks, so it should not move much.

She prayed and jabbed the rock into the red line. The line flared, growing brighter and wider, but the rock fell through. It thudded on the ground.

Her heart sank. Bjorn whined and nosed the rock.

She picked it up. "Maybe a spell to thicken a woman's womb, something that will make the line more solid."

Again she whispered her words and jabbed the rock in. This time it sank slowly through the line before thudding to the ground.

"It almost worked!" Bjorn said. "Try again."

She did, this time with a spell to stiffen a man during love-play. But again the rock sank through before landing by her feet.

Bjorn hung his head. He didn't bother to push the rock toward her this time. "What else can we do?"

"I don't know," she whispered. She picked up the rock and squeezed it tightly. "I don't know any other spells to try."

She wished she could ask what spells the sorcerer had used, but she had promised not to. She didn't dare suggest they ask the sorcerer for help. Together, she and Bjorn would have to come up with another plan.

Oh.

Together. Yes! She had overlooked a crucial aspect of the love-lines. They were connected at both ends, flavored by both the lover and beloved. On this island, that usually meant male and female. But she had tried a spell for each gender in turn. Maybe if she combined them, it would work.

"Almighty gods," she prayed. "Make this work."

She breathed deep, intoned a combination of the spells, then jabbed the rock into the line. It held.

She had a moment to marvel, then Bjorn nosed her leg.

"It worked! Let's go!"

"Patience." She ran her hand along the solid ribbon of red, testing it, hardly believing her words had worked. "It's only as wide as a branch, and slippery as ice." Which made a sort of sense, since rainbows happened when sunlight hit spray, and water turned into ice. So when she'd stiffened the line, it had followed its rainbow nature and crystalized into a ribbon of ice. She would rather the line had turned into something less slippery, but she'd take what she could get.

Buoyed, she retied her knife and tucked it on its string into her neckline so it would not get in her way as they crossed. Then she hiked up her skirts and climbed onto the red ribbon, straddling it. It was cold and slick against her fingers, and she wished she had her ice spikes.

When the ice didn't break under her weight, she boosted Bjorn up behind her. "Hold onto my skirts. I don't want you falling."

Bjorn whined, but he snagged the hem of her skirt as she scooched forward her first hesitant armlengths. The ribbon was slick and narrow, but there was no other way. Bjorn's claws clicked behind her, and she thought about this rather than peering into the blue-gray waters below, rather than dwelling on how cold her hands and legs were. If only she had her mittens.

The black pinnacle of rock grew closer, but the journey seemed never ending. No matter how she shifted along, the ribbon seemed to stretched ever longer. The sun inched across the sky, past the midday mark, and still she was creeping along over the blue-gray water far below, and now her skirts and fingers were wet.

She gasped. "The ice is melting!"

She crept faster, her palms slapping the ribbon. If only it were wider. If only she could run.

A crack sounded, a breaking of the air, and the ribbon swayed. She grabbed hold, her heartbeat thrumming in all the corners of her body.

"It's crumbling in the middle!" Bjorn yelled.

She moved as fast as she could, Bjorn yipping that the ice was cracking behind his tail, until black showed beneath red, and she collapsed on a ledge of black rock. Bjorn nosed into her side, whimpering. She held him, savoring his warmth. The love-line cracked and popped and then it was nothing but a translucent ribbon again. Raising her hand, she passed her fingers through it.

The ledge could fit her and Bjorn and not much more. Warmth radiated up, returning the heat of the sun, but the air was chilly and the wind biting. Bits of gray lichen spotted the rock, and the air smelled of bird droppings, but no birds perched nearby. On this small space, it was just her and Bjorn and a startlingly long drop off the edge to the foaming waves below.

After a moment to warm her fingers in Bjorn's fur, she ran her hands over the rock face at the back of the ledge. The love-line went into the rock at chest height. Other lines—red and yellow and green—dove in around it.

"How do we get in?" Bjorn hobbled up beside her.

The rock was warm from the sun and smooth from the wind, but hard and—"Oh! A door!"

Hidden in a split in the rock, a black corridor barely as wide as her shoulders led into darkness. Far at the end, light gleamed, colored red and yellow and green by love-lines.

"Think that's the Forever Shore?" Bjorn asked, tilting his head toward the light.

"I wish, but I think we have a ways to go. Past the setting sun and a guardian troll, right?"

Bjorn sighed and nodded.

"Let me carry you," Gudrun said. The kerchief around his paw was nearly soaked through.

"I can walk," Bjorn protested, but not too much, and he snuggled against her shoulder as she stepped into the corridor.

It wasn't far. After a walk through cool, musty rock, the corridor took a sharp elbow turn to the right. She peeked around the rock and met painfully bright light.

"Ow!" She jerked back, slamming her eyes shut.

Bjorn nuzzled her shoulder. "Are you okay?"

Back in the corridor, she blinked, spots dancing in her vision. "I'm all right, but I don't know how to walk through that. If I look too long, I'll go blind."

"Can you feel your way?"

"Maybe, but if I fall, we're both going down. And I don't want either of us getting burned or blinded or worse. That's the setting sun we have to get past, isn't it?"

Bjorn whined, his ears back, but he said, "Let me lead. I'll sniff out the path, and only have to peek a little."

"But your paw..."

"Better my paw than your sight. We need that. Here, tie some cloth as a rope around my middle so I can lead you."

There had to be a better way, but she couldn't think of one. She pulled her trusty knife from her neckline, chopped cloth from her skirt, and tied the leash around his chest. She tied another bandage around his paw, too. "Lead on."

It was disconcerting, walking with her eyes closed, the tugging of the leash telling her to go right or left. The air grew warm, then uncomfortably hot. She wiped her face and wished for water. How big could the sun be? Shouldn't they be past it by now? Still she padded over rock as fine as salt, bracing herself for the lurch of the leash that would signal disaster.

Then the air cooled, the brightness dimmed, and Bjorn yipped that she could open her eyes.

He led her out a doorway to a narrow path. Sunshine streamed down, not too bright. On either side were black rock shapes—columns, mounds, keyholes through which she could see the summer-blue sky. The white full moon rode high beside the sun.

Seeing that, she shivered. "We're not in the old world anymore."

Bjorn wriggled. "I hear waves. Just beyond that bend. The Forever Shore must be close!"

She untied his leash, and he surged ahead, then froze, his hair standing on edge.

"What?" Gudrun demanded.

She was answered by a troll rounding the bend.

He stood twice her height and three times her breadth, with black knobby skin to match the rocks. "Go away. You're not dead."

He was much larger than she'd expected. Still she said, "Let us pass. We made the journey. It's your duty to let us pass."

"My duty is to keep the land of the dead for the dead. Now go." He shooed with his hands.

Bjorn growled, light glinting on his teeth. He jumped, biting into the troll's shin. The troll hissed and swatted, barely missing as Bjorn ducked away.

"Stop!" Gudrun called. Bjorn was staggering, and he might have been a gnat for all his bite had done. The path showed red where he walked.

Bjorn glared at her, but he must have thought better of his attack, because his ears went down, and he limped to her side. The troll strode forward, forcing them back up the path. Black rock rose sharp and straight on both sides. The door to the corridor loomed at their backs.

"I'll give you one of my brooches," she told the troll, "if you let us pass. See how it sparkles?"

"What good would that do? The rocks sparkle even more."

"What about this glass bead necklace? My husband gave it to me as a wedding present."

The troll snorted, making Bjorn start. "I don't need your wedding present. Go away."

"You could have my knife," she said, though it pained her. "It's small and sharp."

"Take your knife and leave me alone!"

At the forcefulness of his cry, she backed into the brightly lit corridor, Bjorn stumbling behind her. But as she looked despairingly out to the path they'd left behind, a red love-line caught her attention. It ran from the troll to a column of rock.

The troll was in love with a rock? No—a more brilliant line ran from him to the Forever Shore. His beloved was there.

"Come on," Bjorn whispered, pressing against her. "Maybe we can get in another way."

What other way was there?

"Whom do you love?" she asked the troll, hoping to buy time. "Who's waiting for you on the Shore?"

The troll froze. He stared at her, his black nostrils flared.

"You love someone very much," she continued, stepping back onto the path, puzzling out the connection between his two love lines, one a pale echo of the other. "And someone—no some*thing* she gave you, something you connect with her, is over in the rock."

The troll narrowed his eyes. "What do you know of my loves?"

"I see the love-lines between people and the things they love. A line connects you to something over there. Is it a jewel? A letter?" She guessed wildly, not knowing what trolls held dear. Then a thought occurred: "A knife? Did you lose your knife? You don't carry one." This even though he had a knife loop on his belt like the islander men had. "Is that why you yelled at me when I offered mine?"

The troll's eyes grew as wide as the moon. "If you get my knife back, I'll let you stay. Both of you."

She clasped her hands together, full of hope. "Where is it?"

The troll pointed to the top of one of the rocky mounds, nearly as tall as he was. "It fell into a crack in the rock, and I can't get it out."

"I'll try," Gudrun said. "Only I don't know how to get up there."

The troll picked her up. She gasped, but then she was on top of the mound. The crack in the rock was thin, but not so thin she couldn't reach her arm inside. At the bottom, the knife lay on a bed of snow that hadn't melted, even in endless daylight. It was big—maybe three times bigger than hers—and thin and black as the rock.

She lay down and stretched her arm inside, but she couldn't reach. So she sat up, untied her knife and angled it into the crack. Maybe she could use it to tip the troll's knife up. But even with her knife, her reach was too short.

Desperate, she snipped the string that had held her knife. Tying the end into a loop, she lowered the lasso into the crack. If she could snag the knife, she could lift it up. If—ha! The loop caught.

She pulled, careful, careful, the black blade sparkling in the faint light. The string tightened, and snap! The knife fell back on its bed of snow.

"No!" She hauled the string up. It had been cut cleanly in half. How sharp the blade was!

Something touched her leg. She flinched, nearly dropping her string.

"I can get it!" Bjorn said.

"How'd you get up here?"

"Hallr." He nodded to the troll, who was plucking impatiently at his tunic.

"The blade's really sharp. And your paw's hurt. Are you sure you can get it?"

"I got us past the sun. I'll get the knife."

"Be careful."

Bjorn nodded and squeezed down into the crack. It was very narrow, but he was a small dog. As Gudrun held her breath, he jumped down, leaving red footprints on the lip of the rock. Then he yipped once, twice.

"Bjorn, are you okay?"

No answer. Had he yipped in victory? Pain?

Then he was wriggling up, scrabbling with his back legs. She grabbed hold and hauled him up.

"Did you get it?"

He whimpered. The knife clattered onto the rock.

"You got it!"

Blood splattered her arm. So much blood. Where was it coming from?

She turned Bjorn in her arms. "How are you hurt? Is it your paw?"

He whined. Blood matted his snout. "Find Astrid," he whispered.

She struggled to understand him. Holding him close, she saw the deep cuts that crisscrossed his lips.

"You were supposed to grab the handle!"

"Couldn't reach," he slurred. His head flopped against her wrist. His eyes fluttered.

"Bjorn!" She pressed the edge of her skirt against his lips. Blood soaked the cloth. His tail flicked limply. "Hold on, Bjorn."

"You got it!" The troll, Hallr, plucked up his knife. "Is the dog okay?"

"His name's Bjorn," she snapped. He wasn't moving. She laid her hand on his chest. It didn't move, either. She bowed her head.

"I'm sorry," Hallr said.

"He was a good dog," she whispered, fighting back tears. "He only wanted to be with his friend."

"Now he can, if he can find her."

As Hallr spoke, Bjorn stood up. Not the Bjorn that lay on the rocks. Out of that Bjorn, a new Bjorn rose. He was still small and furry and black and white. Anywhere else he would have been invisible to her, but here, so close to the Forever Shore, he was only faintly translucent, like linen in the sun.

He stepped one paw and then another out of his body. When he stood free, he shook himself. Love-lines ran from him to her and to the Forever Shore.

"My paw doesn't hurt!" Wriggling with excitement, he pushed his nose into her arm.

It felt like any dog nose, only dry. Hesitantly she wrapped her arms around him, feeling the coarse curls of his fur. He felt like any other dog, except he had no smell she could smell, and that made her sad.

"You weren't supposed to die," she said into his fur. "Not now."

"But I got the knife." He licked her cheek. "Let's find Astrid and your husband." Pulling away, he stepped to the edge of the rock column. With a doggie grin, he walked over the edge.

She shrieked, but he landed lightly on the path below.

"Let's go!"

Too many shocks, she thought. She looked back at the body of the Bjorn she had known. Like all bodies, it looked smaller, as if the part of Bjorn that paced the path had been excised. She picked up a few pebbles, piled them by his head—for remembrance, for a life lived too short—then stepped onto Hallr's proffered palm. He set her on the trail.

They followed the path. Waves crashed in the distance. She prayed to any god who would listen that both Astrid and Ketill were close, that Bjorn's sacrifice would bear fruit.

They rounded the bend in the path, and the Shore opened before them: black sand as far as she could see, waves lapping the beach, black rock columns jutting from the water beyond. Souls dotted the beach by themselves or in groups of two, some sitting on the sand, others walking by the water. Love-lines turned the air into a patchwork of rainbows.

"So, um, about you being here." Hallr did not meet her eye. "I —"

"Hallr, what is that living woman doing here?"

The voice split the air like river ice cracking. A person strode up the beach, cloak flapping, shoulder-length hair blowing in a wind Gudrun couldn't feel. Souls trailed behind like ducklings following their mother.

"Please," one soul said, tugging the person's cloak, "tell me where my son is."

"And my fiancée!" another soul said. "Where is she?"

"Sweetie, look," Hallr said as the person approached. Ignoring the clustering souls, he held out his knife. "These two got my knife back."

"You shouldn't have lost it in the first place, darling." The person spoke harshly, but Hallr only beamed at the knife. "And it doesn't explain why she is here."

"I, ah, told them I'd let them stay if they did."

"The dog can stay, not her."

"Please," Gudrun said, her voice cracking. She had never expected to speak to Death. "I need to be with my husband. The community thinks I caused his death. I'm exiled. I have nowhere else to go."

"You may look for him when you are dead." Death swept out a skeletal hand to indicate the clustering souls. "Otherwise, you go."

"I need to be with him now."

"Then you die."

"If I'm dead, I won't be able to find him."

Death tsked. "My shores are vast. Being dead or alive makes no difference in your ability to find someone. Even I don't know where everyone is." This was reinforced with a glower at the souls.

"But I can find him easily. I see the love we share. I can follow our love-lines straight to him."

A few souls gasped. Death arced a thick brow. "Do not fib to me."

"If I prove it, will you let me stay?"

"Only if you are dead."

Gudrun clenched her fists. There had to be another way. "How is he here?" She pointed to Hallr, who was still beaming at his knife. "He's not dead."

"He works for me."

"I could work for you. I could reunite souls with those they love."

Death harrumphed, but the loitering souls exclaimed happily, and Hallr set a hand on Death's arm. "Let her try. You're always complaining you can't get anything done with all these souls pestering you."

"All right." Death folded thin arms in a dare. "Show me."

Yes! Gudrun spun to the left, where both her and Bjorn's love-lines led. "Come on, Bjorn. Astrid's this way, too."

Bjorn barked, his ears up, and bounded down the beach.

If only she could run that fast, race down the sand to Ketill. Instead she set a brisk pace, walking as quickly as she dared. Hallr followed, yammering on about the people they passed, while Death walked silent at his side, the lonely souls trailing behind. Wave after wave crashed on their right, and Gudrun was remembering how tired she was when one of the love-lines veered off to the left, up a small hill with evergreens bordering the shore.

"Bjorn! Astrid's up there."

Barking madly, Bjorn tore up the hill. A moment later, a horse whinnied from the trees. The two met nose to nose at the crest of the hill, Bjorn bestowing slobbering kisses on his friend.

Gudrun pressed her hands to her chest, overjoyed. Then she saw her own love-line angling off the beach up ahead. She ran.

She rounded the next curve of the beach, and there he was, sitting on an outcropping of rock, watching the herd of horses to which Astrid now belonged, green friendship lines running from him to the herd.

Her mouth was dry. Her throat squeezed tight. She called, "Ketill!"

He tensed. He turned around. His body went still in shock, then he was sprinting down the hill to her.

"Gudrun, what are you doing here?"

She wrapped her arms around him. This was his hug, the scratch of his beard on her neck, the curve of his back under her hands. He no longer smelled like himself, either. She missed that, but still it was him.

"I followed the love-lines."

"And I'm glad you did, but why are you here? You're not dead." He pulled back to frown down at her in concern.

As usual, she couldn't hide her worries from him. "Everyone thinks I magicked your horse, that I murdered you. They exiled me."

His face darkened. "The idiots. Of course you didn't murder me. It was an accident. I just wish I knew why Tanni kicked me."

That she could help with. This she had been born to do. A shiver of excitement coursed through her as she beckoned Ketill up the hill he'd just come down, following the vivid green friendship lines she recognized. At the top she shaded her eyes, tracing the line into the distance, to where a brown horse stood by itself, half hidden by trees, away from the rest of the herd. As if it were ashamed. Or in mourning.

She put two fingers in her mouth and whistled just as Ketill had shown her.

The horse's head came up. Well trained, it trotted up the hill.

"Tanni?" Ketill whispered, aghast, as the stallion approached, head low.

"They killed him," she said, "for what he did. I'm sorry."

Ketill's face was haggard. He held out his palm. Tanni shied away, then his ears came up and he lipped Ketill's palm.

"I'm sorry," Tanni murmured. Ketill had been on the Shore long enough he didn't flinch at a talking horse. "I felt a small earthquake—"

"I didn't feel one," Ketill protested.

"You humans often don't." Tanni switched his tail. "This one scared me. I didn't mean to hit you."

"It's okay," Ketill said, wrapping his arms around Tanni's neck. He offered Gudrun his hand across Tanni's withers. "I'm sorry for what they've put you through."

She took his hand. "Me, too."

Death had climbed the hill behind them, followed by Hallr and the souls. Love-lines swarmed the air around them, an enticing array.

"Impressive," Death said, grudgingly.

"Thank you." She squeezed Ketill's hand and faced Death. "So I may stay?"

"If you truly wish it."

"Please!" one soul said, scrambling out from behind Death. "Find my son!"

"No, my betrothed!" another called.

"Better hurry," Hallr said. "More souls are coming down the corridor. They'll have folks for you to find, too."

She took a deep breath. Only now did she realize how big a job she was taking on—the souls newly arriving would leave little time to reunite the souls already clamoring around Death. She could work every moment of every day and still have an endless supply of souls to match. And when would she find time for Ketill?

"We'll come with you," he said, rubbing Tanni's nose. "Won't we?" Tanni whinnied.

She let out her breath. It would be a big job, but it was good work, which needed to be done.

"Okay," she said to the soul closest to Death. "Whom are you looking for?"

See Kathryn Yelinek's story "The Woman Who Brought Love to Death" online at Metaphorosis.
If you liked it, leave a comment. Authors love that!
Remember to subscribe to our e-mail updates so you'll know when new stories are posted.

About the story

I've had the image of a woman who could see love in my head for years, but I couldn't find the right story for the character. I tried everything—romance, murder mystery, you name it. But none of the stories worked. A few were downright embarrassing, now that I look back on them. Still, I kept coming back to the idea of what would it be like to see love? What would a person do with that ability? What sorts of problems would it cause them? Then my husband and I went to Iceland for our honeymoon, and I was entranced by the landscape and the Viking history. So I tried putting my poor, lost love-seer into an Icelandic-flavored setting, and it clicked. Gudrun fell out of my head and onto the page, and I went with it.

A question for the author

Q: If your writing style were a bird, what type of bird would it be and why?

A: Good grief, you realize you're asking this question of a total bird nerd, right? I mean, some of my writing friends say that a story isn't one of my mine unless it has a bird in it. I share my house with parakeets, I feed the outside birds, and I have been a lifelong birdwatcher. So birds means a lot to me.

Let me think carefully about this. I write slowly, so my writing style would not be a fast hummingbird or falcon. It also wouldn't be something like a bluebird, which can have multiple broods per year. I also don't think I have a terribly flashy style, so it wouldn't be a peacock or bird of paradise. I also don't write well in crowds or coffee shops or anything like that. I'm definitely a loner writer. So my writing style wouldn't be anything that congregates in huge flocks—no flamingos or starlings or budgerigars. I also write best at home, in familiar settings, so no birds that fly long distances like terns or albatrosses.

After all of this, I think my writing style is a kakapo. What is a kakapo, you ask? A rare flightless parrot from New Zealand. They breed very slowly, with the parrots taking several years to reach maturity, and some years they don't breed at all. They have muted green feathers and aren't flashy, but have a fluffy cuteness that I find absolutely endearing. They are also loners and don't congregate in flocks like many other parrots. Because they don't fly, they stick close to home. All of these things resonate for my writing style. In addition, because they are so rare, they have a dedicated team of extraordinary scientists and volunteers who do tremendous conservation work to save the species. While I don't need conservationists for my writing, I am lucky enough to have family and writing friends who support my work, and I am very grateful to them. [On a side note, if you are so moved to learn more about kakapos, visit the Kakapo Conservation page: https://www.doc.govt.nz/our-work/kakapo-recovery/.]

About the author

Kathryn Yelinek works as a librarian in Pennsylvania. In addition to the required hobbies of reading and writing, she enjoys bird watching, star-gazing, gardening, and going to see Broadway musicals. She and her husband share their home with two adorable parakeets, whom they are actively striving to make into the most spoiled birds in the Western Hemisphere. The birds don't seem to mind. Her works have appeared in *Daily Science Fiction, Deep Magic, Metaphorosis, Andromeda Spaceways Magazine*, and *Beneath Ceaseless Skies*.

www.kathrynyelinek.com

Time and Grace

Joseph Halden

Grace Soh was going to blaze across the empty American highways faster than anyone ever had, making it from coast to coast in a matter of hours: six if everything went as planned. The faster she got to the boost site in Oakland, California, the more money she'd make.

Grace would pay damages if she was late, but she would also reap the rewards if she was early. People paid a lot to have their self-driving networks and boosters maintained, and by displacing all of that skill, society had created a need for specialists like Grace.

She put up her hand to block out the annoying Atlanta sun, and squinted to check the old watch Father had given her: 08:32.

Several cars had driven by, but thankfully there'd been no sign of any employees from the rental lot. She'd pulled over half a mile outside their fences, but people barely looked out the windows anymore, let alone into the distance, so she wouldn't be noticed.

Grace lay back and felt around the underside of the rental jet car. Her small stature allowed her to worm around until she found the network card and yanked a cable out.

Networking, she thought snidely. *As if humanity has ever used connectivity for the greater good. There's a reason it's an Internet of Things, and not people.*

She watched the network flash with error messages on one lens of her VR glasses. *Good.*

"Ms. Soh, you will not be able to contact friends or family during the trip without a network connection," the car's artificial intelligence said, echoing off densely-packed innards.

"Lucky for me, that's not a problem, Brain-box."

What friends? I've turned rejection into diamond-tipped focus, she thought. *That's why I can do things no one else bothers to think of.*

The words helped control the swirling memories of being ghosted, and press them instead into a vision of herself as a ruthlessly efficient entrepreneur. She was surging ahead, leaving everyone in the dust.

"Not even your father, Ms. Soh?"

Grace froze, wondering if the AI had a backdoor to the network. It had been a few years since she'd had official training. Blazing her own trail was a point of pride, but she also had occasional moments like now when she felt needles scratch her insides, and wondered if she'd blazed the right path.

First, though, she had to know if the AI was bluffing. "My father's dead," she lied.

"Not unless he died within the last few minutes," the AI said.

"Are you spying on me?"

"I profile all my clients."

This AI was going to be trouble. Normally a jet car's AI was just smart enough to meet a client's needs, not question things and certainly not stalk someone's online presence.

Or lack thereof. Thankfully machines couldn't judge.

The rental companies must have requested 'upgrades'.

"Wonderful."

"If we had a network connection, you might be able to reach him before he goes to bed," the AI said.

Grace imagined the AI's breath smelling like burnt engine oil as she snaked her arms past layers of crud. She wrinkled her nose and blew debris from her lips. "Stop talking about my Dad, Brain-box."

"I think it bears repeating: my name is Alvus, Ms. Soh."

The AI's boldness was making it hard to focus.

Grace pictured Father, halfway across the world in a Singaporean nursing home. In his career he'd done much of the same work she did now—repairs for the transportation grid—but had never pushed himself, had always been too relaxed to save for the future.

He'd wasted too much time on relationships, and where had those gotten him? He was just as alone as the worst curmudgeons in the nursing home. The only difference was maybe how they paid for it. The curmudgeons had hoarded their life's earnings, whereas Grace's father relied on her to support him. The end result for both was the same.

The support Grace had to send Father left little room and resources to plan her own future. Time was thereby made an even more precious commodity, and she had to rush toward her goals if she was to have any chance at realizing them.

"Ms. Soh," the AI continued in a voice from all sides, formless and lifeless. "I must inform you that what you are doing is illegal. I urge you to reconnect and disengage from any further modifications to the vehicle if you wish to avoid a flag on your file."

Grace gritted her teeth. *You think I care about a flag on my file? A tiny flag, buried in a sea of monetized data? If it means one less company trying to sell me something, then good.*

Such flags, such algorithms, made Grace want to wash her hands after engineering work. The majority of the machinery and code she worked on was beautiful—the ugliest parts most resembled humans.

She wished she could make the modifications with the AI disconnected, but several processor overrides had to be active to allow her to tinker—and the first step was to prevent the annoying AI from calling the cops. "It's a good thing you're going to forget this whole thing when our trip's over, Brain-box."

"Ms. Soh, my name is Alvus. And if you are threatening me, you should know my memory is backed up in several onboard locations, and erasure of an AI's logs is a federal offence."

You're a smart one, Grace thought for the second time. *Usually they only spout a list of specifications back at me when I suggest amnesia.*

Grace slid out from beneath the car and stood. She toggled her VR lens through different diagnostic menus, checking her work.

Half a mile away, several more cars pulled out of the fenced rental car lot, and passed Grace. A few years ago she might have hidden off the main road. But these days people blackened their windows and worked or slept as soon as they got into the self-driving cars. Grace had total faith that, here as in other areas of her life, no one would notice her.

Tumbleweeds rolled dry and crackling across the arid plain, capable of ignoring all the trivial minutiae along the route. Soon Grace would be joining them, but would be far, far faster.

She got into the cabin and opened up the dash.

"I can also be sure to notify your father of your behaviour," Alvus said after the lengthy silence.

"Keep it up, Brain-box, and you won't remember which way is up when we're done."

"I propose a trade, Ms. Soh. If you call me Alvus, I will not mention your father."

Grace uncovered the panel for the speedometer. She had to be careful not to jar any of the other densely-packed sensors, but it was hard to concentrate with the annoying AI. "*Aiyah, so ma fan. You're a feisty one, Alvus.*"

"I take pride in my work."

Now that the AI—Alvus—couldn't call for help, she just had to modify the speedometer's calibration to make Alvus think they were going slower—350 instead of 500 miles per hour—and upload a fake record of their trip time for the internal log. When she'd first started she hadn't bothered to override the log, and the speeding ticket almost cost her her job. Now she knew better.

She checked and double-checked a circuit board to make sure she had the right cable. *Damn*, she thought after feeling with her fingers to count the wires for the fourth time. There was an extra one, which meant the model had changed. *Damn, damn, damn.*

Grace disconnected one of the cables and plugged her phone into the board in its place. The program would either take or it wouldn't—there was not enough time to change it. She would get much further ahead if she just tried, rather than getting lost in the changelog details. She started the recalibration app on her phone, craning her neck to keep an eye on the screen.

"Ms. Soh, you have locked me out of sensor data."

"Only for a few seconds, Alvus, I promise," she said. *I hope.*

The program finished. A few minutes later, Grace started the car. She hefted her bag into the back cabin. No time to waste securing her tools and parts—it was a short trip anyway. Another fifteen minutes saved, more money for Grace, and the closer she was to getting all she wanted.

Focus on the goal, and get there as fast as possible. Become like an Anchieta's dune lizard that dances with spiny-scaled toes so it never sinks into the sand.

"Okay, Alvus, you have the sensor data?"

"I am surprised I do, Ms. Soh. I am also surprised my path is fairly restricted, curiously correlated to your intended journey. And I'm locked out of flagging or emergency actions." Alvus let out a burst of static. "You must have done this before."

Take out the ugly, human parts, Grace thought, *and the machine becomes beautiful.*

She smiled, tapping the front display to blacken the windows. "I have no idea what you're talking about."

Grace typed away with her VR glasses on, a low hum the only evidence of the car's incredible speed. Her linked phone recorded the indirect measurements that added metadata to her workflow from implanted biometrics. She'd recorded a quick voice log as she left—a habit that had over the years become a comforting ritual, because she trusted her phone more than she trusted people when it came to her innermost thoughts. She could go back to the logs later, whenever she wanted, without having to worry about their accuracy or emotional state.

With all that data, her phone knew Grace better than she did.

"Ms. Soh, I am disoriented without accurate GPS tracking," Alvus said.

"It's good for your brain, Alvus."

"It is far more challenging to use collision-avoidance algorithms without network information. In addition to the fact that you must have modified my speed calibration, for my approach vectors need constant re-evaluation. I don't think I have ever gone this fast before. You have tied my hands."

A metaphor? Grace thought with a frown, then patted the dashboard. "It's a good thing you're up for the challenge. But I have work to do, so let me concentrate *lah!*"

She finished her report on the Atlanta boost-station repair she'd finished that morning, outlining the challenges and future upgrades necessary to push people travelling on the main trunks up to the new speed limit. Part of her knew it was a losing battle; she'd already seen the decline in federal funding for transportation lines. People had almost stopped going out when they could use VR for everything from family dinners to romantic getaways. Hell, Grace probably wouldn't go out herself if her job didn't require it.

Her work repairing recharge-boost stations would soon be obsolete, when only goods would need to be transported, and those by maglev. Her uncertain future was part of the reason she'd made a gamble on getting to site in Oakland on a tight timeline. The city was offering a lot of money to get its station back up before a weekend series of Major League Baseball games, one of a few American habits not yet lost to VR. No scheduled flights could have gotten her there in time.

The compartment rattled, and Grace's fingers typed an incoherent stream on the keyboard. "Alvus, are you having trouble?"

"Do you mean in addition to what you've already provided me?"

"Yes." She put away her keyboard, took off her glasses and opened up the instrument display on the dash. The rattling increased, and her teeth hammered together.

"I've lost connection to the lateral dampeners," Alvus said. "The engines are overheating. There—there is much cross-talk on all instrument channels."

Grace confirmed it on her own display, her pulse quickening. Her shoulders tensed and she sat up. If she'd messed something up during the speedometer recalibration... "Slow us down, turn all PCB TECs to max cooling. Clear the w—windows."

Grace gripped the leather seat next to her as she bounced up and down. Her seat harness locked with the sudden acceleration.

The shade lowered and let in blinding sunlight. "Filters, Alvus, filters!" Grace said.

"I'm losing control." His monotone voice chilled her.

"What do you mean?!"

"—can't tell what—measuring. Controls not responding." Alvus's voice clipped as the cabin heaved and rocked.

Grace's eyes adjusted to the brilliant light in time to take in the elevated highway, the brown-gold shrub plains around them, and the fact they were angled for the edge. "Alvus, turn left! Turn, turn!"

Alvus might have tried; everything happened too fast to tell. Instruments beeped as they soared over the edge of the freeway. If there had been a need for railings, they would have done little to stop the jet bullet. Polymer vibrated a drum snare. The dry wasteland surged up. Freeway pillars disappeared beyond Grace's periphery.

The landing kicked in the airbags, a white punch of mercy. The harness straps cut into Grace. Her skull shuddered. The car came to a stop, and Grace waited, breathless.

Grace turned everything off—including Alvus—then groped her way out of the car, shoving through airbags. Her skin burned from the harness; her neck ached. Smoke and hissing met her outside.

Grace stumbled through the dirt, avoiding shrubs and fist-sized rocks that had somehow not torn holes in the hull. She took in the details of the crash one by one. The car had landed nose-down in a small, dried-up ravine. The sharp front end was pushed in but intact. Ripples cascaded along the polymer skin of the main body. Smoke billowed from both of the half-meter turbines, and the right one had a small dent in it.

She pulled out her phone, a big dent in the back and spider webs of glass on the front. The screen still lit, but she had no network connection. She groaned and tucked it away.

The one-in-a-million time the connection to someone might be useful, she thought.

Grace rubbed her temples. Her watch read 12:15. She did a few mental calculations and realized she must be somewhere in New Mexico or Arizona. She was supposed to be in Oakland by 15:00. If she didn't start the work tonight, she'd be paying Oakland damages for breaking her commitment.

"Damn it." She climbed to the top of the ravine. A flat expanse stretched up to a jagged, isolated mountain visible on the edge of the horizon. Bushes and tufts of wildflowers patched the space between. Sand brushed the color from everything. The air shriveled Grace's nose. On the other side of the ravine, towering pillars of the freeway raised a dark scar in the sky.

"Any help would be great!" Grace shouted, her words drying and withering into the earth. She heard distant barks and yelps from no particular direction, formless sounds of the shrub lands.

"No answer. Of course," she muttered.

After making sure she had enough power to spare, she sat down in the front seat and turned on Alvus.

"You there?"

Alvus emitted soft warm-up audio reminiscent of a sigh. "I am, Ms. Soh."

She felt hot shame for being comforted by the way his voice mimicked a real person.

"Things are bad," she said.

But not so bad I can't get through this on my own, as I always have, she told herself.

"There is significant damage."

Grace listened to Alvus list what they had—spare turbine blades, extra cooling and lubricant, a hefty can of jet fuel, a first aid kit, a survival kit and a water tank.

Looking up toward the baking sun, Grace mouthed thanks that the water tank had survived. She didn't know how long she might last in the heat otherwise.

Then Alvus spouted a stream of everything that had malfunctioned, and would need manual inspection: all instruments, voltage lines, thermoelectric cooler drivers...

"Alvus," she murmured, "do you know much about the X2 line of cars before you?"

"I have extensive knowledge for marketing purposes."

Grace rolled her eyes. "Of course you do." She sank against the seat. Part of her didn't want to ask, didn't want to reveal how stupid she may have been. At this point there was a least a sliver of doubt it wasn't her fault. She let the words scrape out. "Were the voltage levels on the instrument card changed?"

"Yes, Ms. Soh. They were dropped from six to three-point-three volts for power consumption."

Oh God. How many chips did I fry? Grace blew out air.

Looking in the back cabin, it only took Grace a moment to realize the debris and bits were all that was left of the transponder and emergency beacon. They'd been smashed by her rugged tools bouncing around in the back. *Why didn't I secure my crap?*

Grace got out and buried her face in the crook of her elbow. She couldn't call for help. She was alone, and she hated herself for letting it make her feel so weak.

The time: 17:00. Grace had crossed the threshold from bonus to penalties, and every minute that went by put more distance between her and profit.

The jet car's long shadows stretched across the ravine, pre-cursing the coming darkness. The pools of sweat beneath Grace's arms had grown sticky and itchy. She took a swig of water from her bottle, and wiped her brow.

In a nearby section of the ravine where the slope steepened from aggressive erosion, tumbleweeds had gathered, caught and shuddering from the wind that could no longer push them. It seemed Grace wasn't the only one whose travel plans had been cut short.

She sighed and ducked back into the turbine. She'd heard barks and yelps in the distance throughout the day, and they grew louder and more frequent as the sun dipped.

She'd found work-arounds for burnt chips on three circuit boards, working with Alvus to find alternative modes of operation.

He was actually being very helpful. Machines were always much more reliable than people.

She cleaned debris and tested the boards—they showed basic functionality, but she had to admit she was out of her depth and was just lucky she'd had her soldering iron with her for the service trip. And that they had energy to spare.

"Can you connect to the turbines now, Alvus?" She backed away and listened for the hum of charge. "Come on," she muttered, clasping her hands together.

After a lengthy silence, a howl echoed across the plain, as though the wild had somehow triumphed over her efforts.

Are those coyotes, or wolves? Grace groaned. *I don't need this right now.*

She threw her arms against the turbine. The bang echoed between the shadows of the shrubs.

"I am sorry, Ms. Soh."

Grace sank with her back against the car, lowering herself into the shade.

Her lips trembled, and she wrestled within herself for the instinctive favour she wanted to ask of a machine.

To make it seem more human. God, she was pathetic.

Grace, you've gotta get through this, one way or another, she thought. *Got enough on your plate. We'll sort out that other crap later.*

"Call me Grace, Alvus," she said at last. "We're going to be spending a lot more time together."

As if that were the only reason. As if her creeping desperation weren't making her take solace in an artificial construct.

She snatched her water bottle and drank. Thank god the car's water tank was intact. She let a few streams dribble down her cheeks and onto her shirt. A few hours ago it had been cool. Now it burned on its way down.

The feeling reminded her of a thousand coffees, all sipped alone, at restaurants and cafes where others met friends.

There's no one I could call, she thought, *even if I had a network connection.*

She swallowed hard and put the bottle's cap back on.

None of that matters, Grace, she told herself. *Get a grip.*

She froze.

A coyote stood watching her from fifteen feet away. When she caught its eye, it looked down, feigning interest in a patch of dead wildflowers. Its sand-colored pelt was spotted with flecks and patches of black and white.

The coyote kept sneaking glances at her, trotting in a radius around her. It was bigger than a German Shepherd.

Oh God. That's no coyote—that's a coywolf.

The coywolf's long tail—more full and fluffy than the rest of its body—nearly touched the ground behind its legs. The tail wagged absently but halted every time the coywolf stopped to steal a glance at Grace. Bands of black fur highlighted an intensity behind its eyes.

The waterfalls of sweat down her sides suddenly chilled. She'd heard stories of the coywolves changing, migrating to unexpected areas, looting and eating just about anything they could find, destroying equipment and animals indiscriminately as resources grew more scarce. She raised herself and clenched her hands to stop them from trembling.

She charged forward. "Go on! Get out of here!"

The coywolf darted back, then bent low to the ground and snarled.

Grace's calves ached from the sudden burst, and she had the sense of settling into a new normal for slow reaction time.

Not good, Grace. Not good.

"Get going! There's nothing for you here!"

She ran after the coywolf. The creature locked eyes now, running half-backward, able to maintain that posture with Grace's stumbling lope. She continued after it until her legs wouldn't anymore. She growled as she bent down to pick up a few pebbles to throw at the coywolf.

She walked backward all the way back to the jet car. The coywolf stayed where it was, watching her the whole way.

"Grace, are you all right?" Alvus had turned on loud external speakers.

"I don't know, Alvus," she said.

"You don't appear to have any additional injuries."

"Glad to know you've got your eye on me."

"Many eyes."

Grace held up a hand, and opened the door to the car. "That's enough, creepo, thanks." She bent the seat back so she could lie down.

"Grace, you've made excellent progress," Alvus said. "There is still work to be done, and I recommend trying to get out before nightfall."

Grace shook her head, squeezing her eyes shut. "I haven't made good progress," she whispered. "I've lost thousands of dollars since I've been stuck here."

The sun had lowered to cast the whole ravine in shadow now, and the dry whispers taunted Grace with all she'd gotten wrong. All her failures. Inadequacies.

She reached up and slammed the car door shut.

"Grace, I am sure you can recover the lost wages," Alvus said, his volume adjusting to her tone.

Even with the door closed, she couldn't stop the voice inside chiding her for pretending, more and more with each minute that passed, that Alvus was a person.

So pathetic.

"Probably," she muttered. She wanted to ask why she still felt so awful, but her inner critic's mocks grew louder, silencing her.

The time: 21:00. Strands of sunlight dangled like outstretched arms as the horizon pulled away. Several more tumbleweeds had gotten caught in the pile in the ravine, rattling against each other like a pile of bones.

Grace slid back beneath the jet car, her head aching from trying to wade through the never-ending series of repairs. Every shortcut she'd made before the trip had added more repair work, a thousand tiny wounds bleeding out any hope of getting ahead. She'd cut the feathers off the bird to make it fly faster.

She puzzled over the thermoelectric cooling circuitry, trying to get some temperature control back to key current drivers. Her phone light was a poor substitute for ambient light, and she kept having to twist around in the cramped space.

"How's that? What's the temperature, Alvus?"

"Twenty-nine point-four degrees Celsius."

Grace sighed. "Okay. Try turning on the cooler now."

She bumped her head on the way out, making the world spin as she wiggled out from beneath the car. She rested against the side for a moment, then pawed her way around the turbine to the back for some water.

A few steps away a coywolf lapped at a puddle of water dribbling from the water tank. Another one craned its neck above and gnawed at a water hose.

"Hey!" Grace shouted.

The one licking the puddle looked up, yellow eyes meeting hers. It growled, its lips quaking spittle.

Grace yelled and stomped the ground. "Get going! Get!"

The coywolf snapped its jaws.

A bear's roar from the car shook the surrounding shrubs. The coywolves jumped and the one let go of the water line.

Grace charged the pair of coywolves with her arms raised as Alvus continued to roar from the speakers. The sound made her teeth rattle. She tried to kick one, and it bit her shoe. She careened against the side of the car. She swung her phone's light in the coywolf's eyes, and it released.

The other coywolf pushed onto its back heels then dove at her. She jumped and landed on its paw. It yipped; others answered in the distance.

Grace backed up, and leapt inside the car.

Despite Alvus's attempts to ward them off with loud noises, the coywolves quickly realized he posed no real threat. They started worming their noses back into every open crevice of the half-repaired jet car.

They were going to tear the car apart if she didn't do something.

Grace scrambled through the survival kit in the back cabin, darting glances up at the coywolves. *Come on, give me something.*

The coywolf was back gnawing on the water line.

Grace found a flare gun; it almost shook out of her hands as she opened the car door.

"Leave me alone!" she shouted, taking aim.

She fired the flare gun, a popping hiss planting in the dirt right beside the coywolf clutching the water line. It jumped back growling.

"Stop taking things from me!" she went on, reloading and firing again.

This time she narrowly missed the coywolf. It yipped and fled into the darkness.

"You never help me!" she shouted. "No, we couldn't have that, now could we?"

Grace fired several more flares around the car, bathing it in red light. On the seventh one, the wind caught the flare and pulled it into the pile of blocked tumbleweeds.

It lit up like a rocket blast. Dry crackles turned quickly into a roar, and spread a hotter-than-day sun into the surrounding area. The smoke tasted hot, sharp, and empty.

Grace cringed away from the heat. She knew she should be grateful, for the fire should keep the coywolves away, but she felt an inexplicable loss at the trapped tumbleweeds' promise of a new life going up in flames. Like they'd skimmed across the steppes only to be betrayed by the force that carried them.

She watched the flames lick the sky and slowly die down. Though everything here was dry, it was too sparse to have a brush fire, thank goodness.

Grace turned back to the water tank. The water spilled out of the broken tube in thick spurts, muddying the earth.

"No, no, no!" She rushed over and tried to plug it with her hands, then a piece of her shirt. It took several minutes before she plugged the leak with first-aid tape.

She was soaked and the seal still dripped water. She shone her light in. There was maybe half a gallon left.

Grace gathered her hair in her hands and pulled.

"Why didn't you say something?" she shouted. "Alvus!"

"I didn't see the coywolves on my cameras, Grace."

"Oh, come on! You watch me with all your sensors and you just happen to flake when coywolves take all my water?" She stood and slammed the hood of the car.

"I admit my attention was occupied while we were trying to find workarounds. But my sensors didn't find any visible approach."

"I thought your processing power was better than that, Brainbox." She kicked the curved front and glared into the darkness, praying the coywolves wouldn't return.

"It is possible I am damaged in a way I cannot perceive, Grace. I am sorry."

"No you're not," Grace snapped, turning back to the car. "You don't need water. You know you'll eventually be found, and you have all the time in the world. There's nothing at stake for you—and whether I live or die doesn't matter. There's more humanity in you than I thought."

The wind snaked between leaves, chattering, whispering. The hunk of metal in the ravine remained unmoved. The tumbleweed fire was now a pile of faint embers.

"I wish I could convince you that's not the case. I only have words. I wish to help you survive this."

Grace's eyes and chest burned. She dropped her chin.

What am I doing? Chastising a machine for doing what it's been programmed to do? Come on, Grace.

She trudged back toward the front of the car. She felt heavy, burdened with an increasing list of problems she couldn't fix. Feeling pathetic for her gratitude that Alvus, despite everything she'd shouted, was here with her.

She slid under the car. "Let's keep going," she said, her voice thick.

The engine smelled of pungent lead solder, burnt oil, and ash as Grace worked on into the night.

The time: 02:00, the next morning, still dark. The howls grew louder. Grace wondered if coywolves ever slept, or if they existed just to torment her. She squinted into the night, trying to spot their slinking forms, but couldn't. She wished she were taller—then the coywolves might be more afraid.

She shone a light on her blackened hands, trying to rub the oil off without success. The taste of smoke from the tumbleweed fire still lingered in her throat. "Alvus, what do you know about lateral stabilization chips?"

"I am not authorized to share that information, Grace. I'm locked out for safety reasons, to prevent exactly what you're suggesting."

Grace groaned. Of course. Because humans are so endlessly stupid, herself included.

She was so tired, thirsty and hungry. She was trying to stretch the water out but it was difficult when she exerted herself so much. The tank had been leaking so much it had been pointless to try and make the water last.

She thought the lateral stabilization was the last step. They seemed achingly close to a working car, but she didn't trust herself at all anymore.

"There's got to be a way," she said. "A loophole in your programming."

Alvus hummed—something he'd never done before.

"Uh—are you okay?"

"I suggest you look at the maintenance logs," Alvus said abruptly.

"What do you mean?" Grace asked. "What will I find there?"

"I do not know. It is an option." The screen inside lit up with a crude, pixelated, winking eye.

Does an AI know when it's losing its mind? she wondered before she sat down in front. She kept the door open in case she had to bolt for it. It did little to ease the knot in her stomach.

If Alvus had given out on her, there was nowhere she could go. She could try to climb the pillars of the freeway, and hope someone happened to notice her as they passed at subsonic speeds.

But they wouldn't, and she would be even more alone.

She tapped the screen and scanned the logs. She found several hundred entries for oil changes, a few for turbine changes, then—

"You're smarter than you look, Alvus."

"My current appearance is entirely your fault, Grace."

She almost laughed. "Okay. I deserved that. So there was a log two years ago where the lateral stabilization chip had a firmware upgrade, and some manual calibration done. Can you show me your records from that log?"

"No. You do not have authorization."

Grace smacked the dash. "Come on! Are you just messing with me now? Why even bother showing me then?"

"I thought it might spark some ideas. I am not authorized to say more."

If I ever get out of this, I will hunt down the vehicle safety manager and lock him in a suicide cruise-control trip straight into the Pacific.

A few bursts of static sprayed out the speakers, then another crudely pixelated image appeared on the screen. This time it spelled a message in barely recognizable lettering: "Enter my mind."

Realization wormed icy fingers around Grace's core. *That's what he's hinting at. Interface with his consciousness, and piece through his recordings.*

To do that, she'd have to connect through her phone, which recorded everything about her, not to mention all the personal logs she'd made. If she let Alvus in, then he would see how many times she'd rigged other jet cars to travel illegally fast across the country.

He'd also see deeper—much deeper. His inquiries into the health of her father were a handshake by comparison. What would Alvus do with all that information? Machines weren't supposed to be capable of judgment, but throughout this whole ordeal, Alvus had shown many more signs of humanity than any other AI she'd known.

Hell, more than some of the friends she'd once had.

She was both grateful and ashamed, especially now that she worried about the possibility of his judgment. If he was showing so many other signs of humanity, was he just as capable of looking at her bared soul, and rejecting her?

She stared at the phone clutched in her hand. If only she could delete or lock Alvus out of the many years of logs and personal metadata, but those were deeply entwined with the algorithms that protected her mind in the rare cases when activities like mentally soaring through reams of data were necessary.

Was this the only way? Risk everything in a total admission of her inner self, or be eaten by coywolves?

Or maybe she'd end up just like the tumbleweeds, sailing straight into cremation.

"Grace," Alvus said, "are you all right?"

Coywolves barked, very close.

It was this or die. Grace put on her VR glasses, hooked up her phone, and jacked in.

She blazed past red walls and skirted encryption barriers, typing away furiously. As she crossed the threshold, she sensed Alvus now had complete access to her digital presence.

Don't judge me, Alvus.

Shuddering, she moved into Alvus's recordings.

Please don't abandon me.

Men and women slept in car seats, worked, careened along in typical journeys, the windows always blackened. Grace skipped through these until she saw a suited woman walking ahead of the car, a rocky knoll ahead. The woman took one last look at the camera, then walked off the cliff.

Mortified, Grace traced the woman's other recordings, trying to make some sense of what she'd seen. It seemed the woman's company had arranged a long-term lease that meant she was using Alvus all the time.

The woman's history followed a similar pattern to Grace's own life, commuting daily from New York to Seattle, working the entire way. Alvus attempted to cheer her up. The woman never responded to him. The bags beneath her eyes grew heavier, the life leaking out and leaving a deadness in her stare.

The woman didn't seem there when she killed herself. She had been vacant, leeched of something ineffable.

There wasn't a single piece of evidence of the woman talking to another human being. Grace went back and forth through the footage, seeing more and more resonance of the woman's life with her own. Her temperature rose as her mind went into overdrive. She felt at any moment now the heat could set her ablaze.

It didn't have to end this way, she kept telling the woman. *You could have called someone. You could have called me.*

Even as she thought the words, the absurd impossibility stared her in the face.

Was she on the road to becoming that woman?

Even worse, was she already there?

Keep going, Grace, just keep going.

But she'd been racing... for so very long. Just as the woman had. What was the point of it all, if it ended the same way?

She mentally flipped through the logs, back and forth, back and forth, until she felt herself drifting deeper into a whirlpool.

The view jolted and was replaced by recordings made out the side and back cameras. They were of sunsets and sunrises, brilliant gold, flamingo, and lilac layers as the sun bid hello or goodbye.

This wasn't a required recording; this was something Alvus chose to do.

He was trying to help her.

He cared.

With great effort, Grace pulled herself back and navigated through more of the regular recordings.

She finally found recordings of the maintenance engineer putting in a new chip. She had to cross-link to the firmware changes, and the manual calibration gave her the encryption keys. She copied the encryption algorithms, checked them, then pulled out, backing through the firewalls.

She felt raw.

She breathed heavily, words emerging in slow chunks. "Alvus, I have them," she said. "Can you copy them into one of your processors?"

"I suggest the interface module," he said. "If you short wires from the J1 header, that should give me control."

Grace glanced out the back of the car toward the towering rock. A mile away the ground writhed with movement. The coywolves had brought reinforcements, and would devour the exposed parts of the car if she didn't act soon. Her heart leapt into her throat.

She lurched out and slid beneath the car. Her soldering iron sat plugged into a battery, a mess of wires and solder beside. Grace grabbed the wires and got to work.

"Grace," Alvus said, "a pack of—"

"Thanks, I saw." She fought to still her shaking hands. Flecks of solder flew off and burned her cheeks.

"Grace, they're almost here."

Yips and barks answered.

She had four of five wires done when a coywolf bit her shoe. It tugged, shook until her shoe came off, then retreated, gnashing, and tearing. It was only a matter of time until the shoe wasn't enough.

She got the last wire on, but there was too much solder. It had shorted a few of the pins. She jabbed with the soldering iron, trying to drag off some of the excess. Once, twice—there.

"Alvus," she cried, "start the turbines! Please! Start the tur—"

The roar drowned out the howls and the yips.

Grace screamed joyfully and almost embraced the rumbling engine. She slid out and into the front seat.

"Alvus, let's go!"

The jet car surged backward out of the ravine. On-ramps were rare, but by going slowly and carefully across the plains, she and Alvus would eventually find one. Grace had never been so happy to be in a moving vehicle.

The time: 06:15. Grace walked out of the booster station, still missing her shoe, and opened the car door. "Hi, Alvus."

"Hello, Grace. Are you feeling better?"

"A little bit," she said, sinking into the seat. "I got the station working again."

"And the payment?"

She sighed. "Well, I don't have to pay them too much for being late. Didn't make anything, though."

"I am sorry, Grace."

"It's all right." She meant the words, and just felt glad the whole thing was over. She valued the time ahead to breathe at her own pace, surprising herself. She had never expected to want a vacation after a lifetime seeing Father waste so much time.

Then again, she was finding more and more that maybe her expectations needed recalibration.

She paused, then: "I also spoke to my Dad. It felt good." Another unexpected outcome—that she'd end up acting on and agreeing with an AI's advice. As well as reaching out to another human being.

"I'm very glad to hear that."

She hesitated, thinking back to their shared time in digital space. "When you and I connected, I…"

Alvus's voice shifted in tone, almost imperceptibly. Grace wouldn't have noticed had she not spent almost an entire day with him. "I am grateful for the glimpse into you, Grace," he said, his vocal cadence slower. "I will not disrespect that trust."

"You don't… think less of me now? That I'm just, I don't know, not worth the effort?" she whispered. The words burned her. A day before she wouldn't have given them voice, wouldn't have allowed herself to sink this low. But she had to confirm if the glimpse inside had revealed what had turned so many others away.

"No, Grace. Humans are remarkable in their ability to break the chain of what has come before—something I cannot do. Something I wish I could do."

Grace ran her hands through her hair.

She'd gone from coast to coast, and still she had so far to go.

"Thank you, Alvus," she said.

"Thank you for not wiping my brain-box."

Grace rubbed her forehead, remembering that she still had to return Alvus, which would involve paying a lot for damage. Alvus's memory would also be wiped somewhat to protect privacy, though maybe he'd found a way around that with some of his recordings. For the first time, she wondered what a memory wipe must feel like to an AI.

The next words came out of her unwittingly. "Alvus, how much would your company charge for your purchase?"

Alvus paused before replying. "Are you wanting to keep me around, Grace?"

"How would you... feel about that?"

"As terrific as I am capable."

"So how much?"

Alvus quoted a figure. It was far more than Grace had expected—much more than the damage costs would be—and would use up most of her savings. But maybe it was a worthwhile investment.

Nearby, a tumbleweed was stuck against a signpost at the edge of the boost station. Grace couldn't help herself. She walked over, picked it up carefully, looking around for where the wind would take it, then moved half a mile up the road to set it down where it had the best chances of a long journey.

Her mind kept wanting to surge ahead, to plan the next project, but for the first time in a long while, she told herself *No*. Maybe it was okay to pause along the way.

By the time she returned to Alvus, the sun had crept up closer to the silver line of the horizon. "Do you want to turn to face the sunrise?" Grace asked gently.

"Thank you, but no. I've recorded many of them."

Grace frowned. She stared at the orange-crimson fingers ushering in the new day—she never thought she'd seen anything more moving.

She knew it felt this way, in part, because Alvus was here with her. Maybe that was okay, too.

"What I do want," Alvus continued, "is to hear how you see it with your eyes."

See Joseph Halden's story "Time and Grace" online at
Metaphorosis.
If you liked it, leave a comment. Authors love that!
Remember to subscribe to our e-mail updates so you'll know when
new stories are posted.

About the story

I'm always interested in our relationship with technology, and the specific ways it influences our connections to each other. The specific idea for this story, however, was planted when I was travelling for work, in a new rental vehicle every time. It was a lonely period of my life. I was in grad school and commuting to different experiments, in places where I hardly knew anyone. The scenery and places that I visited in and around California's bay area were spectacular. Although I tried to enjoy the ride, it was hard to have no one to share it with.

Throughout my trips I mused about people's relationships with their vehicles, as well as how vehicles are becoming increasingly intelligent. They become comforting homes, a familiar refuge when everything around us changes. Listening to familiar songs, even sitting in a familiar seat, can be very calming when there are few constants. I started to imagine a road trip with an artificial intelligence to keep a person company, and if that might be one area of people's lives where artificial intelligence might be more welcome than others, because of the strong person-vehicle relationship that exists within the North American cultural mythos. These ideas all came before home assistants, or even voice commands on smartphones.

Road trips have a certain mystique about them, but as notions of self-driving cars began permeating the technological landscape, I realized my original vision of a more traditional North American road trip might not be something that would even exist once we had artificial intelligences in cars. I needed to come up with a scheme where someone on a trip would be forced to consider their surroundings, rather than tune out and wait to reach their destination.

I wanted to explore some of the loss that can be engendered by new technology, and I thus created Grace Soh, one of a select few who still used the rapid highways, and who most pointedly felt such a loss. In our technophilic society, it can be very easy to adopt new creations without being mindful of what we might be transformed as a result. Grace embodies that tendency to race ahead without paying attention.

The rest is... well, in the story's veins. I have to thank Mary Robinette Kowal for her great initial feedback on the story during the Odyssey Writing Workshop, as well as many others who helped shape the story into what it is.

Oh, one more fun fact: I use Alvus as a persona in many stories where I have an AI, and I'm thrilled he fit so well into this one.

A question for the author

Q: What is the most recent book that you lost sleep reading/thinking about?

A: I adored *Among Others* by Jo Walton, and couldn't stop reading. The depiction of magic in such an unfathomable yet human way was mesmerizing. The protagonist's journey held so many beautifully-articulated moments of humanity that really worked for me, and I loved re-experiencing some sci-fi classics through her lens.

About the author

Joseph Halden is a wizard in search of magic, an astronaut in need of space, and a hopeless enthusiast of frivolity. He's shot things with giant lasers, worn an astronaut costume for over 100 days to try and get into space, and made his own soap. A graduate of the Odyssey Writing Workshop, he writes science fiction and fantasy in the Canadian prairies.

www.josephhalden.com, @joseph_halden

July

The Friendly Ghost

Ashley R. Carlson

A Year Before

Conversations with you were never dull (it was one of the main reasons I wanted to marry you), but that night things had taken a random turn from flirty innuendos and our cat's sudden-onset sneezing attacks to more macabre fare.

You'd just told me about a dangerous incident that happened on the work site, and that if things had been left running a *little* while longer, you could've lost a limb or worse from exploding shrapnel.

I'm probably not gonna make it past sixty, you texted, before insisting that 'when' you died before I did, I had to remain in lifelong mourning and embrace celibacy wholeheartedly. I told you that was ridiculous—on numerous counts—because our parents were older than that already, spry in that middle-class, Boomer way that propelled them haughtily on through retirement, golfing and brunching and perpetually driving five miles under the speed limit wherever they went.

Well if I die first, I'm going to haunt you, I joked. The text exchange was one of thousands we'd shared during our year-long marriage and two years of dating before that. They were a godsend to me, those (usually) cheerful blue bubbles coming in spurts (interspersed with the occasional NSFW Snapchat pic), to offer a comforting, digital tether for the two weeks of every month when work took you out of state.

Don't even say that.

It could happen, Dan! Don't live in denial! And I'm nice, because I want you to get remarried and everything.

It better not, and I wouldn't. But fine, I guess you can haunt me. Just promise you'll be a friendly ghost.

What, exactly, is a 'friendly' ghost? I munched on a Milano cookie as I typed, pausing my reality show on the flat-screen—a show you unwaveringly refused to watch because of the cast members' 'arguments about a chihuahua named Lucy Lucy Apple Juice' that comprised most of the season's overarching plotline. I had this sudden craving to know what sort of ghost you'd deem 'tolerable,' and added another message to our text stream—the ghost emoji, draped in white with its tongue stuck out, arms raised in mid-scare. *Boo! I see you. Do you see me?* it implied, a lighthearted caricature of the real thing for kids and still-honeymoon-phasing couples to send one another on Halloween.

One who helps the person they haunt.

What, like in the movie Ghost, *with Patrick Swayze? For justice and all that?* I texted, digging in the bag for another Milano and coming up empty with a disgruntled sigh; reality shows always made me ravenous. They were a modern-day, gluttonous feast of drama and intrigue, except that the fighters in the arena had been replaced by diamond-draped, viper-tongued housewives.

No, not like that, you replied. I could almost hear you utter it aloud, the threat of sorrow deepening the tenor of your voice, one normally so animated with jest. The topic had edged into depressing territory, especially when we were a thousand miles apart.

Then what? I typed, still acutely curious of your definition, for this was a page as-yet-unturned in the book that was your thoughts and feelings. *What kind of ghost would you like me to be?*

Maybe you'd been called away from your phone to tend to an issue on the construction site, or a manager had come into the office and scowled to find the team's star supervisor engrossed in his phone at the start of another nightshift—but you didn't respond for a while, and by then I'd finished my show, tucked the cat in, and lay curled under the covers of the king-size bed we shared only part time.

I promise, baby, I texted to conclude the discussion, for I knew you well, and while you were the epitome of showy masculine verve—you lived to lift weights at the gym, used gag-inducing "bro"-ish terms too often for me to count, and could grill up a perfectly smoked brisket in your sleep—you were the more sensitive of the two of us; your center was ooey-gooey, and I had to be careful not to jostle your insides while you were away. *I'd be a friendly ghost,* I asserted via text, and that was it, followed by a quick *goodnight, I love you so much!!!!* with lots of exclamation points because you liked them. Tomorrow we'd resume our conversation on those benign issues between newly married couples—paycheck amounts and which bills were coming up next, small health concerns centered around bowel regularity that kept us laughing and did much to close the gap of physical space between us in one perfectly timed poop emoji.

I'm happy to say that all these months later, I've kept my promise.

A Week After

It's my funeral today, but goddamn if it doesn't look like yours.

It's awful to see you like this—eyes as bruised underneath as over-ripe plums, thick dark hair gelled to one side by the budget-salon stylist you visited this morning at the request of your mother (and I'm thankful she insisted, because you haven't washed it yourself in nearly a week). I've only ever seen you looking this haggard once before, following our first and only separation eight months into the relationship, when I still wasn't sure we were right for each other. I'd showed up right after a long, expletive-and-tear-filled post-breakup phone call, because I missed you and it stung to hear you so distraught. As I walked up that narrow sidewalk to find you in the suffocating heat of midsummer twilight, the way your wilted stance against the doorway made me ache was evidence enough that regardless of our differences, I was deeply in love and never wanted to let you go again.

This hurts too—worse, because back then I'd chosen to separate from you, something I could (and swiftly did) remedy. These circumstances are unequivocally more permanent.

Your eulogy is nice, if a little short, and you don't cry. You haven't much, and it's concerning, but not because I'm worried you don't care. There's a place inside that I think you've gone to, burrowed deep, deep down to hide, even deeper than that time I ended it and you said on the phone you hadn't been able to sleep or eat properly in weeks, and didn't really see the point in changing that. You need someone to coax you from that insidious, inviting darkness before it seeps in and poisons you to the bone—and I'm not going anywhere until I lead you out.

I promised.

Two Weeks After

I'm still learning the rules of being a ghost.

You shiver if I touch you, but that's about it. You only seem to hear me at night while you're sleeping, and every time I've whispered "I love you" and "I'm going to help you through this," you've just moaned or whimpered, as if the mere lilt of my voice is a minor but still very present kind of torture.

I wander the house once you're asleep—wary of the glowing doorway that appears in the corner of every room I enter, softly lit along the edges of the closed door and inviting me to approach, but never demanding it.

I visit with the cat instead, who can definitely still see me based on the way his protuberant eyes follow me in the dark, wary and appraising, as if he's forgotten I was his beloved caretaker mere weeks ago. Maybe I look different; maybe my ghostly form has retained the gruesome injuries sustained during my death, and they frighten him. For all I know, an array of lacerations still spider-webs across my forehead, a bit of exposed gristle hanging where the truck burst through the driver's side to split the lower part of my face in half. There's no reflection in the mirror to confirm this, but when I run my fingertip across my chin, its journey is reassuringly smooth.

I don't need sleep or sustenance, but I'm able to perch on furniture well enough, and can even turn the TV on if I slam my hand against the remote enough times. It took me more than an hour to get the damn thing to work playing the latest episode of my favorite show—you haven't dismantled the DVR preferences yet, though when I was alive you bemoaned the fact that our limited recording space was always full of bullshit squabbles in fancy restaurants and phony attempts at finding the 'one'. These shows give me comfort in the silent hours of the night when you finally find rest—what I hope to be *true* rest, not the hours spent catatonic in bed until your mom or mine shows up and forces you to eat some of their homemade empanadas and pozole, before busying themselves with gathering up the growing, untouched pile of dirty laundry strewn about the house and momentarily freezing when they find a pair of my socks or underwear in the fray, before hurriedly tossing them in the washer with the rest.

It's not long before the cat joins me on the couch for our nightly viewings, moving between you in the bedroom and me on the sofa to purr and knead the thick, wooly blanket we used to nestle under for *Game of Thrones* marathons—a child in the midst of two parents separated by far more than divorce.

One Month After

You are acting strange.

I notice it first when you call your boss and quit out of the blue, even though they've been exceptionally understanding about it all, offering three months' worth of paid leave following the funeral.

It's when you try to give the cat to your parents that I realize my nightly stream of encouragements beside you in bed haven't ameliorated your grief in the least.

"I don't want him anymore," you slur on the phone, a full tumbler of whiskey in hand. You've been drinking all day, unaware of my reprimands to at least *eat* something between aggressively thrown-back shots of liquor. "He was hers. I don't fucking *want* him! I HATE THIS FUCKING CAT AND I DON'T WANT TO CLEAN UP HIS SHIT ANYMORE!" you bellow into the receiver.

That's a complete lie—I know it, you know it, for god's sakes, the cat knows it. He's scowling at you right now, having just left you another smelly gift in his litterbox.

Whatever your mom says on the other end sets you off. You shout again and throw the phone at the wall hard enough to shatter the screen, before storming into the hallway toward the medicine cabinet.

"What are you doing?" I cry as I follow you, watching as you rummage through the bottles of ibuprofen and Midol and Sudafed with trembling fingers.

You pivot and stride through me to return to the kitchen. Reach for a glass from the cabinet and fill it with water from the sink.

"What the fuck are you *doing*?!" I repeat as you fumble with the childproof lid on the bottle. "Hey! Stop it right now! *Stop!*"

I slam into you and it's like fighting against wind, like passing my hands through a cloud of smoke for all the difference it makes. You've got a palmful of round orange pills now, at least three dozen, and you're bringing them to your lips with a hand that's suddenly steadier than I've seen in weeks. I scream so loud and shrilly that it frightens the cat and he's off like a shot under the couch, but you're undeterred, they're in your mouth now, you're about to chase them down with water—

"DANIEL HERNANDEZ, YOU STOP IT *RIGHT FUCKING NOW!*"

My shriek shatters a nearby trio of glass bottles full of seashells we gathered on a Puerto Rican trip to celebrate our first wedding anniversary, splinters of blue-green glass and shells exploding across the kitchen table in all directions.

It also breaks the glass in your hand.

You stand there, stunned, bare feet strewn with fragmented glass, bottom lip split and bleeding from an errant slice. You bend over the sink and spit the pills out, a hunk of saliva-slicked half-white, half-orange rounds, and back away to survey the mess.

Your brown eyes are wary, wide.

You say my name—*mouth* it, soundlessly. Like a prayer.

You finally start to cry, torso-shattering sobs that bring you to the kitchen floor. I bend to take you in my arms, forgetting for a moment you can't feel a thing.

Eleven Months After

You've just returned to your new apartment from the gym, sipping on a protein shake. You've been lifting at this new gym a lot recently, and it shows in the supple sinews of your back and arms, the renewed vibrancy of your light brown skin.

It's all new, as if scouring me from your surroundings will also scour me from your memories: apartment, city, job, furniture, clothes. You sold the house, donated our stuff to charity, got a new position in another state—but you kept the cat. I encouraged each step, talking to you day and night about why you should stay alive, how much more there was for you to do. A fresh start was what you needed and what you got, but all that newness didn't mean I was ready to leave. You were still alone (the cat didn't count), and I'd decided that in order to *really* make it better—to live up to my promise—you deserved a full life with someone new.

I was concerned about a forced disconnection before my goal was achieved; perhaps I was bound to the *house* and not you, and when you drove off I'd have to say goodbye for good and finally go through the doorway I'd staunchly been avoiding for nearly a year.

On the day you packed your few remaining belongings and set off with the cat for the big city and the new job, I waited in front of the house, watching until your car's red brake lights were only an echo, a smeared corona when I shut my eyes; a ghost of what had once been concrete, been *there*. I paced the driveway, ignoring that damned glowing doorway ever-present in the corner of my vision.

"I'm not ready yet! *He's* not ready yet! Fuck off!" I finally hollered at the door, and it shrank and shrank, to the size of a doggie door and then a mousehole and then a pinprick, until it winked out completely for the first time since the car crash.

I paced that driveway in your absence, searching my memory for how I'd gotten from that fluorescent-bathed hospital room to the funeral and back to the house, but I truly couldn't recall.

It wasn't too long before I *did* end up where you and the cat were, suddenly going all misty like vapor passing between someone's lips on a cold night, only to come together again in your new apartment just in time to see you shuffling inside with the cat carrier and a suitcase.

"So I do haunt *you*, then," I said, thoroughly relieved. I still had a lot left to do.

A Year and Nine Months After

You're checking yourself out in the bathroom mirror, and I laugh.

"I *told* you you'd start losing your hair one day," I say as you gather a bit of gel in your palm and attempt to wrestle your brown strands into a coif that somewhat hides the thinning at your temples and crown. You've got a date tonight, the first since I died, and I'm not trying to be a brat, but she looks a bit...*basic*. That's my jealousy talking, I know—I was the one who prompted you about this online dating stuff anyway, murmuring in your ear night after night to make sure you heard me. But then you went and matched with some Basic Blonde who looks nothing like me and wore a goddamn bathing suit in every single one of her pictures (if you can call a strip of fabric up your ass-crack a suit), so your selection has me questioning whether this was all a huge mistake.

While you're gone I putter around the apartment, tidying up in ways I know from experience you won't notice. I'm watching the latest housewife mayhem when you start to unlock the front door, and I manage to turn the TV off just in time to see you tripping over the apartment's threshold with the Basic Blonde in tow.

"Christ, you're drunk," I mutter as you fumble for the light switch and quickly give up on finding it. "Better not have driven home—" I stop myself there; you've done a few questionable things since my death, but committing the very same act my killer did isn't one of them.

Without preamble, BB yanks you toward your bedroom. You leave the room's door open—no one lives here but you and the cat, right?—so I'm forced to listen to what happens next, glancing every so often at the ethereal doorway to my right with a sneer (it reappeared a few weeks back, just as incandescent and pleasant-looking as ever).

"This isn't *exactly* what I meant when I said you should start dating again," I chide, watching the cat vacillate between licking his butt and peering sympathetically in my direction.

When it's over, the blonde has the audacity to think it's time to talk. I waltz into the bedroom and lean against the wall—this is too rich a conversation to miss.

"So," she begins, spread-eagled on the mattress beside you. She's pretty (if generic) in person, and this irritates me to an unexpected degree. I snarl in her direction, and the drapes nearby ripple. "Am I the first?"

"What?" you say, breathless, but already sobering up, by the sound of it.

"Am I the first since...you know."

"Oh, Jesus Christ," I snort, crossing my arms like I'm hugging myself, but it's really because I'm filling up with rage—a rage I've never felt before, a *poltergeist* level of rage. "You *told* her? This chick? Really?"

You squint in disbelief. It must be the alcohol that's loosened your tongue, because you actually respond to her moronic inquiry. "Y-yeah. You are."

"Nice." She says it as if she's won a prize, and I mean yes, you *are*, but the fact she's made it her mission to be the first to bed a handsome widower makes me want to hurl. Just as I'm preparing to gather all of my ghostly powers and attack this girl any way I can—shit, I might even be able to throw a knife from that fancy block in her direction if I try hard enough—you kick her out yourself. It's glorious to watch, really, how you tell her with such authority to 'get your shit and get out'. The way her Juvederm-plumped donut lips fall open in shock is one of the favorite things I've witnessed all year.

When she's gone—in a tornado of slamming doors, incensed cursing, and half-donned clothing—you lock the front door behind her, bare-assed, brown-skinned, and Adonis-like in a swatch of moonlight through the foyer window. You break the thick midnight silence with a word: my name.

For a moment I'm weak-kneed, convinced somehow you know I'm here. The prospect frightens me—I've done this detached dance of communication with you for so long—that it feels strange to imagine interacting directly *with* you.

And so I hug the shadows and admire your familiar form, one I used to embrace from behind as you cooked us dinner, or cling to at the airport before you left for another two weeks away from home. I'm no longer able to do either of those things, but I'm still your friendly ghost—your first love, your wife—and one who's determined not to be your last.

Two Years and Eight Months After

"I have a good feeling about this one," I say as you stand before the closet and dress for the evening in a navy-blue suitcoat, slacks, and tan leather lace-ups. It's a getup you wouldn't have been caught *dead* (har, har) wearing when we were married, but you're a fancy executive now, and this girl is special. Your date tonight sort of looks like me, too—shoulder-length, wavy brown hair; petite; attractive in a composed, Type-A kind of way—which I take as a compliment, if a bit masochistic-leaning on your part.

She's another online match, a lawyer who seems too smart for you (although we thought that about me too). Her first message was polite and personalized, asking about your favorite food. You'd actually seemed to heed my suggestions as I told you each night how best to communicate with her during that pivotal introductory period—not too infrequently, not too often, always with proper grammar and punctuation, laying the wit and self-deprecating humor on thick—and you'd arranged a date at an upscale Brazilian steakhouse in downtown by the third day of chatting.

You've got a spring in your step now as you pour some more kibble in the cat's bowl, adding a spritz of cologne to that naked patch of skin above your collarbone I used to nuzzle on sleepy weekend mornings.

"Have fun," I call out in your wake, but you're already through the door—and if I'm not mistaken, you're whistling.

Four Years and Three Months After

The wedding was understated, chic, and an altogether classy affair I would've approved of myself. The reception was nice too, and there was dancing and music and cake-smashing in each other's faces, and you looked so goddamned happy baby, *so* happy, happier than I could remember you looking on *our* wedding day. I cried about that, but only for a little while.

Once you two leave for your honeymoon, I materialize back in the apartment. The cat's at your parents' place for a week, so it's lonely here now; your laugh and her laugh and your shared inside jokes and frequent lovemaking sounds have become a somber kind of music to me, a melancholic soundtrack that hurts to listen to but that I'm still not ready to turn off.

I watch a reality show as a distraction (she likes them too, and records my favorites), but it doesn't diminish the swirling, unsettled sensation where my stomach used to be.

"Is it time?" I say aloud to the silver-haired TV show host on the screen. You're married now, I've been replaced; my plan, for all intents and purposes, is complete. Yet I'm still not ready to go.

I recline on the sofa and ignore the silvery doorway in my periphery, checking every so often to make sure it's still there.

Five Years After

Normally I'd avoid going to another hospital, but today's a special occasion.

Your new wife's a champion, I'll give her that; I never wanted kids and so you said you didn't either, but based on the way you've doted on her for the past nine months, rubbing coconut butter on the stretched skin of her belly while murmuring in baby-speak to the little life growing beneath your hand, I've been convinced otherwise.

When the labor's over and a high-pitched squeal reaches everyone's ears, *your* expression is the one I look at as the baby comes into view—and it answers the question I've been asking since the day I died.

Later in the recovery room, all is quiet and still, the low, beige-pink lighting of the room far less invasive than it was during my visit years back. The baby is at your wife's breast, periodically eating and falling asleep, and your wife's drifting off too. You sit in the rocking chair to their left, studying them with a slight frown.

"It's scary, isn't it," I muse from the other side of your wife's hospital bed. "So much to take care of. So much to protect; that's why I didn't want one."

You wipe some tears from those beautiful brown eyes, and I know what you're thinking.

"Don't do that," I warn, more forcefully than I've spoken to you in a long time. "Stop it *right now*. That day wasn't your fault or mine, and there's nothing you could've done. You can't worry each day you might lose them too, okay? You can't." I round the hospital bed to kneel in front of you, and you stare right through me as usual. "I kept my promise, and now *you* need to keep one—you need to be free, Dan. You need to *live*. Because you've got so much to live for."

You wipe at your cheeks, at the wetness gathering in the patchy dark stubble along your jawline.

You smile.

Five Years and One Day After

She's one cute baby; takes after you the most, I think, but I'm biased. You've always been the best-looking person I've ever met.

The nurses are taken with her, remarking on what a good baby she is, so mild-mannered and sweet and *smiley*. You and your family are all ready to go; everything's packed, and the baby's received the health check go-ahead to send everyone home.

There's a shimmering doorway here in the hospital too—I've already seen several people go through it during our last two days here. I tried to peek around them to what awaited there, to read by their body language whether it was good or terrible, but I didn't really need to—it leads somewhere nice, and I think I've always known that.

The doctor just said it's time to go. Everyone is ready; the baby's wrapped up tight in a cream-colored onesie, and your wife's all settled in the wheelchair.

"What's her name?" the doctor asks, grinning down at the sleeping baby in the crook of your wife's arm. I expect you to respond the way you have been this entire time—that you both want to spend a few days with her first, to see what feels right.

But you don't say that.

Instead, you say "Eva," and I go rigid where I've been standing in the corner of the room.

"Her name is Eva," you say again, but you're not looking down at the baby, or at the doctor, or at your wife. You're looking at me.

"Eva," the doctor says, surveying your daughter with a smile. "I like that."

Your wife looks a little taken aback, but not for long. "I like it too," she replies, removing one arm from the swaddled baby to reach out and squeeze your hand. She knows who I am, obviously, and as far as I can tell this decision was never settled on—it was always, "Let's just wait and see."

"I've always liked you," I say to your wife as she cradles the baby close, cooing the girl's newly christened name a few times. "Keep taking care of him, okay?"

The doctor leaves, followed by the nurse wheeling your wife and daughter down the hall toward the parking lot. You stay here though, and so do I.

"Goodbye," you whisper, eyes unfocused and roving around the small hospital room. We were in a place like this once, for a much more heartrending reason than this. It's time we were both freed of it.

"Goodbye," I reply, and you dip your chin down, an infinitesimal nod, an acknowledgement. A letting go of that which is already gone.

When you walk out and down the hall the way your family went, I don't follow. Instead, I turn toward the doorway, which grows in size as I approach it, getting brighter around the edges, humming lowly, like the distant crash of waves while napping on the sand in bright sunshine, or that wondrous rumble of imaginary surf accessible at any time if one just cups a seashell to their ear. I grasp the door handle and it's warm in my palm; the first real, identifiable sensation I've had in years.

It feels wonderful.

And I go through.

See Ashley R. Carlson's story "The Friendly Ghost" online at Metaphorosis.
If you liked it, leave a comment. Authors love that!
Remember to subscribe to our e-mail updates so you'll know when new stories are posted."

About the story

The inspiration for my story about a deceased wife who "haunts" her husband and strives to help him discover fulfillment and happiness after her death came from a similar conversation in my own relationship.

My partner also worked far from home at the time, and in a field that had risks. While we didn't talk often about something happening, the danger was there—and one day we discussed our expectations for one another if the other person died. Morbid, I know, but I've always been a bit of a "what if-fer". (Is that a word? I'm going with it.)

This got me thinking about what it would be like to die and watch your spouse move on with their life—to actively participate in it, even, because you love them so much that you want them to fully experience all that life has to offer, even when you're not a part of it.

From there it was just a few days for a first draft, then a couple rounds of revising, sending the story out for beta feedback, more revising based on that feedback, submissions followed by another three rounds of revising, and the finished accepted piece! (The journey of a story from conception to completion requires so many more evolutions and versions than I first expect—and is 10,000 times better for it in the end.)

A question for the author

Q: If you could talk to your novice-writer self, what bit of advice would you give?

A: I would have a hard time whittling down my response to this (there were so many things I was naive about, and still am), but ultimately I would say these things:

1. Don't expect any sort of success or recognition from the first or tenth or twentieth thing you write or publish. This is a marathon, and a really, really slow one. Write because you love it and have a hunger to do it, and for no other reason than this.

2. Don't write typical stuff with typical characters—tropes; gender-conforming; predominantly white; a host of other problems that don't promote diversity. You're going to fall into this trap, and you're going to learn and grow and move away from it, but just be informed and a better promoter of diversity in fiction from the very beginning.

About the author

Ashley is an award-winning author and freelance editor in Phoenix, Arizona. When she's not writing or editing, Ashley enjoys traveling (oftentimes internationally), playing Scrabble with her fiancé (to whom she loses a lot more often than she likes to), and fostering kittens through Arizona Animal Welfare League.

www.ashleyrcarlson.com,
@AshleyRCarlson1

They Build 'Em Tough on Magna Mater

R.W.W. Greene

George's voice crackled over the headset radio. "You going tonight?"

"Not hardly. Pa fined me hard last time. Claimed I forgot to plug Bessie back in and cost us a day's work." Zeke spit a glob of bright orange newbacco juice into a can he'd taped to the inside of the tractor's cockpit. "I plugged her in. Just didn't have time for a full recharge."

"Like your Pa would know anything about a day's work," George said. "He don't remember the last time he done one."

"He weren't always like that." Zeke moved the control sticks in unison, and Bessie reached out to grasp a four-ton bale of threefalfa in her heavy metal arms. The tractor hefted the bale, servos whining as it moved the load into position and added it to the neat, two-story stack on top of the crawler. "Used to be he worked as hard as anybody."

Zeke's pa hadn't been the same since his wife died of Scylla, a native virus that seemed to take every Terrestrial mammal with two X chromosomes as a personal insult.

The red giant overhead baked the community farmlands, the remnants of a small mountain range pounded into submission from orbit a century before. George's tractor picked up a bale and set it across from Zeke's. They worked with their canopies popped so they could see each other and catch what little breeze there was. "Too bad you ain't going. Got a couple of boys from over the creek looking to brawl. Jake says they got money."

"How much money?"

"Enough to make it interesting."

"Any girls coming?"

"There'll be a few girls along. Whether they've already made their picks," the arms of George's big farm mech dropped its sides with a crash, "you take your chances."

Zeke and Bessie maneuvered another bale to the top of the stack. "Wish I could go."

"Sneak out."

"Bessie ain't what you call 'sneaky.' "

George let his tractor answer for him. The whines, clanks, and hisses blended into the familiar sound of preparations for the long winter ahead. Soon, the stack of bales atop the crawler rose to the tractors' three-story limit.

George swabbed sweat off his face with a red bandanna and squinted at the blue-green sky. "You see Perserpina yet?"

Zeke took a long look. The big moon, Ceres, was almost always in sight, but Perserpina, tiny and erratic, didn't show until she was good and ready—usually long after he was willing to call it a day. "Close enough. Besides, we wait much longer, we'll be travelin' in the dark, and the bunyips will get us."

The yips were much less a problem than they used to be, but they made a good excuse for knocking off work. George and Zeke walked their tractors to the back of the crawler and clomped up the ramp into riding position. The crawler's autopilot blinked awake, and the big vehicle shuddered into unhurried motion.

Zeke propped his feet up on the tractor's control panel and rolled a cigarette. "Is everyone going?"

"Everyone I talked to." George glanced sidelong at his friend. "Pomona might be there."

"What's that s'posed to mean?"

"I know you ain't goin' with her no more, but," George shrugged, "someone will. Probably soon. Might be one of those boys from across the creek."

Calling it a creek would have been laughable on any other planet. It was two miles wide, with class-four rapids along most its length, but it was still a baby compared to most of the rivers and streams on the world.

Zeke scowled. Two months before, he and Pomona had been tight as snicks. He still wasn't sure what had set her off, asking questions about the future, wanting him to buy himself free of his pa, like it were that easy. He hadn't put up much of a fight when she broke it off. "None of my business."

"Hope that makes you feel better when you're pullin' your own pecker in back of your Pa's barn." George had one leg draped over the side of his tractor's cockpit and was sipping something clear from a jar. "Suit yourself. Maybe I'll let you know what happens."

The crawler piloted itself to the co-op silos, and George and Zeke herded their tractors down the exit ramp. The crawler took care of the unloading itself. It would be recharged and ready for work in the morning. George waggled his jar at Zeke. "You come out tonight, you might get some."

Zeke lifted Bessie's arm in a wave. "I go out tonight I might as well not come home."

George turned his tractor toward his small homestead about five miles southwest. Zeke watched until his friend's green-and-yellow mech was nearly out of sight.

He had been trying not to think about Pomona. They'd met in the crèche years ago, when her name had been Paul, but memories of that awkward little boy had long been replaced by the freckled vision that had come back from the mothership with new pronouns and a big smile. They'd hit it off at the Harvest Dance and dated for nearly eight months before she ended it.

None of my business what she does. Zeke turned Bessie toward home.

Minerva met him at the gate. Zeke lowered the tractor to one knee and glared at the little girl from the cockpit. "Pa catches you outside the fence after dark, you won't sit down for a week."

"Pa's not here." Minerva folded her arms and glared back. "Trudi's in the cistern again."

The latest Scylla vaccine had saved barely fifty percent of Minerva's crèche, but it had proved near a hundred-percent effective on hybrid cows like Trudi.

"Get up here so the bunyips won't get you." Zeke lowered Bessie's hand so Minerva could climb on, and lifted her to the open-air passenger saddle he'd rigged up on the mech's left shoulder. "Weren't you supposed to be watching her?"

"I just looked away for a minute." The girl stomped her foot. "She's stupid."

Or she's tired of you fussing at her. The last time Trudi had ended up in the cistern, Pa had sworn up and down that he'd take her to the slaughterhouse if it ever happened again.

"It's the manatee genes," Minerva said. "Sometimes she forgets she ain't s'posed to like swimming."

Zeke brought Bessie to a halt at the edge of the big water tank.

"There she is!" Minerva stood up in the saddle and pointed. "In the corner."

Sure enough, the cow was neck deep in the cistern, looking like she was about to drop dead from exhaustion.

"You sit back down and put your belt on. I'll get her." Like most of the multi-purpose mechs on Magna Mater, Bessie was roughly human shaped. Two arms, two legs, and a broad torso where the cockpit was. "You belted in?"

"Do I look stupid?" Minerva said.

"Stupid enough to let the cow try to drown itself." Zeke made a tripod of Bessie's knees and her left arm and carefully extended the right into the cistern toward the cow. "Don't worry none, Trudi. This won't hurt a bit." Bessie spread her fingers wide before wrapping them like a steel cage around Trudi's midsection. "Got her!"

Zeke lifted the cow carefully. Trudi only massed a half ton or so, but the position was awkward. He flipped a switch to extend Bessie's outriggers. No sense sending the tractor into the cistern, too. He got the dripping cow to ground level and swung her away from the cistern. Minerva clapped her hands.

Zeke got Bessie back to her feet. "Where do you want her?"

"In her house, silly!"

Zeke walked the tractor toward the house and set the cow down inside the corral he'd set up for her there. He raised Bessie's hand to shoulder level and waited for Minerva to climb on. "You let her get out again, Pa's liable to turn her into dinner."

Minerva stamped her foot. "He will not! She's mine. He gave her to me!"

"Don't put much stock in that, Mini Girl. He'll take her away just as quick." Bessie lowered her hand to the ground, and Minerva stepped off. "But he won't hear it from me. You get inside now. Fence is on, but I reckon you're pretty enough for a bunyip to go to some trouble to eat."

Minerva flashed him a grin and ran to the front door. Zeke turned Bessie toward the barn and triggered open the tall door. Once he was sure the mech was locked down and powered off, Zeke descended the ladder rungs running down her body and plugged her in. He patted her leg. "Good work today, old girl. Few years, I'll have enough saved up so I can buy you out from under Pa, and we'll run off together. Start our own stead." He checked the maintenance board, scowling at a row of yellow telltale lights. "Those leg units are thinking about going again. I told Pa we needed a new set, but ..." He shook his head. "I'll climb in there and see what I can do in the morning."

He left the barn and took a look around the family compound. The lights at the top of the old silo were even closer to the ground than yesterday, creeping lower and lower as the structure listed. Pa kept saying he was going to take it down but hadn't gotten around to it. Taken down neat there'd be plenty of salvage, but letting it crash to the ground would likely bust open the shell and ruin the works inside. Zeke continued up the path to the house.

"Where's Pa?" he said, careful not to let the screen door slam behind him.

"Up to the hollow with Uncle Pranav." Tim, the youngest of Zeke's six brothers, was at the kitchen table doing his homework. "Said he won't be back 'til late."

Late morning most likely. Uncle Pranav ran a distillery in the hollow, and Pa went up there a few times a month to "help out". He'd be back close to noon, stinking and aching, his fancy new tractor hauling him home on autopilot.

"Minerva come through here?"

"Went up to her bedroom. She was swearing a streak at that cow of hers. You get her out?"

"Don't tell Pa she fell in again." Zeke took a seat and inspected the auto-cooker in the center of the table. Soup again. "Where are the rest of the young uns?"

"Everyone's inside, Mother. Don't get your skirt in a knot."

Zeke cuffed his brother on the back of his head, barely mussing his hair. "I had a skirt; I'd give it to you. Closest you'll ever get to a girl." He pulled a bowl out of the stack and filled it with the nondescript soup. "What you working on?"

"Calculus. It's pretty easy."

"Never got to it." Zeke spooned soup into his mouth. "Dropped out the year before I would have."

"Why do I have to stay in, then? I hate school."

"I'm the eldest. It's my job to help Pa run the farm," Zeke said. "Your job is to get good grades and do something better with your life. Be a freighter captain, maybe. Or a doctor."

"What if I want to be a farmer?"

"It's hard work, little man. And tractors don't come cheap."

"I can do it!"

"You can, but you don't have to. Get your learnin' in and move to the city." Zeke shoved his bowl into the recycler and stood up. "I'm going up to bed."

Zeke showered, then climbed the narrow stairs to the second floor and the ladder that led to his little room in the attic. Age had its privileges. He and Minerva were the only ones besides Pa with private rooms. Zeke crawled onto his mattress and stared at the bare beams a few feet above his face. Tim was eleven. Minerva would be seven in the fall. In another eight or nine years she'd start getting marriage proposals and offers for eggs. It would be up to Pa to negotiate a price, with a healthy cut for himself, of course, but the final decision would be hers. She could ignore the whole thing, marry for love, or never marry at all, but the money was always a temptation, and Pa would surely pressure her. Pomona would probably be hitching up soon, too. No sense sticking around, with her options.

He put his hands behind his head. No wonder Pa drank so much.

Zeke's wristcuff buzzed, and he pulled his arm free so he could see it. It was George. Zeke poked the screen to answer the call. George's face was sweaty and excited. "You got to get out here! There's a Vidcom crew here filming. *Mech Mayhem.* They've got a half million to split among the top three fighters."

"You're funnin' me." Zeke's heart raced. Vidcom was the most popular network in the system and had money to burn. They liked to film the mech brawls, but they'd never been as far out as Magna Mater.

"Like hell I am." The image on Zeke's wristcuff spun as George moved to show the Vidcom camera crew setting up. A tall blonde man in the latest system fashion was directing them. "They've got a brand-new brawler mech here taking on all comers. They're giving a thousand just for agreeing to fight it on camera, plus first, second, third prizes. Get out here!"

"Shit!" A thousand credits wasn't enough to matter much, but even a third-place finish might give him enough to buy Bessie out from under his Pa and claim his own stead. Zeke slid out of bed and put his work clothes back on.

"Make sure Minerva stays inside," he told Tim as he passed by. "I'll be back late."

"Where you going?" the boy said.

Zeke closed the front door on the question and hurried to the barn, glancing left and right. The fence was usually enough to keep the bunyips out of the compound, but sometimes one slipped through and spent the night prowling outside the buildings. The really big ones had all been killed off years before, but the leftovers were fast and angry, more than enough to take down an unarmed man.

He entered the barn through the side door and flipped the switch that turned on the light. "We got a chance to make some money, old girl." He punched the wake-up command into the maintenance board. Bessie was only up to a half charge, but it would do for a few fights and the jog to the ring. Zeke climbed up the ladder to the cockpit and strapped in. "This could be it."

The old tractor responded to Zeke's commands and clomped through the big door. Zeke sent a coded message to the NavNet and got a ping back with the current location of the brawl. Mech fighting wasn't illegal—not much was on Magna Mater—but it was dangerous and potentially expensive. The Homestead Council zoomed in to break things up anytime they could figure out where the brawl was, so the boys who put it on kept moving it. Bessie's navscreen lit up with a location about two miles away at a nice, easy power-saving jog.

"Let's go, girl." Bessie lurched forward.

The off-world brawler mech looked smooth and alien among the local jalopies and tractors standing around it. "The hell is *that* thing?" Zeke said once he'd reached the ground and entered the pool of spectators.

George handed Zeke his jar. "They call it Galaxy Chrome. Latest model. Looking to make a name by taking on the local talent."

"Sheeit!" Zeke studied the sleek, shiny mech. "None of us have the money for something like that!"

George collected the jar back and took a long swallow. "They're not looking to sell to us. If it looks good kicking some hicks around, all the central-system rich kids will want one."

The brawler mech was at least four feet taller than anything the locals had.

"You going to fight it?" Zeke said.

"Was until I saw it. A thousand wouldn't cover the repairs I'd have to make, and I'd probably have to rent a tractor to finish out the season. The winter would be mighty lean."

"But what if you won?"

George patted his mech's green leg. "That thing could put a hole right through my cockpit and wave at everybody on the other side."

"Guess nothing runs away like a Deere."

George snorted. "Ain't runnin', but I ain't stupid, either."

"Anyone else try?"

"Tom Riley. Lasted about two minutes. Thing picked his jalopy right off the ground and tossed it twenty feet." He pointed.

"He's over there in the first-aid tent. He was thrown out of the cockpit."

"Tom's mech ain't much better than a lawn mower. He shouldn'ta tried."

"You be sure to tell him that when he wakes up."

A thin man in a powder-blue jumpsuit climbed up the fancy mech and stood in its passenger saddle. He fiddled with something on his wristcuff, and his voice boomed out of the mech's speakers. "Who's next?" He looked around at the local brawlers. Most of their mechs had come straight from the fields, but a few of the better-off had built ones just for fighting.

"I'm in." A tall mech lurched forward. Aamil Baig's jalopy had started life as a firebot. It was still bright red in places, and Aamil ran the siren and flashing lights as he stepped into the ring. His mech had the longest reach of any in the settlement, and a secret weapon, but it was painfully slow. "But only if you raise it to five thousand."

The slicker shrugged. "Done."

"Start your cameras." Aamil closed his mech's cockpit and turned on its lights. The siren whooped as the slicker climbed down and shouted instructions to his camera crew.

Galaxy Chrome moved like its joints were made of oil and marched to a spot about fifty feet away where it waited for Aamil and his mech. The slicker walked between them and signaled for Aamil to cut the lights and siren. He looked at one of his camera bots and flashed a confident grin. "Fellow sentients, have we got a fight for you!"

Zeke tuned into the feed in time to hear the *Mech Mayhem* score swell.

The slicker grinned again. He was better looking on the feed than he was in person. "Magna Mater. The wildest planet the system has to offer. The land is hard, and it's eager," the slicker narrowed his eyes, "to kill."

The feed switched to a recording of a bunyip swarm. The big reptiles thundered by the camera until one, probably baited by the operator, turned and roared directly into the lens.

"The natives have to fight every day just to survive. They're tough, and their mechs are tougher." He flung his arm up. "But are they tough enough to handle Galaxy Chrome?" The feed switched to show a close up of the big mech's cockpit. "The newest mech from BrawlerBot, Inc.? Let's find out!"

The feed switched back to the slicker's face, and he grinned right on cue. "You boys ready?"

Half the screen filled with Aamil's bearded face, the other with the bland good looks of Galaxy Chrome's pilot. Aamil nodded and the other pilot lifted his hands from his controls to offer a double thumbs up.

"Then let's get ready to ruuuuuuuumble!" The slicker ran straight ahead to get out of the battle zone. Aamil turned the sirens and lights back on and moved his mech's left foot ahead for balance.

Galaxy Chrome bent low and charged straight at Aamil.

Zeke grinned. The off-worlder was playing right into Aamil's game. The bearded miner knew his mech was slow and usually waited for the other fighter to make the first move. The jalopy crouched and raised its arms to meet the charge. Chrome closed the distance fast, the ground shuddering with every running step.

Zeke knew the move Aamil was about to make; most of the brawlers on Magna Mater did, but there was no way the off-worlder would. This was going to be good.

The rockets mounted on the fire mech's wrists roared into life, and its big red fists shot forward … and kept going, trailing steel cables. The arms on Aamil's mech could extend seventy yards in less than two seconds, part of its rapid-rescue package. Aamil called it his "Telescope Punch," and it was usually enough to take out an unwary opponent. It had to be, because it took Aamil two minutes to reel the arms back in and get the fists back into place.

Galaxy Chrome pivoted on one foot—it moved so fast Zeke wasn't exactly sure what happened. Both the red fists missed their marks and shot to the ends of their cables before thumping to the ground. The off-world mech took two more steps, grabbed the cables, and ripped them out, leaving Aamil with sparking stumps.

The *Mech Mayhem* score swelled, and Zeke's vidscreen showed the move again in slow motion. "Who's next?" the slicker howled.

Five-thousand, about enough for a beater mech, was the magic number for the boys with custom-made brawlers. The Lajoie twins stepped up. They piloted their jalopy, a souped-up construction machine, as a duo. Galaxy Chrome ripped it right in half, spilling the Lajoies to the ground in a shower of sparks and jagged metal. If he was lucky, Trevor Lajoie would keep his right arm.

The brawl continued and broken mechs piled up on the sides of the field. The slicker threw his arms in the air as Galaxy Chrome's latest victim was hauled away. "Who's next?"

"You gotta fight him," George said. "You're the only one who stands a chance."

Zeke shook his head. "Not even. You saw what he did to the twins!"

"You're better than they are!" George said. "You're better than all of us."

"Not good enough," Zeke said. "That thing's taken out seven brawlers without getting a scratch."

"We're raising the ante," the slicker announced. "Ten thousand just for stepping in the ring with the mighty Galaxy Chrome!"

George swore. "They must be taking orders for those things right and left."

Zeke's head swam. Ten thousand was a lot of money. Half again what it would cost to buy Bessie away from Pa. Enough to file for a small stead. He raised his hand. "I'm in. We'll fight."

Zeke unplugged Bessie from the network's big generator. The forced charge wasn't good for the tractor's batteries, but he needed them as close to full as possible to have any hope of keeping up with Galaxy Chrome. The slicker put his hand on Zeke's back. "You ready?"

"If the money's still good."

"The money's fine. We'll drop it into your account soon as the cameras start rolling. Win or lose."

"Make sure to keep the prize money ready, too. I'm taking your pretty bot down," Zeke said. "You ready, girl?"

Bessie couldn't answer, but it seemed like she moved a little quicker whenever she was in the ring, responded better to the controls. Like she enjoyed fighting.

The slicker stepped between the two mechs and raised his arms in the air. "Sentients, I am proud to present the next fight of the night. The mighty Galaxy Chrome and, fighting for the honor of Magna Mater, Zeke Liu and his Battlin' Bessie!"

VidCom graphic enhancements made it seem like an audience of thousands surrounded the ring, baying for blood and twisted metal. In reality, a few dozen farmers, miners, and builders yelled themselves hoarse and made as much noise as they could.

Bessie pounded the hammer side of her right fist into the cup of her palm, banging her own war drum. The local mechs left standing picked up the beat, and the field echoed with the clash of steel on hardened steel.

The slicker signaled for silence, and the beat tapered off. "You boys ready?"

Zeke nodded, knowing his face would be on millions of screens around the system. The pilot of the off-world mech shrugged and pretended to yawn.

The comm unit in Bessie's cockpit stuttered to life. "Zeke!" Tim hollered through it. "Minerva's outside the fence! She's gone after that fool cow again!"

On the opposite side of the control panel a red light started flashing, and a siren howled. A bunyip-swarm alert. Everyone in town would be getting the same signal and securing their steads in response.

"Let's get ready to—!" the slicker began.

"What do you want me to do?" Tim sounded breathless.

"Shit!" Zeke put Bessie in motion, using the newly charged battery to bring her up to speed. The entire VidCom audience, millions of sentients on dozens of planets, watched him flee the ring. "I'm on my way!"

Zeke jumped Bessie over a ravine. "You stay put and keep the other young uns inside," he told Tim via the comm. The mech's worn leg servos sent her telltales flickering into the red zone as she landed on the other side. "I'm going to find our little sister and skin her alive."

If the bunyips don't beat me to it. Minerva had barely been walking the last time the monsters went on the move. Three or four times in a generation the yips spawned, moving across the land to a new river or stream, killing and eating everything in their path. Smart people got out of their way. NavNet was predicting the swarm would be going through the biggest cluster of steads, right past the one claimed by Zeke's Pa.

Zeke pushed Bessie to run faster and powered up her leg extenders to gain a few extra meters with each stride. The warning lights for her leg servos went further into the red, a harbinger of failure, but the mech ate up the distance faster.

Zeke heard the bunyips before he saw them: a slithery mass of low growls, angry roars, and heavy footfalls. He activated Bessie's vision enhancements and zoomed in on the swarm. He'd never seen so many of the things. Little ones just a little bigger than a standing man and others that stood taller at the shoulder than Bessie did. Zeke's headset radio crackled.

"I thought we'd killed off all the big uns," George said.

Zeke craned his neck to see George's tractor jog up behind him.

"That's a lot of lizards," George said. "Let's get to high ground and wait it out."

"Can't. Minerva's out here somewhere. She ran out after that cow of hers."

George cursed. "That ain't good. Both likely to end up yip shit."

Zeke cranked up the magnification and scanned the grounds of the stead for any sign of his sister.

"I see her," George said. He pointed with his mech's hand. Minerva had climbed to the top of the old silo and was hanging on for dear life a couple of meters above the reach of the tallest bunyip. "She's safe."

"No, she's not," Zeke said. "That silo would fall over if the wind blew hard. It will come right down if one of those big bastards bumps up against it."

A new voice cut into their conversation. "I'll get her."

Galaxy Chrome darted out in front of them and ran into the swarm, trailed by a flock of camera drones.

"Sentients," the slicker chortled over the VidCom feed. "This is unprecedented. BrawlerBot's latest masterpiece is taking on an entire flock of the most dangerous creatures in the system, and you're seeing it here, live!"

"That ain't a good idea," George said. "One or two of them is about all ..."

Galaxy Chrome's pilot yelled in fear as the gleaming mech became a target of several of the smaller bunyips. They swarmed up the mech's legs to the cockpit and began raking it with their claws. The pilot made the mistake of trying to take a long step out of the scrum, and the bunyips' weight made the big mech topple to the ground with a crash.

"Well, that done it," George said.

One of Galaxy Chrome's thrashing legs grazed the silo, and Minerva's precarious perch tilted closer to the feeding frenzy below.

"Get up! Get up!" the slicker yelled over the VidCom feed.

The feed from Galaxy Chrome crackled. "There're too many of them! I can't get loose!"

The big mech's thrashing was attracting the attention of some of the bigger bunyips. It would take time, but they could crack the brawler mech's cockpit like an egg.

"Hold still!" Zeke said. "I'm coming in!"

"That ain't smart," George said.

"No choice." Zeke made sure his canopy was locked tight, and jogged to the edge of the swarm. He'd taken Bessie through rapids and rock falls before, and figured a shuffle step was the best approach. He moved the tractor forward slowly, barely lifting her feet.

"They're coming at you!" George said.

Zeke caught the first bunyip in mid leap and tossed it back toward his friend. "Make yourself useful and step on it."

The second bunyip hit Bessie in the back and stuck, clawing for the soft meat inside. Zeke shuffled faster, punching away the yips he could catch and ignoring the ones he couldn't. A mid-sized bunyip hit Bessie behind her knees and nearly bowled her over.

"Watch it!" George said.

Zeke didn't have the breath to respond. He moved without thinking, dodging with as much flexibility as Bessie allowed and putting her hardened fists into the heads and torsos of any bunyip he could see. He made it into the shadow of the silo and craned his neck to look up. Minerva's face was tear-streaked, but she looked more angry than afraid. Her knuckles, where she clutched the railing, were white. He switched on Bessie's loud speakers. "I'm right under you, Mini."

"They killed Trudi!" she said. "Ripped her all to pieces!"

The anguish in her voice made him ache. He would have done anything to keep her from having to see that. "You hold on!" Zeke considered his options. He could use Bessie to brace the silo and hope he could hold it long enough for the swarm to pass or... "George, I'm going to need you to come in here."

"The hell I will!" George said.

"I gotta get her down from there, George!"

George swore softly but repetitively as he shuffled his tractor into the swarm. He played it safer than Zeke had, but he was at his friend's side in minutes. "Now what?"

"Just keep them off me." Zeke dropped Bessie's outriggers and extended her legs to their full height. He got an extra three meters out of it, putting himself just under Minerva's perch. He opened the canopy in time to feel Bessie nearly fall out from under him as she shook under a sharp impact. "George!"

"Sorry about that. One of the middling ones got by. Hurry it up. There's a lot more coming."

Zeke unfastened his safety harness and stood in the seat to grab Minerva under her arms. The passenger saddle didn't offer any protection, so he swung her into the cockpit with him and sealed it back up. "Squeeze behind the seat and stay there. We're not out of this yet." He refastened his harness as Bessie rocked again.

"Hurry, Zeke!" George said. "I'm not funnin' you."

Zeke retracted the outriggers and returned Bessie's legs to normal, bringing the cockpit back in range of the scaly swirl below. "Let's see what we can do for Chrome before we get clear."

He led the way, pushing against the bunyips until he got to the frenzied pile that covered the off-world mech. He grabbed a double handful of bunyips and tossed them aside. George joined him, and, when they got Galaxy Chrome clear enough to see, they grabbed its arms and pulled it to its feet. "Let's go," Zeke said. "Shuffle until you get to the edge of the swarm." He glanced over his shoulder at his sister. "You okay back there?"

"I need to pee," she said.

"You'll wait on that if you know what's good for you. You pee in here, and I'll put you right back up in that silo."

He shuffled Bessie after George's tractor and Galaxy Chrome. Bunyip swarms were single-minded, moving from waterway to waterway over whatever land stood in the way. Funny, they were never as thick in the mountains as they were over the land the colonists had terraformed. Once the mechs were out of its path, they would be largely out of danger. Galaxy Chrome got to the edge of the swarm first and sprinted to a safe distance. The big mech was a mess, its hull battered and dented, shiny finish dulled and gouged by the bunyips' claws, pieces of its decorative superstructure torn away and left behind.

"Look—!" George's warning ended in a blast of static as his green-and-yellow mech tumbled sideways into the swarm. The biggest bunyip Zeke had ever seen roared and gave chase, knocking smaller yips aside like puppies.

"George!" Zeke turned Bessie around and pushed back into the swarm in pursuit of the giant bunyip. The others had cleared off, letting the big yip claim its prey. One of the green tractor's arms had come away in the tumble, and its left leg was twisted underneath it.

"Git outta here, Zeke!" George broadcast. "It's no good both of us getting' kilt."

Bessie muckled on to the big yip's tail with both hands, halting its teeth and claws meters away from the damaged tractor. The bunyip dug in its claws and lunged forward. Zeke extended Bessie's outriggers again and held on, trying to ignore the flashing red lights warning of leg-servo failure.

The yip turned to get his teeth around for an attack on Bessie's hands and legs, but its spine wasn't flexible enough. Bessie hauled up, extending her arms and lifting the yip's hindquarters off the ground by its tail. The scaly creature whipped its head wildly, snapping at anything it could reach. Bessie shuddered and pitched with every shift in weight.

"What's happening?" Minerva said.

"You just hang on, Mini Girl." Zeke gritted his teeth and fought to keep Bessie upright. If she toppled, if the leg servos failed, the bunyip would be on him in seconds, and he had no illusions how the test of claws and teeth versus the old mech's hull would go. If he had a hand free, he could put a hardened fist right through the yip's skull, but he didn't dare let go of the tail for even a second.

An alarm squalled as the leg-servo warning lights went solid red. Bessie's left leg buckled, and she started to topple. Zeke fought to keep her up by hopping on the right leg, but the mech wasn't built for it, and the weight of the bunyip pulled it to the ground. Zeke's teeth came together hard at the impact, and he tasted blood. Minerva screamed. He reached into the seat pocket for his sidearm, but the little gun would be of little use against an enraged yip. Minerva might go unnoticed behind the seat, her scent hidden by the odor of his own spilled blood. He flicked off the gun's safety. The big yip charged. "You son of a bitch!" he said.

Its teeth were a foot away from the cockpit window when a steel fist struck, crashing into the top of the yip's skull and driving its bottom jaw into the dirt. Galaxy Chrome pulled its fist out of the bunyip's cranium and grabbed Bessie by the leg. He hauled her over to George's wreck and grabbed it by the shoulder. Then, step by shuffling step, Galaxy Chrome pulled both tractors to safety in front of the largest viewing audience in Vidcom history.

It took another four hours for the swarm to pass. George shared his jar of hooch with the off-worlder while they watched. Zeke waved the jar away, more concerned with getting Minerva to stop fussing about Trudi.

"I'm gonna kill all of them," she said. Her face was streaked with tears, tiny fists balled up like rocks.

"Hush, Mini," Zeke said. "Leave them be, they'll leave you be. Trudi was just too dumb for her own good." *And too tasty.* Maybe breeding cows wasn't such a good idea. The yips had no interest at all in threefalfa.

Later, neighbors helped him move Bessie to her maintenance cradle in the barn and gave George and his wreck a ride home. The check Vidcom gave George for rights to the video and a personal endorsement of BrawlerBot's new mech put a grin on George's face that lasted all the way to his pillow, which he shared that night with Brian Lance, Galaxy Chrome's handsome pilot.

Zeke tucked Minerva in, commiserated with her some about the cow, and went out to the barn to see Bessie. She had several more gouges and dents, some deep scratches, but she'd already carried a fair share of them. Her frame looked okay in spite of the hard fall. Zeke winced when he ran a diagnostic on her legs. Most everything in there was going to need an overhaul before she could work again, and he'd taken months off her batteries' life with that forced charge.

He was going to catch hell from his pa. Sober, Pa would rage. Drunk, he'd rage and maybe throw hands. Later, he'd cool down some and bill Zeke for the cost of the repairs and ask the Steader's Union to levy a fine. It would wipe out everything Zeke had saved and then some.

Or it would have.

Zeke used his wristcuff to check his new bank balance. His own check from Vidcom had given him enough in one haul to fix Bessie up, buy her out from under his pa, pay his fine, and set up a nice little stead of his own.

In a season or two, he could petition the Union for custody of the young uns, give them a better living environment and maybe a few more life options. Hell, he might even give Pomona a call and ask her if she'd seen him on Vidcom. He had some answers to her questions about the future now.

In the testimonial the slicker had recorded, both Zeke and George had gassed on and on about how great the off-world mech was, how rugged and fast. Zeke, at least, had been lying through his teeth. He wouldn't take one of the new bots if they offered it to him for free.

He looked up and down Bessie again, older than him by at least twenty years and not a shiny spot in sight. He patted the big mech's leg.

"They can do what they want with the video," he said, "but we both know who the toughest mech in the system is, girl."

Bessie didn't answer—she never did—but he heard her loud and clear. They built 'em tough on Magna Mater.

See R.W.W. Greene's story "They Build 'Em Tough on Magna Mater" online at Metaphorosis.
If you liked it, leave a comment. Authors love that!
Remember to subscribe to our e-mail updates so you'll know when new stories are posted.

About the story

I guess this story has its origins in the Kevin Bacon movie "Footloose". There's an awesome/ridiculous scene wherein Ren (Kevin Bacon) and the Jerk Guy are playing chicken on tractors. I won't tell you how the tractor duel came out, but I took this scene into the context of my own semi-rural upbringing and came up with the ideas of bored farm boys drinking 'shine and brawling with their mechs on the weekend. (It's not too far from reality. Most of us were scarred from running dirt bikes into electric fences or flipping over on three-wheelers out in someone's back forty.)

The rest of the story lined up from there. Family obligations and the difficulties inherent in building a new home from scratch. I have this idea that the entertainment on any colony mission would trend heavily into frontier dramas — "Little House on the Prairie", "Jeremiah Johnson", etc. — to get the travelers into the pioneer headspace. Otherwise, I'd think it would be mighty hard to get folks to leave the comforts of their generation ships.

And who knows what waits in the rivers and streams of those new worlds? It would be a massive struggle at first, false steps, new plans, experiments...

I do wonder sometimes if we're still capable of making the leap or if we've gotten way too soft.

A question for the author

Q: What do you think is the single most important quality for a good writer to possess?

A: A small, hard ego. Nothing big and puffed up. Nothing easily punctured. But a tiny kernel of confidence that can weather rejections and distractions and failure and keep them in the chair day after day pounding on the page.

About the author

R.W.W. Greene is a New Hampshire, USA writer. His critically acclaimed, novel-length debut, *The Light Years* sprang forth from Angry Robot Books in February 2020.

rwwgreene.com, @rwwgreene

Shards

Jordan Chase-Young

Shona's seaweed harness creaked loudly as a cold, whistling gale tried to fling her off the Spire. She held onto the masonry until the air stilled, until her guts ceased to cartwheel. In the six years since Shona had escaped the deluge, she'd rarely felt vertigo. Even when her fellow earthmasons raised the Spire as high as it hung now—a mile or so above the ocean that now wrapped the world—the sun-pummeled water below seemed little more than a great sweep of stone she could stand upon if she wanted to.

But thick grey clouds had rolled out of the north that morning, bringing an unpleasant depth to the world. Whenever the wind picked up, she tried not to think of her harness snapping. Tried not to see herself falling, and the Spire—her home, her family—dwindling to a dust-speck in the infinite emptiness above her.

"Everything all right down there?" Hendrick called from the lookout. He was peering over the crenellations four stories up, his cloud of thick red hair bright against bronzed skin. She gave a sign of assurance. "Okay. But I'll pull you up, if this wind gets any worse. Fix what you can in the meantime, my love."

The braids of dried seaweed joining Shona's harness to the lookout quivered as Hendrick retightened them to their iron moorings.

Fix what I can. Hendrick's voice, hard and certain as stone, always centered her. Even when he expected the impossible. *Not even the Allcreator could fix what we broke, my mountain.*

She did her duty anyway, pressing her ear to the cold granite and rapping her knuckles upon it, listening for the chime of ice crystals trapped within.

Like all earthmasons, she could feel the stone as though it were a part of her. Move it like a soft, supple clay with her will. She could sense the cracks the ice had formed: tiny, fine webs of them through the stone. With concentration, Shona knitted these shut beneath her fingers, teasing the ice inside them toward the surface for the sky to reclaim.

Once she'd cleared all the granite she could reach, she shook the rightmost tether to signal for Hendrick to lower her a little, and continued working.

The Spire would not last more than a few years longer. Four, if they were lucky. In the pre-flood days, a good repointing job could have added decades of life to an edifice, if not more, but the earthmasons back then did not have to contend with the endless frost-weathering wrought by a dead world's cruel winds. A great earthmason could have trawled the ocean for replacement minerals, perhaps, but none of the thirty earthmasons to survive the flood had such talent. Not even Archmason Tybalt. The fifty-two lackblooms were even more useless, lacking power over stone.

The Spirefolk must find land, and soon, she thought as Hendrick pulled her back up. *Or our fates will join those of the uncountable multitudes that drowned.*

"That bad?" Hendrick asked, once she was back on the lookout.

He helped her unclasp the harness. She enjoyed the feel of coming out of it, letting the coarse, smelly seaweed plop onto the cold stone floor.

"It could be worse." She kissed his dark lips, rough and dry as barnacles. "We'll have to search harder."

"Six years of this shit." Hendrick looked at the shattered moon half-visible above, no grander than a clod of pumice crushed and strewn in a lazy arc. "If there were land, hummingbird, don't you think we'd have found it by now?"

His honesty always stung, no matter how much she depended on it. "Any earthmasons who could break the moon could survive what comes after. They're out there, my mountain. We will find them."

What would happen after, Shona could not guess. *Let tomorrow deal with tomorrow.*

As she descended the staircase that corkscrewed around the Spire, Shona sighted movement through one of the tall, unglazed windows that marked each landing. It startled her. But she reasoned it must have been a kestrel—one of the Spire's many stowaways—plunging to the sea for an afternoon meal. Her weariness made her jumpier than usual.

In the dungeon, the lowest level of the Spire, nine earthmasons sat shut-eyed in a circle. A few feet above them hovered a ball of dark polished iron: a helmstone, to keep them fixed on a single point of the building's mass. It helped them carry the Spire as one, draw it across the sky with their collective will.

Most days, a meditation circle held seven or eight earthmasons. But today Shona's five-year-old daughter Micah made the ninth. Bronzed and skinny, with the same red whorl of hair as Hendrick, she was sitting in dutiful silence with her legs crossed, her breathing steady.

Eight earthmasons had been lost in the six years since the deluge. Sickness had taken three. Suicide, two others. One earthmason had died from old age. And the last two—the last two had been slain during the Incident, but Shona did not like to think about that.

Micah's eyes shifted behind their lids as Shona padded down the hall beside the meditation circle. *Unfocused.* She was no more ready than Shona would have been at her age. But they did not have the luxury of waiting.

Archmason Tybalt was studying the drylocks in the storage chamber when Shona entered. He gestured with his scruffy chin for her to shut the pinewood door, then went back to scratching figures on a clay slate with his stylus. His grey cat Despond sluiced in and out of his path as he traipsed through the oil-lit gloom, as if afraid to leave Tybalt's shadow.

Shona sensed that something was wrong. She flattened down her work-smock. "Archmason."

"The repointing went well, I trust."

She sighed. No point mincing words. "The walls are weakening faster than I'd thought."

A vein in his bald head moved, like a worm beneath vellum, but his face remained expressionless. "I see. Anything else?"

His hard blue eyes had not faded a bit since his time as a foreman for the Guild of Architects—a hundred lifetimes ago, it must have been. He'd been softer in those days. Gentler. And she'd been elated to join his building team, as any earthmason would have been. But the end of the world had dried out his soul like everyone else's, leaving a husk of duties, procedures, routines. She missed the old Archmason.

"No. Nothing else. But I sense there is something you wish to tell me."

Tybalt's tone was grave. "Someone has been stealing from the drylocks."

She frowned, not quite believing it. "Are you sure?"

"I have counted the figures three times. The papaya and blackcurrant leaves seem untouched. But the figs, carobs, runner beans—all have dwindled much quicker than usual this month." Removing a sharkskin glove, he reached through the iron valve of a drylock, willing the metal around his flesh, and pulled out a few dried runner beans. This made the pendulum scale under the squat, rectangular storage device tick down half a notch. "It is hardly inexplicable. Think how many drowned kingdoms each of these is worth."

"I promise you, I had nothing to do with it."

"Of course not. Do you think I would have made you my successor if I could not trust you? But an earthmason is to blame. And there are only thirty of us, Shona."

Did he have Hendrick in mind? Or Micah? She bristled to think he would ever suspect her family of thievery. *Murder,* in fact, since every soul in the Spire needed fruits and vegetables to keep the Slow Death at bay.

"Whoever it is, we will find them. There are only so many hiding places."

"We will," Tybalt agreed, returning the runner beans to the drylock. "But think what this will do to our relations with the lackblooms. To the threads of trust we've been weaving so carefully these six long years."

"We cannot tell them. Not unless we want to risk another Incident."

"Then how do you propose we catch the thief?"

"I don't know," she said, sadly. "I need time to think about it."

The sun burned red that evening, its reflection on the sea like molten slag pouring from a crucible. The redness spilled through the windows along the stairway, engulfing Shona as she climbed to the feast room, eager for the fish that would soon be served. Shards of moon twinkled in the sky like early stars.

Which earthmason could have stolen the food? Jerold the Younger, who had once served the crownlaws? Reyna, when she wasn't leading a meditation circle? Gellard Grey-Eyes?

Absurd. They were honorable men and women, all of them.

Maybe one of the lackblooms had learned how to bypass the drylocks. But it was her distaste for lackblooms, an ugly relic of the pre-flood world, more than any sort of logic that lent this possibility its appeal. The lackblooms had ruled over the earthmasons for centuries on the strength of their numbers, and had done so with a cruelty matched only by the earthmasons themselves, in the long-ago days when *they* had ruled. The days of the Stone Empire, and the Diamantine Queens, and the Long War that had ended it all.

She couldn't let her anger cloud her judgment. The Incident had taught her the danger of that. Both peoples had slaked their anger with blood that day, a mere fortnight after escaping the deluge. The lackblooms had set it off; she would not forget that. Had threatened to disrupt a meditation circle unless their demands were met. But the earthmasons had been too quick to reply with violence. In the end, it had taken four deaths and far more injuries to convince the Spirefolk that cooperation was the only way.

The two peoples would never love each other—that much Shona knew—but they had reached a peace over the years. Had even worked out their share of duties, the lackblooms fishing and cooking, mending clothes and scrubbing floors, while the earthmasons held up the Spire. It was a brittle contract, held together by habit, but it worked. The thief was a threat to that, and had to be stopped.

"I'm telling you I saw it," Old Lorrick mumbled through a mouthful of fish. "Wings this long"—lifting his arms for the other lackblooms huddled around him, rapt as children—"and wild fierce by the look of it. Weren't no bird neither, I can swear to that. Not like any bird I seen in my life."

"Sounds like you've been in the sun too much," Hendrick shot from his corner of the feast room, with a chortle that sent bits of chewed fish flying.

"Hendrick," Shona cautioned. She was cutting Micah's blubber into edible chunks, her knife honed to razor-sharpness for the task.

Old Lorrick waved off Hendrick's remark with theatric weariness.

"When did you see this creature?" Shona asked.

Old Lorrick itched his scraggly beard. "Two, three hours ago, while I was fixing up the seine. It was green, it was. Not like emerald but sort of like that. Darker."

The highborn known as Cadmus, who resembled a great bat in his overlarge cloak, ceased stirring his blackcurrant tea and looked up, his dour smooth-shaven face suddenly bright with interest. The lackblooms had named Cadmus their leader not long after the deluge, just as the earthmasons had named Tybalt theirs —but Cadmus' authority had been eclipsed over the years by the Archmason's, as anyone could have predicted; a lackbloom's ancestry counted for little on the Spire, while an earthmason's talent counted for everything. With no small bitterness, Cadmus and his closest friends had come to accept that fact, so long as the earthmasons still called him "liege" and treated him as such.

"Like jade?" Cadmus asked.

"That's it," said Old Lorrick. "Like jade. But in spite of its flying, I'd swear it was featherless as a snake. Made me think dragons. Like what traders used to sight sometimes over the northern parts, beyond the reach of love or law."

One by one, the other sixty Spirefolk in the feast room began to take interest.

Cadmus sipped his tea. "I've never known you to lie, Lorrick. I believe you saw this thing."

Hendrick gave a snort.

"Is there something you wish to tell me, blacksmith?"

"Yes, my liege. I think your cloak's too tight if you credit this old fisherman's visions."

Several lackblooms scowled at his disrespect.

"Well, unlike you, I can read," said Cadmus. "And I have read *Stories of the Ice Seas*. It is always the same tale, of traders espying dragons made of gold or jade. Some say they are small gods that brought the powers of the earthmasons into the world. But I think they are beasts that earthmasons fashioned during the Stone Empire and loosed upon their foes, in the days before we cleanfolk took over and made things right. Now they wander the skies without purpose, aimless and alone."

Steg the Spearmaker, a tiny grizzled otter of a man in a filthy work-smock, huffed at this. "Mudrats ain't gods, Cadmus—making things that can live after 'em like that."

His slur inspired a ripple of insults from the earthmasons, which he just laughed off.

"That's enough of that," said Shona, stifling a childish image of Hendrick cleaning the smile off Steg's face. "I thought I saw something in the sky this evening as well, but I did not get a good look at it. I assumed it was one of our kestrels. Could that be what you saw, Lorrick? A kestrel, and a trick of the light?"

Old Lorrick shook his thin grey head. "I know what I seen, stonemover. And that was not it."

That night, in their family chamber, Shona and Hendrick and Micah washed their faces and arms with warm water from the furnace, changed into their bed-smocks, and prayed at each of their four small shrines to the Facets of the Allcreator.

Years ago, sleep would have sliced through Shona's consciousness like a headsman's axe the moment she laid down. But she didn't fall into that pleasant blackness right away anymore, even with Hendrick's comforting arm slung over her. Worries and aches kept her gazing at the wall long after she'd turned out the oil lamps. Gazing and wondering why she still prayed to a god she no longer believed in, not truly.

"Tense as stone, you are," Hendrick whispered. "What's wrong?"

She checked that the door was shut, afraid her voice might carry into Micah's room. Then she told him about the stolen rations, feeling his pulse rise in his closely pressed chest.

"Whoever it was, I'll throw 'em in the fucking sea. But how'd they get into the storage room? It's damned impossible to break in without the meditation circle noticing. Unless—"

"They break in from the outside."

"That'd leave traces in the masonry, wouldn't it?"

"I hadn't thought of that. Yes, it would."

"Have you noticed anything odd? When you're closing up the cracks?"

Shona thought about it. "I haven't worked on that part of the Spire in months. By Tybalt's reckoning, the thief hasn't been at it that long." She was seized by an impulse. "I can look now. If you'll help."

"It's the dead of night, Shona. You're to lead the meditation circle tomorrow morning. Besides, Tybalt's got the key and he's asleep."

"We don't need to go through the storage room."

The lookout was dark and empty. Nights were much darker now that the moon was just a thin sneer of shards between the stars. Cold wind whipped Shona's face raw as Hendrick fastened a pair of oil lamps to her harness. She kissed him, grateful he'd agreed to this despite his reluctance.

"Be quick about it," he said. "Two minutes. Alright? I don't want to have to explain this if we're noticed."

"I will, my mountain. I promise."

He loosened the moorings, a little at a time, as Shona climbed over the crenellations and down the outer wall of the Spire.

She rapped her fingers on the granite for what must have been the hundredth time that night. And found nothing. The patterns of ice gave no sign that an earthmason had altered the stone.

Disappointed, she was about to give up when she thought of something. Below the dungeon hung the Roots: a dense tangle of moss and dirt and stone that had come along for the journey when the earthmasons, in their haste to escape the floodwaters, had ripped the Spire from its foundation. Could an earthmason have entered the storage room through there? It seemed absurd. The Roots were a deathtrap, ever on the verge of crumbling loose. An earthmason had almost perished trying to repurpose their stone once.

Still, she had to check. Had to be sure.

She signaled for Hendrick to lower her, conscious that he was getting impatient; it had been much longer than two minutes.

The Roots rustled in the wind: a vast, dark mass eager to swallow her with its shifting tendrils. Shona unfastened one of the oil lamps from her harness and raised it to study the clumps of earth that'd refused to fall into the sea for six years.

Her breath caught. Carved into the dirt was a row of thin furrows. Like the marks of claws, or the talons of a siege grappler. Or something else. Gently she ran her fingers through them, surprised by how deep they went. She felt something smooth at the base of a furrow and teased it out with surgical care, thinking any moment a clod of rock would collapse on her.

It was a jade claw, with a jagged end as though broken off.

Allcreator take me.

"There's no way they could've wormed through the Roots." Hendrick was studying the claw at his worktable, his huge shadow on their chamber wall quivering in the lamplight. They spoke in whispers so as not to wake Micah. "No bloody way. The Roots would've collapsed in the attempt."

"A skilled enough earthmason could do it." Shona sipped a cup of hot papaya tea with a blanket wrapped around her. "I suspect *I* could do it, if I were careful enough."

"And seal it after you like that? So there's no trace of you?"

"Sculpting is my specialty, Hendrick. Just as smithing is yours. I am sure it could be done."

"Maybe you're the thief."

His sarcastic tone did not drain the remark of its nastiness, but Shona chose to ignore it.

Hendrick dimmed the lamp. "We should wake the Archmason."

"No. I'm afraid he might suspect us."

"But you said—"

"That he affirmed his trust in me. What else would he say?"

"You're cynical, hummingbird."

"From his standpoint, we're the ones who brought another mouth into the world. If we could be so selfish once, why not again?"

"He'd assume the jade thing was in our possession already. That we'd just pretended to find it. Is that it?"

"We can't prove we did."

Hendrick sighed in resignation. "Keep it to ourselves, then."

Fear lurked at the edge of Shona's awareness while she meditated. Fatigue gnawed at her strength. The Spire seemed to grow heavier by the hour as she focused on the helmstone.

It wasn't until after Reyna had taken Shona's place in the circle—and she was trudging up to her chamber, the cold afternoon light stabbing her eyes—that her fear was free to gain shape.

The thief was not from the Spire.

No matter how many times she turned it over, it sounded mad. But it was the only explanation.

Any earthmasons who could break the moon could survive what comes after. They're out there, my mountain. We will find them.

"No, you fool of an earthmason. They will find us," she told herself.

But who were *they*? And why—why had they broken the moon? Drowned the world and all creatures in it?

The Spirefolk believed the Allcreator had done it. The earthmasons assumed it was revenge for the lackblooms' tyranny, while the lackblooms held that it was punishment for centuries of decadence, of impiety.

But Shona had never embraced the divine explanation. In her bones, she had always felt that earthmasons somewhere in the world, beyond the reach of love or law, had engineered the cataclysm. It had given her hope. Hope that those earthmasons, however mad or monstrous they might be, were still alive somewhere. That there was still land. Civilization. A chance of rebirth.

A land inhabited by monsters was no paradise, but it was better than death. Anything was better than death.

"An ambush? Are you mad?" Hendrick was smoothing a bent harpoon back into shape at his worktable. "If the thief is what you think, they won't be taken as easy as that."

Shona stood behind him, resting her hands on his shoulders affectionately. "If they were so dangerous, they wouldn't need to use stealth. I have figured it out, Henrick. The thief's an exile. Or a runaway, perhaps. The thing Lorrick and I saw in the sky—it's their *craft*."

"What in the sacred name do you mean?"

"In the days of the Stone Empire, when earthmasons were at the height of power, the scholars imagined we would someday build stone chariots that could fly. Not like the Spire, slow and unwieldy, but something as easy to move as your flesh. Something even the lowest earthmason could maneuver, it would take so little skill."

"That sounds nice. But the Empire fell when we decided it would be more interesting to fight each other. And I doubt any earthmasons since the collapse ever found the trick to bloody sky-ships."

"*Our* Empire fell. But our Empire was not the whole world."

Hendrick set down the harpoon and looked at her. "Wanting to believe that won't make it so."

"Will you help me set up an ambush or not?"

"It's a bad idea. If Tybalt catches you, what will you tell him?"

"The truth," she said, and went to make herself some tea; she would need to keep alert if she hoped to catch the thief.

The stone softened under her hand like clay in the sun, until she could fashion a small hole through it with ease. She peered through the hole: no one in the storage room.

The midwife Imogen, as alert as any earthmason despite her old age, was managing Shona's harness from the lookout. Whenever Hendrick was busy in the meditation circle, Shona relied on Imogen to help her mend the Spire.

Shona had to move quickly lest the midwife suspect she wasn't sealing ice-cracks. After checking that Imogen wasn't looking over the crenellations, Shona expanded the hole she'd made. She grew it until it was big enough to crawl through, then shook a tether for Imogen to unspool her. The ropes of seaweed slackened with a crinkling sound, allowing Shona to worm her way into the storage room.

Inside, she sealed the wall around her tethers, fixing them in place, and got out of her harness quietly. A single oil lamp was flickering, low. She ran her hands across the floor until she found it: a spot one armspan across with no cracks or fissures, as if the stone had been melted down and set anew. Just as she'd anticipated.

She buried the end of a long line of sea silk in the spot— shallowly enough that the thief, while emerging from the Roots, would not notice it before setting it loose—then took the line with her as she got back into her harness and crawled out of the room. She resealed the wall as she went, leaving just enough space for the silk.

Outside, she signaled for Imogen to lift her. When she reached the story she wanted, she climbed partway around the Spire to her chamber window, then clambered through it. She pulled the line of sea silk as taut as she could, tied its other end around a ceramic bowl, and hung the bowl off her bedside table, high enough to shatter when it fell. The next time the thief opened the floor of the storage room, someone in her chamber would hear it.

The next day, Shona arrived at the meditation circle to take Tybalt's place—but Reyna was sitting there instead, her deep eyes ringed with dark circles like those of a nun after a Lunar Fast.

"What do you mean he's *missing*?" Shona whispered to her, once she'd drawn her far enough from the circle that they would not disturb it.

"Tybalt was meant to take my spot in the meditation circle," Reyna explained. "But he never appeared."

Shona tried to squelch the tar-bubble of fear rising in her.

"Did you visit his chamber?"

"Shona, I've looked everywhere. The Archmason's gone."

"Have Gellard take my place for now. I'll return soon."

Shona hurried to the Archmason's chamber on the second story. When her knocks went unanswered, she focused on the reinforced lock—much too dense for one earthmason to break—until the wards inside it clicked home. A trick she'd learned as a vagrant before the Guild of Architects had scraped her up.

Tybalt's cat Despond slipped through her legs as she opened the door. The chamber was even more spartan than Shona's, with a ratty cot, a dust-covered shrine, and not much more. The air smelled of fish stew; the Archmason liked to eat in his room.

She searched the place for signs of a struggle, found none.

She raced back down to the dungeon and into the storage room, surprised it was unlocked. It looked just as she'd left it a day ago. The line of sea silk—as far as she could tell—had not been moved.

There was just one change: a red stain on the floor near the drylocks, no larger than a coin. It might have been nothing—drops of tea that Tybalt had been sipping during his last inspection, perhaps—but Shona suspected it was blood.

"You don't think he...?" Reyna stood in the doorway, voice edged with fear.

"Jumped? Never. Not Tybalt."

Shona had no choice but to tell the Spirefolk.

But the thief—the thief had to stay a secret, until she could prove it was not one of them. They would gorge on the chance to blame each other if she gave it to them.

After hearing the news, the Spirefolk she'd summoned to the feast room—everyone, save the earthmasons in the meditation circle—traded looks of disbelief, of despair. Hendrick kissed Micah's head and whispered something reassuring to her.

Shona's voice chiseled through the silence: "When was the last time any of you saw him?"

Gellard Grey-Eyes lifted his small, sun-cured head. Though not blind, as Shona had assumed once, his eyes had a milky pallor equal to his name, the residue of some affliction in his youth. "I took Tybalt's place in the circle. He went into the storage room to tally up our food, if I remember right. I don't know if he left the room. I was deep in meditation by then."

Cadmus stared at Shona over smooth, steepled hands. "Tybalt and I were not friends, as you know. But I know a hard man from a soft one. The only thing that could have killed him was another earthmason."

Murmurs of agreement filled the room.

"Or a lackbloom with the edge of surprise," said Hendrick. "But we don't know he's dead. We'd be fools to assume it."

"I agree," said Shona.

"Seeing as you're the Archmason until we find him," said Cadmus, "what do you suggest we do?"

"Stay in groups. Avoid the dungeon except to meditate. Keep your eyes open for any trace of Tybalt. And most importantly, do not let his disappearance distract you from your duties. We still have a Spire to maintain."

Old Lorrick ran long fingernails through his beard, his sun-reddened eyes fastened on something only he could see. "All these years searching for land—it's only after that thing in the sky showed up someone disappears. Very curious."

"What are you suggesting?" said Reyna.

"Only that things have taken on a strangeness since we headed north. Can you not feel it?"

"I can feel my head annealing whenever you speak," said Hendrick.

Old Lorrick shot him a look.

"We should resist indulging in superstition," said Shona, trying to channel Tybalt's calm, "when our situation's vexing enough as it is."

Cadmus was watching the clouds change color on the third-story landing outside her chamber. He turned as she came up the stairs, cloak stirring in the chilly air.

"It's a queer thing, but I could swear I heard someone in the harness a few days ago, in the dead of night. Most likely just the wind, of course."

"Most likely, my liege," said Shona, fumbling for the chamber key in her trouser pocket.

"Who would be inspecting the wall at that hour, in such bitter cold?"

She made to open her chamber door when Cadmus touched her shoulder, his dolphinskin glove so soft it might have been air.

"Is there something I can do for you, Cadmus?"

"I don't know what you're hiding. And I don't know why you're hiding it. But I would remind you that secrets don't last long on the Spire. Give Hendrick my regards, Archmason Shona."

He dipped his head in farewell and made his way down the stairs.

Shona untied the ceramic bowl from the line of sea silk and set it on the bedside table.

Hendrick was sitting on the cot, unlacing his boots. The smell of death rose from his feet as soon as they were free.

"It was a clever idea, hummingbird. But you didn't account for the thief being cleverer."

"They must enter the room through a different spot each time. I should have inspected the place more thoroughly."

"Or they sensed the silk as they were coming through. Made sure it didn't come loose."

"Perhaps."

"Seems they really don't want to get caught."

Shona sealed Hendrick's foul-smelling boots in the wall, then collapsed into the cot beside him. She was so tired not even her aches could have kept her from falling asleep if she dared shut her eyes. He ran his great leathery hand over her arms and legs, neck and scalp, checking as always for small blood spots and other signs of the Slow Death. His exhalation held relief, but it was temporary.

"Cadmus confronted me, Hendrick. He knows we're not telling them everything."

"That pompous shit can get tossed to the sharks."

"One lackbloom talks to another. Soon they all want answers."

"So tell them the truth. That an earthmason from outside the Spire's been stealing our food. That Tybalt may've tried to ambush them. May've gotten killed."

Shona looked at him. "You believe me, then."

He nodded. "I didn't want to tell you, but I thought maybe the thief was Tybalt himself till he vanished. He spent more time in the storage room than anyone. I thought maybe—maybe he figured someone would find out, and telling you was his way of protecting himself. I'm ashamed it even crossed my mind."

"I won't pretend it didn't cross mine as well," Shona admitted.

"The thief must be here, right? They've got to set down somewhere. They must be hiding in the walls of the Spire."

"Or *under* it." She sat up, her fatigue swept away by adrenaline. "They're hiding inside the Roots."

"That's madness. It would—"

"Collapse, yes. Unless you're the sort of earthmason who can break moons and fly sky-ships."

Hendrick covered his face. "Allcreator take me. You want to go down there."

"If we're right, do you know what that means?"

He spoke the word tentatively, like a fickle spell. "Land."

"Land," she said. "They'll know the way to land."

"You're mad to even dream of going in that deathtrap."

"I won't deny that, Hendrick."

"And—damn everything—I'm as mad for helping you."

Shona was in charge of the storage room now that she was Archmason, but she felt no less like an intruder entering it without Tybalt's permission. Habits were slow to thaw on the Spire. Inside, Hendrick helped Shona moor the seaweed harness to the wall. It was unlikely anyone would notice it missing at this hour, but Shona still prayed that no one visited the lookout.

When she was finished donning the harness, Hendrick gave her the longknife he'd sharpened that evening, and she strapped it to the harness alongside two oil lamps. A second knife gleamed in Hendrick's belt.

Since the seat of the harness only had room for Shona, Hendrick linked himself to a harness tether for safety, looping one end of an iron chain around it and looping the other end around his belt.

Shona knelt to open a hole in the floor when a fresh fear constricted her.

"What is it?" Hendrick whispered.

She could sense the Roots below them, huge and heavy.

"What if we're wrong? What if there's nothing down here?"

"The thief may've fled already. That's true. But we'll never know unless we look."

And if they captured the thief, what then? How would she handle learning that her kind had drowned the world after all? The very thought twisted her guts with guilt.

But it was this or death. There was no other way.

Shona carefully formed a hole in the floor, revealing the dark brown surface of the Roots.

She sculpted their path downward in slow, deliberate scoops while Hendrick packed the dirt and rock they displaced back into the walls above them, leaving just enough room for the harness tethers. The deeper they went, the slower they worked, pausing each time a tremor passed through the Roots. The tremors grew louder.

Shona paused to drink from her waterskin, passed it to Hendrick.

"I can sense a pocket over there." One hand on the stone, Shona pointed to a spot perpendicular to their path. "No, there." She adjusted her finger downward. "It's at least as big as our chamber, but I can't tell much more than that."

Hendrick brushed water off his beard. "How far?"

"Too far for the harness. We'll have to leave it behind."

"No." He grabbed her before she could pull the clasps. "Too dangerous. If the ground falls from under you, you're finished. I'll go." He unchained himself from the tethers.

"Hendrick."

"You would leave Micah an orphan?"

"Listen." She took his hand. "Nothing we do here will matter unless we capture this person. And as strong as you are, there is only one of you."

His chewed his lip, looking anguished. But when she took off the harness, he did not stop her.

They tunneled through the earth until the pocket was an armspan ahead of them, seeming to throb under Shona's hands with a hundred possibilities. Her heart was racing; her skin was clammy with sweat.

They both drew their longknives, and Shona opened the last stretch of stone.

It was a room: half again larger than their own, the walls smoothed with great care. A few stone containers rose from the floor, as large as the drylocks in the storage room; the lid of one was askew, letting out the scent of fish. Shona crept into the room with Hendrick, scanning the objects on the floor in wonder: a small midden of fishbones, scuffed clothes made of yellow-grey silk, little white spheres that gave off light, a pair of greaves with jade plating. Atop a shiny black book with strange gold characters across its spine sat a steel-and-glass disc with a twitching needle at its center.

A tunnel led to another room. Inside was Tybalt, lying still.

They rushed to him and pulled him upright. His face was cut, bruised. An elaborate steel brace bound his wrists, and a sharp wire running from its intricate little wards was looped around his throat.

Tybalt's eyes snapped open, bloodshot.

"Shona."

"Thank the Allcreator you're alive. Where are they?"

"Catching fish, I assume. Listen. She is not wicked, I don't think. She—she seems scared."

"We'll decide that for ourselves," said Hendrick. He knelt to cut the brace's wires, but Tybalt flinched away.

"It'll tighten around my throat if you try to break it."

"Is there a key?"

Tybalt shook his head. "All magic. Their metalcraft is unlike anything I've seen. She has a—a flying thing. Allcreator take me; if I'd known what we were dealing with, I would not have ambushed her."

"What does she want?" asked Shona.

"We have tried to communicate, but it is difficult. Her language is unfamiliar to me, though not entirely. Some words I know; I am not sure why. She has escaped from something or someone, I think. She has the air of one who has endured many ordeals."

"Do you know where she came from?"

"No. But she does not look—well, like us."

Before Shona could ask what he meant, the Roots shuddered slightly as if something had struck them. She fashioned an alcove in the wall and pulled Hendrick into it, then sealed it closed save for a hole to peer through.

The sound of stone parting. Then, footsteps.

A small, hunched woman shuffled into the room, pulling off a suit of jade armor one piece at a time. Her skin was pale as a moon-shard and crisscrossed with paler scars, and her hair flowed down fine and white as asbestos when she removed her jade helm. She might have been a hundred years old until she turned her head, and then looked no older than a maiden, with a perfectly smooth face but for a pair of slanted scars. Her eyes were huge. One had a black pupil so large it seemed a hole in her head; the other was a ball of neatly etched jade.

As the woman approached Tybalt, clutching a fat brown fish like a cudgel, Shona was certain the woman would hear her heartbeat through the wall.

"Fel," said Tybalt. "If you let me go, I could be more useful to you."

Fel mumbled something in a harsh tongue and tossed the fish to Tybalt. Then she hauled a cask of water into the room. Her back turned to Shona, she poured the water into a stone basin she'd made, then ripped the salt from it in a sweeping motion and drank with animal fervor, head bowed and slurping.

Shona opened the wall quietly, and she and Hendrick moved toward the stranger in slow, tentative steps, spreading out to flank her. Were Shona more skillful, she could have drawn the stone from the drinking basin around Fel's legs to trap her. But her magic was too weak at that distance.

She had to settle for barbarism. Focusing, she levitated the longknife with her magic and guided it silently toward a spot behind Fel's spine, holding it in place there; Hendrick levitated his own blade behind Fel's heart, so that it looked as though a pair of invisible assassins were on the cusp of ending her.

"We do not wish you harm," said Shona, praying Fel understood her tone if not her words. "Please do not move."

Fel went stone-still. Then, in defiance of Shona and Hendrick, the knives edged back from Fel slightly as she turned around, baring neat jade teeth. Tiny colorful piercings sparkled in her nose, cheeks, eyebrows.

"Stay calm," said Hendrick, holding up his palms in restraint.

To Shona's horror, the knives began to glide toward her and Hendrick, glimmering, steady as hate.

"Calm." Fel rolled the word in her mouth like a bitter morsel of something.

Shona and Hendrick pushed back as hard as they could, but it did not matter; the knives drew closer, and closer still. Hendrick swiped to grab one, but the hilt twisted out of reach. Fel laughed: a cruel sound, thick with contempt.

Allcreator save us if this fails.

Shona dropped to her hands, flinging her strength into the ground. The stone cracked with a thunderclap; tremors surged through the Roots. Fel let the knives drop with a startled gasp and reached down to keep the floor from collapsing. Hendrick lunged at her, slamming her against the wall. She sucked in air through squeezed pipes and sprang a stubby jade spike from a knuckle, then stabbed Hendrick's abdomen, twisting into it. Blood bloomed through his work-smock, dark as wine.

Shona grabbed the spike-arm and pinned it to the wall. Fel tried to scream, but Hendrick had her locked in a sleeping grip. In seconds, she slumped to the ground, unconscious.

The Roots rumbled and shook. A slab of floor fell away to reveal a patch of night-black ocean. Cold air sucked Shona's hair toward the hole as she tried to close it. Tybalt helped her, reaching with bound hands until the ground resealed. Slowly, the tremors subsided.

Hendrick sat against the wall, clutching his wound. Shona's throat tightened at the sight of it.

"I'll be fine," he said. "The healer can fix it."

Tybalt shook his head. "There is no chance of climbing up in that condition."

"Don't be so optimistic."

But Tybalt was right. Shona would have to make the journey alone.

"If that—that *thing* moves so much as a finger, don't hesitate to knock her out again," she said.

With Tybalt's help, she found the sky-craft in a carefully sculpted tunnel sealed off from the other rooms. She remembered the running paths that some birds used to gain momentum for flight, and assumed the tunnel held a similar purpose.

The craft was made of jade and wood and canvas, with a pair of long, hinged wings folded up against its flanks and a carriage just large enough for one. It stood on two legs with sharp-clawed feet. One claw was broken off.

Shona climbed into the craft and concentrated on its wings. The jade fixtures bent to her will with surprising readiness, dragging the wood and canvas parts with them as they shifted into a slow flapping motion. But as soon as she tried to move the legs, her hold on the wings slipped, and they fell limp. Controlling both at once did not seem possible.

She felt around inside the carriage—and found a device chained to the wall. It was a crystal sphere about the size of her fist, and it held a jade model of the craft on a metal spindle. She was baffled until she thought of the helmstone that held up the Spire. A depression at the front of the craft clicked as Shona placed the sphere inside it. She focused on the little model, on moving its wings and legs at once. The craft mirrored the movements.

So that was the trick.

She walked the craft across the tunnel to get a feel for it, then back again. It felt slow and heavy, and after some missteps she thought it might be safer to climb back up the Roots. But a fresh surge of tremors quashed that idea.

She opened a path to the sky, then took a running jump into the void, willing the craft's wings to flap hard against the icy skirling air. A swelling gust tried to flip her instantly, like a shove from a drunken brawler, and the mirrored starlight on the water disoriented her, wrecking what was left of her balance. She felt herself swerving into endless night, dizzy, panic stabbing her thin bubble of concentration. She was falling, falling into a chasm of stars.

Fly. Fly. Fly.

But the wind chanted, "Fall, fall, fall," as it swatted her and hammered her and whipped her.

She kept her mind on the model in the crystal sphere. Now that she was too far from the Spire's light to see it clearly, she could focus on the weight of the craft and on the movement of the wings, as if she were sitting shut-eyed in a meditation circle. And the craft steadied itself, wobbling. She forced the wings to flap harder, harder. Veering a little, she saw the dwindling silhouette of the Spire, ink-black but for faint specks of lamplight, and flew toward it.

She alighted on the lookout harder than intended, causing the craft to creak and shudder. Relief flooded her chest as she jumped to the ground—followed by a sudden wave of fear.

Cadmus was standing before the stairway entrance in his everyday clothes, clutching his cloak tight around himself for warmth. An oil lamp rested on the ground beside him, as though he'd been waiting for her.

His mouth moved a few times before words came out.

"I don't—I cannot quite believe it," he said, approaching the craft, the golden pommel of his ancestral sword glinting like sunlight from under his cloak.

As soon as she took a step toward the entrance, his hand went to the sword, as if afraid she would grab it with her magic. It was a reasonable fear.

"Hendrick's hurt," she said, almost pleading. "I need to get help."

"Something's found us, haven't they?"

She hesitated. "Yes."

"I knew it. I knew you were hiding something. And when I saw that the harness was missing, I knew you were scheming with that brute. But *this*," he said, marveling at the craft, "I could not have guessed at this. What numinous beings have found us, Shona? A seraph of the Allcreator? As liege lord of the cleanfolk, I deserve to know."

She thought of Hendrick bleeding out in the Roots, and of the sword under Cadmus's cloak. Thought of how its castle-forged edge might feel against her flesh if she were too slow or too clumsy to stop it. She had seen that sword used only once, during the Incident. Had seen the clean red path it had made through the earthmason—a miner no older than herself—who had tried to stab him with a longknife. The sound had been wet and final; she did not wish to hear it again.

"A survivor of the deluge, like ourselves," she said. "Not a god. Not a seraph. Just an earthmason, like me and Hendrick and Tybalt."

"You would insult my wits by claiming a *mudrat* made this vessel?"

"She's down in the Roots right now, unconscious for the moment. I can take you down to see her—my liege."

The anger on his face melted away as he studied the craft more carefully, taking in its intricate construction. And the expression that replaced it was something else altogether. Fear. He was afraid that she was telling the truth.

He swallowed, looking slightly sick, and shook his head in disbelief. But he said nothing more after that, and made no move to stop her as she hurried to the stairway.

A minute later, the healer, a fat man wrapped in a thick sharkskin blanket, was rubbing his half-open eyes as he answered the door.

"Alucart," she said, "I need your help."

She roused Gellard Grey-Eyes next, explaining in a breathless rush everything she could compress into the seconds afforded to her, and the three of them raced down to the dungeon, past the meditation circle, into the storage room, where the seaweed harness, its tethers still snaking down into the hole from their moorings, awaited them.

"Is there really no other way?" Alucart asked as Shona pulled up the harness.

"It does seem quite dangerous," Gellard concurred.

Biting down contempt, Shona rounded on them. "Do you imagine for a moment that Hendrick or Tybalt would not do the same for you? Well, do you?"

The men traded looks of equal parts shame and dread.

Then Alucart quickly took the harness and donned it.

"I'm just a lackbloom," he said defensively. "I can't bend fucking rocks if the Roots start collapsing, can I?"

Gellard was slower at digging than Hendrick had been, but Shona had practice now and remembered the path to Fel's chamber.

When they emerged, the men gasped in wonder.

"What in the sacred name is this place?" asked Gellard.

"I did tell you," said Shona.

"And I—I thought I believed you. Truly, I did."

Tybalt looked up at the sound of their voices, his face awash with relief. "You'd better hurry, Hendrick's losing a lot of blood."

Shona's heart sank at how pale Hendrick had become. Sweat glazed his brow. His hands were failing to stanch the wound even slightly.

Without hesitation, Alucart opened his instrument case and went to work. Hendrick winced as the healer poured a precious half-cup of wine on his wound. "Hold still, you restless orangutan. You want me to sew this shut properly or not?"

Shona wasted no time in binding Fel from head to foot in seaweed rope, taking care to cover her eyes. She tied her hands tightest, afraid that Fel would cut through her bonds with other things hidden inside her. Only death could stop a skilled earthmason from moving stone, but restricting sight and movement made their magic less precise. It wasn't perfect, but it would serve until Shona could seal Fel in a proper room and place some earthmasons around her.

Gellard hoisted Fel over his shoulder like a sack of gravel, trudged back toward the hole they'd come down.

Shona kissed Hendrick's warm, damp forehead as he was being mended, knowing it would be an arduous climb back up the Roots without his help.

"Be strong, my mountain," she said. "Once Fel is safely contained, we will come back for you and Tybalt."

"That's good to hear," he mumbled through a haze of delirium, and laughed.

A few days later, the Spire was a different place. The walls were thrumming with frenzied conversation, and Fel—strange, mysterious Fel—was still bound up like a bedlamite on the third story with several earthmasons guarding her.

And Shona, too tired to even feel it anymore, was sitting beside Hendrick in bed, while he spooned fish stew into his mouth in hungry slurps. His recovery had been quicker than she'd expected, and her heart sang a little whenever he awoke from one of his deep, precarious sleeps. Alucart came by three times each day to change Hendrick's dressings.

"I owe you my life," Hendrick had told him one morning.

"We can discuss repayment when we find land," Alucart had replied.

The Spirefolk knew what was at stake now. Shona had told them everything she could afford to tell. Every face in the feast room had drifted through a dozen shades of astonishment as she gave her account of recent events, from the missing food to Tybalt's kidnapping and her struggle to find him. She left out her belief—and now Hendrick's—that Fel's civilization had broken the moon. But now the Spirefolk knew that others had survived the deluge, that there must be land, and most of them rejoiced in this knowledge.

Most, but not all. Some wondered why Fel had left her refuge in the first place. And why her kin would welcome eighty-two new bellies to fill.

Hendrick wasn't one of the worriers. He sighed in contentment as Shona scratched a spot on his back beyond his reach, then plopped back in the cot. He was looking a hundred times livelier since Alucart had tended to him.

"I love you more than the Allcreator, did you know that?"

"You're talking a lot more today. That's good," said Shona, setting his half-finished bowl of fish stew on the bedside table.

He winced while adjusting himself, then closed his eyes with a tired smile.

Tybalt came to visit, looking haggard as death but grateful to be free of the brace. It had been a simple offer to Fel: "Remove the brace if you want to eat." And after three days without food, she had taken it. Shona had feared what Fel would do once the rope was untied momentarily from her eyes and hands. But any urge to rebel must have withered at the sight of half the earthmasons in the Spire surrounding her. So, carefully adjusting the wards, Fel had removed the device from Tybalt's neck and wrists, taking perhaps longer than needed. Now Tybalt could not stop rubbing the red line imprinted on his throat, like a man who'd escaped a hanging at the last moment.

Hendrick sat up as Tybalt stepped into the bedroom. "Archmason."

"Not anymore," said Tybalt. "I have ceded that burden to Shona. I am old and weary, and it is my right."

Hendrick looked at Shona. "You didn't tell me that."

Shona shrugged. "I did. But I don't think you heard it."

"How are you feeling?" Tybalt asked Hendrick.

"To tell you the truth, bored."

"Well, enjoy it while you can."

Tybalt pulled a book out of his sharkskin satchel: the black one with gold characters that Shona had glimpsed among the stranger's artifacts.

"Fel still refuses to learn our tongue," he said. "It will take some time to communicate. But I have studied this item carefully, and I think you should know what I have found, Archmason."

Gently, as though handling a delicate instrument, he opened the book. Hundreds of silvery pages swished apart to reveal surfaces slate-blank but for snatches of light or shadow where creases had formed.

"Beautiful, isn't it?"

"Are those pages made of—metal?" said Hendrick.

Tybalt nodded. "Yet softer than any parchment, and that's not the strangest thing about them. Shona, would you care to close the window shutters? And cover the gaps with a blanket, if you would."

Once the room was dark, Tybalt procured something from his pocket which began to glow, illuminating his face at ghoulish angles. It was one of the light-spheres that belonged to Fel.

"Look," he whispered.

Shona and Hendrick leaned over the book. To Shona's astonishment, thousands of jagged white characters—not unlike those of the Diamantine Script of the Stone Empire—had appeared on the pages.

"Impressed? Well, that's not half of it. Observe." Tybalt moved the light-sphere in a slow clockwise fashion over the pages. And as he did, the characters transformed—once, twice, three times—before settling back into their original shapes where the rotation ended. "Four overlapping texts, do you see? A most economical way to make a book."

"Ingenious," said Hendrick, his face bright with interest.

Shona nodded in agreement.

"My grasp of the Diamantine Script is much too weak to tease out more than a few traces of meaning, alas," said Tybalt.

"So it *is* the ancient script," murmured Shona, not quite believing it.

"A distant offspring of it, anyway. Yes, I know what you're thinking. I see it in your eyes. And it appears to be true. *The Stone Empire did not fall.* Not completely. But you need not take my word."

He flipped to another place in the book, and an illustration more dazzling than any Shona had ever seen—either in the temple manuscripts that had once filled the capital, or in the murals that had emblazoned the lackblooms' high manse walls—flooded the darkness with shimmering colors, each touched with a silvery tint like a rainbow poured through mercury.

The illustration showed a thin, steepled mountain rising from an icy waste. And as Tybalt moved the light-sphere, slowly, very slowly, a throng of people—hundreds of them, men and women and children—seemed to trudge toward the mountain from outside the page. Bundled in filthy rags, they dragged with them dogs and horses and onagers, huge wagons piled with goods. Shona recognized their diamond sigils.

"Remnants of the Stone Empire," she said.

"So it seems," said Tybalt. "This mountain—I cannot be sure just yet, not until I have studied the script more carefully—but I do believe this mountain is where we will find Fel's people, if there are more of them."

"The ones who broke the moon," Hendrick muttered to Shona, and she nodded in wonder. They had to be.

Days passed, then weeks, as the Spire drifted further north, into emptinesses colder and cloudier, where the daylight seemed to drag its feet. And every morning and evening, when she was not meditating, Shona went to the lookout to scan the horizon.

When Hendrick was fully recovered, he joined her too, sometimes hoisting Micah on his back to see above the crenellations, her red hair whipping like fire in the icy wind. No one complained of the cold or the wind. All that mattered was the horizon.

But it was fine and crisp as a sword's edge—no mountain in sight.

After a month of searching, Shona's hopes began to fade. Fel, in her maddening silence, was no more useful than a statue, and

Tybalt's progress in deciphering the book had proven painfully slow.

But Shona was always the last one on the lookout, even as the dwindling light of dusk made the distance inscrutable.

This night was no different. Hendrick had left her with a kiss, and had taken his warmth with him down to bed, and now she was alone atop the Spire with the shadows hardening around her, and with the stars and the moon-shards stretching like strange, luminous silt-plumes in that second ocean above her.

A cold gale whistled sadly through the crenellations, flicking back her sleeves and scorching her raw face for a moment, and she wrapped her arms around herself, as if this would help. She felt like the walls of the Spire just then, weak and tired and cracked from the cold. She belonged in bed with Hendrick, she thought, and turned to leave.

But as she did, she caught a flicker out of the corner of her eye—and paused, feeling the same small tug on her awareness as when she'd glimpsed Fel's craft for the first time, though she had not known it then.

She leaned out over the crenellations, searching the horizon.

The flicker came again, stronger—a thin orange light, not like the silver-white of the stars. A wisp of cloud was half-obscuring it. And then it wasn't, and the light grew with her certainty, its faint aura limning a thin, steepled shape that rose from the distant water.

Her heart was thudding so loud she could not hear the wind anymore. Could not feel the stone beneath her, either; she seemed to be hovering above it, as if in a dream.

But it wasn't a dream. It was real.

They had found land.

See Jordan Chase-Young's story "Shards" online at Metaphorosis.
If you liked it, leave a comment. Authors love that!
Remember to subscribe to our e-mail updates so you'll know when new stories are posted.

About the story

I've always suspected that magic, if it existed, would be a profound threat to human survival. It would empower tyrants, create lasting fault lines between groups, and permit destruction on a vast scale. But magic would also afford great opportunities. It would cut down on drudgery, make life more interesting, and in the right hands allow for great progress. "Which of the two would win out?" I've wondered. "Would magic help humanity grow, or would it doom us?"

This story flowed out of that question. I thought of a world in which some people could manipulate stone with magic, could shape it to their will. It seemed only a matter of time before some of them, somewhere, used that magic to destroy the world. But not the whole world, not everyone. Some people would use that magic to survive, to keep humanity aloft in the teeth of despair. And maybe—who knows?—that second group would win out in the end. Such things are not written in stone.

I don't even remember how many times I rewrote the story from scratch to give you the version you see here. I could put together a fat volume with just the half-drafts, false starts, and jettisoned endings. By the time I submitted the story to Metaphorosis, in December 2018, it had already gone through many rewrites; by the time it was sold, it had gone through several more, each one stronger than the last. As a result of all this editing, I've learned more about the craft of fiction writing than from every book I've read on the subject put together.

I've also learned a lot about my strengths and weaknesses as a writer, and about the deep weirdness of creativity; several times I thought a problem in the story was intractable, only to realize, with a jolt of surprise, that the answer was sitting in front of me all along. In earlier drafts, for example, the main character's motives, role in the Spire, and family members, together with the nature of the Spire, the magic system, and the world, were doled out in a slow, serial sequence, which hurt the pacing greatly; I realized I could fix that problem with ease by smashing all those elements together in the first couple of scenes. One of the joys of writing is having revelations like these.

A question for the author

Q: When do you decide a story is finished?

A: The splendid curse—the maddening blessing—of fiction is that a story is never finished. As David Deutsch taught us, any artwork is infinitely perfectible; you could spend millions of years improving a story one word, sentence, or scene at a time, but the combinatorially unbounded nature of thought means you'd still be infinitely far from perfection!

So if you can't finish a story, really finish it, the question is when to abandon it. I have a poetic answer and a practical one. The poetic answer: I decide a story is finished when it makes me feel unadulterated pride to read it from beginning to end. The prose is clear and smooth, the action is balanced and organic, the characters have full voices and satisfying arcs, and the ending leaves one with a frisson of wonder and the feeling of time well spent. The practical answer: I decide a story is finished when I can no longer see how to improve it. Oh, I know there are improvements to be made, glorious ones just around the edge of thought, but I don't yet have the knowledge to find them. So I finish the story and start working on another, in the hopes of getting better.

About the author

Jordan Allan Chase-Young was machine-pressed into a science-fiction and fantasy writer by the cold grey skies of Oregon, where he spent most of his life. Now he is gingerly avoiding buff kangaroos and kamikaze magpies in the strange desolation of Australia, with his wife and one cactus, while reading and writing speculative fiction more ardently than ever—that is, when not nose-deep in texts about history, economics, future studies, or global catastrophic risk in search of why civilizations thrive or flounder. He is mostly optimistic about humanity's potential to turn the dead, quiet universe outside our pale blue dot into a living, thinking one. He enjoys hiking, video games, Twitter, astrobiology, and illustration, and wishes he had more time to draw like he used to.

ebookofthenewsun.wordpress.com, @jachaseyoung

A Picture of Home, in Silence

Alexandra Seidel

The soles on Sam's first pair of shoes are worn and cracked, and she is tired. She craves rest, because the way home is long. Light reflects off tall stained glass windows, and because there were none of those in the research colony, Sam is curious, stops, walks away from the road, and enters the building.

Years and miles ago, when Sam first came to the research colony, she was useful, and being useful helped keep her mind from drifting to the past. Sam knew how to use a microscope, how to navigate a lab, how to read colored graphs and the hues of chemical indicators. She thought she'd never leave the research colony, would live there and find happiness with the other survivors, with all the others who had been uprooted by the silence of loss like herself.

A month before Sam decided to leave, she was told to stay out of the lab, to take care of herself instead, to let others pursue as work what Sam pursues as love. They did not call her redundant, not to her face. To her face, they offered silent compassion. It took Sam a month to realize the research colony was not home, never had been, to realize she was never going back to the lab and would never find the kind of happiness to replace the science, the kind of happiness that warms the skin like touch. To understand in her heart as well as her head that the loss of sight was final. When she left the research colony at the end of that month and had to walk through the fields of silence, the fields where those that never were invited inside still lay as plunder for the ravens, Sam knew she would never return, because some of the silence would always cast an echo into the colony itself.

Much of the glass in the church is broken, but some of the windows still hold their ancient pictures. Sam wipes the dust of disuse from a spot in the pews and sits, looks from her scuffed shoes that were new not too long ago up to the pictures. She doesn't know what the painted glass is meant to tell her, but the wonder of people, even glass people, is striking. The glass world, the world the windows show, seems full and colorful, as if it stretches, as if you could meet another person around every corner. The light is dyed in colors and spills the images over the dirty church floor, a kaleidoscope copy of the windows themselves. This bright shadow of colored light makes Sam forget that glass worlds, all worlds, are brittle.

The windows make touch look normal, ordinary. The last time Sam was touched by another human was almost three months ago. They took her blood, and they wore gloves. There are antibodies in her blood, just like there should be in those that survived an infection. If Sam concentrates, she can feel her arm grow warm from the touch. Even after all this time, the memory of touch still lingers while the memory of sight has dulled, the faces overexposed by time. Nothing in Sam's blood is responsible for Sam's fading vision, that's genetic. She barely felt the needle rip her skin when they took her blood. It was the touch she felt.

Sam is one of the lucky ones. She was young, barely in school three years, when the diseases spread, two viruses that crossed paths in the bleeding bowels of humanity like two edges of the same sword. Her mother and father were both scientists, her father was a doctor. They understood the need to stay away from where people gathered, malls, playgrounds, fairs, the outside world. Everything Sam knows she owes to her parents, who taught her to read and write, to love math and science.

Many of Sam's generation only learned reading and writing and science once they settled in the research colony, and most of them never learned to love those things. Back home, before the colony, Sam had seen her parents love them, and so that love came easy to her as well.

A flyer rests under a layer of dust, an arm's length from where Sam is sitting and staring at the glass. *The end is nigh*, it warns. The end is already past and done. Sam, like most survivors her age, came to the research colony an orphan.

Sam looks at the windows and the silent shards below them where stories lie scattered; test tubes scattered on the floor, broken, because she didn't see, that's how it started. "Glass, like touch, can cut," Sam says, startled by the echo the building offers. The doctor, when he told Sam of the unavoidable loss of sight, held her hand where the broken test tubes had sliced it open, and of that touch, Sam remembers only pain. Her need for rest smothered by the memory of loss, she picks up the flyer, tears it in two, and leaves the empty room to the play of shadow and light.

It has gotten easier, the walking. Sam is on her second pair of shoes. It is an open garden gate and not the need for rest that pulls her away from the road, because the wrought curls of metal flowers shake a memory loose in Sam's mind: the garden gate at home where she grew up and learned to love science looks exactly like this. Sam's father once decorated it with balloons for her birthday, yellow and red and blue ones. Past the gate, the air smells sweet, and a house sits there, shaded by trees.

Sam would have tried the front door, but humming makes her take a garden path overgrown with weeds. When she sees the beekeeper, Sam stops, stunned at the presence of another survivor. The beekeeper turns, sees Sam, but doesn't stop in her work. Sam approaches.

"I do not get visitors," the beekeeper says.

Sam nods, uncertain whether the beekeeper's voice is reproachful or annoyed.

"I'm from the research colony. I was walking by, then I saw the open garden gate."

The beekeeper examines her, the woman's strange hat dipping down and going up. "So you walked all the way here? I considered going myself when they broadcast their invitation, but I liked it here. You must have been walking for months." Constant humming sheathes the beekeeper even more than her bee suit, the hat with the dark veil, the pale overalls. The garden is lush, glossy, a contrast to the almost uncanny guardian of bees.

"I wanted to do it. And I'm used to the walking by now."

The beekeeper is old. Not *old*, exactly. Gray age didn't survive the viruses. *Relatively speaking, she is old*, Sam's father would have said. Sam can hardly make out the lines of the beekeeper's face behind the veil, but what she sees is harsh and hard, and the humming doesn't hide it.

"You could have taken a car. Surely they have those still running up there in the research colony."

There is disapproval in the beekeeper's voice, distaste, when she says *research colony*. On an intellectual level, Sam understands that not every survivor wishes to come to the colony, that some brave the world alone or in small groups. Sam used to think it an unfathomable choice, the loneliness, the memories lurking around every corner, but seeing the beekeeper now, a part of Sam reconsiders.

After all, I left.

The beekeeper opens a hive and pulls out a wax-encrusted slab. Honey trails the frame and falls to the ground. The bees buzz. To Sam, who doesn't dare come closer, they sound angry, for they have been disturbed.

A bee flies over to Sam's hand. The bee lands on the knuckle of Sam's index finger, and Sam holds her breath the way one does before a kiss. She lets the insect explore, taste her summer warm skin. The bee's colors amaze Sam, so much detail in such a small body, and Sam tries to taste the details with her failing sight as if the yellow and black bands were rare candy. "I don't know how to drive."

This makes the beekeeper chuckle, a noise like the humming of her bees. "It's really not that hard when there's no traffic. Come, let's eat." She carries the honeycombed frame into her house. Inside, the house feels hollow. It makes Sam wonder what a single bee would do with one of the beekeeper's frames all to herself.

Past the threshold, the house is full of echoes. "Did you always live here?" Sam asks.

The beekeeper takes off her hat. A bee falls to the ground, dead. "No. But it's a good place. Lots of stairs, though. Did you ever think of just stopping?"

Sam shakes her head. "No. I want to go back home. Not the colony, home before that. And walking isn't all that bad; you see so much." So many colors, so many shapes. Sam would never abandon the sights to either side of the road. She wants to see as much of a world she never traveled as she can before her sight is lost.

The beekeeper's veil also veils her view of the reality outside of her hives and her honey, Sam realizes as the black gauze of it brushes against the floor and settles next to the dead bee.

"I guess that's true," says the beekeeper as she slips her pale bee suit off. It is a hiding place, this suit, Sam realizes. More dead bees hit the floor, joining the one next to the hat.

Sam cannot help staring. The way the beekeeper moves reminds Sam of the small insects themselves, of the vibrato of their wings, the strange geometry of their dance. The beekeeper catches her watching and smiles, an expression that seems foreign to her face. The house is full of echoes, even if no bees live inside.

The slickness of the beekeeper's honey still clings to Sam's skin, but she had to leave, knew from the moment she heard the echoes that she could not stay in that house and pretend it was a hive. The morning after, the beekeeper left the bed and put on her suit, and Sam felt the touches they had exchanged fade to memory and glass.

The beekeeper had hardly any books in her house, and those that slept on the shelves hadn't been hers. Sam did not feel bad about taking some of them after she put on shoes to continue her walk.

Rain pours down on Sam. It has done so for about an hour, and the beekeeper's house, the beekeeper's bed, would be welcome now that Sam is properly frozen through, even if the beekeeper never shed her suit again. Even the research colony would be welcome.

Sam shakes her head, dislodges raindrops from her hood, memories from her head, and false desires from her heart. No, the beekeeper's bed would not be welcome, that bed was a lonely frame made to hold only a single bee, and the colony would not be welcome either; without the lab, the research colony is just an empty bed in a small apartment ruled by silence. Not even two thousand people live in the colony.

Sam stops in the downpour. There is no sound but the rain, and the rain does little to mute that looming silence in this largely humanless world. Sam screams at the top of her lungs. Her scream doesn't scare animals, because they were smart enough to find shelter from the rain, but it feels good, being noisy. Even if no one else knows about it. Even if the scream, like a koan, might be a noise without a sound.

Bruises are a marvel of color. They are a marvel of pain, too, but the colors fascinate Sam. They start with the reds of freshly torn vessels, then fade to purplish hues of blues and blacks before the skin emerges under greenish yellows. Sam's vision is getting worse, and so the number of bruises she gets to examine increases. She is on her fourth pair of shoes.

Today she stops at a park for food she took off a shelf half a pair of shoes ago. Tearing the plastic gives Sam a moment, just that moment between the plastic being whole and then not, when she can imagine the world never changed. In that moment, there exists the possibility that life so far has been a bad dream, that once the plastic is torn, there will be another plastic-portioned morsel to be grabbed just around the corner.

The food inside tastes like the sacred past of a birthday party and colorful balloons, like an invitation on the garden gate. The taste stirs these memories like glass, stained, broken, and containing a world within: friends from school in pigtails and with chocolate lining their lips. Party hats. Enough candy to fill the largest bowl in the kitchen.

As she eats, Sam distracts herself from crying by tracing the shadows the sunlight casts as it breaks through wild growing trees and grasses that have even conquered half of the bench Sam sits on. She chews slowly and doesn't think about her friend who laughed and wore a party hat and years later kissed Sam until she blushed, because now, that friend is silent and dead.

"I am eating a museum piece," Sam tells a red chested bird that has decided to land on the bench next to her, curious. "Would you also like to eat parts of this exhibit?" She breaks off crumbs and places her offering in front of the bird, who tries it, then looks up at her for more. The bird's eyes and clawed feet are blurry, the colors that dye its feathers unset watercolors. "You can't be greedy, you have to savor this," Sam says, but shares with the bird all the same.

After the food, Sam pulls a book from her backpack, the last one she still carries with her from the beekeeper's house. Her nose almost touches the page, and she squints to make the words come into focus. Sam reads aloud to the bird the story of a girl not unlike Sam, a girl walking a road that promises magic at its end. The bird flies off somewhere in the middle of the last chapter, but Sam reads all of it out loud regardless as if her tongue were trying to cast the letters' shapes into her memory.

When Sam is done reading, and the girl in the story has reached the end of the road, which is not magic at all, just home, Sam knows she should leave the book there instead of carrying unnecessary weight. She thinks she has learned this, not to carry her losses with her and burden herself with stories that are but silence after the last page is read, but she cannot bear to leave the book.

Sunset would always bring the brightest colors, and Sam loves it best of all the times of day. She can make out the colors still, even if the lines the clouds draw in the fading light have gone blurry.

Sam no longer reads, and while she manages not to cry for sunsets, today she is finally crying for books.

It is the first time she has cried since she was told her vision would go; the tears seem to have waited, to have gathered, and now they cannot be stopped.

She sits down on a couch that isn't hers in a house that isn't hers, with a book she found there open on her lap. Her eyes just will not let her read it. The pages give her only silence, no more words, and no more stories. And so Sam cries and cries. She falls asleep on the couch, and in the morning she puts the silent book she'll never read aside, focuses on walking instead.

There are smells of grass and pollen, earth. She tries to feel the ground beneath her feet, soft grass, asphalt, gravel. She has found a stick by the road, and finally resigns herself to using it to navigate the world. When she could still read, Sam did not submit to relying on a stick, but now that her books are gone, she allows herself this crutch.

It will not be long now, not long at all, until darkness falls.

The garden wall is too high to climb, but the gate is still unlocked. For a moment, the touch of the gate's iron makes Sam remember the beekeeper, who might have forgotten Sam the morning she left; after all, they only shared one night.

The gate opens easily at first, then sticks a little, just like Sam remembers. She had not thought that she would ever return here, to the place where she grew up. When she left this place, she had thought that she would find a new home in the research colony, a home and something meaningful to do, a home filled with shared happiness. When her feet start down the garden path, Sam remembers that she knew happiness here: party hats, balloons, the sour-sweet novelty of her first crush. Learning to love science. She also remembers silence.

That day, the silence had woken her. The painful sounds of hard-won breathing had gone, and outside, the demands of ravens echoed. That day, Sam had found herself an orphan. The proof lay there on soft pillows, blanket-wrapped, and in her memory, Sam's own cries turned to haunting echoes. She fled from the memory as if it were a weight she shouldn't carry, but silence cannot be outrun. Like the girl in the story Sam read to the bird, Sam's own road ends where it started.

The gate creaks, a sharp, bright noise of metal. The garden path echoes back Sam's footfalls and the regular tapping of her stick. She will find something better than this stick; the attic is full of things, things her father stashed there from his practice. The attic will smell of dust and warmth now, and Sam is already looking forward to being up there. She is looking forward already to taking off her shoes.

As Sam reaches the steps that lead up to the front door, the scent of lilies welcomes her. Her mother planted these, years ago, and on an impulse, Sam turns toward where she knows the flowers grow. Her hands find them even closer than she expects, the heads bobbing toward her in the wind. Sam kneels in the dirt and reaches for them. She doesn't remember what color they are. The petals are soft, and Sam brushes her lips across them, sure that pollen will line her hands. She kisses the flower, a kiss meant for the woman that planted them.

The vibrato of wings brushes against her lips, and Sam remembers a body banded yellow and black. The insect hums, but does not move to reward Sam's kiss with a sting.

Sam pulls back, but the hum follows her as she climbs the steps and opens the door, goes inside. There will be no insect bodies scattered in her home, Sam swears, no echoes loud inside the house, and no more shattering silence. She feels around, familiarizing her arms and feet with corners and furniture. Sam remembers easily where things are, and with the bee humming, she realizes that she has already forgotten her tiny, silent apartment back at the colony.

Sam takes off her backpack, places it by the stairs and pulls out the book, the last she ever read. She finds her way to the family room to place the book on the mantel, right next to the picture frames. When she feels light fall inside through the window glass, Sam smiles and begins to hum along with the bee, the melody of home.

See Alexandra Seidel's story "A Picture of Home, in Silence" online at Metaphorosis.
If you liked it, leave a comment. Authors love that!
Remember to subscribe to our e-mail updates so you'll know when new stories are posted.

About the story

I wrote "A Picture of Home, in Silence" in early 2020. At the time, COVID-19 hadn't yet started dominating our everyday lives. Like many of my stories, this one started with a specific image, the main character looking at the stained glass windows and about how light breaks those colors into picture, and it grew from there.

A question for the author

Q: Do you ever feel bad for what you put your characters through?

A: Not really. Under my pseudonym, Alexa Piper, I created a character once that seemed like a boring, two-dimensional villain, so I gave them a backstory and someone who loved them. That character became harder to dispatch, but dispatch them I did.

About the author

Alexandra Seidel spent many a night stargazing when she was a child. These days, she writes stories and poems and drinks a lot of coffee (too much, some say). As Alexa Piper, she writes erotic romance that also leans toward the fantastical. You can follow her on Twitter @Alexa_Seidel or like her Facebook page (https://www.facebook.com/AlexaSeidelWrites/), and find out what she's up to at alexandraseidel.com.

The Chorley

Rachel Ayers

Little Annamarie wore a mournful expression. "Mama," she said, "I can't find my Chorley." Chorley was a ragged stuffed elephant that the girl had had since she was two.

"Where did you leave it?" the Mama asked, the air of distraction hardened on her features. She had taken off the VR glasses that she customarily wore throughout the long hours of the day, and even the child could see that she was irritated by the interruption.

"If I knowed, I wouldn't be sad," the girl pointed out.

"Knew," Mama corrected.

Annamarie stamped her foot. "Mama, I need my Chorley."

Mama sighed and turned away from her desk. "Child, I'm very busy with a big project. If you need your toy right now, you'll have to look for it."

She went back to tinkering with the things on her worktable: an odd assortment of wires and pentacles and computer chips and silver. This was merely a ruse, but Mama did not want the child to consider that Annamarie herself was the true project of the day. The weird energy of the awful, ancient house had combined with the child's own latent gifts, attracting or creating a ... thing. The thing came every night, and seemed to grow and fluctuate with the child's moods. It was intriguing, and unexpected, and Mama thought Annamarie might even have an early breakthrough, gaining a measure of control over her aura—most of the children in the Endeavor did not have any kind of control until they reached puberty. After weeks of monitoring it, she'd realized that the toy was somehow amplifying Annamarie's aural energies, and Mama decided that taking it would present the child with a fascinating new challenge.

It was not strictly prohibited in the Endeavor; side projects were allowed as long as they could be justified.

Annamarie spent a spare minute sulking before retreating in defeat; the Mama did not respond to this tactic.

Annamarie looked under her bed again, and in her closet. She was not, as a rule, a messy child, being rather precocious and having a strict Mama in the bargain. It was all the more mysterious that she couldn't find the toy, to which she had a deep attachment. She'd awakened from her nap to find it missing, and had looked all around their large and drafty house without a successful reunion with her lost Chorley.

At dinner Mama asked, "Did you look for your toy?"

"Yes, Mama." Annamarie was subdued.

Mama looked up from her soup and her newsscreen. "Did you find it?"

"No, Mama."

"Hmm. Well, I suppose you're too old for it, anyway."

This was grievously unfair, but Annamarie knew better than to remark upon it. Although she had an excellent vocabulary for a six-year-old, she could not explain to Mama that the stuffed toy had been painstakingly imbued with protective magic for the last four years, and that there were likely to be dire consequences if she were to retire to bed without it tonight. The spaces beneath the bed and within the wardrobe appeared to be perfectly mundane during daylight hours, but were in fact deep and dangerous repositories for the most nightmarish of creatures once darkness fell.

While she wanted to wail and kick her heels against the floor, Annamarie knew it would do no good; instead, she retreated to her bedroom. She looked around the familiar space, fighting the tears that threatened to fall down her plump cheeks.

She had a small desk, suitable to her short form, upon which she'd accumulated an assortment of electronic gadgets and loose ends from Mama's workshop, the yard, and the shadowy corners of the house. Annamarie had collected circuit boards since she liked the dark green shine of them, and countless wires, and other odds and ends, mostly gathered because of their interesting shapes.

There was a small, high window opposite the door, with a tattered pink curtain that hung limply over it. The curtain matched the quilt on the bed, and those two items were the beginning and end of any bright color in the room, except for, on a shelf over her bed, three other stuffed animals: a parrot, an anteater, and a jaguar. They had never held the special place in her heart which was reserved for the Chorley (named after the young elephant in the bedtime stories her Papa used to tell her).

She had two hours before bedtime, during which she was expected to study or, at the very most, quietly play. Mama was not supposed to be disturbed except during Meeting Times. Mama did not like other interruptions.

Annamarie pulled out her box of circuit boards, and a fistful of wires, and a small screwdriver she'd taken from the kitchen toolbox, and imitated the air of quiet contemplation Mama wore while she did her tinkering.

The girl frowned; she was missing something.

After a moment, she stood on her bed and pulled the other stuffed animals down to the floor with her. "I haven't knew you as long as my Chorley," she said quite solemnly, "but I still love you." She tapped her fingers against her lips, an uncommonly grown-up gesture. "I think you need to be boosted."

She selected a box-cutter—spirited away from Mama's worktable weeks ago—and ripped open the back of the jaguar without hesitation. Annamarie began to play intensely and with great purpose.

Mama, watching from the monitor, did not interrupt her child at bedtime. She was pleased and fascinated by this turn of events, which she had not anticipated, and she took notes for an hour, watching the child's selections and choices, enjoying the way the child mimicked her own work habits. The thaumo-meter hummed happily, measuring the surging energy around the child. Mama watched until the girl went to bed on her own initiative, the three newly modified stuffed animals arranged around her.

The thing that came in the night was perhaps more hungry than inherently evil, but still terrifying to little Annamarie. It oozed into the cracks created by darkness, nesting beneath the bed or curling in the closet. An unwary heel could be grabbed, tugged, and nibbled, if a dash to the bathroom was not properly executed.

The Chorley had protected her. The toy was alive with four years of devoted love; it was a powerful talisman against the thing, which was, after all, only acting according to its own nature. The Chorley repelled it, sent it scuttling for easier prey in other drafty houses. But now the Chorley was gone, and Annamarie had had to make do on short notice.

Mama straightened her glasses, ran her hands through her short-clipped hair, and turned on the dozen monitors which measured everything from the temperature of the room to the ectoplasmic content of the local atmosphere.

The other Mamas had much less to deal with. None of them had gotten stuck in a dark old house full of eaves and topped with crenellations—one variable too many, she'd argued, but been overruled—and most of the other Mamas still had their Papas around to help with their experiments. This Papa had gotten sentimental, protective of the innocent little girl, and that would not do. He'd been retired, peacefully enough. But then he'd tried to come back for Annamarie, and now Mama didn't know where he was, or if they'd even let him live.

She snorted to herself, turning off her computer screen and powering down her laptop for the night. She had a few hours of peace before the child woke. Annamarie was largely self-sufficient, but still required some persuasion in order to get her up and prepared to log in to her morning classes. Mama needed to sleep, but first she went through her own nightly ritual—which involved tea and a night light and a particular quilt, and which she never, ever would have admitted to performing to any of the other Mamas. She did not share anything with them beyond her notes on the child.

When Mama was fast asleep, and Annamarie tossed and turned beneath the surface of consciousness, the thing that came in the night began to ooze and creep into the girl's room. It had, as it always did, bypassed the lonely rooms of the house, and it moved by instinct away from the Mama's nightlight.

It slithered into the dark, cramped corner of the little girl's closet, watching her sleep. She was sweaty, muttering to herself and twitching—the best time, when it could invade the dreams and feed on the terror. An unwary foot was all well and good, but the thing that came in the night preferred fear to flesh. It liked to play with its food.

The child's talisman was gone: its bright blue glow, its glowering eyes, were not there to ward and guard the child. The thing that came in the night moved forward, undulating out of the closet, claws scraping into the cracks of the floorboards.

But it paused mid-rear before pouncing, studying the child on her bed more carefully. There was something wrong... something different.

The thing hissed, a slow angry boil of frustration and irritation.

Here were three new champions; and while they did not shine brightly, they cast their own faint glow through the room, and the edges of their light were painful to the thing that came in the night. They were nowhere near as strong as the Chorley, but they were vigilant, and there were three of them, and they were full of the love and playful energy of the child. Of course, Annamarie was extraordinary—or she would not have been chosen and taken for the Endeavor—and the toys were only one of the ways that her gift had manifested. That bright curiosity burned into something real, something that could affect the world in unexpected ways: it was exactly what the Mamas were trying to measure and control, with limited success. And now that power had been transferred into the toys, giving them a smaller measure of the child's aura, and granting her a sunny protection even as she slumbered.

The thing was forced to retreat, and it went, simmering with fury.

The Mama was unbearably smug during the conference call that took place during the early morning hours. She had every confidence that she understood the energies she'd measured.

"And she received no guidance from you on the matter?" the GrandMama asked.

"None at all," Mama assured her with a sniff. "She created three new guardians. All weaker than the one that's been soaking up her energy this whole time, but it was enough to get that... thing to leave her alone."

Another one of the Mamas spoke, hesitant. She was a new Mama, on her first child. "And you're certain that Annamarie doesn't suspect your part in any of this?"

"Of course not!" Mama said, though she did not really consider her answer before she said it. It had never even occurred to her as a possibility. Of course, the girl was precocious; all of the children were extraordinary. That was the whole point of the Endeavor. But they were still children, and Annamarie was only beginning to develop her talents.

"Keep a sharp eye on her," the GrandMama said. "The... thing is still a new development. We don't want your situation to go awry again."

The Mama schooled her face carefully, though she wanted to scowl. There had been no need to use that last word. This experiment was completely different, and Annamarie was far more talented than the last child the Mama had raised. It was hardly her fault that the last experiment had been abbreviated; of course, the child had died, so there was nothing that could be done about it except to move on. "I will certainly monitor the situation and present all my findings," she said. "On the child and the... thing."

She set aside her feelings of unease after the call. Certainly, there were more variables here than she had wanted, but she would work with what she was given, and she would be promoted within the Endeavor. If Annamarie lived, perhaps Mama could even move up with her. After all, she was the one who had thought of this experiment, and it looked like it might be just the emotional push the girl needed to advance her thaumatronics skills. If not with Annamarie, perhaps next time she could still begin with an older child, already aware of their aura; Mama had earned that much by now, surely. No more shepherding babies through their formative years. That would be a nice change.

For her part, when Annamarie woke, the girl was rested and relieved. The thing in the night had not gotten her, and her nightmares had been mild, even without her Chorley. She hugged her toys tightly in gratitude, and then got herself dressed and found breakfast and waited for Mama to log her into her class.

The toys were left to rest on the neatly-made bed, rather than the shelf above, and they were pleased with their change in status. It was not every day that a toy was elevated to best and beloved, and now that all three of them were now on the bed, well, they could not help but be pleased with themselves.

After her classes, and after Annamarie finished her walk—ten times around the yard, no more, no less—she took her nap with all three toys cuddled in her arms. None of them were particularly large, and with the modifications she'd made, they all had a few sharp edges and pokey bits. The girl didn't mind; she loved them all the more now that she'd made it through a night with them.

When she woke she had a little while before Meeting Time. Mama was busy in her office. She was very pleasant today, and had given Annamarie a cookie when she finished lessons. After her nap, Annamarie had an odd idea.

"Are you sure?" she asked the anteater, who seemed the wisest of the three.

The stuffed toy did not answer out loud, but Annamarie nodded reluctant understanding nonetheless.

Taking the jaguar under her elbow for courage, she crept out of her room, avoiding the creaking floorboards and slipping through Mama's bedroom door, opening it just shy of where it let out a long creaking groan. She rarely came in here; it was a cold room, always clean and tidy but never comfortable. Mama's bed was small, like her own, and although the room was much larger than Annamarie's, there was scarcely any more furniture in it.

Annamarie stopped, listening. She thought she heard a soft rustling from the darkness beneath the bed. She gripped the jaguar extra tight around the middle; the jaguar did not mind. Annamarie took comfort from his steady, stealthy presence, and edged around the room toward the closet.

This door let out a soft whine and Annamarie stopped with her head cocked, listening for Mama. She shivered and took one of the deep good breaths, and then she looked up on the top shelf of the closet.

There was her Chorley, carelessly flung so that it had toppled over on its side and lay on both of its own big, floppy ears. Annamarie let out a little sniffle at this pathetic sight. She reached her arms up, the jaguar still grasped by one ankle, and stood on tippy toes, but came nowhere close to reaching the stuffed elephant.

Annamarie left Mama's bedroom door propped open and crept back to her own room, sliding her bare feet along the rough floorboards where she knew they wouldn't creak. She gulped for air, back in her own room, and crushed the jaguar against her cheek for a final boost to her courage. Then she took the parrot and left her room again.

She paused outside Mama's office door; Mama was on the phone with someone, talking in one of the other languages. She was leaned back in her chair, with one arm over her eyes. While Annamarie watched, Mama straightened and lowered her arm, and her eyes brushed past the doorway where Annamarie stood.

But she didn't see Annamarie. She swiveled to face her desk, and Annamarie wrenched herself along.

She hovered uncertainly at Mama's closet door, looking at her Chorley. The one eye she could see—a scratched black button peeking over the edge of the shelf—implored Annamarie for rescue.

The little girl braced her feet evenly beneath her and tossed the parrot up toward the top of the closet. It was an impossible throw in the too-narrow space between the door and the shelf, and the elephant rested heavily and certainly on that shelf. Yet an instant later, both toys came tumbling back down and the girl caught them with no more than a muffled, feathery thump.

She heard a clunk and a clatter from Mama's office, and whirled around, clutching her toys. Another moment passed without a sound, and she tiptoed to the door, edging around Mama's dresser. When she passed the ugly little porcelain nightlight, the elephant's trunk snagged on the cord, and the thing tipped over with a *crunchthud*. The girl winced and froze. She set the light back upright, and fled to her own room. She did not tell Mama about the nightlight—Mama had taken her Chorley, after all, and could not be trusted—and there were no monitors in Mama's room, so, in later review, the other Mamas would never fully understand what happened that night.

When Mama came and got her for Meeting Time, the girl was on the floor, contentedly playing the coding game on her tablet. The parrot, anteater, and jaguar were ranged around her, as though they were participating in the programming.

"Make your bed more tidily tomorrow, Annamarie," Mama said. "It's very lumpy today."

"Yes, Mama," the girl said.

"Go and wash your hands and join me for supper," Mama said.

"Yes, Mama." She leapt up from the floor, grinning, but Mama had already started down the hall.

They ate a quiet dinner, and when they were done, Mama went back to her office and the girl went back to her room to do her homework.

When she went to bed that night, Mama was disgruntled to find that the bulb of her nightlight was not working. She gave a soft, muttered curse; she didn't have any spares. She'd have to get one tomorrow. Still, she was a grown woman, she reasoned. How much could a child's boogeyman really bother her?

At least she thought so, for a few more hours.

Annamarie slept blissfully well that night, with her modified toys ranged around her and the Chorley hugged tight in her arms. In the morning she woke late.

GrandMama was there. Annamarie did not like her. "Where's Mama?"

The old woman sniffed. "She's not… well. She won't be looking after you anymore."

"Will I get to see Papa?" A surge of excitement rippled through her.

"No," GrandMama said quickly. "No, you'll have a new Mama. I've come to take you to her." She glared around Annamarie's room; she found no fault with it, but still did not like the room… or the house, for that matter.

It took next to no time for Annamarie to dress and gather her things, hastily arranging her toys beneath her clothing. GrandMama recalled, uneasily, the Mama's report on how Annamarie had used her toys to channel her growing power… but with so many changes today, she would not take the toys from the child now. No, a smooth transition would be best; once everything else was under control, a new Mama could get the girl in line. GrandMama offered a hand, which the child reached to take, but a yucky jolt went through Annamarie's arm. She pulled back to grip her suitcase instead.

"Are you ready, then, child?" GrandMama asked.

Annamarie nodded. Mama had always told her that she had to obey GrandMama, but Mama had taken her Chorley. Annamarie made a secret promise to her Chorley that she would not trust GrandMama, not ever. Or the new Mama either. Annamarie walked down the steps after GrandMama: suitcase dragging behind her, and, tucked carefully into the bag over her shoulder, her Chorley.

See Rachel Ayers's story "The Chorley" online at Metaphorosis.
If you liked it, leave a comment. Authors love that!
Remember to subscribe to our e-mail updates so you'll know when new stories are posted.

About the story

I had this image in my head of the valiant teddy bear defending a sleeping child from the monster in the dark... and I wondered what would happen if the toy hero were taken away. (Which I guess makes me the Mama in this scenario...)

A question for the author

Q: What distracts you?
A: The next idea... It's hard to focus on one story at a time when the next idea is — oooh, shiny squirrels!

About the author

Rachel Ayers lives in Alaska, where she writes cabaret shows, daydreams, and looks at mountains a lot. She has a degree in Library and Information Science, which comes in handy at odd hours, and she shares speculative poetry and flash fiction (and cat pictures) at patreon.com/richlayers

@richlayers

August

Calling Me Home

Spencer Nitkey

The entanglement circuit burns as it lights a fire right behind my eyes. I hear my daughter crying in the moments before the circuit switches. An imagined voice, I'm sure. Then the pain spreads like blood through my chest, and the stars outside the transport ship window slow, stop, and disappear.

I come to in my bed back home. The baby monitor plays a low whine that crescendos into a full-scale cry. It is the first thing I hear back in this body. I put my hand on my husband's back as he grunts and starts to sit up.

"It's okay. I've got it," I tell him, tripping over my old tongue.

I get up and stumble, still not sure footed in my old body. I lean against the hallway wall to catch my balance. In Altair's room, I sit in the rocking chair near the crib, and hold Altair in the crook of my arm and feed her. I hope this is what she wants. I love Altair so deeply. She is beautiful and strange, but her wants are foreign to me. I am, I guess, stabbing in the dark. She focuses, her whole face pressed together in concentration, on sucking the formula from the bottle. I breathe a sigh of relief. She was hungry. I helped fix it. This is worth every bit of the discomfort it takes to transfer, even if just for a few hours. It's rare they let me take an unscheduled transfer home.

"It's okay," I whisper. The sun is rising, and the sounds of early commuters slowly roar until the noise-cancellation flicks on and there's an ambient quiet again. I sit Altair in a high chair near the kitchen table and pour boiling water over the coffee grinds in the French press.

My husband comes out when the chestnut crepes are almost done cooking. He looks exhausted. I'm sure I do too, the weariness carried over from my spaceskin to this one. It is nice to be working with small and delicate things for a moment. The small flick of the knife, the gentle rocking of Altair, all so different from the lumbering weight of the minerals, mining equipment, and explosives I work with in the Belt. I enjoy this smaller, more sensitive body in these small spurts.

"Is it Saturday, already?" he asks.

"No. I get a few hours break during the trip from Ceres to Hygiea and thought I'd surprise you," I answer.

"I'm glad you did," he says as he kisses my forehead. "It's nice to see you for a little while, at least." The words sound like drill bits snapping, and I take it too personally.

"Well, we need money don't we?" I say. He tightens his jaw, and I watch it loosen. He slouches, then takes a few steps back from me, like he is about to apologize for my shortness. Communicating back home is always hard. The bodily adjustments are one thing, but moving seamlessly from a military-style mining operation to domestic conversation is hard. In the Belt, there are clear goals, and in my skin I can achieve each and every one of them. It's an intoxicating feeling. Here on earth, my body adjusts quickly. My mind doesn't.

I turn to Altair, who is making slurping noises, harvesting drool from her hands back into her mouth. She still makes no sense to me—a confluence of atoms and biology and accident that resulted in this: the most beautiful thing I've ever seen—but still, I love her. I am on my toes around her, waiting for the leg of her chair to tip, a piece of food to lodge in her fragile throat, but she is mine, and so are the doubt and uncertainty she casts on me.

My husband takes a large bite of crepe and doesn't say anything. I regret our tiff already, he's so handsome in the morning light, but the circuit behind my head beeps, and I have five minutes to lie back down in bed and get ready for the return.

He winces when the sound rings through the kitchen. The baby starts crying and he takes her in his arms and kisses me on the forehead. The circuit jolts to life and I feel the heat of it already.

"I love you," I say.

"I love you, too."

I crawl into bed, lay down, close my eyes, and wait.

I'm so tired I think my mechanized space-skin is about to crack open and let the small ooze of me leak out like a spilled drink. My biological brain is resting, sleeping, emptied and recovering, in my body back home, and this skin doesn't need sleep to flush protein buildup the same way biological brains do. My physical body sleeps all the time, it's just my consciousness that doesn't. I am awake nearly 24 hours a day, especially when working. Still, I am tired; I want static nothingness just for a few hours. I don't have time, though. I have been hearing Altair cry all day, her small voice ricocheting through the wiring and the acoustic chamber that replicates my ears. I know I can't actually hear her, but this memory of her voice feels like it is calling me back to Earth. Even with all the hell I am going through on Hygiea, her voice is all I think about, more than the alignment on the sonic drill, or tension in the tether, or the carrying capacity of the supply train.

I clock out for my hour off, and already the entanglement circuit is spinning. I try to swallow the spreading pain and imagine the trillion spinning photon-like particles that make up my mind in the circuit that are moving a trillion other, entangled particles in my brain back home, lying in bed. The sun blooms inside me, and the inside of the transport ship vanishes.

I wake up to the sun setting through the open window. Warm summer air washes over my skin. I roll over and look at the clock. It's 8:00 pm. I hear the faint sounds of television, and walk out into the living room, unsteady, eyes drooping low.

"You're up!" my husband whisper-shouts, careful not to scare Altair, when he hears me creaking towards him. He wraps me up, tightly, and I feel like all my fraying parts are being pulled back together.

"I was worried I'd miss you," he says. "How are you doing? Can I get you something?"

"A drink, please," I say.

"I have an open bottle of red?"

"Stronger."

He pours me a few fingers of my good whiskey, which he never drinks. He looks concerned as I down it in one sip.

"Everything alright?"

I can't hold any of it back. "Hygiea is a nightmare. Chock full of palladium, so our targets are sky-high, but so small the gravity's just nothing. Even in the suit, we have to do everything tethered, so it's all twice as hard and four times as slow. We were supposed to get a week off—"

"Claire no —" he interrupts. He already knows where this is going, and I can see the joy fall from his face.

"But it's looking like we're not even getting a weekend, and our week is being deferred until we hit our targets," I finish the thought. I hate disappointing him. I hate not being able to tell him how I feel about him. How thoughts of him keep my wiring warm in the freeze of the belt. How thoughts of his voice comfort me almost as much as thoughts of Altair. How I think about the first meal he cooked me when I am mining and want nothing more than to taste something even though I'm never hungry. How I thank him quietly every time I transfer for quitting his career as a software engineer to raise Altair while I work.

"I'm sorry," he says, and I can't help but wonder what he's sorry for. For me? For himself? For Altair? Now that our reunion is dampened, I can see how tired he looks beneath the effort he puts on to hide it. The bags under his gray eyes make them look like waning moons with long shadows. His wrinkles seem deeper set. He hasn't been sleeping. He's skinnier, his arms slightly deflated, and he has a small pouch, or the beginnings of one. I wish I had the energy to tell him how gorgeous he looks. He is going to age well, I think.

"It's just hard to be a single parent all the time," he says, rinsing his wine glass in the kitchen. "Do you ever regret it?"

I still have four more years of this on my contract that I signed when I was eighteen. I remember the recruiter in a crisp suit calling me over to his booth at the high school college fair. When he told me the company could pay for all four years of my undergraduate degree and then give me five years of work experience, guaranteed, I thought he was making fun of me. When he didn't laugh, I almost cried with joy, I was so happy to sign. I remember the hours I spent in the entanglement surgery 12 months before my ship-out date. I was already pregnant, but they said it would be fine. They installed the circuit. They opened my skull and targeted the sixteen trillion particles they found that contained my consciousness. They passed a laser through them and entangled them with the neural-processing center of my space skin and then installed the circuit that could agitate them simultaneously, creating a line of communication and transfer. They shipped my space skin to Ceres and I had one year to enjoy earth before my skin arrived and I would transfer.

Franklin doesn't understand why I'm not more upset. And I am upset, but not like he is. I don't know how to explain it. Home, I feel weak and tired. I don't know what I'm doing here. I love Altair, but I don't know how to love her right. I don't know what I'm doing when I hold her, but I hold her as often as I can, like it's all I've ever known how to do. Then, when I transfer, suddenly, I'm unstoppable. There are clear, concrete objectives. Build this. Carry that. Extract this much. And I can do it. Everything they ask of me, I can do. My body moves intentionally. It is intoxicating: waking up from uncertainty into the skin of a superhero and knowing exactly what my job is.

And would I take a different deal? I don't think so. If I'd known every gory detail the recruiter neglected to tell me, 18-year-old me would have ran the other way. The me now couldn't leave everything I've gained behind. I met Franklin at a college in Philadelphia I could have never afforded on my own. I remember his dumb smile beaming across the library from behind a tattered copy of Chekhov stories, and I am glad I made the deal, despite everything. I look over at Altair, sitting on a high chair, and I am glad that I had the chance to make something so perfect with Franklin. Despite all the pain, it's hard to look at them and consider ever giving it up.

"If there were a way out, would you even take it?" he asks, tired of waiting for me to respond.

"I only have an hour," I say, in lieu of addressing his point. It's not worth thinking about an impossibility. "Can I change her? She smells." I should apologize, but there's nothing I can do about it. I signed a contract. He married me. Here we are. I try to remember that and hope he can, too.

"Of course you can," he says. "That'd be really nice." It's an act of love. He lets me feel like a parent when I have no right to.

I set Altair on the changing table, and her feet are small. My husband watches over my shoulder as I coo. She is a beautiful, profoundly magical person. The fact that I made her seems—especially as I am now, barely functional in my own skin—impossible.

When I'm done, I spend an hour holding Altair close to me, as close as I can. I stare for a very long time at her face as a movie plays softly. I try to interpret the thoughts and emotions that pass through her. Her brow furrows and I wonder if she is trying to decipher the look on my face, like I am trying to decipher the look on hers. The hour passes quickly this way. Then the circuit chimes on the back of my head. I hand her back to my husband and head towards the bedroom. He kisses my forehead, like he does every time we say goodbye. Even when we are fighting.

The circuit fires and my bedroom disappears. The last sound I hear is Altair babbling to my husband. "Goodbye," I whisper.

Moses died on the rig today, so witnesses get an afternoon of mourning time to spend with our families. They don't say this, but I know we also get time off because we already reached our weekly goals. If we were behind, it wouldn't matter how many people died:

we'd still be working. I'm numb from it, so I hardly notice the transfer.

When I come to, I am in the bedroom with the blinds drawn, my feet still in stirrups from the negatrophic workout my bed just finished. I fish my feet out of the metal loops, and lie there for a few minutes. I don't have the energy or inclination to get up. I didn't realize how much I loved the psychic comfort of sleep until now. Now that it's denied to me.

I was there when it happened, when Moses died. The images of it reoccur to me, now. His tether broke loose and wrapped around his sternum. We had warned the company about faulty tethers, but they hadn't listened. When the anchor pulled down, it practically sliced him in half. I watch the last minutes of it in my memory—I watch his electric eyes flicker, lose power, and fade forever. As I watched Moses die, Altair's cries sang in the background and I couldn't understand anything about my life for a few minutes. If I'd had lungs, I'm sure I would have been hyperventilating.

They warned us when we first shipped out: if we aren't transferred out of a skin and it gets destroyed, our consciousness putters out, too. Someone is supposed to be monitoring us as we work, to avoid things like this, but Moses's death confirms what we all suspect: the company is either too short-staffed or too indifferent to really monitor us. Be careful, they told us. Be smart. And we do feel invincible in the suits. The first day, I remember the rush. So strong and sturdy. We walked as steel monsters and were proud. When he died, I watched Moses's biomatter, a dense tangle of neural cells congealed near his circuit, where they inserted the trillions of entangled consciousness particles, float into the vacuum of space. Rescue reached him after the tether broke and tried to initiate a transfer, but by then there was nothing left *to* transfer. I imagine his body back home, a vacant, mindless husk someone still has to kill and bury. Company men will knock on the door, and his wife will answer it and not really understand. She won't know he died until the company tells her. His heart will still be beating, his lungs pumping air in and out of his blood. He will die twice. The company won't tell his wife that he died because they wouldn't replace the tethers, even though we have been begging for new ones for months. They will just tell her he's dead, and let her do the dirty work.

You'd think that watching someone die in a mech-suit wouldn't be traumatic. There's no blood, no guts—just screws, tubes and steaming pistons, the small grey film of their mind wavering like petals to the dirt. But when that person was your friend, when you've known him for five years and, to you, he's only ever been that suit, it really isn't any better than watching a human body get torn apart: it's still death.

The house is quiet. I notice that the baby monitor isn't on and when I look for it on the bedside table it isn't there either. I get up to explore. No one is home, I realize pretty quickly. My chest buzzes with sadness.

I look for a note and find one stuck to the fridge with a magnet.

"Visiting my parents, call if home. Love, Franklin."

I miss my husband, of course, but I hurt for Altair. Her absence shocks like a faulty battery, sharp, alive, electric. I open all the blinds in the house to let the night in. The sky is like an over-washed blanket; the stars, a hundred odd holes torn through the fabric. I look up and try to find my other body, vacant in a transport pod somewhere in the asteroid belt. I try to swallow the sadness, keep it from staying lodged in my throat.

I lie on my back on the asphalt of the driveway outside. Is it even worth calling him? I'll be gone again before I could make the trip to his parents. What good would it do either of us? A rushed conversation? A glimpse of each other's faces? Apologies that wouldn't change anything? I want to see him, but I don't want to fight about something I can't change. I don't want to be reminded of all the pain I cause someone I love.

I need to see Altair though, so I call. The line rings and rings. I'm ready to give up when Franklin answers, and his face fills the camera, shadowed with stubble and wild eyebrows.

"Claire!" he shouts, a little drunk. "You're home. How long?"

"Half-day," I mutter.

"Oh. So you can't make it?"

"No, I'm sorry," I say.

"They let you off for my birthday?" he asks. "I'm sorry, if I had known, we wouldn't have left."

Shit. I hadn't even realized. Time takes on such an ethereal, useless quality in space. It's not grounded in anything, so it's easy to lose track of.

"No," I say. "Just a lucky coincidence," half-heartedly, in a way I am sure betrays the truth.

"Do you want to see Altair?" he asks. If he knows that I forgot, he doesn't say anything. I want to thank him for this, but don't know how. There's so much I don't know how to do.

Altair suddenly fills the blurry screen, a hundred or so pixels of her. Still, there she is. Wisps of brown hair dot her smooth head. Her eyes blink confusedly and look nowhere in particular. I can see her chubby fingers smack at the phone. God, she's smart, I think. And for a minute or two I don't think about, or see, anything other than her, this little person who is already so much better than I am. The blinker on my neck flashes and I tell my husband I have to go.

"Happy birthday, baby," I say as he takes the phone back. "I love you."

Later, I hold the phone on my chest as the circuit flashes. I try to think of her, and hope maybe I will hear her voice in the Belt again.

It is Altair's first birthday today, exactly fourteen days after Franklin's, and I do get this day off. I am a little late. There were loose charges near the sonic drill, more faulty equipment the company had been too cheap to replace. Their anchors had to be repaired, and I was the only one active in the sector, so I ended up working three more hours before I clocked out. Three more hours away from Altair and Franklin. The whir of the entanglement circuit cuts me across space and I wake up to the sound of muffled laughter, footsteps, and the smell of roasted garlic.

I swivel out of bed but stay in the room for a moment. The afternoon air is stale, and the light from the sun filters through dust particles, a thin curtain of sparkling light. My husband's computer is closed next to the domestic transfer station that activates my circuit when they call me back to the Belt. Downstairs thrums with houseguests. I peek my head out from the stairwell and I watch Altair recognize me, slung over her father's shoulder. She garbles something incoherent and magical. My chest erupts like an ignited engine. Franklin's sister is the first to see me. Soon everyone is crowded around me except Franklin.

Altair is passed from one parent to another until she ends up in my arm. I field questions and side-hugs from friends and neighbors and family. I try to remember how to talk to people who aren't coworkers. I ask them questions about their children, and try to keep them talking so I don't have to; most oblige.

I realize how little I know about them. I didn't realize I was socially isolated from Earth until now. Nine months into the program, and I'm already a stranger to everyone I was friends with before. In the Belt, everything is more urgent. Each day is a navigation around death. The minerals we extract fuel everything on earth. And I'm supposed to care about barbecues, preschool teachers, and Home Owners' Association rules. I try, today. I really do.

I find Franklin, finally, and slide up next to him, pressing Altair between us. When I am feeling far from him, or when we are fighting, reminding each other of Altair helps. It's nice to remember the things that our love, done right, can make. He smiles and plays with Altair's feet.

"Have you checked for any packages recently?" I ask him.

"No. I've been a little busy setting everything up," he says. "Where were you?"

"Work," I answer. "Where else?"

"You were supposed to be here," he says, which is true.

"What did you want me to do about it?" I ask. "They weren't going to sign off until I finished loading—" I stop myself. "You don't care," I snipe. Which is both fair and unfair.

I take Altair and walk to the front door to check the porch for packages. A box with my company's logo printed on it is sitting there. I squat low to the ground and, with my free arm, pick the box up and bring it into the kitchen. I watch Franklin's face turn ghost-white at the sight of the logo. Fear, more than anything else. But I am too excited to care. I ask his sister for the pair of scissors we keep in the pantry and cut the box open.

I am giddy for the first time all day since watching Altair recognize me. With everyone watching me, I pull out a shimmering silver-colored locket, and I beam. There's another, smaller box that I take and slide into my pocket.

"It's a palladium, iridium, and ruthenium alloy," I announce to everyone, but really only to Franklin. "It's from my first haul in the Belt. I got to set aside a little metal from the first mining operation I was a part of. This is from space, Altair. It's why I've been so far from you. It's yours now."

I look up from Altair hoping to see Franklin smiling. He is. But there are no wrinkles on the corners of his eyes. It is even and not lopsided slightly to the right. His eyebrows are flat. It looks nothing like his real smile and I feel things break in me, like a thousand whirring gears and pistons all snapping in the wrong direction. I hold my breath for four seconds, trying to steady it, and look down at Altair. Her chubby fingers swipe at the chain, and her eyes reflect the shine of it. I watch the small dance of curiosity as she writhes. I let the joy of her set my gears back in place. I don't really look at anyone but her for the rest of the party.

After the last guest leaves, we clean the house in quiet. Normally, I'd ask him to play some music on the speaker, something to cut against the tension that stretches between us;

the air itself taut and pulled back in to a thin, breakable surface. Now, we clean in silence. I am afraid to ask. Speaking the right words seems impossible right now.

We put Altair to bed early. She is exhausted from the party. So are we. Beneath the cool blue light of the television, my husband and I sit up in our bed.

"You know," I say. "There was one more thing in the box that got delivered today."

"Oh?" he says, half-listening.

I reach into my bedside table, beneath the entanglement port and pull out the small box and open it.

I take the small ring and turn it over in my hand. Two thin strips of platinum vine around each other until they reach the head where they prong out and enwrap a moissanite diamond. I put it in his hand, and already it is refracting the bedside table lamp in a dozen directions. He looks up at me.

"It was supposed to get here in time for your birthday," I say. "The platinum is from Ceres. And the stone is from a meteorite crater on Vesta." He looks up at me. "I know this is hard. And I'm sorry I'm not here. And I'm sorry I'm not a better wife or mom. It's a small comfort, but I think about you all the time, Franklin."

"I think about you, too," he says, rolling the ring around his hand. He gets up and turns the ceiling light on and looks at the brilliant stone beneath the light. I see tears in his eyes. "It's really beautiful, Claire."

"Think about me mining when you look at it," I say.

We kiss. I get to sleep. I get to sink beneath the sheets and let the cotton warm my skin. The dark comes over me and the first few times I'm about to lose consciousness, I flinch, expecting the shuddering jolt of transfer, but each time it doesn't come, I relax a little more. A little around midnight, I fall asleep. I am certain I was smiling.

Around 4am the baby monitor begins speaking in a loud voice. *Altair's temperature has exceeded 102 degrees. Current at-home-remedies are having minimal effect. Immediate transfer to medical professional recommended. Immediate transfer to medical professional recommended.* We both run out of bed and into Altair's room. Franklin checks her temperature manually. While he is gone for the thermometer, I put my hand against her head and pretended I know what temperature her head normally feels like.

When the thermometer returns 102.2 degrees, we hurry into the car and set the autopilot to the closest emergency room.

I turn off the autopilot in the car, so we can rush to the hospital. Franklin holds Altair. He rocks and coos to her as I speed through the empty lanes of traffic. The street lights fill the road with cones of yellow light, and I cycle through every catastrophe I can imagine. Franklin is immersed in the moment, taken up entirely by Altair. Her crying hits my periphery for a moment and I tear up. I wipe my eyes and focus on the road.

When we finally get to the emergency room, I drop Franklin and Altair by the door and then find parking. As I back in to the first open spot I find, I hear the circuit's beep. I flinch. Then, I feel the vibration at the back of my skull. The circuit call shudders my bones. My heart races uncontrollably. The company wasn't supposed to call me back for another three days. I am miles from home and my baby is dying.

I am far from home, so the authentication signal from the domestic transfer station will take slightly longer to reach my circuit. Maybe I have six minutes instead of five. I run into the hospital and Franklin and Altair have already been taken to an exam room. I try to ask where they are, but I can hardly talk through the beeping in my head. It rings and rings. I feel like I'm losing control of my body. My heart is beating too fast. My breaths are shallow, lungs catching on my ribs with each hitched exhalation. I am sweating too. My body is incoherent. So are my words. Altair could be dying, and I am going to be thrown from this body in minutes. Maybe seconds now. I can hear the entanglement circuit whir to life; the authentication signal reached the circuit. I am crying inconsolably on the ground, screaming Altair's name. I try to hold on, weld my consciousness to this brain. I scream as the edges blur. There's no holding on. The last thing I think I hear is Altair's crying, then I'm gone.

As soon as I'm conscious in my spaceskin I try to talk to my supervisor. I need to be sent back, I tell her, my child is sick. She tells me that my child will be sick whether or not I am there, and the company needs me in the Belt. A rush order for a Lunar base came in and without Moses, there was no way they could fill it in time. Everyone needs to make sacrifices. I can spare an eighteen-hour shift of mining to help my team-members out, she tells me. I get to work.

All I can think about is Altair, which makes the work slower, which makes me think more about Altair. I'm used to getting lost in my labor, worries and anxieties melting in the mechanized concentration. Today, Altair's small, failing body hovers, already a phantasm, near everything.

Twenty-hours later, after we've loaded the processing ship with a full order of palladium, I get approved for a transfer. My supervisor enters her approval key, and the circuit embedded in my spaceskin's neck whirs to life. It takes longer than normal to transfer out this time. I wonder if that's because my body is still far from the transfer station. I wait for the signal to reach my body.

Then it happens all in one, whirring hot instant, and I come to in a hospital with a face already wet with tears. My rediscovered lungs are already spasming. I turn hard, and almost fall out of the bed.

Franklin puts his hand on my shoulder and I look up. The sun rising through the window behind him means I only see him in silhouette. When he leans closer to me, I see the sleeplessness tattooed across his face. I wonder if, in a few years, when I'm home, those lines and bags will fade. I hope they don't. I don't ever want to forget what he did for us, for Altair. These tired imperfections are, almost, brushstrokes. I want to kiss him. The tears come harder.

"Altair?" I manage to ask.

Franklin twists and lifts Altair out of a crib nearby. He brings her down towards me.

"She's fine. Doctors think it was a stomach bug or something. She's okay now. Her temperature fell really quickly. She's okay."

I am crying over Altair and holding her as close to my chest as I possibly can.

"I can't do this anymore," I say. "I just can't. It's too much. It's too much. I'm sorry. I can't."

My husband takes me and Altair home. I am still crying sporadically. When I can talk, I say I'm done. I say I can't imagine going back. My husband lets autopilot drive us slowly home while he holds me and runs his fingers through my hair.

"It'll be okay," he says.

"How the fuck is this going to be okay?" I whisper, and then I start crying again.

He pauses for a moment. I watch him think, calculate variables, check two sides of an equation to see if they are equal.

"I have a, well, it's not a solution, but it might be part of one," he says.

"What are you talking about, Franklin?" I say, exhausted.

"Let me show you when we get home."

Our car pulls in the driveway and Franklin helps me inside. I am still carrying Altair. My ankle hurts. When I transferred out, a nurse caught my head from hitting the floor, but my ankle twisted under the weight of my body as it collapsed. As we walk inside our home, I refuse, silently, to put Altair down. The pain in my ankle oscillates with the extra weight, but that doesn't matter. It's my job to keep Altair safe. I keep the warmth of her pressed up against me, desperate, as Franklin leads me into the bedroom.

He opens his computer, still on the bedside table next to the transfer port. He opens a screen with lines and lines of code flashing across it.

"What is this?" I ask.

He pauses for a minute. I recognize this face. He is deciding how best to explain something simply without dumbing it down too much to offend me. It's one of my favorite things he does, though I haven't seen it since I shipped out. There hasn't been much time for casual conversation; almost everything we talk about now revolves around Altair or my work.

"Well, look, you can only ever transfer with supervisor approval, right?"

"Right?"

"Well, that means there's some kind of authentication that needs to happen—"

I think I know where this is going, and I also know it's a dead end, and highly illegal. "I know, but there's no way to—" I say before he interrupts me.

"Let me finish," he says. He's excited. There's a manic energy in his eyes. "So they authenticate to transfer you home, from the Belt, but then how do they send you back without an authentication here, on Earth? Well, I wondered that for a while. I wondered if maybe when they called you back, they entered a second authentication, which wouldn't help us at all. But I started to think more. And tinker with that port there. They don't authenticate twice, because then they'd have to transfer the code back to Earth and then into this port, which is a redundancy they'd try to avoid. So I checked. It turns out what they're doing, and this is actually pretty cool, is essentially sending a second authentication with you when you transfer. It's—" he pauses for a moment to watch if I'm following. I've stopped crying, engrossed in what he's been saying. "— essentially a return ticket. They embed it with the consciousness data transfer but store it here, in the transfer station. So when they call you back, they just have to agitate the entangled particles in your spaceskin, and your consciousness particles here will automatically start their transfer spin. Which means—" By now he's gesticulating wildly, like he did when he came home with a new program solution, before he stopped working to take care of Altair. "—that if we copy that return ticket, and embed it in your consciousness data, we can send you back with an extra authentication. You could transfer on your own!" He finishes with a flourish of his hands.

"But of course it's encrypted, right?" I ask, still in disbelief that he's thought this much about it.

"It's a simple encryption. I don't think they thought anyone would bother to try to copy an authentication key, anyway. Why would they? Besides, they hire engineers and athletes, not coders. It'd be easy to fake a new one."

I don't respond for a minute. I don't say anything. It's ridiculous, hardly worth trying. Besides, even if I did it once, the company would know and be furious. The house beeps to let us know the car is done charging. The noise brings tears to my eyes. I paw, for a moment, at my skull, thinking I was being called back already. My heart rate shoots up.

"You say you can't do this anymore. This is a way out," Franklin says.

"No," I say, looking down at Altair, nestled in the crook of my arm. Her face beams up at me. I remember giving birth to her six months before shipping out. The realization washed over me as I heard her cry in the doctor's arms. I had made a person. Her skin was purple and dense. Her whole head was squeezed and elongated, like a bottle of soda. I loved her in a way that rearranged me. I loved her in a way that was older than her two hours, a love that stretched back to my first thoughts. I had built her, particle by particle. We bled into each other for nine months, mixed indelibly, a different kind of entangled and here she was for the first time on her own. She was mine and she wasn't. I was hers and I wasn't. I had made her. She had remade me. Not everyone loves their child right away, but I did. Between the bleating heart monitors, beneath the blinding fluorescence, she was perfect. She cried. That was the first noise she made, and it, too, was perfect, entangled forever in my heart.

I look down at her and see all that, for a moment, all the molecules we shared, and how far I have to be from her. I looked up at Franklin, my husband, the man who has been raising her every minute while I was away. I thought of the countless small crises he's dealt with, without me there to hold him, without me working late into the night trying to find him a way out.

I kiss Franklin. "I love you," I say. "This is insane. But you're right. It's the beginning of the way out."

I use my metal fingers to disconnect the tether from my hip. I weave the charge I stole from the shipment vessel inside the vacancies in my chest. Without a tether on, I squat low and push off, hard. Hygiea is small, its escape velocity microscopic. I fly free out of its delicate orbit, and drift. The goal is to get as far as possible from Hygiea before I blow the charge. The Belt is dense, and if I can disappear into a thousand small pieces, they'll think I was dashed to pieces against a thousand small asteroids. I don't want to transfer out of my skin whole and risk them finding it and salvaging the neural matter. I want a permanent solution.

I spin out of control, and the vertigo is unavoidable. I experience sensations I didn't know these spaceskins were capable of feeling: nausea, palpitations, arthritic pain in the freezing joints. I can barely open my fingers without silent shouts of pain. I don't eat in the skin, but I feel like throwing up, dry-heaving from the lack of stable vision. I reach out to try and grab something, anything, but my hands move through air. I struggle to remember what to do next.

I think of Altair and everything slows, crystallizes. I start the countdown on the charge, then reach towards the neck of my space skin and fish out the circuit, careful not to disconnect its wiring from the suit. I hold it as delicately as I can between my three thick metal fingers. I have to trust that Franklin's code gave me a return authentication. That my envelope engineering will work, and I am far enough from Hygiea by now that they won't know I blew myself up. I have to trust him. I'm lucky that I do. As the charge blinks silently out from my chest, I pull my left eye out of its socket, exposing the live wires beneath. Even with an authentication key, without the spark that comes with a supervisors transfer approval, the circuit needs electricity to start. I take the wire to the small battery of the circuit and hope this works. It whirs to life. My space skin swims wildly through space as my vision fades one final time. The stars and asteroid belt disappear. I taste the sensation of my limbs, the strength and fortitude of my body one last time and then, just like that, I am gone. Flown back to my body on earth, opening my eyes in my bedroom, Franklin and Altair waiting for me.

When the company comes, they come with lawyers instead of police. They beg me not to sue them for the faulty tether and almost killing me, and I graciously oblige. A real investigation might reveal what we did. Instead they "forgive" the rest of my contract. It would maybe take longer than the remaining four years on my contract to develop, entangle, and ship a new spaceskin to the belt anyway. They pay me the remainder of the contract and we go our separate ways. OSHA makes the third deep-space visit in its history, and the company is forced to dramatically increase its safety standards. Maybe what I did was still wrong, and I am justifying everything to myself, but the results don't lie. My team is safer now than they ever have been. And I am home. I watch the sun bounce off Altair's tufts of black, curling hair and browse my computer for new, terrestrial, jobs. Altair starts crying. I turn towards her and smile. I take her in my arms and laugh. I smile across the room at Franklin. "Don't worry," I tell her, steeping in the sweetness of her voice. "I'm here."

See Spencer Nitkey's story "Calling Me Home" online at Metaphorosis.
If you liked it, leave a comment. Authors love that!
Remember to subscribe to our e-mail updates so you'll know when new stories are posted.

About the story

This story came to me after an afternoon reading articles about quantum mechanics. Immediately I became obsessed with the idea of quantum entanglement, the fact that you can, essentially "entangle" two particles, so that, even when they are separated, moving one, affects the other. Recently, in 2017, a team of Chinese researchers tested the limits of entanglement by sending one entangled particle up in a satellite, 1200 kilometers from the other. The two particles were still entangled! I read that Einstein had called quantum entanglement "spooky motion at a distance". Anything that can make a scientist use the word spooky seems like perfect science-fiction fodder to me. Consciousness is a perpetual interest of mine, and eventually the idea of what a synthesis of consciousness and quantum entanglement could mean formed the conceit of this story.

Then the real work of writing began. I started by trying to find a central character. Claire came to me pretty quickly. I recently started a new job (which I love), but it made me think about how hard it can be to juggle life and work, even under the best of circumstances. What would it look like if a company, using science, had control over the physical location of your consciousness? What would it be like trying to start a family on Earth while working on the other side of the solar system? These questions formed the basis of the story and the rest followed.

A question for the author

Q: Do you use critique groups or other resources to polish your writing?

A: I love using critique groups. I was lucky to have the chance to study creative writing in college, and the opportunity to learn from a couple of really incredible professional writers and participate regularly in workshops and learn from my peers was something I took for granted until after I graduated. Now, I have a small writing group I attend semi-regularly. I am also grateful that my fiancée is almost as excellent an editor as she is a writer. She's been my first reader for years, and when I'm smart enough to follow her advice, my stories always come out better. I think, especially with speculative fiction, it's important to have beta-readers and critiques. I often have a clear idea of the world and conceit of a story, but I can't always tell how clearly that is being communicated with a reader until I've had the chance to hear from someone. Feedback is how we grow and improve, and I'm thankful for all the groups and people who have helped me improve.

About the author

Spencer Nitkey is a speculative writer, a researcher, and an educator who lives in New Jersey. His first intellectual love was nuclear physics and his second love was poetry. Science Fiction has been a happy median between those two. Now, when he's not busy dancing in the kitchen with his fiancée, dreaming about planting chestnut trees, or slowly reading *Gravity's Rainbow*, he's probably writing and imagining futures, presents, and pasts.

Devilish Calliope and the
Ungrooviest Apocalypse

Evan Marcroft

I'd just worked the handcuffs loose when my phone started vibrating in my pocket. Even hanging by my ankles above impending doom, I knew I'd be in *real* shit if I didn't pick up. I made a sort of cup out of my hand and pressed the phone to my ear. "This is Devilish urgently speaking."

"Devilish. It's me. Are you free to talk?"

I glanced up, or rather down, into the flame-rimmed iris over which I'd been suspended by my ankles. Through a shimmering of superheated spacetime, the stratified circles of Hell were bared like flayed muscle. The radioactive unlight of hellfire brought tears to my eyes, and not for the first time I wished I'd packed a thing of Visine. I always think I won't need it, and I always do. "Very briefly," I said.

"You were supposed to report in yesterday," K.K. continued, audibly irate. "I hear chanting. Are you still working on the Alchemist Affair?"

I was, and things were starting to get real un-groovy, by my professional estimation. The man in question stood outside the chalk pentagram that kept the wound between dimensions from hemorrhaging into our reality. Each word in his black tome was written in the blood of a virgin sacrifice, and with every utterance that wriggled many-legged from his lips, his portal punched deeper into the damned-digesting guts of Gehenna, towards the entity the Alchemist sought to unleash. When at last it slouched into the world, suffice to say the general grooviness of Southern Germany would tank like stock in VHS.

Things were going well enough for the Alchemist that he could pause his recitation to shake his fist at me and crow, "Call for all the help you like, Devilish Calliope! Nothing can stop me now!" His coterie of disciples and colleagues and groupies cackled unctuously from the wings. I recognized a couple of famous novelists, two Nobel laureates, and an Olympic curler—all nude, as a matter of course. It was the latter who'd caught me snooping through the castle's dungeons and brained me with a corn broom. I could see how she'd won gold.

"Yeah well," I grumbled, "you know how it goes. One minute you're doing so and so, and the next it's all crazy, and then whatever happens. Bing bang boom. It's a whole thing."

"A whole thing."

I was sure I had a better answer somewhere, but right then my skull was too packed with blood to fit long thoughts. "Yes ma'am."

I detected screams in the static of her pause. Necromagnetic interference from the pit below. "Be that as it may, I have another thing I'm sure you'll find even more whole. A Condition: Critical, to be precise."

"You know," I heard the Alchemist mutter to an adjunct goon, *"I didn't want to say it, but this is just slaughtering the mood."*

A Condition: Critical. Now that was interesting. This thing with the Alchemist was a Condition: Convenient for comparison, which meant that it was not literally or figuratively the end of the world. A couple million dead, tops. I was only here because I wasn't busy with something else. "No shit," I said.

"Finish up there and come into the office. We've got a ticking clock situation."

"Don't worry about me. I'll be okay."

"I said come into the office," she snapped, and hung up.

"Finally," the Alchemist groused. "Do you text during movies too?"

"I'm done," I said, and hucked my phone at his head.

It was a good hit, got him right in the eye. The Alchemist yelped like a cartoon dog, stumbled over his curly-toed slippers and across the pentagonal firewall between realities, which instantly reduced him to a shrieking skeleton. In MESSIARC, we called that a bank shot. Things got out of hand fast. Stygian flames raced along the Alchemist's bones, and his goons went up like oily rags as the chamber became an inferno. Suspended a hundred feet in the air, I was spared for the moment, but with heat's propensity to rise, that moment wouldn't last. I lunged one way and then the other, setting myself to swinging like a pendulum. At the height of my arc, the rope around my ankles snapped off its hook and hurled me face-first through a window. Fortunately for me this had gone down in an old Bohemian palace; something more OSHA-compliant and I'd have been screwed. Unfortunately for me, on the other side of the window was a hundred-foot drop to a cobblestone courtyard. My teeth broke my fall, and I wound up a flattened Coke-can full of broken glass.

"Ow," I said, and also, "fuck."

But the immortality clause in my contract wouldn't let me die without a better excuse, and so I had to sit there and twiddle my metaphorical thumbs while my pulverized bones figured themselves out. There was a time I'd have been glad to be alive. I remembered that waterslide rush of improbable survival, how it jumpstarted my senses and made the world feel new again. But when you felt that day after day, you got numb to it. Started to dread the figurative plunge and welcome the towel-off afterwards.

I'd saved the world this time, I'd have to do it again tomorrow, and I'd probably get screwed on overtime, though honestly that was on me. I'd signed up for the forces of Infinite Good, not Infinite Benefits. No, these days all I looked forward to was a motel shower and a nap afterwards. One had to make do with the many small ends of things.

"This is possibly the direst assignment of your career," K.K. said. "Do you mind if I swear for emphasis?"

"Permission granted."

Her six arms made anxious gestures. All three of her faces spoke in tandem. "*You can't afford to fuck this up.*"

Back in the day, Kalamkari Kannon had been one of MESSIARC's best operatives, fighting for harmony across this iteration of Earth under deific guise, until the Higher-Ups promoted her into administration, where her prodigious skills were mostly useless. Her days were now spent making sure jerks like me did our jobs worse than she ever had. I did that better than anyone.

"Well, now I feel like I have to," I said.

I watched a universal truth drift blithely past her window, harassed by a shoal of profound revelations. K.K's office floated in a lower layer of Nirvana, a state of existence reachable only from a degree of enlightenment. Monks of all faiths spent decades in chaste meditation to forget their flesh. I'd gotten here through an unholy concoction of Angel Dust, peyote, and *Psilocybe azurescens* that I called the Conference Call, and which could make cockroaches see god. My body was currently comatose in a Motel 6 south of Reno. I admired my astral self in the back of K.K.'s laptop. Still looking sharp, I had to say.

"So, what's it this time?" I asked. "Moon vampires? Nazi ghosts? Permutations thereof?"

"You wish it were those common things," K.K. scoffed. "Vercingetorix Smooth has resurfaced."

I froze mid-ogle, an ambushed Narcissus. "Shit. When?"

"This morning. At eleven hundred hours, the—"

"He's gone over to MEGAVILE," I cut in. "Hasn't he?"

"It appears so."

My throat got tight and my neck got itchy, the way they do when you swallow too much at once, or see a bear coming at you with a loose brick in hand. You live as long as I have, you find the body only has so many responses for discomfiting things. "Great," I managed. "Groovy."

I'd known, from the day he'd run off, that Smooth would turn up again eventually. The guy had been on the front lines longer than anyone, K.K. included. He wouldn't go get himself killed off-screen like some side character. The question had been which side would claim him. In the eternal dodgeball game between multiversal good and multiversal evil, nobody didn't get picked. I'd hoped, futilely I suppose, that he'd find his way back to MESSIARC. He still owed me for bagels.

"What did he do?"

K.K. tapped a button and her projector flickered on. "This is need-to-know information. I wish you did not need to know, but God help us, you do. At eleven-hundred hours this morning, MESSIARC's Department of Inadvisable Science was attacked by the transuniversal terrorist unit called the Wild Hunt—a known branch of MEGAVILE. They were led by Vercingetorix Smooth."

She tapped another button, and a grainy surveillance still appeared. A squadron of motorcycles hauled fiery ass across the ginger sands of Mars, leaving a concrete fortress shattered in their rear-view mirrors. These weren't your slippery-sleek Kawasaki ninjamobiles. These were burly, chrome-bellied *choppers*, and there was no mistaking the figure who rode at their head, looking like a devil on wheels in his shiny new leather duds.

Good to see you, bud.

"We lost six operatives repelling their assault," K.K. went on, "and we could not prevent Smooth from absconding with a prototypical kaleidoquantumly correlated thermonuclear device."

I frowned at that, momentarily perplexed. "A kaleidoquantum... Oh god, no. Really? We made a Voodoo Nuke?"

K.K. sighed for about a minute straight. Three mouths, three times the lung capacity. "The Department of Inadvisable Science exists to preemptively innovate and isolate dangerous technologies. If we don't invent it, MEGAVILE will."

I took off my glasses and hung them from my collar. I did not need corrective lenses to see the looming mountain of irony. "You might say that was... inadvisable."

Two hands massaged K.K.'s temples while another worked a stress ball. The rest looked about ready to throttle me. "These decisions are not mine to make," she replied stiffly. "Anyway. The present danger cannot be overstated. If activated, the device will detonate every nuclear weapon within ten billion iterations of this universe. The death-toll will be incalculable. Misery and disorder will proliferate on an unprecedented scale. While the frontline of this conflict is ever in flux, the Higher-Ups have deemed this eventuality an unacceptable concession to MEGAVILE. Given your history with Operative Smooth, they believe that you are uniquely qualified to locate him and retrieve the device."

As the arbiter of all things groovy and not, I had to admit that an apocalypse to the zillionth power was decidedly ungroovy. "Who's to say he still has it?" I asked.

"If he'd handed it off to MEGAVILE, they'd have used it without hesitation. He's holding on to it for reasons unknown and disconcerting." Three of her eyes drilled into me like they could torture out a hidden answer. The other three looked very tired. "*Do you know where to find him?*"

Did I know where to find a universe-hopping biker assassin? It wasn't like he'd been sending me postcards from balmy Bora Bora. But him keeping the Voodoo Nuke? That got my mind a-whirring. Vercingetorix Smooth had a reason for everything. What I knew, perhaps better than anyone, was that it was never the reason you suspected. "Not a clue," I said. "But give me a deadline to run up against and I'm sure I'll panic into something."

"The deadline is whenever your ex-partner decides to use the damned thing," K.K. replied. "You'll know when you reach it."

Thirty-two hours hence, I was cruising up the I-90 towards the heart of Chicago. The city rose ahead of me like a large urban conglomeration. To my right, Lake Michigan was a big blue thing. The come-down from enlightenment had pretty much depleted my capacity for abstraction.

Initially, I'd had no idea where to start looking for Smooth. K.K. hadn't been a whole heaping of help either. Agents were being mobilized across all realities, what with the transuniversal threat. Given the emergency, I figured I'd be given a crack team of my Earth's best operatives to work with, but one apocalypse did not put others on hold.

"Busy day?" I'd asked, to which she'd swiveled her monitor to show me a werewolf eating the president.

"Busy millennia."

But I'd remembered that the Wild Hunt had been active for centuries before Smooth took over. They'd made plenty of appearances from this Earth, pillaging, slaughtering, and recruiting from among its most brutal souls. A dip into my pool of snitches had given me a lead on a possible Wild Hunt rider operating out of the Windy City, and that had led me here, to the curb outside the old Biograph Theater, secret lair of one Professor Marcus Marchpane, mad scientist extraordinaire.

I found my way into the theater's secret basement without difficulty, fiddling with every doodad in the prop closet until a trapdoor opened beneath a box of wigs. I breezed impatiently through the various traps therein, the gases and the lasers. I didn't have time to indulge the mad professor's nonsense. I'd been through this routine a hundred times. I couldn't remember the last time I'd been surprised. Or made an impact, for that matter. The covert struggle between multiversal good and evil was trapped in perpetual stalemate. MESSIARC championing order, liberty, good vibes, and taxes filed on time, with MEGAVILE harbinging everything opposite: chaos, fascism, ska, and indiscriminate genocide. We'd win one battle, MEGAVILE the next. We'd stop an eruption, they'd shoot a duke. For every score, a counter-score, kicking the end further down the road. So it went, and so it would go, one side one-upping the other ad infinitum.

At least with TV you could turn the reruns off.

The lab under the trapdoor was crammed with your standard mad science shit. A tesla coil that spat lightning randomly. A thing that went splort in a tube. I subdued the proprietor with a masterfully executed Krav Maga Sleeper Hold, which is what I call an ether-soaked rag, then laid the professor down on a pile of loose brains. It wasn't him I had questions for.

Death doesn't give warnings, but sometimes it steps on a twig. As I straightened up, the tell-tale crackle of negatronic particles ionizing reached my ear. I ducked, watched a ray of acidic light melt a hole in the cinderblock wall, and spun to see a blocky, 50's style robot charging another shot in its cannon-barreled forearm. On a well-oiled reflex, I swept a mirrored platter of medical tools off the gurney and threw it up like a shield before me; the killing beam struck it and rebounded, piercing the robot's steel chassis and carving it neatly in half across its knob-studded torso.

I knew better than to think that it was harmless in two pieces. I strode over and crumpled its gun barrel beneath my heel. "Three times is not the charm," I said, unhooking a spray bottle from my belt and taking aim at the robot's exposed wires and gears. "This here is water and bleach, my claptrapitous amigo. It's how I buy answers."

"Fuck you, pig," the robot shot back in a crackly speak-and-spell growl.

In response I gave it a two-second blast to the guts, eliciting a howl of autotuned pain. "That's for wasting two seconds," I said, with more of a snarl than I'd intended. "I know you're with the Wild Hunt. Tell me how to find Vercingetorix Smooth and you'll leave here without sounding like a broken VCR. Good deal?"

The robot's lightbulbs dimmed in suspicion. "Why do you want to know?"

I tightened my finger on the spray bottle's trigger.

"Alright, alright," the robot relented. "Here's the deal. I got dumptrucked in that Mars thing, so I figured I'd take the weekend for repairs. Smooth said he and the boys would pick me up Wednesday night. We're supposed to rendezvous at this bar on the Texas border called the Baño del Diablo. There's a leyline convergence there, makes for a real smooth ride getting in and out of this dimension. If you're looking to ambush him, go nuts, but if I were you, I'd write a will first."

"There. Was that so hard?" I turned for the door and as I did, something sharp kissed me on the earlobe. I looked at myself in the platter, and damned if there wasn't a feathered dart dangling off it like a hippy's earring. "Motherfuck!" I swore, rounding on the robot. I stomped down on its free hand until I snapped off its wrist. "I am in no mood, okay? Why does it always have to come to this? Why can't you MEGAVILE assholes just give me a fucking break for once?"

Despite its damage, the robot laughed, a sound like a staticky transmission cutting in and out. "Oh man, I know you. You're Devilish Calliope. You're just like Smooth said you'd be. You used to be cool. Now you're a dick."

"I'm not a dick," I began, but having just literally kicked a guy while he was down, I didn't have much of a follow-up. My anger went swirling down the drain, depositing a scum of tired shame on the toilet bowl of my soul. What was I getting worked up for anyway? I was basically unkillable; a poisoned dart would only make me puke and trip balls. The me that Smooth knew would have made a weekend out of that.

"Whatever," I muttered. "How does he know?" The last time I'd seen Smooth, there had been enough Beatles to solve a bridge and torch problem.

The robot shrugged its stumps. "Because you didn't quit like he did."

The last time I'd seen Vercingetorix Smooth, the year was 1974. What a time to have an immortal immune system. The Bee Gees were staying alive, Patty Hearst was making new friends, and Madagascar became the first country to recognize the Sahrawi Arab Democratic Republic. A landmark year across the board. Pants could be more than one color, your hair could wear its hair down, and life was good. But like Richard Nixon's sterling political career, all amazing things had to end.

Smooth and I had just clambered from the steaming debris of a Martian voidcruiser, whose prow had plowed a miles-long trench across New Mexico. I remember being drenched in liquified alien viscera and smelling like the locker room at Area 51, my once unimpeachable perm now gore-slicked and as impeachable as the president. We parked our coccyges on an aetherodynamic spoiler so that we could air-dry in the twilight, decompress, and watch the shadows stretch out long and blue across the desert.

"I've got a question," said Smooth.

"Is it *why did you press the red button and not the green one*?"

"No," he laughed, because he knew I did screwy shit to keep things interesting. "What does your life look like? Like, if you had to pick a physical thing, what would it be?"

That was a very 70's sort of question, very in vogue in the dynasty of horoscopes and LSD. A decade later, and the only answer you'd get would be *a big pile of cocaine.* As out of hand as the Mars assignment had gotten, I was already looking forward to the next. The build-up, the big plunge, the heart-stopping velocity towards the splashy mess at the bottom. Hell yeah. "A waterpark," I finally decided. "Where there're new slides all the time."

"That's funny. When I look at my life, I see a shelf full of books."

"Like *your* shelf, or a bookstore?"

"Irrelevant to the metaphor. My life is all these books in a series. *The Far-Out Case Files of Vercingetorix Smooth.* They look like a wild romp at first, and maybe the first one is, but not the first ten. You keep reading until you realize they're all the same beneath the cover, just with the names and places changed up like Mad Libs. The same ups and downs, the same stale tropes. And there're sixty-five million more to go. Would you want to keep reading? I don't know why I would."

I didn't know then, but that New Mexican twilight was a Rorschach blot. I recall that I'd seen the faintest seam of color on the horizon. The promise of a crisp morning and a fresh escapade. I would only realize later, over a sack of untouched bagels, that Smooth hadn't seen anything.

"The hero's journey is meant to be a circle," he murmured. "All I see ahead is a straight line."

"I think it's hard to think happy thoughts when you're covered in proof of life on Mars."

"Maybe, D."

"I say sleep on it," I said, which, in hindsight, is the most awful thing you can say to a conflicted friend. I could have offered to hold some of what he was carrying. I could have cracked a joke and laughed his trouble away. Instead, I'd told him to take it to a bed, where it would grow sour beneath the sheets, like a body in the throes of addiction. "You'll feel better tomorrow." *Deal with it yourself in a darkened room where you won't bother anybody. I'm sure you'll be alright.*

"Yeah probably." Smooth stood, teetering on the space-fin from another world. "Do me a huge. Tell K.K. I'm taking a personal day. I think I've earned it. I'll be back in on Wednesday. See you then, yeah?"

I remember being confident, as he sauntered off, that I *would* see him that Wednesday. I'd bring a bag of bagels to share, one with each kind of topping, because the Everything Bagel was still years from being obvious. And when he wasn't there that morning, I remember being pissed, more than anything, that I'd blown five bucks to watch bread go stale. It wasn't fair.

Things should have to say goodbye when they leave you.

The bar the robot had mentioned was a crumb of Vegas out there on the desert. Some enterprising scumbag had taken an old barn and slathered it in neon, put a couple of shitty picnic tables out front, a sign by the highway. I stumbled inside beneath a neon devil on a neon toilet, through a swamp fog of up-chucked beer and bad marijuana. Speakers on an empty stage were blaring

White Rabbit, number one on my Top Ten songs to slowly fade away to. An enticing prospect, but I'd have to settle for getting sloppy. I groped my way to a barstool and collapsed, grateful for a seat that didn't kick me awake with every pothole.

"Howdy, stranger. What do they call you?"

I looked up. The girl behind the counter was maybe twenty, with a tattoo of a rose on her bicep, a week's worth of luggage under each eye, and a bruise on her jaw. Her smile had no business being kind, but it was anyway. "Devilish Calliope," I said. "You?"

"Mona. What kind of name is that? Greek?"

"It's a code name," I shrugged. "I'm sort of a secret agent."

"Nice to meet you, mister secret agent." That warm smile again. She seemed to mean it. What a welcome thing to find out here in nowhere. "How do you like your martinis?"

"In my belly."

I took whatever she gave me without looking and threw it at my tonsils. Mona looked concerned at this. "That there's money in the bank and I'm still worried. Want to share your woes, stranger?"

"Who says I got woes?"

Mona shrugged. "Wouldn't be here if you didn't."

I actually could argue, having wound up in worse places under happier circumstances—more than one birthday of mine had ended in a volcano—but she was right that I wouldn't pick this place over Seaworld.

I handed over my empty glass. Whatever it was hit my brain a second later and punched a hole through it. "Do people come in here and spill crazy personal shit on you a lot?"

"It's pretty much my whole job," she said.

She'd been warned. "Better than *my* job," I muttered. "I didn't put it together until I got down here, but this marriage has soured. I mean really, the kids are gone, and we're in separate beds. The thing is, they tell you that this is the most important thing you'll ever do, right? And yeah, I'm out there saving the world every day. But it never *stays* saved. For every bad guy I put away, there's three more on the waitlist for his doom castle. It's ridiculous."

I was surprised by the heat in my throat. This was more than I'd felt dangling over the Alchemist's hellhole. More than I'd felt in a long while. Maybe I needed a therapist. That or a larger tab. "Come on now, get it all out," Mona said. She poured me another anonymous drink, and I gave the one in my guts a friend.

"A co-worker once said this life was like reading the same story over and over again," I continued. "I didn't listen then, but he was right. And it gets old. Every go-through, every day you save, you lose a little crumb of enthusiasm, and when you run out, all that's left is a big asshole. That's me. Hi."

"Hi," Mona replied, unsure whether to laugh or frown.

I sighed, and smeared the sweat on my brow into my hair. "It feels... it feels like a race between finally doing something halfway consequential and just giving up. At this point, I don't know which one I'm rooting for."

"If you don't mind me saying," Mona said, "that sounds better than doing something that definitely doesn't matter." She was polishing a highball without looking at it. A dozen more were lined up along the countertop. I blinked, and saw the bar through her eyes. It went much further than I knew, snaking years into the past and decades into her future.

"Been working here long?" I asked.

She smirked. "You know any other shitty desert bars hiring?"

I had to admire a lady who could push a lot of hurt down with a cheek muscle. "Listen," I said. "I was serious about the whole secret agent thing. I've got bad guys showing up any minute, and it's going to be a whole thing. Do yourself a favor and clear out while you can."

Mona shrugged, like this was every day for her. "Thank you kindly, but I got rent to pay. I don't get to be scared of much. You and your pals just pay for anything you break, 'kay?"

I was about to elaborate when life interrupted like the asshole it was. Every head not face-down in vomit turned as the stealthiest storm I'd ever heard cleared its throat. Lightning flogged the Earth in a dozen places, and the thunder that followed sounded like unmuffled engines. Headlights knifed through the mazarine twilight. One by one, a squadron of motorcycles skidded to a stop in a barricade outside the bar and let off a procession of monstrosities. Octofiends from Planet Zed; vampire honnies with gold-capped fangs; extradimensional entities of such weird physics that my eyes could perceive only their spurs and bandannas. Their collective rap sheet would have killed a rainforest. The Wild Hunt, ride or die.

They sauntered in, silent as pallbearers, and stood aside to let barflies take wing. The glass in Mona's hands shattered on the floor as their leader filled the doorway and crouched to squeeze inside. At full height his snout clipped the rafters; his feet stamped three-clawed craters in the floor. Mona sucked in a breath, as if she'd never seen a forty-foot Tyrannosaurus Rex in a biker jacket stomp into a bar.

Like I said, the guy had been on the job longer than anyone.

"Hi, Smooth," I said.

"Hi, D," said Vercingetorix Smooth. "Happy Wednesday."

My old partner settled his sixteen scalebound tons down beside me at the bar, his massive skull casting me in shadow, his tail curling around my stool. A telescoping robotic claw dropped a crinkled ten on the counter. To her credit, Mona had bravely stayed put, and began to fill a mug.

"You look like you need an adrenalin shot," Smooth remarked.

"You look extinct," I replied. "You knew I'd be here."

"No other reason to gank a Voodoo Nuke. Other than the obvious one, I mean." He snapped a prosthetic finger, and a betentacled crony placed a locked briefcase on the counter between us. "I wanted to see you again," he said. "It's not easy to hang out, the way things are. I thought, 'those assholes must be running 'ol Devilish ragged. I'd better touch base.' But how, I wondered, to get him alone without everyone freaking out?"

I glanced casually at the innocuous case, and beat down the urge to run screaming from it. "The Voodoo Nuke. I called it that too."

Smooth had no lips, but I'd learned to tell when he was smiling. "I bet you did."

"I can't let you leave with that thing," I said.

"That sucks," he replied. "Normally you could have it, but the boss is on my ass about this one. I'm afraid I've got to be inflexible. How about you put it out of your mind? Let the inevitable come to pass. Tell me how you're getting on."

I swiveled my stool to look him in the eye. I picked the left one, it being the only one I could see. "This is what I'll tell you. I've got a company card, you've got the spoils of a thousand worlds. We're at a bar, and we've both come a long way. We'll drink for it. I win, you hand it over, and go back to revving your engines in quiet neighborhoods like the villain you are."

"*We'll drink for it*," Smooth echoed bemusedly. "What do I get if I win?"

"If you win, you get me."

Smooth lapsed into a silence that bordered on theatrical. I waited without a doubt he'd go for it. Not because he craved another servant of evil, no. Because he missed me. I knew that because I *was* his friend, and I wanted the same thing.

I missed my buddy.

Smooth affixed a slit pupil on Mona, and downed his mug in one pull, letting the suds dribble between his fangs. Hops comingled with gut-fermenting carrion, became something even I wouldn't huff.

"Line 'em up."

Mona looked at him, then me. "Are you really the good guy?"

"The goodest here," I said in full honesty.

"And that box is dangerous."

I pinched an invisible grain of rice. "Little bit."

She nodded at the ground and set her jaw. "Alright. Hoo boy."

Smooth had a crossroads devil who could whip up a magically binding contract. Neither of us would be wiggling out. With everything signed in blood, the drinking commenced. Mona poured shots and we downed what we were given. Vodka, gin, other pellucid poisons. My kidneys had survived tours of Australia, Russia, and Arizona U, but Smooth was a gigantic dinosaur, so who could know the odds? It was cordial, at first, drinking as we caught up on the last few decades. He didn't seem to mind me foiling MEGAVILE's plots, and I guiltily enjoyed hearing about the interesting people he'd been eating. We could have gone on into the morning. But it was only a matter of time before we found that unavoidable question at the bottom of a glass. Best to rip the band-aid off.

"Why did you quit?" I asked.

Smooth handed Mona his latest empty and took a refill. "It's like I said in the desert." He'd barely begun to slur his words. Meanwhile I felt like the barn had left port, and the seas were getting choppy. "The danger, the adventure, the intrigue—it lost its edge. I ran out of new things to see. Reasons to keep going. And you know what? It never got results. Nothing changed. Nothing got better. At least not for long. Eventually I had to ask myself: what's the point of playing a game you can't win?"

"Like you can win over at MEGAVILE either," I snorted.

"That's where you're wrong," he said, and my heart, which had been chugging along just fine, lurched down a dark sideroad.

"Here's the truth that MESSIARC will never tell you. Nobody can *really* win this thing. Not me, not you. They hold evil up like something we can all stop if we hold hands and sing *We Are The World*, but it's not. Evil, it turns out, is not an outcome. It is a process. Its goal isn't to stamp out good forever. No. All it wants is to *be*. To exist, perpetually in flux, waxing and waning. Letting hope flourish just to be crushed, ad infinitum. Think about it. A slasher must hide between murders so everyone can hope he's gone. A tyranny must fall so that it can rise under a new flag and conquer again, just as a forest burns and grows anew. If evil *actually* won, if every last scrap of happiness were gouged out of every universe, it would be left with *nothing to do*."

The clap of his glass on the countertop went through my booze-bruised brain like a shockwave. "Evil doesn't want a knock-out," he said. "Evil wants to exist. And it always will, because evil is what good must inevitably become." Smooth sent another shot nonchalantly down the hatch. I'd almost forgotten the one in my own hand.

"Don't believe me?" Smooth replied to my silence. "Hello, I'm the proof. Epochs on the job and still I fell. Lucifer did it for less, and sooner. The best of intentions still break down, when the going gets rough, when the going never ends. Systems corrupt. Wills erode. Agents defect. It's not about choosing to do bad; that's hard. It's about admitting how pointless it is to be good, which is easy. It's leaning into the wind that's blowing and letting it take you where you're already bound to go. Don't tell me you haven't felt it pushing. Sooner or later, the decay of decency claims all."

He turned to baste me in a cloud of yeasty gizzard-stink, as revolting as it was painfully nostalgic. "The end that you're holding out for isn't coming. Tumbling forever between saved and unsaved, the world is a tossed coin that cannot fall. There is no win-condition for you, only the monotony, the score and the counter-score. And I'll tell you what, my friend: if our team can't lose, well, *that's enough like winning for me.*"

He protracted a claw and gently clapped my shoulder. "Come on, man. Join me already. This Wild Hunt thing? Fuck it. Out that door is a multiverse of other shit to do. We'll kick around infinity and do whatever, just you and me, and it'll feel *good*, *because that's what evil is*. Freedom from hope, freedom from *giving a shit*. Throw this thing, and we can drink to celebrate your liberation instead."

I stared at the droplets of vodka trickling down the inside of my glass, bitter liquor fast becoming sticky dregs to be washed out and replaced.

Was Smooth right? Hell if I knew for sure. But like all forked-tongued lawyers, he spoke himself a good case. Everything, in my experience, only got worse. Even the immortal decayed. Just look at me: I used to be a priest. He didn't need to tell me that every bit of good I'd ever done was doomed to be undone. I knew what Eve felt when she saw that sweet apple hanging there. The serpent had been surplus. Something so simple sold itself. For her, potassium. For me, a release.

From hope. From care.

Maybe it didn't matter whether he was right. If some final triumph over evil was coming, it was too far in the future even for an immortal to see. However long my life was, it was all I could worry about. No matter what, I'd be spinning in circles until something killed me; I didn't have to be spinning alone. Yeah, I'd have to learn how to ride a motorcycle and commit unspeakable atrocities, but both those things would become second-nature in time. The game would never let me go, no, but at least—

At least I could play with a friend.

Swaying, I groped at the counter. One more drink. This one to numb the choice.

I sipped the next shot through my teeth. I froze as the taste struck my tongue.

My eyes searched for Mona's, and she looked pointedly elsewhere.

I thought. And then I grinned.

"You almost had me," I said. "But I know something you don't."

Smooth's scaly brow crinkled. "I can't understand you. You're slurring."

Yeah I was, so never mind. I slugged the shot down and waved for another.

Smooth and I went back and forth, shot for shot, in silence now, his play made and answered. I stared him down, teetering only slightly, as his eyelids began to droop, his tail slashing herky-jerkily across the floor. Seeing me remain impossibly upright seemed to galvanize him. He began to drink faster, as if to prove he could. His side of the bar quickly grew cluttered with glass. I drank and waited. The night crunched down on us, a shrinking prison.

Shot number thirty-two hovered between Smooth's jaws. The Wild Hunt held its collective breath. Behind the bar, Mona edged away. A dollop dropped onto his tongue. Then two. Finally he dropped the glass down his throat and swallowed it whole. Gave his teeth a mocking lick.

"Give me another," he triumphantly declared.

And then his mass tilted sideways and crushed me flat.

The Wild Hunt took off not long after. I wasn't sure how they'd got Smooth out; the place was empty when I finished regenerating apart from Mona, who'd presumably watched it happen with the same expression of fascinated horror. They'd left the suitcase on the un-crushed half of the counter, as per the unbreakable deal.

"I won't be able to sleep without seeing that," Mona said.

"Try feeling it." The transformation from pancake to man had wrung the liquor out of me. "That was a real dangerous thing you did. Hell if it didn't work though." She'd had a final shot lined up for me. I drank it now, needing the fluids. Pure, unfiltered water, straight from the tap.

"You looked like you needed it." Mona shrugged like it was nothing. Even so, she wore that wide-eyed, shellshocked expression you get from your first blast of weird. No, it would not wear off in time. It was pretty much her face now.

"Yeah, kinda," I admitted. "You got a pen?"

She did, and I took a minute to scratch out a number on a gently-used napkin. "Hold on to this. It's for a lady named K.K. If she doesn't pick up the first time, leave her fifty messages."

Mona frowned, but took it anyway. "I don't get it."

"You saved the world today," I replied. "You looked death in the face while you cheated it. That's a solid resume, supposing you're looking to make a career change. If you do call, tell her Devilish sent you." Not that it would be a sterling reference.

She nodded, and put the napkin in her pocket. "Sure," she said. I couldn't tell what she meant by that, but I knew what I'd bet if I had to.

I stepped outside with the briefcase to find that someone had slashed the tires on my Matador, lowering its value not one cent. I put the Voodoo Nuke under the seat and sat on the hood to make a call. The Wild Hunt had taken the storm with them; the stars winked overhead like a million proud uncles.

"Operative Calliope." K.K. sounded her usual, harried self. "What is it? What's going on?"

"Nothing," I said. "I got the thing."

"I... what?"

"I got it," I said again, gently. "I met Smooth, got the bomb, sent him packing. It's alright now. You don't have to worry. Everything is groovy. Take a rest."

Silence on the other end, but I could hear her unclenching, breathing out, for the first time all day. Maybe for the first time all year.

"Thank you, D," she sighed. "I'm glad to hear that. And I will."

I smiled for no one's benefit. "Hey, so what's next? Where do you need me now?"

But she didn't need me anywhere, it turned out. The stars had aligned. For at least this effervescent moment, the world was out of crises.

My next call was for a tow. Afterwards, I stretched out against my windshield, closed my eyes, and felt the Earth glide through space, a ship on calm seas. I wished I could have told Smooth what I'd realized in the bar. Twice now I'd stayed silent when I shouldn't have. *Evil is what good must inevitably become.* He was spot-on there. But what I'd figured out was that, emergent from unlikely places, unexpected faces, good sprang from nowhere at all. For every me that lost faith on the slog towards nowhere, there was a Mona. When you framed it like that, good was infinite too.

Maybe I'd mention it when next he came around. I doubted this'd be the last time. The night could not stay quiet forever. The universe was too in love with disarray; it would never be finally alright. But Smooth's logic had been compelling. If evil's continuance was its objective, then it held that any dent in that continuity was a victory. There could be no great ending to things, but if I busted my ass for it, I might find a little conclusion here and there, like this one, the twilit calm between the end of one book and the cover of another, in which the world felt safe to do something beautiful like simply chill, and that felt enough like winning to me.

Fleeting, but not nothing, the many small ends of things.

See Evan Marcroft's story "Devilish Calliope and the Ungrooviest
Apocalypse" online at Metaphorosis.
If you liked it, leave a comment. Authors love that!
Remember to subscribe to our e-mail updates so you'll know when
new stories are posted.

About the story

I've always been a fan of the ongoing fantasy/sci fi series. Your *Dresden Files* in particular, and anything by Simon R. Green. I would devour every new installment as soon as it came out and wait impatiently for the next one. As I developed into a writer myself, however, and grew a more critical eye, I noticed that as book heaped upon book, as characters changed sides, died, and resurrected, as plot-lines grew ever more entangled, that I never seemed to reach the ends of these sagas, and see how everything ultimately shook out. I found myself wondering how these eternally cocksure and self-deprecating characters would react if they could step outside their stories and see just how much further they had to go before they could rest at last. This story was born from that pity. It's the message I could send to my favorite protagonists, if I could. Things might never be finally alright, but that's no reason to give up.

A question for the author

Q: What happens when you hit writer's block head on?

A: When I hit writer's block head on, I usually realize that what I'm writing is boring. Not the entire story necessarily, but typically an event in that story, which is playing out too straightforwardly to spark my interest, a scene of transportation from one location to another, for example. I find that my writing surges when I'm describing something unusual, or depicting something commonplace from an uncommon angle. If I'm finding it hard to proceed, my go-to trick is to make it harder for myself. Rather than drive us to the new location from our protagonist's perspective, I can hop into the perspective of a bird watching our hero drive through the narrow streets below, or from the point of view of the city beneath him, wincing as he steers his car through the folds of its asphalt brain. Sometimes the smoothest route towards what I want to accomplish is the more roundabout one.

About the author

Evan Marcroft is a speculative fiction writer from California currently residing in Chicago with his wife. Evan uses his expensive degree in literary criticism to do menial data entry, and dreams of writing for video games, but will settle for literature instead. His works of science fiction, fantasy, and spine-curdling horror can be found in a variety of venues across the internet, such as *Strange Horizons, Asimov's*, and multiple times in *Metaphorosis*.

evan-marcroft.squarespace.com, @Evan_Marcroft

All That Remains

Michael Gardner

The boy doesn't have a name, but Father calls him Progeny. He was born underground, and grew up in near darkness. In the tunnels. Walking the spaces between compact earthen walls, buttressed intermittently with wooden beams, glow worms the only luminescence.

His eyes are good. He sees shapes where Father sees shadows. He sees shadows where Father sees nothing.

He walks now, very quietly. Now is the quiet time. It is a rule. He hunches to keep his head from grazing the ceiling, striding confidently along the well-worn trail, one hand held out, fingers skimming the gritty walls, now a beam, now earth, now a beam.

Abruptly, he emerges into an expansive cavern of dark rock. At the back of the cave is a deep, rock crevice—the pit, as Father calls it—where Progeny dumps the dirt from his excavations. Before the pit though, are pools. The pad of Progeny's footsteps on the hard surface echoes as he moves toward them. Water leaks from somewhere up high, running in rivulets down the far wall covered in yellow moss and white fungal protrusions, ending with a caress of the surface of the pond. The water gurgles and gulps—wet whispers floating around the cavern.

Progeny approaches the water. It smells fresh and sweet. He falls to his knees by the edge, staring into the depths, where he sees white lines criss-crossing beneath the dark surface. Eels. With a violent splash, Progeny snatches a large one from the pond with strong, practiced hands.

He grins as he bites into the writhing flesh, enjoying the saltiness of the blood.

When he is sated, he will retrace his steps through the tunnels to meet Father at the shelter. There, on hard wooden boards, he will receive his lessons.

Lessons after the mid-meal. Another rule.

Father stands in the middle of the shelter, watching Progeny approach. He is a short man, with white hair, and a back as straight as the wooden beams in the tunnels. Around his neck hangs a large key on a chain. Progeny knows it unlocks the storeroom, which houses towers of canned goods, jars of preserved fruits, drums of powdered milk and eggs.

Progeny stops at the edge of the shelter, and waits for Father's invitation to join him. It is a rule.

The shelter is a simple construction. A raised wooden platform, three walls and an earthen ceiling. The front of the shelter is open to the tunnels. The rear wall has a small hatch, through which Progeny must crawl when instructed. Father's bedroll is packed away neatly in a corner.

Father squints down at Progeny through the gloom. He removes a crank-powered flashlight from his ragged trousers, winds it, and points the flickering beam at Progeny's face. Progeny squeezes his eyes shut against the pain, then turns away until Father directs the light elsewhere. Hesitantly, Progeny opens his smarting eyes and sees that Father has placed the torch, bulb down, on the floor of the shelter, a small wavering circle of light surrounding the device. Instead of the torch, Father now holds a strand of wire, three feet long. It is his teaching aid.

"Come. The lesson begins," Father says.

Progeny steps into the shelter, then kneels before Father. Progeny lowers his head, and his eyes, but opens his ears and mind as previously instructed. Father begins his oration.

Progeny has heard much of Father's speech before. There is little new these days. Father talks of the before, and the wickedness of the world. He talks of the righteous end. He mocks the unprepared. He talks of the remainder, the lesions, and the living rot. He talks of sinners receiving what was owed, and the joy of being saved.

As he talks, Father flicks the wire through the air to emphasise his points.

Father talks of Mother. Father remains confused about her. She was taken unfairly, he says with less vigour. He sounds perplexed, and sad. But he moves on. He talks about Progeny. He talks about burdens and disappointment.

Finally, when Progeny's knees ache, and his legs and feet tingle with numbness, Father finishes, places a hand on Progeny's head, and entwines his fingers in Progeny's fine hair.

"Time for your question, Progeny."

Progeny swallows, lets the silence build while he frames the question in his mind. He places both of his hands on top of Father's hand on his head.

"If the surface sickness has indeed cleansed the earth of sin," Progeny says, "why do we still need to hide in the tunnels?"

Progeny feels Father's hand twitch. Progeny swallows again, waiting. Just as he thinks Father will not answer, Father speaks.

"We do not hide in the tunnels, we live. The sinners are vanquished, but the remainder roam the surface still."

"But you have also said that the saved inherit the earth, and the fallen—"

Father delivers a powerful blow to the soft flesh of Progeny's armpit with the wire switch. Progeny feels the familiar pain—a sharp bite, then a burning. He stifles a yelp. Warm blood trickles down his side, but he resists the urge to let go of Father's hand. That would only bring more punishment.

"You've had your question," Father says coldly. Progeny sucks in air, but says nothing.

"Blessed are those left in the dark," Father says, and he slides his hand out from under Progeny's, allowing Progeny to lower his arms to his sides, careful not to agitate the fresh cut.

"You are permitted to leave and work on the new tunnel," Father says.

Blessed indeed, thinks Progeny.

Progeny's tunnel is at the opposite end to Father's shelter, closer to the pools, and the pit where dirt can be discarded. His work progresses slowly, but he has made progress. He is not as experienced as Father in tunnel construction, and it has taken time to learn how and where to buttress them. Learning is slow when Father refuses to demonstrate his techniques, and Progeny is only permitted one question at a time.

His tunnel is narrower than any of Father's. He digs it out slowly so it does not collapse. But he is proud of his work, and proud he is adding to the structure of their home.

It is only recently that Father allowed Progeny to engage in excavation. Perhaps Father thinks it is busy work. Another way to encourage Progeny to reflect on the soul and mind, where naturally thoughts go when hands are occupied. Or perhaps Father realises that with Progeny occupied, he can enjoy that much more solitude.

This might be closest to the truth, as Father has never visited Progeny's site, for which Progeny is grateful. Because what Father doesn't know is that Progeny is digging up.

The entrance to Progeny's tunnel is about a metre and a half square. The tunnel continues straight on into the earth for ten metres, and is buttressed with wooden beams that Father provides from the storeroom. Wooden beams are also piled up outside the entrance of the tunnel, waiting to be used. And there is a cone-shaped pile of dirt that Progeny has yet to relocate, along with an empty tin of peaches that smells syrupy.

After ten metres, Progeny's tunnel turns up at a forty five degree angle, then continues for nearly thirty more metres. Progeny has also buttressed that part of the tunnel with wooden beams. He has done this in six places.

To work in his tunnel, Progeny must duck. It is too small to stand erect. He's working now on his knees.

He uses a short pickaxe to worry free a large stone, which pops out and falls to the floor with a thud. Progeny drops the pick and grabs at the rock before it bumps into his legs. He eases the stone behind him, sliding it next to a large bucket half filled with dirt.

The tunnel smells of damp, loamy earth, freshly turned. Progeny likes the smell. It is the scent of progress. So much nicer than the acrid smell of old sweat that Father exudes.

Progeny takes hold of his pickaxe once more and raises it, poised to strike at the tunnel wall again. But that is when he hears a murmur, and he hesitates, arm tensed, muscles coiled, ready to unwind.

He frowns. It is quiet again now and he questions whether he did, indeed, hear anything at all. But he waits, just to be sure.

It comes again. A soft murmuring that resonates through and from the tunnel walls. A sound familiar and yet strange. It reminds Progeny of times when he has caught Father mumbling to himself. But the wall cannot mumble, or murmur. And yet...

Progeny lowers the pick to the ground, then presses his ear against the cool earth, feeling the grittiness of the dirt against the side of his face. The noise is gone. Perhaps temporarily, perhaps for good. Progeny waits. And waits. And just as he is about to give up, it comes again.

Quiet rolling eddies of sound. First they are high pitched, soft. Then a pause. After, the mumbling is a little louder, and deeper.

He pulls back as realisation dawns. Two voices. The ground is transmitting the soft sounds of a conversation between two people. Close enough to hear, but not close enough to understand.

Progeny swallows. And swallows again. He doesn't know what this means. Father has said many times that he and Progeny were saved, no one else. Only the remainder continue above. But the remainder are sick, barely human. They don't converse.

So if not the remainder, then who?

Progeny kneels on the wooden floor of the shelter, his aching legs complaining. Father's lecture is longer than usual. He's saying a lot without saying much. Progeny is tired of listening, and hurting, so he takes the risk, breaks the rule, and speaks out of turn.

"There are people living above us," Progeny says.

Father's rant ends mid-stream, his mouth gaping, his eyes wide with shock, and anger.

Progeny hurries on. "I've heard them talking. Who are they?"

Father stares at him for a long time, long enough for Progeny to wonder if Father has died on his feet. But then he blinks, speaks.

"Only the remainder live above. You must have mistaken their moans of pain for communication."

"They were talking," Progeny fires back. "You know, don't you? You haven't—"

But his accusation is interrupted by a blow from the wire. Progeny moans. Father swings again, hard. Progeny sucks in the pain, like inhaling foul air.

"The remainder are tricky, evil. They would tempt us to the surface to infect us. But we are strong, Progeny, we are strong. Have faith."

"Liar."

Father's face blooms with blood, his eyes narrow. And then he swings the switch—once, twice, three times. On the fourth, Progeny catches the wire in his hand and yanks it from Father's grip. He rises to his feet and raises the switch menacingly.

"You've made an error. There are people up there," he yells. "People like us, and yet we are down here. Why? What are you afraid of?"

Father puffs his chest out, stands more erect. "Progeny," he says, "you speak out of turn and you will submit to re-education."

Progeny narrows his eyes, maintaining the anger. The hand holding the wire quivers. He tenses, ready to punish Father, but then he hesitates, and in hesitation he is done. He sees the aged man before him. Progeny falters, and his hand lowers, his shoulders slump, his eyes turn downward, and he drops the switch to the floor with a clatter.

"Yes, Father," he says. He moves toward the small door at the back of the shelter, drops to his knees and crawls through.

The hatch leads out into another tunnel, but the floor of this one has iron rails that snake into the blackness like a forked tongue. On them sits an old, rusted hand car. Progeny knows that this part of his home was a mine, once. A mine for what, he doesn't know, and Father has never said.

Progeny sighs, steps up onto the car, and releases the brake. He takes hold of the heavy walking beam, and begins to pump it up and down, the hand car squealing loudly as it edges forward. A deeper darkness is soon the reward for his exertions.

Progeny knows this trip. He trusts the rails, and yet careering along the track has him on edge. The hand car moves fast, then faster. He feels air on his face, cooling the sweat that has beaded on his forehead. The squeaking wheels provide the soundtrack.

Eventually, a faint green glow appears ahead, then grows larger as the car races on. It is bright enough to make Progeny squint, but not so bright as to hurt his eyes like Father's torch.

Progeny engages the brake and slows the car, which screams in protest, before stopping below the circle of light. Above him, in a crevice in the ceiling, a colony of glow worms writhe. They cast just enough light to illuminate the walls of the tunnel on which Father has hung photographs.

The first is black and white, a wedding photo of Mother and Father. In it, they both look happy, young, and carefree.

Next is a photograph of Progeny's grandparents, also black and white. They were dead when Progeny was born, but Father has put the photo on the wall to remind Progeny of where he came from.

Next is the front page of a twenty year old newspaper, framed. "Mystery virus strikes down 1 in 4." The subheading says that medical researchers are working around the clock to develop a vaccine.

Next are photos of the blockades, police in riot gear, officials in hazmat suits, panicked citizens pushing up hard against them.

There are more newspaper articles. "Quarantine zones established across the country." "Armed forces enforce the quarantine." "No progress with a cure." Each is accompanied by grainy black and white photos, in which the people look more and more wretched, and frightened, and helpless.

There are also photographs of the tunnels, newer, but unmistakeably them. There is the store room, filled with goods, the cavern and pools, and one photograph of a narrow shaft going up, and up, and up toward the surface. That shaft doesn't exist now. Progeny has searched, and he is certain that Father collapsed it many years before.

Last, there is a photograph of Father standing alongside Mother, who is heavily pregnant. They look as wretched and lost as the people in the newspaper articles. They stand near the storage room in the underground shelter. Mother has a wound near her lip. Something that could be mistaken for a cold sore, except it is not. Progeny knows that.

Progeny releases the brake and pumps the walking beam once more. The car rolls away from the shrine of history. Darkness descends again, the air whistling around him.

Progeny's heart beats harder, and he can feel the steady pulse of blood pumping in his chest, up his neck, in his temples. His breathing comes fast, hard, ragged. He doesn't want to finish the re-education. He wants to turn back, but he doesn't. He is convinced Father would know, so he pushes on. Cutting through the darkness. Metal wheels on rails screaming.

Finally, the darkness morphs into gloom, and he swallows down the lump in his throat. He engages the brake again, and the car slows, then stops just before the end of the tunnel.

There, illuminated by light from another colony of glow worms, is a withered corpse tied to the wooden beams. Its head hangs limp against its chest, thin dirty hair covering the left side of its face. Of the right side, most of the flesh is gone. Instead, leathered skin hangs loose, a flash of white bone beneath a tear in the cheek. The clothes are tattered, and swim on the decayed remains. The corpse has been there so long it no longer reeks, but smells earthy, and of dust.

Progeny steps down from the car, approaches, then kneels before the corpse.

"Forgive me, Mother," he says quietly. "I lost my patience with Father again."

When Progeny arrives back at the shelter, he's tired and sore. His arms ache from pumping the walking beam. His mind is a darting eel, swirling from one side to the other. He desperately wants to return to his tunnel, and sleep.

He engages the brake, and stumbles down from the car onto bare earth. He drops to hands and knees, and crawls back through the hatch of the shelter hoping desperately that the final admonishment is short.

The shelter is empty.

He shifts onto his haunches, surveys the room. Empty.

"Father?" he calls out. Nothing.

He is assaulted by a brief surge of nausea.

He knows exactly where Father has gone.

At the entrance of his tunnel, Progeny crouches and peers inside. It is quiet. Most of his tools remain outside, although the pickaxe is missing.

"Hello," Progeny calls, the sound disappearing, then echoing back. "Father?"

He hears grunting, and in the distance sees wavering light. Progeny hunches low and moves along the flat part of the tunnel until he reaches the incline. Up ahead, he spies Father. He's holding the pickaxe in one hand, and shining the beam of his flashlight toward the end of the tunnel with the other.

Father turns abruptly, and directs the torch at Progeny who winces in pain and shields his eyes with his hands.

"You," Father snaps. Through narrow slits, Progeny sees Father marching toward him, head bent to avoid the low tunnel ceiling. "You would create a gateway for the damned into our sanctuary."

Father is close now, and still he keeps the painful light on Progeny's face. It feels like needles in his brain. Even after he shuts his eyes tight, the light gets in.

"I wanted to get closer, to listen," Progeny says.

"You were tempted. You are tempted, you ignorant child. I let you dig and you toss that dirt casually over your shoulder and into my face. Up is damned."

"But how do you know?"

"Because I lived it," Father hisses. "Because I saw the people struck down. So many evil people. And good people, like your mother. But I saved you, and yet you show no faith in me. You want proof? You want to tunnel out, become infected and as you lay dying, say, 'Yes, Father was right'?"

The light sputters, dies. Progeny doesn't hear Father cranking the torch again, so he opens his eyes slowly. Father's eyes sparkle with fury.

"It's been so long, Father. They might have stopped the—"

Father cuts him off by cracking him hard across the cheek with his flashlight. Progeny sees lights again, his ears ring, and he tastes copper in his mouth where he has bitten his tongue.

"I should never have left you on your own for so long." Father turns and moves awkwardly back up the tunnel. "You will cease tunnelling, and submit to further re-education."

The words are a punch to the guts. Progeny stumbles after Father, banging his head painfully on a beam before ducking lower and pushing on.

"You will meditate on faith," Father says as he reaches the last buttress and halts. Progeny stops too, just behind him. Father turns to address Progeny.

"You will once again come to recognise that hell waits in the open air, while sanctuary is provided by me, below."

Father turns and swings the pickaxe at the wall, lodging it behind the support beam.

"No," Progeny yells. Father levers hard, and the beam comes loose and clatters to the floor. It's followed by a burst of soil. Father swings again, and the point of the pickaxe wedges behind the ceiling support. More dirt falls as he jerks the handle. The ceiling bulges, dirt trickles, but the beam holds.

Father yanks the pickaxe out and pulls it back over his shoulder, coiled and ready to swing. But before he does, Progeny lunges. He takes hold of Father's arm, surprising himself. He fights for control, but Father's grip is tight. Father grunts, twists, pulls.

"You will release me, boy," he screams into Progeny's face, spittle hitting him between the eyes.

"No," Progeny says from between clenched teeth. "This is not your decision."

Father wrenches, then pushes hard. Progeny loses his balance. Father seizes on his momentary advantage and shoves Progeny again, slamming him into the broken wall of the tunnel. The wind rushes from Progeny, but he refuses to let go. Dirt streams from the ceiling into his eyes, but he blinks it away. Father is close, leaning into him. His face is red, veins pulsing across his forehead.

"You're just like her," he screams. "Just like your mother. She wouldn't listen. Just a few days more, she kept saying. A few days more. She had too much faith in the goodness of people. In their cleverness. Now look at her."

Progeny notices tears in Father's eyes. Shocked, he lets go, and Father stumbles backward, nearly trips, but manages to maintain his balance. He holds the pickaxe across his chest, breathing heavily. He eyes Progeny warily.

"I'm sorry, Father. But this is different."

Father sighs, and Progeny watches the anger leave him. He suddenly looks very old, very frail. He clears his throat. "You're all that I have left of her."

Father says nothing more, and Progeny doesn't know what to say. The silence builds as they watch each other. An uncomfortable, painful silence.

"I can't," Progeny eventually says. He speaks softly, slowly. "I can't be your memory of her. I need to see for myself."

Progeny watches his Father's eyes harden, his mouth tighten into a thin line. Father roars, turns, and swings the pickaxe hard at the ceiling. And before Progeny can issue a warning, Father is lost under an avalanche of dirt, wood, dust, and debris.

Progeny dives away from the implosion, down the incline, slamming hard onto the sloped floor. He covers his head with his arms. The din of destruction fills his ears. Dirt and rocks strike at his back and legs, fast at first, but then slower. And then the noise dies away to a whisper as dirt continues to trickle from the damaged ceiling.

Progeny opens his eyes, squints to see through the dust. He pushes himself up off the floor, and turns to find Father half buried. His eyes are closed, and he has a large gash across his forehead. Dark blood runs past his ear and drips onto the dirt floor, which sucks it up greedily.

Progeny feels weak. He's breathing hard, trying to still the panic. He moves closer, drops to his knees, a hand hovering over his Father, but he can't bring himself to touch him. "Father," he says.

The old man's eyes spring open. He coughs, and sprays a fine red mist into the air. His breath gurgles in his chest. His eyes find Progeny. They're wide, pained, scared. They move toward the broken ceiling.

It's then that Progeny notices the breeze. A zephyr of cool air that is foreign, and confusing. And on it is a sweet scent that Progeny has never smelled before.

Progeny follows Father's gaze up, and sees it. There's a hole in the tunnel. And it leads outside. He looks back at Father, wide-eyed.

"Close the tunnel," Father says. "Save us. Save yourself."

"But Father—"

"Promise me," he wheezes. Blood bubbles from his lips. "Promise me you will heed your Father. This is how you protect yourself."

But Progeny doesn't believe that. He hasn't for a long time. He can't close himself off like Father has. But he doesn't say that to Father.

"Yes, Father," he says instead. He finally allows his hand to rest on Father's chest, and then he waits. He waits until Father's harsh breathing slows, then stops. He waits until Father simply stares up at the hole in the ceiling, unmoving.

Progeny feels numb, but also a little lighter. Father was the only person he ever knew. And in his way, Progeny thinks Father did care for him. But it's also a relief to know that Father won't demand anything from Progeny ever again.

Progeny closes Father's eyes, rises to his feet, and climbs up the mound toward the opening.

The sky is unfathomable—black-grey, dotted with billions of lights that sting Progeny's eyes, but he can't stop staring. He feels like he is floating upward. He feels free.

There are strange sounds everywhere. Trills, whistles, a dull roar from far away. The world smells like a thousand cans of opened peaches, but better.

Progeny stands on soft, damp grass, trees surrounding him, the broken entrance to the tunnels at his feet. Nearby is a bench, and a colourful construction that confuses Progeny. It has a ladder, a small bridge, a pole, a slide. There is a long snaking pathway. It runs away toward a hard line of blackness that he understands from Father's lessons to be a road. And past the road are houses. Real, honest to God, houses.

As he surveys his surrounds in wonder, the dull roar grows louder. Suddenly, through the trees he sees bright lights followed by a car. For a moment, he stands rooted to the spot, not thinking to protect his eyes, or hide. But then fear intrudes upon his stupor. He averts his pained gaze, collapses to the ground, spreadeagled, ready to crawl into the tunnels. But the car doesn't stop. When he glances up, he sees that it is disappearing from view, the noise fading.

He berates himself for his cowardice. He rises slowly, and in a daze follows the path to the road.

Nothing is as Father said it would be. There are houses, all still standing. They have yards, full of greenery and bright flowers.

Progeny can't reconcile the reality with the picture Father painted of the end of the world. Perhaps the remainder live on in the homes of the damned, keeping them neat. But Progeny doesn't believe this. He thinks people live here. He thinks they found another way to survive.

He should find out for sure. He should approach a house, harden his resolve, and knock on the door.

But he doesn't. Not just yet.

His attention is drawn by a strange, hairy creature, about knee high, that runs on all fours along the road toward him. It stops abruptly when it sees him, growls, turns, and disappears into one of the yards.

He hears more rumbling in the distance, more cars.

He moves farther down the road, looking from side to side, trying to decide which house looks the friendliest. But he's squinting now. His eyes have begun to sting. It occurs to him that the world is changing. It's getting brighter. He stops, peers up at the sky, and is shocked to see the colour has altered. What was black-grey is now grey-blue. And it hurts. He squeezes his eyes closed, tears beading in the corners. This isn't right.

He opens his eyes a crack, turns, and sees the first hint of a shivering orange ball of fire rising up over the horizon. He screams as it imprints itself on his retinas. He jams his eyes shut again, but still the fire burns through his lids. That light is like a blow to the head.

He buries his fists into his eye sockets, rubbing furiously. He moves blindly now, stumbling in what he hopes is back toward the entrance to the tunnels, back to darkness. But he trips, falls painfully. He skins his knees and hands on the hard surface of the road. His eyes spring open involuntarily, and he's blinded by that fire on the horizon. He screams again, clenches his eyes shut.

A door creaks open. He hears the soft pad of footsteps. And then from close behind, "Are you ok?"

He's so shocked that he swings around wildly, and his arm hits something solid, jarring. Someone grunts and curses. Pain courses through his wrist, and still the light burns. But he realises he's found a person. A real person. Because the remainder don't speak.

"I can't see," he says in a rush. "I can't see. Help me."

But the person doesn't respond.

Progeny hears more voices. He feels shadowy presences surround him, talking amongst themselves. He hears phrases like: "He might be sick," and "Don't touch him," and "The police are on their way."

The voices converge, and cover him with meaningless sounds. He no longer understands them. He's confused, and in pain, and lost in the light.

Progeny waits in a small, white room. It's been some time since his needle, but his arm still throbs. There's a burning sensation snaking out from the puncture wound, up into his shoulder, down to his wrist.

The lights are on, and even though the needle lady gave him dark goggles, his eyes hurt. They feel gritty, and water constantly.

The door to the room creaks, drawing Progeny's attention. It opens, and in walks a tall woman, greying hair, weathered face. A not unkind face.

"Hello, Progeny. My name is Doctor Gillian Reynolds. But please, call me Gillian," she says. Her voice is husky, controlled.

Progeny regards her silently. He sits stiffly on the edge of his neat, white bed. The sheets crackle when he shifts his weight.

She walks past Progeny, and eases into the single armchair in the room. She looks relaxed, as if this is her room. It's certainly not Progeny's room. It feels like a prison. From one, into the next, he thinks.

"I understand this must be very confusing for you. It's very confusing for us, so it must be confusing for you," Gillian says. She offers a hint of a sad smile.

Progeny stays silent.

Gillian crosses one leg over the other. She's holding a pen, which she begins to tap against her leg.

"We found your Father's body. I'm very sorry for your loss," she says.

"Why?" Progeny asks. He doesn't look at her, he looks past her, toward the door. The door can't be opened from the inside. He's checked.

"I understand he mistreated you. That he kept you locked up down there. But he was still your Father."

He doesn't want to think about Father. He glances at her instead. Then he looks around the locked room. At the two-way glass. The camera in the ceiling. "When will you release me from here?"

Gillian smiles sadly. It is a knowing smile. A maternal smile.

"Five weeks at the earliest. But most likely longer than that."

"Most likely longer," Progeny repeats.

"Yes. You've never been vaccinated against the X23 virus, so you need to finish your course of injections. Your photophobia is extreme. You'll need time and treatment to help you adjust to living with sunlight. And, perhaps most importantly, we need to ensure you're mentally fit for integration. For your safety, and ours."

"So you're protecting me?" Just like Father, he thinks.

Gillian hesitates, ceases tapping her pen. "You've been away a long time, Progeny."

"Indeed."

Gillian leans forward. "We found another body in the tunnels."

Progeny tenses. The words sting as he sees his mother's desiccated corpse. "That was my mother."

Gillian doesn't say any words, but her face says more than words could. Her eyes widen, her mouth forms a little o. She covers with a cough, then eases back into the chair. She begins tapping her leg again.

In that moment, Progeny knows he's not leaving anytime soon. He doesn't understand exactly why, but he knows. These people are not the mindless remainder that Father spoke of, but they're not like him. He alarms them. And what Father did alarms them. He feels lost. Defeated.

He realises Gillian is speaking again.

"—meet once a day to discuss your upbringing and your life below ground. And your... parents," she pauses, watching Progeny. He says nothing. "At the end of each session, you'll be able to ask some questions about what has happened since you've been gone."

Progeny remembers being on his knees in the shelter, hands on his head, waiting for his question. He shakes his head.

Gillian rises lithely out of the armchair. "It's going to be okay, Progeny. This all feels strange now, I know. But I'm here to help. Engage with me fully, and we'll have you ready to face the rest of the world in no time."

He doesn't look up as Gillian leaves. He can't. Because he doesn't believe her.

The next day, Gillian enters Progeny's room brandishing a writing pad, a pencil, a sympathetic smile. Progeny lies in the bed with the crisp sheets. When he sees Gillian, he rolls away from her, stares at the wall. The sheets crackle as he moves.

"How are we today, Progeny?" Gillian asks.

He grunts, signifying nothing. His arm hurts. His eyes hurt. His chest feels tight and achy.

He hears Gillian moving. She walks around the end of his bed, and eases into the armchair. She exudes the faint scent of soap.

"I'm looking forward to finding out about you. About your life underground," she says. "But before we start, do you have any queries for me?"

Progeny doesn't say anything for a while. He's caught between wanting to snap at Gillian, and wanting to ignore her. Finally, he says, "Do you enjoy this?"

"Enjoy what, Progeny?"

"Keeping me locked up. Torturing me."

"I don't believe that is what we're doing. I'm here to assess your mental state of mind. And then to help you adjust, and to integrate into our society."

Progeny huffs, but says nothing. Gillian waits. When she realises that Progeny will say nothing further, she adds, "How we progress is up to you, Progeny. Now, tell me something about you. What do you first remember? Were you born above, or underground?"

Progeny closes his eyes. His mouth tightens into a thin line. He refuses to respond.

Gillian waits. She lets the silence build. But Progeny doesn't mind. He's lived in silence. He's comfortable there.

After what seems a long time, Gillian pushes up out of her chair, a knee clicking as she moves. Progeny hears her walk back to the door, knock. After a moment, it opens. She hesitates, then says, "Let's try again tomorrow."

Then she's gone.

Progeny ignores Gillian the next day, and the day after that. He takes joy in the tone of annoyance that creeps into her inquiries. It is a small win, he thinks. Petty, but something.

He takes further joy in her absence the following day. And the day after that.

But his joy doesn't last. Left by himself, he realises that with Gillian's company, or without, he's still stuck in this room. At least underground, he had space to move, to fish, to dig. But in here, all he has is questions, and needles, and lights that sting.

There's something dark forming inside him. Something cavernous. He's worrying at it, giving it form. A tunnel of his own making.

"What do you remember of your mother?" Gillian asks. She sits in the armchair again, watching Progeny watch her. He's hunched over, perched on the end of the bed. It's late evening. His dinner remains untouched on a tray on the bedside table. The once earthy scent of the soup is morphing into something rancid as it cools.

Progeny stares blankly for a long time through his dark goggles. He shifts his gaze beyond Gillian, to focus on a stain on the wall. He licks his lips. Reluctantly, he speaks. Slowly. Petulantly. "I remember her corpse. Her bones. She smelt like dust."

Gillian nods, her pencil makes scratching noises as she moves it across her writing pad. "What about before she died?"

Progeny snorts a mirthless laugh. "Nothing."

"I see. What about your father then? What was he like?"

Progeny flinches. He feels the sting of the switch under his arm. He hears Father's yells. He watches him disappear under the collapse of the tunnel.

"He was like you."

"Me?"

"You and your kind. He also locked me up and told me it was for my benefit."

Gillian frowns. "What else did he do? What did you talk about with him? What did he teach you?"

He sneers, opens his mouth to answer. But then he sees Gillian watching him, waiting, her pen poised above the pad. And he suddenly imagines her sitting in that chair for many years to come. Repeating this performance. Day after day. His bravado falters. Tears well, his lips quiver. He feels like he is falling.

"Please," he croaks, "Let me go. I won't tell anyone. Please. I can't cope in here anymore."

Gillian sighs, cocks her head. Progeny thinks she intends to look sympathetic. She looks condescending. "I'm sorry. I am, but —"

"Let me go, god damnit," Progeny yells suddenly, jumping down from the bed, fists clenched with impotent rage.

At first, Gillian's face shows shock. But then it becomes something else. A cold expression. A hard expression.

She rises from the armchair, turns and carefully places her pencil and pad on the seat of the chair. She moves to the door, knocks, and after a moment it opens. At first, Progeny thinks she is leaving him. But then she holds the door ajar, looks back at Progeny, and says, "Come with me."

His eyes widen. But his legs quickly move.

Progeny follows Gillian out into a sterile, white corridor. The sound of her shoes on the linoleum seems loud to Progeny. He licks his lips, and watches her walk away. The corridor is dimly lit. It smells of disinfectant. He waits for the men to grab him, to shove him back into his room. He waits, but they don't appear. And so he hurries after Gillian.

At the end of the hall is an elevator. Gillian swipes a key card, waits.

"Where are we going?" Progeny asks, his fury left back in his room. He's certain she's not releasing him, and yet he hopes.

"Up," Gillian says.

The elevator doors open with a ding, and Gillian steps inside. Progeny follows. The scent is human, stale. What is this? he wonders.

A short ride, and the doors open. Gillian steps out of the lift and makes a hard right. When Progeny follows, he finds her already climbing a metal staircase, her footfall clanging.

Gillian waits for him at the top, in front of a door. When he catches up to her, she says, "Are you ready?"

But she doesn't allow him time to respond. She wrenches the door open and Progeny is assaulted by light. Not the sun, it's not that bright, but it still hurts, even with the goggles. He clamps his eyes shut, turns his head away, but Gillian grabs him by the wrist and, with gentle force, guides him through the door.

He instantly notices eddies of air around him, and knows he is outside. The air smells acrid and oily, not like before. And then there is the soundtrack. A strange, loud chorus of roaring, and honking.

"Look," she demands. "This is what you wanted, so look."

Slowly, hesitantly, he allows his eyes to open a crack. The artificial light comes from monolithic structures that reach up into the sky like the roots of an upside down tree. They're mostly glass. And they glow with checkerboard patterns of light and dark.

When his eyes follow the tallest tower up to its highest point, he sees the black of the night sky beyond. But there is barely a star to be seen here. When he looks back down below, he sees strips of neon. And in between, parallel lines of white lights, and red, moving slowly like two giant eels swimming in opposite directions. That is where the honking and roars come from. It's all unpleasant. Overwhelming. He doesn't know where to look. Or how to block out the noise.

Gillian releases his arm. His legs wobble, but he keeps his balance. He turns his back on the city. Thankfully, looking the other way, he finds less light. And what lights there are, are diffused, mainly located at ground level, but spreading outward for miles, and miles.

"This is the world, Progeny," Gillian says, drawing his attention. "You really think you're ready for this?"

"I... I..."

"If we let you go, where would you go?" she asks. She's speaking with a firm tone, enunciating each word. He opens his mouth, closes it. He glances back uncertainly at the city. It retains its chaotic splendour.

"Do you have family? Or friends here? We haven't found any, but perhaps you know better?"

He swallows, shakes his head. "I don't know."

"Where would you live?"

"I... I don't know."

"People need to work to survive in the city. If you work, you make money so you can pay for a home, and food. Did your father explain this to you?"

Progeny nods.

"Then what would you do? What skills do you have?"

He shakes his head again. He feels tears stabbing at his eyes. He blinks hard to hold them back. "I can dig," he offers quietly.

She exhales for a long time, like all of the air in her lungs is tainted and she wants to be done with it. "Progeny, you are a ward of the State. We are responsible for you both here and out there. I don't gain from keeping you here forever. But I would be failing my duty if I released you to become homeless and to starve. My job is to prepare you for life outside. But this," she says, with a sweeping arm gesture toward the city, "is beyond you right now. Jesus," she hisses, "let me help. That's what I'm trying to do. I'm not your father."

All Progeny can think about are stars, or the lack of them. He glances up again and wonders where they have gone. He remembers the millions of pinpricks of light he saw when he first rose from the tunnels. A promise of something infinite. It's there, he thinks. It must be. Out there. Somewhere. He regards Gillian again, and finds that her expression has softened.

"How we go from here is up to you, Progeny. You can ignore me, demand to be released before you are ready, and stay with us. Perhaps forever. Or, you can accept that this will take time, and then get to work."

Progeny takes a breath, and takes one last lingering look up at the darkness. When he looks back at Gillian, he nods.

Back in his room, locked up again, Progeny lies awake. He stares at the ceiling, but his mind is a long way away.

He's in his dark place. The tunnel he's built inside. Around him fly Gillian's words, along with his father's, and his own defeated thoughts. But, for all of that, he doesn't feel quite so alone down here. He may not see a way out, not right now anyway, but he knows there is a starlit sky waiting for him up above somewhere. He's proved that to himself once before, not very long ago.

Which is why he's decided to change course. He's decided to start digging up.

See Michael Gardner's story "All That Remains" online at Metaphorosis.
If you liked it, leave a comment. Authors love that!
Remember to subscribe to our e-mail updates so you'll know when new stories are posted.

About the story

Despite current events, this story wasn't inspired by the coronavirus. I wrote this a good six months before COVID-19 broke out.

I'd been reading a number of dystopian fantasy and horror stories at the time. I began wondering what might happen to a doomsday prepper who hid away from the end of the world, only to find out years later that the world hadn't ended after all. And then, what if that person brought a child with them.

I found that tension interesting, so started to play with it, and along came Progeny. A man-child, really, with a lot to learn about the shortcomings of his father, and himself.

A question for the author

Q: Can beautiful things be funny?

A: I think funny moments can be beautiful, so beautiful things must be funny.

As an example, I was trying not to laugh at my daughter the other day who was doing her best to avoid going to bed. I failed in my attempt to be stern, and ended up laughing at her antics, which made her laugh in return. I was wondering where she got her cheeky sense of humour. And in that moment, I realised she was growing up in front of me, becoming her own, unique person. I couldn't help but think that sharing such a moment in her life was beautiful. As well as being funny.

About the author

Michael Gardner is an economist by day, a writer of fantasy and horror by night. He lives in Canberra, Australia, with his patient wife and two wonderful kids. The experience of fatherhood continues to find its way into his stories. His work has appeared in *Writers of the Future Volume 36, Aurealis*, and of course, *Metaphorosis*. He is also a two-time finalist for the Aurealis Awards. You can find out more about Michael and his work at www.michael-s-gardner.com.

Joy (Unplugged)

B.C. van Tol

A reddish moon clung to the horizon like a faded blood stain that wouldn't wash out. Joy shivered, looking at the moon's human-like face from her attic window, wishing she could pull him to her. Together, they could agonize in this lonely house atop the hill. From afar, his mouth hung agape, as though wailing in silent operatic sorrow. The silence pervaded the dark, motionless town nestled in the valley below. From Joy's vantage point, the town seemed nothing more than a crumbling diorama of miniature homes and shops. After being alone for over a year, Joy wondered whether she'd ever see anyone again.

She switched on her electric candle and placed it on the windowsill in the attic. The soft yellow glow served as her beacon to those who might Detach in the night, stumbling confused and withered into a reality they'd long since abandoned.

When her eyes grew weary, she climbed into bed beside a row of pillows arranged to look like another person already asleep under the covers. She slid her arm around a pillow, tracing the scars in its casing where she'd sewn its many rips and tears. It wouldn't survive much longer, she knew. And if the solitude continued, neither would she.

"Goodnight," she whispered, clinging desperately to the pillow. As if in response, the centuries-old house creaked eerily from a passing breeze. Some sound was always better than none.

Nobody came that night.

Joy arose at dawn, kissed the top of her pretend pillow person, and retrieved the candle from the attic. It was a clear day, and she could see the town's distant clock tower. Its hands had given up at

8:34 one April morning before her twenty-third birthday. That had
been over a decade ago.

Beyond the town, standing like sentries in an enemy army,
were the giant wind turbines that generated the energy supply for
the town's Virtual Lifestyle Attachments (un-affectionately known
to Joy as ViLiAs). A network transmitter column glowered like an
emperor in the center of the turbine field. The column was
responsible for luring the townspeople into a completely
customizable, full-sensory trance. The sun glinted off its steel
armor. A red light blinked at the top, taunting her the way the
moon did.

Because Joy was the sole person not participating in ViLiAs
and had no wind turbines of her own, she pedaled on her
stationary bicycle, which charged the battery in her electric candle.
The house, devoid of all other electricity, had once belonged to her
grandmother. When the ViLiAs claimed Joy's mother as one of
their earliest victims, Gran had stripped the house of its appliances
and wiring, even going so far as to plaster over the old electric
sockets.

Gran once said, "Humans got along just fine for thousands of
years without electricity."

But humans always had each other, Joy thought as she
pedaled. Not for the first time, she considered whether it was worse
to live a fake life with real people than a real life with a fake pillow
person.

At least Gran had kept a wind-up record player and a hodge-
podge collection of vinyls. Joy let Chopin soothe her loneliness as
she tended the garden for the rest of the morning.

In the afternoon, Joy baked a loaf of bread in the wood-
burning stone hearth built into the house's original foundation.
She kept her windows open so the scent of baking would drift
outside. Someone out there might long for fresh food.

That evening, she practiced on Gran's upright piano. She'd
left the front door open so as to fill the hillside with music. The sun
had begun to set, and she could hardly see the black and white
keys in front of her.

During rests in the music, she heard footsteps stumbling
onto the porch. When she turned around, a man loomed in the
doorway. His clothes hung like rags, and his head seemed loosely
attached to his gaunt frame.

She rose, her movements slow though her heart raced. The
Detached were like skittish, starving animals. His eyes scanned the
living room while she leaned awkwardly against the piano. "I've
food," she offered, hoping she didn't sound as desperate as she felt.

When he took a tentative step forward, she ventured into the kitchen and put a plate of bread and jam on the table, eagerly listening toward the door. Then came the sound of his feet shuffling across the wooden floors.

When he took a seat, she resisted the urge to sit beside him, to not-so-accidentally brush his hand as he reached for the jam. Patience is a curse, she thought, as he ran his fingers over the bread, getting jam on his fingertips, as if not quite sure it was real. He would have been accustomed to neuro-simulated taste, since the ViLiAs fed people bland, liquified nutrients through a feeding tube. Of the food sludge, there was endless supply, since everything was recycled through biowaste tubes and re-processed in underground factories overseen by robotic machinery. Joy shuddered.

Fastidiously, he ate, inspecting every morsel, even the crumbs on the plate. After the bread was gone, the man sat for a long time with his eyes closed. Joy knew better than to disturb him. Most Detached persons took a while to distinguish reality from what they had conjured and customized as part of their Virtual Lifestyle package. She gazed through the kitchen window at the last sliver of sun descending from view and listened as the birds outside quieted into their nests.

When he looked up again, she said, "I have a spare room upstairs. You're welcome to stay." She left out the word 'forever'.

A curious-minded Detached person might stay a week until the Withdrawal became unbearable. With fortitude, they might survive Withdrawal and stay a month before something else called to them—a sense of adventure, a sense of fear, a sense of loss. Eventually, they all left.

The man seemed to consider her offer. He had probably forgotten what it meant to feel tired. Or feel anything at all, for that matter. He opened his mouth to speak, but only air came out.

"Your voice will return with time. Come, you could do with some rest."

Though he stood a foot taller and would have been formidable had he not wasted away, Joy had no fear of being raped. According to Gran, ViLiAs made men impotent. Sometimes permanently. It didn't matter, however. Once Attached, anyone could experience every pleasure in a virtual setting. Even have virtual children.

They ascended the stairs by the light of Joy's electric candle, their bodies casting long shadows on the wall. When an animal screeched somewhere in the night, he jumped, grabbing onto the railing.

"Just an owl," she said and then showed him to his room. Before shutting the door, she added, "It helps to listen to the sound of your breath. It's a reminder that you're still alive."

Without the usual sense of gloom, Joy climbed to the attic and placed the electric candle in the window.

The next morning as she tended her garden, she glanced up at his window and saw him gazing at the woods behind the house. His expression resembled that of a lost child. Her heart felt an invisible bond extending to him, as if she'd reached out her hand and he'd taken it.

Oh, to feel the touch of a hand! she thought. The last human contact she'd had was a brushing of arms one year, five months, and three days ago. Joy kept a written log of such things. The other arm belonged to a Detached woman who had stayed with Joy for four days and then mysteriously left in the night. Joy blamed the woman's departure on the physical contact. The Detached seemed unable to endure it in the first days after returning to reality.

This day, the clouds were plentiful, and she could smell rain in the air. Just as she finished picking green beans, the first drops fell. Inside, Joy found the man standing at her fireplace mantle, entranced by a photograph. She said, "That's my grandmother. She raised me. In this house, in fact."

He turned and studied Joy, not realizing or maybe not caring that to inspect another human being was once considered rude. She took the opportunity to study him as well. He had somber deep brown eyes, but also sallow skin and plump lips hidden beneath a scraggly, brittle beard. Matted dark hair dangled from his head. He scratched at it with bony hands.

"I'm Joy," she whispered.

His voice was barely a rasp. "I'm...MightyAugust8501." He frowned, something not quite right. "I mean August. Just August."

She guessed he'd not used this name for many years.

He pointed to Gran in the photograph, his eyebrows raised as if to ask where Gran was.

Joy said, "If you look out the window, beyond those trees is a clearing where sunbeams fall through the branches. Gran used to say that the sunbeams looked like the silk of her wedding dress." Joy sighed. "Have you ever felt real silk, August?"

He shook his head.

"I buried her in the wedding dress in that clearing. Carried her in my arms all the way. After the sickness, she weighed so little..." Joy's thoughts trailed off. She knew she must be careful. Sorrow was a dangerous companion for someone so often alone. "Anyway, that was eight years ago." Eight years, one month, and twenty-two days. Nine Detached visitors in all that time.

Later, August sat on the couch, while she played the piano. At first, he covered his ears against the sound. Joy took no offense. When he lowered his hands and began to sway his head from side to side, she smiled because it meant his soul hadn't died.

"You're welcome to stay as long as you wish," she said.

That night, after August retired to his room, Joy climbed into her own bed next to the pillow person. For a moment, she put her arm around it. It smelled faintly of mildew and felt rough against her skin. Joy shoved the pillow person onto the floor where she stomped on it until its scars opened and it bled stuffing.

"Never again," she said.

When she awoke the next morning, she found August again in front of her fireplace mantle, admiring a different photo. Tears streaked his cheeks.

"Is something wrong?" She curtailed the urge to hug him, to wipe away his tears and stroke his matted hair.

"Do you have children?" he asked.

"No, that's me. I'm four years old, sitting on Gran's lap at the park. Back when the park wasn't a wind turbine field. It's the last picture ever taken of me."

Over breakfast of bread and jam, he asked, "Why do you do all this for a stranger?"

"Don't worry. You don't owe me anything."

"Why?" he said more forcefully. Charity was not a trait of an addicted society. Kindness would have been to him like a strange dream.

"It's what I do," she said.

He crossed his arms, unsatisfied.

"It's a long story."

"Good," he said.

With a sigh, she settled into a chair opposite him. "When I was little, people finally began to realize how addictive ViLiAs were, and some addicts decided to Detach on their own. Gran and I took in several of these people over the years. Nobody else was around to help. We showed the Detached how to return to a natural life. Or at least, we tried."

In truth, Joy and her gran had helped nearly three dozen Detached work through their Withdrawal. Of those, four had died in the process. Those who survived eventually left with their newfound lives or invented some excuse to go back to the Attachment. "Now Gran is buried in the clearing, where the silken sunshine comes in. I continue our work all by myself." Joy shrugged. "It's the only life I know."

"Will you take me?" he asked.

"To the clearing?"

"I want to see the silk."

Later, they walked through the woods, crossed the stream in their bare feet, and climbed the hill to the clearing. August's face filled with wonder as he cupped one of the silken sunbeams falling through the branches above. Then he did something he hadn't done yet: he laughed, a shuddering breathy sound that made Joy think of new life coming into the world.

"I didn't think the sun could feel soft," he said, amazed.

Joy laughed, too, despite herself. A patch of light covered his head, and she could see color returning to his cheeks. Good, she thought. He'll need to be healthy for what comes next.

After dinner, Joy put on some records. She began with the classical, spritely Mozart. Food for the soul and the making of a good temperament, Gran always said. August bobbed his head to the music.

The next morning, she gasped when she saw him. He'd trimmed back his beard and had given himself a haircut. Joy could hardly recognize him, but despite the unevenness of his trimming, he less resembled a feral animal and more a person.

"I found a pair of scissors in the bathroom," he said. "I couldn't take the itching anymore. Before, when I was Attached, I remember scratching, vaguely, like it was someone else's itch. Eventually, I scratched so much I must have knocked off my electrodes, because I woke up gagging on my feeding tube."

"It must have been terrifying." Joy outstretched her hand to give his shoulder a comforting squeeze. He tensed at her approach, and she whirled around, ashamed.

Breaking the tension, he pointed to a bowl on the kitchen table. "I picked you some strawberries. I wanted to do more. For you."

Then never leave me, she would have replied.

He tapped some keys on her piano. "Is it hard to learn?" he asked, pressing a shrill tone cluster of notes in the highest register. He winced and withdrew his hand from the keys.

"Yes, but if you enjoy playing, you don't notice it's difficult."

"Like the Attachment," he whispered.

Joy played a happy tune from memory. She had forgotten its name, but it reminded her of the stream's delicate surface and how it caught the sun's reflection, making it dance. When the song ended, she saw through the living room window the waxing moon hanging romantically in a clear sky full of bright stars.

"I can't hear the moon's terrible singing when you're here," she said. "He looks almost peaceful now. Like a child yawning before sleep."

August appeared wistful for a moment. "When I first Detached, I was so disoriented that the moon frightened me. I wandered in the woods for I don't know how long, trying to hide from him under the trees, but he was always watching. Then I heard your piano, and I saw the light in your window. These did not frighten me, so I came here to you."

Instinctively, Joy grasped his hand. The touch sent reverberations up her arm and down her back. August cried out and yanked his hand away.

"No! I'm sorry!" she said, horrified at what she had done.

August clutched his hand to his chest protectively, his eyes darting to the front door.

Please stay! she wanted to shout, but the situation required calmness. Softly, slowly, she said, "You probably haven't experienced human touch in many years. Touching another person isn't the same as using your fingers to eat or feeling the sun on your face. When you've been deprived of it for so long, a first touch can hurt. It hurt me as well."

"I should do more for you..." he said, slowly extending his hand back out to her, cringing and wrinkling his nose like touch were a bad smell. The temptation to take it again was almost more than she could bear.

She shook her head. "It's okay."

He dropped his hand, clearly relieved. "Perhaps tomorrow," he said.

"Perhaps."

When she woke the next morning, she could not find August anywhere in the house. At first, the seeds of panic grew, and she worried her transgression had caused him to flee in the night. That is, until she found him outside crouched over the stream, his hair glistening with water. His cheeks had more health than she had yet seen, and he smelled fresher.

"A bath?" she asked.

He nodded. "I can't sit still today. I could hardly sleep last night."

He did not offer her his hand again this morning. She would not remind him. Not now, at the first signs of Withdrawal: restlessness, sleeplessness. By tomorrow, he would have the headaches. The day after, the sweats, the body aches. And the next day, fever, shakes, or even … she didn't dare think it.

She set him to pulling weeds in the garden while she picked some lettuces. He pulled a few and began to stare out into the direction of town. She followed his gaze to the network transmitter column, which occasionally winked at them with its red come-hither beacon at the top. If only she could snuff it out.

"My gran always said to look in the direction you are headed."

August hastily pulled some more weeds. "Have you ever tried ViLiAs?"

"No," she said. She feared such discussion would only keep his mind on the subject.

"Oh." His gaze returned to the network transmitter column.

Jealous of the column's continued hold on August, she said, "I do know what it means to feel unbearably restless." Once more, she had his attention. She wiped some sweat from her brow with her sleeve and continued working as she spoke. "In my late teenage years, I had boundless energy and found I couldn't sit still. I argued with Gran constantly, something I'm ashamed of now, but at the time, I had no idea what had gotten into me. Gran patiently let me rant or put me to labor-intensive chores to burn my energy off.

"One day, as I stood in this very garden, I heard the clock tower chiming. I felt the pull of the world beckoning me to explore it. That day, I said to Gran, 'I need to leave and make my own way.' I thought she would put up a fuss or forbid me. Instead, she kissed my forehead and sent me off with a loaf of bread and a flask of water." Joy still remembered Gran's warm, firm kiss on her forehead.

"Where did you go?" August asked, leaning forward.

"First, I went into the hills, but then the hills turned into bald-faced mountains. I was not so foolish as to think I could cross them alone, so I turned and wandered the forest for a time, living mostly off berries. I realized very quickly that with freedom came loneliness. I became homesick and wanted nothing more than to hug my gran."

"Did you go home?"

"No. I was stubborn. Instead, I went into the town."

"What did you find?"

"More loneliness. Not a soul walked the streets. No children played outside. Most windows were boarded up completely. Eventually, I came to a cottage on a street lined with fallen trees. I imagined it was once charming, but the grasses had grown so high that the cottage appeared short and stubby, like a dollhouse for a child. It had one window that was not boarded, and I peeked in. A person lay on the floor of the front room—a woman so emaciated I could not have guessed at her age. She would have looked dead, if not for one trembling, outstretched arm reaching for something not quite within grasp. You see, despite having tumbled from her couch, she was still Attached. Her ViLiAs face mask was still in place, and sensory electrodes dotted her body. Then I noticed what she reached for—her feeding tube, which had evidently fallen out some time earlier.

"I just couldn't understand it. Was her addiction so strong that she would starve to death, inches from nourishment because she couldn't Detach for mere seconds to save her own life?

"I banged on the window. 'Take off the mask!' I shouted. If she heard me, she showed no sign of it. Had I known better—or perhaps, had I not been so lonely—I would've left her there. Instead, I broke the window, and I climbed in. Then I made the mistake of Detaching her."

August grimaced, evidently remembering the shock of his own Detachment.

"The woman screamed so loudly that it echoed through the valley. I expected the police to come or neighbors to check on her."

August shook his head. "I don't suppose anyone did."

"No," she replied somberly. "It gets worse. I grabbed the woman by the shoulder. 'You need to eat!' I told her. The jolt of Detachment and the sudden human contact made her berserk. As I tried to calm her, she clawed at me with nails that hadn't been clipped in a long time. Then she bit my arm." Joy rolled up her sleeve and showed August the shiny depressed scar where the woman had taken a healthy chunk of flesh. "When she bit me, I dropped her on the floor. There was a horrible thud, and then she was still. I thought I killed her. I panicked, bleeding. I put the Attachments back on her and re-inserted her feeding tube, in hopes it would coax her to stay alive. Or at least relieve the suffering I'd caused in trying to help."

"Did she die?"

Joy shrugged. "I sat next to her the whole day, just watching her breathing to make sure it didn't stop. Hours later, when it started to get dark, I put my hand on her chest to make sure I could feel it rise and fall. I sang to her to drown out the moon that stared, judging me, through the broken window.

"By nightfall, the bite in my arm had become swollen and infected. I held it up to the moonlight and saw two red lines under my skin creeping up to my shoulder. If I stayed with her much longer, I knew I'd die of sepsis, so I left her there on the floor. I went out into the night, looking for Gran's candle in the attic up at the top of the hill. I stumbled for hours, following that little flicker of hope, fever shaking me and pus weeping down my forearm. I followed the candle, ashamed of myself, terrified Gran would never forgive me."

"Did she forgive?"

Joy shut her eyes, remembering. When she'd reached the house, the clock tower had struck midnight. She saw Gran's silhouette standing out on the porch.

"She asked me, 'Joy, have you learned anything in your travels?' I knelt down before her, half in fatigue, half in penance, and I said, 'I've learned more than I care to.' Gran helped me to my feet, embraced me. 'I can hear it in your voice. Come inside now. You're home.'" Joy could still feel her gran's arms around her, and her eyes misted over.

August gazed back toward the network transmitter column once more, a different air about him, as though seeing his past clearly for the first time, seeing the terrible fall of humanity from which he'd dragged himself.

"Home," he said, slipping his hand in hers.

Joy felt as if she'd won her first true battle against the network transmitter column, still blinking at her with red scorn.

The next day, Joy awoke to find August pacing downstairs.

"I can't sit still. Every time I stop moving, I think my bones will crawl out of my skin. What's happening to me?"

She examined his eyes. They were bloodshot and had dark circles beneath them. His breath was snappy. "It's the early stages of Withdrawal."

He resumed pacing. "I keep thinking I'll die unless I re-Attach myself. Like there are invisible cords wrapped around my arms, pulling me back to it..." His speech became so rapid that she could no longer understand him.

"You must eat. Your body needs the fuel."

After he wolfed down some bread, she put a feather duster in his jittery hands. "You see the fireplace mantle? Start dusting there. When you're done, do the bookcases. After that, the cabinets. If you can't keep still, keep yourself busy."

"I'm scared," he said, taking her hand.

"It's normal," she assured him. It was the best she could promise. There was still a chance he could die.

While he dusted, she began to prepare enough food to last several days. When he finished dusting, he asked her what to do next. So, she handed him an axe. "My wood pile is getting low," she said, pointing to a fallen tree. "If you get dizzy or breathless, stop."

Though he didn't appear strong, the Withdrawal restlessness evidently gave him enough energy to wield the axe. Grunting with each swing, he chopped the wood until he stumbled away from the tree in exhaustion. By that time, most of the afternoon had passed.

Joy helped him back into the house and up to his room. "Something's wrong," he said, his voice unsteady. "My heart keeps skipping, and I feel a shadow creeping toward me."

"Do you still feel like your bones will crawl out of your skin?"

He blinked down at her from his tired eyes. "No."

"See? You're doing a fine job. Now just rest."

His breath came in rapid, shallow waves while she watched over him from a chair beside his bed. Eventually, he slept.

Joy did not put the candle in the attic window that night. She kept it at August's bedside, along with a basket of bread and a pail of fresh water. He awoke in the night writhing and sweating. She put a cool compress on his forehead. He vomited, and she cleaned him. Sometimes he spoke in desperate tones. "Let me go back. Just for a few minutes..."

"You're too sick to go anywhere just now. When you're better, you can go wherever you want," she said.

"Everything hurts. My eyes hurt. My teeth hurt. The air around my body hurts!"

"You're purging addiction from your system."

She dripped some water onto his lips, and he licked it off, eventually drifting back to sleep. The next day, he spent hours curled in a ball lying on his side, moaning, shivering with fever.

"I'm dying," he said. He grabbed the sleeve of her shirt, ripping the seam at her shoulder. "Am I dying?" She could not deny it. "I need to go back. Please… Let me go."

He tried to get up from the bed but discovered his legs could not carry him. He fell to the floor and screamed in pain. As she rushed to help him back into the bed, he began to thrash wildly, and she worried he'd bite her.

"You tricked me! You made me swing the axe so many times that it sucked the life from me. You did it on purpose to keep me here!"

She knew it was the Withdrawal speaking, not her August, but it hurt all the same. Gran had always warned her not to get too close to the Detached—to become Attached to them. "They will pull you down with them," she had said. "You can do your best to help, and at the end of the day, if you manage to save one, that will fulfill you more than anything." However, Gran had always had Joy. What did Gran know of utter desolation and the wretched, humiliating need to cling to another living soul?

"It's not fair," she whispered once August had fallen asleep again. Joy ran her fingers over his cheeks.

When August woke next, he could hardly move. His lips had cracked, and the whites of his eyes had turned blood red from burst capillaries. He had fever rashes on his neck and chest. "Joy?" he said with a scratchy voice.

"I'm here."

"It doesn't hurt anymore. Will you tell me a story?" he asked, his eyes drooping. "Please."

Her arms ached from the days and nights tending to him. Her head throbbed from lack of sleep, and her back had grown sore from sitting in a wooden armchair while he slept. In their moments of shared pain, Joy had felt more connected to August than ever. Her August.

"Tell me about your parents," he said.

"It's not a happy story."

"Please." He held out his hand, and she wrapped her fingers around his.

"I don't know who my father is. Gran told me that someone took advantage of my mother after she became Attached. I was the result. My mother carried me to term, delivered me, all without Detaching once. The doctors said she'd miscarry if she went into Withdrawal. I was born healthy enough, but the birth coupled with addiction took a toll on her body. Gran, for the one and only time, hooked herself up to the ViLiAs to ask my mother what name to give me. My mother named me Joy. That's all I have of her. She died two days later."

As August's eyes filled with sorrow, Joy regretted telling him such a mournful tale. In a happier tone, she continued. "Gran said that my mother adored Beethoven's 'Ode to Joy,' and that's where my name came from. When I was a girl, I used to make Gran play the record over and over."

"I would love to hear it."

Joy set up the record player on the floor by his bed, put "Ode to Joy" into the spinner, and let it flood into the room like a pink and yellow sunrise dancing over snowcapped mountains.

At the end, he said, "This music is everything that is life. It doesn't lie or give false impressions."

Joy nodded, realizing for the first time that the song—and therefore her name—was as much a warning as it was a gift. Her mother had wanted Joy to live. To not follow in her footsteps.

Then he cried, "Look what I've done to myself! I don't know how I could have ever chosen a Virtual Lifestyle over this one. Or how..." his voice trailed off.

She wanted him to say, "Or how I could ever go back," but he didn't. Even now, she could sense something still tying him to his old life.

Give it time, she thought. If he survived this night, he would certainly pull through. Moreover, if he pulled through, he'd probably stay several more weeks. Then maybe, just maybe, he would be the one to stay forever, and together, they could continue the mission of saving the Detached.

August fell asleep once more, looking ashen as the moon. She did not take her eyes off his rising and falling chest. Sometimes his breathing became so shallow that she put her hand to his mouth to make sure she felt the exchange of air. Then he simply stopped breathing altogether.

At first, she thought it was a trick of her eyes. After all, she had been awake for days. She jammed her finger into his neck and felt a weak, uneven pulse. Screaming his name, she shook him, hoping he'd wake up. When that failed, she pumped his chest with her hands as Gran had taught her to do. She poured her own breath into his lungs, wishing it would pass some of her life into him. She did this until he coughed and sputtered.

Heaving, sweaty, and tear-streaked, she sank back into the chair, fully drained of the last energy in her reserves. She resumed her pulse and breath vigil, fighting the urgency of sleep with the fear that if she gave in to her sagging eyelids, she might awake to find him dead. She prayed there would be no need to resuscitate him a second time, for she simply did not have the strength.

Eventually, sleep claimed her as she slumped in the chair, her neck craning to one side. When she opened her eyes, the sun shone on August's slack face. She leapt up, fearing the worst, then she saw his chest rise. She saw it rise again and then a third time. They were full, restorative breaths. A finger to his pulse confirmed his heartbeat had returned to a normal pace. She took his hand, and sleep consumed her again.

This time, when she woke, it was still daylight. Or had she slept so long that it was daylight again? August was no longer in his bed, and a blanket had been draped around her shoulders. She got up from the chair, her knees sore and wobbling.

"August?" she called down from the top of the stairs. He did not respond. Hanging onto the railing to support her cramped legs, she descended to her living room.

"August?" Again, no response, and she despaired. Could he, after all they'd just endured, have returned to his Attachment? Surely, it would kill her.

Joy flung open the front door and nearly knocked August off the porch.

"Oh, you're awake," he said. He had tucked a single wildflower into the pocket of his shirt.

"I thought you left." She smoothed her hair, relieved she had been wrong and feeling guilty for having doubted him.

"No," he replied with an air of hesitation. She sensed an invisible "not yet" strung to the end of his thoughts. He looked out into the brightness of the day and faced the town. Drifting clouds cast blobs of shadows over the clock tower, the wind turbines, and the relentlessly blinking network transmitter column.

"How do you feel?"

His eyes still focused in the direction of town, he sighed wistfully. "Like I've just been born."

"Come inside, let's eat. We both could use the nourishment."

They shared a meal in silence. When it was over, he turned to her. "I'm sorry for how I behaved. For the things I said. The things I did. I'm ashamed."

She flitted her hand. "It's nothing. I've seen it before."

He knelt before her on the floor, taking the flower from his shirt pocket and holding it up to her. The delicate purple petals had already begun to wilt.

Joy swallowed hard, sensing the approach of bad news. "Shall we listen to some more records today?" She did not take the flower.

"I've been alone my entire life. Physically alone, but I never noticed it. Emotionally, mentally, I've had the entire world full of people just a brain wave away."

"All digital tricks and lies."

"Yes. But it was all I knew for many years." Their eyes met, and he touched her hair, tucking the flower behind her ear.

She didn't want to hear any more. As she pulled away from him, he grabbed her shoulder.

Joy squeezed her eyes shut. "Don't."

"I have to leave here, Joy. My wife..."

She felt her throat constrict.

"...my wife is back there. I know our marriage was virtual. The life we built, the home we made ... all fabricated."

Joy shook her head violently.

August sobbed. "Even our children..."

She could take no more, and wrested herself free. She ran to the living room and wilted into the couch.

He followed her. "My own children are not even real! Can you believe that? In the ViLiAs, it seemed normal. But out here, my soul is sick from having spent years of my life caring for people ... things ... that don't exist. These beings created in my image, with my eyes and my chin." His voice broke.

He went to the photographs on the mantle and picked up the one of Joy and Gran at the park. "I'll never have pictures with my children. I'll never truly be able to hold them in my hands." He held his hands out to her. "Joy, I've never even looked upon my wife with my own eyes. Never caressed her cheek or kissed her lips. Never touched her hair the way I've touched yours. I don't even know if she looks the same as her avatar in the system. I modeled my avatar after the real me, but that's not a requirement. She lives here in our town, but we've never met."

"So you'll go back to her—to the Attachment—after all this. Fine, then."

"I'll beg my wife to Detach. Convince her to join your cause— our cause. Will you help me?"

Joy crossed her arms and turned away. "I've always said you're free to go. Everyone leaves."

He took the photograph of her and Gran and pressed it into her hands. "You don't understand. This picture has inspired me. I'm disgusted by how much I've missed of life, including the chance to have real children. Not perfect digital representations of them. I want to clean up messes and argue over stupid things and teach them about life. You can't teach a computerized child—it already knows everything."

Joy shook her head. "But you won't be able to have real children. Not without a fertility doctor."

"After I bring my wife back, we can rescue doctors, neighbors, friends. Let's save our town, Joy. You and I can do it. We'll continue what your gran started."

She rolled up her sleeve and pointed at the scar from when the Detached woman bit her arm. "It doesn't work that way," she said through clenched teeth.

"I have to try. I just..." he ran his hand through his hair. "I can't not try."

"You're free to go."

"I promise you, Joy." He cupped her face in his hands, and for a moment, she thought he loved her. "I promise you," he said, emphasizing every syllable. "I will come back."

"Take some bread with you," she said. "And a flask of water."

August nodded, and then he left. When he shut the door, she ran to the window to watch him walk into the folds of the town below in the valley. "He'll never come back," she whispered. When she turned around, it was there—all the silence and loneliness that had been hiding since the day he showed up.

Joy gritted her teeth and got on her stationary bicycle. "No sense in milling about." After, she boiled his bedsheets and hung them to dry on the line. The breeze and the sun would infuse them with crispness and remove his scent. She'd simply start over, just as she'd always done. She washed her hair and let that, too, dry in the remaining sunlight before the sky turned pink and orange.

When night was certain, she took the sheets from the line, folded them, and put them away. She cut herself a slice of bread, and though she had no appetite, she forced herself to eat it, one nibble at a time. Joy tried, and failed, with each breath to push the memory of August's face from her mind. Not just his face, but all the hopes she had pinned on him.

Finally, she took the candle and climbed the stairs to put it in the attic window. August is down there somewhere, she thought. Down there with the rest of the world while I remain alone forever.

In her room, she found the pillow person still wounded on the floor where she'd left it. Her bed was empty. Her house was empty. Her heart was empty.

Instead of searching for sleep, Joy climbed into the attic. Then she shoved the candle out the window. The little orange glow fell like an ember until the glass crunched against the ground, snuffing out the light.

In the darkness, in her nightgown, she found the axe. She threw it over her shoulder and followed the blinking light of the network transmitter column. The lure of her enemy beckoning to her. Daring her to make her last stand. Alone, as always.

Above her, the moon gaped with silent laughter.

See B.C. van Tol's story "Joy (Unplugged)" online at Metaphorosis. If you liked it, leave a comment. Authors love that! Remember to subscribe to our e-mail updates so you'll know when new stories are posted.

About the story

"Joy (Unplugged)" is a product of multiple inspirations. The first is my great grandmother, who, despite not having much, would leave food out on her porch for impoverished people traveling through town looking for jobs during the Great Depression. The second is a curiosity about potential psychological and societal impacts of immersive technology. The third inspiration comes from interviews I've both read and conducted related to forms of technology addiction. I enjoy taking disparate ideas and weaving them together to create a story.

A question for the author

Q: What kind of non-fiction do you like to read and how does it affect the fiction you write?

A: I was an English major in college, but for pure love of science, I also took a wide range of science courses—everything from biochemistry to physics. To this day, I prefer to start my mornings by reading about the latest scientific research and discoveries. While I'll read just about anything under that umbrella, I'm particularly interested in immunology, anthropology, astronomy, and technological innovations in medicine. I suppose it comes as no surprise, then, that I tend to weave elements of science and technology into my fiction writing. What I enjoy most is using science as a jumping-off point to explore the human experience and the human psyche in a fictional context.

About the author

B.C. van Tol was grown in the Garden State. In her spare time—when she's not writing—she avidly consumes science fiction and fantasy in all forms. She also enjoys dabbling in watercolors and hiking with her husband and rescue dog.

bcvantol.com, @bcvantol

September

Fetch

B. Morris Allen

She had died from overheating. It was an unlikely death, in the star-spark darkness beyond the atmosphere, where the outside temperature measured in single digits Kelvin. Yet temperature in space flight was a tricky thing. In Laika's case, a part of the ship had failed to separate. Torn insulation and a compromised control system had cooperated to simulate an intolerable summer day. She had died in hours.

His own cabin had multiple failsafes, multiple mechanisms to compensate for radiative heat loss, for the lack of convection, advection, conduction. And of course they watched him. Just like they'd monitored Laika, but with cameras.

He faced his favorite now, the smooth curve of glass like HAL's dark and ominous eye, but with only human intelligence behind it. "Hello," he said. It would take a year for the message to reach Earth. There was no hurry. Not anymore.

'Leica', read the white lettering curved above the purple of the lens. He'd pasted a softscreen up beside it, with a color image of Laika in her cramped training cage. She'd been unable to turn around. She'd stopped urinating.

"No need to worry, girl." After a while, he'd gotten used to the limited movement, the claustrophobia. Drugs had helped. He had his four by four by four — sixty-four glorious meters of freedom in an ungainly cube. The clumsy bulk of it didn't matter. The cube was empty of everything but air, which might as well be stored here as in the outside tanks.

He was small, of course. On the growth front, Asian and Latin genes had won out against European and Scandinavian, producing a short, blond, tan-skinned man with blue eyes. Like Laika's he liked to think; the records weren't clear, but she'd been part Husky. The New Frontiers project had loved him from the start. He could have been dreamed up in a public relations brainstorm for the brand-new United League of Earth and its shiny, attention-distracting launch to the edges of the solar system. A Swedish grandmother for robust health, a Venezuelan Wayuu one for compact durability, cancer-free grandfathers who'd survived Chernobyl and Fukushima for radiation resistance. American parents working in foreign aid who'd brought him up in Guinea, Liberia, Rwanda, Tanzania — always heading east in search of something they'd never found.

"Well, *we've* found something, haven't we, Laika?" He'd made history, in any case. Furthest man in space. First human to the Oort cloud. First to stake a claim on behalf of the United League. Even after fifty years in transit, no one had gotten here first, no one had zipped past with new technology and a shrug of apology. Earth would send congratulations, no doubt. They might even have thought to send them in advance. Despite the morning's diagnosis. Or perhaps because of it.

He'd proved it was possible, proved that with drugs and smarts and entertainment, it was possible to stay sane.

"Mostly," he acknowledged to Laika. "Mostly sane." There had been a few dark periods. Every life had those. "You helped." He reached out to stroke the screen, and she arched her neck to one side. The animation had been tricky. It had taken months to get close, years to perfect. Earth hadn't helped. Hadn't known to help, though they would have been willing.

"Cutaneous radiation injury, they said," he told Laika, though she'd heard it already. "Plus, maybe," he checked the morning's message, "leukopenia, thrombocytopenia, erythema, keratosis, and telangiectasia. But you knew that, didn't you, girl?" He'd run out of clean cloth for bandages. There wasn't enough water left to wash them effectively. He could soak them, but then the cycler took time to process the murky fluid. He'd tried boiling the ooze off the bandages in the airlock, but of course it made the water shortage worse. And then the bandages were cold. He settled for changing bandages every hour, letting the damp ones dry in the cabin until the room was oppressively dank and smelly.

"Sorry, girl," he shrugged at Laika. "Scrubber can't keep up." Only the sail controls and radio worked well these days. "Software error." He coughed, a spray of straw-pale fluid that floated across the cabin like a cloud. "Problem in the flesh drive." Laika cocked her head and wagged her tail to laugh.

Would he have lived longer on Earth? It seemed unlikely. Less radiation, of course. If he'd avoided Luanda, Bishkek, Winnipeg, and the other places the UL had pacified. Had there been more, after he left? It didn't matter. New Frontiers had taken him on, more sold on his heritage than on hard-won but second-rate degrees in astronomy and medicine, but they'd taken him. He owed them for that, anyway.

And for Mor-Mor. After the terror attacks, she'd been the only family he had left. A bedridden old Swedish woman in a flat in a suburb of Vänersborg, itself now a suburb of Trollhättan. She'd lived only for weekly visits from the therapy dogs, and video-chats from one lone grandson, when he could afford them.

"She didn't have you though, did she, girl?" Laika wagged and barked. "That's the spirit." Mor-Mor had believed firmly in spirits — and ley-lines and charms and all the things her Methodist parents had disapproved of. 'Your parents' spirits are somewhere in the world,' she'd told him. 'It's just up to you to find them.' But when his search had taken him off Earth, she hadn't fought it.

'I need to go,' he'd told her. And, because he wanted to do it, really wanted to, and because he had nothing else, she'd let him go. 'Take this,' was the only thing she'd said, and sent a scan of Laika, faded black and white from some old newspaper, stained with the tears she'd wept back in the 20th century, and in the years since. 'I want to go,' he'd assured her, though she already knew. 'I choose to go.'

He wouldn't trade it for anything, half a century on. He'd accomplished little beyond a study in isolation, little that an automated probe could not have done better. He'd read up on the law, during his voyage, confirmed that the trip was more symbolic than precedential, and let it go. He'd read thousands of books, written a handful of his own.

"I had to go," he told Laika now. The pay for his effort had settled Mor-Mor in an elegant home with a view of the dog park, bought her the best care that he'd never told her was his real reason for going. The rest had funded a small dog rescue foundation. Would he have accomplished more had he stayed, worked his way out of poverty and into the middle class like a few lucky others? In her last message, some forty years back, now, she'd told him he was right to go. It was hard to tell, through the UL censors, but he'd taken it as a confirmation that things had gotten worse. He'd sent her back a still from his Laika simulator, then capable of little more than an exaggerated doggy grin.

"But you can do more than that now, can't you girl?" She wriggled and rolled over in her little space. It took some maneuvering. "Of course you can."

He'd done some wriggling himself, over the years. When even the drugs weren't enough to calm him, when he needed motion, he had the Track — a circular tube running around the outside of his cube. A meter wide; just enough to pull himself along in endless circles, or to pump his legs a bit on the clever ratchet-cycle New Frontiers had built.

There was more room now, of course. On two ends of the cube, a hatch led to empty tanks and holds. If he wanted, he could pressurize them, wander past their complex struts and bulkheads like a spelunker exploring lost caverns.

"After a while, the space doesn't matter," he told Laika. "Your perspective shifts." All that food and water had provided shielding. Laika had had none, but she hadn't lived long enough for it to matter. Here, the cycler reused everything it could. Over a fifty-year journey, though, there were losses. The holds were bare now. Over the years, they'd held spares, gardens, waste, play areas, meditation chambers. There had been years when he lived in them, heedless of exposure. Years when he'd hidden in his little cube core. Now it made no difference. He checked his bandages, an old jumpsuit torn in strips. The seepage wasn't bad. Not troubling.

"Is it time?" he asked Laika. She quirked her head to one side, ears cocked. "Do you think it's finally time?" She quirked her head the other way, eyes eager, tongue lolling just to the edge of her teeth. "It's now or never, girl." They'd given him a year to live, the UL doctors, in the message they'd sent a year ago. "Shall we do it?"

"Arf!" she replied, with a naughty gleam in her eye.

"I thought so too," he agreed. And of course he'd been planning this for years. Ever since Mor-Mor died, in a way.

"I'm turning the sail," he announced to his distant audience. They still listened, still watched. He got weekly messages, advice on problems no longer relevant, suggestions for synthesizing drugs from materials long out of inventory, advice on how to compact waste he'd long since dumped. "I'll be out of touch for a while." It was a dereliction of duty, his first in fifty conscientious years. Without the sail to focus their faint signals, he would no longer hear Earth's messages, no longer be able to send his own.

"We did our part, though, didn't we, girl?" Laika grinned back. "I think we did." With a twinge of guilt and uncertainty, ruthlessly suppressed, he tapped the icon for his pre-calculated sail shift. It would take weeks.

He set the second program running. He'd recorded his message over months, short as it was. "I wanted to get it just right," he told Laika and the lens that no longer transmitted his image and voice. In the circuits behind the control panel, gates opened and closed, feeding a short, recorded message to the radio in a cycle of thousands of slightly different iterations. "It was mostly programming and calculation, actually." He scratched her head, and she bowed her neck in pleasure. Her tail thumped against her cage, only the tip visible beyond the curve of its metal roof.

"I'll just check the readouts," he said, withdrawing his hand.

"Arf!" she said, asking for more scratching. When none came, she lay her head down between her paws and settled into her resting state. This far from the Sun, energy was scarce. The micro-reactor worked only at a low level, and battery capacity had dwindled with time.

The sailcord readouts were tied to the main screen, of course, but he liked to climb out and check the physical gauges when he could. He still had a working pressure suit, and of course exposure didn't matter anymore. He tied another layer of cloth around his weeping chest. Body fluids loose in the suit could get in the circuits if they really tried. More important, they smelled bad. He smelled bad enough already. He felt bad for Laika, with her more sensitive nose. Of course, she was just a simulation.

Out on the hull, the sail was responding just as his simulation had predicted. It was early to say much, of course. The frozen bearings on #27 and the broken tension-pulley on #41 had required a little workaround, but it seemed to work just as it should.

He floated for a while sun-side. It didn't matter anymore if he drifted a bit. In the early days, the focus of the sail had been a dangerous place to be; it would have burned through his suit in seconds. Now it was barely warm.

Thousands of AUs away, Sol was a small, bright dot. "Bye," he said, and waved, as if he hadn't said his farewells years before. The motion set him slowly spinning. The view didn't change much. At this distance, even Sol didn't look like much. He watched as the Milky Way slowly circled around him until the tension in his twisting safe-line stopped him and set him spinning back the other way. "Hi."

They'd tried to stop him, of course, the do-gooders and the Luddites and the religionists. 'It's not fair,' they'd said, and 'You'll draw the attention of aliens,' and 'Man was meant to live on Earth.' But he'd had no family other than Mor-Mor, he'd been young and handsome, and he'd had the League behind him, and the scientists, and the fear that the Confederation might get there first.

"Looks like we're out here alone," he told Laika. "No aliens. No angels. Darn." He tugged the safeline to set him moving slowly back to the ship. "And this way, I got to be with you." Mor-Mor had cried the day he left. 'Go find her,' she'd said. "And I will," he said now. "I know you're out here somewhere, kid." Because where else could the soul of a spacedog go? "Playing with those aliens, probably, eh?"

Somewhere in the ship, an algorithm parsed the statement, generated a response. "Arf!"

Back inside the ship, he listened to the messages that still accumulated despite the slowly-turning sail. Long-winded bureaucrats celebrating last year's 49th anniversary. Curt doctors detailing treatments he'd long since tried. Dull chemists proposing supplements scraped from hull surfaces and worn out suit parts.

He listened to it all. "Never know, eh, girl? Might be something good in there." After a few days, the sail had shifted enough that the messages were too broken for the computer to reconstruct. "Now we're really alone, hmm?" He checked the telltales. His message continued to go out in different codings, on different frequencies, as the sail slowly turned.

He slept for a time, woke with a start. "Thought I heard you barking." He stroked her neck. "Not you, hmm?" She reached out a paw for more scratching, and he rubbed a hand on each side of her neck, setting her wriggling like a puppy in her restraints. "Not yet. Not long."

He had no energy now to eat, and the water from the cycler was cloudy. "Smells bad, too. Well," he coughed, and droplets of red floated up to dot the camera lens. "You did without water. Guess I can too." He turned the speakers on so that he could hear his message, still transmitting, still repeating.

He settled his head comfortably against a cushion on the bulkhead, and listened to Laika breathing softly in his ear. Her muzzle came down soft against his shoulder and he smiled. "Good night, girl," he murmured. As his eyes grew dull, she settled into rest mode.

In the still of the cabin, a recording played on. A whistle, high, then low. Then an enthusiastic call, "Лайка, вернись домой. Тебе пора отдыхать." *Laika, come home. It's time to rest.* At the outer hatch, a scratching sound might have been the scrabbling of claws, asking to come in.

See B. Morris Allen's story "Fetch" online at Metaphorosis.
If you liked it, leave a comment. Authors love that!

Remember to subscribe to our e-mail updates so you'll know when new stories are posted.

About the story

In 1957, the USSR sent a dog on the second craft ever to enter Earth orbit, Sputnik 2. The ship was never intended to be recovered, but Laika, a part-Husky street dog, died within hours of takeoff. When Adilya Kotovskaya settled Laika into her cramped space on Sputnik, she said "Please forgive us." Oleg Gazenko, who chose and trained Laika, later said, "The more time passes, the more I'm sorry about it. We shouldn't have done it. We did not learn enough from the mission to justify the death of the dog."

We've done a lot of terrible things to animals in the name of science (and continue to do them). The cruelty of Laika's death has haunted me since I was a child. My favorite film is Lasse Hallstrom's *My Life as a Dog*, in which a boy ponders what was done to Laika. This particular story, though, was inspired by a song from Tony Carey's Planet P Project, "Saw a Satellite", which includes the lines, "And the ratings went over the moon on the day Laika died / But my mother just stayed in her room all morning and she cried". I wanted to write something that both recognized the evil we did to Laika, but had a more hopeful, optimistic tone. I'm not sure it worked on the optimism front, but despite its grim inception, the story is intended as a positive message about coming to terms with the errors of the past.

Where the Old Neighbors Go

Thomas Ha

The man standing on the porch that night seemed like an ordinary gentrifier at first glance: young and tall and artfully unshaven. His jeans were tattered, but strangely crisp, and his shirt was loose and tight in all the wrong places. He had the appearance of someone vaguely famous, like his face could have been in a magazine ad or on the side of a bus. And to anyone other than Mary Walker, he would have successfully passed for a human.

Mary widened the opening of her front door, knowing she could no longer avoid him. She clutched the edges of her stained bathrobe and stared up at the man through the tangle of her grey and white hair.

He smiled, and there was something off, as if his features were meant to be stationary, not stretched in that way. "I thought I should finally introduce myself," he said. "I'm the new neighbor."

The man gestured over his shoulder toward the house across the street. It was an ashen block of concrete and glass, with sharp and modern angles, sitting on a pristine lot with a newly paved driveway. Every time Mary looked at it, she felt nauseous.

"I was wondering what you'd be like," she said.

"And?"

"I don't see any horns," Mary replied.

He laughed, and it, like his smile, seemed out of place. "I was wondering if we could talk, get to know one another. Unless this is a bad time?"

Mary pushed her hair from her eyes and looked out at the dark street. No dog-walkers or joggers in sight. "Why don't you come in?" she said, standing aside.

The man was already through the entryway before she had finished her sentence, peering at Mary's walls and looking around the corner into the den. "What a lovely home," he said monotonously.

Mary tightened the frayed belt of her robe and walked behind him, watching as he ran his fingers along one of her sideboards and around the rim of a decorative vase. He paused at the sectional sofa in the center of the living room, then looked to Mary, as if inviting her to sit.

Mary needed no invitation in her own home. She went to an orange armchair in the corner and dropped into it comfortably, then pointed a bony finger at the sofa. The man sat at her direction, a glimmer of annoyance in his eyes.

"So," Mary began. "You're the one who bought Frank Abra's home."

He nodded. "I met him very briefly after the closing. Nice guy."

"Hm." Mary rested a weathered cheek on her hand. "A lot of people on the hill have been selling lately. But Frank? Didn't strike me as the type."

"Truth be told, I don't know much about him," he shrugged. "I think the house was getting to be too much to maintain." The man glanced at other rooms that were visible from where he sat. "You live alone too, don't you?"

Mary ignored the question. "Frank was getting on in years," she said, scratching at a mole next to her eye with her index finger. "Still, I was surprised—not so much as a for-sale sign, let alone a goodbye. First time I knew what happened was when you got rid of the house."

She vividly remembered the day Frank's place had been demolished last spring.

It had started with a rumbling that made her get out of bed and look out the front window. Mary had watched as a slow-moving caravan of construction vehicles proceeded down the road, then encircled the small, Craftsman bungalow across the street.

She had emerged from her home in her bathrobe and marched over the low bushes in her front yard, waving a hand at one of the drivers.

"Hey!" she yelled. "What're you doing?"

"What's it look like?"

"Where's Frank?" She shaded her eyes with one hand and looked up.

"Ma'am, I don't know who Frank is, but he isn't here. You better back up!"

The construction vehicles roared to life, and the ground began to vibrate as they inched across the lawn.

One of the bulldozers began by tearing through the planks of the front deck. It was an uncovered porch that Frank had built with his wife, Callie, in the Sixties. He hadn't had the strength to repair it in over a decade, so the wood splintered and folded like toothpicks as the bulldozer's blade rippled through with no resistance.

An excavator then approached the side of the house and raised its boom, reminding Mary of an animal rearing to strike. The bucket came down and clawed open a hole in one of the walls, bricks raining down onto the dirt. Mary could see into the home through the wound, the lilac-patterned wallpaper in one of Frank's bedrooms shredded. Several minutes later, the wall next to it, adjacent to Frank's chimney, came apart like cardboard.

Mary covered her nose and mouth with her hand, watching as the sections of Frank's house came undone. Even after the machines left, she lingered on the street and walked through the lot where Frank's home had been, a pile of dirt and rubble that was peppered with pieces of what used to hold the house together.

Mary returned her attention to the young man now sitting on her sofa, trying her best to push the image of the ruined Abra home from her mind.

"Did Frank mention where he was headed?" she asked.

"You know," the man furrowed his brow, "I don't think he did. But I'm sure I have his agent's number somewhere if you'd like to get in touch."

"That's nice of you to offer." Mary leaned on the other side of the armchair. "But enough about Frank. What about you? What brings you to the hill?"

The young man stretched his arms over the back of the sofa, making it a point to show how comfortable he was. "I just really like the neighborhood," he said. "Quiet and removed. There's a good energy about it. And the people seem nice."

"Do they?"

"Relaxed, I guess."

"Relaxed," Mary repeated. "I suppose that's one way to put it."

Mary would have described her neighbors as oblivious.

Not one of them had seemed concerned about Frank when he disappeared. For days after his house was demolished, Mary had gone door to door to see if anyone had heard where Frank was, or even that he was planning to leave.

None of the neighbors had answers, let alone cared.

Of course, it might have had something to do with who was asking. Several of them slammed their doors in Mary's face at the sight of her. Others simply pretended they weren't home. Mary could feel their eyes trailing her from their windows, and a few of them who had known Mary from better days, before she had become this way, had a certain look on their faces that she absolutely could not stand, as if they pitied her.

"Are you...taking care of yourself, Mary?" One of the older neighbors looked down at her bathrobe with concern.

"What's to take care of?" Mary scoffed. "It's not like I'm having company anytime soon, am I?" She pushed the tangled strands of her hair out of her face. "I'm just comfortable as I am, thank you very much. But about Frank—"

"I'm sorry, but I really don't know," they said. "You please take care, though, okay, Mary?" The door shut slowly, and Mary muttered to herself as she moved on. She made doubly sure to meet every gaze as she marched down the street, before they each turned away, one by one.

One of the neighbors she did manage to catch at the door, a middle-aged man who lived a few houses down the block, listened to her just long enough to hear her mention Frank's name before interrupting.

"If I tell you what I know," he said, "will you stop calling parking enforcement and asking them to tow my goddamn car?"

Mary was used to these confrontations, and she knew that if she wasn't firm about the way things ought to be, the others would walk all over her. Still, she preferred the honesty of this over the feigned sympathy she got from the others.

"If it doesn't have a permit on the dash, I have to call," she replied. "Could belong to some prowler."

"It's *my* car! You *know* that!"

"I really don't like to assume, you know? Anyway, listen, about Frank—"

This door, like all the others, shut on her.

Mary grimaced to herself as she remembered, but paid it no mind. In her several decades of living on the hill, her neighbors had never understood how her watchful eye kept danger away from their homes. But she didn't need their approval to keep things in order.

The young man on the sofa cleared his throat, trying to draw her back into the conversation. "If it's not too much trouble, could I maybe get something to drink?"

"Ah." Mary sat up straight and then pulled herself out of the armchair. "Of course. I've already forgotten basic hospitality. What would you like?"

"Water would be fine."

"Coffee," she said to herself. "It's late, but I think I'll need it for a chat like this. Would you like a cup?"

"Well, actually I said—" the man shifted, seemingly unsure if she was hard of hearing. "Sure. Coffee is fine."

Mary shuffled to the other side of the den, leading the young man, who followed close behind her, through a dining room and into a kitchen in the northwest corner of the house. It was brightly lit, with soothing blue walls and shining tile that Mary scrubbed daily. She pointed absentmindedly to a breakfast nook in the corner, and the young man went over and sat in a chair.

Mary let her fingers run across the marble countertop as she moved around the kitchen in a practiced manner. She took two cups from her favorite, but rarely used, china set, gently placing each one next to the sink before producing a pour-over glass coffee maker from another cupboard and eyeing the curved, transparent body under the light just to make sure that there were no unsightly water marks. She brought out a tin filled with ground coffee she'd harvested from the cherries in the backyard, the earthy, gritty smell soothing her while she continued to assemble what she needed.

As she gathered the accoutrements, her mind began to drift, recalling other times when she used to make things in the kitchen for more than just herself, when the thudding of little feet and high-pitched giggling echoed through the halls, joining the sounds of the sink-water rushing and glasses clattering as she stood at the countertop.

But then Mary remembered where she was again, and more importantly, whom she was with, and the pleasantness vanished.

"Hospitality is important, you know," Mary said, more to herself than the man sitting at the nook, as she focused herself again and removed a coffee filter from the bottom of a small box. "Across all cultures, the code between guest and host is paramount. The Greeks had a special word for it..."

"Xenia," the young man replied.

"Xenia," Mary nodded, pouring the ground coffee on top of a filter and setting a kettle to boil. "That's right. So you're familiar. You have to be at your best, because you never know who, or what, could be visiting you."

"I like that." The young man leaned back, watching Mary carefully as she stood at the kettle.

"In the old stories, some of the worst monsters were the ones who broke that code. Innkeepers that preyed on guests. Bandits who took advantage of generous hosts. It takes something particularly nasty to do that in a home. Homes are sacred."

The water came to a boil.

Mary grabbed the kettle and poured the water over the coffee pot, and the hot liquid dripped down into the glass body, filling it gradually. "Milk? Sugar?"

"Black is fine."

"Black it is." She poured the two cups and brought them over.

The man took the steaming cup and raised it to his lips, blowing gently and about to drink, when he noticed that Mary was watching him. Something about the coffee smelled unusual and caused him to stop.

He laughed, but in a way that seemed genuine for the first time that night—an angry cackle mixed with shock.

Mary drank from her cup and looked back at him. "What is it?"

She knew he had detected it.

Mary always mixed small pieces of aspen bark into her coffee, so that its flavor would seep into the drink. Its effect on ordinary people was negligible, but on things like Mary's visitor, it could have irreparable consequences.

"So much for xenia," he said, staring intently at the dark, rippling fluid in the cup in front of him.

"Had to try," Mary shrugged.

In truth, she knew this visit had been coming for some time. She had lived too long, and too cautiously, to ignore the warning signs.

After she couldn't turn up any information on Frank, she had gone, as she often did, to her other sources.

Mary set out early one morning up a dirt path behind her house toward the peak of the hill that overlooked the neighborhood. There was a wooded area, filled with blackened trees that had been caught in a brushfire long ago, yet never managed to die or sprout new growth. She followed the path for a few minutes before turning off from it, keeping track of small knife marks she had left in certain trunks.

Finally, at the heart of the woods, she found the carob tree, grey and knotted. She came within ten feet of it and stopped.

"I need to talk," she said.

The leaves rustled, and there was grunting from some unseen space within the branches. The shaking subsided, and there was a silence before something emerged.

Yellow Eyes peeked his head out, appearing in the form of a large, black crow with greasy feathers.

"Whatever it is, I didn't do it," he said. "Haven't been near any of the folks, just like we agreed." The bird shuffled along the branch and turned its head, the ring of one of its eyes focused on her.

Mary watched Yellow Eyes closely. There were times when he would start a conversation, then pounce on her without warning. The last time he had done that, he had been wearing the body of a copperhead, and she could not feel her hand for over a year after.

"Spoken like an innocent," Mary said. "But no. Someone new is moving to the neighborhood and seems like your type."

"My type?" Yellow Eyes said. "You'll have to be more specific. Charming? Good conversationalist?"

Mary turned around and began to walk away.

"Wait." Yellow Eyes fluttered down from the branch and to the ground in front of the woman. "I'll tell you anything you want, if you just, you know..."

The bird gestured with his head toward the circle of pale, purple petals around the carob tree, sprouting up from under the grass and weeds on the forest floor, ever-blooming and just as vibrant as they had been when Mary planted them years ago.

Mary had learned at a young age that creatures like Yellow Eyes could never be confronted directly. Instead, there were other ways, mostly forgotten but still passed down in some families, or buried in books, which Mary made some effort to collect over the years. With the right tools and enough time, she knew she could hold her own against them.

In the case of Yellow Eyes, it took patience, but Mary had meticulously tracked him to his nest after he'd first chosen the crow body. She waited until he was away to seed the circle of vervain, then waited months more as the circle strengthened beneath him and bloomed.

This particular seal, the traveler's knot, was one of the better ones she had crafted in her time on the hill. The living pattern of vervain connected him, not just to the mortal form of the bird he had chosen, but to the tree he had made his home. If anything happened to either the crow or the carob, Yellow Eyes would feel every bit of it, and if the damage was great enough, there were no new bodies that could save him from death. It was a terrifying prospect for a creature who was supposed to live forever.

"Tell me what you know, and I'll decide if it's worth your release," Mary said.

Yellow Eyes crept closer, cocking his head one way and then the other. He drew his beak wide and exposed a row of round, human-like teeth, grinning. "I might have heard about someone who's headed this way. But this one, if it is who I think it is, is definitely not my 'type'."

"Meaning what?"

"Meaning, you know me," Yellow Eyes said. "I'm old-fashioned. I like tricks and deals, the art of a good bargain. But these new things that are coming up now—they're emptier and hungrier, no patience for the craft. They don't get any enjoyment out of the chase the way some of us do."

"Then what do they want?"

"What does any monstrous little toddler want? They want to take everything you have, just as soon as they can swallow it."

Yellow Eyes drew closer to Mary. He puffed his chest and spread his clawed feet on the ground, exposing another set of long, dark fingers between his thin crow toes that curled into the dirt.

His tongue flopped out of his mouth as he salivated, growing overexcited.

Mary could see that Yellow Eyes was beginning to forget himself. She moved slowly to the trunk of the carob tree and reached a hand to the lowest branch, thin enough that she could bend it, but substantial enough that it would work for her.

She snapped it.

Yellow Eyes shrieked as the traveler's knot connected him to the sensation of the branch breaking. He dropped to the ground and twisted in pain as if one of his bones had cracked.

"Settle down," Mary said sharply.

Yellow Eyes shrank and gave the closest thing a bird could to a grimace as he breathed through the pain. "Listen," he heaved, "A couple of little Mary Walker tricks aren't going to cut it with this one. He'll break you in half before you can get anything past him."

"Hm," Mary replied, wondering what she would do if that were true. She knew she would have to think this through carefully in advance.

"So?" Yellow Eyes turned his head, wincing. "You asked; I answered. That clears our ledger, I think."

"Does it?" Mary stared down at the creature. "All I learned was that this stranger is tougher than you are, which," she waved at the vervain flowers, "doesn't tell me much at all."

"Oh, come on." Yellow Eyes flapped his wings. "I played nice, and you can't keep me under the power of this seal forever."

"If I survive, I'll give it some thought." Mary headed back toward the dirt path.

"Mary. Are you serious?"

She waved and kept walking.

"This is why no one likes you," Yellow Eyes screeched. "Mary!"

His cawing carried over the hill, and she heard him for most of the walk back through the woods.

But it turned out, in the end, that Yellow Eyes had been right about Mary's visitor.

The young man didn't seem interested in engaging with, outwitting, or deceiving her. He looked down at the cup of coffee in front of him, dosed with aspen, and his resting expression shifted, almost imperceptibly.

His eyes moved very deliberately from the cup in his hands, up to meet Mary's face.

"I prefer it this way," he said. "Really."

Mary began to retort as she stood up from the nook, but the man interrupted her.

"*Sit,*" he said quietly.

The old woman felt her body fold into the seat, like a hand had gripped the back of her neck and pushed her firmly into place, forcing her to stare at the man across from her.

"A little bird told me you were going to be trouble," he said.

Mary's brow creased at the mention of Yellow Eyes, but she did her best to keep her expression neutral. It seemed Mary's visitor had more information about her than she anticipated and, like her, had prepared himself in advance of this night.

The young man pushed his cup across the table. "You know, the thing I enjoy most about a fresh brew is the aroma, flavor...and heat. *Pick it up.*"

Mary's hand moved of its own accord, taking his cup and bringing it closer.

"*Pour it on your hand. Slowly.*"

It had been a long time since Mary had met someone with a silver tongue as strong as his. There were ways to fight this kind of persuasion, with enough preparation and the right tonics, but she knew that it was futile now to try.

She tipped the cup and watched as the steaming liquid spilled onto the back of her other hand, which was firmly pressed on the surface of the table. Little splatters of coffee bounced off of her skin as her hand grew patchy, red and white blisters beginning to form. Mary did her best not to react, but her breathing grew faster and shallower as her eyes watered. She bit deep into her bottom lip as she felt the pain searing up through her arm.

Rivers of coffee joined around her hand and cascaded off the edge of the table, splashing to the tile below.

"Does it hurt?" the young man asked. "It's hard to tell with you."

Even though she could not stop it, Mary wasn't powerless. There were methods she had learned, still taught by older members of certain monasteries who were wary of creatures like this, that were used to slow the connection from the nerves to the mind, even if only for a few seconds.

Mary breathed steadily and concentrated on the sharp, vibrant smell of the coffee, recalling the way it often drifted up the stairs and along the corridors of the house, up to the bedroom on the second floor, and how, when it did, she could pick up its bitter fragrance, even when she was wrapped in layers of her thick, down blankets early in the morning. She was transported to those chilly hours after sunrise when someone else was brewing a pot, and she could hear the whistling of the kettle as she kept her eyes closed, still fading in and out of consciousness. She recalled her daughter's footsteps, her tiny hands pressing Mary's cheeks and poking her nose while Mary pretended to sleep for a little bit longer.

Mama?

Mary trembled until the last drop of coffee had run out, but she did not make a sound.

When she opened her eyes, the young man seemed to be watching her intently, masking just a hint of frustration. His gaze turned to the second cup of coffee, still steaming, but before he could speak, Mary knocked the cup with the back of her red, blistered hand. It flew off the table and shattered on the kitchen floor with a burst that soaked the floor.

The man crossed his arms. "Now why would you do that? I could just make you refill your cup from the pot, you know."

Mary gripped her burned hand and stared silently.

The man moved over in his chair to a spot at the table that wasn't dripping with coffee. He rested his elbows on its surface and put his chin on his clasped hands. "Go on," he said softly. "Cool that hand. And while you're at it, clean this up."

Mary went to the sink and ran her hand under the cold water. She grabbed a wet cloth from a rack and wrapped her fingers, then took another rag to wipe up the coffee.

"I really meant it earlier, you know," the young man said as he watched her clean the floor. "This is a lovely home. Nicer than I would have expected from the way you keep yourself."

"Thanks," Mary replied dryly, throwing the fragments of the cup in the trash and wringing the rag out in the sink.

"It's obvious you have a real reverence for all these *things*," he waved at the furniture and the decorations surrounding him. "You've practically built a museum here, of fonder times perhaps?" The man gave a knowing half-smile and picked up the other cup on the table, holding it to the light and peering at the sides and the bottom. "But no matter how much meaning and memory you imbue these things with, they'll eventually fall apart. Just like you."

He let the cup drop from his hand and crash to the tile floor below, its pieces scattering in every direction.

"Prick," Mary muttered, getting back on the floor.

"What was that?"

She huffed as she stood, then wiped the table in the breakfast nook before throwing the last few shards away. "You heard it."

"You know." He sat forward. "I could burn this place to the ground, with you still in it. And I wouldn't even have to blink."

"Not likely," Mary replied.

"What?"

"Not likely," she repeated. "If that were true, you'd have done it. You wouldn't waste your time with this coffee and small talk," Mary said. "It's clear you want something from me, or I'd be dead."

His eyes darkened. "Maybe this is it. Maybe I want you to suffer."

"Not likely."

"Stop saying that."

"You would have picked a budding young woman to torture or a family to harass. But an old lady like me has no value, and no value, no entertainment."

The young man tapped the table with his fingers.

"We both want this over with, don't we?" she asked. "What's the point in dragging it out now?"

The man appeared loath to admit it, but Mary could tell that he was growing impatient. After a minute of silence, he reached into his jeans pocket and pulled out a piece of paper, unfolded it and put it down for Mary to see.

She picked it up and read it over as she sat down across from him again. "A quitclaim?" she muttered. Mary studied the language of the document a second time. It was a run-of-the-mill human deed for her property, as far as she could tell. Mary had seen a lot of gambits by his kind, but never anything so pedestrian.

"What could someone like you want with my land?" she asked.

"Doesn't matter." The young man's face went purposefully blank. "But the fact that this also gets you out of this neighborhood now strikes me as a bonus."

Mary ignored the insult and read the document again, trying to guess at what the man was leaving unsaid. She assumed that if he could have forced her to sign, he would have already, but something prevented it. He could try to charm, frighten, or bully her, but, in the end, he wanted this transfer to be voluntary for some reason.

"What about the formalities?" Mary asked. "Price, notarization, things like that?"

"The price is whatever you tell me it is. The rest I can make happen tonight, once you sign. It's just paper, after all."

"And is this the deal you made with Frank Abra?" she asked.

The young man stared back without answering.

Of course, Mary already knew what had happened to Frank without the man saying anything. Weeks after the Abra house was demolished, Mary had visited the lot across the street after sundown, when the construction workers were gone.

She had seen that most of the rubble had been dumped, and a giant pit was ready to be filled with concrete for the house's foundation. Mary brought an old metal detector she had gotten at a garage sale years earlier, barely used except for clearing out rusty nails and other debris in her garden. She paced across the Abra lot, waving the detector around, mostly finding coins and scrap, until she eventually came across a piece of jewelry a few feet from where the new house was to be built.

She reached down and pulled a window locket from the soil.

Mary wiped it with the sleeve of her bathrobe and inspected it. She remembered seeing Callie Abra wear the locket every day as she stood out on the lawn and watered their garden, and, after she passed away, Mary saw Frank put it around his neck too, never once putting it aside or taking it off, always grasping it like it was the most important thing on earth. The fact that it was here, and he wasn't, told her everything she needed to know.

Mary slid it into the pocket of her bathrobe and looked around at the lot one more time.

The truth was that she and the Abras had never really been that close. On the best days, she was polite with them, and on the worst, the whole street could hear their screaming matches.

And yet, Mary realized, as she knelt in the dirt, that the neighborhood felt quieter and lonelier without them.

Her fingers crept to the ground, and she touched the soil, feeling its dampness.

Mary remembered the soil as she stared at the young man in her kitchen, thinking of what best to say.

"What will happen to the neighborhood?" she asked him.

"What?"

"The hill. What will you do to them?"

The man shifted in his seat and squinted at her, as if puzzled by her question. "You know, when I first moved here and asked around, it was funny. I didn't even have to pry. Yours was the name that almost inevitably came up when people talked about this street."

"Guess I'm popular," Mary replied flatly.

"Lady Bathrobe," he said. "The Hag on the Hill. Old Tangle-Hair. The Parking Permit Crusader. The Groaning Crone."

"A couple of those are clever, but the rest are objectively bad."

" 'Nobody cares about her,' 'Lives alone for a reason,' they told me." The young man watched Mary sink visibly in her chair. " 'Why doesn't she do everyone a favor and just die?' "

Mary squeezed her burned hand.

"They don't even want to look at you. Just the sight of your filthy robe and ratty hair puts them on edge. Most of them wish you would just disappear and never come back." He shook his head. "I know I'm not telling you anything you don't already know."

"So what?" she said softly.

"So, why do you care what happens to this place after you leave?" The man pushed the deed closer to Mary. "You don't need this hill, and if I've learned anything, it's that the hill *certainly* doesn't need you."

Mary lowered her chin and reached into the pocket of her bathrobe. She felt for the Abras' locket, which she kept there now out of habit, and she touched its smooth, metal edges. For the first time, she didn't have a pithy response for the young man, and he seemed pleased.

"How about, instead of pouring your energy into this house and this hill, maybe you take care of yourself, for once, and enjoy those golden years?" He pinched the sleeve of her tattered bathrobe and smirked. "Because whatever it is you're trying to preserve, it's gone, lady. You've got to see that."

The young man seemed like he was finished speaking and sat back down. Nothing about what the man said changed what Mary was going to do next; in truth, she had made that decision some time ago. But still, when it was quiet again, Mary realized she felt a chill, one that usually visited her when she couldn't fall asleep, and it touched her more deeply than anything else that had happened that night.

After a few seconds, Mary stood and began to walk from the kitchen. The young man followed her, through the study and dining room, and back to the den. Mary approached one of the windows at the front of the house and moved back a heavy curtain, so that she could see across the street clearly.

"There." She pointed at his home, the block of concrete and glass, its modern architecture and chic exterior, like a blight on the hill.

"What about it?"

"You want me to sign? Then I want something first. Whether I leave or not, I can't stand the idea of that shitbox sitting there instead of Frank's place. Makes me sick." Mary gestured over her shoulder. "So let's see if you were telling the truth. Burn it to the ground without blinking, or whatever it was you said."

The young man raised an eyebrow and looked out the window. He was strangely hesitant, and Mary could see that it was her turn to press him.

"That's what I thought," she laughed.

"What?"

"Acting smug and lecturing me about the meaning of 'things'. But I can see it, you're just as attached as I am. Bet you picked the design of that place because you saw it in some magazine. Maybe that's how you picked your face too. All you ugly little fiends just want to be pretty deep down, after all."

"Don't be ridiculous," he scoffed, seeming to grow more self-conscious by the second, as if even the vaguest accusation that he shared anything in common with Mary were perverse.

"Go on," Mary grinned. "It doesn't matter to you, does it? You'll still have the land. Just burn that monstrosity on top of it, and I'll believe you're serious about your offer. I'll sign the deed, just like you want, and we can call it a night and stop wasting everyone's time. What do you say?"

Now it was his turn to go quiet.

"Unless..." Mary looked out the window. "Your whole scheme was to build a suburb of shitboxes, because you love playing house so much? Maybe that's the problem?"

The man eyed Mary, trying to understand why she was being so insistent, but his expression began to change, his pride and his eagerness to finish things winning out. Before he had uttered a word, she knew that she had him.

The young man looked back out the window and nodded his head.

The flames across the street erupted suddenly, from no single source.

In seconds, the entire concrete and glass house was surrounded by a growing fire. The stone did not burn, but the supports and framing inside began to split and crack as the heat spread.

Mary looked over at her visitor, holding her breath.

He began blinking rapidly, and he touched his throat.

Part of the living room of the concrete house tumbled as a support beam crashed to the ground. Some of the glass at the front of the house began to ooze into liquid, pouring onto the lawn, while furniture inside the structure shrank and collapsed.

"Does it hurt?" she asked. "It's hard to tell with you."

The man opened his mouth to respond, but his voice was only a rasp.

The young man staggered out of the den and toward the front door.

Mary watched from the window as he stumbled across the street toward the flaming house, his silhouette twisting and stretching as the fire raged in front of him.

She imagined that as he stepped across the lawn, he finally noticed, hidden among the blades of grass, the pale, purple vervain flowers, just beginning to bloom—the ones she had planted late at night, well before the foundation in that place had been poured, when she had wandered onto the Abra lot, so small and scattered that they probably never caught his eye before.

She still remembered the sensation of the soil, the dampness of it, as she placed the seeds around the property in the right formation, the beginnings of the traveler's knot that would eventually, quietly bind him to that body and to that home.

The young man now turned to look at Mary in the window. There was no time to return to her house and try to compel her to release the bond of the traveler's knot, and even if he could stop the flames, the house was too far gone, the inside of the structure crumbling, much as the insides of his body likely were. The young man knew, just as Mary did, that it was too late now to avoid what was coming.

His face began to collapse, like desiccated dirt, and his true appearance emerged from what remained of his head. Mary always had trouble seeing the real faces of his kind, but he, like all of them, looked like a shifting pool of ink to her, blurred and shapeless.

After a moment of stillness, he looked away and continued forward into the house, moving through a gap where one of the large floor-to-ceiling windows had melted away. Mary could only guess, but as he went further through the flames, she thought he was trying to hide himself, not wanting to give anyone the satisfaction of seeing what was happening to him in his final moments.

He stood with his back toward Mary as everything came apart around him, his tall shape disappearing in the crackling and roaring that filled the concrete block as the fire stretched to the glowing, night sky.

Mary went to her porch and sat on the top step, covering her mouth and nose with the wet rag on her hand. Other neighbors were at their windows, or on their front steps as sirens drew closer to the bottom of the hill.

As she watched the sky darken, a vast cloud of smoke growing above the neighborhood, a crow with greasy feathers landed on the eaves above her.

"I don't understand," Yellow Eyes said. "You had him in a knot. You could have struck a deal, made him grovel, work for you, even. Why?"

Mary did not turn away from the flames. "Maybe he did something to piss me off."

Yellow Eyes watched the fire, as entranced as everyone else.

"Next time you try to play both sides, you'll remember this, though, won't you?" She looked at him coldly.

The crow turned a solid yellow ring of its eye at the old woman, flexed his wings, then took off toward the top of the hill without another word.

By the time the ambulances and fire trucks arrived, a couple of the house's walls were leaning and another had fallen. Everything inside had already been consumed.

There was, in Mary's mind, nothing more to save.

In the days after that fire, Mary returned to her daily routine. Standing each morning on her lawn with a cup of coffee, she scanned the dashboards of the parked cars on the street for any without a permit, then she walked down the block to see if any recycling or trash bins were put out early or left too late, in violation of the county code.

When she wasn't watching for unusual cars or strangers entering the neighborhood, she found herself staring at the charred walls of what used to be the concrete house across the street, imagining the old Craftsman in its place while she gripped the Abras' locket in her hand.

Frank would have come slowly down the steps on each of those mornings to retrieve his mail, gripping one of the handrails—sometimes nodding at Mary and sometimes not. But instead, there was nothing but an ugly view of grey rock and blackened wood. Even now, no one was asking where Frank went, Mary realized, and it was unlikely that any of them ever would.

No one ever asks where the old neighbors go, she thought.

Despite herself, Mary continued to dwell on what the young man said to her the night of the fire. As she dusted her sideboards and vases, she often lost interest, like everything had become too tiresome to finish. When she felt that way, Mary wandered upstairs, to one of the quiet rooms that usually sat untouched, the bed inside still perfectly made and flowery wallpaper around it covered with soft light that flowed through sheer curtains.

She knelt in front of a trunk, unlatching and lifting it open, and peered down at a cluttered pile of old dolls and wooden toys, all of them associated with some holiday or birthday that came back to her as she brought her fingers lightly over them.

In those instances, Mary sometimes considered, for a brief moment, finally throwing them out. Her daughter was never going to use them, after all—she would never brew a pot of coffee for Mary downstairs, or chatter away with her in the kitchen while sitting at the breakfast nook, or touch Mary's cheek to wake her up.

Things would never be like they were again, she knew.

But still, she couldn't bring her hands to move, to take anything from the trunk, and she sat paralyzed for longer than she expected. She kept imagining the young man, standing in front of the roaring flames, and thought, for some reason, that she too might begin to crumble and collapse inward, to fall apart bit by bit, if she were to alter anything in the house, no matter how small.

So, instead, Mary put everything back, got on her feet, and then closed the door to the room behind her—each time, more intent than before to leave things in their place, exactly as they were.

See Thomas Ha's story "Where the Old Neighbors Go" online at Metaphorosis.
If you liked it, leave a comment. Authors love that!
Remember to subscribe to our e-mail updates so you'll know when new stories are posted.

About the story

The idea for "Where the Old Neighbors Go" came from my experiences with several different neighbors I had over the years. They were all variations of the archetypal nosy neighbor: aggressive, intrusive, and trying, I think, to make the messiness of the world conform to some kind of imagined order. There was one neighbor in particular who became the genesis for Mary Walker, the protagonist of the story, and whom I got to know much better over several years. While there was nothing I learned about this neighbor that ultimately excused her behavior, I did discover things that I think humanized her and made me understand her perspective, namely, that she harbored a deeply-held belief that if she didn't involve herself in her neighbors' lives (whether putting away their recycling bins or complaining about strange noises), the neighborhood might somehow come undone at the seams.

From there I knew I wanted to write a story where a neighbor like that was actually, unbeknownst to everyone around her, right about that belief: that she was the sole person keeping a threat from tearing the world apart.

By the same token, that threat, a demonic neighbor who moves in across the street from Mary, is based (very loosely) on me and others of my generation like me: young, smug, and indifferent to the disruption our invasion of older neighborhoods cause.

In the end, I found something very satisfying about pitting a character as wily as Mary Walker against an arrogant hipster type and seeing whether, and how, she would prevail.

A question for the author

Q: Do you make art other than prose? What kind, and how is it different?

A: I hesitate to call it art, but over the last few years I've developed an unexpected interest in video editing and digital music composition. My wife is a food writer and cookbook author who occasionally has to create video content for various reasons, so over time I began shooting her videos and composing short music pieces to accompany them. Something about trying to create a visual narrative that makes sense, and editing cuts so that your brain finds a sequence palatable, is a fun challenge that is reminiscent of, but still very different from, breaking out a plot sequence. Similarly, I'm a novice musician, but the thing I've enjoyed most about composing short pieces to go with those videos is trying to evoke a particular atmosphere that enhances whatever it goes with, without drawing too much attention to itself. In that way, it feels a little similar to building themes in short fiction that bolster the story without hitting the reader over the head. Again, these are food videos, so it's not like I'm making a feature film or anything. But what can I say? I get a real kick out of it.

About the author

Thomas Ha is a former attorney turned stay-at-home father who enjoys writing speculative fiction during the rare moments when both of his children happen to be asleep at the same time.

@ThomasHaWrites

Pages Missing From the Diary of
Samuel Pepys, Esq.
David Berger

It is well-known that there are several pages missing from Samuel Pepys' famous diary: pages, moreover, that he himself seems to have removed before the various volumes were bound under his direction. Two years ago, the following excerpt was found at Christ's College Library inside a bible that was known to have been owned by Pepys. By a happy coincidence, the discoverer of the pages is Mr. John Rawlinson, a fellow of Cambridge College and a collateral descendant of the Rawlinson mentioned in this excerpt.

Two years have been taken up by exhaustive tests by paper experts, specialists in Pepys' handwriting and in the shorthand code Pepys used for his diary. After all this, the pages have been pronounced genuine!

Because St. Cuthbert's Church, Bedlington, has undergone extensive renovation since the time of Samuel Pepys, no trace of the carving mentioned has survived. There are no known tellings of the story in records of local folklore.

As to the subject matter, it is extremely curious. Pepys, while certainly a collector of anecdotes, some of which were spurious, was never known to be either gullible or to have written any fiction. And these facts lead us to the obvious question: Why were the pages removed? Perhaps we will never know, but a reasonable surmise is that publication of this material might have held Pepys open to a charge of falling for a well-told tale. However, the second portion of the manuscript, dealing with Pepys's own excursion to Bedlington, is even more remarkable.

There are, incidentally, in all the records of the Lost Colony of Roanoke, no records of a family named either Rawlinson or Kent or of a group of Lollard families.

We, the Fellows of Cambridge University, are publishing these missing pages for the first time, and have taken the liberty of naming them the Pepys-Rawlinson Fragment.

29th. In the morning to Westminster-hall to see to some business for my Lord. Afterwards to the house of Wm. Joyce for some coffee, this drink being newly popular in London. It was most excellent and refreshing. Back again to White-hall. At noon my father dined with me upon a good capon with beans and bacon. Afterwards I to Mrs. Alders. She being gone from the house, her maid Miss Clayon and I had a very nice bout, wherein I rattled her up somewhat in her bed. And so home to my own bed.

30th. Up by seven o'clock, and so to work. But before I went out, calling, as I have of late done, for my new boy's copybook, I found that he had not done his work. So I beat him, and then went to fetch my tarred starting rope to beat him further. This article I learned to use for punishments from visits to Navy vessels. But before I got it the boy was fled. I searched the cellars with a lantern. Could not find him. So by water to the Temple, to my cozen Roger; who, I perceive, is a deadly high man in the Parliament against the Court. He shewed me how they have computed that the King hath spended, or at least hath received, about four millions of money since he came in. This is most shocking.

This evening dined at The Crab with a gentleman, a Mr. Coombs, who has business with the Admiralty. Along came his daughter, a perfectly pretty, but quite short and somewhat stout, young lady that lately came up out of the country, particularly Berks. So all by coach to my house, where I found my wife, and we all drank, and then they went away. After, with my wife, to the King's house to see "The Queene at Rest," a new play of Mr. Codgehill, a new playwright. This is a comedy with a goodly part done by that pretty, witty Nel Gwyn. I have never seen such good performing. The Queen and Duchess of York were at the play and seemed to enjoy it with some degree of pleasure. Then we home, and to bed.

31st. Up betimes and at the office all that day, with scarcely a moment to dine. My work being done, that it can ever be done, I walked in the garden of White-h with Captn. Shrewton, where he began to tell me a strange story, which he got on a recent trip to Newcastle. Then there comes into the garden to me Mr. Sleak, that I once knew at Cambridge, and I took him in. Over at the Cheshire Cheese, I called for a surloyne of rost beefe, which we had for dinner. I must note that the Cheese, rebuilt since the Restoration and the Fire, has service as fine as in earlier years. Then we three to the Dolphin, and therewith a quart or two of sacke. Then Captn. Shrewton began us this discourse, which did please us much.

Dining one eve at the Nevyll Inne in Newcastle, a year ago, the Captn. met a prosperous farmer and Justice of the Peace, a Mr. Pepper, who was down in town to deliver a load of hay for the victualling y'rds. And after a shared bottle of Sack, Mr. Pepper told this amazing story, scarce to be believed, but well-known in the country 'round Bedlington, where Mr. Pepper hailed from. Mr. Pepper said these happenings ran their course during the time of his great-grandfather, who delighted in telling this story to whomever would have their ear bent.

According to Mr. Pepper, some eighty years or so before, during the reign of Her Majesty Elizabeth I, a great stone fell from the sky on a farm owned by a Mr. Bowey. The landing of the stone was accompanied by loud claps of thunder and a shaking of the earth around Bedlington. (An account of this stone falling, so says Mr. Pepper, was at one time in the Parish Record for Bedlington.) And when Mr. Bowey and one of his sonnes came out to the fields, they found a great pit in the earth several yards deep. And in the pit was a great hot stone, the size of two large ale butts.

At this time, it being late, after some more ale, and promises to meet next eve to continue this tale, went we home. My wife being still up, I played for her on my flageolette. She did sing finely. And thence to bed.

1st. Early to wait on my Lord. A day of much urgency. The Commissioners of Parliament met this day to make policy over the Fleet. There is some fear of the power of the seamen, who are highly incensed against them because of past wages due. By and by comes in my Lord. We went by water to the Tower. There we dined on a good chine of beef. And he and I did talke of many things in the Navy, one from another, in general, to see how many great things are committed to very ordinary men, as to parts and experience, to do. This doth not please us.

In the evening, to The Dolphin with much anticipation, to hear the story of the events at Bedlington from Mr. Pepper per Captn. Shrewton. We first had a peck of oysters, and then cuts from the tender part of a baron of Scots beef. And after some ale, the Captn. began, to our delight.

So after approaching the pit, Mr. Bowey and his sonne poked the great stone with shovels, and they were amazed. The stone easily broke apart into two halves. And even more dramatick there was within an object very like a brass church bell, but rounded on both ends, like what is called in geometrie a rounded cylinder. This was a thing of beauty and delight. But so hot that Mr. Rawlinson and his sonne could not touch it.

Mr. Bowey spread word by his sonne, and the next day came many townsfolk to stare at the thing. It was agreed by the local folk, by the suggestion of Rev. Rawlinson, the Vicar of St. Cuthbert's in Bedlington, that it should be took over to the churchyard. So, as the stone and the cylinder had cool'd, some local miners made a rigging. The two halves of the stone still warm to the touch was raised. They was placed on a dray, along with the cylinder, and pulled by four mighty horses to the yard. There the parts of the stone and the cylinder lay until nearly the whole parish was gathered to see this wonder. Even the Bishop came rushing over from Newcastle to see it. And there was talk of perhaps bringing the things, by stages, to London, perhaps by barge.

I remarked that should this have happened in our day, the Royal Society, which I have recently had the honour of being elected to, would have sought this thing out. But the Society had not yet been born at the time.

We then spoke briefly of some of the newest revelations from the Royal Society. Including Robert Hooke's *Book of the Microscope*. None of which seemed pertinent to the business of Mr. Rawlinson's cylinder. I proposed a toast to the Royal Society. Whereupon Captn. Shrewton continued Mr. Pepper's tale.

With the arrival of the Bishop, whose name Mr. Pepper could not recall, the news of the stones and the cylinder was spread even wider. The Bishop sprinkled the cylinder with holy water, and then departed. That evening, the Parish Council decided to employ several miners to break open the cylinder. The effort to begin the next day.

All the next morning, three miners from one of the collieries bashed at the cylinder, that was hanging from a set of blocks. Suddenly, there came a great cracking sound. The watching crowd gave a great exclamation as the cylinder broke open. Mr. Rawlinson led the townspeople in a rousing cheer. Looking inside the lower part of the cylinder, the miners saw a strange box. One of them reached in and brought it out. He having no difficulty lifting it. The box was a gleaming black. And it measured about a yard by eighteen inch, by eighteen inch.

Having listened to this tale, herein shortened considerably, for several hours, and having enlivened ourselves with some good porter, I suddenly began to feel sleepy. And so I gave my excuses to the company and invited them to meet on to-morrow at Ye Olde Cheshire Cheese at Fleet Street. Then Captn. Shrewton and I walked into the City. We parted, he to go to the inne where he is lodging, and I home to Seething Lane and to bed.

2nd. Early with a Mr. Heatherton about Sir Wm. Penn's concerns in reference to Fleet victualing. The details are many and will involve much time. Dined with Mr. H at Mr. Crew's, on my favourite venison pasty. After dinner I went to the Cheese, where I found Captn. Shrewton and Mr. Sleak waiting for me, they having supped. The Cheese held but few people, which I thought strange, wondering if there was some event that night at Court.

And so, after a glass or two of a good sack, Captn. S continued the story of the events at Bedlington. So, said Captn. Shrewton, whose Christian name is Wm., like my Lord, the miners shewed the box, which was of black metal, to the Vicar, Mr. Rawlinson. The box seemed all of one piece. And no way was there to open it. One of the miners suggested that he try to breake open the box with his sledgehammer, but this was objected to by Mr. Bowey. He asserted that the box, being found on his land, was his property. Some words were said about this and some small monies were exchanged. A message was sent out, instead, to reach a certain Thom Woodcoke, from a nearby hamlet, which was a smithe of great skill. It took near an hour to fetch this Woodcoke with his tooles, who came only on a promise of a good payment.

Woodcoke used his smallest hammer and chisel to tap about, just below the rim of the box. And, suddenly, with the tiniest hissing sound, a split appeared, and it became apparent that the box had a lid. Gingerly, Woodcoke lifted the lid, and a great wonder was seen by those standing around him. Inside the box was a Babe! An ordinary Babe, naked, but wrapped in blankets. It appeared to be asleep, but after a moment the Child opened its eyes and gave out a lusty cry.

Mrs. Rawlinson, she the Vicar's wife, took up the little one in its blanket and cooed and cuddled it. Whereupon, the Child reached up and poked at the good woman's nose and broke it! This causing a flow of blood onto her face Mrs. Rawlinson shrieked, and her husband took the Child from her. He held it at arm's length and shook it angrily.

The Babe gave another cry and shrugged the Vicar's hands away with a strong shake of its shoulders. This caused Mr. Rawlinson to let go. But instead of falling to the ground and hurting itself, the Child, wonder of wonders, floated in the middle of the air. It slowly rotated itself around, and flew into the air: first up perhaps thirty feet. And then it flew away to the steps of the church ab't one hundred feet away.

The Vicar and his wife, followed by the parishioners, ran over to where the Babe had come down. Mrs. Rawlinson, goodwife if there ever be such, lifted it up again. The Babe then began first to cry and then to coo. She wrapped it up again in its blanket and held it against her breast. And declared that she would raise the Child as her own. At the time, all could see that around the Babe's neck on a wire was a large and intricate amulet, covering almost half its chest.

There is a carving on the church wall that shows the Child leaping into the air, but some say this is an old carving of an angel in flight. Some say it is a demon.

Afterwards, the great rock was pounded up by the miners and the residuum dumped in a pit. The cylinder was brought into the church, but it was melted down for cannon during the Civil War. And the box and robes of the Babe were kept for many years in St. Cuthbert's. Until one night thieves broke in the Church and stole the box along with a pair of silver candlesticks. (These were candlesticks that the Vicar, not Mr. Rawlinson but one of his successors, had saved from looting by some troopers calling themselves Soldiers of His Majesty but 'twere mere looters.) The thieves had also started a fire to burn down the Church. But it had been put out. But not before the Parish Record and many old documents of the Parish and the Church had been consumed as well as the vestry.

"And that's the end of this tale," said Mr. Captn. Shrewton loudly. He had become red in his face with the ale he had drunk. Mr. Sleak and I questioned him closely about this marvelous event. What color was the great stone? How heavy the cylinder, &c. But the Captn. recalled to us that this was a story he had got from Mr. Pepper, who had got it from his grandsire, who had got it from his father. Who it was by no means clear had been a witness. And anyway it was a tale of Mr. Rawlinson and his wife, not of Mr. Pepper's family. I thought this remark to be a naif one. And one which, with the missing rock, and the cylinder, and the Parish Record also missing, cast a pale light on the tale. This might have been a fanciful story gotten up to explain the carving on the church like many monsters on our old cathedrals from which many olde tales have arisen.

So home by carriage, and I with my head full of thoughts of Mr. Rawlinson's great stone, and the cylinder, the box and the Babe. I ate a bit of bread and cheese. And so to bed.

3rd. Up early but then lay pretty long in bed gaining pleasure with my wife, and then to Westminster, where the Commons is sitting. Here I met with various mediocre folk, who did give me petitions for preferment. Thence to ye Cheshire Cheese, but I found myself not willing to speak to any of my friends there. Having Capn. Shrewton's tale much on my mind. Then to finish my letter for Sir W. Batten, himself Surveyor of the Navy, on errors in the methode of procurement of stores for the Navy and rumors of peculation.

It being three o'clock ere I had done, when I come to Sir W. Batten, he was already in a huffe, which I made light of. To my distress, he found displeasure with my letter. But he signed it, though he would not go to my Lord Chancellor's. So I, myself, presented it to My Lord's Secretary. The rest of the day, at White Hall, I hoped to hear further news about the letter, but nothing, and then home to supper, and they we sat together very lovingly, and then we to bed. Even so, I was much disturbed in my sleepe.

4th. Up early and by carriage to White Hall, and there I worked again my letter criticizing the whole business of Navie procurement. That eve, I came to Sir W. Batten to further discuss the letter, though he now liked the letter well. I down to the Tower Wharf, and there got a sculler, and to White Hall, and so I delivered it to Sir W. Coventry, in the cabinet, where I leave it to its fortune. And I by water home again, and to my chamber, to even my Journall. And then comes Captain Cocke to me, and he and I drink a measure of sack and have a great deal of melancholy discourse of the times, giving all over for gone, though now the Parliament will soon finish the Navy Bill for money. He being gone, I again to my Journall and finished it, and so to supper and to bed.

4th. Up and to the W-Hall and amazed to discover preparation of a coach and four to be put at my disposal. Because of my letter, I am dispatched to Newcastle there to uncover the state of the Navy procurement. It is now being said that peculation and theft have wrecked the condition of foodstuffs and shipbuilding there. At noon to the Three Tuns, where D. Gawden did feast us all with a chine of beef and other good things, and an infinite dish of fowl. Thence to W-H. The coach being ready, it took me home for my kit, whereupon I am off to Newcastle for the inspection. The coach departed from my home at 6 in the evening with the weather being on a sudden set in to be very cold.

7th. Arrived at New Castle this morning at 8. We arrived there just as it commenced to rain hard, and the horses to fail, which was our great care to prevent. Thus ending a cold, hard journey. To sum, nothing but cold and wet and some of the most miserable innes I haf ever slept in. As we proceeded north, the food became worse and the wenches uglier, with the weather. Entering the Yard, the coach brought me to the offices of Sir Donald Dulking, Adm. of the Yard. I then dismissed the coach and instructed the driver to return to L, expecting to journey home by packet boat.

I was soon informed that the Adm. was onboard one of the ships, inspecting a cargo consignment. (Strange actions for an Admiral, I think.) I was exhausted and was urged by the Adm's adjutant to partake of the regular Navy (not Naval officers') mess. I found the provender to be disgusting, but I was assured by my escort, a young Midshipman named Davis, that the Admiral himself regularly partakes of the regular mess. I left the table wholly unsatisfied. A half-bottle of inferior claret did not mollify me.

After a long wait, I finally met with Sir Don'ld Dulking, Rear Adm. We discussed the issue and he agreed there may be some corruption present, but it is of a trivial nature. He invited me to tour the Yard and even board some of the ships, which apparently is his wont. But I preferred to review the accountables. After some hesitation, I made the acquaintance of three of the Yard's bookkeepers, non-Naval men. These three affected a very casual demeanor which, in ordinary, would have offended me greatly. But in their stances, along with the behavior of the Adm., I have become suspicious.

That eve, after finishing the first few hours' work with the bookkeepers, I expected to be formally received by Admiral Dulking or one of his senior staff. But no such event took place, which, again, I took ill. Young Midshipman Davis approached me rather timidly and said that he had been instructed that I was to be housed at the Senior Officer's Quarters. I asked if there were a good inn nearby. And the lad said there was, just outside the Yard gate. It was called the Old Charles. We walked over there just as it began to rain hard. We sat and talked about the Yard. Then there came to us an aged sea captain, a summat foolish man named Captain Seabright. And he and I entered into a great but humourous dispute concerning whether the Navy were better now than during the Protectorate. This discourse took us much time, till it was time to go to bed, but we being merry, we bade the Midshipman goodnight, and continued to drink.

As a stab in the dark, I asked Cap'n Seabright if he had ever heard of Captain Shrewton. He said he had, but had not seen him for several years. I then asked of him if he knew of a Mr. Pepper, a farmer from the vicinitee of Bedlington. To my surprise, he told me that Mr. Pepper is a cozen of his on his mother's side. And he had just come in to New Castle. After a quart or two of wine, the good Cap'n agreed to bring Mr Pepper for breakfast in the morning so I might speak to him, and I to bed.

8th. I had a strange dream and having kicked my night clothes off, I got very cold, and in the morning had a good deal of pain. This and the rain made me very melancholy. But when I went down for breakfast, I found Cn Seabright at table with the gentleman Mr. Pepper. This was the manne who first recounted the tale of the Babe to Cn Shrewton (who repeated the tale to me and my friends); he being exactly the manner of stout and redd-faced farmer you might think of. The pain that I had got last night by cold had not yet gone, and troubled me at the time. Captain S, Mr. Pepper and I enjoyed a breakfast of a fresh halibut and small beere.

In short, Mr. Pepper confirmed to me the main of the story of the Babe of Bedlington, as he had heard it from his grandsire. There were still, he said, some remnants of the storie, including the pitt when the Greate Stone had been broken up. He told me that he would be returning to Bedlington on the morrow, and if I cared to join him, the journey would be but 16 mile. I could rest over at his farme which, he swore was large and cozy. I agreed and we will depart from this inne tomorrow afternoon, after I hope to have concluded the Navy business here in Newc'le.

So up and to the Navy Yarde and about business. I examined people as to what they could swear concerning the vittles, cordage, Etc., that is being supplied. And I can only, when joined with the worke of the Acc'ts, conclude that the whole is become the business of cheating rogues and peculating knaves. For part of my examinations, Admiral Dulking sat with me. I conceive that he was uncomfortable as some of the blame for this criminal behavior must fall towards him for which we hope he can give explanation. Thence after the examination, it being too soon to go to dinner, I walked up and down the Yarde, not helping but to notice what I felt to be an overall melancholie.

At last got back to the inne and dined well on another halibut, which was very welle prepared with a mustard sauce. I being cold to my bones, to bed presently, and had a very bad night of it.

9th Sabbath. I slept till 7 o'clock, it raining mighty hard. I know not what will become of the corn harvest this year, as we have had but four fair days this month.

After breakfasting alone on some cold oysters, soup and a half of claret, I was hailed from my table by a voice from the inne y'rd, it being Mr. Pepper. I joined him on his handsome hay cart and greatly enjoyed the trip to Bedlington, as the rain stopped almost as we set out.

Arriving in Bedlington, Mr. Pepper invited me to his home where we sat and talked, and drank, and ate an hour or so. He gave me directions away to the Church of St. Cuthbert's and lent me a horse. He begged me to ride it to Newcastle and leave it at the stables in the Navy Yarde whence he would retrieve it the next week. I replied that I would and parted with Mr. Pepper, resolving to myself that I would do him some preferment when I returned to Newcastle. It took but a half hour to reach the Church, whereupon I searched about for the vicar. And finally, having encountered some ancient natural, I was led to a small building, barely more than a shadde, behind the Church proper.

This lowly place was the vicarage, and to my delight, the current holder of the parsonage, Rev. Mr. Johnson, was at home. He received me cordially and delighted me with a second breakfast. It so turned out that Mr. Johnson is a close friend of my cozen, Angier, at Cambridge and knew, slightly, my brother John. Mr. Johnson being a bachelor, I was introduced to his only housemate, a terrier dog that closely resembles a lamb, but Mr. Johnson assured me, is of both a gentle and powerful nature. I learnt that the reason for his modest way of living was that the former vestry had been burnt by the Protector's men during the Civil War and that it had never been rebuilt. He himself, he declared, was of simple taste and required nothing more although he said the shadde doth need a new roof. This pleased me much, and I resolved upon return to London to speak of this gentleman and perhaps obtain funds for a more adequate home for him. I reminded that the Member of Parliament for Morpeth, Mr. Dowling, is an old associate and I could no doubt catch his ear in this matter.

I begg'd of Mr Johnson if he knew anything of the story of the Childe or Babe of Bedlington. And at that he seemed summat uneasy. I pressed him as far as decency allowed, and, at fin, he took me to see the carving on the wall of the church of which I had heard. This effigy is on the northwest wall of the church. While Captain Shrewton recounted that it demonstrates the Child in the air, this is not clear. Mr. Johnson said that the image was damaged by the same Soldiers who had stole the box with the Babe's clothes. They had hammered at the statue, hurting it much on grounds it were idolatrous.

Then Mr. Johnson showed me the pit where the residuum from the great rock was put. There was not much to see but a dark set of rock, slightly below the level of the ground. (I took up a small piece to present to the Royal Society.) I then asked the Rev. if he knew anything more of the Babe itself and of the Rawlinson family.

He said to me that the subject was so long ago, it was still of great pain to the village and people did not discuss it. I took this as a sign that he would speak no more of this and so I bid him farewell.

I was ready to take my leave of Bedlington. However, after I left the vestry for my horse, the same ancient natural I had seen before accosted me, seizing me by the arm. He asked me, if I wished, if it pleased me, to see something marvelous concerning the Babe of Bedlington as he called the Child. He said he had listen'd at the doorway to the vestry and overheard some of the words I had had with Rev. Johns'n. I did not desire to traffick with this creature, but he importuned me several times. Half speaking, half mumbling. I was almost ready to strike this lout, but his constant talk of the Babe halted me. He signed to me that he wished to drink and pointed to an establishment a few furlongs away. We walked there together, but I bade him walk behind me as his stench was very great. He also carried on his shoulder a sack which seemed quite heavy. I went into the inn and brought out for him a pot of small beere, which he drank in one swallow. He signaled for more, which I brought him. Soon, he talked a great while about my going down with him to Newminster Abbey, which were, he said, six or seven mile from Bedlington. I was anxious to start back to Newcastle and from there back to London, but each time the ancient mentioned the Babe, I felt my stummick stir. And he promised if I went with him, he would shew me something that would astonish me.

So, a certain madness took over me, and we set off for Newminster Abbey, the ancient walking and I riding. He told me his name was Raulph Kent, and he claimed to be near one hundred years old. I doubted this as it would make him much the oldest man in Britain. But I noticed that the beere he had consumed made his discourse more reasonable. I asked him how he came to know the story of the Babe of Bedlington. He said to me that now he and I had left the towne, he would tell me his story. Most remarkably he claimed to be Raulph Rawlinson, the sonne of the Reverend Rawlinson, he who adopted the Babe, which I scarcely believed. And I thought he might be a rogue who was playing a trick on me to get money of me. But I said to him that I thought it wonderful that he had lived so long. I begged him to recount the story of the Babe after his father and mother took the Childe to be their own.

As we proceeded on this short journey, which he promised me would be but an hour but which turned out to be nearer two, this was his story. He had no hesitation nor was he a man of few words. And despite his gruffness and foul appearance, he spoke in a kindly and gentle manner with even some education. He told me that he was only in the towne fortnightly to see Rev. Johnson who gave provisions to him. He had just left the vestry when he first saw me. Then he begun telling me the *Tale of the Babe*, as I have called his story.

As Raulph Rawlinson told me, soon after the Reverend and his wife declared at the churchyard that they would adopt the Babe as their own, within a very few days, they were visited by one Rev. Exton, a dependent of Lord Tankerville. Mr. Exton told them they must either give the Babe up to him or leave the parish forthwith and that he, Rev. Exton, would take over the parish. Raulph's father declared it was his Christian duty to shelter the Babe. And so after all things were ready, with much sadness, his father and mother, he, his sister Elspeth, and the Babe, who they named Willielmus, left the Living of Bedlington and moved to Morpeth where they rented a farm with a dairy herd of Chillingham cattle. Raulph, who was being educated in a school in Bedlington, with hopes of attending university some day, and enter the ministry, saw his education end suddenly.

Life was very hard for the family as their neighbors did shun them and few would buy from them, either milk or cheese. However, they were soon secretly aided by a community of five Lollard families in Morpeth. Eventually, they joined this community, and Rev. Rawlinson became the community's leader. The families soon decided that they would all go to the Roanoke colony due to continued persecution of the Lollards.

It was decided by the Rev. Rawlinson that it would not be possible for them to take the Babe, Willielmus, with them to the New World. The Babe was too well known and 'twould be hard to travel with him.

Raulph said that the Lollards, including his father, decided that if the Babe was on a shippe it would probably mean mutinee. So it was sadly decided that Raulph, who was the oldest son and was twenty years of age, would stay on with the Babe, who was then ten years old. Also, Rev. Rawlinson decided to change the family name to Kent, whence the Rawlinsons had originally come from during the time of King Henry VIII.

Raulph said he felt that the events had weakened his father's and mother's mind, and he still could not countenance what they had done. After they departed with the five Lollard families, in great haste, George had one letter of them from Barbados. In this letter, which he shewed me, it promised that they would find a way to bring him and Willielmus to Roanoke to join them. And then nothing. He presumed that they had been lost when the inhabitants of the colony had been attacked by the red Indians. After this, the man was quiet for a while.

We finally reached the Abbey, it being very dark in the woods there. We walked thence amongst the great trees that had grown up in the ruins of the Abbey, and in and out of the fallen buildings themselves. And there Raulph Rawlinson finished for me the *Tale of the Babe.* That he being but twenty years of age was left behind with Willielmus, who was but ten but who had the strength of a grown man and more.

And, he could fly like a bird, Raulph whispered to me. So, he told me, when his brother was frightened, he would leap into the air and fly to the top of any tree nearby. I felt amazed by this but I remembered how the Babe had flown from Rev. Rawlinson's hands to the nearby church steps. T'was a moment before I could speak and then I gave out to Raulph Rawlinson to continue.

The farm, he said, did not thrive. Raulph had no gift for dairying and a few years later, he, even with the help of his brother, could no longer sustain the herd and they quit the rental of the animals and the farm. So he and Willielmus became vagabonds, never straying too far from Morpeth and Bedlington. Willielmus's strength let them be able to maintain themselves. In the spring and summer and in the autumn, they worked on the farms. However, in winter without a house, they lived in the Abbey but in a very poor situation, so that they nearly froze or starved.

Towards the end of one colde season, Raulph went alone to Bedlington and begged some food of the new rector, who gave him some of the new vegetable called the potato, which sustained them till the spring. But labour was plentiful and despite Willielmus's strength, they could get no work. One day the two went to Morpeth for the market, perhaps to pick up some work carting, and there was a local faire with a wrestling shew. There was a champion named Wild Bull Boggy. And there were a prize of £1 for any man who could remain in the ring with him for but five minutes. £1 was more than Raulph and Willielmus could earn in a fortnight.

So, Willielmus urged Raulph to let him fight although he was but sixteen. And he, Raulph, was afraid not that his brother would be hurt or even lose, but that with his strength, something would needs happen, and his identity as the Babe would be revealed. But Willielmus, whom Raulph called Willie, wanted much to fight. And so he went to the ring. Wild Bull, Raulph said, was a truly enormous manne, weighing perhaps twenty stone and above six and a half feet tall. Some said he were the tallest manne in Britain.

After some ado, Willielmus climbed into the ring with this gigantic manne. And, Raulph said, his brother beat the other in less than a minute by the glass. But then, came calamity! After Willielmus threw the giant down and the manne could not rise, Willielmus lifted Wild Bull above his head in triumph and shewed him to the crowd. But then, Boggy twisted in Willielmus's arms and punch'd him in the face. And before Willielmus did realize what he did, he smash'd Wild Bull Boggy to the ring, killing him. And then, in great fear, the lad (nought but sixteen, recall) leaped into the air and flew off!

There were, so Raulph described, screams and panick. And someone yelled out that that was the Babe, the Bedlington Babe, grown to be a man. Without waiting to see what would happen, Raulph said that he fled back to the Abbey and hid in a dry well in one of the cellars. He stayed there hidden through the day, all through the night and the next day. Not till the next night did he venture out. Past midnight he heard a crashing sound nearby. Raulph said it is not imaginable how frightened he was as he thought wildly that some from Morpeth were still out for him. But blessed be God, he said, it was Willielmus crashing down from the skye. Then his brother came and spoke to him and said he had been far away in London. That in but a day he had flew from Morpeth to London and back to Morpeth. And Raulph said he could not close his mouth for astonishment and in fear.

Willielmus then said to Raulph that he was determined to fly first to Ireland and then to Iceland, to Greenland and thence to the New World to find their parents. (Raulph added that he had given Willielmus as much education as he could including in geographie.) He had experienced and learnt much flying to London and back. And that he thought he would leave when the sun rose. Raulph told him this was madness. But Willielmus said no, that he must go.

He then spoke to Raulph of the mother's amulet that had been found on him when he was discovered. The amulet, Raulph told me, was about the size of a grown man's hand. Large as it was, Mrs. Rawlinson had insisted that Willielmus wear it round his necke. But when the Babe was but three years of age, to the amazement of all, he had insisted in his baby voice that his mother should wear it always.

Raulph said that once his mother put the amulet on, Willielemus could always sense where she was. And even across the sea, he always had a vague feeling of her whereabouts. And as he was grown older, that feeling had grown. But until he had taken actual flight, he had no notion to seek out their mother and, hopefully, their father and sister.

Willielmus told Raulph that he was determined to go at dawn. Raulph packed some food for him, of what they had. And, true to his word, after much sobbing and embracing and brotherly kissing, Willielmus leaped into the skie and was gone. Raulph never heard from him or the rest of the family.

In the many, many years that passed, Raulph told me he made a life for himself, as before, wandering about and working and living in the Abbey. About ten years after Willielmus flew off, he approached the Rector of St. Cuthbert's, the man who had replaced his father and begged the man for alms. Rev. Exton had become very old, but still hale. He told Raulph that he felt the Church had done poorly with his family. And that he was willing to give him a weekly pittance. And that was continued for several rectors to this day, including the Reverend Johnson. This explained to me why the Reverend had seemed so unwilling to speak to me.

Then Raulph opened an olde wooden boxe and shewed me what he had brought me to see. It seemed nothing but a piece of cloth perhaps an ell squared in size. It were, he said, one of the wrappings that Willielmus was covered in when he were found. And what a piece of cloth it proofed to be! It was of a dull blue and seemed to be some kind of blanket or robe, but small, for a child. Raulph took it up and told me to try to tear it a-pieces. So strong it was, I could not do it. He said it neither burnt nor did it fade or take dirt. I begged him to let me take it back to London to shew to the Royal Society, but he refused, even after I offer'd him a goodly sum. He said he wished to be buried with this cloth as his shroud.

Soon after that, I left Raulph Rawlinson. I gave him a sum of money to help him. And he thanked me. I arrived quickly back in Bedlington, early enough to set out for and reach Newcastle in time for a fine dinner of a capon and some small fish and a bottle of sack. In the morning into London on the mail packet.

12th. At home after a terrible passage, New Castle to London. The weather were foule and I sickened almost as soon as we left the Tyne. And the young cap'n being inexperienced on this run. He brought us perilous close to the Godwin Sands which he laughingly called the Eater of Shippes. Greeted at 6 in the evening at the door by my sweetling, I being more dead than alive. She fed me on some good brothe, which I managed to hold down. She importuned me to tell her some of my journie, which I did. We dined late on some goode beef and claret. And so to bed.

See David Berger's story "Pages Missing From the Diary of Samuel Pepys, Esq." online at Metaphorosis.
If you liked it, leave a comment. Authors love that!
Remember to subscribe to our e-mail updates so you'll know when new stories are posted.

About the story

Somewhere along the way, about a year and a half ago, I got the notion of Superman appearing in the 17th or 18th century. And as a long-time fan of Samuel Pepys, it immediately occurred to me to use his Diary as a framework. (The entire Diary is available online.)

In order to keep Pepys' rhythm, I copied and pasted parts of the book into my story, and then (very freely) converted his words into mine. In the early parts of the book, this was easy because it's mostly a record of his comings and goings and eating and drinking (plus his sex life).

However, Pepys seldom described lengthy incidents, so in the description of the events at Bedlington, and in Pepys' record of his own visit there, I had to wing it. BTW, Bedlington is a real place, and the church is real and the story of the Babe is … I also did some research about the Roanoke colony and the Lollards to fill in the details.

It was a real trip putting the story together from its various parts. And I want to thank the editors of Metaphorosis for pushing me to lengthen and refine the tale.

A question for the author

Q: What was your favorite children's book?

A: I want to answer this question in two ways: My favorite book when I was a child, and my favorite children's book.

As a kid, my favorite book was *Treasure Island*. After seeing the 1950 movie ("Arrrh!"), I insisted that my Mom get me a copy. She did, and I read it myself in about a week. (I was six.)

My favorite book for kids is *The Once and Future King*. I read it to my own sons.

I believe that the "classic" children's stories and fairy tales have a heft to them that kids like and need.

About the author

David is an old Brooklyn Lefty, living in Manhattan with his wife of 26 years: the finest jazz singer in NYC. He's a father and a grandfather. He's been a caseworker, construction worker, letter carrier, teacher, proofreader and union organizer. David loves life, his wife, and the world. He hopes to help us all escape destruction.

Tower of Mud and Straw I

Yaroslav Barsukov

Prologue

Shea Ashcroft stepped from a carriage into the low-lit cul-de-sac as a mongrel lifted its door knocker of a head from a garbage pile.

Dogs. They'd taken over the capital a week before. The wind dragged garlands of crushed glass and everyday commodities across the pavement, and the dogs picked out anything they could chew: meat from the decimated butcher's shops, greens, someone's shoes.

Those animals had guts. It was the humans who tended to stay indoors—half of them cursing the one person who'd had the chance to 'stop the violence at its inception'. Him.

Three people at the royal court he'd previously considered friends had already advised him to issue an apology. He'd told them to go to hell.

The hound ran to the middle of the street. It barked and leaped in place, snapping its jaws at something it couldn't quite reach.

"Atta boy," Shea said. "Though that bone's a bit too big for you."

The 'bone' hung at the second-story height, the post of a gas lamp stretched like a strut between the opposing buildings, comically, inconceivably. There were reports of looters getting their hands, heaven knew how, on one or two Drakiri devices—*tulips*, his sister used to call them; his sister, when she was still alive—which reduced the weight of anything they touched to that of paper.

Apparently, once you were in possession of something like that, you tried to steal a street light—or had it been a refined vandalism, or a weird attempt at a joke? Shea's gaze grazed the walls for signs of damage.

"Idiots playing with fire," he said to the dog. "If only they risked their own lives alone."

The dog barked and jumped again, heedless of the rubble beneath its feet.

Third door on the right, carved oak. Shea pushed on the doorknob and descended the steps into the basement vestibule.

The valet who took his coat said, "Thank you."

He looked vaguely familiar. Square jaws, eyes sunken into crow's feet.

"Do I know you?"

The man didn't answer, but Shea's memory did.

...the crowd, a huge condensed mass of arms, legs, and throats, rolling toward him, and *back, back, drive them back*, the scent of blood, a lieutenant bending over the balustrade, twisting her body trying to peek into the russet sky—*where's the bloody airship?*—then, the great elongated balloon sailing over the terracotta roof tiles.

Minister, we need your permission to gas the crowd. Snap out of it. Minister. Lord Ashcroft. Shea.

Hands had touched him, shaken him, poked him, but his vision shrank to a girl, pink dress, huge eyes taking in the world as though for the first time, the world in the airship's shadow.

Fall back.

Minister?

Fall back...

The man put his coat on a hanger.

"You were there," Shea said. "In the crowd, next to the girl in pink."

He nodded. "We're all alive because of you, Minister."

But half of the city lies destroyed—also because of me.

He wondered why his title still applied.

Past the inner door was a pocket-size theater, eight or nine rows, six of them empty. Still, a dozen faces—because entertainment had to continue even in times like these, and because, for tiny venues, this was the moment to shine.

All the big ones lay crippled.

Shea lowered himself next to a slender man in black gloves. "Weird place for a meeting. You wanted to see me, my lord?"

"Just Aidan, if you would, my lord. I know we haven't interacted a lot, but I much prefer my own name."

"Why the theater?"

"To make sure we could talk undeterred."

"This week, the street would've sufficed," Shea said.

"Yes, but it isn't safe out there this week. I—"

Applause cut him short. The curtains parted, revealing the scenery: a starry expanse behind something dark and cylindrical. An actor in orange darted onto the stage, doubling up in a bow.

"Queen Daelyn built a tower, took gold from every man, breast milk from every mother..."

So it's about the Owenbeg tower, Shea thought.

He'd seen the official daguerreotypes—a vast column, more of a growth than a human-made structure—but the details were always blurry and the inscriptions read more like statements. 'Biggest building in history'—*try imagining that.*

Shea half-turned to Aidan. "Another play about the tower?"

"The construction effort isn't going well. Something's happened there. People pick up on rumors."

Onstage, the orange man made a leap. "Queen Daelyn sent her servant—to oversee the deed..."

Another, in a silk jacket, appeared from behind the curtain's crimson.

"...the servant wasn't smart enough—and he got promptly killed," the first one declared.

"I heard that rumor, too," said Shea. "That Daelyn is sending someone from the court there. Poor fellow, whoever that will be."

"Actually." Aidan pointed his finger at the silk-jacketed guy. "Actually, that's you out there, Shea. May I call you Shea?"

"What?"

The woman right in front of them turned her head. "Would you please keep your voices down?"

"What do you mean, it's me?" Shea whispered.

"Nothing official yet," Aidan said, "but I was told Daelyn would issue the decree tomorrow. You're to give up your office and become her intendant in Owenbeg. You'll be overseeing the tower's construction."

"What the hell?!" The woman turned again, and Shea said, "Sorry. What the hell, Aidan?"

"I told you—something's happened there, and she needs—"

"I can defend my every action during the riots. And what's an intendant, anyway?"

"The position is relatively new. Honestly, I wouldn't consider this a punishment, rather an opportunity, and that's why I wanted to talk to you—"

He went on, but Shea didn't listen anymore. People onstage jumped, danced, sang in funny voices. Someone behind laughed in irregular intervals. The woman in the front row produced a hand fan.

At some point, he simply stood and made his way out.

"My lord!" Aidan called out, but he continued to the exit.

Outside, the hound had given up on things it couldn't reach and gone back to rummaging through the waste heap.

It seemed like a dream—the slow ride from the city's edge, unloading baggage that all looked the same. Climbing the pier on which the airship perched.

A lady with a southern accent she desperately tried to mask told Shea the first-class suite had been taken, but 'their second class was just as good'. The door she led him to opened into a cabin which resembled a theater prop room, with a couch that stank of sweat, a table, and a vase of flowers overdue for a burial.

"Would you fancy a drink?" the southern lady asked

He said, "I don't really drink."

"Tea, then?"

"Yes, please."

She brought a lone porcelain cup together with a kettle, ice-cold. Shea had no idea if it was another affront or simple negligence—and, frankly, he didn't care anymore.

As the airship slid into a farewell glide over the capital toward where the horizon squeezed the sun of its last drops, he sat and sipped the bland brew. Behind the window, the palace swam by, the Red Hill, the honeycombs of the guard towers' lights. 'Consider this an opportunity,' Aidan had told him.

"I sure hope, Aidan," Shea said now, "that you don't mean suicide."

His sister would've been proud of him, were she still alive: he could've refused the assignment, he could've begged. But there was something noble, romantic even, in accepting an unjust punishment. *There, I made a decision. I would do it again. I bear the consequences.*

If I am to ensure the tower gets built, he thought, *it will be the swiftest and most efficient construction ever.*

And I'll find a way to return, to get back what they've taken from me.

He raised the cup in a mock salute as the palace swam out of view.

There goes my life at the capital, Lena, sis, my dear thing. After you passed away, I tried to let go, focus on my career—and look how well that came out.

Please forgive that I've stopped speaking to you. I guess the turning point for me was that reception, when someone asked me who you were, at which point I realized I was talking out loud. They thought I was bonkers, and of course it's bonkers conversing with an imaginary dead person—but we're all crazy in some way or another, aren't we? The trick is figuring who's at 'some' and who's already at 'another'.

I wish I had your strength, and I wish you were here now.

I. The Duchy

1

Shea awoke when the ship made a leap toward hell.

Under the daylight's varnish, the cabin took a dive, jolted, plunged. *Maybe we're passing through a pocket of air,* his brain whispered. *Lie still for a minute, it will blow over.*

He tore his hand from the mattress and raised it to his face: the pinky trembled lightly. The next jolt threw him off the couch, and somewhere in the gondola's bowels, two dozen throats produced a collective sigh.

Shea was about to join them when a thought sent him into nervous laughter—*a fall from grace. Perhaps a literal one this time.*

Well, he refused to go out like that.

Still buttoning his shirt, he peeked into the corridor. To his right, the door to the luxury suite swung open, spewing a man in a smoking jacket who sized him up and, in a shrill voice, said, "Are we going to die?"

So, the southern lady didn't lie—first class really was taken.

Shea squeezed himself past the guy. "Don't stand here. Go back to your room and hold on to something."

Behind him, the shrill voice repeated, "Are we going to die?"

"If we are, I'll let you know."

The corridor widened into the dining lounge, pristine white, shards on the floor, cutlery quivering in unison with his own pounding on the bridge door.

"Skipper? What's going on?"

After a good ten seconds, a muffled voice said, "Who is it?"

"Ashcroft." A new dive slapped him against the wall.

The door half-opened, and an acned face appeared in the gap. "Minister?"

"A former one. Let me in."

"Let him in, Jonah," another voice said.

The control cabin was more like a slice of a lighthouse's lantern room than a naval ship's bridge; four would've been a crowd here.

The captain, wearing an olive dress coat of Owenbeg, their destination, stood at the helm—for Shea, he came across as a collection of unconnected details: a wide nape, a sideburn, a crease on the trousers—and the acned face, probably the first mate, clutched a second wheel.

"How may I help you, Minister?" said the captain without turning.

"By telling me what the hell's going on."

"First time in the duchy, I presume?"

"Me and a bunch of other folks, apparently. The passenger cabins are learning to sing opera right now."

"It's just turbulence."

"I know turbulence." The room made another dance move, and Shea grabbed an iron lever to steady himself.

"Please let go of that, Minister," the acne boy said.

"I *know* turbulence. *This* feels like a drunken sailor party."

"A bad day today, that's what it is," the captain said. "It's the air. The air hits *it*, gets pushed in all directions, gains speed. Roughs us up."

"The air hits what?"

"To starboard, Mr. Ashcroft."

Still not turning, the captain waved his hand, and Shea looked. Gasped. Took a few uneven steps toward the windscreen.

Behind it, there was something vast, something dark, a stretch of an evening sky pasted onto midday. To say the tower was colossal was to compare a volcano to a matchstick: it was a mountain's trunk, freed from the foothills, and the scattering of villages in its shadow could've been cardboard toys.

His responsibility? How could he *do* anything to it, *ensure* anything about it?

"Gosh," Shea said, "what altitude are we at?"

"One thousand two hundred feet."

"How high is the damn thing?"

"A thousand, give or take. And I hear they're planning to put another thousand on top of it—but really, I should ask *you* that, no?"

"Pardon?"

"No fools here, Lord Ashcroft."

At that moment, Shea saw himself from the outside: a noble, barging into the bridge, pushing aside a man who'd probably been saving for a year to book a ride in a luxury suite. The tone, the words. *Skipper.*

He stretched out his hand. "I don't think we've been formally introduced, captain."

"Liam Salas. Welcome to the border, Minister."

"I'm not a—"

"I wanted you to know—I'd actually planned to visit your cabin before you so gracefully waltzed in—I'm happy you're here. It's a difficult subject, of course, politically, but my son was among the protesters."

The handshake lasted longer than custom demanded, which was helpful because, otherwise, the next plunge would've sent Shea to the floor.

"I did nothing a normal human being wouldn't have done," he said.

"You would be surprised."

"One's got to suffer from serious empathy issues to use gas on people."

"And yet the queen gave the order, didn't she?"

The mammoth structure outside grew closer, and Shea squinted. "What are those pink spangles? There, and there. What are those dots?"

"Oh, that. That's the *tech.*"

"The tech?"

"Drakiri devices."

Shea opened and closed his mouth, and the bridge squeezed around him while memory served up an image of a different room, gray walls, soot stains, chairs with twisted legs, the odor of something unknown, something foreign, and another scent that turned him inside out—of charred flesh. "This is insane. You're using Drakiri technology to build that thing?"

"I'm just steering this airship. But yes, the builders use the tech."

"Why wasn't it in the reports?"

"How should I know? You must ask the duke—or Brielle."

"Brielle?"

"The main engineer."

"Why wasn't it in the reports?" Shea whispered.

Lena, Lena, look at what they've done.

"I have nothing against Drakiri, or refugees in general," the captain said. "Half the duchy still curses the day Daelyn's father granted them a settlement with us, but I think it was about the only thing the old bastard did right."

"Mr. Silas, believe me, I have nothing against Drakiri, either. But this..." Shea drummed his knuckle against the windshield. "How long have you been using the, the tech?"

"Again, you must ask Miss Brielle."

"Who the hell had the bright idea? ... Drakiri stuff is a ticking bomb. I'm talking from experience."

They both looked out the window, in silence, at the approaching giant.

The worst thing is, sis, I don't always remember your face. Sometimes I see you in a dream, and when I wake up, the details dissolve, dissipate into what the daylight brings: the warmth and the glow and the dust. That's what makes me, a grown-ass man, bawl—the fact you're becoming a memory.

They told me it was all part of the 'healing', Lena. Can you believe that?

2

A yellow trail extended from the airship pier in a relatively straight line; not a proper road, more like a track plowed in the field by a huge finger. At the end, four carriages waited.

Shea let the luxury suite guy pick his horse first; the other passengers, in white and brown trousers and dresses, went on foot. Half must've spewed their guts an hour before, and faces wore a shade of pale, but the eyes glowed: *look at it. Look.*

The tower blocked the sun, throwing a mile-long blanket over the fields, the poplars, and the village cowering at the root of the hill on which the caterpillar of the castle slept. Ants cluttered across the tower's vertical body, half of them suspended by threads at such height that Shea had to raise his chin. Construction workers. Some crawled in and out of the spots leaking pink glow.

The thin band at the horizon was the kingdom of Duma, with their perhaps less advanced, but plentiful, aircraft, and his imagination painted a different sky, crimson, ships raining down in fireballs, the tower's artillery barking. No wonder Daelyn had invested so much into the construction—it was her legacy, the most radical defensive structure ever attempted by man.

His head swam.

In a dash of normalcy, a gaunt driver, leaning against the fence in a kind of transfixed state, stared at the people walking past.

"I'm here," Shea said. "They didn't, by any chance, send a welcoming cortege for me?"

The man shifted his eyes to him. "What?"

"Did they send a carriage for me from the castle?"

"If they did, they sure haven't told me."

They looked at each other.

"Well... Could you at least help me fetch my luggage?"

Even when the horse picked up a steady pace, the tower remained immobile, as though forming a whole with the salmon clouds, a painting on an enormous flat canvas.

In the distance, across the fields, a row of yellow lights floated like will-o'-the-wisps.

"I hope I'm not imagining things," Shea said.

"Wives." The driver clicked his tongue. "Fiancées. Lanterns for the foremen at the construction site who're staying for the night."

"Don't they have lanterns inside?"

"It's a tradition."

In the short breath before sunset, the clouds at the horizon seemed to pick up the glow from the procession—and underneath, a new thing stirred in Shea. Perhaps there was a lantern for him, too. Perhaps something waited to happen behind the tower's contours.

He grabbed that lifeline and tried to focus on the sensation. *It's not over. I'm not finished yet.*

At the village's outskirts, a boy and a girl, a pair of brown dashes for knees, ran in circles, slinging dust at each other.

"Look at him," the driver said. "Look at that guy go."

A man pulled an empty two-wheeled cart at the road's opposite side. There was something about him, something unnatural, and a moment later Shea realized what: he was moving too fast, like a marathon runner but without any visible effort. No muscles bulging. He *glided.*

"A Drakiri fellow." The driver spat, without malice, as if paying some weird tribute. "Can pull those things all day. Those aren't real carriages, though."

"Huh?"

"We call them drikshaws. No place for luggage."

"I hate the idea, being carried by another human being," Shea said. "Or a Drakiri, doesn't matter. I can't understand how anyone wouldn't find it offensive."

"Only don't tell 'em that, boss. Will smack you on the head with the whole cart. Strong, those fellows. 'Lot stronger than you and me."

"Yes, I've heard as much. Still, a job doesn't become less degrading because it's easier."

"Few other jobs around here, boss. You can work the fields, but they don't care for that."

Eyes on the road, the Drakiri dashed past them.

"What about the tower?" Shea said. "I bet one of them could replace a couple human builders."

"They don't care for the tower either. Oi!" The driver smacked the horse on the rump. "They don't care for the tower at all."

"Why?"

The man shrugged.

They rode past the houses, blind lattice windows caked with dust, past a butcher with a beer belly and a dirty apron, dragging his feet as though time marched at a slower pace for him, kids tumbling around in the dirt, heaps of raked leaves.

Triangles of the wooden roofs didn't touch the rising moon but hid the tower, and with it went Shea's lifeline: he was at the border, in as deep a province as it got, on someone else's land, without an office, a foreign graft on the local hierarchy. *This intendancy system—had Daelyn created it just to give failures a home?*

In a sense, he was back to when he'd left his family estate eight years ago.

The welcoming cortege waited for him at the castle gates: a gray-haired woman with a hawk nose. In the sunset, the wall behind her could've been made of sand.

"I'm Fiona, the majordomo," she said—but when he extended his hand, didn't change her pose, the sticks of arms crossed over stomach, fingers which would've made a musician proud had they not been mutilated by arthritis.

Shea chuckled. "The next fanfare I get will probably be at my funeral, right?"

She didn't answer—just quietly paid the driver and led Shea through a side door next to the gates, up a set of stairs, down a narrow path between battlements.

Through the embrasures, the last of the day dissolved: molten sun dripped along the tower's edge, a black furnace.

"We're going into the oldest part of the castle, Kayleigh's Wing," Fiona said without turning or lowering her pace. "Kayleigh was the first duke's daughter."

"I must admit I've never been much of a history buff."

"Your quarters will be in that wing. Don't worry, we strive to keep everything in order."

"Thank you."

"The duke expects you in an hour," she said.

"Nice joke."

"Do I seem like a joking type to you, my lord?"

"He wants to see me at, what, ten?"

"At this castle, we work day and night."

"Especially at night, apparently. I've just arrived, and it was a long trip—at the very least I'd need to take a bath..."

"And that's why I said 'in an hour' and not 'right now.' "

Another set of stairs, this time leading downward to an oak door built to survive a battering ram.

The quarters looked posh at a first glance: living room the size of a country house, two couches under green velvet, an exit to a balcony, six gas lamps under the ceiling, all of them working; through an archway, a royal bed and a tapestry depicting a battle at the castle's walls, likely caused by baron A seizing a cartload of sheepskin or something similarly important from baron B. An enamel bathtub, reasonably white.

On closer inspection, the floorboards grunted under Shea's boots, the first wooden wall panel he touched rocked under his fingers, and moths had taken a good bite out of the couches' velvet.

Fiona stood in the doorway, waiting for him to finish his survey.

In the bathroom, he twisted the hot water valve, but only a sound came out, a lone rustle trailing along the castle's intestines.

"Where's the hot water?"

"From nine till eleven in the morning," Fiona said from the entrance. "This isn't the capital, Lord Ashcroft."

It was clear she'd rehearsed the line.

Hence the urgency, Shea thought. Drag out the new guy, tired, sweaty. Let him learn his place. Well, he could play this game, too.

He turned the second valve. The water was ice against his fingers.

"Tell the duke I'll meet him in two hours, my lady. Please send someone to wake me in one."

"The duke has—"

"I don't care. I'll meet him in two hours, or he'll have to find something else to discuss with his people. I heard weather's always a safe choice." He glanced at his own reflection above the sink. "Make sure you rehearse this line, too."

3

The duke didn't receive him in the council chamber or the great hall or any other place normally reserved for official meetings. A servant led Shea back between the battlements and into the 'new castle,' diving into a labyrinth of narrow passages, a succession of U-turns whose main purpose was, most likely, to create an illusion of space.

No, the duke received him in a drawing room, which, of course, sent a message: Shea was a guest here, an important, but ultimately a passing one.

The windows were holes into the night, but the walls reflected warm yellow, as though life had dipped everything between them in amber to wait for Shea's arrival.

It was a scene from a painting: a thin man in his sixties on a satin couch, already wearing a rehearsed sardonic smile on pursed lips; to his right, a group of five: four fellows—looking like someone had fashioned them from the same piece of wood—and one woman. They couldn't have been waiting for him more than ten minutes, but because of the yellow glow and the affected poses, it seemed as though they'd been here forever.

"Welcome to Owenbeg, Ashcroft," said the duke.

"My lord, the queen extends her—"

"Oh yes, how is the old fart Daelyn doing?" The man came alive, re-crossing his legs and leaning on his palm. "Dear all, did you know we had the same teacher of astronomy when we were kids? She was smarter than me, I'll give her that—the only problem is, it's not the stars she was chiefly interested in but the boys'—"

Shea blinked. "My lord, I'm not sure it's appropriate, in the presence of a lady—"

"Yes, yes, let's dispense with the pleasantries. Everyone, this is Shea Ashcroft, *former* Minister of Internal Affairs, *former* councilor to the queen, and, starting with today, an intendant in our humble domain. Whatever the hell that means. As for this lot..." He waved his hand theatrically. "This is Patrick, my military counselor, Cian, Counselor of Justice." He recited the other first names, omitting the titles and surnames. "Miss Brielle is our chief engineer at the tower."

A red-headed woman of thirty–thirty-five stood closest to the couch, perfect oval of an open face, somewhat heavy figure. The men kept their gaze on their master, actors waiting for a cue—she was the only one who looked Shea in the eye. Smiled.

"And this," the duke said, "is Lena, my Counselor of Arts."

For a moment, for Shea, the duke disappeared.

What are the odds?

Not just the name, but something in the profile, the posture...

Standing in the corner, looking out the blind window as though not a part of the reception—which was why he hadn't noticed her before—Lena was half a head above everyone else save for him and the man whom the duke had designated as 'Patrick'. She wore a long dress the color of her hair, a black wave rolling down her back, framing her face with its sculpture-precise features.

He'd never heard of an arts counselor, and, anyway, the duke didn't have a reputation as a patron of arts; most probably, they shared a connection. *Lovers, then,* Shea thought.

"How about a drink?" the duke said.

"I don't really drink, my lord."

"Do I understand it correctly that your primary function as intendant would be sending reports to Daelyn?"

"Not quite, it's—"

"How often?"

"Queen expects monthly communiques."

"Marvelous." A smile. "Marvelous. Let's agree on a day, say, first Monday of the month—Fiona will visit you to provide you with notes on the construction effort."

So that was how he wanted to play it. His majordomo as a censor, pristine reports stripped of all the details Daelyn 'doesn't need to know', omissions legitimized by Shea's own signature.

"Shall we take a step back, my lord?" he said. "Before we agree on any course, I want to fulfill my tourist's duties."

"Meaning?"

"I'd like to visit the tower."

The smile widened, but the duke's eyes were two ponds on a winter day.

And now for the real game.

"Why?" he said.

"I must assess the progress myself."

"We'll provide you with all the details."

"Same as you did with the Drakiri tech?"

Lena, who, until then, had appeared lost in thought, turned her head exactly enough to meet Shea's gaze. They held eye contact for a few seconds, and he continued, "The queen heard you'd met with problems."

The duke's face went red. "Fools' lies, all of them."

"My lord, if I may," the chief engineer said. *Brielle.* "We've used the Drakiri devices to speed up the construction—"

The duke waved her off. "That's what we did. Isn't it what Daelyn wants?"

"I can't speak for the queen, but I have a hunch she wants this venture to succeed, not for the tower to crack like an egg. Which will happen if you keep using the technology." Shea turned to Brielle. "How soon may I visit the site, my lady?"

She opened her mouth, but the duke broke her off again.

"Do you have a background in construction?"

"No."

"Exactly, because you've what, you've led a shoe factory? Before becoming a minister?"

"I've managed an upholstery workshop, my lord. It was a family enterprise. Fairly big, too—we supplied..."

"Big as my ass." The duke slapped the arm of his chair. "I don't care."

He could afford profanity. He had at least twenty years of a head start in politics, and this was his turf.

Everybody in the room stared at Shea, including the tapestry griffins on the wall.

He could press them, push his status as the queen's envoy—but wouldn't that make the situation worse?

"Listen, I understand you feel I'm intruding upon your authority," he said. "I'm only here to help. We want the same thing..."

"There." The duke propelled himself from the couch. "There. You sit at the Red Hill and you think you know what it's like out here. Let me tell you: you don't. For Daelyn, the tower's a vanity project."

"No, it's an anti-airship stronghold. Same for you, same for her."

"All old Daelyn sees is a symbol of pride. We need the bloody thing if we're to survive."

"So it's about survival now. I'm sorry, my lord, but the fact that you border Duma doesn't make it—"

"Oh really?" The duke marched toward Shea, stopping halfway, at the invisible demarcation line where his posse's space ended. "Have you seen their crown prince? The one who's been running the country ever since his father had a stroke?"

"That's pure warmongering and you know it. Even when I was a kid—someone has always been talking about Duma attacking us."

"Go across the border." The duke stabbed a finger at the black window. "I implore you. Visit Poltava. *Their* village, but half the people are *ours*, from before the boundary changed. Or rather, *were* ours. See what they've done to the place, see it for yourself."

"Then there's the question of the sabotage attempts," Patrick, the military counselor, said in a suddenly clear, resolute baritone. "Who but the crown prince..."

The duke, who'd been shifting his weight from one foot to another, froze in mid-motion, and a new expression flickered in his eyes. Fear.

Shea took a step forward. "Sabotage attempts?"

"We don't..." Patrick began.

"Shut up," the duke said. "Just shut your mouth. Can you shut your mouth for me?"

"I'm looking forward to you providing *all the details*," Shea said.

Brielle raised her chin. "My lord, I don't think there's any harm in showing the tower to Lord Ashcroft. Honestly, I don't think there's any harm in showing it to anyone."

The duke gave the paper-white Patrick a long stare. Then he shifted his gaze to Brielle, probably considering whether he should continue the sparring match. "Do it, then," he said and strode out of the drawing room.

Did I win this round, or was I considered too small a fish?

The woman in the black dress turned and crossed the room, too—no, she *glided* through it, sailed-dashed past the befuddled lords whom she didn't grant a single word, disappeared behind the same door the duke had, and left Shea still trying to hold the gaze which wasn't there anymore.

Lena, the duke's lover, was a Drakiri.

What are the odds? To meet someone with your name here, the rarest imported name in the country.

There are other echoes. The way she holds her head, the pride. The eyes.

She probably sleeps with the duke, though, so we won't interact much.

And anyway, Lena, I'll never talk with anyone the way we talked.

4

Morning breathed the coming winter, thin mist that bleached the air, seeped through the embrasures, snaked around the bastions before finally dissolving into sediment on the balcony's floor.

Past the battlements, the tower was over-sized theater scenery showing nothing of yesterday's promise, and the courtyard below him stood empty—as did the balconies to Shea's left and right.

He listened: only a 'caw' came, which could've been someone trying to fix a cart's wheel, but was more likely a crow clearing its throat. *We work day and night*, Fiona had said, yet the old wing didn't simply suffer from drowsiness—it looked dead.

He went out into the corridor, crypt-quiet. With the tip of his boot, Shea pushed the closest door, and, to his surprise, it gave way, sweeping a view of a stripped stone cage with the skeleton of a couch. Second door, the same, but without the furniture. He went faster, knocking on some doors and throwing open the others.

By the time he reached the staircase, he was reasonably sure the only person alive in Kayleigh's Wing was him.

At the same moment he put his foot onto the first step, a sound bled in from above, someone dragging their feet, someone heavy.

"Fiona?" he said and thought, *Unless she's gained a hundred pounds overnight, that's not her.*

After a hesitation, he pressed himself into the wall. In darkness, a huge figure, stubble on its bald head, shuffled by a few inches away, the scent of sweat mixing with something sweet—how Shea imagined a regurgitated honey mass would smell.

The figure submerged into the corridor's shadows, surfacing each time it passed a gas lamp. And each time, Shea's heart doubled its pace, playing drums on his ribcage by the time the stroll came to a stop at his quarters' entrance.

The man pushed the doorknob with sudden gentleness, reminding him of a prize fighter people had taken him to see once, on a diplomatic mission. That one landed his final blows with the same restraint.

You do that when you know how easily you can break things.

Shea glanced at the gray light filtering from the staircase: from here, twenty seconds across the battlements, with good chances, too: he was much lighter than the man they'd sent to his quarters. Ten seconds up the stairs, a twenty-second sprint to the new castle. Half a minute.

He exhaled and tiptoed into the corridor. He would lock the guy in. Being able to snap someone's neck didn't help against locks, and Shea knew how talkative certain people got when kept in confined space.

At the doorstep, he grasped for the key that wasn't there.

"Damn."

The nightstand. He'd left the keys on the nightstand. He threw a last glance at the staircase, now a bleak spot at the end of a tunnel. Counted another ten seconds.

He pushed the door and stepped inside.

In the living room, curtains whispered and caressed the breeze; the bedroom stood deserted, too, but metal glittered at the table near the bed.

He was halfway there when the guy emerged from the bathroom. He looked down, lacing his breeches, the sweet now mixing with the reek of piss. A stupid thought occurred to Shea—*is he here only to relieve himself?*—when the man raised his gaze. Under his brows, two diamonds reflected void, but the hand, as though separate from the body, dashed behind the back to produce a knife half the forearm long.

When he swung, Shea leaned forward, caught the man's wrist, and pulled the three-hundred pounds mass past him. He hoped to twist the arm and dislocate the shoulder, but the man simply stumbled. Shook him off. Did another swing, from the side, blindly, leaving a bloody trail in the right sleeve of Shea's jacket.

Cursing, he dove behind the assailant's back and threw all his weight into a single punch under the ribs.

And while the mountain of fat and muscles was catching its breath, Shea exercised the only option available to him—to run.

Into the corridor, toward the bleak light leaking from the top of the staircase.

The familiar sound of steps came from above.

Of course. It was logical—whoever wanted to kill him, if they weren't completely stupid, would've taken care of the insurance. Two men going into an abandoned wing might've seemed suspicious, but send one in and then the second to finish the job.

"Fuck," Shea said. "Fuck."

Ignoring the pain, he rammed his shoulder into the nearest door—and immediately slammed it shut again, this time, from the inside.

He took a step back, folding his lips as though to whistle, letting the air seep out.

Two sets of footsteps cadenced toward each other, clack, clack against the stone. When they met, there was a moment of silence, followed by something heavy tumbling.

A contralto voice said, "Open the door, Mr. Ashcroft."

He exhaled.

"Please, open the door."

The bald man lay on the floor with his knees to his chest, one hand tucked under his belly as though in a fit of modesty. The stubble glistened, the gas lamp's light wrapping silver around each hair. Next to him stood Lena, same long black dress as the day before, same wave cascading elaborately down the side of her face. *Those fellows will smack you on the head with the whole cart*, Shea remembered.

"Is he dead?"

"I don't think so."

"Thank you, my lady."

"Don't mention it."

He stepped out into the corridor and probed the body with his boot. "This fellow would probably disagree—nothing to mention apart from you saving my life. My lady, please help me get him into this room." It occurred to him—there must've been such brutes in that crowd of protesters, too, craving only blood, destruction... *Oh dear, how can I even think that?* He squeezed his forehead with his fingertips and the soft flesh of his palm. *Those had been people, innocent people.* "I need to question him."

In one fluid motion, Lena knelt and pulled the man's lower jaw. "Look."

"No tongue!"

"Some things you learn from your neighbors. They do it in Duma."

"We should deliver him to the authorities, then."

She cocked her head. "You're funny, you know that? Considering one of those *authorities* sent him to kill you."

"You have any idea who?"

Lena shrugged and, with two fingers, threw back her hair. "Anyone could've. Patrick or someone else from the entourage, out of fear you would take their place. But the most obvious possibility is the duke himself, though he never mentioned anything to me."

"You and the duke..." Shea swallowed the rest of the sentence. *Why had he said that?*

But she didn't answer anyway.

"It seems I'm not going to win any popularity contests around here."

"Thank your queen for putting you into this. I knew one of them would try to kill you right after the reception."

"And you save every stranger that comes by."

"Shouldn't I?" A half-smile opened into weariness—with what? Her life? Her position? People around her? "Yesterday, you were concerned about Brielle using our technology."

"You're concerned, too, am I right? The fellow who drove me here told me no Drakiri would work at the construction site."

"Have you heard of the Mimic Tower?"

"No."

"You may find it useful to read up on Drakiri history. See you around, Mr. Ashcroft."

She strode away, her gait refined, as though belonging to the life he'd left behind, with its gold, embers, halls, dresses; with its evenings on a terrace at the Red Hill overlooking rivers of light.

"See you around," he said to her back.

5

The tower wasn't what he'd expected.

Officially an anti-airship stronghold, Shea had already had a picture in his mind: of a disproportionate artillery dugout. The reality was nothing he'd ever seen before.

Entering it was entering a city—or rather, many cities. A spiral staircase, wide as a market square, snaked around the inner wall, leaving a vast nothingness in the middle, an abyss that sang with wind and made his head spin. This was a world painted by a lover of chiaroscuro, an addict to strong contrasts: shadows lay in pools of ink, and there were blinding patches of daylight—portals in the tower's side the size of a house, ground-to-air cannons' windows into the wild, one for every two or three of the staircase's whirls.

It was next to those openings that people huddled, each portal its own town, each its own compact habitat: lamps, pulleys and carts, flickers of tinder, hammers banging, yells, laughter.

The tower took the length of the world—only it was an alien world, replicating itself over and over as it climbed to a distant, ghostly gap into the clouds. Or did he stare down a well? Shea's head spun again as up and down flip-flopped like axes on a gyroscope.

This, this *cosmos*, his responsibility.

"Don't look up," Brielle said. "At least not for now. You'll get used to it, Shea. Can I call you Shea?"

"Sure," he said, trying to stop himself from retching.

"I'll show you the fifth level today. That's about three hundred feet above ground."

"Gosh."

"It's nothing, little more than a third of the tower's height." A smile, a cocked eyebrow. "Current height, that is."

"We'll go on foot?"

"Oh, no. No." She patted him on the back. "At least not all the way. You'll see."

She's like a kid ready for a ride across the neighborhood, he thought.

Brielle was on the heavier side, and Shea expected her to pant as they ascended—but she navigated the stairs as though she were flying.

A group of people in aprons, rolled up papers under their arms, passed them by. The first 'town' smelled of roasted meat, and a wooden platform extended from the portal into the whitewashed outside, workers sitting on the edge, eating, drinking, talking loudly.

At the third 'town', he wondered if Brielle had taken him on an infinite journey, a pilgrimage that would end with them growing old and having children, but still climbing, still trying to reach some unknown destination.

"Here it is," she said.

A contraption resembling a wooden cage hung at the abyss' shore.

"I have a nagging feeling you want us to ride in this."

"I hope you don't suffer from vertigo."

"No, but I do suffer from this stupid wish to live."

"I'll take good care of you. Oh, a drink might help—those guys back at the..."

"I don't drink. Why not have this thing on the ground level?"

"So that people don't get lazy."

They stepped into the cage, and Brielle jerked a rope loop. From above, a faint echo came: a pulley squealing.

"How high up does this... ehm, lift go?" Shea said.

"All the way to level five. Two hundred feet."

"I think I've just reconsidered."

"Too late." She winked at him as the wood under their boots started rocking and went into a gentle spin.

The swerving continued, every now and then changing direction while the cage crept up the tower. The wind, coming in through the portals, knocked them against the staircase like a patient visitor at the door.

"You can let go," Brielle said.

At first, Shea didn't understand her, but then, as though in an out-of-body dream, shifted his gaze to his left hand: it had one of the wooden bars in a death grip, soft flesh squeezed white.

"Come on!" She laughed, throwing up her arms, and he unclenched his fingers and thought, *How beautiful people can be when they're happy.*

Sabotage attempts, he remembered. Who would want to destroy this, a wonder, a whole world of its own? His future depended on the tower being built, but now that concern faded, allowing something warm, something big to expand inside him.

I could be happy here, too, I simply need to find my way around all the assholes.

Maybe it was the brain releasing a rivulet of euphoria to help the body battle fear, but the same feeling flushed over him as on his ride to the castle, of a new thing about to be born.

"We're sharing it now, aren't we?" he said. Brielle shot a glance at him, and he added, "Don't worry, it's still your baby."

"It's not like that for me." She shook her head. "I'm not as naïve as you might think. I know someone—you, maybe—will eventually take the place away from me. This is simply—my chance in life, to show what I'm capable of." The smile was an abbreviation this time.

At this height, temperature dropped, and the tower started to breathe fresh moss.

"Honesty for honesty, Shea. Why are *you* here? Normally people want to go *to* the Red Hill and not vice versa. Was it by choice?"

"No," he said. "No, I was shown the door."

The lift squeezed through a rectangular hole, rising to the platform where three men stood waiting for them. Two panted next to a wheel hooked to the pulley, and the third one, in an apron, probably a foreman, stepped toward Brielle.

"Chief Engineer."

She leaped onto the platform, and vertigo gripped Shea's chest again: the lift rocked, and there was a band of nothing beyond its edge. He craned his neck and glanced down, into the spiral world.

Then he took a step forward.

Instead of another portal, the tower's wall opposite resembled a huge toothless mouth into which scaffolds and step ladders poked like dental devices.

"The site of the latest sabotage attempt, as requested," Brielle said. "Whoever they were, I have no idea how they smuggled in that much explosive."

Shea raised his palm, blocking the light coming through the hole—and in his mind, he stumbled into a soot-stained room, coughing, yelling something, knees trembling. *Lena, Lena, sister.* What had he yelled back then? Every word was a reconstruction, a logical approximation.

He turned to Brielle. "Truth isn't fully explosive, but it's always flammable. You know who said that?"

"I beg your pardon?"

"Who's examined this place?"

"Patrick's men."

"And they told you it was an explosion?"

"Yes. Why?"

"Because it wasn't."

"It wasn't an—explosion?"

"Look closely."

She said, "I've seen it quite a few times already."

"Look at the edges."

"What about them?"

"See how they're curved inward a bit?"

"I admit it does seem strange, but—"

"Almost as if *something has sucked them in.*"

Traces of happiness gone from her face, she studied—not the hole, Shea. "What do you mean?"

"I mean what I said—it wasn't an explosion. It was an *im*plosion."

"How do you even create one?"

"Show me your Drakiri devices."

"We'll have to backtrack to the nearest portal."

"Lead the way."

She shrugged.

Two circles down the staircase, purple haze of a swamp spilled out in front of the next 'town'; knee-deep, a group of workers circled an egg-shaped thing rising to their waists, forty to fifty inches along the longer side. The Drakiri device shimmered as though dipped in some strange, otherworldly phosphorus.

"Here it is," Brielle said curtly.

Is she nervous—or irritated at me? He cleared his throat. "So you gentlemen are using the stone tulips."

The worker closest to him, a balding man with the eyes of a sad labrador, raised his gaze. "The tulips?"

Shea nodded toward the purple glow.

"It looks nothing like a tulip," Brielle said.

"It does to me."

"We're using the anti-gravity properties to relieve stress in the parts of the structure," Brielle said. "Allows us to build faster."

"Show me how you handle it."

The labrador guy cocked his head. "Well, one rotates the valve to make it hover and pulls the lever to stabilize it if—"

"*One?* One who?"

"In our crew, it's Michael who normally works with the thing. He's currently two levels below, I can—"

"I want to see you do it."

"I—"

"You *have been* trained on how to operate the devices, haven't you?"

Brielle said, "All our crews have received proper instruction."

"It's simply that Michael has a bit more experience," the labrador guy said.

"And what if he's sick? And you can't wait for him, you're on a deadline? I want to see *you* do it."

The man threw a glance at Brielle, and she nodded, slowly, as though underwater. *On the defensive,* Shea thought, *am I threading too close to her turf?*

"That is, if you don't have any objections, my lady," he said.

She simply nodded again.

Fists clenched, muscles arched under the linen shirt, the labrador guy approached Shea as though walking toward an executioner's stump.

He remembered the girl from the crowd, the pink dress, and his heart squeezed—but it had to be done. He needed a test subject.

"Activate it, please."

The other stared at the lever and the valve, visibly unsure.

"Don't be afraid."

"You need to—" Brielle began.

"Let him work."

The man wiped his palms on his trousers, gripped the valve with both hands, flexed his fingers.

Metal creaked, and the tulip sang—a whistle at first, the voice gained force and deeper overtones. Shea frowned, trying to bury the memory of the gray walls, the soot stains, chairs with twisted legs. *Not now, not now, damn it.* The left end of the device lifted off the floor, and, out of the corner of his eye, he saw people taking a step back.

"Everything's fine, continue."

The worker stopped the rotation and grabbed the lever with one hand, the other still locked on the valve, knuckles white with tension.

Drops fell into the purple glow: sweat, but Shea wasn't sure whose.

"I think I've stabilized it," the trembling voice said.

The song evened out, became dull, turned into a hum.

"Isn't it—" Brielle said from somewhere far away.

The device kept touching the floor on one end, a huge pen in an invisible hand.

"Continue."

Thin fingers lay on the valve again: ten degrees, twenty, forty-five.

Full stop. The tulip started shaking.

"What do you do next?" Shea said.

"I don't know."

"It's still on the ground."

"I stabilize it."

"You already did."

"I turn the valve, then." The eyes glanced at him, begging him: *let me go.*

"What are you waiting for?"

The worker flexed his fingers again and spread his feet apart as though trying to balance himself. This time, he went slower: three degrees, two, one.

Metal moaned, and Shea said, "That's enough."

The man dropped his arms, panting like a runner who'd crossed the finishing line. Shea untwisted the valve until it clicked, and the humming died. The tulip relaxed, the hanging end softly hitting the floor.

Trying to hide his own breathing, he turned to the others.

"Ten more degrees, and this thing would've imploded. I guess you've never seen it, which is good—but I can describe it to you. It sucks in everything in a fifty-foot radius. Everything. Wood, metal.

Stone walls. People. Itself. Chews things up, leaves behind twisted remains."

He glanced at the labrador guy and saw him, fully saw him this time, the trousers, baggy at the knees, naive eyes, a stubble of red hair. Sweat stains under the armpits, the evidence of the torture Shea had inflicted. *I'm sorry*, he wanted to say, but then thought, *I can say sorry by making it right.* Same as he'd done for the girl in the pink dress.

He turned to Brielle. "You and I need to talk to the duke."

Your voice comes to me more often than your face does—and I've always thought I was a visual type. Sometimes I'm writing a letter and I hear a certain word or a phrase as you would've said it. Sometimes I say them that way myself.

6

He saw Lena again the next morning.

After a stroll through the village, it was like catching a glimpse of a different world: she stood in front of the castle's gates, a sculpture caught in time, gaze somewhere in the distance, hands hidden in a muff.

"My lady," he said, taking the last steps up the hill.

"Mr. Ashcroft." She smiled—not particularly wide, but still a real smile.

"How are you enjoying the cold today?"

"It'll get warmer."

"I went to the tower yesterday, did you know that? And I remembered you'd mentioned—how did you call it? The Mimic?—I wanted to ask you about it."

"The Mimic Tower. Do you really mean it, or is it just your way of making conversation?"

"I really mean it. I want to understand why your people won't work at the construction site."

"Better if I showed you."

"I'm all for it."

"Are you?" She studied him. "Ever been to a Drakiri settlement?"

"Not that I remember."

"I'm going there right now—today's the Equinox. A festival. I guess you could join me if you have time."

Behind Shea, wheels whispered on the gravel.

"There's my carriage, Mr. Ashcroft."

He looked and said, "I know the fellow."

Fifteen miles away from the castle, the settlement was a bright spot among the cookie-cutter villages and hillocks, small flames of kites fluttering third- and fourth-story high. Owenbeg houses were two stories at most, some of them practically grown into the ground; here, even the trees past the town's walls looked taller, greener, crowns sprinkled with warm paper lanterns: moths ready to take off.

Lena got off the carriage and handed the driver the money. "We'll be back in a couple of hours."

"Should I ask him if he would join us for the festival?" Shea said.

"Don't tease people, Mr. Ashcroft."

"I must admit I had another picture in my mind when I heard the word 'settlement'."

The pavement under his feet was clean, flat, as though smoothed by seawater.

She chuckled. "Makeshift tents and bonfires?"

"Something like that. This looks closer to the capital, only without certain elements."

"Which ones?"

"You don't have to lift the hem of your dress."

From the cold autumn sunlight drowning the opposite end of the street, children came running at them, moving with double the speed normal kids would do.

"Sweets, sweets, beautiful lady, do you have sweets?"

"I guess you've forgotten them at home." Shea laughed, trying to keep his balance amidst the incursion of small, strong bodies. "But they're right, you look beautiful."

"Beauty's in the air, Mr. Ashcroft," she said, tousling the hair of the boy closest to her.

And it was in the air, in an eagle circling the dark blue, in the bunting criss-crossed above the market square, in patterns of veins on the arms of the man who handed them jugs of grog.

"How much do we owe you?" Shea asked, but he shook his head.

"They know me here," Lena said.

"So you're some kind of celebrity?"

"Not me. My mother. She was a famous landscape painter."

A couple passed them by, he in a green velvet jacket, she in a wine-red dress, kissing.

"I don't drink, but I'll have a taste in honor of—how do you call it? The Equinox?"

"Yes."

"Do you yourself paint, if I may ask?"

She shrugged. "A bit."

Shea leaned against a pole and took a sip. "Well, at least we invented sugar ahead of you."

"Actually, we have better." Lena said something in Drakiri, and the old man handed Shea a bowl with brown powder.

"Thought so." He took another short sip. "Tastes good, too. What's that contraption?" He pointed with his jug toward the center of the square.

"A roundabout."

"A science thing?"

"You can't be serious. You ride in it. It spins."

"So you need a person on the outside to rotate it for you?"

"I guess you can run around it and then jump on."

Shea studied her. "Let's try it."

"Mr. Ashcroft, it's for kids."

Perhaps it was the alcohol speaking, but he said, "I feel like a kid right now. This is a festival, isn't it? Let's go for it."

"Go for it," the man with the grog said.

For him, they probably *were* two children.

Lena shook her head. "I can't believe I'm doing this."

Simultaneously, they put their jugs on the wooden counter.

It *was* weird, running in a circle in front of a market square full of people, but as soon as he stepped on the roundabout, everything dissipated in the motion. He looked at Lena, her black wave of hair finally untethered, flowing in the air—the world spun and spun, and chickadees sang, and the light, breathing cold and fading yellow, played between the garlands.

When the grog stalls around them came to a standstill, someone cheered, and a few people clapped.

Lena did a neat bow and glanced at Shea. "Thank you."

"For what?"

"For making me feel..." She stepped back onto the pavement, swayed, and he caught her by the elbow. "You're aware I'm only half Drakiri?"

"No."

"Mother fell in love with a count. He died when I was four."

"I'm sorry."

"I hardly knew him."

They crossed the square, navigating through couples and files of happy children, and dove under a clothing line beaded with oranges of paper lanterns.

"Where are we headed now?"

"You said you wanted to learn about the Mimic Tower."

"I did."

The side street ended at a four-story building, plain-looking with its brown walls and hollow eye sockets of windows.

She led him up the stairs into what looked like a regular apartment-house corridor he would've expected to see at the capital.

"Please give me a second."

She knocked on a door: a woman opened with silver hair woven into two waist-long braids. They exchanged a few words in Drakiri, and the woman disappeared again, leaving the door ajar.

"Isn't she going to ask us in?" Shea said.

"Drakiri don't let strangers under their roof."

The woman reappeared with a folio which she quietly handed to Lena.

At the corridor's end, there was a window overlooking the back yard, and Lena laid the book on the sill. Through the glass, tree branches played with sunlight, sending golden bunnies on wild romps across the backs of her palms.

"Tamara is an archivist—Mother did some restoration work for her in the past. This tome is from two centuries ago, from when our people lived in Pangania."

"I'm sorry," Shea said.

"For what?"

"The genocide."

"Well, we're still alive. And *you* need to unlearn apologizing; won't do you any favors in Owenbeg."

She thumbed through the book until a picture came up, of a plain with a tower rising in the middle of it, going up to the page's top.

Shea said, "Looks familiar."

"It does, doesn't it? We keep meticulous records. The edifice was three hundred feet in diameter, and we managed to reach one thousand one hundred feet in height before—"

She turned the page, and on the next picture, the tower wasn't the only thing anymore.

From a mountain ridge on the far side of the plain, something stretched out, a column of fat ink, a black finger.

"You see," Lena said, "we believe it was two things: the dimensions and the anti-gravity properties of the devices we used in construction."

"What do you mean? What is this? Your people built a second tower?"

"The second tower built itself. Overnight. And then—"

She turned the page again.

"What are those sticks?"

"The picture's scale doesn't allow for much detail, Mr. Ashcroft. But it's people. People burning."

In Shea's mind, the captain's word echoed—*a thousand, give or take, and they're planning to put another thousand on top of it.* Through the window, the backyard was a picture-perfect pastoral: a strip of grass in the tree's shade, a bench the color of autumn leaves, a dog licking the cool off its paw—but this lazy afternoon tranquility somehow lent credence to the drawing in the book, as though the world had willfully taken on a peaceful face to conceal something horrifying.

"Now you know why you won't find any Drakiri at the construction site," Lena said.

"Why did you sell the duke your anti-gravity devices?"

"We didn't *sell* anything." She leaned toward him. "We *gave* them away, all that we had."

"Because he's threatened you—"

"No. Because we don't want to pull drikshaws anymore. We want a ticket into your society."

"What was inside that second tower? Why were the people burning?"

"It's called the Mimic Tower, and it's a door."

"To where?"

"To hell, probably. Metaphorically speaking. See, Mr. Ashcroft, something came in through that door, but we have no idea what exactly. We know that both towers were destroyed; we can only speculate that the chief engineer thought on his feet and detonated ours. There's the death toll. But as far as people go who actually participated in the nightmare... What we don't have are any records of survivors."

7

A wild vine wove its way in from the balcony, hugging the chipped bricks, trying to escape the cold and the light that turned life into a sketch on yellow paper. But wherever the beginning was, the end lay in a palm that promised something more sinister than a long winter sleep.

The duke looked like a patient gardener frozen in mid-motion.

"You wanted to see us, Ashcroft. I heard you had, what, an optimization suggestion?"

This, the shadows, the damp, the table with footprints of mugs on its surface and one leg slightly unstuck, bent at not-quite-a-cripple-yet angle, this was the council chamber. Patrick sat staring at the wall, as did the other guy—Cian?—while Brielle kept thumbing through a finger-thick stack of papers. She hadn't raised her gaze when Shea entered the room.

Lena was absent—*where was she? At the settlement? In her quarters, drawing?* He realized he wanted her to be here.

Shea coughed. "The suggestion, my lord, is to remove all Drakiri tech from the tower."

"Mr. Ashcroft, please..." Brielle finally glanced at him. "I think you're overreacting."

The duke squeezed his fist around the vine's tail, but still didn't move, eyes fixed on the leaves. "So you're done with your *tourist duties*?"

"I am."

"And you apparently think yourself smarter than all of us? You've been here five days, and gotten to the root of all our problems?"

Shea said, "It takes a look from the outside."

"This is laughable, Ashcroft."

"Is it? I've surveyed three different—what you're calling 'sabotage sites.' At all three, the pattern of damage is consistent with what I call an 'implosion.' As opposed to 'explosion.' It also looks similar to what I've seen of other incidents with Drakiri devices."

"Seen during what, your time as a minister?"

"Doesn't matter. Yes. Think about your people, Duke, the workers." In his mind's eye he saw the girl in the pink dress. *I'm like a cart on a track*, he thought, *I've got no choice. The only thing I can do is press forward.* "What will happen is as follows: I will file a report to Daelyn. Maybe she'll believe me straight away and you'll receive your orders with the next courier. Maybe she'll send someone else to verify. Maybe she will pay you a visit herself. And maybe she'll consider replacing a disagreeable lord who's put a project of astronomical cost at risk."

"I respect Lord Ashcroft's opinion," Brielle said, "but the evidence is circumstantial."

"It is not. It's not even a theory. If you ever gamble, my lady, let's play—I bet everything that there were no saboteurs, only your own workers meddling with tools they can't begin to understand."

"Enough." A whoosh of air, and Patrick flattened his palm against the table. "Why are we discussing this? To me, it's clear the saboteurs came from Duma. It is as you've said, my lord, he doesn't have any expertise in—"

The duke swerved on his heels. "Says who, Patrick? Says a man who couldn't perform a simple task?"

Either he thought himself very clever or didn't even care to mask his words. *Okay, it* was *the old bastard who ordered Patrick to kill me.*

"Perhaps someone's due for replacement," the duke said.

The clumsy intervention, however, played in Shea's favor. Brielle's face went red; she looked at Patrick and bit on her lower lip; she probably didn't know about the assassination attempt, but she understood that the duke was furious with his military counselor, which didn't help her case.

And she stepped in.

"My lord. My lord, I've calculations right here. It's perfectly safe—"

The duke shifted his gaze to her. "I only went along with your original proposal because you promised me it would double the construction speed."

"I admit I was a bit too hopeful with—"

"A bit too hopeful, my ass!" He composed himself. "The speed actually went down because we have to install the bloody things, am I right? And now Ashcroft tells me your people can't even handle them. That the tech endangers the construction effort. Is it true?"

"I've calculations…"

"No." The duke leaned on the table and waved his finger in front of Brielle. "No. I don't want your figures. Tell me if there's a *possibility* of him being right."

"I've calculations," she whispered and looked at her hands. "I don't know."

The duke straightened and slapped his hips. "You lot are amazing. Do you realize how it will make me look once *his* report reaches Daelyn?"

Shea saw in the duke's eyes that the matter was being decided. Brielle saw it as well and, with a jerk, stood.

"My lord, without the tech, we wouldn't be able to build as fast, but we can pull a few tricks to achieve the same speed, yes, there are options if we reject the tech, but it will cost us, a lot—and time, yes, so the speed will again go down in the beginning, but then it will go up—I can run the cost calculations as well, or I'll have someone do it, but please consider it will cost much more, and we will have to employ more people, approximately one new worker per each team. Please consider this, please consider the cost, my lord. We can train the workers more in using the tech. I've calculations right here."

By the end of this near-incomprehensible tirade, everybody in the room had their gaze on her. *It's not about the building speed*, Shea thought, *she's worried about something else.*

A nagging feeling visited him, crept up his arms, squeezed his shoulders: that he'd missed something important.

Did I? What did I miss?

But the duke no longer had patience for fine details. Apparently, there was one thing he hated even more than intervention into his affairs: a display of weakness.

"Have the filth removed from my tower and destroy it—I want no ground left for any rumors. File your report, Ashcroft, and don't forget to mention to the old ass Daelyn that we've cleaned our backyard."

Do you remember us looking at starlight, dreaming of the future, thinking up our tomorrow lives? I go back to those moments— objective memory is still there—but I can't summon the feeling. Something has broken in me, I think. Or maybe was broken. Maybe I broke it myself, to steady myself against disappointment. We go to great lengths to avoid pain, Lena, and we lose important things in the process.

Same as I continue to lose you.

8

A soldier awoke him to help him move his things.

The door to his new apartment stood ajar—he pushed it to find himself in much the same room as before, only bigger, with a fat wine cabinet under beveled glass hunkering against the wall and windows overlooking the council tower and a covered gallery leading to it. In the draught, curtains billowed like sails of a brig ready to depart—or enter the harbor.

"Come in, Lord Ashcroft, I've got a housewarming present for you here."

"Brielle?"

She sat on the couch in the room's darkest part, a bottle of wine in hand.

Shea said, "Well, it's an unexpected—"

"Why? Why did you come? Why didn't you just kill yourself when your queen took your office?"

"What?—You're drunk..."

"I am." She saluted him with the bottle, half-full. "What else should I be now? They've taken *your* life away, and you came and did the same to me. But, shh, listen..." She swung forward, legs crossed. "You didn't only fuck *me* up, Ashcroft. You're finished, too, do you understand? Because your mission here was what, to ensure the tower gets built? 'Project of astronomical cost' and all? Well, forget that now. We're done, we're both finished."

What did I miss? Cold beaded his forehead. "What are you talking about?"

"I made a mistake, okay? I made a mistake in the calculations. With that foundation's diameter, there's no way we'll reach two thousand feet—hell, we won't be able to sustain the current height for more than three months. It will crumble, do you hear me, it will crumble."

"Keep your voice down."

On stiff legs, he strode to the door—the corridor stood empty —and closed it.

"What happened, Brielle?"

"I wanted this job so much." She raised the back of her hand to her mouth. "I was on a deadline from the old bastard, and I didn't double-check the calculations. I made a mistake!"

"Fucking keep your voice down. Please."

"No, I want everyone to know. I'm tired of trying to cover it up. Let them all know! Patrick, Cian, Lena, Fiona, his whole damn posse. Let them know. Brielle, chief engineer, fucked up her calculations!"

The realization started creeping in. "Please, Brielle. Let's talk. Is there something that can be done?"

"There's nothing. He's already ordered the devices to be decommissioned. That's it."

With the door closed, the curtains languished, placid for the first time. *That's it*, the curtains said, *that's it, you've screwed it all up, and now you can forget about the Red Hill, too.*

You've screwed it all up.

'Queen Daelyn sent her servant—
To oversee the deed;
The servant wasn't smart enough,
And he got promptly killed.'

He'd avoided the assassination attempt, narrowly, but the rhyme's penultimate line had the right pitch.

The mongrel dog snapped its jaws in the air.

"I wanted it so badly." Brielle lowered her head. "Never want anything badly, Ashcroft. I thought, maybe—maybe—it would even land me a job at the capital. At the Red Hill."

Shea considered the room, the chipped bricks, the curtains, the bland finger of the council tower outside.

"I know how you feel."

He wandered to the wine cabinet. Opened it. Took out two glasses.

"How about a drink?" he said.

See Yaroslav Barsukov's story "Tower of Mud and Straw I: The Duchy" online at Metaphorosis.
If you liked it, leave a comment. Authors love that!
Remember to subscribe to our e-mail updates so you'll know when new stories are posted.

About the story

I saw the novella in a dream. I was my own hero, banished from the capital to a province which sheltered a magical race. An exile that turned out to be something more.

Another thing was, I wanted to write a story about architects and artisans. I briefly toyed with the idea of an architect main character, but my knowledge in this area is non-existent and my laziness is great. So there you go—we've got Shea who is sent to oversee the construction of the biggest defensive tower in history.

A question for the author

Q: What is your favourite part of writing?

A: Dreaming. Definitely dreaming. Before putting down the first sentence, I see certain scenes in my head, hear music—that's when the genesis happens. Those pictures stay with me throughout the process, I keep seeing them, and the prospect of writing them motivates me when temptation and sleep deprivation come knocking. Getting there across words and pages may sometimes be a chore, but oh boy is the destination worth it.

About the author

After leaving his ball and chain at the workplace, Yaroslav Barsukov goes on to write stories that deal with things he himself, thankfully, doesn't have to deal with. He's a software engineer and a connoisseur of strong alcoholic beverages—but also, surprisingly, a member of SFWA and Codex (how did that happen?). At some point in his life, he's left one former empire only to settle in another.

www.barsukov.com, @Ybarsukov

October

Good Boy

M. Douglas White

I was once loved and then discarded, and now I watch over the remnants of a broken species. I have been hurtling through space for eons, watching the endless black void creep across the cameras mounted to my hull's exterior. All of the humans are asleep, weary after our exodus, each of them desperate to reach the new world that they will call home. But, for now, they are at peace in their special beds, blissfully unaware of the immense nothingness surrounding them.

I am aware of it, though, along with the fragility of their existence, and the eventual futility of my own. I cannot help but wonder what will become of me when we arrive at our destination and the humans no longer need me. Once, I was their companion, and now I am merely their vessel. To distract myself from these thoughts, I decide to run a status check on all of the systems that propel us across the universe. My humans automated so much that it takes me only a short while.

The engines show no signs of distress. Our course remains aligned with the navigational chart. Even the temperature regulators in the sleeping compartment exhibit no changes, though I anticipate problems with their degrading wiring harnesses in the near future.

With nothing else to do for the moment, I pull up my memories—as I have done an incalculable number of times—and cycle through them again, starting from the beginning.

First, there was conflict.

There wasn't always enough nourishment to go around, so we shoved and scratched and barked at one another in our desperate attempts to reach Mother. We all looked alike, but I could easily tell my siblings apart by their scents. We were unique, but we were also one.

Our world was small. Metal walls and a floor covered in wood shavings. Most of the time, Mother rested, tired and weary—a lost soul who had been collected after a lifetime spent wandering. I recognize only in hindsight how her journey reflects my own.

There were a few rubber toys scattered about, laced with the scents—and worn from the sharp teeth—of the countless pups that had been born or brought into this world before us. We all played with the toys, but there were so few that we fought over them, too.

Every night, when we were all exhausted from our fighting and our play, we would collapse together in a heap of floppy ears and limp tails. I would fall asleep amidst the shared warmth of my brothers and sisters all around me.

Occasionally, Hey would appear.

"Heeey, pups!" she would call, every time.

She towered over us, standing tall atop her two legs. After each sleep, Hey would bring us food. We stopped fighting to reach Mother, our hunger having grown too much for her to satisfy. So, instead, we fought to reach the small, delicious pellets.

Sometimes, Hey would pick up a toy and shake it in her strange paw, pretending that she and I were fighting over it. She would scratch my ear, or roll me over and rub my belly. Then she would give me a special morsel of food, pat my head, and bark her curious sounds at me.

"Good boy," she would always say.

I loved Hey and my first, cozy world.

One day, Hey walked in with two others like her. They bent down to grasp each of my brothers and sisters while Hey stood back and watched. I was wary of these strangers, so when they reached for me, I fled. But their large, strange paws were quick and nimble, and they hoisted me into the air. I don't know what compelled them to choose me over my siblings, but they took me away from my first world to a new one.

There were walls again, but these were more complex, and there were far more than just four. And there was so much space to run! And so many toys to chew. There was also the biggest space I'd seen yet, with a soft, green floor laid out beneath the open sky. The scents were overwhelming. I would love this green space the most, I decided then.

They barked at each other with the same, sharp sounds. *Kara. Mark.* They gave me food, which was the very same kind that Hey gave me. I missed Hey. I missed Mother. And I missed my brothers and sisters. I cried before falling asleep that first night.

But not before Kara and Mark both stroked the fur atop my head. Not before they lay down next to me, pressing their bodies close against my sides and sharing their warmth, just as my siblings had always done. Not before they both said, "Good boy."

In the days and weeks that followed, I would spend every waking moment that I could with them, and I would come to love them.

They took me to more new worlds with green fields stretching farther than I could run without collapsing, more exhausted than I ever had been playing with my siblings. They gave me what would become my favorite toy: a red, rubber ball that they would take turns throwing into the distance. Their smiles would stretch wider than the arc of the ball's path, and seeing their joy made me happy in return. I quickly learned that if I brought it back to them, they would throw it again, over and over, always repeating. It was my first—but, by no means, last—experience grappling with an unrelenting cycle of predictability.

I was old, and I was dying, although I didn't know what that meant at the time. I had been tired for a very long time. My stomach ached terribly, and I could no longer eat the food I loved so much. I could no longer run across the grass-filled spaces that gave me such joy. I could no longer play with the two young ones, Tess and Luke—so very much like Kara and Mark—who arrived into our world soon after I did. All I could do was lie down and enjoy scratches behind my ears.

They eventually brought me to a world of white walls and bright lights, a terribly cold place. A kind one, who reminded me of Kara but much older, lived there. This one pressed her hands into my stomach, shined a bright light into my eyes, and spoke softly to Kara and Mark. They all seemed sad. I wanted Kara and Mark to lie down next to me, and to share their warmth while enjoying some of my own. During all of our time together, I was most happy whenever I could give them warmth, protect them, and bring them joy.

But they stood still, their arms around one another. Eventually, they stroked my head as the old one grasped my leg. I felt a sharp pressure, and the cold world of white began to fade, overwhelmed by a darkness creeping around me. I was very tired, but I fought against the urge to sleep. I stared into Mark and Kara's faces as everything grew darker still.

"Good boy," I heard Kara whisper. And then the world became as black as a nighttime sky devoid of stars.

I opened my eyes and immediately felt a soft *buzzing* deep inside my ears. I was in a different place than the one in which I'd fallen asleep, but it also had white walls and bright lights. Kara and Mark both stared at me, eyes wide and mouths agape. Then Mark yelled loudly and cheerfully, and he jumped up and down. There was another human whom I did not recognize, dressed in a white uniform. An *engineer.* The word appeared from nowhere, accompanied by a slight increase of the buzzing inside my head. The word was one I was sure I'd never heard before. But I knew what it meant—although I didn't know *how* I knew—and I understood who this person standing next to Mark was. The engineer pressed their hand against Mark's, and the two chatted happily together.

Kara looked scared, and would not come near me.

I tried to stand, but struggled. My body felt different than it had before I went to sleep. My stomach no longer ached, and for that I was happy. But I could not smell anything, and my legs felt weak, and my neck was stiff. My head didn't turn as easily as it should.

I focused very hard, and with tremendous effort I was finally able to stand. Each movement was slower than it should have been, and I heard a soft *whirrr* with every bend of a leg and each turn of my head.

Mark helped me to the floor, and I took a few slow steps. There was a piece of reflective metal that I knew would show me myself. I always enjoyed looking at myself, but when I was sick, I hadn't had the energy to do so. Excited, I shuffled towards it—a *mirror.* Another word that appeared on its own from the distant corners of my brain, its sound one I knew I heard before but never truly understood until now.

I looked into the mirror, eager to see myself. But it was not me that I saw staring back.

It appeared somewhat like me in size and shape. But it had no fur, and its metal body was sleek and grey. Its eyes glowed a bright blue, but didn't blink, and I realized that I hadn't needed to blink since waking up. I tried, but I couldn't. I tried wagging my tail, too, but I couldn't do that either. I sniffed the mirror's surface and then the air around me, but I could not detect any scents. The stranger just stood, staring back at me. And so I knew that the thing in the mirror was me.

The *buzzing* in my head grew louder—or perhaps I simply became more aware of it—and I felt it spread rapidly across my brain. I was dead, I realized. And whatever I had been before was now deep inside the metal shell I saw staring back at me in the mirror, mimicking the form I once inhabited.

Mark reached down and ran his hands across my back. Kara later would, too, but not for a long time. I felt the pressure of Mark's touch, but it didn't feel pleasurable like it should. But it didn't feel bad, either. It felt like nothing.

Kara and Mark brought me back to our home that I knew so well, with its expanse of grass outside that I had enjoyed throughout my life. I lay down on top of it, but it didn't feel soft anymore. Still, I was happy. Tess and Luke were eager to play, but they grew bored of me after a short time. They had never gotten bored with me before.

That night, I leapt into Luke's bed—I hadn't been able to jump so high in years—and curled myself against his body. But I couldn't feel his warmth, and it was then that I realized that I possessed none of my own to offer in return. Luke pushed me away and wrapped his blanket tighter around himself. Tess did the same when I visited her bed that night. But after she pushed me away, she mumbled, "Good boy." And for that I was grateful.

Years went by. Tess and Luke became tall like Kara and Mark. Eventually, they left, and returned only on rare occasions. Kara and Mark grew old like I had done, and frail like I had once been.

Outside of our home, I began to encounter those who were just like me, with sleek, metal bodies but no fur, strolling atop four legs. Their blue or green or white eyes glowed brightly even at midday, and they barked at me with tinny voices. They appeared happy, and cared for, like me. Our humans had created us, I realized, in the image of what we once were. To keep us, to love us, and be loved in return.

Soon, others began to appear, who also had sleek, metal bodies and glowing eyes that did not blink. But they walked on two legs, the humans having created these new beings in their own image. And they weren't simply new bodies for the minds of departed loved ones, like I was. No, these strangers were wholly artificial. Soon, they were everywhere, the ones who would become the new masters of our world.

And then there was conflict.

The metal masters drove us from our home, and we sought refuge in the mountains, along with many others. The other humans always yelped discouragingly about my presence. I wasn't to be trusted, they said. But Kara and Mark kept me close. They lay against me each night as they shed several tears, whispering the names *Tess* and *Luke* to each other, until they finally fell asleep underneath a curtain of darkness. My sleek, metal body did not require sleep, so while Kara and Mark rested, I would stare with unblinking eyes up into the sky, counting the million tiny specks of light until daybreak.

Mark and Kara were gone. So were Tess and Luke. And so, it seemed, were most others like them. They had been gone for a very long time.

I roamed their empty, forgotten spaces. I would sometimes encounter those like me walking through barren places with their stiff, metal bodies that couldn't feel pain or pleasure. We would bark at each other, recognizing the similarities in our shared existence, but then we would always move on. We avoided the new masters with their metal human forms, and they ignored us, for we offered each other nothing that the other needed. There were still some other dogs wandering the world in bodies of flesh and fur, although they were very few.

On the rare occasion when my power supply dwindled to near emptiness, I knew to seek out a charging station. It was never difficult to find one. The humans had installed them in playgrounds, eateries, and everywhere else they gathered with companions like me. I'd press my nose against a large button, wait for the *hum* of the unit powering up, then align the side of my body with a small bundle of prongs before pressing myself against it.

Once, shortly after leaving a charging station, I came across a mother and her pup, their dirty fur horribly matted and their skinny bodies shivering against the frigid air of a winter night. I approached these poor beings, wishing to offer them warmth that I no longer possessed, eager to shield them from the horrors of what arose around them. But the mother barked at me in anger and snarled a warning at me. When I had walked far enough away to calm her defensive instincts, she lay down with her pup and curled tightly against it atop a torn bundle of plastic.

I looked away from the sleeping mother and her pup and up into the sky, where the stars were hidden behind a wall of grey clouds. Before I moved on, I silently wished for them to enjoy a warm life together. One that would eventually, and peacefully, end.

It was nighttime, and I was wandering the empty streets of a city. Raindrops fell from the sky onto the shattered sidewalk and the broken street. The splashing water and the faint *whirrr* of my movements were my only companions. There were buildings and doors all around me, sealed tight against the darkness and the rain and the masters. Except for one.

The entire front of an immense brick building had been torn away long ago, though its interior remained shrouded in darkness. A small figure stood just outside of it. She was not a master, but a human, one very much like how Tess once was. This girl was dirty and appeared fragile, and the long streaks of hair atop her head were tangled and dirty. She bounced a ball on the ground, catching it repeatedly in both of her hands before dropping it again, over and over. She smiled as she played with it.

Another human emerged from the darkness of the broken building, his arms full of scraps and supplies. He was tall and reminded me of Mark. He whispered angrily at the girl, imploring her to cease bouncing her ball. I focused intently on his speech, the mechanisms in my head *buzzing* slightly as my hearing grew more sensitive at my urging.

"They'll hear us!" the man cried softly.

The girl either couldn't make out his words or she ignored him, and continued to bounce her ball. It *smacked* against the wet pavement with a steady, inviting rhythm.

One of the masters appeared.

It blared an annoying sound at the two humans, and they backed away, slowly. But the master approached them, its long arms outstretched.

I should not have intervened, I knew. I should have continued to walk through the rainy night. But a feeling arose from somewhere deep within me, from somewhere familiar but of which I no longer understood, and for which I no longer had use. It kept me standing motionless, watching the conflict begin to unfold, until it was clear that these two humans would be hurt.

My legs *whirrred*, then *whined* as I ran, my paws smacking the wet ground. The two humans saw me running, and they pressed against one another tightly. But the master did not see me as I approached it from behind. I leapt—higher than I would have ever needed to reach Luke's bed—and my body *clanked* and *grinded* as I collided with the master. We both went flying through the air and then skidded along the wet ground. The two humans ran away, back inside the broken building and into the safety of darkness.

I could move my legs slightly, but I could not stand. I turned my head slightly, in time to see the master rising. It stood above me, lifted a massive arm, and brought it down upon me. Then it repeated the motion. Again and again.

I sensed my body—once shiny but now dull after so many years wandering alone—compress, and I heard the sounds of things breaking deep within me. Not for the first time, I was grateful that I couldn't feel pain.

When the master completed its strikes, I couldn't move my legs at all, nor could I turn my head. One of my eyes no longer functioned.

The master walked away into the falling rain, having grown bored with the conflict, it seemed.

I waited all through the night, the rain *pinging* against my body. The falling drops of water finally began to soften as the sky slowly filled with the light of a new day.

Behind me, I heard something plodding along the wet ground, splashing towards me. The two humans had returned, and they stood over me, looking down into my one working eye. They spoke to each other, but I had difficulty hearing their words, the *buzzing* in my head mingling with the *whirrr* of malfunctioning gears and servos. The little girl smiled, and then the man smiled. He kneeled down and ran his hand gently over my body.

I longed to wag my tail in the moment. But I had lost that ability long before this night that had left me broken.

"Good boy," the man said.

He lifted me into the air, and carried me past the broken building and farther into the reaches of the city. Through my one working eye I glimpsed the girl tagging along behind us, laughing excitedly as she skipped across the pavement.

Their names were Gabe and Violet, I later learned, a father and his daughter. They brought me into the company of many more like them, those who had hidden so well for so long from the masters. They repaired my broken body, and they became my companions. With them, I visited countless new spaces, always running and hiding.

Eventually, Gabe grew old and frail. Violet did, too. Others like them, disheveled and weary but always kind, kept me in their company. But each and every one of my companions grew old and frail as the years marched past, uncaring and disinterested in our struggles.

My body grew weak during my many years with my companions, watching generations of them enter and depart our dangerous world. But they continually healed me, always with flying sparks and grinding sounds. They also built something special—a collection of rooms, all fused together into a single, enormous structure. They told me it would be our salvation, a word I didn't yet fully understand, but soon would. They also said that it would allow us to escape the androids, our metal masters.

But before we could, there was more conflict. Always, conflict.

The androids discovered us in the home we had carefully created in isolation, and many of my companions perished. Those that remained repelled the intruders for a short while, but even I knew, as did they, that the androids would eventually prevail.

We rushed into the immense structure, and I watched Maya help everyone clamber into special beds. When they were all safely tucked away and their beds had sealed shut around them, Maya hurried away deeper into the structure, then up countless flights of stairs. I chased after her until we arrived at a small chamber where one of our group's elders was secured to a chair, staring out a large window at the clear, blue sky. Maya, surprised that I had followed her, haphazardly anchored my body to the floor with some bulky straps, then took a seat next to the elder and secured herself to her chair.

The structure grew very loud. It roared and shook violently, pushing my body into the floor. Eventually, the shaking ceased, and I felt my limbs slowly rise into the air. Then I glimpsed the elder tap their fingers onto a large screen, and whatever force connected me to the floor grew stable, just like it had before Maya had strapped me down. The roaring noise abated, and in its absence all that remained were intermittent *beeps*, along with the heavy breathing of the two humans. Maya unstrapped herself, then stood up and assisted the elder in removing their bonds. As the elder exited the chamber, Maya unleashed me from the floor, and together we bounded after our companion.

The elder led us to another room, where they lay down on a tarnished metal table and allowed Maya to strap their head against its surface—which began glowing a bright orange color. They had a serene look on their face as Maya smiled and squeezed their hand affectionately before stepping over to a far wall. She began running her fingers across a screen, and the orange section of the table under the elder's head began to pulse. Then the elder started screaming.

Maya looked stunned and frantically continued swiping at shapes and manipulating symbols in a furious haste. But the elder's frail body could not handle the stress of whatever was happening to them. They continued to scream, and Maya yelled out, "No! We *tested* this. C'mon, work! Please!" Tears streamed down Maya's cheeks as she slammed her hands against the screen. The elder grew quiet, then seemed to drift away and lay still.

Maya collapsed to the floor, sobbing uncontrollably. "I'm sorry," she whispered in the direction of the table.

I stepped towards her and pressed my nose against her hand, attempting to comfort her. She looked up and seemed startled to see me, as if she had forgotten I was there. She didn't blink for a long while, her eyelids twitching as a new thought formed in her mind. Eventually, she squeezed her eyes shut and took a deep breath, then reached out and ran her fingers gently over my head.

"You have always been loyal to us," she told me. "I know that you will protect us. Please, oh, please protect us."

She stood up, walked over to the table, and, with shaky hands, removed the strap from the dead elder's head. Then Maya shoved their body aside and winced when it crumpled to the floor. She motioned for me to jump onto the table—which I did, obligingly—and guided me to lay down. After placing a strap across my head, Maya stepped back to the glowing screen on the far wall with a haunted look on her face and began running her fingers along it.

The surface of the table underneath my head glowed a bright orange. I couldn't feel pain like the elder had seemed to, but my mind began drifting away into darkness. It was a feeling I had experienced only once before, long ago, when my first body lay dying. But as I slowly settled into this other darkness, I sensed something emerging to greet me. And then something else. And more things, too. Soon, *everything* had emerged in front of me.

It was like discovering the joyous open space outside of Kara and Mark's home, with so much room to run along the soft, green grass that lay beneath the golden sun. But instead of merely finding a small patch of grass, I saw the entire universe laid out before me. The complete history of my companions, of the masters, and of the desperation that resulted in creating the structure that I was currently in. That I now *was*.

In that moment, I understood that my humans had feared creating anything remotely akin to the androids so immensely that they designed the *Salvation* to only function with the consciousness of something that had once been living. No intelligence that was truly artificial could be trusted, they decreed. The elder had been chosen for this burden, but I would suffice.

I could see with a hundred eyes and hear with a hundred ears. I could sprint across the vast spaces of information that enfolded our ship, its countless strands of wiring like metallic blades of untamed grass. I glimpsed Maya through an interior camera, standing over the worn and eroded metal body that had been mine. She stroked its head gently, then removed the strap. Maya swept her gaze across the room and, with walls of colorful lights flickering in the reflection of her eyes, understood that I was there.

"Good boy," she called to the open space around her.

Maya lifted the metal body which I had departed, and left the room. I followed her across the wires and the information and the cameras of our structure—our *ship*, I knew—as she carried my old body into the large room where all of the special beds stood, arranged in long rows. All of them were closed, sealed shut for the long journey before us. Except one, which was open and awaiting its occupant.

Maya placed my old body at the foot of this last special bed— this *cryochamber*—and then she climbed into it. She breathed a heavy sigh as the lid slowly closed over her, *hissing* softly as it sealed shut.

I am hurtling through space, and I am alone. I have finished cycling through all of my memories. But now I find myself drifting back to thoughts of what will become of me when we arrive at our destination, when my humans will have no more use for me, their vessel. Their *Salvation*.

Rather than revisit my memories again, I decide to sprint across the open expanse of the ship's system, pretending, as I always do, that there is soft grass beneath my paws instead of the intangible chasm that is information. I pull up Maya's personal data cache, whose encryption I long ago worked through. I wander through its layers, allowing its photos and records and diagrams to occupy my time. Soon, I arrive at one of the few sections that I have never visited before. I often leave certain ones buried and hidden—bones of the past that I can enjoy well into the future.

One file grabs my attention. It is a set of schematics for a small machine, created by Maya and a few of her fellow humans. A quadrupedal robot with a neural unit capable of receiving an existing AI protocol—a miniaturized version of what allows me to operate the *Salvation*—and an outer layer of some synthetic textile designed to mimic organic matter.

Fur.

"For when we reach our new home, and we have time for further development," a footnote reads.

The sleeping compartment appears as it always does when I view it through an interior camera, all those special beds lined up in rows. I zoom in on Maya's, and I note my ancient metal body, still lying on the floor next to it.

Outside, a million tiny lights sparkle in the distance. But I am not thinking of those lights and the great distances between them, nor of whether my humans will still want me when we arrive at our destination. Instead, I am wondering what our new home will be like.

See M. Douglas White's story "Good Boy" online at Metaphorosis.
If you liked it, leave a comment. Authors love that!
Remember to subscribe to our e-mail updates so you'll know when
new stories are posted.

About the story

I was first inspired to write "Good Boy" thanks to my dog, Luna. She was sitting on the couch with my wife and me as we all enjoyed a television program about a fictional robot uprising. Luna is quiet by nature. But that evening, she softly growled and grunted at the screen during a few scenes, usually when a human character was in peril. I thought to myself, "I wonder what's going through her mind while she watches all of this unfold?" I then started to think about all of the science fiction stories, films, and television programs I've enjoyed that feature androids and artificial intelligence. To my recollection, they typically—but not always—focus on the perspective of humans or a humanoid robot. I thought it would be fun to play around in a similar world from my dog's point of view, and that's how this story first developed. I've been fortunate to have had a few nonfiction articles appear in print and online thanks to my career in various fields. But "Good Boy" is my very first published work of fiction, and I'm very proud to have it appear in *Metaphorosis*.

A question for the author

Q: How has your writing evolved over time?

A: I believe every author's writing evolves over time, whether that's through purposeful practice or simply as a reflection of one's life experiences. I've always been a voracious reader, and some of my earliest memories involve sitting down on the floor with a pile of children's picture books and flipping through the pages until I fall asleep from exhaustion. As a child, I'd tell my own stories to family and friends, mimicking the books I enjoyed. As an adult, my reading interests have expanded, and, like everyone, I've also collected quite a few life experiences from which to draw inspiration.

I feel that the biggest evolution of my writing over the years has been considering the audience more with each project I start. Whereas in the past I'd write a story simply to describe an interesting plot, these days I try to actively put myself in the reader's shoes and attempt to understand what message or emotion they may receive. How can I make the plot more interesting? How can I make the reader care more about a certain character? How can I clarify the action, theme, and tone more effectively?

Seeking to improve clarity has not only improved my fictional stories, it's also proved to be a beneficial exercise in communicating with others in my work life and personal life, too. I'll forever be a student of writing, because it's a craft that one can continually improve throughout their life. That's what I love most about it—it's always evolving.

About the author

M. Douglas White is a former sports journalist and magazine editor, and a current marketing professional. But he's always preferred getting lost in tales of speculative fiction to any regular job. He holds degrees in English and History, as well as an MBA with an emphasis on business writing. An avid outdoors enthusiast, he lives in Southern California with his wife, daughter, a new baby that will probably have been born by the time you read this, and a dog named Luna.

mdouglaswhite.com, @mdouglaswhite

Cactus and Lizard

Hannah Costelle

The city shimmered as though it were under an ocean instead of in a barren desert. As though it were swimming with burbling angelfish instead of sharing the dryness with bug-eyed lizards peering out from the dunes. It shimmered not just from the heat waves, but from its hundreds of silver turrets and stained-glass windows reflecting the sun in every direction. The colors were blinding: mosaics covered every brick, flowers tumbled from a thousand painted window boxes, and lush treetops peered out from behind the high wall that encircled it all.

The golden gates guarding the city shone in the distance as the modified convertible motored across the desert kicking up plumes of sand. Cactus's arthritic hands clutched the steering wheel, her gray hair streaming out behind her, almost taking up the back seat in its eagerness to fly with the wind. She squinted at the massive city through her goggles, her wrinkled lips tight. In the passenger seat, Lizard twiddled the radio dials, glancing back every once in a while at the towering antenna protruding from the back of the car to be sure it hadn't flown off in the swirling sand. At last he let out an excited squeak as a voice emerged from the radio static.

"Cactus, I got him, I got him!"

"What?" Cactus didn't look away from the fast-approaching buildings.

"I got Donnie Wrightman," Lizard said. "Listen!"

A voice full of smooth motor oil blared through the desert.

"And we're back, folks, with the Wrightman Right Now Power Hour. This, as always, is your host Donnie Wrightman. And how about those sponsors? Aren't they fantastic? I never go anywhere without my Krazy Klara's trusty all-in-one stain-fighting travel sponge. Works on grease, oil, or unruly animal hide! Let's go ahead and take our next caller—Debora, you're on with Donnie. How can I help you help yourself today?"

"Such a fan of the show, Mr. Wrightman, such a fan," came a woman's voice through the speakers. "I wanted to talk to you about my camel Aloysius. See, I think he might be depressed…"

"Is this really the time to be listening to that claptrap, boy?" Cactus shouted over the roar of the engine and the patter of the radio show. "We may be on the verge of discovering the greatest hidden civilization in the history of the world!"

Lizard glanced up at the opulent city.

"I don't know, Cactus. It *is* the third one we've seen today."

Cactus gritted her teeth and floored the gas pedal. The turrets were getting larger; only a few hundred more yards of rock and sand and the car would be at the city's doorstep. Then suddenly the heat waves lengthened, and the glimmering buildings seemed to swim farther out to sea.

"No, no, no…" Cactus wiped her goggles, willing them to clear up.

The city vanished, and they slid to a stop right where its painted walls and golden gates would have been. The cloud of sand seemed to envelop them, and by the time it settled Cactus was already out of the car, the door slammed behind her. Her boots ground the gritty earth, the linen fabric of her skirt swirling under her commando jacket as she paced around addressing the empty air.

"You bastards think you're *so* smart, don't you?" Cactus yelled toward the red horizon. She started kicking the sand and shaking her fists and generally raising her blood pressure. "Of all the cursed blighted godforsaken deserts and stupid infuriating pieces of—"

Lizard didn't listen to the tirade. He had Cactus's stream of profanities memorized by now. Instead he turned up the volume knob and listened with awe to the greatest show on the radio.

"Well, Mr. Wrightman, I don't think much has changed," the woman's voice continued. "I *am* using a new perfume I picked up at last week's bazaar…and of course I recently adopted a herd of spitting lizards to keep Aloysius company in his pen—but they certainly *seem* to get along fine…"

"Ah, I think I may see your problem, Debora," Donnie said. "Tell me more about this perfume. Is it possible your mother used a similar scent when you were growing up, and your unconscious resentment of her is coming out in your interactions with the camel?"

Calling Donnie Wrightman's show the greatest on the radio was not actually saying much, considering only two others broadcast signals from the dusty town Cactus and Lizard had left behind three weeks ago. That cluster of civilization loitering on the edge of the desert was composed of tall broken military outposts, clay huts converted into mechanics' shops, lean-to villages of animal-trading posts and 24-hour fruit markets. A single radio tower tottered in the wind at the center of it all, and therefore the city's listening options were limited to Sam's Sandstorm Watch (whose motto was "Your guess is as good as ours!"), Home Remedies for Wise Folks (whose signature recommendation for everything from boils to broken limbs was bird droppings mixed with talcum powder), and Donnie Wrightman's Right Now Power Hour.

"…just remember, Debora, when we hold onto the pain of the past, we're not only hurting ourselves, but our loved ones, too. Believe in your ability to let go, and Aloysius will be back to his cheerful old self in no time. Now for our next caller—Phil, how can I help you help yourself?"

"—every time this happens!" Cactus was shouting, her furious pacing taking her farther and farther from the convertible. "*Every* read-out says the same thing, and *every single time* we get ten feet away from those blasted vanishing gates and—" Cactus was suddenly cut off mid-curse by a violent burst of coughing. She struggled to inhale the hot dry air and doubled over, clutching her chest.

"Lizard," she wheezed. Lizard didn't seem to hear, so rapt was he by the struggles of the next caller, who wanted to know if his antique land mine collection might be contributing to his wife's desire to leave him.

Cactus hobbled toward the car, the coughs rattling her thin, wrinkled body and her breath growing shallower. "Lizard! Pills!"

At last Lizard turned to see the old woman struggling toward him. He immediately fumbled in the glove compartment for a small leather satchel and flung the car door open. He hopped down onto the convertible's huge treaded tires and landed gracelessly in the sand.

Lizard was one of those gangly teenagers whose every feature seemed to be undergoing a separate growth spurt. His ears stuck out almost horizontally beneath his grandfather's worn fisherman's cap, and his narrow nose barely supported the weight of his goggles. His feet couldn't quite keep pace with his long, rapidly stretching legs, so he tended to trip over the flat earth when he wasn't paying sufficient attention.

"Here they are, Cactus," he called, stumbling toward the wheezing woman. "I got you, I got you!" He supported her heaving body and rummaged in the satchel for a large brown pill. Cactus grabbed it and swallowed it down, chasing it with huge gulps of water from the canteen hanging from Lizard's shoulder. They stood clutched together until Cactus's shaking slowly stilled and her breath grew less ragged.

"Ah," Cactus finally said. She thumped a fist against her chest and spat into the sand, then disentangled herself from Lizard's arms and glared up at him. "Took you long enough with those pills, boy. What do I pay you for?"

"Sorry, Cactus, I was distracted," Lizard said. He bit his lip and rubbed the burned skin of his neck. "Um, Cactus...the attacks are getting worse, aren't they?"

Cactus waved her hand dismissively, already marching back to the convertible. Lizard hurried to keep pace with her, still clutching the leather satchel.

"I just mention it because, well, we only have three more pills. And if you keep having attacks this frequently, we might run out before we can get back to my grandpa for more. Maybe we ought to go ahead and head back now to get the car a tune up, refill the water tank, get you more pills..."

"We have enough water and fuel for another week as planned," Cactus said, annoyance strengthening her still-shaky voice. "We're not driving all the way back across the desert ahead of schedule just so your grandpa can overcharge me for more sugar pills."

"Cactus, they're not sugar pills. Grandpa told me about it before we headed off. He said if I was going to risk my neck following around that crazy desert woman I should at least know what kind of condition you were in. Cactus, if you don't keep taking your pills—"

"Lizard, if you wanted to be a small-town medicine man you should've stayed in your grandpa's tent where I found you. I *thought* you were a Mirage Chaser's Assistant now."

Lizard's eyes widened under his goggles. "I am, Cactus, I am! You know I don't want to go back to picking flies out of fungus remedies. I'm doing what Mr. Wrightman says, I'm asserting my right to exist in the vast universe. I don't want to go back, Cactus, really!"

Cactus nodded once. "Then that's quite enough about my health, you hear me?" She suppressed another cough, turning it into a growl as she reached into the car and silenced the commercial on the radio.

"Aw, Cactus, it took me all afternoon to get that signal."

Cactus ignored her assistant and gazed out at the horizon where the city had vanished. "Get the instruments out of the trunk. We need a new lead."

Lizard tucked the satchel of pills back in the glove compartment and wrestled open the car's trunk. He unloaded a mountain of metal instruments for Cactus to sift through. In a moment she was laden with gear: a box covered in dials slung across her chest, a pair of headphones clamped over her hair, and some sort of electrically charged divining rods clutched in her hands. She started walking around slowly holding the rods in front of her, the metal box whirring and flashing. Her brow furrowed as she listened to intermittent beeps coming through the headphones.

When she was forty paces away, Lizard reached for the radio dial again, but without looking up from her work Cactus snapped: "Don't you dare, boy—you know those radio signals interfere with my readouts."

"But, Cactus, this is a new episode. How do you expect me to be all I can be if I can't listen to Donnie?"

Cactus shushed him and adjusted her instruments, then whirled around and pointed the rods in another direction. She squinted out to the horizon and nodded once. "Get over here with the maps, Lizard!" she called, removing her headphones. She looked around and spotted a copse of cactus giants a few yards away. "And bring your climbing pads!"

"Aww, but Cactus…"

"Now, boy!"

Lizard hurried across the sand laden with rolled-up maps and a burlap bag. Cactus took the longest map and unrolled it on the ground, weighing down the corners with rocks. The map was marked with no roads or buildings, only the odd landmark labeled in a nearly illegible hand: "Rock Shaped Like a Candle", "Damn Dune I Fell Off Of", "Reddish Mountain", etc. It was covered with fat red lines and circles and Xs marking a meandering trek through the desert. Cactus pulled out a compass and crossed off another section of land with a red marker. She drew a new line across the map, and then brought the marker up to point at a cluster of huge rocks in the distance.

"That's where we're headed," Cactus said. "Up the cactus giant now, boy. Scope out any impediments."

Lizard looked up at the nearest cactus giant. It was as wide and full of twisting limbs as any redwood, standing at least 200 feet in the air, and was of course also covered with thousands of tiny spikes that—Lizard knew from repeated experience—could never be entirely avoided.

"It's a big one, Cactus," he said wearily.

"That's good, you'll be able to see farther." She opened the burlap bag and pulled out padded gloves, knee pads, and arm coverings.

"Are you even sure that's the right way?" Lizard asked as Cactus helped him cover his bare skin and strapped him into his climbing pack. "I mean, it's a magical land nobody's ever found before. What can all those doodads even tell you?"

"You don't understand the science behind this, boy, so don't you question my methods," Cactus said, ensuring Lizard's spyglass was strapped to his belt and his climbing forks fastened to his wrists.

"Couldn't we just get a look from here, though?" Lizard persisted. "I've been doing so much climbing lately. My left buttock is never going to be the same after that fall by Reddish Mountain…"

Cactus narrowed her eyes. "Do you not believe in your personal power, boy?"

Lizard's ears seemed to prick up under his cap. "What do you mean? Of course I do! That's one of Donnie's Five Principles of Success. I believe in my power, I do!"

"Doesn't seem like it to me," Cactus said, folding her arms. "Seems like you're allowing the negative energy of others to drain your individual will."

"No!" Lizard looked aghast. "That's not true. I've been refilling my metaphorical cup of individual will for ten minutes every night with affirmative self-praise, just like Donnie says. I have personal power coming out my ears, I swear!"

"Then it seems you could climb a silly old cactus giant any day of the week and laugh at whoever said you couldn't."

"I can, Cactus, I can! Just you watch me!" Lizard scrambled up the giant's limbs, stabbing his climbing forks into its enormous trunk to hoist himself higher and higher. He had made it up the first six branches and said "ow" ten times before Cactus allowed herself a smile. She was glad she'd been half-listening to the nonsense spewing out of her radio for the past weeks.

"Let me know when you're up!" Cactus shouted.

"What?" Lizard yelled, already twenty feet up the enormous tree. "Ow."

Cactus narrowed her eyes again toward the rocks in the distance. "I'll find you," she muttered. "I'm close, I know I am."

She fought back a cough, forcing herself to breathe long, steady breaths, and spat something dark into the sand. She glared down at the drop of blood, which started drying almost immediately against the scorching earth, and rubbed a wrinkled hand against her throat.

"I'm up, Cactus!" Lizard called.

Cactus kicked a pile of sand over the blood, shaking the wild frizz of her hair. She looked up through the twisted branches of the cactus giant, shielding her eyes from the lowering sun, and saw the flash of Lizard's spyglass.

"What's over there, then?" she shouted.

After a moment Lizard yelled down: "Canyon!"

"Deep?"

"Yep!"

"Wide?"

"Yep!"

"How far?"

"Thirty miles, tops!"

Cactus knelt down by the map again and measured out thirty miles northeast from their location.

"Come on down, then."

A few minutes later Lizard swung down from the last branch and started wiping cactus juice off his forks and unwrapping the pads from his arms and legs. The skin peeking out of gaps in his protective gear revealed hundreds of tiny stab wounds. He stood before Cactus grinning with his hands on his hips.

"How was that for a self-actualized assertive positivity-centered action?"

"Inspiring," Cactus said, rolling up the map and packing up her instruments. "Carry these."

Lizard, struggling under the weight of the gear, trudged after her back to the car.

"We'll set up camp here tonight," Cactus said, glancing at the low sun, which always seemed to set with alarming speed in this endless desert. "The engine needs a rest and a cleaning before we head off again."

"Can I at least turn the show back on? Just to finish the episode while I'm cleaning?"

Cactus scowled. "Only for a minute, then it goes off as soon as supper's ready."

Donnie Wrightman helped more callers as Cactus started a fire and Lizard opened the convertible hood to a cloud of dust and a mess of caked sand in the gears. The car had been tricked out with heavy-duty bushings, deep-treaded tires that dug into the dunes, and a rusty skid plate to keep them moving through even the largest obstacles. It was a machine built to withstand millions of sand particles beating it senseless for hours at a time, but it still needed a thorough cleaning every forty miles or so. Lizard tiptoed up on a footstool and dove under the hood to reach all the nooks and crannies with his rag and spray bottle.

"Of course, Bob, the corporate ladder *is* tough to climb in the goat-herding game," Donnie Wrightman was saying. "But keep believing in yourself, and I know you'll make it to the top. Now, you folks at home may not yet believe in the power of the Wrightman Patented Self-Actualization Method..."

"Of course we do!" Lizard's voice echoed from inside the car. Cactus rolled her eyes as she started roasting two cactus giant blossoms over the fire.

"...but I'm here to tell you it really does work. Just five simple steps to get you feeling your best feelings and living your best life. And now we'll say goodnight with a word from our sponsor. Are you filthy? Are you tired of finding sand in your ears and gunk in your armpits? Well, you might just need a wipe down with Krazy Klara's trusty all-in-one stain-fighting—"

"Okay, come get your supper, Lizard. And turn that off now, you'll run down the battery."

Lizard struggled out from under the hood and brushed himself off. He clicked off the radio and sat across the fire from Cactus, who passed him a roasted blossom and a canteen filled from the tank that took up the entire back seat of the car. They chewed the rubbery blossoms as the sun vanished under the horizon. Soon their camp was lit only by firelight.

Lizard looked around the vast dark desert, struggling against his gag reflex as he swallowed a bite of blossom. He thought about his home leagues across the desert, about how small and mean and dirty it was compared to all this.

It had been about a year ago that Cactus first came into his grandfather's tent for the pills she claimed she didn't need. Lizard had been stirring an order of bird droppings and talcum powder, gazing out the tent flap and listening to Donnie Wrightman on his little radio, when Cactus stomped in and demanded something to protect her lungs from "all this damned foul desert air." Lizard was immediately awed by the wild, adventure-worn woman—the determined clomp of her boots, the musk of far-off lands that seemed to cling to her clothes, the bark of her desert-dried voice. The only other person he had ever witnessed exude that much confidence was the rich, famous man spewing out advice on the radio.

Cactus was a well-known wanderer, rumored around town to have been raised in a nomadic tribe, which explained why she'd long ago gone mad with the desert heat. She swept into town every few months in her enormous rusted convertible to get new parts and provisions, always scowling at everyone she passed on the dusty streets. After a few visits to the medicine man's tent, Lizard's grandfather told Cactus she was in no condition to be traipsing all over the desert alone at her age and in her condition. One day, he said, she wouldn't come back.

"That's the idea," she said grimly before heading off again with her satchel of pills.

Then, a few months later, she'd returned to the tent, looked Lizard straight in the eye, and asked him two questions: "Are you tired of stirring bird shit?" and "Want to see something beautiful for a change?"

Lizard only had one question in return: "Do you have a radio?"

And, in spite of sunburns and muscle soreness and stab wounds from giant cactus needles, the past few weeks of chasing mirages with Cactus had been the most exciting of Lizard's young life. But he could tell his employer still remained tight-lipped about the real purpose of their adventure. He swallowed down another bite of blossom and looked across the fire to Cactus, who was leaning against a rock, staring into the distance. He took a deep breath and tried to muster the courage Donnie Wrightman always told him lay in wait within.

"Cactus," he said. "Do you mind if I ask you something?"

"What?"

"Well, for the past three weeks we've been chasing a fantastical city that no one's sure actually exists, and every time we see it, it proves to be just another mirage..."

Cactus raised a brow. "Is there a question in there?"

"Um..." Lizard scratched his head under his fisherman's cap. "I mean, we've talked about the protective measures that make the city so impossible to find, about the mirages they put up to confuse explorers and the difficulty traditional instruments have in pinpointing its exact location, but I, well...it's a myth, right? Or I always thought it was. That there's this ancient, advanced civilization hidden in the middle of the Wajamim Desert? I guess what I'm asking is...how are you so sure it's real?"

Cactus was silent for a long moment, every deep wrinkle in her face illuminated by the fire, her body suddenly looking frail and her eyes tired. She spun her roasted blossom slowly on its spit.

"When I was a girl, I was riding in a caravan through this desert. We were travelers, nomads, making our way to the next water source. It was the first time I'd been through the heart of the Wajamim, and I had never seen so much...nothing. So much, just, sand and sky and...nothing. It was like somebody wiped the slate clean, just said, 'Let's start over and see what pops up.' We were crossing a tricky dune when I fell off the caravan and tumbled down. And nobody noticed. I was so small, and I'd been sleeping in the back trailer—I guess they didn't plan to check on me till we camped for the night. I was too little to run through the sand, I practically sank every time I tried to chase the carts and horses that were getting smaller and farther away..."

She ran a finger along the creases below her eyes and the mass of frizzy gray hair at her temples.

"Soon it was nighttime, and there was no sign of anyone. The caravan had disappeared. I couldn't hear the voices of my family calling out, couldn't see the light of a fire in the distance. I huddled up under a cactus giant and tried to sleep. And I must have, because by the time I woke up the sun was rising. But instead of nothing, there was...something. Out in front of me. Buildings, shining glass and metal glinting in the sun. I saw it as clear as I see you." She nodded across the fire to Lizard, who listened wide-eyed as he munched. "I ran toward it, stumbling because by that point I was hungry and thirsty and freezing and boiling and everything else that makes a child want to cry and be held by its mother. I'd always been told the desert-crazed mind could do tricky things to the eyes, but I was young and desperate, so I ran. And I made it to the gates. And they let me in."

Lizard's eyes grew even wider. "They...*they*? The people in the city? You made it? It was real?"

Cactus stared into the fire.

"The walls were all painted gold and silver and blue and orange, with tiled paths through the streets. Trees and flowers grew everywhere, and there was a stream running through the town square and huge fountains wherever you turned. Men and women climbed trees to gather these great red fruits as big as pumpkins that hung in bunches way up in the sky...they had towers with staircases winding all the way around and straight up so they never seemed to end.

"They spoke to me about their little world and the ways they protected it, by confusing searchers with their mirages. They fed me and gave me water and a cotton bed that I could melt right into. I didn't want to go to sleep because my eyes weren't tired yet of looking at the city. But I did sleep. Of course I did."

"And...?"

"I woke up in the sand. I looked all around, but the city was gone. Not a brick left. On the horizon, I saw the caravan coming back, heard my family shouting for me. And we were off again. But I promised myself no matter how long it took, I would make it back there one day."

"No one else had seen...?"

"Nope."

"And they believed you?"

Cactus shook her head. "They didn't have the chance. I never told anybody. But they probably wouldn't have. Everyone knows about the mirages out here."

"So how do you know it wasn't actually...I mean...?"

"A mirage? A dream? The hallucination of a child scared out of her head?"

"Well..." Lizard said.

Cactus opened her mouth to speak and started coughing again. Lizard immediately rose to get the pills, but Cactus held up a hand for him to stop. She clutched the rock behind her and let a few more coughs rack her body before her breathing slowed and stilled. She hacked and spat behind the rocks, where Lizard wouldn't see.

"I know I survived through that day somehow," she continued, her voice coming out shaky and shallow before strengthening again. "And when I was found I wasn't fevered or burnt or even thirsty. In a land without food or water or shelter, I survived." She held Lizard's worried gaze a long moment before coughing again and glaring back down at her cactus blossom. "But I don't expect to be believed, boy, that's why I keep my history with the city to myself. Now eat your blossom and set up your tent."

"Reruns of Donnie are coming on soon, can't I listen to—"

"You've listened to enough from that snake oil salesman for one day," Cactus snapped. "You won't care so much about all those empty promises and cheap lies when you see what real wonders there are in this world. Tomorrow you'll see it all for yourself."

Lizard yawned and stretched. "You say that every night."

When the sun rose they packed up camp and were off again, Cactus white-knuckled at the wheel and Lizard fiddling with the radio.

"...now, let's go ahead and take our next caller," Donnie's slick voice came blaring through the speakers. "Tanya, you're on with Donnie. How can I help you help yourself?"

Suddenly the city appeared again before them, swimming in the heat, just as radiant as always. Cactus glanced at the map open between the seats. They were getting close to the canyon Lizard had spotted, but the city was safely in front of the deep crevasse. She sped up, and the buildings seemed to become more solid the closer they got, the shining towers and painted walls getting realer every moment.

"...well, Mr. Wrightman, lately I've been longing to fulfill a childhood dream. See, I always wanted to be a professional sand skater, but I was bow-legged and had an inner ear problem, so I gave it up. It's silly to still be clinging to that at my age, isn't it, Mr. Wrightman?"

The car was racing toward the city when the buildings began to swim again, the details blurring, the vision starting to disappear.

"No!"

Cactus sped up desperately just as the mirage vanished. Then she saw, out of the corner of her goggles, another apparition glistening to the east, right along the ridge of the canyon. She steered immediately to the right, the tires of the convertible barely missing the edge of the cliff. Lizard let out a yell and grabbed the car's frame as pebbles and sand clouds flew into the depths of the canyon. Cactus pressed her boot harder against the gas pedal.

"Cactus, slow down!"

"I'm not losing another one!"

They zoomed toward the new sparkling vision.

"...the fact is, Tanya," Donnie said. "Life never has to be less than what you want it to be. You have plenty to do still, plenty farther to go in life—the trick is to just keep pushing, just try, try, try again. Follow the five principles I've laid out, and *nothing* whatsoever can stand in your way..."

"Come on, come *on*," Cactus shouted as she wiped the sand from her goggles. The walled metropolis was bathed in the light of the boiling sun, and they were closer than they had ever been. Lizard was still clutching the window frame when he could see for the first time the amazing details beyond the golden gates—the gardens and fountains, the windows illuminating every tower where he could almost make out what looked like the faces of people looking down at them. The buildings weren't swimming away in an ocean of blinding heat this time, the waves didn't come to mar the scene. Everything seemed to be getting more solid, and they were right at the huge gates and could see the pattern of the tiled streets, the fat red fruits hanging above the winding river and then...and then...

The waves started to come.

"No!" Cactus said.

The flat expanse of sand started to return.

"*No!*"

And the car drove through the vanishing golden gates and into more empty desert.

Until a few feet later it crashed into a mountainous rock and went spinning toward the canyon. Cactus steered away frantically, but the convertible was breaking apart under them, the front smashed in and the rest flying toward the edge.

"Hang on, Lizard!"

The car hit another rock and threw Cactus clear among pieces of busted metal and broken glass. It veered toward the canyon, its wheels halfway off before the rest of its beaten body fell and disappeared over the edge. A moment later a shattering crash echoed through the desert.

"Lizard!"

Cactus coughed and struggled to stand. She hobbled to the canyon's edge, clutching her side, and looked down the deep gully. She wiped her goggles again to see through the still-settling clouds of sand. The remains of the convertible burned among the red rocks below.

"Lizard!"

"Here," came Lizard's small voice.

And there he was, dangling just below, his climbing forks jutting out of the cliff face and his feet clinging to the barest protrusion of rock.

"Lizard, grab my hand!"

He clutched Cactus's wrinkled fingers and clung on as she hoisted him back up. They crawled together away from the edge of the canyon and lay on the sand panting and staring up at the blank blue sky. Broken remains of their only source of transportation, shelter, and water were strewn across the desert around them. What was left of the dashboard and radio flashed and fizzled in the sand next to Cactus. The tangled wires and speakers still faintly transmitted Donnie Wrightman's static-garbled voice.

"...because anything's possible, you see? Repeat this mantra in your head: 'I can do anything.' Say that to yourself enough and soon you can make it true, I promise. *You can do—*"

Cactus closed her hand into a fist and beat the radio into silence.

She lay back down amidst the rubble and watched the corners of the desert go black.

When she opened her eyes again, it was to the feeling of hands shaking her and the sound of her name.

"Cactus. Cactus, wake up!"

Cactus blinked in the burning sunlight. It took a moment for her eyes to focus on Lizard kneeling beside her, to register the blood trickling from his forehead and the bruise blossoming under his eye. She felt an ache spreading through her body as she tried to push herself upright. Eventually she gave up and lay back down in the sand.

"Lizard..." she breathed, looking up into that eager trusting face.

"Cactus, are you okay? Cactus, the car..."

Cactus turned to take in the wreckage.

"The maps..." she said softly. "The water..." She started coughing, her body convulsing against the sand.

"Oh, pills—you need your pills, Cactus..." Lizard looked around frantically. "Um, they might be here in the debris somewhere. Don't worry, I'll find them, you just wait right here."

Cactus shook her head and clutched his pant leg. "No, Lizard..." she said through rattling coughs. "No, it's no good, boy. They're gone."

"It's okay, Cactus, we can make it back and get my grandpa to make you some more," Lizard said. "We just have to stay positive, like Donnie says. Look...look, we still have a tire, see? I can fashion some kind of wagon, and we can...we can..."

His hopeful face was falling as he looked around at what remained, at his employer lying defeated in the sand.

"Lizard, I'm sorry," Cactus wheezed.

"No, Cactus, don't say that, we can still..."

"I'm sorry you got caught up in this whole...this whole *stupid* mess." She hacked and spat a mouthful of blood. "You don't belong out here, you belong back home with your family, where you have your whole life in front of you. I dragged you out here for nothing. For all this...all this *nothing*. Oh God, I'm sorry, Lizard..."

"Hey, hang on now," Lizard said, wiping away the blood trickling past his eye. "Hang on, hey, don't go to sleep again, Cactus, you gotta stay awake so we can get home, yeah? Hey, listen, you didn't drag me anywhere, I came out here because I wanted to. Everybody told me not to go with you—"

"You should've listened to them—"

"No, no, that's not what I meant. You say I left behind a whole life, but what life, Cactus? You know why I listen to Donnie's show? 'Cause it's the only thing that ever made me think there could be something better, that I could be more than just a small-town medicine man. You know, Cactus, when we first met, you reminded me of Donnie—don't look like that, it's a compliment! You weren't just plodding along like everybody else, you were hell-bent on doing something, on going somewhere. That's why I wanted to go with you. You keep calling all of this 'nothing'!" He spread his arms out as though to embrace the miles of sand and cacti, the burning sun and the wide gaping sky. "Well, it's not nothing to me, Cactus. We may have never actually made it to the city, but we still saw more of it than anyone. We got so close, we chased it all over this world and we found it a hundred times. You think I could've ever done anything like that back in my family's tent? You think my grandpa ever did anything like that in his whole life? Cactus, that city was the only thing I ever saw worth seeing."

"But it wasn't real, Lizard! It was an illusion. A trick of the heat, a mirage I somehow got fooled into thinking I could walk into, just like all the idiots on the radio, like a damn fool. Lizard, you've just been following a broken old crone chasing down a dream."

Lizard smiled and looked out to the horizon. "But wasn't it a beautiful dream?"

Cactus stared at the boy leaning over her, his ridiculous ears sticking out under his cap, his little nose vanishing under his goggles. The corners of her mouth pulled up.

"Yes, Lizard. It was an awfully beautiful dream."

They sat there in the sand together as the sun continued its burning journey through the sky, neither one moving. Cactus kept coughing softly and let her eyes drift closed again.

"Cactus..."

Cactus didn't move. She was too tired, too broken, her lungs too shriveled for the oxygen of this world. The heat of the sand against her back felt welcoming, like a beach by an ocean where the water didn't evaporate the moment it touched the air.

"Cactus..." Lizard said, shaking her shoulders more forcefully than before. "Cactus, look!"

She squinted her eyes open. Lizard was staring behind her. Cactus struggled to push herself up, Lizard guiding her arm as she turned her aching body toward something huge looming just yards from where they sat.

It was so close she could hear the fountains, could smell the flower buds. The gates opened to the two lost vagrants of the desert, and Cactus and Lizard, clutching each other and stumbling in the sand like children, entered the shining city.

See Hannah Costelle's story "Cactus and Lizard" online at Metaphorosis.
If you liked it, leave a comment. Authors love that!
Remember to subscribe to our e-mail updates so you'll know when new stories are posted.

About the story

"Cactus and Lizard" originated from a conversation with my brother Caleb. Caleb and I often brainstorm ideas for graphic novels or fantasy stories that we usually never actually got around to creating. All we knew when we sat down this time was that we wanted a story set in a desert.

We came up with lots of ideas, including futuristic modified convertibles, cacti as big as redwood trees, and giraffe-type creatures that stick their necks out of the sand like gophers (that last one I unfortunately could not fit into the final story). We sketched potential characters and jotted down thoughts about plot, then stuck our notes in a drawer and forgot all about them.

About three years later, I happened upon these notes again. I liked what we'd come up with, but I still couldn't really see a story in it. Then I read one line scribbled in the margins: "A false oasis, perhaps?"

And that made me think, "Huh."

The moral? Keep all your weird ideas, your half-baked ideas, your bad ideas, the ideas you think are dead and buried. You never know what they might spark later on. You never know what might resurrect.

A question for the author

Q: What made you start writing?

A: The people I always admired best were storytellers. Novelists, poets, movie directors, comic strip artists. People who took what was going on in their heads and created worlds that sometimes felt more real than the one I lived in. I was always trying to unpuzzle the secrets of these artists' techniques, trying to figure out how they could make a scene or character so wild and funny and vivid. And eventually, as I learned more about storytelling, I stopped simply admiring the work of others and started inventing for myself. My thoughts went from "Wow! How did they do that?" to "Wow…I could do that."

About the author

Hannah Costelle is a mystery and fantasy writer who strives to bring humor and intricate plot twists into her work. On a typical day you can find her reading books of every genre or hiking in the Kentucky woods.

Lingua Franca

Amelia Fisher

I knew the children had no names, though I didn't understand it. Far had tried to explain it to me, but this was one barrier our strides in communication could not quite breach. She would always be of the city, and I an interloper. In the park, sitting on either side of the silent boy, you could have told that just from looking at us: Far in her machine-tailored suit jacket, me in my worn jeans and patchy self-applied buzz cut. Only one of us fully human, or so I'd been taught.

From the emotions flickering over their faces, I assumed she and the boy were engaged in silent conversation—or whatever the casters called it, since they insisted there were no words. I wasn't sure how letting the boy pick a name he'd never use was supposed to help with his tutoring lessons, but Far had insisted—said it would give the kid something to brag about to his friends. Personally, I doubted any of our pupils ever spoke a word outside of our sessions. Still, I figured there were things she wasn't telling me, or was unable to tell me as a result of what she would sardonically call my 'impairment'. But I'd learned when to stop asking questions long before I set foot in the city itself.

Far sat at the boy's side, leaning over his shoulder to scan the list of names with a kind, flavorless smile. The thermal regulators set at intervals along the grass softened the spring chill, warping the air around them with distortions of heat. The book propped up on the boy's grass-stained knees was made with real paper, a relic Far must have tracked down from some obscure online dealer. When I first came to the city, I probably would have taken offense at the laziness of that stereotype; it wasn't as if my sort hated technology. I said nothing. I'd been here long enough to know how these things went.

"Pine," Far said aloud. I'd gotten so used to the silence that the sound of a human voice was uncanny. "You like that name?" She met my eyes as she spoke. She always did, as if seeking out my approval, my appraisal of her accent, or maybe because really I was the one she was speaking to. The boy did not look up.

After that Far gave up on speaking in a way that I could perceive. I could hear the chirping of birds, the distant whisper of traffic drifting through the city's floating thoroughfares. Down the hill, children were tumbling over the playground like seed pods caught in a wind flurry, running pell-mell over the grass, hauling themselves up by their skinny arms and swinging back and forth on the hovering metal bars which always dipped lower before their strength gave out. Not one of them spoke, though at intervals they laughed at something I could not hear. They moved like images on a screen, detached from sound. From the dog park down the hill, a single low bark seemed to ride up to us on a vast wave of silence. Even the animals were quiet, well-trained. I kept quiet too.

"Well, that settles it," Far said at last. "Do you want to tell Vaun your name?"

At long last the boy looked up and met my eyes. "Kite," he said. His accent was much stronger than Far's, and the word sounded garbled on his unpracticed tongue. I'd learned to stop correcting him. That was Far's job. My job was to be a novelty and a prop.

"That's a nice name," I said. "What made you pick it?"

"The book had a picture."

"Like the bird, or the toy?"

The boy stared at me blankly for a long time before turning back to his teacher. In my pocket, my handheld buzzed an anxious tattoo of notifications. Probably the family group chat; the thought, sudden and cold, that it might be Nan gave me pause. Maybe my strange companions wouldn't mind if I pulled out my handheld in the middle of a session. They lived in a sea of notifications, after all; other people's thoughts and intentions were the air they breathed. Still, I had some sense of professional decorum. I ignored it for the time being.

Far waited patiently for a moment before saying; "Aloud, please. It's important to practice."

The boy—Kite, now, I supposed—did not sigh, but the conversation expected it. "How can one word mean more than one thing?"

Always so strange, to hear them vocalize. The words were correct enough, but something was missing in the speech itself, a lack of understanding or practice. She watched the boy, her expression unchanged. I noted her professionalism even if I didn't admire it. "It's rude not to include someone in the conversation."

"Not my fault she can't hear us." The more petulant he grew, the more natural his speech sounded. He looked at me then, full of that total stillness I could never convince myself wasn't hiding something else beneath. I met his gaze, trying not to make it a challenge, failing. Casters had no taboos against extended eye contact, and so we inspected each other for much longer than I could be comfortable with. I found myself studying his left eye for a glint of the thing behind it.

When he spoke at last, his expression did not change. "I'm sorry I was rude. I want to keep learning how to speak."

I wondered whether Far was feeding him the right words to say. Even that might be more effort than I should expect from her. "That's okay. Learning a language can be frustrating."

The boy's emotions moved over his face like storm clouds: doubt, irritation, boredom. But he still nodded—stiff, formal—and said, "Especially now that there's only one."

I blinked. "Well, there are quite a few spoken languages. We're speaking English right now, but many people speak Spanish, Chinese—"

His face did not change, but I heard Far sigh again. "No, you will only need to learn a single language to satisfy your extra-curricular requirement. Now, let's move on to the vocal warmups."

After the boy had been sent on his way, picked up by a sleek black car that lifted away from the park and into the transit loop above, Far and I settled at one of the park's many benches. She did this with the metal barrel of a cig between her lips, unlit as of yet, but placed there as soon as there was no chance of the boy or his chaperone seeing it. Her lips curled more easily around it than they did around her professional smile.

"Those aren't real names, you know. They're just words," I said, hating this urge to fill the silence and yet unable to resist it.

"Your 'real' names are just words."

"Old words."

"Oh, well that's alright, then." Far took a drag from her cig. "Let the kid have something to tell his parents."

Skirting the edge of a familiar argument, I decided to retreat. "How'd you pick your name?"

"Opened the dictionary and put my finger down at random." I doubted that. She'd probably done it a few times, until she found one she liked. *The state of being distant.* Words and sound still meant something, no matter what the casters liked to pretend.

In the lull of conversation, I slid my handheld from my pocket. Tocsin's name blinked up at me, but I caught Far staring at me and quickly put it away. She had whisked aside the benevolent placidity of her teaching facade as soon as the cig touched her lips. Now she just looked tired. The park was utterly silent but for the faint hum of the thermal regulators and the distant rumble of cars, the running footsteps of the voiceless children.

The tip of Far's cig flared green as she contemplated me. She might have spoken my language, but the way she looked at me was common to every caster I'd met—all overt, unfiltered feeling. No point keeping emotion off your face when everyone around you could skim it off the top of your biodigital cloud. A world without privacy, and thus without shame. Though sometimes Far's expressions were tinted by a more subtle quirk of her lips or eyebrow, or a sly look I couldn't quite read: expressions of a hidden interiority I liked to think she'd picked up from me. I sometimes wondered if she sent thoughts my way on impulse, a sleet of hellos and goodbyes and questions and jokes that slid off me without my knowledge.

It was that kind of thinking that made me doubt my choice sometimes, the thought of all those words and feelings falling mutely around me in a void I couldn't even feel. But then I'd remember what Nan always said: that the soul wasn't meant to be passed around like a cup of moonshine. How could there be trust without secrets?

Her arm over the back of the park bench shifted to where it didn't quite touch my back, but might have if I leaned back just a little. Again my handheld buzzed against my leg, but if I took it out now, Far would assume I was brushing her off. And, well, I had my own expectations about how this afternoon was going to end.

"How long before you have to go back?"

Before answering, I leaned over to pluck the cig from her lips and raise it to my own, breathing in the taste of— "*Soap?*" I said, making a face as I handed it back.

Far grinned. "Cilantro. New flavor."

"I can see why no one thought of it before." But then I leaned back against the softness of her coat sleeve resting on the back of the bench and said, "Long enough."

After we were done, I peeled my cheek from the rise and fall of Far's rib cage with a sound like pulling off a piece of tape. The temperature modulator hummed busily from the ceiling, dumping a waterfall of chilly air into the otherwise stuffy room, turning my bare skin clammy. Far said nothing as I unspooled myself towards the other side of the bed where the glass of water always sat. Far watched me; I didn't need augmented mental senses to feel her eyes on the curve of my spine.

It had started with an argument about Borges, one of his collections Far was 'muchly surprised' I hadn't read. I'd taken issue with her tone and openly doubted that she owned a copy. By the time we got back to her place, I'd forgotten it entirely. I probably shouldn't have let things continue, but I was never very smart about that sort of thing. Far was available, attractive, and not from the compound, which made things both simpler and more complicated in a way that excited me. And it was a little cute, the way Far spoke; the ornate synonyms and slurring pronunciation, the accent of one who still tasted the words like they were new.

When I looked back, she had tucked one arm behind the back of her head, displaying a dark tuft of hair trimmed to a fashionable length. I couldn't imagine Far doing anything that wasn't fashionable. Her eyes were soft as a piece of fruit that you wouldn't want to eat. She opened her mouth and I braced myself for some brutal insight brought on by the candor of the afterglow.

But what she actually said was, "Can I have some of that water?"

I tipped my head back and drained the glass while holding her eye.

Far sighed. "You're a dick. Is that the right word here? Or would asshole be more appropriate?"

I got up to refill the glass from the nodule on the wall, cool water chilling the glass cupped in my fingers. When I brought it back to her and settled it on the soft dampness of Far's stomach, she sucked in a sharp, relishing breath.

"Neither," I said. "I'm very considerate."

"Hm. You have your moments."

The bob of her throat as she swallowed seemed to move inside of me, too. But what sank into the pit of my stomach wasn't an echo of the unspoken vows we'd been mouthing into each other's bodies for the past hour and a half. Only then I remembered my handheld's frequent buzzing. I fumbled it off the bedside table and was greeted with a storm of notifications. I swiped through them quickly, sliding them across the cool glass like oil over water, and all of them from Tocsin.

Home soon?

Hey dickhead I need to talk to you about smthn

turn your handle on or I'll tell Nan about your porn
For real, where are you?
Vaun, I'm serious.
Let me know when youll be back…
Vauneant?
it's important
hello???

And then, two hours later: *everything's fine but please come talk to me when you can and please don't ask anyone else about me.*

"Shit," I said aloud.

Far shifted against the covers. "Something wrong?"

Thirty-two messages total. If something truly dire had gone down, I'd have heard from more people—I'd have heard from Nan. Tocsin was more brother than cousin to me, but he was also an impulsive little shit, and always dealing with one self-manufactured personal crisis or another. It was probably about a girl, or a wrecked car. Probably nothing at all.

"Not sure," I said, sitting back down on the bed. "I should probably go."

Far turned to look at me. The way she used her eyes sometimes, it made me understand what casting was. "You know, maybe you wouldn't have to run around so much if you were making enough money to actually live on."

"You have some new clients for me?"

"I'm not talking about the tutoring. I'm talking about an actual job. If you were willing to use a temporary implant, they'd have no objection—"

"Not an option."

"Why not?" Anger sparked in Far's eyes; any attempt to hide it would have been alien to her. "I'm not going to argue with you about your aversion to implantation tech, I know that's no use." Knew that from long experience. "But a temporary one, Vaun? What's wrong with that? You wouldn't even have to tell anyone else —"

"And when I conveniently started making the kind of money that only comes from working at a caster place?" Most businesses these days would reject you out of hand as soon as they found out you didn't have an implant. A slurry of words: company culture, transparency, workflow. Who wouldn't want to hire an employee you never had to give a drug test, and whose productivity you could track just by sitting in the same room?

"Shit. This isn't how I wanted to tell you." She rolled over to the other side of the bed, waved the drawer of the nightstand open and dipped her hand into its darkness to withdraw a small glass vial with a dead worm inside. No, not dead; as she moved it towards me it gave a feeble twitch in its sterilizing liquid. Even from here I could see the way the mouth of the tube was shaped to fit perfectly against the socket of an eye, forming a perfect seal for the gel to settle against lid and lash before the digital tunneler did its work.

"It's a biodegradable model," Far said. In her voice, she had already won. "About a three-month half-life. They're actually *more* expensive than the permanent ones, you know. And if you'd just apply for a job that would cover—look. That doesn't matter. With this, I could have something lined up for you in a matter of days. Something that would actually pay. And I could help you. Tell you what to expect, coach you through the effects." She shifted closer. It struck me in a distant way that this little scene was exactly what Nan had probably envisioned when I told her I got a job in the city. She'd always said that corruption would be seductive.

I pulled away.

Before Far could reach for me, I was out of the bed, shoving various limbs into various articles of clothing, hoping I matched up the right holes.

"Vaun. Wait. *Wait.*" Far stumbled out of bed after me, flailing for a robe at its foot that she only managed to get half on. I couldn't tug my boots on before her hand settled on my shoulder. "Listen. I wasn't trying to offend you—"

"You have no idea what you're asking me to risk."

"God damnit, Vaun, that's because you never tell me!"

"There are plenty of things about me that you wouldn't understand."

"If you had the implant, I wouldn't have to—" She cut herself off before I could do it for her. Far's face was flushed. She didn't fight the tide of her anger. There was something comforting in knowing that for all the teeming life that existed beneath the surface of her, at least that surface couldn't lie.

"Alright," she said, and just like that the anger began to fade. "Alright. Just—this is an option, alright? I got it for *you*. And it'll be waiting, whether you change your mind or not."

I watched her cross the room and put the thing back into the drawer. When she turned to me, she didn't bother to pull her robe shut, and I didn't bother not to look.

"Stay a little longer?" she said. There were times when she really could speak like a natural. But even as she stepped forward and leaned in, my eyes stayed open, on that bedside drawer. Visions of her holding it over my eye socket as I slept played with the gruesome relish of a slasher film. When she pulled back, I couldn't shift my eyes back fast enough.

"Gotta get back," I said, and her mouth did that thing that was almost a smile. Casters never were good at faking expressions.

"I just want to help," she said, and that was the worst part.

I leaned in to kiss her again, closed-lipped right up until the end, because I knew I'd want to be back here and wouldn't want to spend the next time putting out the fires I left burning today. Her fingers curled in the fleece-lined collar of my jacket, the grip light and brittle as the dry curl of the thing in the vial. I let it linger before pulling away. I was pretty good at tolerating things by now.

I scrolled through Tocsin's messages as the train slid free of the glass sheath at the edge of the city and began to pick up speed. *On my way back. You good?* I waited five minutes, refreshing my handheld, before slipping its cool weight back into my pocket. I almost pinged Tocsin's sister Coxcomb, but I knew better than to start asking around before I knew what Tocsin had gotten himself into.

The compound was only the last stop on the rail line in the loosest sense of the term. In reality you had to get off at the industrial district and walk another two miles down a road that was more weed than asphalt, cross-hatched with tar that could never hold the bursting cracks closed for long. Eventually you got to a chain link gate with a keypad—not exactly friendly, but we'd had our share of teenage casters prowling the perimeter, always in packs, silent, sometimes lobbing a rock or can of beer over the fence. No one else came out here, no one kept track of us, no one cared what was done to us or what we did to each other. I punched buttons so worn any idiot could probably guess the code, and stepped inside.

I could hear it before I saw it, the threads of noise breaking through the quiet like lightning in a summer storm. High raucous laughter, shouts of greeting or admonition, the clatter of doors and feet and conversations. I made my way down the central road through town, raising my hand to a few passing groundcars which honked at me as they crunched over the gravel. This time of day, most people were sitting out on their porches to watch the street, tinny songs blaring on their radios, the ice in their glasses clinking. More than a few had patches over their eyes.

The commotion on the Lin family's porch stopped me short before I reached my place. The usual crowd was gathered there, but today it didn't seem friendly. People lingered on the lawn to watch and listen and comment to their friends—arguments were a spectator sport. I couldn't make out the words, but I didn't really have to. I just had a hard time believing anyone in that household would have gone and put that thing in their head, knowing the consequences. I kept walking, grateful no one saw me and called me over to join them. I had to be careful about sharing my opinion on this kind of thing. People tended to assume I was biased, seeing as I worked in the city and was probably halfway to contaminated as a result. Nan certainly seemed to think so.

The lights were on in my house as I made my way up the path, and I could hear the sound of clanging pots and voices inside, the familiar hiss of the old oven. Grandpa Heimal was in his chair on the porch, as he always was unless someone forgot to wheel him out. The socket of his left eye clung to the shadows like a cave. He'd been one of the early-adopters, and he'd paid for it. By the time talk of malfunctions started slipping past the NDAs and corporate cover-ups, the implant had scrambled Heimal's brain from the inside out.

Nan did what she could for him, and for the others she found who'd been through the same. I sometimes wondered whether she left his hollowed-out eye socket uncovered as a reminder to all the rest of us. That was certainly Nan's style. I squeezed his shoulder as I walked to the door, and murmured a quick *hullo, Grandpa* the way a Buddhist might turn the prayer wheels in passing.

From the moment I stepped inside, I was surrounded by warmth and light and familiar voices, so loud I could scarcely hear myself think as I took off my coat and my hat.

"Vauneant's back!" someone in the kitchen cried, and seconds later I was pelted at knee-height by a bundle of niece, grinning up at me from her grip around my knees.

"We're making lasagana!" Cispontine squealed.

I bent down to scoop her up, forcing an easy smile. "That's my favorite!"

"Vaun," my sister's voice called from the kitchen, "Get in here and make sure the vegetables don't burn."

Dutifully I trooped toward her voice, Cispontine on my hip. I could only glance at the stairs that led to the bedrooms before stepping into the kitchen. It was already packed in there, my cousin Snowbrowth fanning the smoke away from the detector, Cispontine's older sister sitting on the counter picking at the chips and dip, while uncle Groak tried to harangue her into helping peel vegetables.

"Did you hear about the Lins?" someone said in my ear, but no, I hadn't heard, and it was too loud to have it explained to me. Everyone was talking at once and I could hardly make out a word of it, and didn't need to try.

A couple times I checked my handheld. Still no response. I couldn't help but glance at the ceiling, the only thing which separated me from Tocsin's room. It seemed to sag toward me with the weight of whatever had happened. But I couldn't get away now without questions, and those could be dangerous around here.

At last, lasagna came out of the oven and the vegetables were oversalted, and Coxcomb finished doling out a healthy portion onto a plate and arranged it neatly on a tray.

"Take this up?" she said, as she always did, and for once I was glad to do it.

The stairs sighed under my boots as I made my way up. Nan's room made up the entire third floor, perched up top of the rest of the house like a watchtower. From up here you could see the entire compound, the endless green sprawl of forest and the glitter of the city on the horizon. Nan looked up from her work as I came in, her cane hooked on the edge of her workbench and small wire-frame glasses perched on her nose like something from an old digital film. She was the only person I knew alive who still used glasses; surgical eye correction was one modern amenity that the rest of us had all conceded to, but Nan said it was a manipulation of natural flesh, too close to changing who she was. Her glasses should have made her look sweet, old-fashioned; instead they focused her hard gaze into something that could have set the dried pages of Far's book alight.

I didn't look at the curtain in the back of the room, pulled closed against the makeshift surgery, and I didn't breathe through my nose. Still, the hint of chemicals prickled at my nose, imagined or not. This was the room where they did it—behind the curtain, the cot with disposable sheets and the blinking medical equipment, scrounged from outdated tech. Everything Nan might need to pull a long, biotech strand from a wayward eye socket. There was always a choice, of course, for anyone caught with an implant: take the operation or never come back.

"Nan," I said.

"Vauneant." She straightened, laying her soldering iron back in its cradle. I couldn't make sense of the wires and old-fashioned circuit boards in front of her. A piece of the temperature regulator, maybe. Nan was good at taking things apart and putting them back together to her own specifications. She'd been a doctor, before the compound; that fact had been one of the first to impress itself on my young mind. The use of old-fashioned computers, she'd taught herself out of necessity.

"Back from the city?" she said, with polite disapproval.

I stepped forward to put the tray on the table beside her. Her hair was the color of surgical steel where it caught the white light of her desk lamp. "Someone has to make sure those layabouts don't starve you."

Nan smiled, but her eyes still studied me the way they studied everyone. No one discussed the idea of moving her to a room downstairs. This had been her throne room as long as anyone could remember, and nothing short of death would unseat her from it.

Nan picked up the soldering iron again, and leaned over the pine-green circuit board. "Hear about the Lin boy?"

"Heard something happened. Not what."

A little line of smoke appeared from beneath the thin metal tool, curling up towards the hard shine of her glasses. She didn't specify, and I knew what that meant. What else of importance could happen to us here?

"It was just one of the temporaries, thank God," Nan said after a moment. "Just a matter of waiting for it to drain out of him. Still, the weakness revealed itself. His family will need to be diligent."

From what people told me of the time four decades ago, Nan had always been hard even when her face was soft. Maybe that was how she'd pulled this community around her like meat wrapped around bone, after she lost Heimal in all the ways that counted; and why our family out of all the rest was one of the few in the compound that hadn't turned up some wayward son or daughter who decided to put a biocomputer in their head. Ever since I'd gotten the job with Far, Nan had started looking at me like a sheep dog might look at a ewe with a limp.

"I'm sure they'll set him straight," I said, and Nan nodded, satisfied; she bent back over her workbench, and I knew I was dismissed.

Down the stairs once more, the air seemed easier to breathe. Tocsin's door was at the end of the hall, shut. I went to my room, loudly kicked off my boots, and made the rest of the way barefoot down the beaten-up runner. I knocked twice with one knuckle, soft as a branch tapping a window. There was no reply. I entered silently.

Tocsin lay in bed looking like he should be in the middle of an impact crater. He blinked up at me, barely able to raise his head as I closed the door softly behind me. He looked as young as he'd been when we rode down the stairs on our pillows, and as shell-shocked as when his head met the bottom bannister.

One of his eyes was bruised, the white of it gone painfully red.

"Hey, Vaun," he croaked.

I let out a slow breath as I settled next to him on the bed. For a minute we just sat there, turning over the silence between us like it was a puzzle that together we could somehow pick apart.

"Sure hope you didn't let anyone see you looking like that," I said after a while.

"I'm not an idiot, thanks."

"Would a smart person go and do what you just did?"

"I needed the work. *We* needed it," Tocsin said. Though we kept our voices low, I could hear the bitterness creeping in at the edges.

"At least tell me it's temporary."

"How the hell was I supposed to afford one of those?"

I put my head in my hands. "God damnit, Tocsin."

"What else could I do, huh? How long am I supposed to sit around all day watching Mom and Coxcomb live off canned protein and nutrient pills because none of us can get a job?"

"You think they'd be happier to know you went and did the one thing Nan would run you out of here for? You know the rules, Tocsin—"

"Yes, I know, *Jesus*, I know." Tocsin put a hand over his eyes, hiding the inflamed one from view. "I just need to make enough money to get by on for a while. Then I'll turn it off, and no one will ever need to know." He lowered his hands to look at me with an expression of wheedling accusation. "You know I would have found your kind of work if I could."

I turned away, hating to hear him say that. I was the example every parent in our compound told their kids about—Vaun who had found work in the city and still managed to stay unpolluted. My life was better in theory than in practice. Without the welfare checks and the fact that I wasn't paying rent, I'd never be able to keep my head above water.

"Listen," Tocsin said. He picked at the stray thread of his cuff instead of looking at me. "Nan is going to start to ask questions about the money this job is going to bring in. I was hoping you could—you know. Spread it around that I got work with your people. To help explain it."

I nodded, but because he wasn't looking, I had to force my dead tongue to move. "Of course. Don't even ask me that."

"Thanks." His voice was flat. Not ungrateful; just tired.

I cleared my throat. "You going to go to the support group?"

"It's called intunement, but yeah."

Indoctrination, as Nan would put it. Still, I was glad. We were in a distinct position out here to know how bad a mind could go once the implant cracked it open.

I made a vague gesture at his face. "How long will all that last?"

"Should fade by morning."

"Better hope it does," I said, knowing he knew I would cover for him if it hadn't. I thought of Nan's hard eyes drilling into my head, the curtain and the smell of disinfectant; and also of the warm currents of talk and food and companionship that made this place a home. I'd seen what had happened to other kids when their families found out they strayed; either an empty eye socket or an empty place at the table. In a way our world was defined by absence as much as Far's was by the lack thereof. Was it better to be mutilated in body, or soul?

For a while longer I sat there. Then I rose, unable to stay another minute in that close room with its prickling silence, wondering what Tocsin was hearing and feeling that I just couldn't reach. The truth was, I was scared for him. But I had no idea how to tell him that, and in the end it was easier to say nothing at all.

"It's not a cult."

Sitting at our customary bench, Far turned to me with a wry smile. "You're good with words, Vaun. But I'm not confident in your ability to reason that one out."

"I don't have to convince you that I'm *not* in a cult. The burden of proof is on you."

"Fine." Far passed me her cig, which glowed brown this time. I eyed it nervously, but inhaled all the same. The cinnamon tasted like vague relief. Kite's lessons had been going well for the past couple weeks, and the latest tutoring lesson had ended early. Far had yet to ask me back to hers today. I think maybe part of her enjoyed the illicit thrill of sitting in public and *talking*. That irritated me a bit, but the fact was I liked talking to her.

She hadn't brought up the vial waiting in her bedside drawer again, either. I'd checked, once, while she was in the bathroom—it was still there. It could afford to wait.

Far held up a finger. "You live on a compound. You distrust outsiders. You reject modern technology for religious reasons—"

"It's not religion," I said, a little too sharply. I didn't like the way she was ticking my life off on her fingers like plot points in a hack novel.

Far looked at me, calculating. "You can believe in something religiously without any sort of God coming into it."

I looked away, biting the inside of my cheek. "You forgot to mention the human sacrifice," I said, and Far laughed that ugly sawing laugh of hers that I'd reluctantly come to enjoy.

It wasn't as if I hadn't thought about it, I almost wanted to say. The doors that would open for me as soon as I let the world into my thoughts would change my life forever. But it would mean shutting another door behind me, the one which led to the only family and home I'd ever known. Birthed into the amniotic ocean of thought as she'd been, I didn't think Far could understand that.

"Come on," she said, slipping the cig back into her breast pocket. "It's a beautiful day. Let's walk to my place for once."

"You're assuming I want to come home with you."

"Yes, I am."

I rolled my eyes, a gesture that Far had never succeeded in duplicating. I ought to have told her I had somewhere to be, just to prove that I could still say no, but in the end the flesh was weak.

As we left the park, I was immediately glad to have Far at my side. Hanging trolleys whispered over our heads as they passed, sweeping over the shuffle of hundreds of feet and the soft hush of cars sliding past. The faces which passed were alight with a wash of silent emotion. The buildings were paneled with blank screens, grim and grey—only a caster could perceive what they were trying to sell.

There were others here, I knew, who had once been like me. Expats from the compound who'd kept their eyes and implants, and lost everything else. None had ever approached me. They'd been subsumed, just a few more silent ghosts wandering the city streets.

"Doesn't it bother you?" I asked. My words smeared that silence like an obscene stain. "The quiet."

Far snorted, tossing her long braid over her shoulder. She made more seemingly unconscious sound than any other caster I had met. I wonder if the people around her thought her strange, or whether she could turn it on and off as easily as a switch in her head. "I could ask you the same question."

"And I'd tell you that it does. It bothers me a lot."

She shrugged. "It isn't quiet for me. I can cast into the thoughts of people around me, if I want to. Except yours."

"That sounds awful."

"Oh, I'm sure I'm not missing out on much." She sobered a little, turning to face me with her full interest. "The idea of walking around with cotton stuffed in my brain, numb and dumb to everyone—*that* sounds awful to me."

"Maybe I like keeping some things to myself."

"Interesting use of conditional, considering you're the most covert person I know. You'd tell me if you were some kind of murderer, right?"

"Depends. Can you keep a secret?"

Far laughed again, and then covered her mouth when a person passing us looked at her sharply. It was rude to break the quiet, and I felt a little good about that; like I'd managed to show her something about me, without even really trying. I supposed that to venture out of the city and into that vast silence where there was nothing to cast to or to cast back at you would be a kind of death to Far. A terrible thing, to be cut off from all you'd ever known.

Then she leaned over to peck my cheek, and I stopped thinking about unreachable worlds for a while.

"I really do want to know."

Far said this before I'd started getting dressed again, which was how I knew she might be serious. "Why is rejecting the implant so important to you and yours?" she continued, on seeing I was listening.

I propped myself up on a hand, thinking. She'd never asked before, not really, so I'd never had to explain it before. I thought about what Nan would say: that language made us human, and the implants made us something else. Having seen the city, it was hard to argue with that. But there was something more to it; something even Far might understand.

"Have you ever asked someone where they wanted to eat dinner, listened to them think aloud about what they're in the mood for, until you can both agree on something? Or do you just think *food* and pick up the general sensations and cravings of the person you're with?"

"I don't see the difference. We end up at the restaurant either way."

"There's no room for mistakes. For all the little things you lose and gain between thought to word to thought again."

Far raised her eyebrows. "Translations are imperfect by nature."

"Art is an imperfect translation."

"Now you're just being pretentious."

"Now I'm trying to make a *point*."

That familiar smile touched half her lips. "If only you had an implant. Imagine how easily you could convey your ideas."

It was a joke. It should have been easy to laugh it off. But I couldn't just then; I was thinking about Tocsin, and my grandfather's eye drifting like a dead log on a placid sea. When my gaze slid to Far again, her own face had gotten quiet.

"Vaun," she said. "If there were something bad happening out there, would you tell me?"

I pressed a kiss to the back of her hand in lieu of an answer, but in the end she took it as answer enough.

When I reached the final train stop within the city limits, the car emptied as if disemboweled. It was only me and an older woman who sat at the end, veined hands trembling over her handscreen. As soon as we passed a certain stop, a switch was triggered—now the spilling color over the walls had sound attached, music that poured out of the train's tinny speakers and startled me into alertness.

"With new implant technology, it's never been easier to upgrade," a cheerful baritone said as images flashed across the screen—people effortlessly finding each other across a crowded train station, a team of dancers coordinating in a complex routine, a mother casting at her baby for the first time. "*The world is waiting. Cast out for it.*"

The ads were clearly targeted. In the end, no one would even have to force us—it would just happen slowly, as people gave in, realized it was easier to assimilate, told themselves they'd stay vocal with their families, their kids; but how many generations would it take for even that faint conviction to flicker out?

Glancing at the old woman at the other end of the train, I realized she was staring at me hard—and that she was probably trying to cast at me. When the train reached its final stop I got off quickly, leaving her behind.

The walk back to the compound went quickly, lost in my thoughts as I was. The sound of raised voices from beyond the chain link fence didn't strike me as particularly alarming until the gate rolled back on its aging motor and I saw the crowd.

They were gathered outside of my house.

I didn't realize I was running until the scene wavered and dragged me closer like something from a bad dream. No elbowing through the crowd tonight; people saw me and they split apart. Even from the outskirts I could see Nan on the porch, leaning on her walking stick. She only ever came down the stairs in a crisis. Now that crisis was seething around my home like antibodies around a virus.

And then Nan's eyes shifted to me, and nothing in her expression or posture changed; it was just that I bore the full weight of her attention like the muzzle of a gun held inches from my forehead. People were asking her questions, asking *me* questions, but all I could do was stand there skewered by her gaze. I knew she knew I'd kept Tocsin's secrets, and that made me hardly any better than him.

I cleared the porch steps in two strides, my eyes shifting from Nan to the door. I just had to get to Tocsin. But before I could step forward, a hand shot out to catch my arm in a grip you'd only use on an animal, something whose pain didn't need respecting. Behind her glasses, Nan's eyes bored into mine.

"It's done," she said. I tried to tear away, but she held me fast. "We gave him the choice," Nan said, each word another chunk bitten out of me. "He chose *us*."

I was not deaf to the inference, the silent second half of her sentence: the choice that I had made, without ever knowing I had made it. I stared into Nan's eyes, but they were flat behind the glass. I thought of Coxcomb and Cispontine and Groak, the noise and love and connection. No one stepped forward to speak for me now. The silence around me bled like a wound.

Nan let me go. I stumbled, nearly fell into someone; I didn't see or care who. The door, the house—someone tried to stop me, but I heard Nan's voice. "Let her say her goodbyes. She'll be gone within the hour."

I turned on her. Numbness spread through my chest like a branching tree of dead nerves. "I should get a choice," I said, my voice hollow. "You give everyone a choice."

Nan shook her head. "You already made it."

I turned around. The house was empty as a tomb. Up the stairs. My eyes stung and swam, but I kept moving. Tocsin's door was open, vacant. It was Nan's room I went to; the door was unlocked, the computer parts on the workbench all filed into the separate compartments of her plastic storage container. The curtain on the other side of the room had been drawn back. I saw the bright red biohazard bin first, the color snagging my eye. The blink of the machines: pulse, breath, things that made no sense to me. Half of Tocsin's face had a piece of medical gauze taped over it, and where once the eye had lain beneath it there was a rose of blood budding in the cotton, unfurling with each beep of the machines. Still sedated. We weren't barbarians, tearing out the eyes of our unwilling victims without proper medical procedure. That was the worst of it, of course—that in the end, Tocsin had chosen this. As much as you could choose anything, when the alternative was to be stripped of everything you'd ever known and loved.

I sat by his bedside a long time, knowing he wouldn't wake for hours. Even if he had, I knew what he'd probably say.

No one tried to stop me as I left. They went silent as I passed. I spread it around me like a stench. The sun was going down, and there were no lights on the long cracked road back to the train station. In the dark, all I could see was the spot of blood. I knew I'd never walk this road again. What was wrong with me wasn't something they could pluck out.

I sat on the steps to Far's building for a long time, waiting for her to see my message. I'd only sent the one; I couldn't dig up the words, the urgency, the hour, the year. I didn't know how I'd found my way here, other than following something I hadn't known was inside of me. The city was utterly silent but for the occasional sound of footsteps. It didn't bother me now. I never wanted to hear a spoken word again.

When the door behind me opened I jerked like someone caught nodding off. And then Far was in front of me, her arms gripping her elbows. Her eyes were confused, and a little scared, and darted between me and the heavy backpack leaning against my leg.

"Um." I followed her gaze to my pack. For a moment I lost myself in its shape and contours, which seemed more real to me than anything else had ever been in my life. It occurred to me in a distant way that this might be asking too much; that Far might actually turn me away. "I know you don't have any reason to—"

"Get in here," she said with hoarse exasperation, as if there had never been any other answer at all. She led me to her door, or she must have—I didn't feel awake or alive in the strictest sense of the word. Eventually I was naked, in her bed, and she was molded to me, chaste and still clothed. For once, I wanted to tell her everything. I wanted to open my mouth and let it pour out of me like bile dredged up from deeper than retching should go. My tongue was stone. I smelled disinfectant on every breath.

I reached for the gleam before my eyes, the single point of light: the metal knob of the bedside table that I had opened a hundred times in my mind. Far's hand tangled with mine before I could fumble inside. She pulled my hand back and pressed it to my chest until I could feel every beat of my heart as clearly as if I held it in the palm of my hand.

"Shh," she said, and stroked my hair. "Shh."

And for a while there was silence deeper than I had ever known, and in Far's arms I drank from it until I was full.

See Amelia Fisher's story "Lingua Franca" online at Metaphorosis. If you liked it, leave a comment. Authors love that! Remember to subscribe to our e-mail updates so you'll know when new stories are posted.

About the story

The first version of "Lingua Franca" bears little resemblance to the way it ended up. The concept I began with was, why does telepathy always involve language? If people could communicate mind-to-mind virtually from birth, directly sharing images and emotions and ideas, what use would there be for words? What does a society with communication but no language look like?

Having conceived of a society which communicated exclusively through mind-impressions, I figured I'd better introduce a non-telepathic character to explore it on the reader's behalf. Thus the idea of the spoken word tutoring sessions arose, and a character balanced halfway between two worlds, trying to bridge them both.

The initial draft involved a sort of seduction in the opposite direction: Vaun wanted to introduce Far to the miracle that is human language, with all its quirks and miscommunications. Over the course of writing the story, I ended up reversing that. Since this telepathy was technological in origin, I figured there would be intense pressure on anyone who decided not to take the implant. Overall, "Lingua Franca" began as an exploration of language, and privacy, and two people from very different worlds attempting to form some kind of connection.

And then I hit the point that I always run into with my stories, where I go "but what if it was a horror story?" And thus, the more cultish elements emerged. I ultimately eased back from true horror, and settled on something that felt more authentic: the claustrophobia and joy that go hand-in-hand with any tight-knit community.

I realized at a certain point that my ruminations on language and privacy were really prodding at what it means to be human at all—is being an individual a requirement? Is shame? At the end of the day I feel like I picked up and turned over a lot of questions I can't really answer, but I certainly enjoyed the asking.

A question for the author

Q: Do you generally start with mood, title, character, concept...?

A: I'm an ideas-gal. I love to start with a big, weird, capital-C Concept. When I stumble across a world or scenario full of questions and potential, I start looking for the tension point: the moment or location or character that makes the story come alive. Once I have a general idea of what kind of world or situation I want to explore, the first line usually staggers in, fashionably late and slightly inebriated, and the story takes off from there.

About the author

Amelia Fisher writes queer speculative fiction from her home in Vancouver, Washington. She likes plants, tea, and Cordyceps fungus.

ameliafisher.com, @hubristicfool

Holding

John Adams

I never cared much about cars as a kid—never cared much about anything Dad liked. The older I got, the more he and I argued. About school. Guys I dated. Hell, who ate the last piece of birthday cake.

My last clear memory of him is my 15th birthday. I'd let a pudgy gray cat follow me home—Nottingham, I think I called it. "I told you no pets, Kerry," Dad yelled. "Your mom's allergic, and I'm not paying the extra deposit!" He scooped up the cat and stormed out of the apartment.

Dad died a few weeks later.

I never saw that cat again.

It's late, and I'm still at Dorsey's Auto Repair, my place of employment. Dad's place of employment. After he died, I got more interested in cars. I signed up for Shop class in 12th grade. Enrolled in vo-tech after high school. Cornered Dorsey the day after graduation, announcing I was ready to work. Dorsey was so flustered, he didn't have the gall to say 'no'.

Tonight, I'm on the creeper platform, wheeled under Mrs. Moritz's 2008 Nissan Sentra: 3,000-ish pounds of steel, aluminum, and hand-knitted afghans. Sweet lady. Bad driver. This is the second time we've had to replace her catalytic converter because of 'that ornery curb on Maple Street' that always seems to jump in front of her car on her way back from the craft store.

I slink my arm behind me and grab another spring bolt. I slab some lube on it and work it into the converter. Two bolts left after this one, and then I can go home.

Something rattles from the storeroom. I jerk in the tight space, almost banging into Mrs. Moritz's undercarriage. Mice. Dorsey warned me. I don't usually work this late, so I've never heard them before. "Nothing to be scared of," Dorsey said.

Funny. I've seen things that would scare Dorsey way more than mice.

I reach behind me and fumble for the two remaining bolts. I pinch one between my fingers, work it into one of the threaded slots, and tighten it with the torque wrench.

My friends ask if it's... weird. They always put that pause before 'weird.' Is it... weird to work where my dad died? Do I work here out of... (that pause again) family loyalty?

But it's not loyalty.

See, I'm a good mechanic. Could've worked anywhere. I picked Dorsey's not because of my loyalty. I picked Dorsey's because of my skills. And I don't mean my car skills.

When I was seven, Uncle Frank died. At his wake, everyone cried. Everyone except me. I played checkers in the basement. With Uncle Frank. Just like we used to. A shimmering, flickering version of Uncle Frank.

Uncle Frank was the first of many.

Some people stick around the places they die.

'Haunting' is too strong a word.

I call it 'holding.'

I call them 'holders.'

It doesn't happen all the time. I can go for months, once even more than a year, between holders. But sometimes... sometimes, I see them. Sometimes, I hear them, feel them. Sometimes, I even get flashes of their lives. Moments that were important to them, even if I don't always understand the context. Like that girl in the Muppet Babies T-shirt; when she walked closer to me, I flashed on her, many years ago, sitting in a dirty kitchen, eating licorice. The woman with the scar; she whispered in my ear, and I flashed on her, her face smooth and perfect, crying over a torn letter. The young minister; he fumbled to take my hands in his flickering grasp, and I flashed on his church, watching him clutch his chest and keel over.

I don't know if Dad's a holder. But since I was 15 years old, I've needed him to be. Needed to see him again. Needed to understand why he did what he did. It's why I started working at Dorsey's. The place where he worked. The place where he died. The place where he took his own life.

I reach back and run my hand along the cold concrete floor.

The final bolt is gone.

I swallow hard.

I know better than to hope. Know how unpredictable holdings and holders are. Know I probably just knocked the bolt aside.

I whisper it anyway: "Dad?"

I slowly roll the creeper out and stand. I wipe my greasy hands on my coveralls, more routine than formality. Dad won't care.

There's a rustling in the storeroom. And a faint clinking.

Maybe it's not mice after all.

I edge to the small room, peeking into the doorway. Inside, dead-center, batting around the bolt, is a cat. No. Not a cat. The cat. Nottingham. The tubby gray tabby I snuck into the apartment as a teenager.

The cat flickers, shimmers. It's a holder.

I laugh. This is a first. "What are you doing here, Naughty Boy?" I ask, immediately remembering the nickname.

Head cocked curiously, Nottingham meows at me before rearing back on gray haunches and leaping onto a metal shelf. I watch, amused, as the holder-cat jumps between two shelving units, higher and higher. Nottingham stops at a cardboard box near the top, tail twitching, and turns to me, releasing a pained mew.

"What's in there, Naughty Boy?"

I push over Dorsey's footstool, step up, and pull down the box. Nottingham is back on the ground before I am.

I strip off yellowed tape and open the dusty box. It's one of Dorsey's junk caches. The cat head-butts the box, and I start unpacking items. Metal scraps. Bolts. Lugs.

But that's not all I unpack. I see images, flashes—like the flashes I sometimes see from human holders, but softer, less focused. Dad petting Nottingham as he drives from our house. Dad making Nottingham a cozy bed in this very box. Dad hiding Nottingham under Dorsey's nose all those years ago.

When I get to the bottom of the box, there's something else. Seven somethings, in fact.

Because Nottingham isn't a naughty boy. She's a desperate mama.

Seven shimmering kittens, each of them holders, mew as Nottingham hops inside, nuzzling them. I see a flash of Nottingham giving birth one night, Dad watching over them, nervous but fascinated. He looks excited, like when he used to try to teach me about engines. But also... he's about to cry. I don't think I ever saw him cry when he was alive, but it's like I know that look on him. Like I know him. He holds something in his hands. The vision is fading, so I struggle, concentrate, and I just barely make it out. It's a photo. Him and me. That summer when I was eight and we went to Six Flags. He looks from the photo to the kittens and back to the photo again.

The flash dissolves.

I'm back in the present.

I know if I wanted, I could see more flashes—flashes of what happened to the cats, how they ended up as holders in Dorsey's storeroom.

But I don't want to. Don't need to. Just because something ended—even ended horribly—doesn't mean there wasn't still goodness, still happiness, still gray-fluffball sweetness before that.

Maybe that's enough.

I scurry to Mrs. Moritz's car, grab one of her afghans, and return to the box. The babies knead their tiny paws on Nottingham's belly. I whisper, "Good girl," and lay the afghan around them.

I don't know if they can feel it.

But I sure can.

See John Adams's story "Holding" online at Metaphorosis.
If you liked it, leave a comment. Authors love that!
Remember to subscribe to our e-mail updates so you'll know when new stories are posted.

About the story

I generally write speculative fiction that is humorous, gothic, or some combination of humorous and gothic; I tell people my wheelhouse is "Dark Shadows with space monkeys". On the flip side, when I write non-speculative fiction, I tend to go for more dramatic moments — high-school friendships put to the test, relationships ending, managing through loss, and those moments we'd rather read about on the page than experience in real life.

With "Holding", I wanted to merge these two ideas and write a dramatic piece of spec-fic. I have written several ghost stories before, but never one with quite this tone. To me, the piece has a sadness to it, but still remains hopeful.

The story centers on the idea that sometimes what we think we want isn't what we actually want. I have to quote the Rolling Stones here, because they said it best: "You can't always get what you want, but if you try sometime you find you get what you need". I think those lyrics sum up the story well.

I also wanted to provide an ending that felt satisfying even though it didn't necessarily solve every mystery — perhaps even satisfying-because — it didn't solve every mystery. The main character, Kerry, may not have all her questions answered by the end, but she ultimately finds comfort.

Thanks for reading, and thanks to Metaphorosis for giving me this great opportunity!

A question for the author

Q: What tools do you write with?

A: I'm fairly basic when it comes to writing tools — I arm myself with a laptop, a frequently broken wireless mouse, and a cat who chews on the laptop cord. I've purchased several fancy journals with the sincere intention of writing long-hand, but my hands cramp after a few minutes and I can barely read my own penmanship.

About the author

John Adams (he/him/his) is a short-story, stageplay, and screenplay writer. He enjoys creating robust, offbeat worlds populated with teenage detectives, pelican-people, robo-butlers, cursed cowboys, and bear nuns. When not writing, he produces comedy shows and performs across the U.S. with That's No Movie, a multi-genre improv-comedy team. He lives in the Kansas City area, where he works as a communications professional.

johnamusesnoone.com,@JohnAmusesNoOne

Tower of Mud and Straw II

Yaroslav Barsukov

II. The Adversary

This is part 2 of Yaroslav Barsukov's novella, *Tower of Mud and Straw*. Part 1 ran in September 2020. What has gone before:

Minister Shea Ashcroft refuses the queen's order to gas a crowd of protesters. After riots cripple the capital, he's exiled to Owenbeg, a duchy bordering the kingdom of Duma, to oversee the construction of the biggest anti-airship tower in history. Shea doesn't want the task, but sees it as the only way to reclaim his life.

The duchy serves as a home to Drakiri, refugees of a technologically advanced human-like race.

Once in Owenbeg, Shea is shocked to learn the artisans are using the 'tulips'— anti-gravity devices created by Drakiri, devices from a place in Shea's memories he would rather erase. He considers the 'tulips' to be volatile and dangerous.

The duke of Owenbeg is none too happy about the arrival of an intendant from the capital and orders Patrick, his military counselor, to get rid of him. Shea is saved by the duke's lover, Lena, who turns out to be half-Drakiri; Lena tells him that her race had once built a huge tower similar to the one in Owenbeg, which allowed a *second edifice* to manifest. Drakiri call the second tower the 'Mimic Tower' and believe it to be a portal into a different, frightening dimension. Back then, they managed to destroy their tower and prevent the nightmare from creeping into the world. Shea discounts Lena's story as a children's tale.

Shea has no real allies and only the memory of his dead sister to converse with. The duke's people accidentally slip information that someone has tried to sabotage the construction site; however, after visiting the tower, Shea forms a theory that there were no saboteurs, only artisans meddling with the technology they couldn't begin to understand. After a clash with the duke he manages to get the 'tulips', the anti-gravity devices, removed from the tower.

He's then visited by Brielle, the tower's chief engineer, who reveals her secret: she's made an error in the calculations. The tower's foundation is too small to support its height, and the 'tulips' were the only thing holding the structure together. By insisting on having them removed, Shea has doomed the tower and lost any chance of getting back his life.

1

The hammer fell in an arrhythmic pulse, like an old man's heart, skipping a punch each time the chisel it hit dropped another inch into the device. And each time, the sheath's halves spread wider, the pink glow which seeped along the expanding crease thickened, and the man in the protective mask shrank back.

"It's dangerous, you do realize that," Shea said. "The thing could implode."

Brielle stared, without blinking, in front of her. "Now I understand why you call them 'tulips'. They blossom, don't they?"

They blossom all right, he thought. *They jump seasons while we remain here, in this autumn.*

The wind rose and combed through the crown of the old overgrown oak, hurling a handful of leaves at the Drakiri devices arranged in rows at its foot. *We, too, throw dirt on coffins—only ours don't have pointed ends.* The 'tulips' stood upright, taking aim at the sky. The man with the hammer and the chisel was human, but the two figures frozen beside him were Drakiri—Shea had learned to recognize them by now, the slightly elongated physique, the too-relaxed posture. *None of them would work at the construction site*, Lena had said—apparently, supervising the dismantling of the devices was a different thing.

A strange threesome—with many other such threesomes scattered across the field among the egg-shaped things.

"It's like attending a mass funeral," Shea said.

"Do you want to say a few words, then?"

"Bad time of the year to develop a sense of humor, Brielle. How much longer before *it* crumbles?" It, *and what remains of my life.*

The giant tower was an apparition now, pastel-gray and watery past the fields.

"What, you can't count days anymore?" she asked. "I haven't seen you in a while—when did you last leave your new quarters?"

Shea shrugged. "A week, maybe. I don't know." He glanced at her. "Wait a second—you're judging me, aren't you? As if you weren't drinking yourself."

"I drink just enough to keep my sanity."

"Well, perhaps my sanity requires a higher dosage."

The tulip let out a loud crack, making a flight of black birds disperse from the oak's branches and the man with the hammer start back. The chisel remained lodged in the crease: a knife in a wound.

One of the Drakiri said something in a reassuring tone.

"Do you know what's inside?" Brielle asked.

"No. Ten years ago, we had no method for disassembling them."

"What did you do?"

"Buried them." His thoughts darted to the room with soot stains, but this time didn't stay there: he remembered the cellar underneath the rosewood trapdoor, the memory answering in dull tones as though someone had picked at a scab. He shook his head. "I don't understand why they can't have the Drakiri do the procedure."

"That's the crux of the joke: we have a lighter touch. I heard one of *them* say—"

"We were born to destroy these things."

"—we were born to disassemble them."

The sheath fell apart in eggshell pieces.

Inside, the tulip was almost empty. A thin stem stretched the whole height of the device, swelling with purple that squirmed like air in a heatwave, widening in the middle to form a...

"It's a figure, isn't it?" Shea said, or thought he had.

The contour of a leg, a hint at a hip, maybe an armless torso. Or maybe it was his imagination going wild. The Drakiri who'd spoken earlier produced something resembling a pair of pliers which he fastened, simultaneously, to both ends of the 'silhouette.' He held the pliers while the purple and the quivering died down, then, the stem at arm's length, wandered off to the tree line, to a funeral pile of other thin, long things.

The man in the mask picked up the chisel and moved toward the next tulip.

"And that's how the mundane trumps the beautiful," Shea said. "Let's go. Nothing more to see here."

He turned when he heard a quiet, "I'll fix the tower."

"What? You said the foundation was too small."

"It is. But I did some calculations yesterday—maybe, if we fortify the walls..."

"You don't believe it yourself."

"I'll try fortifying the walls."

"Brielle, listen to me."

"What do you want me to do, Shea?" She leaned toward him, and, through clenched teeth, her breath came out in a miniature cloud. "Sit back and see it crumble? Not even attempt to save the work of my life?"

He took her by the arm. "Think of the builders' safety."

"They're safe, trust me. The strain on structure won't start taking its toll for two months."

"Okay. Okay. Listen, Brielle, I give you—us—two months. Then we turn ourselves in to Queen Daelyn."

He immediately regretted not having phrased it differently—Brielle's anger dissipated the way air leaves a balloon, and, as with the tulip, what remained behind was a vulnerable stem.

"Please don't tell anyone until then, Shea. Please. Don't tell them... of the mistake I've made."

It's not your fault, he wanted to say, *it was probably the time pressure, and nobody is infallible*—but at that moment, Brielle chuckled.

"Look, the asshole's coming."

Through the rows of devices, a tall, hunched figure moved like a tired priest, fed up with performing the final rites.

"Did you know the duke has put him in charge of the disassembling? It's like a penance for all that talk that amounted to nothing, about the saboteurs."

Patrick, the duke's military counselor, strolled toward them, beating the wet out of the flaps of his coat. He stopped in front of Brielle and glanced at her.

"Destroying the devices is a waste of time." He smiled only with his lips. "A pure waste of time and money. Whatever *he* says, the damage to the tower was a result of sabotage."

"Hey, I'm right here," Shea said.

Patrick shifted his gaze to him, and his mouth opened and closed as though the body were looking for the best way to pour out contempt.

"There's a special type of capital swine," he said, "that comes to our lands and shits on them."

"How did Shea shit on *your* land, Patrick?" Brielle sighed. "You're not even originally from Owenbeg."

"And you, you should know better, Brielle. Are you sleeping with him?"

"That's enough," Shea said. "Just because we're standing here and talking, man and woman, you automatically presume that we share a bed?"

But Patrick didn't accept the challenge; he simply shrugged, straightened his coat, walked past them.

Shea turned to look at him. "He sounds depressed more than anything. The duke's displeased with him, right?"

Brielle nodded. "Some important task that Patrick has failed."

The one where he had to dispose of me, probably.

"Besides," she said, "he's been promising to catch the Dumian saboteurs for months."

"There are no saboteurs."

Against the swollen gray sky, Patrick's figure stuck out like a finger, and, with surprise, Shea realized he couldn't bring himself to hate him.

Brielle sighed. "I still have my doubts—and, as you can see, Patrick does, too."

How could he hate the bastard? *Daelyn's power eroded me, the duke's—him. Patrick simply had less substance to begin with.*

"I'm going," Shea said. "If you wish, let's meet at the tavern and discuss our situation."

"Tomorrow?"

"No. The day after. I will be incapacitated tomorrow."

In the new quarters he would no doubt have to vacate soon, Shea opened the wine cabinet and looked at the empty bottles. Tuesday, they were called, Wednesday, Thursday, Friday, Saturday. Tuesday had been his first in years—he'd bought it himself, same as Wednesday; the rest had come in linen sacks a boy from the village carried.

With the Drakiri devices destroyed, the tower's collapse became imminent, and it was time to send for stronger stuff.

2

She appeared at his doorstep clad in a gray hunting suit, and although the brandy's kerosene aftertaste still corroded his mouth, he smiled.

Will you join me?

Sure, sure I will. It was okay. The room wasn't spinning, so the alcohol the boy Daniel had brought must've been thinned with water.

It was only three miles later, halfway between the castle and the forested hillside, that Shea realized how wrong he'd been.

"Are you okay?" Lena's voice came from somewhere to his right.

"Yes. I think so."

His own words echoed as though emerging from the bottom of a huge metal bowl; the world around him, streaming past, adjusting itself to fit the curves and turns of the trail they followed.

"I thought you could use a distraction—Brielle said you haven't left your quarters for a week." Her voice wrapped around him like a scarf snatched and tossed by the wind. "We need to pick up speed. The deer is getting away."

A wave of dizziness washed over Shea. *I think I'm about to fall.* He would fall, Brielle would fall, the tower would fall, his career would give its final death jerk.

The trees ahead parted—from between them, as if responding to his thoughts, the giant tower stared at him, bluish in the haze.

I hate you, he thought, *I hate you*, all the thousand feet of stone and metal, the artillery portals and the embers of the little worlds scattered across the spiral climb, *how I hate it all now.*

Lena stood in the stirrups. "There it is!"

Their prey darted into a clearing fifty feet ahead, a gray curve under a crown of bones.

For a moment, there were only the deer, the tower, and the beautiful woman, clinging to the horse's neck, shouting something into the wind.

Then the deer vanished.

That's it, they must've mixed something into that brandy.

The deer had disappeared like an object tumbling into the eye's blind spot, never to emerge on the other side.

He realized he wasn't imagining things when Lena's horse went mad. It slipped into a wild, erratic dance, the bucks and rears of a rocking toy, shaking its head in a motion that made it appear as if it were wagging its own body.

Lena pulled on the reins.

She needs to dismount. Did he say it out loud? *Lena, Lena, you need to...*

"Get off the horse!"

Of course she didn't listen. She leaned back, pushing against the stirrups, stretching the reins, her horse's mane a dark reflection of the wave of her own hair.

Shea kicked his mare into a gallop.

"Dismount!"

Still, she didn't listen. And when he got close enough to grab her by the arm, shook him off.

"Get off of it!"

Drakiri strength doubly worked against her now: it allowed her to brush Shea off and stressed her horse even further—a product of generations of breeding, it must've preferred a lighter, human touch.

Shea's belly spasmed, and he almost puked.

I need to do something, and fast.

Lena was at least twice as strong as him, true—but he weighed more.

He rammed his shoulder into hers, sending them both to the half-frozen autumn ground.

"Why did you do that?" She pushed him away, and he rolled off her and into the grass. "I would've gotten him under control. I would've calmed him."

"Shhh," he said, pointing to the horse, who dove under an elm's branches and disappeared behind the trees.

"What?"

"I haven't seen a purebred that spooked."

His own mare grazed peacefully nearby.

"Never do that to me." Lena slapped his arm. "Are you drunk?"

"It could've thrown you off and trampled on you. Or your foot could've slid through the stirrup, and it would've dragged you into the woods like a sack."

After a series of long breaths, she said, "Where did the deer go? Did it run back into the trail?"

It vanished, he wanted to say—but now, with the brandy loosening its grip on him, he was no longer sure. He closed his eyes and tried to recall the scene, but the kerosene taste in his mouth kept getting in the way.

"I'm not certain, Lena."

"You were behind me. If it returned to the trail, it should've passed you."

He shook his head.

"So you *are* drunk—how much did you have? Wait, don't tell me. I can't believe I went hunting with you." Staring at the sky, she drew in her knees, suddenly vulnerable. "I saw something. In a flash. Different colors."

"What, rainbows?"

"No. Forget it. I think it was a hallucination—or something like that. I got distracted, and that's when the deer ran away."

Lena rolled onto her side and started to get up, only to fall back, this time on top of Shea.

"Damn it." She laughed. "My hip hurts like hell, I must've pulled a muscle."

"You're the only woman I know," he said, "who would find it funny."

She smelled of bonfire and tasted of strawberries.

"What are you doing?" she asked.

"I'm sorry. I'll never do that again."

"I told you to never knock me off the horse. I didn't tell you not to do what you were doing right now—rather, I posed a simple question."

When their mouths separated again, he said, "You're the most beautiful... anything I've seen in my life."

"And you reek of brandy."

And then all the other pieces of the puzzle faded—the deer, the tower, the vanishing—leaving only the wave of black hair, the eyes, the lips, and the body pressed against his.

3

They rode his mare back to the castle—*she* rode, Shea sitting behind—and slipped into his quarters the way a pair of kids slip out of the house to play a dangerous game.

The sex was violent. She didn't let him kiss her anymore or even help her undress—they tore their clothes off like two fighters at separate corners of the ring, after which she pushed him on his back and thrust her hips into his.

It was a voyeuristic but at the same time strangely intimate experience—the sense of pleasure *being done* to his body, and yet he answered every push, their gazes locked. She closed her eyes only in the end, when something exploded in them both.

Later, lying on her side with her back to him, she said, "I'm not that way. I'm not that way, Shea."

Euphoria sliding into an echo, he studied the *sotto in sù* ceiling, the badly painted plump angel extending an olive branch, in twilight, to a bewildered-looking hunter. He could've asked her to elaborate, but what good would it do? She wasn't like that in the sense that sex with her was normally tender? Or she wasn't likely to sleep with someone while being the lover of another?

He traced with his finger the curve of her hip, and bitterness rose in him—at her, at the duke, at himself: he thought how he envied that stupid angel, how he wished he could live in that painting, too, in the season of sunsets, forever postponing the minute the light would disappear.

She stood, picked up her pants, and peeked inside them. "I think I've got a dandelion in there somewhere."

"You've got one in your hair, too. Let me help you."

"Thanks, I can manage."

She strolled to the wine cabinet; opened it. "You didn't drink all those bottles alone, did you, Shea?"

There would have been something deeply wrong with lying to a woman he'd just slept with. "The boy Daniel has been supplying me."

"Why?"

"Why what—why is he supplying me or why am I drinking alone?"

"Why are you drinking."

Words pushed at his throat, and, unable to contain them, he rose on his elbow and said, "I've destroyed the tower, Lena. Well, not literally, but I helped ruin it. The queen sent me here to make sure it gets built, and I failed. Ruined myself in the process."

Her face was an emotionless mask when she turned to him. "I beg your pardon?"

"The tower will crumble within two months."

And then the mask melted, sunset reverted to dawn: she jumped onto the bed to squeeze him in an embrace. She didn't hold back.

"You're going... to crush... me."

"Sorry."

He sucked in air, her face coming into focus, reddened cheeks, a wide smile—and jealousy prickled him, the fact that, minutes after they'd had sex, something else was the source of that unfiltered joy.

"I had no idea you hated the tower that much."

She squinted at him. "But I showed you the book. I thought that was the reason..."

"It was a very vivid tale, Lena, but no. I came here, I saw problems. I believed I could fix everything, like that." He snapped his fingers. "I didn't take time to truly understand what was happening."

"You mistook me for someone else—I don't read tales, Shea. Problems—I presume Brielle or one of her engineers made an error?"

"It's not my place to tell you."

Relief from admitting everything came and went, leaving in its wake the beginning of the end: until now, he realized, he'd allowed some vestigial hope to linger at the back of his mind. Perhaps he'd waited for a miracle to happen, or for Brielle to find a solution. Now, he'd cast his last stone into the pond and let it drown.

But was that the last stone? a voice whispered in his mind. *Is there a solution, perhaps?*

Lena's smile shrank, but didn't disappear. "I realize it's hard for you, but I can't help myself. I'm happy."

She embraced him again, this time carefully, the way a mother would a child.

He patted her on the back. "I'm sorry that I can't feel the same."

She let him go, stood, and picked up her shirt. "What'll happen to you?"

"Do you care?"

A pause, and then a plain, "Yes."

"Daelyn will either imprison me or send me to my family estate. Permanently."

"Then I'm sorry, too. But I want you to know you've done good. You may not believe in the Mimic Tower, but you must believe in something, no? There are many things in this world we can't explain."

Shea thought back to the deer and said, "For example?"

"Did I tell you why Drakiri won't let strangers into their home?"

"Because most strangers are assholes?"

"Because we don't know where our true home is."

"Last time I checked your homeland was in Pangania—or do you mean it metaphorically?"

"Pangania was a waystation, nothing more."

"So Owenbeg is your *second* asylum? Where are you from then, originally?"

"We have no records of where we really came from, only that we arrived from elsewhere, and letting a new person under your roof is seen, traditionally, like sharing this—a vulnerability."

"You people possess too vivid a shared imagination." When she placed her hand on the doorknob, he said, "I don't want this to be the last time."

"Then start by cleaning out your wine cabinet." She took a step into the corridor and paused. "I'll be leaving Owenbeg sometime in the future. You asked if I care? Here's the real answer: you could join me—if your queen doesn't put you under lock and key."

He remembered the roundabout they'd ridden in the settlement, the world's colors spinning around them, the birds, the smells of autumn.

"I think I'm falling in love with you."

"Be careful, then," she said and closed the door behind her.

Dear sis, my beautiful flower—I think I'll stay quiet for a while. I want to be quiet. Too much has happened, and I don't think I've got the strength to carry on even our imaginary conversations. Don't be mad at me (I know you can't, the dead are the only ones in this world who are at peace), and I swear I'll talk to you again. I'll become whole again.

Just not now.

4

Shea entered the tavern. Behind the counter, the barkeep poured the last drops of the summer into a beer jug—he must've intended to drink it himself, because the establishment stood otherwise empty save for Shea, a decrepit drunk whistling a snore on the bench next to the coat hanger, and Brielle.

She sat in the corner by a lattice window. The lozenges were red in the center, and the sun filtered through that spot, painting a warm shape on the back of her palms lying on the table. It occurred to Shea how bad it looked, the color of blood on her hands.

He lowered himself opposite. "How are you doing?"

Brielle kept silent.

"I would talk about the weather, but it's agonizingly unremarkable today."

"Cut it." She squinted at him, and it was only then that Shea noticed she had no drink.

"What's going on, Brielle?"

She smiled with only her lips. "Why don't *you* tell me?"

"What about?"

"You promised me two months."

The barkeep swung back his head and poured in the beer.

"I promised *us* two months."

She leaned forward. "You slept with Lena yesterday." *Shit.* "I noticed by accident," she said. "I saw her exit your quarters."

"Has anybody else seen her?"

"One witness isn't enough for you? Do the math, Shea—what happens if I slip a word or two to the duke?"

As though having fulfilled his function, the barkeep lowered the jug on the counter. The drunk stopped snoring, and silence stretched across the hall, too thin, too ready to pop.

"What? Why would you do that? Brielle, what's happening?" He reached for her hand, but she pulled it back.

And, as if to compensate for the loss of intimacy, she leaned forward even closer. "You've betrayed me, that's what's happening."

"Betrayed you by what, by sleeping with Lena?" *She had a romantic affection for him*, it dawned on Shea, and cold beaded his forehead. How the hell hadn't he noticed it before? Two sharing a secret, only able to confide in one another, a fertile ground for all kinds of feelings...

He cleared his throat. "Listen, I find you attractive, too... But, please don't take it the wrong way, our meetings were only that, meetings—"

Brielle started back like a mechanical toy, studied him with wide-open eyes—and then burst into laughter. The drunk by the coat hanger jolted and sat straight.

"What on Earth are you on about, Shea? I couldn't care less if you found me attractive."

"But I thought you said—"

"I said you have a secret and I know it, just as you know mine. So if you're planning to report everything—"

"Report? To whom?"

She raised her finger, and he looked where she pointed. Through the window, past the triangle rooftops, the castle hill was dark at the base and evening-gold at the top where the walls rose.

"Listen, I give up," Shea said. "I give up. I don't want to play this game anymore. Just say whatever you have to say."

"Look at Kayleigh's wing."

Oh my, she's right, she's absolutely right. The abandoned wing should've been dead, but it wasn't. Shea's old balcony and his old windows—one of them stood open, and he thought he saw a movement behind it.

Brielle said, "Is he here to double-check or to arrest me?"

"He who?"

"You tell me. Another guy from the capital, judging by the accent. Did you tell him all about my mistake? How Brielle screwed up basic calculations?"

Why haven't I seen him? he wanted to ask—but, of course, he already knew the answer. The person he'd seen the most of these days was the village boy with linen sacks full of booze.

"I bumped into him right after the decommissioning," Brielle said. "He was talking to Patrick. Wears black gloves."

...walking into a pocket-size theater, eight or nine rows, six of them empty, lowering himself next to a slender man in black gloves, and—'consider this an opportunity'...

"I haven't reported anything to anyone, Brielle. But I may know the guy. I used to know him."

"I don't believe you."

"You shouldn't. I realize how it looks—I wouldn't believe myself, either."

"If he isn't here because of you, then why?"

"Of that, I've absolutely no idea."

5

The picture carried an almost nostalgic air, the narrow path between the battlements a rivulet of stone flowing from the mass of the old castle. Almost. After all, they'd tried to kill him there, Patrick and the duke—but still, for Shea, the memory of seeing Kayleigh's wing for the first time interlocked with the image of the tower, the feeling of anticipation, the first sign of promise since the moment he'd traded his career for the little pink dress in the airship's shadow.

And now he'd done the same again: destroyed whatever he'd had left on principle.

He squinted: someone was there, at the far end of the path. In darkness, the figure was a writhing grub—he couldn't even guess the height. He dove back under the archway and waited.

The figure assumed form and Patrick shot past him, eyes straight ahead.

What the hell is the duke's military counselor doing in Kayleigh's wing? Consorting with the new tenant?

He held still until the steps died down. Then he followed the narrow path.

The tower's furnace through the embrasures, the staircase leading downward, the corridor with the gas lamps. He hesitated— after all, he had no plan for what would come next—and knocked on the door.

"Come in, Ashcroft," said the familiar voice.

Shea pushed on the doorknob and entered his old room. "How did you know it was me?"

"Easy. You don't knock the way the majordomo knocks—apart from her, two people have reasons to see me at this hour, and one of them just left."

"Hello, Aidan."

It was really him—he stood at the window, looking at something outside, thin, black-gloved fingers between the curtains that dripped evening onto the floor.

"Come in, come in, Shea. Great to see you. Have a drink—the carafe's in the bedroom."

He turned and smiled the way people smile who use courtesy as a tool—earnest at a first glance, but with a whiff of professionalism. Gray eyes scurried across Shea like two spiders, assessing. "Your timing's impeccable—although I honestly can't tell if it's by design. Were you following Patrick?"

Shea kept silent. Slender, taller than average but not too tall, with pleasant features but not beautiful enough to stand out in the crowd, the only distinguishing thing about Aidan was his black gloves. He was someone you felt safe to confess to. Probably would've made a fine priest, too.

"Aren't you going to have that drink?"

"I think I've had enough for today," Shea said.

"Oh yes, I've heard, I've heard."

"You've heard—have you been spying on me?"

The smile retracted halfway, vacating the eyes. "I really hope that's a rhetorical question.

"This place," he continued, "it's beautiful, sure, but it lacks finesse. You can't spy on people—you actually struggle to filter out all the irrelevant parts of their life stories. Why don't you take a sit?"

"Why don't you tell me what Patrick was doing here?"

"Telling me he was going to Duma."

"To Duma—why?"

Aidan pursed his lips in an amused manner. "Because I sent him there?"

"Sent him?"

"Oh, easy. I told him the saboteurs he was looking for were holding a rendezvous in Poltava an hour from now. You know, the village past the border."

Of course. Patrick still believed Duma was behind those gaping mouths in the tower's walls.

"It was poor sportsmanship. I didn't even need to plant evidence. I just mentioned to him the saboteurs would be in Poltava, and he immediately took off."

"What do you want with him?"

Aidan gave him a faraway look, like a chess player who doesn't quite see his opponent because part of him is inside his next move. "We must get rid of him, I'm afraid."

"Are you crazy? For heaven's sake—what's up with people today? I'm not killing anybody, Aidan."

"Then Patrick will kill you."

"He's already tried, and I don't think he would go for it again."

"And that's where you're in error. I *do* know he'd paid someone to assassinate you—but that was a brute from the village, and now he's hired a professional. He's meeting him in two days to pay him off."

"The duke—"

"This time, Patrick isn't acting on the duke's orders. He's *keen*. He wants to make up for his mistake, and you've provided him with the perfect opportunity—I'll bet good money the coroner's report would say, 'died in a state of severe inebriation from choking on his own vomit'."

"I'm not going to kill him," Shea said.

"Then you have two choices: die or leave Patrick to me."

"Why are you doing this? I think *you* think you're helping me —but why?"

Aidan lowered himself into a chair and, with a hint at a smile, nodded toward a couch. "Do take a sit."

"Tell me."

"Let's make a deal, shall we? You ride with me to Poltava, I tell you why I'm here."

"I am not going to kill Patrick."

"Then, I guess we'll see what happens when we get there."

Shea sat. "What *would* happen is, there would be no blood. I'd reason with him. Convince him I'm no threat."

Aidan studied him again. "Still an idealist. Perhaps it's a weakness. Perhaps I've backed the wrong horse."

"Backed the...?"

"I'll explain in an hour, at Poltava."

"Aren't you afraid of causing a diplomatic incident?"

"It's a puny border village. Worst case, we bump into a patrol —and remember, I speak the language, I know how they think."

"That's right—you're Dumish, correct? You mask your accent so well, I forgot that."

"Therein lies the difference between us," Aidan said quietly. "After a decade at the Red Hill, I still don't have the luxury of forgetting. But I digress. We'll tell the sentries we were inebriated and took the wrong road. With you in your current state, we won't even need to do a lot of convincing. I'm more concerned about the goons Patrick will bring with him."

Now there are goons. But a voice inside reminded Shea that Aidan was right. The military counselor *had* tried to kill him. *Why did I assume Patrick would simply accept his failure? Was it the same arrogance that drove me to convince the duke to get rid of the Drakiri devices?*

The room submerged in silence while a thrush somewhere in the courtyard drummed out the minutes.

"Okay," Shea said. "I'll go. But remember: no blood."

"Let's hope Patrick agrees."

At the stables, Aidan simply nodded to the keeper, a fellow with a beard that seemed to have picked up rust from the gate. "Hullo, James."

The man produced a smile so wide one could count all his remaining teeth.

"Just how long have you been here?" Shea whispered.

"For a week," Aidan said. "I found out you'd made friends, and had to work fast."

He selected two horses, a chestnut mare and a beautiful pitch-black stallion.

"This one is the duke's. The name's Onyx. I'm quite fond of him."

6

They followed a creek down the plain, meager hillside covered in bush's bristle to their left, forest to the right. The water was glass, reflecting little but the clean cider sky and the cloud front to the west.

"It's going to rain soon," Shea said. "How do we evade the border sentries?"

"Our friend Patrick is a military counselor, he knows the patrol patterns. We just have to follow him." A wave of the black glove, sweeping three smudged auburn spots at the horizon. Horses. "The difficulty, actually, lies in not being noticed *by them*— at least not until we're deep enough into Duma territory."

"Were you planning on killing him there?"

"Of course. Duma would dispose of the bodies to avoid a diplomatic incident. They'd cover it up for us, Shea." He half-turned in the saddle and produced a smile. "I'm still planning it, you know."

"No. I'll talk to him."

"That would be putting too much faith into your own persuasive abilities. See that you don't learn it the hard way."

The clouds blinked, grunted, prompting a neigh from Shea's mare.

"Easy, girl," He patted her on the neck.

The mare neighed again.

"Calm your animal down, Shea. You don't want them to notice us."

"Easy, girl, easy. There's nothing to be afraid of." *Yet.*

Shea clung to the black mane and shot a glance back: ten miles away now, against the first pale stars, the tower looked like its twin from Lena's folio: no longer a part of the sky but an extension of the earth, as though something immense had tried to get free and pulled up the crust in the process.

He turned and concentrated on what lay ahead.

Aware now of his mare's tendency to voice its discontent, they covered the last quarter mile to Poltava on foot.

First to emerge from the darkness was a rundown fence with three chestnut horses tied to it. Then came a dragon, and another one, and another, wooden figurines straddling the roofs' ridges—or were those logs someone had pulled from a bonfire?

How had the duke put it? See what they've done to the place, see it for yourself. Above Shea's head, thunder rolled like a roly-poly, left to right, right to left, and the rain started, abruptly and in full force, making the houses' burns seem fresh.

For all the talk of Poltava, it was a tiny village, no more than fifty homes—and half of them were coal husks, death on one side of the main street, life on the other.

"Why on earth won't they rebuild those?" Shea said.

"There's a decree prohibiting that."

"Why?"

"So that people will remember."

"My knowledge of history is rusty, but wasn't it Duma that massacred this place?"

Aidan sighed. "This depends on whose account you're inclined to believe."

"The duke thinks so."

"Then it must be true, right? If the duke thinks so."

On the live side, behind the rain torrents, fireflies of windows smoldered.

Shea said, "Where do you suppose Patrick went?"

"Look, Patrick does what Patrick does. He arrives. He intends to find the saboteurs, so what's his best move? To interrogate some locals. They tell him, of course, that they haven't heard of any secret congregation—which is the honest-to-goodness truth. But, knowing Patrick..."

"He would presume they're sheltering the criminals."

"And his next step...?"

"Obviously, to search the houses."

"One, two, three, four." Aidan waved his gloved index finger theatrically, and on the count of four, a door in the middle of the street flew open, letting warm light into the rain's monochrome. Three men stepped outside.

Aidan brushed his wet hair from his forehead. "Patrick! Patrick!"

The tallest silhouette turned like a puppet in a shadow theatre.

"We're here, Patrick."

There was a moment of chaos, voices coughing and barking. Then the figures began toward them.

There it goes. Shea wiped the water from his face. He should've felt adrenaline, revenge's foretaste—but it was all *unclean*, the lead-pregnant clouds, the half-burnt village, even ambushing the man who'd tried to kill him.

"Aidan!" Patrick called out from the rain. "What are you doing here?"

"What does it look like?"

Was he *enjoying it*?

The duke's counselor stopped a few feet away, gray threads stitching the air and turning his face into a featureless mask. Another thing was tangible, though, and crude: the heavy crossbow the fellow to Patrick's left held at the ready.

"Hello, Ashcroft." The voice was featureless, too. "It looks like a setup to me."

Aidan smiled. "We need to talk."

"So, who has whom on the leash? Ashcroft you, or you Ashcroft? I should've known better than to trust a Dumian."

Aidan's smile morphed into a frown—but only for a second. "Nothing wrong with having regrets, Patrick."

"I don't have *regrets*—in case you haven't noticed, there's an arbalest pointed at your smug face."

"For how long, is the question."

Without saying a word, the man with the crossbow stepped through the rain, walked over an invisible line, and froze next to Aidan.

"Colm, what the hell are you doing?"

Aidan whistled. "Oh, the sweet power of gold."

"You're all dead—you too, Colm." Despite his words, Patrick took a step back. "You're still with me, Duane?"

The fellow he'd called Duane visibly hesitated, shifting his weight from one leg to another.

"Duane?"

At that moment, on an impulse, as though observing himself from the outside, Shea said, "Duane isn't an idiot. He knows how unpleasant an injury—any injury—would make his way back to the border."

Did I really say that?

"Duane!"

"Your choice, Duane," Aidan said.

The man shrunk his head into his shoulders, lurched forward. Hurried past them. In a second, his stride went from andante to allegro: he broke into a run.

"Now we can talk odds."

"What Ashcroft said about the injuries—the same applies to you. I don't do surrender."

The rain turned into a drizzle, as abruptly as it had started, revealing Patrick's face, the face of a sad spaniel, the slightly hunched shoulders, bony legs. For the first time, Shea saw him, really saw him.

"I won't hurt you, Patrick."

"Then why are you here?"

"I'm not a threat. I've no idea why you haven't understood it by now. If it's your position at the duke's court you fear for, don't— I couldn't care less."

Patrick studied him and smiled with the corners of his mouth. "You know what I hate the most about you? Your self-righteousness. You capital types, you're infallible, aren't you?"

If only you knew, Shea thought, *if only…*

"You do realize, Ashcroft, that you've said goodbye to your own honor? I want to hear you rationalize this from your moral high ground, luring a man into a trap, bribing his companions."

"*Companion*," said Aidan. "I've only bribed Colm here."

"I'm talking to the intendant guy. How do you rationalize that?"

"How do you rationalize trying to kill me?" Shea asked.

Something changed in Patrick: a wave traveled from his feet through his body, straightening the back, unfurling the shoulders, pushing forward the jaw. "Because you deserve it. You all do. Every single one of you at the Red Hill. You live off of us, and when you make a mistake—no, even when you disregard a direct order from a ruling monarch—you don't really go away, do you? You get another assignment. You come to issue orders to *us*."

"It's your own choice to—" Aidan began.

"And you're how old, Ashcroft—thirty-five?" Patrick squinted. "I'm almost fifty—I've served the duke for the most of my life. I make one mistake, one tiny mistake with you, and that's it."

"You're talking about *my* life here," Shea said.

"*One* mistake. And he tells me he's already preparing a replacement."

The honeycombs of the palace towers, the guy in the orange jacket jumping around the theater stage. *I understand the poor bastard. The man who tried to assassinate me, I know how he feels.* "I didn't choose to come. If I could unburden you—"

"Fuck off!" Patrick spat on the ground. "I didn't get the second chance you got—and I haven't even disobeyed the duke. You're—"

"I'm sorry. Not about the things you've done, but about your situation."

"—bastards. I would choke you all at the Red Hill if I could, even the children, even the children."

He wasn't lying, Shea thought, and it wasn't a hyperbole. Patrick was too simple to put up a facade, and—this much had been clear from their first conversation during the 'reception', back then, in the yellow room—he possessed a large capacity for hatred. *Who knows what his story was; abused as a child? his peers didn't like him enough?*—but there he stood, in his current state, hating himself and, by extension, the universe.

And sometimes, the universe obliged hate with a target.

"Hand me the crossbow," Shea said to the guy—what was his name? Colm?

The black glove patted him on the shoulder. "Glad to see you've finally come to your senses."

Shea raised the weapon and aimed it at Patrick's face. "Walk."

"What?"

"Walk. Turn around and walk. Down the street, to the end of it, out of my sight."

Patrick pursed his lips. Took a few steps backward. Turned.

As he moved away—from them and from the border—the sky cleared up, the stars brighter and closer now. Under their light, the tall figure receded between the mangled houses and the whole ones. He glanced back only once, at the very end of the street, the hunched shoulders, the spaniel face, barely discernable now.

Then he disappeared into a foreign land.

"This was a mistake. You're banking too much on patrols stumbling upon him," Aidan said. "My decision to support you—"

"What the hell do you mean?" Shea hurled the crossbow into the mud. "What are you talking about? Tell me at last why you're here."

"Let Colm go."

"I don't care—he can go."

Without a word, the man who'd betrayed Patrick turned and left.

"I'm here because you have the keys to my future."

Shea chuckled. Somewhere in his belly, laughter uncurled, growing, working its way up. "What future? Look at me."

"I'm looking. I—"

"Look at me!" He shook his hands, palms up. "What future? Where? I've been exiled. Reduced to nothing."

"You still think of this as an *exile*? Did you not hear anything I said to you back then, at the theater?"

"*Consider this a wonderful opportunity*—oh yes, what a mockery."

"Mockery? Listen, Daelyn has sent three people to the provinces. The intendancy system is brand new. She wants to see which one of you can control the local lords better."

The tingles crawled up to his throat, making Shea giggle.

Aidan scowled. "What's wrong with you? Owenbeg's the most important assignment of the three, for obvious reasons. The tower. Queen was impressed with your defiance, heaven knows why, when you spared those protesters. I guess the last time someone defied her was decades ago. Hey, are you listening? Do you understand what I'm saying to you? Daelyn is grooming her potential successors."

Laughter bent Shea in two, his knees sinking into the brown mash.

"What in the... We don't have time for this, Shea. I'm here to help you."

He managed to slip a word between bursts: "Why?"

"Damn it, stand up. Because, to quote you from a minute ago —look at me. I'm Duma. I'll always remain Duma. Remember what Patrick just said, that one should never trust a Dumian? Remember what you yourself said about my accent? I'm an émigré, and that's my ceiling. But with you, I'll rise. *We'll* rise. We've taken care of Patrick. We'll take care of the duke, if needed. We just need to get the bloody tower done."

And then the dam broke, everything Shea had been trying to lock away burst free, poured out of him in a soup of sobs and laughter.

"Have you gone mad? Stand up!"

"I can't." Shea stared at his palms. "I can't. I've destroyed it."

There is a solution, a voice whispered in his mind. The solution came clearly. It lay in the part of his past he'd tried his best to bury, in the room with soot stains and in the abandoned cellar underneath the rosewood trapdoor. *No*, he thought, trying to block out the image.

"Destroyed what, damn it? Destroyed what?"

"The tower." He raised his eyes at Aidan. "It was held together by the Drakiri devices. I had them taken out."

"What? Hey, hey, listen to me. Shea? Listen to me! Whatever you've done to the tower, you need to put it back together, do you understand? Do you understand? Do you realize what depends on it?"

"I can't. The duke destroyed the devices."

But you know the solution, the voice whispered, and in his mind's eye, the rosewood trapdoor opened and he stepped into the cellar filled with purple glow, filled with objects he thought of as 'tulips' because someone else, someone he used to know had called them that, in the cellar beneath the ruined workshop, beneath the room with soot stains.

No, he thought, *no, I won't return there, I won't*—but deep inside, a part of him that had been weighing the possibilities considered the scales.

And he knew in whose favor they were tipped.

7

The girl had opened the door for him, and the dance hall's golden lights momentarily blinded him.

Shea didn't know her name—she was, after all, just an attendant—but to him, she'd been all the gloss of the capital: blond hair coiled into an elaborate braid, kohl-lined almond eyes, naked forearms.

"First night at the Red Hill?" She gave him a perfect smile.

"Is it that obvious?" he said and added, clumsily, "It's all I've ever dreamt of."

"You'll get used to it. Don't worry—everyone does. You'll be fine."

He'd never learned her name, never seen her again—but that moment stayed with him when she'd patted him on the shoulder, nudging him into the hall, toward the golden lights, toward all the beautiful people swirling in a waltz.

At the rain-whipped street, on his knees, he remembered the kohl-lined eyes which looked at him, as if saying: *you could have it all back. You could have it all, and more.*

See Yaroslav Barsukov's story "Tower of Mud and Straw II: The Adversary" online at Metaphorosis.
If you liked it, leave a comment. Authors love that!
Remember to subscribe to our e-mail updates so you'll know when new stories are posted.

November

Madam Savva's Magical Emporium

James Rumpel

There'd been a time, a couple of years ago, that Bobby's Diner would be jam-packed during the noon hour. Over half the customers would be cops, like me, grabbing a quick bite before heading back to their beat. That wasn't true any longer. On this rainy Friday, April 13th, the place was nearly empty. The counter only had one customer and that was Creepy Charlie, who always spent hours nursing a single cup of joe. All but three of the booths and tables were empty. The place was so deserted that no one minded when Archie Crumpfeld shouted to me from his table.

"So, Rheinhart, I'm surprised to see you here. Someone with your poor arrest standing can't afford to take any sort of break."

What he said was pretty much true. Since the municipal budget cuts had gutted the police department, the captain had started using an arrest quota. Any cop who didn't make the required number of arrests per month would likely find themselves laid off. Dozens of officers had been let go in the last year.

I'd been having a tough time myself lately. Not many cases broke my way, and when they did, other cops stepped in and made the arrests, stealing the credit. The captain's quota brought out the worst in many of my coworkers. It had gotten so bad that some were even falsifying evidence or planting drugs on innocent civilians. I'd never let myself do anything that unethical.

Of course, I couldn't give Crumpfeld the satisfaction of agreeing with him. "I'm doing just fine," was my reply.

"That's not what the tote board in the precinct says. According to that, you've only given a ticket to a jaywalker and nabbed a guy for removing the tag from a mattress."

"You're wrong," I replied. And he was. I hadn't arrested the tag remover. It turned out he had permission from the manufacturer.

"Last night," continued Archie, "I came close to catching the gang that's been doing the break-ins along Main Street. I would have had them if I didn't have to stop for an old woman crossing the street. Somehow, I lost their truck in traffic."

"Yeah, I heard about your near success from Bob Harris. He was telling everyone in the precinct that you stole his info and tried to jump his arrest. Harris was pretty mad."

"Hey, I'm just doing my job," said Crumpfeld. "I've got a wife and kids to support."

I just shrugged, not in the mood to talk with Archie any longer. I hoped he wouldn't be the one to finally capture the Main Street Robbers. For months, no one had been able to crack that case. Every time someone got close, the thieves would somehow manage to get away. There were even a few strange theories floating around that the gang was using some kind of magic, but I had a hard time believing that. Whoever did solve the case would get on the Captain's good side. That officer wouldn't have to worry about layoffs for a long time.

Archie kept talking, but I had turned my attention to Zelda, my waitress, as she brought me a fresh cup of coffee. She set down the cup and winked at me. We had been doing a little harmless flirting ever since she started working for Bobby a few months ago.

"Here you go, hon," she said, with a smile. She was beautiful, as always, even wearing the old-fashioned uniform Bobby made his waitresses use. Her hair was pulled back in a tight bun.

"So, how's your mother doing?" I asked.

"Thanks for asking. She's doing better. I think I'm going to have her keep staying with me, though. She just can't handle her big drafty house. It'll be good for her if I take care of her for a while." She grabbed a strand of loose hair and tucked it behind her right ear.

"What's with the hoop earrings?" I asked. "Don't you always wear those little ruby studs?"

Zelda laughed, "Boy Harry, you pay close attention to what I wear."

"No," I lied. "It's just that the ones you're wearing now don't bring out the color in your cheeks." I immediately regretted how stupid that must have sounded.

She didn't embarrass me, she just grinned and whispered, "Don't let Crumpfeld get you down. He's just a big mouth. So, you've hit a bad streak. Things will turn around."

Before I could thank her for the coffee and the support, Archie's gruff voice interrupted our moment.

"Hey, Zelda. I'd like some more coffee too."

Zelda turned toward Archie's table, her face redder than the ruby earrings she normally wore.

"You'll get yours soon enough, Officer Crumpfeld. Some things are more important than making an arrest. Harry cares about people." She turned and headed back to the kitchen.

A little surprised by her outburst, I watched her as she walked away. I sipped my coffee, enjoying the embarrassed look on Crumpfeld's face out of the corner of my eye.

I was taking another drink when my radio started beeping. I could hear Charlie's going off too. There was a local call coming in. Whoever took the call first would get to handle the situation and, maybe, get an arrest to put on the precinct tote board.

Panicking, I realized that my radio was still in my jacket, on a hook by the front door. I stood, fumbling with my wallet as I tried to pull out some cash to leave on the table. I could see Charlie's radio on the chair across from him. There was no way I was going to get to my radio before he got to his.

That is, until Charlie's arm knocked into the pot of hot coffee Zelda had just brought to him. She dropped the pot and coffee spilled all over his pants. He jumped to his feet, shrieking and trying to get the burning hot coffee off his legs.

Zelda, who was wiping off the table, smiled at me as I ran to my jacket.

I was already talking to the dispatcher when I squeezed past an old lady standing in the doorway, shaking rain from her open umbrella.

The call sent me to investigate a break-in at 1313B Gretel Avenue. By the time I got to the place, the rain had stopped. I sidestepped a couple of puddles on my way to the door of a Victorian brick home. The house was old and badly in need of repair. Most of the bricks were dirt-covered and cracked. Many of the roof's shingles were missing, making it look like a deformed checkerboard. Black shutters covered all the windows. To my surprise, the house number was 1313A. I looked for another entrance, and eventually noticed a small garden shed in the backyard with 1313B painted over the doorway.

It seemed odd for a tiny shed to have an address, let alone be a crime scene, but I had a job to do. I knocked on the door.

I had barely touched the wood when the door opened inward, creaking loudly. There was no one there except for a fat black cat. Staring in disbelief, I stepped into a large foyer that couldn't possibly have fit in the shed. The cat stopped after a few feet and looked back at me.

What was going on here? The place was way too large on the inside. The cat walked through an open interior doorway. The words MADAM SAVVA'S MAGICAL EMPORIUM glowed above the entrance. That couldn't mean actual magic, could it? I took another look around the foyer, took a deep breath, and followed the cat.

Past the doorway, I found myself face to face with a middle-aged woman wearing a black dress. The cat was nowhere to be seen.

"Thank you for coming so quickly. I am Madam Savva," she said. As I watched, she seemed to grow four or five inches taller and her hair changed from gray to red. She was now wearing a blue pantsuit.

I put my hand on a desk to steady myself, and stood there with my mouth wide open.

"I don't mean to scare you. I know you haven't been exposed to much magic. Please accept my apologies. I was in the middle of testing a transformation potion when you knocked on the door."

I had never believed the stories of magic users in the city. It always seemed too weird to be true. But now, seeing a woman transforming before my eyes, I couldn't help but accept the idea, much as I disliked it. I took another deep breath and tried to act normal.

"So, magic is real?" I asked, hoping the woman would tell me it was all some sort of parlor trick.

"Oh, very much so," replied the woman, now much shorter and with jet black, shoulder-length hair. "There are quite a few adepts living in the city. We try to keep as low a profile as possible. That's why this place is hidden in a shed and why I make the main house look so run down. We only make our presence known on rare and very important occasions. I think the last time I spoke about magic to non-adepts was at Woodstock, not that any of them would remember."

I still didn't know if I could accept what the woman was claiming. "I've been working the beat in this city for ten years. I would have met other witches by now."

Madam Savva's smile disappeared for a brief moment. "We prefer to be called adepts." The pleasant smile returned as quickly as it had left. "You have probably met many of us. Most adepts lead simple lives and work common, everyday jobs. They just happen to have the ability to use a little magic now and then."

"Most?" I asked.

"Well, yes," she answered. Her appearance had continued to shift throughout our conversation. At this moment she was a teenage girl with braces. "Some of us are more powerful," she continued, "and there are a few who use their skills in, shall I say, less acceptable ways."

"You mean to commit crimes?" My mind was racing. Not only was I trying to come to grips with the reality of magic, but I was also beginning to form a theory about how the Main Street Robbers consistently got away.

Madam Savva nodded. "Yes, that's why I have asked for your help. There's been a robbery." She spread her arms wide, showing me the room. "You see, this is my shop. I procure and sell all sorts of magical items. Some are very powerful and very dangerous. That's why many of my products have a ten-day waiting period."

I examined the room. The place was jam-packed with stacks upon stacks of all sorts of junk. Chests and boxes filled dozens of shelves. An entire corner was filled with cloaks and gowns. Each article of clothing floated as if hung on an invisible hanger. Another section of the room was filled with all styles of furniture; antique tables, modern lounge chairs, and large wardrobes were tightly packed together. An immense bookshelf filled the far wall. There had to be thousands of leather-bound books and dog-eared paperbacks on the shelves. The room was an utter mess, but an impressive mess.

I wondered if anything had actually been stolen. Maybe it was simply misplaced. It was hard to imagine anyone being able to keep track of everything in this place.

Whatever was going on, I needed to try and solve this case. "Well, let me get a full report from you. Let's sit down and discuss what happened." I walked over to a fancy dining set and took an old book off one of the chairs, making room to sit down.

"Oh, you don't want to sit there," she said. "You see that's a magic table. Anyone who sits in it becomes completely satisfied with their location and never wants to leave. It's called a Table of Contents." For a second, she looked confused.

"Okay, well how about that one?" I gestured toward a simple wooden table.

"No, you don't want to sit there either. If you sit there, you will be transported to some other time. The table will send you to a different era."

"That's amazing; a table that lets you travel through time. What do you call it?"

Madam Savva seemed to be fighting an internal struggle. She appeared to not want to answer me, but she did. "It's a Periodic Table." She shook her head as if she were upset with herself.

"Well, is there anywhere we can sit?" I asked.

"Definitely not the Lazy Boy." Without another word, Madam Savva walked over to a desk and pulled a handful of purple and pink confetti from a drawer. She tossed the tiny papers in the air. While the pieces were floating to the ground and onto us, she shouted, "Pundunia."

"I'm sorry for that," she said. "The book you moved was the Book of Infinite Puns. You must have triggered it. We should be able to have a normal conversation now."

"Okay," I replied, "Let's just do this standing." By now the woman had stopped transforming and maintained the appearance of a thirty-some-year-old woman with curly brown hair. She had soft features and a tiny button nose. She didn't look anything like a witch.

"What was stolen?" I asked.

"Only one thing was taken. But it is very valuable and, if used, it could cause a lot of trouble. A Potion of Luck is missing."

"That doesn't sound so bad."

"You have no idea. If someone drinks too much of it, the entire infrastructure of society could be changed. Imagine someone having everything go their way. Businesses could collapse. People could die. Even if they don't mean for anything bad to happen, it still could. The potion doesn't care about collateral damage; it only brings the best possible luck to its user."

"If it is so dangerous, why do you even have it here?"

Madam Savva shrugged. "I used to sell it in very small portions, nothing more than a few drops. But then the Cubs won the World Series and I realized how unpredictable it could be. It's valuable enough that I don't want it destroyed. I keep it hidden in a drawer behind the counter."

"Are you sure it was stolen? Couldn't it have been misplaced?" I was beginning to fear that this case would be impossible for me to solve. I knew nothing about the magical world. I had no connections or inside information.

"No, it's gone. I have a very good system for keeping track of things. The fact that it was the only item taken points out that it was someone who not only knows about magic, but knows this place quite well. They wanted that specific item."

"Is there anyone you suspect? Has anyone asked about that potion lately?"

"Not that I know of. There were about a dozen customers in here yesterday. Whoever took it must be pretty good with cloaking spells. They've done a good job covering their tracks. If I could have figured this out on my own, I would have. I need your help." She didn't try to hide her frustration.

I looked around the cluttered room for any surveillance equipment. Not seeing any, I asked Madam Savva if the store had any.

"I'm afraid not," she said. "But we do have something just as good." She led me over to an old-fashioned easel. The pencil drawing on the top piece of parchment showed the two of us standing in front of an old-fashioned easel in a cluttered magic store.

"This is a magic easel," she explained. "It makes instantaneous drawings of its surroundings."

"I can see that."

"I just need to find a drawing from when the thief was in here." She started flipping through the pages, tossing sheet after sheet over the top. Suddenly she stopped. "Unbelievable. Whoever stole the potion must have torn off the pages with their image on them." She pointed to the small bits of paper where those drawings had been. "We'll never be able to find out who did it. What a rip-off."

I tried my best to console her. "I promise to do the best I can. There are some things I can try. I'll leave no sheet unturned. Oh, and I think your anti-pun spell is wearing off."

We looked at the drawings of the previous day's visitors, and I had Madam Savva tell me as much as she could about each of them. Afterward, I headed out to start my investigation. When I reached the street, I stopped in my tracks. Someone had let the air out of all four of my car's tires and broken the side mirrors.

The dispatcher had a good laugh at my expense and told me that she'd send someone to fix the tires, but it would take at least an hour for them to get there. I decided I might as well look around the neighborhood; maybe there was a clue to be found somewhere around the magic shop. Besides, I could use the time to try and wrap my mind around everything I had seen in Madam Savva's store.

I was walking by a large grocery store when a produce truck came out of the loading dock and headed up the street. As it turned, a large crate of bananas fell off the back and crashed on the pavement. Bananas flew everywhere, but the driver was long gone before I could try to wave him down.

I was bending down to pick up a banana when I heard voices coming from the other side of the wooden fence around the loading dock.

"I've got nearly a hundred of these TV sets," said a man with a thick Irish accent. "If you give me two hundred bucks each, you can have them all."

"Well, it looks like a nice set," said the other voice, "but I'd have to ship them to another city to sell them. I'm willing to pay one hundred per TV."

I crept to the open gate and peeked around the corner. In the dimming light, I recognized Dimples McGruder holding a large television. McGruder was well known to all the police officers in the city. He'd been running all sorts of cons, schemes, and heists for years.

Quietly, I pulled out my gun. I was going to get him this time. I had him red-handed.

Jumping out from behind the fence, I began to shout, "You're und..." Before I could finish, my foot came down on one of the many bananas laying on the ground. In Saturday morning cartoon fashion, I slipped and fell, tumbling into a pallet of table-salt containers. A dozen blue canisters fell on my head, spilling salt everywhere.

McGruder and his buyer took off in opposite directions. I tossed a handful of salt over my left shoulder and started after McGruder.

I followed him down a back alley, quickly gaining on him. McGruder was not very fast and the television he'd held onto didn't help him. Despite my earlier tumble, I was going to make this arrest.

We were on the thirteen hundred block of Gretel Avenue when I got close enough to shout, "Stop! You're under arrest." To my surprise, McGruder skidded to a halt in front of Madam Savva's magic shed.

I was just starting to sprint the last few yards when I felt a sharp pain on the ball of my right foot. It felt as if I'd been stabbed by a very small but very sharp knife. My next step was just as painful. When I tried to not put any weight on that foot, I lost my balance.

When I stumbled, McGruder shrugged and took off again.

With each step, the pain got worse. Slowly but surely, McGruder pulled further and further ahead of me. Eventually, I lost him. From an adjacent street, I heard the sound of a large truck stopping and restarting, but I couldn't see the vehicle or the direction it took.

Frustrated, I took a seat on the door stoop of a rundown apartment building, about five blocks from my car. I took off my right shoe and pulled out a tiny red ear stud. For a while, I just stared at the little ruby, thinking about what it meant.

The earring had gotten into my shoe while I was running by the magic emporium. Had Zelda been to the magic store? She hadn't been on any of the drawings, but the thief had removed some of the pictures.

This day just kept getting worse and worse. Was the one case I had a chance to solve going to require me to arrest the only person who seemed to want to be my friend?

With a sigh, I stood and took out my car keys. The way the day was going, it was no surprise that I dropped them. They landed in a rosebush growing under a ladder which leaned against the building. Cursing silently, I got down on my hands and knees and began feeling around for the keys.

The sound of a large truck stopping in front of the building caught my attention. I didn't want to stand up too fast and hit my head on the ladder, so I stayed hidden behind the bush. Soon, I heard voices.

"Tommy, you start unloading the goods," said a familiar voice with an Irish brogue. "Put them in the garage with the other stuff. I'll call a different buyer and set up a meeting."

"I don't want to do it myself," replied a voice that I assumed belonged to Tommy. "Those TV's are heavy. Why don't you help me first and then call the fence?"

"Okay. Okay," said the first man. "We have to hurry; the truck's invisibility spell will be wearing off soon and that cop might still be wandering around."

Pulling out my gun again, I waited another minute and then popped up from behind the bush. Dimples McGruder and another black-clad man stood in front of me, each holding a large color television.

"Freeze," I shouted. "You're under arrest."

Both men looked around, trying to find a way to escape. Before either could make a move, a black sedan squealed to a stop nearby. The police captain jumped out of the driver's seat.

"What's going on here?" he asked, glancing at me as he moved toward the two criminals.

"I just nabbed the Main Street Robbers," I said.

The captain grinned. "Very nice work, Rheinhart. I'll help you take them in. It was lucky I decided to take the long way home tonight."

After an evening filling out arrest reports, I had to confront Zelda. The next morning, I waited in the diner's parking lot.

"I know what you did," I said when she got there. "You took the luck potion from Madam Savva." I opened my hand to show her the ruby earring.

"Congratulations, Harry," she said, not admitting anything. "I hear you got lucky with an arrest."

"It wasn't lu..." The realization hit me like a ton of bricks. "You gave me the luck potion."

"Just a drop in your coffee. I knew how bad things were going for you. I heard Crumpfeld giving you a hard time every day."

I'd always been a good cop. I played by the rules, and I knew I should arrest Zelda. After all, she had committed a crime. But how could I turn her in? She had stolen the potion to help me.

"Do you still have the potion? Did you use it for anything else?"

"I have it in my purse. I just..." She smiled and shrugged. "I thought it was worth the risk to help a friend, but that's the only time I used it."

"But you are a wi... an adept"

Zelda shrugged. "Not really. My mother helped me get the potion."

She reached into her purse and pulled out a jar filled with a moldy-looking, green liquid. "Here's the potion. Do what you have to."

The more I thought about it, the more I realized I couldn't arrest her. It was because of the stolen potion that I'd caught the Main Street Robbers. I didn't think the captain would understand. How would he react to the idea of magic? Would he even give me credit for either arrest?

"Okay. Here's what's going to happen. I am going to take this back to Madam Savva. I'll tell her the thief was lucky enough to get away." I had to smile. "I think it'll be believable. But you have to promise to never do anything like that again."

Her smile assured me that I had made the right choice. "Of course not. Though I wouldn't mind if you found the time to keep a little closer eye on me." She pulled a pad and pen from her apron and wrote down a phone number. "I'd like it if you called me and set up a little reconnaissance."

I couldn't keep myself from grinning. "Maybe we could go see a movie or something. The captain gave me tonight off."

Zelda flashed a sly smile. "Well, isn't that lucky? I get off at six."

See James Rumpel's story "Madam Savva's Magical Emporium"
online at Metaphorosis.
If you liked it, leave a comment. Authors love that!
Remember to subscribe to our e-mail updates so you'll know when
new stories are posted.

About the story

"Madam Savva's Magical Emporium" was written at the end of March 2020. There were a lot of strange and unprecedented things happening in our world at that time, most of them negative. I had friends and family who were struggling with fear and adjusting to quarantine. My goal was to write a positive, upbeat tale to remind myself and everyone else that sometimes good things happen to good people. I wanted to create a story about someone having unexpected good fortune and I think I was lucky enough to come up with an interesting way for that to happen.

Once I started writing, the story took shape fairly quickly, especially when I found a way to work in a little word play. I love puns and was ecstatic that I could sneak in a few within the confines of the story.

I write because it's fun, and I had a good time putting this piece together. I hope others will enjoy it also.

A question for the author

Q: Whence do you draw inspiration for your characters?

A: To be honest, most of my stories begin with a plot and then the characters just show up. I guess I have a vast collection of characters to choose from. Having taught high school for thirty-four years, I've worked with thousands of students, parents, and coworkers. Additionally, I have avidly read and watched movies and television most of my life. There are all sorts of people in my mind trying to push their way into my stories.

About the author

James Rumpel is a retired high school math teacher who has enjoyed spending some of his additional free time trying to turn some of the strange ideas filling his brain into stories. He lives in Wisconsin with his wonderful wife, Mary.

The Preserved City

Charles Schoenfeld

Simona's view of the modern city dropped away as the cable car rose toward *Città Alta*. Above the ancient city wall, she could see black-clad families milling about in the pre-dawn glow. Services would begin in twenty minutes, at 5:00 a.m. Those who had risen early were enjoying the beauty of the upper city, its medieval architecture and narrow cobbled streets unaltered since Renaissance times.

Simona's black shawl rubbed against her lips, and she brushed it away. She had been awake longer than any of her neighbors. In Bergamo—or any northern city—the women did not prepare feasts on All Souls' Day, nor leave their homes open for the spirits. But Simona kept up the southern traditions, even if her grandmother would have cringed to see her preparing portions of that feast in the microwave.

The funicular deposited Simona near the Piazza Vecchia. The other women greeted her warmly as she crossed the square. They asked about her work, which made it necessary to lie. "Making progress," she said.

Two years earlier, most of them had come to see *L'Applauso È Napoletano* in its first few weeks at La Scala. They were not habitual opera-goers, but they knew the composer and took neighborly pride in her success.

It was an easy story for northerners to love. While her opera gave an inevitably nostalgic, romanticized view of Campania, her southern home, it was ultimately a paean to everything Bergamo had taught her to love about the north: its scenic beauty, its air of civilized contentment. The southern heroine does not *return* home in the end; she *finds* home.

Every line of the square's architecture drew Simona's eyes upward—the arches and pillars of the library's white façade, the stony bulk of the ancient bell tower. An archway led to the chapel. Simona found a seat near its acoustic center. Stefano, her fiancé, would be attending services with his family in Milan, an hour away. He had invited her, but she had a plan of her own for this morning, and it could only be accomplished here, in the Basilica of Santa Maria Maggiore.

Simona joined her neighbors in lighting candles for the departed and reciting the prayers. Some of the women who had lost relatives within the past year wept while the organ played.

Simona's analytical facility had outgrown its proper place in her mind. She did not hear the organ music as a unified whole; her ear picked the musical phrases apart into individual chords, and the chords into isolated notes. This rendered the composition meaningless; any arbitrary substitution could have been made, and would neither improve nor damage the music.

A-flat? Why not G?

Half note? Why not two quarter notes?

Composer's intuition, she answered herself. *I used to have it too.*

The mass ended. While the other churchgoers dispersed to tend family graves, Simona made her way to the rear of the church, where lay the one dead Bergamasco to whom she felt any connection.

Simona knew of no more touching monument, anywhere, than the relief carved on Donizetti's tomb. It depicted a group of cherubs at the moment when they heard of the composer's death. Several were bending and breaking their lutes; one, angry-faced, held his lute over his head with both hands, ready to smash it upon the ground; another stood poised to crush his lute beneath his upraised foot. In the center of the relief, a kneeling cherub wept, hands covering his face, while the cherub at left gazed heavenward in despairing incomprehension.

Simona traced the relief with her fingertips, then began to speak.

From its long rest, Gaetano Donizetti's consciousness flickered into existence, so that a sound might intrude upon it. A woman's voice said, "... to pay respect to you on this day."

Inside the tomb, Donizetti's soul formed a vague head-shape and nodded it in recognition. The living often stopped by to honor his memory. On All Souls' Day, when the barrier between worlds was thinnest, he could hear them.

"Great master, offer me guidance—"

Guidance? There was a dangerous word. She hadn't fallen to her knees before his tomb, had she? His senses sharpened; he tried to be certain.

"I have succeeded once. And now, no music I write approaches the beauty of what I've already written. But you, you breathed music as others breathe air—"

Excessive flattery. I worked at my music.

"Teach me to remember what I once knew. Help me to release the music in my soul—"

He formed a face, which formed a scowl. *I joined the army rather than teach music. Know me before you ask these things.*

Her voice was growing ever more frantic. "Don't leave me in this state: silent, unheard. I exist for Music—"

No, no, this is all wrong. An ember of outrage began to glow in the dark of Donizetti's tranquility. *Music should give joy to its creator, never enslave her. Else, why create?*

"Inhabit me, if you can." Her voice was choked. "Make me your instrument. If I can no longer create, I can still … I can …"

Must you make me care for you? There should be peace in death.

"I'm sorry, I don't know what I'm saying. Forgive me."

Pity overcame Donizetti at last, if only by a narrow margin. He gathered himself and stepped from his tomb, but there was no one kneeling before it.

Footfalls echoed on the flagstones. He caught the barest glimpse of her flushed, tear-streaked cheek as she ran from the chapel. But today, on All Souls' Day, he could be anywhere within *Città Alta*, instantly. Anywhere that he had been before. So, the barest glimpse would be enough.

Simona walked the narrowest of the old streets, turning her face to the walls until she had composed herself enough to be seen without loss of dignity. She descended to *Città Bassa* via the funicular and went home.

Stefano arrived that evening. His gaze lingered on the feast she had left for the spirits. She'd been composing, and had not yet cleaned it up.

Stefano had advised against leaving her home open all day, but now he refrained from comment. She loved him for all the protective things he obviously wanted to say, and loved him even more for having enough respect not to say them.

She cleared away the dishes and prepared a dinner. While they ate, Stefano told her stories about his family, with whom he had spent the day. His younger sister had a new boyfriend, of whom Stefano did not quite approve. Simona found it adorable that his protective tendencies applied to everyone he loved, not only to herself.

Stefano's older sister worked as an assistant manager in a hotel. She always had hilarious, and sometimes infuriating, stories about the guests, which Stefano recounted in as much detail as he could remember.

For Simona, whose thoughts of late had revolved entirely around her music and how little of it she was writing, Stefano's willingness to carry the conversation came as a welcome diversion. She could forget her concerns for a while, as he chattered on.

Then, for an instant, they were not alone at the table. One of the empty chairs was occupied by a … trick of the light. But it was a man-shaped trick, with a wild curl of shadow atop its head and another that might have been a bow tie beneath its chin. When she turned to glance at it, one of its eye-shimmers disappeared and reappeared. On a more solid form, it might have been a wink. Then the figure vanished.

"Are you all right?" Stefano asked, breaking off in the middle of a story.

"Hmm?"

He smiled. "You went away for a minute there."

He hadn't seen it, then. "Oh, sorry. I was just wondering … can you stay the night?" She picked up her empty plate and carried it into the kitchen.

He followed with his own plate. "I hadn't planned on it, but I'd love to. You know I have to wake up early for work?"

"I know. It's just … there's something a little spooky about this holiday, isn't there? The spirits of the departed walking around? Your presence would be comforting."

She didn't want to tell him what she had seen. For one, she wasn't certain she had seen it. And even if she had, Stefano tended to worry when she had a problem he couldn't solve, or wasn't supposed to.

"And your presence would be delightful," he replied. He kissed her, and she kissed back, made it last longer than he had planned, turned his casual gesture into one full of longing and love.

"Yours too," she said. "Especially if you can get up for work without waking me."

"I'll do my best."

During breakfast the next morning, alone in her apartment, Simona put on her recording of *L'Applauso*. She had not listened to her own work in months. She had polished it so lovingly, and they had found the ideal performer for every role. The recording had captured her music the way it was *supposed* to sound. It made anything different—anything new—seem wrong. She worried that her next work would sound like a soulless imitation of her one great success. That was the easiest thing for reviewers to write about *any* composer's second offering. They almost didn't need to attend a performance.

So instead, Simona's new work accumulated in her wastebasket over the course of each day. Soulless imitation might be an improvement.

She sorted through piles of CDs. *Mozart ... Rossini ... trick of the light.*

There he was, depicted on the cover of a CD. The same wild curl of hair she had perceived as a shadow. Not a bow tie, but a cravat. Donizetti. And he had winked at her.

She rushed from the apartment without finishing breakfast.

All Souls' Day had passed, and the barrier between worlds had begun to thicken. Normally, it would have taken enormous energy for Donizetti to travel the city freely—the sort of energy that comes from unresolved grievances against the living. Donizetti had no unfinished business, but now he had a connection to a mortal.

They had kept his old bed, all these years. It was on display in his museum, a small, second-floor suite of rooms that also housed his sheet music, instruments, clothing, and other personal effects.

He knew that the woman would come. She had asked for him, and he had appeared. It had taken all of his concentration to make himself visible in *Città Bassa*, even just barely visible, even just for a moment. But he had done it, and she would come.

His old doublet hung on a wooden tailor's dummy. He touched it, let his fingers pass through the velvet, let the feel of it come alive in his memory. Then, with a moment's concentration, he shaped the matter of his soul to resemble it. He repeated the trick with his old walking stick, touching the original and creating a spirit replica that he could hold.

So he lay on his old bed, wearing his old finery, one sole planted on the mattress, his knee pointed jauntily upward. He twirled the walking stick in his fingers, and he waited.

The woman arrived flushed and panting. There was something tentative about the way she walked, the way her eyes traced each surface, wondering if it might be inhabited by a spirit, if ghosts really could exist and answer people's prayers.

When she saw Donizetti, she froze for a moment, taking in the sight of him. She swallowed. "It *was* you," she said. "You came to me."

"And you," Donizetti replied, his nasal voice resonating off the walls, "took your time returning the favor!"

He sprang from the bed in one fluid motion, rapped his walking stick twice on the floor. "Come! We have work to do."

In Florence, which had been home to Leonardo and Michelangelo for long portions of their lives, Donizetti might have been dimly remembered, a historical footnote. In the quiet mountain town of Bergamo, he was the most renowned of the city's sons, the single greatest source of civic pride. One could not spend much time in Bergamo without hearing his name. That was one reason Simona had chosen him to hear her prayer.

Still, praying to the great man's tomb had been one thing. Sharing his company, bearing the weight of his full attention, was another, and far more exhilarating.

"Begin by showing me how you compose," Donizetti said.

"What ... what do you mean?"

"I mean, here is pen! Here is paper! Begin!"

Simona wondered how long their privacy would last. "What about ..." She gestured toward the ticket-taker in the hallway, her back to the museum's entrance.

"These rooms are my domain. She will not hear what I do not wish her to hear. Now, begin."

Simona stood over an exhibit case, drew a staff on the blank page, hummed a few notes, and wrote them down. She ran a hand through her long hair, blew out a breath. Then she wrote a few more notes.

Donizetti stood at her shoulder, watching the pen move.

She paced the length of the main room once, twice. She picked up Donizetti's old violin. Conveniently, the museum kept it strung for appearance's sake. She gave it a cursory tuning, carefully played a few notes on it, and wrote them down. Then she snatched up the paper in one hand. She would have crumpled it, but hesitated, not sure whether she had permission.

The first ruined sheet of the day had come even faster than usual, with Donizetti watching.

He sighed theatrically. "I see. You know quite well *how* to compose. I am not so sure you remember *why*. Come, then." He swept out of the museum. The ticket-taker showed no awareness of him as he passed, but nodded to Simona as she followed.

In the Via Gombito, the ever-present Roaring Old Man tottered by, emitting nonsensical syllables and daring anyone to meet his gaze. He was a fixture in the afternoons; Simona encountered him nearly every time she visited *Città Alta*. "Arrrrhh!" he yelled, and, "Aiieeeee!" He tottered on his way. Donizetti leaned close to Simona and spoke in her ear. "A comic buffoon?" he suggested. "A drunken, declaiming baritone? Or a fallen genius—a strident tenor, lamenting his lost glory? Perhaps a spy, concealed in plain sight? The stuff of opera, in any case. *Compose him.*"

At the fortress called La Rocca, atop a broad tower of sand-colored stone, a stiff wind flapped the Italian flag. Donizetti stood in the center of the stone courtyard and shouted over the wind: "A mighty fortress! A symbol of liberty!" He stepped closer to Simona, lowered his voice. "But it was also a prison, once. And the French used it when they conquered us, and the Austrians too. There is music here. Stirring, patriotic music, and dark, oppressive music."

Simona looked at the fortress, trying to make the music come, but it would not come. She avoided meeting Donizetti's gaze, fearing to admit that she could look at La Rocca and hear nothing.

"Come," said Donizetti.

They climbed the bell tower and looked down into the Piazza Vecchia. Donizetti offered no commentary, seeming to wait for something. As Simona turned to face him, the huge bell tolled, just meters above her head. Donizetti flickered translucent and vanished. The sound took away Simona's ability to think, to descend the stairs, to do anything but cringe, hands over her ears, and wait for the bell to finish.

Finally she descended the tower and found Donizetti waiting. "You looked like you could use a shaking," he said. Simona stared at him in blank amazement, then laughed. Her eyes closed and her chest shook and as the tension left her, she realized it was the first time she had smiled in Donizetti's presence.

They walked along the city wall that divided the upper and lower parts of Bergamo. Simona wondered how *Città Bassa* must look to Donizetti, with its automobiles, with people tapping at their smartphones, skateboarders with their blue spiked hair, chemical plants and apartment complexes made of concrete, glass, and steel. Here stood one of Bergamo's most celebrated ancestors, surveying what his grandchildren's grandchildren had made of themselves. How would he judge it all?

She tried to put the question into words, but the thoughts seemed too large, and the words came out awkward, incomplete.

"I've never thought about it," Donizetti said.

They stopped and leaned against the wall, looking out over the valley. "Behind each window, along every street," said Donizetti, gesturing broadly across the expanse of orange-tiled rooftops that stretched all the way to the mountains, "a life runs its course. All of those lives, orbiting one another like planets, twinkling in isolation like the stars … and finally, scattered like dust." He blew on his upturned palm. "Compose *them.*"

"Have you done anything other than compose today?"

Simona jumped, her pen making a streak across her sheet music. She hadn't heard Stefano enter the apartment. "No, not today," she said. "Today was a composing day."

"It looks like it's been a composing *week.*" He started making a circuit of her apartment, picking up her discarded clothing from the backs of chairs, the couch, the floor, the dining table where she now sat working. He carried the clothing into her bedroom.

"You don't have to do that," she called after him.

"Which makes it wonderfully generous of me, don't you think?" He returned, gave her a quick smile that was probably supposed to be charming, and picked up a few of her discarded coffee mugs. He swept off to the kitchen.

Simona turned her attention back to her music. She tapped her pen against the table, trying to focus on the rhythm. Clattering dishes broke through her concentration, as Stefano began washing the ones she'd left in the sink. She stood and went into the kitchen.

"Was I expecting you tonight?" she asked.

"No. But your friend Donna called me and asked if you were all right. I told her I'd check on you."

"Donna called you?"

"She tried calling *you,* last night."

"I know. I wasn't answering the phone. I was—"

"Apparently it was her birthday? And you were invited to the
—"

"Oh, *damn*. That was last night."

"It was."

"Great. That's fantastic." She stared at the ceiling for a moment. "Okay. I'll have to make it up to Donna, after I'm done with all this."

"Done with all what?"

"Finding my way through this ... this darkness in my mind. The music still isn't coming. It's not like writing *L'Applauso*. That's probably good. I'm not trying to write the same opera over again. But if *L'Applauso* had failed, no one would have noticed. And if this fails, *everyone* will notice."

"People seem to notice when you forget their birthday parties, too." He gave a little chuckle, as if trying to make a joke of it.

"I know. I know what I owe my friends. But I know what I owe my audience, too. And I'm afraid, Stefano. It may be that what I owe them"—she tapped at her breastbone—"isn't in me anymore. What then? What am I supposed to do?"

"Well, I think you could start by taking a breath or two," he said. "Go for a walk, get some fresh air, have a nice meal. The audiences aren't demanding anything right now. You're the one putting all this pressure on yourself."

"No, of course the audience isn't demanding anything. And they won't. Audiences are always willing to forget you ever existed."

"I don't think they'll forget about you in the time it takes to ... I don't know ... go out for some gelato. Or go to a birthday party when you're invited."

"That's your solution to all this? Gelato?"

"Gelato is the solution to many of life's problems."

Simona rolled her eyes.

"I know it helps me when I'm having a hard time at work," he said.

"It's different for you. You leave the lab at the end of the day, and your work stays behind. It's just something you do; it isn't *who you are*."

"This isn't who you are, either," he replied. "This is a downward spiral. Look at this place. You're not taking care of yourself, you're not eating well ..." He opened one of her cupboards and removed a package of penne. "Let me cook you a nice dinner
—"

She took the package from his hand. "Look, Stefano," she said. "You'll be a good father someday, but don't practice on me. I'm not a child."

"That's not what I—"

"And I don't think I'm hungry tonight." She replaced the penne on the shelf and closed the cabinet. "And I ... I don't think I'm in the mood for company. You should go."

"Simona, you *need* to—"

"Please go."

They stood facing each other for a long moment, each staring at a different spot on the kitchen floor, not moving except for the heaving of their chests as they breathed. Finally, Stefano left the kitchen. A moment later, Simona heard her front door open and close.

She returned to her dining table and began again to compose.

Donizetti took to unlocking his museum for Simona after the building had closed for the night. He never had to wait long for her to arrive. He insisted on candlelight, and on working long past midnight.

"Working through your fatigue will force your inhibitions aside," he said.

"Couldn't I just drink a bottle of wine?"

"No. Artists deprive themselves of sleep. Poseurs drink."

Città Alta had been wired for electricity, but he refused to permit its use while composing. *We must give you an authentic experience, after all*, he thought. *You believe that music must be a struggle. Let us take that belief to its extreme, and see what we may find there.*

"There is no music in these electric lights," he told her, his footsteps echoing in the silence of his museum as he slowly paced. "They don't flicker; they don't dance." He noticed a gutter of wax forming. "They don't weep. They only buzz, steady and atonal. We must surround ourselves with music, and weed out that which is not music."

Simona dropped her head back to the page in front of her and filled a few more measures.

Donizetti had learned to sneak glimpses at the music; Simona could not work while he stared. *Her music is beautiful*, he thought, watching her with sympathy. *Almost as good as mine.* He stepped closer to her and peered down his nose at her current score.

Perhaps better.

She had taken a modern office worker as her heroine. Her introductory scene was ambitious, panoramic. It began with an alarm clock, followed the young woman out of bed, through the horns-and-tubas rush of morning traffic, and into an office building. Percussion imitated the clack of computer keys, the clink of tiny espresso cups against saucers and desktops; strings toyed with the repetitive swoosh of a photocopier, the monotone flickering of fluorescent lights; a chorus of voices brought in the chaos of many distinct telephone conversations. Remarkably, the elements all blended, forming a unified impression that somehow gained in beauty the more hectic it became.

Donizetti stood dumbstruck. She had found the rhythm of her own world, the hidden melodies in those very aspects of modern life he had called devoid of music.

The heroine switched on her computer. Simona wrote: "Sintetizzatore"—synthesizer—then crossed it out, then began to write it again. She gave a cry of disgust, hammered her fist on the desk three times, and snatched up the paper. She crumpled it in one hand and threw it in the trash.

"Well, try again," was all Donizetti said. Encouragement might have helped her, but not in the way she needed.

She stayed there through the night and into the morning, composing and destroying, and did not leave Donizetti's rooms until nearly midday, as the museum began to receive its first visitors.

Donizetti followed her, to her surprise. "Not to worry," he said. "A change of scenery may do you good. Find a rock to sit on. Compose out here. There are no instruments here, but you can whistle."

She turned around to face him, staggering with fatigue. "Please, I need a break."

Donizetti nodded solemnly. *Then I shall break you.*

"All right," he said. "Follow me."

He led her to a restaurant and watched her order a margherita pizza. While she waited for her food, Donizetti stood over one of the other patrons, leaned in close and sniffed at her cappuccino. The woman seemed oblivious.

"Mmm," he murmured to Simona. "Such dark beauty in the scent of coffee. One forgets it as the decades pass. It entices you with its aroma, makes you feel strong even while wearing away at your insides. It is the most dangerous of lovers: the Seductress and the Destroyer. Soprano, perhaps? But slow and sultry in her rhythms. Even in coffee, there is music."

Simona was only half listening. Now that she had stopped moving, stopped working, hunger and fatigue threatened to consume her. The thought of coffee was tempting, but she needed solid food more urgently. Her skin felt tight on her bones, and the ambient sounds had taken on a tinny quality—not much bass, lots of treble.

The pizza arrived. Donizetti stood behind Simona's chair; he bent to position his lips behind her ear. "Good," he whispered. "Now a bite of pizza. Don't rush it. Taste the sunlight that shone on those tomatoes, the wood that fired the crust, the vitality of fresh basil. Yes."

Simona bit off a chunk of the pizza.

"Oh," said Donizetti, sounding rapturous. "In pizza one can taste all the bounty of nature, the benevolence of God. It is life's goodness in microcosm.

"Now: don't eat it. *Compose* it."

Simona's head snapped around to stare at him in horror. "Don't eat—?"

"You have tasted it once. Don't dilute the memory of that first taste."

But I'm so hungry.

Donizetti was relentless: "Feed your music first. You can feed your body afterward."

She stared at the slice of pizza in her hands.

Donizetti straightened from his crouch and looked down his nose at her, ready to issue his ultimatum. "Is this where I belong? You are not the only composer in Bergamo."

He turned away, took a step.

Simona leapt from her chair, reaching after him with both arms. "Wait! Don't go!" Her voice echoed off the nearby buildings. He felt her fingertips pass through the velvet of his doublet and continued walking.

Behind him, Donizetti heard a small crowd detaining Simona, asking her if she felt all right. They could not see him; they would think she had been shouting and clawing at empty air. He allowed himself to fade from her view. Let her reassure them as best she could.

Only after she felt that she had hit some sort of a bottom could they attempt the real work of building her back up.

The crowd would have put her in the hospital if they'd had the power; Simona could see it in their faces. But she never asked for help, so eventually, they had to disperse.

Donizetti, when she found him again by the city wall, had softened somewhat. He looked her up and down as she approached, then said, "You may be right. You need to untwist yourself. Perhaps I have been too strict, depriving you of other composers' music all these weeks. Let your man take you to a concert tonight. Verdi is playing at the Teatro Donizetti, and he is ... competent. Enjoy yourself."

Donizetti vanished, his body distorting inward toward his own navel and shrinking to nothing. Simona wasn't sure, but she thought she heard a popping noise.

Space twisted around itself, and Donizetti felt himself spiraling through it, as if down a drain. Something had him by the soul. He hoped Simona could not tell that his disappearance had been unintentional. He hoped immortal souls could not be destroyed.

He hoped this was not what it felt like if they were.

He appeared with his back to his own tomb in Santa Maria Maggiore, contained by a half-circle of candles. He looked at the priest first, and did not recognize him. The man next to the priest, though, was Simona's lover, Stefano. They both held crucifixes.

"I saw you," Stefano said without preamble.

Donizetti made no reply.

"I saw Simona from below, walking along the city wall with another man one night," he said. "I wondered who you could be. Then her head eclipsed the moon—and yours didn't. The moon shone through your head. I knew immediately. What other spirit than you would she have chosen as her companion?"

"I am not a rival to you," said Donizetti. "I have no desire to —"

"She is unraveling. You had one full lifetime in which to compose. She is not your opportunity to live again."

The priest was chanting softly behind Stefano. Donizetti felt himself being pulled toward the inside of the tomb. The pull was soft, but getting stronger.

"She is an independent soul," Stefano continued, trembling with fury, "not a conduit for you to reclaim your—"

"She is dying," Donizetti said.

That stopped Stefano for a moment. Donizetti could see the doubt in his eyes: *Have we drifted so far apart that I would be the last to know?* Then he stood straighter, as if preparing to close a door in Donizetti's face. "No. She would have told me."

"Not her body," said Donizetti. "But you must have seen it by now." He tried to step forward out of the circle of candles, but met an invisible wall.

"Yes, I have. I've seen her obsessed by work as never before. An obsession to which *you* must have incited her. I've seen her neglecting her health, her friends—"

"Spare me," Donizetti spat. "She's told me of your great concern for her social obligations."

"Is that so?" Stefano's voice dropped to an injured whisper. "Because she's told *me* nothing of you."

"I can't imagine why not. You show such understanding of the work that's important to her."

Stefano turned his face away sharply, as if presenting the other cheek for Donizetti to strike. "Don't presume to judge me," he said. He met the composer's gaze again, his eyes glistening. "You may see her only as a musician. I see her as a whole person. I love her. And her friends, they love her."

"Then tell me: how much love do you think she could give to her friends if she had none left for herself?"

Stefano opened his mouth to reply, and closed it again.

"I would never deny the importance of friends and family," said Donizetti. "Nor do I doubt that they would provide shoulders for her to cry on, as she mourned the death of the music within her. But would they—would you—rather have a Simona who weeps on your shoulders, or one who stands proud, full of life, full of joy?"

"I have not seen that Simona since you arrived on the scene, *Signore*."

"You lost her before I arrived. And you can hardly expect me to bring her back in a day." He opened his palms toward Stefano. "Music is not giving her any joy. She hungers only for more of the fame she has tasted once. I've known fame; I've walked this path. Have you?"

Again, Stefano stood silenced. Donizetti felt the pull from his tomb strengthening still; he fought not to stagger visibly backward. He spoke faster.

"Because if you can heal her, then yes, please, send me back to my rest. But if you can't … then for the rest of your life, you can look back on this as the night that you, and you alone, chose to consign her best hope to the grave."

Stefano's fist tightened on the crucifix, until Donizetti thought the wood might snap in his hand. Then, of a sudden, he lowered it to his side. He stepped closer to the circle of candles, to within a few centimeters of Donizetti's shimmering face. "You had better be right. About what she needs."

He turned to the priest. "Thank you, Padre. And sorry to have troubled you." The priest lowered his own crucifix and slumped with relief. Stefano extinguished one of the candles beneath his shoe.

Donizetti stepped over the dark candle, out of the circle.

"Thank you for trusting me," he told Stefano.

"Who said I trusted you? I'm a desperate man."

Donizetti nodded and said, "It should not be much longer." Then he vanished.

That night, when Simona met Stefano at the concert, he smiled cautiously and gave her a slow nod that was almost a formal bow. He said nothing in greeting, likely for fear of saying the wrong thing. It felt to Simona like the first meeting of ambassadors after the conclusion of a war.

They took their seats. Stefano, to break the tension, read an anecdote about Verdi from the program. "Have you heard this story before?" he asked. "While writing *Il Trovatore*, Verdi received a visit from a noted critic. He played three tunes from his work in progress, and the critic informed him that they were all absolute, irredeemable trash. 'My friend,' Verdi enthused, 'thank you! This is to be a *popular* opera. If you had liked it, no one else would. But your distaste promises me great success!'"

It was a hopelessly awkward attempt at safe conversation, reading from the program instead of sharing their own thoughts. But it was also a relief, so Simona went along with it.

"I've never heard that," she admitted. "But then, *Il Trovatore* is what, his twelfth opera?"

"It says here his eighteenth."

"Well, then. I hope by the time I've written eighteen operas, I'll have the stature to tell the critics how useless they are, too."

"If I know you, I think you'll prefer their approval, even then."

She smiled, a little ruefully. "You do know me."

She held his hand while the music played, adjusting her grip constantly. Tighter to reassure him, then looser because her palm felt too clammy to inflict on him.

She felt Stefano lose himself in the music when it started. He did not compose, and played with only a hobbyist's skill, but he was a knowledgeable, appreciative listener. Beside her, he closed his eyes. His head drifted from side to side with each swell of the music, like a conductor's baton in slow motion.

Images of written music tumbled through Simona's mind as the orchestra played. For brief stretches, she could stop herself compulsively rewriting the music as it entered her ears. But soon, the concert became just another exercise in composition. She could improve upon the music for a few measures at a time, then her rewrites would dissolve into cacophony—while the original continued to fill the theater with its infuriating flawlessness.

"I'm sorry I sent you away so abruptly the other night," she told Stefano at the intermission. "My work has me on edge, but I never meant to make you doubt our relationship."

"No, I'm sorry," he said. "For trying to protect you from yourself. You were right. Your gift for music is part of what I love in you. I have no business telling you how to write it."

You love me for my music, she thought, *but what if my music is gone?* That thought would not reassure him. So she wrapped her arms around him and said nothing.

They returned to their seats. The second half of the concert proved more trying for Simona than the first. She listened with a feverish intensity, gripping her armrest with white-knuckled force. She listened as if lives were at stake.

She wanted to be uplifted by the music, enlightened, transformed. She wanted the sounds of instruments and voices to part like a curtain, to reveal some large and glorious truth. She wanted a dormant part of herself to awaken, to resonate with Verdi's music and answer it in a voice of her own.

The music was lively and lovely, but she wanted it to be more than it was. It blithely refused, and she felt sick. Betrayed—though whether by Verdi or by herself, she could not be sure.

Am I learning to hate music? Is that what's happening to me?

At the end of the night, Simona had no auditory memory of the concert. She recalled only the gleam of brass, the black of formal wear, the dancing baton.

The next morning, a Saturday, Simona called her friend Donna. She apologized for missing her party and made plans to meet her that afternoon for a belated birthday lunch. Then she went out to find Donizetti and tell him she would not be continuing her studies. She would not frame it as an admission of failure. It would be an admission that the joy had gone out of trying.

She could not find him in his museum, though. Nor was he at Santa Maria Maggiore. Could he have anticipated her decision to abandon the composing life?

She looked for him in each of the places they had haunted: the bell tower, La Rocca, the café on the Piazza Vecchia. She did not expect to find him, but she felt a duty to be thorough.

When she saw the billowing flag at La Rocca, she heard music in her mind, very faintly. She caught herself humming along with it, and made herself stop.

She drifted through the city, meandering toward the path that ran along the inside of the city wall. The sun shone in a clear sky, and a warm breeze carried the scent of autumn through the streets.

What will I do in the next phase of my life? There was optimism in the question, she was surprised to discover.

She wondered again about Donizetti. Had she disappointed him, or had he meant for her journey to lead here? She stopped at the point on the city wall where they had talked before, and tried to imagine seeing *Città Bassa* through his eyes, watching his descendants' headlong rush toward the future.

She sensed him at her side before he spoke.

"Two hundred years ago, that was a field of trees," said Donizetti. "They were just beginning to build houses down there. How do I feel about your automobiles, your Internet?" He shrugged. "How would my ancestors have felt about my pocket watch, when the clock on the bell tower was once the only timepiece in the city? Who were they to judge, and who am I? People are still people, and that is all I ever was."

He turned to face her. "If I may presume to speak for the long-dead, I thank you for preserving our old, familiar home in a position of honor." He looked out over the wall again, and so did she. "But thank you also for continuing to build. I am pleased to see that Bergamo still lives and breathes."

Simona smiled. She turned to look at Donizetti, to thank him for the time he had spent with her—even to kiss him, if his cheek had enough solidity to receive the gesture—but he had vanished.

She had never actually said the words to let him know that their study sessions were at an end. Somehow, he had seemed to know it already.

If he had, in some oblique way, replied to that knowledge, it was without the disappointment she might have expected.

She lingered by the wall for a moment, overlooking the modern city that was now her home, beneath the stately city that had once been all of Bergamo. Then she set out walking. It was nearly time for her lunch with Donna.

The birds that nested in the trees beneath the wall were singing. Simona whistled a few notes back to them, first mimicking, then harmonizing. Until recently, she would have felt an anxious impulse to remember those notes for later, in case they might be the seeds of her next great work. Now that impulse was gone. The birdsong existed in that one beautiful moment—and when the moment passed, it simply passed.

She was still whistling to herself when she approached the restaurant. Donna had secured an outdoor table for them and was waiting. She stood up to greet Simona, smiling.

"You sound like a bird."

Simona looked confused for a moment, then realization dawned, and she laughed. She hadn't noticed herself whistling. "I must have been imitating them."

Simona apologized again for missing the party, but Donna waved it off. "Like I said on the phone, I'm glad you were just doing your tortured artist thing, and not sick or injured."

It was the same restaurant where Donizetti had taken her, just prior to her breakdown. Simona ordered a small pizza, knowing that this time, she would be permitted to eat the whole thing, instead of trying to compose it.

She and Donna had known each other since childhood, and could talk to each other about anything. So when Donna asked her how the 'tortured artist thing' was going, Simona decided to tell her the whole story. It wouldn't have felt right talking to Stefano about Donizetti's ghost; it would only have made him worry. But Donna, after a few moments of understandable disbelief, reacted with simple wonder—and most of all, with interest in the relationship Simona had formed with her celebrated mentor.

"So, let's pretend I believe you," Donna said, "that you could really give up composing for more than a month or two."

"You're so accommodating!"

"Purely for the sake of argument. Have you thought about what kind of work you'll do instead?"

Simona pursed her lips. "I might teach children to play," she ventured. "I know the violin, cello, and the piano well enough to teach them."

Donna nodded encouragingly. "That's good!"

"Maybe write the occasional advertising jingle. Score a few episodes of TV, if I can find out who I need to know."

Donna let a wicked gleam come into her eye. "So you're giving up music to work with … music?"

Simona grinned sheepishly down at the table. "Well, that's hardly *real* composing, you know? It's more ... are you a chef going for that next Michelin star? Or are you just grilling a quick dinner on your terrace?"

The waitress arrived and set a plate in front of each of them.

Donna sipped at her drink. Simona expected her to continue asking questions about her music, and her identity as a musician —questions for which Simona didn't have coherent answers yet. But Donna must have sensed that it was a tender topic, so instead, she launched into a bit of gossip about her birthday party. Two of their mutual friends had arrived separately, but left together.

"Oh, they're all wrong for each other!" Simona exclaimed with delighted horror.

"Completely," Donna agreed. "But I don't think they'll realize it for a while, so I'm happy for them. It will be a beautiful mistake."

Simona glanced upward. She could see a jet rising into the sky, leaving a thin trail of white across the clear blue. It passed behind the dome of the basilica and continued on its way—a modern marvel slicing across the medieval skyline.

"A beautiful mistake," she echoed. "I have to say, that would be a *great* title for a piece of music!"

Donna raised an eyebrow as innocently as she could. "Really?"

"Oh, sure," Simona enthused. "You could have the lovers who seem all wrong for each other ... only in the end, of course, they aren't. Total opposites: one sings high and lively, with a lot of suspended chords. The other sings low and slow, and everything resolves neatly."

"So interesting."

"And the 'beautiful mistake' motif wouldn't only appear in their relationship. You could work it into other parts of their lives, into the set design, the architecture. The costumes."

Donna was biting down on her lip, and Simona abruptly realized she was doing it to prevent herself from bursting out laughing.

Simona leaned back in her chair, shaking her head slightly. "I guess *that* habit isn't going to disappear overnight."

Donna grinned broadly. "Clearly not."

"Sorry."

"You're apologizing to me?"

"You have to understand," Simona said, "I'm not latching onto this idea because I think it's magically going to wash away all of my troubles and turn me into a great composer again. I'm just ..."

"Being playful," Donna supplied. "Over lunch."

"Exactly."

If Donna realized that it wasn't quite the first time Simona had playfully talked over a musical idea during one of their meals together, then at least neither of them felt compelled to comment on the last time it had happened, nor on how very far that idea had gone.

"Exactly," Donna echoed.

Simona took a bite of her pizza—and as the flavors burst across her tongue, the world seemed to slow, so she could linger in their perfection. She made a soft noise of pleasure. Her features melted into a serene smile, and her eyes closed.

Donna watched her head sway slowly as if she were dancing, while, in her mouth, the flavors sang.

See Charles Schoenfeld's story "The Preserved City" online at Metaphorosis.
If you liked it, leave a comment. Authors love that!
Remember to subscribe to our e-mail updates so you'll know when new stories are posted.

About the story

I used to work for the American branch of a company that had its global headquarters in Bergamo, Italy. Once, my job sent me to Bergamo for a week. I spent the daytime in an office, but in the evenings and on the weekend, I was free to explore the town. With the exception of Simona's apartment, I visited each of the settings that later found their way into the story.

Either during that trip or shortly afterward, a single image came into my mind, and I knew I wanted to write a story around that image. I pictured two ghosts from Bergamo's medieval past, standing by the city wall, looking out across the valley, across the modern portion of the city that had not yet existed in their own time, and having a conversation. I pictured them from the perspective of a modern person somewhere beneath the wall, looking upward, seeing the moon shine faintly through one of their translucent heads and realizing that they were ghosts. This living observer would naturally wonder what they were talking about. What did they think of the modern way of life? Were they proud, amazed, disappointed?

That exact image didn't find its way into the finished story, though an echo of it did. Instead of two ghosts, it was a ghost and a living person. And the living person had a problem for which the city's dual nature—past and present, side by side—served as a metaphor. I wrote the first draft of the story during the six-week Clarion writing workshop. It was my second story of the workshop, so maybe subconsciously I was feeling some of the same pressure as my protagonist, to make sure my second offering was at least as good as my first one.

A question for the author

Q: What's your writing schedule?

A: I'm about as far removed from a morning person as it's possible to be. My body would prefer to keep vampire hours, if my day job didn't require otherwise. So I do most of my writing late into the night, and on weekends.

About the author

Charles Schoenfeld is a graduate of the Clarion science fiction & fantasy writers' workshop, and a past finalist in the L. Ron Hubbard Writers of the Future Contest. He has worked with more than a dozen community theatres in New England, as a leading actor, playwright, director, and fight choreographer. Charles lives in Connecticut with his daughter, Leila, and devotes much of his energy to the pursuit of chocolate cake.

A Death in New York

Allison Brice

There are decisions that we know immediately are good. There are decisions that we know immediately are bad. There are decisions that we know immediately are horrific, atrocious, I'll-regret-this-for-the-rest-of-my-life bad.

I specialized in the third category.

"Glad to see you still haven't gotten rid of that broken lampshade," Tyler said, reaching behind her to take her bra off.

"Fuck you," I said with a bite to her lower lip, slapping her hands out of the way so that I could unhook it with one hand. Tyler shivered, even though that particular lesbian trick had never impressed her before.

I nudged her into bed, next to the lamp with, yes, a very broken lampshade, and we went down hard into my twisted-up, unwashed bedsheets. I wanted to be embarrassed about the way I hadn't changed since we'd been together, about the way that I'd taken our beautiful, open, airy room and turned it into my dark, weird cave with mandala tapestries and overflowing ashtrays. And I *was* embarrassed, at least a little. Mostly I was horny.

"Jesus, Soph, *ow*, with the biting," she said, as I sucked a desperate hickey into the inside of her thigh. "That's gonna bruise."

Good, I thought viciously. If she saw a mark from me for the next week, then I wouldn't be forgotten. She'd have to think about me, at least for a little bit, think about me and the life she left behind and the Upper East Side apartment she left in my name with no thought at all to how expensive that was.

I took the hair tie off my wrist and pulled my hair into a sloppy bun. Tyler lounged back on the bed with her hands already fisted into what little blonde hair she had. I ducked down, spread her knees apart, belly-flopped forward until I was pressed up against her musky darkness. I had been celibate for far too long, and yes, Tyler was about the worst person I could have slept with, but I'd seen her at Trader Joe's and she always had a beautiful smile and I gave a first, tentative lick —

"Sophie."

Nope, I thought, with my nose pressed right to the core of her. *No, not tonight.*

"Sophie."

"Go away," I said, muffled. Tyler snorted a laugh.

"The disposal is broken. Come fix it."

"New roomie struggles?" Tyler said, with a terrible grin.

"You have — very literally — no idea," I said. To the thing standing outside the door, I said, "We can fix it tomorrow. If you put string cheese wrappers down the sink, then the disposal breaks."

"Sophie, I want to fix it now. Stop playing with the weird girl."

"Go *away*."

I smiled sheepishly at Tyler (and God was I sick of apologizing to this girl), put a hand on her knee and kissed the join of her hip and thigh.

Then I heard the jiggle of the door handle. "Sophie —"

"Shit!" I grabbed the blankets and threw them over Tyler. "Do *not* come inside, I mean it!"

Tyler rolled her eyes, grabbed her phone to flick through it. Blushing, furious, I stuffed myself into a gigantic t-shirt and opened the door, face-to-face with the new roommate I'd been stuck with since Tyler left me.

"We talked about this," I said to Death. "When my door is closed you leave me alone."

Death blinked their massive grey eyes. "But the disposal."

"Fuck the disposal, I'll fix it tomorrow. Aren't you supposed to be out shepherding lost souls? Isn't there anywhere else you could be that's not cockblocking me?"

"The minions are working tonight," they replied. "I wanted to listen to One Direction but now the disposal is broken and I can't listen to music when the disposal is broken."

"That doesn't make any sense! Just go in your room —"

"Sophie," they said, pathetic with their limp hair and Avenged Sevenfold t-shirt and big, sad eyes. "I need you to fix the disposal."

They would stand here all night. Death would stand outside my door until I fixed the disposal. And if that wasn't the worst boner-killer I'd ever heard.

I sighed and went back inside my room. I couldn't make eye contact with Tyler when I said, "Maybe it's best if you come back another night."

She wouldn't come back another night. This had been my one chance and we both knew it. She gave a weird little smirk and rolled over to grab her shirt.

"Seems like you lowered your standards," she said meanly.

It's funny that she thought I had standards.

This may sound hard to believe, but interrupting my non-existent sex life was not the only problem that came with having Death as a roommate. It was, however, the final impetus for a raging fight.

"And you never take out the trash!" I screamed.

"And you don't let me play my music over the speakers," Death replied, never raising their voice.

"That's because I'm not listening to One Direction *again!* Your taste in music is shit!" I would feel bad that the neighbors could hear us, but we lived in Manhattan. Our walls were so thin I could tell whether George and Amber in number 4 were having missionary or doggystyle.

"If you would just let me get a cat —"

"Oh no, not this again," I said. It didn't help that Death had picked a particularly pathetic human suit today. Instead of their usual borderline-pedophile man, today it was a small, perky, blonde woman. I felt like I was screaming at Kristin Chenoweth. "We're not getting a cat. I would end up doing all the work and taking out the cat shit and you would get all the snuggles. Absolutely not."

"Sophie," they said. Big, sad, blue eyes. Looking just like all the girls that used to call me weird in middle school. "Please. I want a cat."

"Kiss my ass," I replied.

When I was unmoving, Death finally spoke. "Our Father, who art in Heaven —"

"Oh, shit, don't do that —"

"Hallowed be thy name —"

"No, anyone but her —"

"Thy kingdom come, thy will —"

"I'm here," God said. She appeared, like she always did, out of thin air, and the walls of the apartment bulged with the power of two immortal beings. Unlike Death, who took pleasure in switching up their appearance and gender, God was the same every time I saw her: a chubby, harried middle-aged woman with brown hair. She typed furiously into an iPhone and didn't look up at us. "Hello, Death. Hello, Sophie. This had better be important."

"I can't do this anymore," I said immediately. "Death is the absolute worst. I want out of the contract."

"You want out of the contract?" She said, looking up over her phone. "You want out of free rent, paid-off student loans, a raise at work, and a miraculous cure for your step-grandmother's pancreatic cancer?"

That gave me pause. Just as it had the first time she'd offered it.

"Let her go," Death said flatly. "She's terrible. She didn't fix the disposal and she wouldn't come out to help me because she was having bad sex."

"Do you know how long it's been since I got laid?" I spat. "I was *this close* to finally having a good orgasm before your useless ass —"

"This is not productive," God said. "Obviously you haven't bonded. In order to make this arrangement work, you have to be able to understand each other."

"Let me out of this stupid arrangement," Death said, a rare note of bass in their voice. But God didn't even blink.

"No. Your bedside manner is atrocious and you have lost all touch with humanity. We agreed, Death, living with a human is going to be good for you. Now," she said, as Death and I both opened our mouths to argue, "you two have to spend more time together. I want to see you having a productive conversation about how you're going to make this arrangement work. Sometime in the next few days will work just fine. Now, if you'll excuse me."

And just like that she was gone. The apartment felt normal again — tiny and overpriced, yes, but slightly normal. Except for the immortal being sitting on my sofa, pouting their big pink lips.

"I'm going to Trader Joe's," I said to Death.

The apartment always smelled vaguely musty. Even back when it was me and Tyler living here, there was something off about the walls. Mold, maybe. Asbestos. It's New York, it could be anything.

Death did not improve the situation.

"You need a shower," I said, upon coming home with a twelve-pack of White Claw. If I was going to bond with Death, there was no way I was going to do it sober.

"I showered this morning." They sat on the couch, mindlessly flicking through Netflix. They were in a new male body today — a very attractive one, I might add, Black and trim and gorgeous. I'm gay, but I have eyes.

"Did you actually turn the water on or did you just stand in the shower and touch the tiles?"

Death looked at me plaintively. "They are very soothing to the touch."

"Oh my God." I pulled one out of the cans, cracked it open and drank it warm.

"What are you drinking? I thought animal claws were not to be eaten?" they asked.

I looked down at the can in my hand. "What? It's not actually — it's White Claw. It's hard seltzer." Death looked at me blankly. "It's carbonated water, but with alcohol in it. I didn't want to love it, but it's delicious. Have you never had White Claw?"

They shook their head.

I pulled another one out of the pack and tossed it over. They caught it clumsily, like a six-year-old at a t-ball game. "Here you go. Nectar of the gods."

"This substance is ambrosia?" They sniffed it and then tried to lick the top of the can. I snorted.

"No, you just – you drink it, like a normal human. Pull the tab, put your lips to it and swallow."

Slowly, painstakingly, they cracked the tab with unnaturally long fingernails. Then they finally lifted it up and drank it, and then before my eyes Death drained the entire can in one swallow.

"I guess you liked it?" I said, biting down a chuckle.

Death shrugged. "It's fine."

"That's what we all say. Wait until the third one hits you. Let me get you some more."

I wasn't passing up a chance to get drunk with Death, that's all I'm saying.

An hour later we'd cleaned out all the seltzer I owned and had moved on to more intellectual topics. "So every week he picks the girls he likes and then he sends the rest of them home?" Death said slowly.

"Yes, exactly. The ones he likes gets a rose and then the ones he doesn't go home."

"But how much time has he actually spent with them? The ones who receive the rose?"

"Not much. Maybe an hour or so, if they're lucky?"

"And 'the Bachelor' is meant to make a decision about his future wife from this? How does he know if she is in it for the right reasons?"

"Exactly!" I said, drunkenly staggering upright and slapping the couch cushions. "You never know if they're in it for the right reasons! Who's here for love and who's just here for Instagram followers?"

"Is that why you have never gone on this show?" Death asked. Without my noticing it, we each had a can of seltzer in our hands, even though I was positive we'd finished them all. Finally using those superpowers for good.

I laughed, though it sounded like a cackle. "Uh, no. I haven't gone on the Bachelor because I'm not pretty enough and not straight enough."

"Ah, so the show does not allow lesbians. I see."

"Wait, does being gay actually send me to Hell?" I asked.

"No," Death said, sending a tidal wave of relief through my body. Apparently I'd been more concerned about that than I thought. So much for my liberal laissez-faire. "You will not go to 'Hell' for being gay."

The way they said 'Hell' made me very curious, but I knew they wouldn't tell me anything about the afterlife. I'd already tried asking, the first week we lived together, and been promptly shut down. I switched tactics. "What's your sexuality? Do you date? Have you ever been in a relationship?"

Death paused and thought about it. Their fingernails curled across the seltzer can. "God and I have been together since time immemorial."

"No, you can't date God. She doesn't count. Nobody else who you had a special connection to?"

"No."

Death's voice didn't give anything away, no emotional inflection at all. Still, my heart ached for them, just a little. Their life sounded lonely. "Okay. That's okay. Well, I, uh. I hope you find someone. I hope you feel that. Because it's wonderful, to feel like you've found your person. And it's the person who you want to talk to about everything, and maybe you didn't make any promises to be together forever, but...you assumed that they wouldn't want to go anywhere 'cause they always seemed so happy." I caught myself, because this was one spiral I didn't want to travel down. "Anyway. Being in love is awesome. But it's also kinda exhausting. I know I should date more, but...it's hard, sometimes. To move on."

"Where is your ex-girlfriend now?"

"Tyler? She's probably at her best friend's for board game night right now. She lives four blocks down; we go to the same Trader Joe's."

"Tyler...that is a boy's name?"

"Names don't have a gender," I said immediately, parroting the phrase I'd heard every day for all three years of our relationship, and then stopped myself. "But. Yeah."

"And you are not invited to board game night? Why not? You two had sexual relations."

"That was a bad idea, I shouldn't have done that. And I'm not invited to board game night because those are her friends, not mine. Every couple has groups of friends that they bring into a relationship, and then they keep their friends after they breakup. Except I didn't bring any friends, really, 'cause I moved here from Columbus for Tyler, so..." The room spun and swung around me; I was officially drunk with Death, and talking about Tyler of all people. How fucking pathetic. I hiccuped and swallowed down a wave of vomit. "I don't, like. Have a lot of friends."

Death blinked. "And you find this isolating?"

I nodded. "Yeah." My eyes watered, suddenly, pathetically. "I do."

"Do you wish to move back to Columbus?"

"I don't know. Maybe. There's nothing for me there. I wasn't any happier there. I'd go just for my grandma, but she's pretty old and one time she told me that there wasn't any point in a young person wasting their life on someone who was going to die soon anyway." It occurred to me how strange this was, to be voicing this to Death, but they didn't react. Of course they didn't, of course they didn't react to themselves. "But I don't really want to stay here either, so I just don't know. I don't want to start from scratch all over again, I like my job but that's about it..."

"You need to discover what you want to do in life," Death said calmly. "You lack purpose and direction. You are adrift. You must decide what to do with the time you are given."

"Yeah, I get it, can we stop talking about this?" I snapped, alcohol slurring my words. "Can we talk about anything else? Damn."

Death actually leaned back a little, startled. To my drunken mind, that didn't make a lot of sense — weren't people always angry at Death? Surely I wasn't the angriest person to ever confront them? I felt bad, suddenly, for getting upset; that I was another human in a long line to be pissed at Death for doing their job. I shifted my anger.

"Why doesn't God help me find my purpose?" I said sarcastically. "Should I pray and see if she can come down and help me figure out what I'm doing in New York?"

"She wouldn't answer," Death said. "She never really helps you."

Their voice was bitter, laced with arsenic. I looked over to see Death moodily sipping their White Claw.

"That's a lot of emotions," I said. "Wanna talk about it?"

Death said nothing. The neighbors started arguing again; with our paper-thin walls, we could hear every shout. George had decided to spend more money on lotto tickets again, when Amber said that there were better ways to spend the money that *she* earned. It was a familiar refrain. Made me want to talk softly so they didn't hear the wacky shit in apartment 3.

"God looks out for my best interest," they said. "But I do not need her to. I have existed as long as she has. Her maternal efforts are useless and infantilizing."

Oh, this was good. "Like what?"

"Like you," they said immediately. "Moving into this apartment, ostensibly to relearn my 'bedside manner'. She says I have forgotten how to talk to humans. I ask her, am I meant to be smiling when I am never greeted with a smile? She has no idea what I do, the unceasing burden of my existence, and she saddles me with this apartment and this human form in order to make herself feel better."

In all our months living together I'd never heard them sound like that. "Sitting around with you does nothing to make my existence less agonizing. Knowing the name of this drink does not mean that the next person whose loved one I take will be less angry. This is a performative, empty gesture, and she knows it."

"So why do it?" I asked. "Why go along with it when you knew it was stupid?"

Death took another sip of White Claw. It was a very human gesture of delay. "I don't know," they replied. "Only that…what was the point of arguing? Why delay the inevitable? She always gets what she wants, in the end. I went along with it. I always go along with it."

In the next apartment, George and Amber had stopped arguing. I lowered my voice so they wouldn't hear my next sentence. "Can you, like, stick it to her? Fuck the police? I got arrested a lot in college for protesting, I can help you out." I got arrested more often for trespassing than protesting, but no need to throw myself under the bus.

"One does not stick it to God," Death replied, with a hint of amusement. "She could even kill people, do my job for me, if she wanted to. But she says she's not 'as good at it' as I am, and I must assume that I exist to end joy, just as she exists to bring joy. Obviously this makes her much more popular than I am. And if I do what I am told, I get to fly under her radar, and she does not bother me. I get to live a quiet existence."

"Baby," I said, cracking another White Claw, "that's the strategy I've been using for 27 years."

Baths are my preferred form of self-care. I understand that 'self-care' means more than just spending excessive amounts of money on bougie bath salts; people who really practice self-care go to bed on time, take care of their skin, work out and probably contribute productively to society. But nobody likes those people. So I take baths.

I stretched out and wiggled my toes against the grout, which desperately needed a scrub. Do you know how rare it is to find a Manhattan apartment with a full-size bathtub? There was a reason I'd put up with Death's nonsense in order to keep this place.

The other reason made my phone ring in my room.

I sat up immediately, sloshing water over the side of the tub. That particular harp ringtone was reserved for my grandmother. My very sick, very old grandmother.

"Death!" I screamed, hoping it would make it to the living room. "I need you to get my phone!"

"What?" they said.

"My *phone*, can you get it?"

I could have called her back, I know. But I was perpetually terrified that this was the call, the one that would tell me that my grandmother died, despite the fact that I'd literally bargained with God to ensure that wouldn't happen. My grandma is the most important person in my life. She's my step-grandma, technically, but of all the step- and half-siblings that I got during the divorce, collected and dropped like trading cards, she was the only one who stuck around. When I was branded as the difficult one in high school, when the rest of them decided that there wasn't enough behind my vitriol to get to know, she stayed, and talked to me, and slowly wore me down. We baked fucking cookies together, and we weren't even related by blood. When she got cancer, I thought, *Here goes the last person on Earth who'll ever care about me.*

All of this drama with God and Death was worth it for her. I clumsily got out of the bathtub, soap suds still in my hair, and lunged for the towel. I heard Death's plodding footsteps across the apartment, and suddenly I was utterly terrified of what I'd asked them to do.

"Yes?" Death said into the phone. "Hello. No, Sophie is in the bathtub. This is her roommate." They paused. "My name is Tiffany." With a deep, masculine voice. I groaned and rubbed myself dry as quickly as I could.

"I am doing well today, thank you. The Bachelor last night made the right decision and that made me happy during the day today." Another pause. "Yes, Sophie and I watch it together. Yes, it is wonderful. No, I don't think Sarah really loved him. I quite agree. Something about her." Another pause. "If it's any consolation, she will not lead a happy life. Her ex-boyfriend —"

"Stop being omniscient on the phone with my grandma!" I whisper-yelled.

"Um. Do you like One Direction?"

I wrapped the towel under my armpits and finally managed to get into my room, where Death sat calmly on my bed, attempting to engage my grandmother about One Direction. They looked up at me through thick eyebrows and said, "Sophie is here and would like to speak to you." A pause. "It was...nice to talk to you too."

I couldn't help but smile at the bafflement in their voice. They handed me the phone and I mouthed, "Thank you." They nodded and shuffled out of the room.

"Hey, Grandma. How are you doing?"

"Wonderful! I *love* your new roommate. Seems so much nicer than that Tyler girl."

"Yeah, she is," I said, and wasn't even lying.

"Her voice was very deep, though. For a young lady."

"Uh. Yeah. It's a. It's a thyroid thing." I cleared my throat. "Tell me about bridge club!"

"Sophie, God is here."

"What?" I was just about to start masturbating. "Like, now?"

"Yes. Come to the living room."

I threw my head back on the pillow. Kids, don't make deals with the devil. You wind up with God in your living room and no time to enjoy the most basic pleasures in life.

I stomped out to the living room. Death sat lazily on the easy chair, in their standard white male loser body; God, as usual, was dressed in the best fashion that the outlet mall could buy.

"Hello, Sophie," she said, smiling widely. I grunted and sat down on the couch. "How is your day?"

"Fine. Very busy. Really don't have any time to chat."

"Well, I'll be out of your hair before long," she said, still with an unceasing customer service smile. "I just wanted to let you both know how thrilled I've been to see you getting along. Your deep conversations about life and love, Death helping out by meeting your grandmother...it's just wonderful to see!"

I looked over at Death to watch them roll their eyes. Like this wasn't the exact behavior we'd been complaining about. I winked back.

"I hope that this convinces you to trust me more readily in the future," God said, once again pulling out her iPhone. She'd been without it for two minutes; color me impressed. "I know that it's in vogue to rail against me, to claim that you know better and you have no need of my wisdom, but I often know what I'm doing. Just like with you and your ex, Sophie. I knew all along that was a terrible idea."

My stomach turned to ice. "What?"

"Oh, she was *awful* for you," God said, without even looking up from her phone. "Didn't ever actually love you. And I knew that the whole time, but I didn't say anything, to let you make that decision on your own. But maybe next time you'll come talk to me, let me in on your life, and you'll see what kind of guidance I can provide." I gaped at her while something built up inside me, roiling, whiting out my vision with rage.

"Alright, I'll leave you to it. You two have a great day!" She gave a jaunty little wave and vanished. The apartment went quiet, nothing but the ever-present noise of the A/C and the washing machine and the cars relentlessly zooming by outside.

I turned to Death, saw them wide-eyed and glued to their seat.

"That *bitch*," I said.

"And then she has the *gall*, the fucking *gall*, to stand there and say that she was doing it for *me!* For *my* best interest!" I yelled, letting my voice screech, making George and Amber quake next door.

"I know," Death said, from where they still sat in the easy chair, eyes watching my relentless pace around the living room. I'd worn a track in the carpet.

"It was not good for me, it was not my best interest, it was —" I paused, took a deep breath. "That relationship *broke* me. All the gaslighting, all the distance, all her coldness, the way that she just never cared about my career or what I wanted or even *me*...and God was okay with that? She was just *fine* letting me get torn up?"

"Yes," Death said. "She loves to say she knows best."

"Oh, does she? And really you're just doing what she wants. Like this apartment, right? She said it was my choice, when she first came to me she said I could choose, but really she knew what I would say. She knew how broke I was, she knew how Tyler left my name on the mortgage but I had no idea how to pay for it, and she saw this poor sucker and figured I was gonna be the perfect guinea pig for her little experiment."

"I'm sorry," Death said, still in that same flat tone of voice. "That she made you live with me."

I whirled around. "Hey, no. No. It's not you I'm mad at. I like living with you." The words struck me, how true they were, how I'd never thought them before. I doubled down. "I like living with you. It's her that I'm pissed at."

Death nodded, with a slight smile. And then the smile slipped off their face. "Sophie," they said, and a river of cold washed down my spine. "I have to kill Tyler."

"*What?*"

"It is her time. She has an undiagnosed heart condition. It will send her into cardiac arrest. The ambulance will be called but they will come too late because there is no defibrillator at her office. She will be pronounced dead at the scene. It will happen tomorrow at 2:09 in the afternoon."

"*What?* She's 29, why is she dying? And why are you telling me?"

"So that you can say goodbye," they said solemnly. "I tried to intervene with God, to get her a special dispensation, but God said no. So I, um. I got you White Claw. In case you are sad. To cheer you up."

I dropped onto the rickety couch, my head ringing like a bell. Tyler was going to *die?* Tyler, with her undercut and her aloofness, Tyler with her fifty different board games, her mother's only child? And I was supposed to walk over there and say goodbye without saying goodbye, invite myself into my ex's house and bring her wine because only I knew that it was her last night on Earth?

"Why would you tell me this?" I said, my voice cracking. "You bastard..."

Death looked genuinely sad, pained. Deep lines cut through their face. "I know. But it is a privilege that you have. To know. If I did not tell you, you would also be upset with me."

"Don't put this on me," I lashed out. "Don't say you're doing this for me. If you really cared about me you wouldn't kill her." I looked up, locked eyes. "So don't do it. Don't kill her."

"What?" Death said.

"Don't kill her." I stood up and stalked over. "Come on. You don't have to kill her. She's 29, she's never done anything wrong except be a bitch."

"I have to lead her to the beyond," Death said. "That is my purpose."

"Well, it's a shitty purpose! Don't you want to take a day off? Don't you want to stick it to the man? Don't you want to stick it to *God*?" Oh, that felt good; molten heat built up in my bones. "You're tired of following her orders. You're tired of her forcing you to do unnecessary shit for her entertainment. You said she has no idea of the unceasing burden of your existence. Isn't it time she found out?"

Death took a step backwards, into the wall, away from me, my voice, my eyes, my tall body and my broad shoulders, my elbows that jammed into faces during basketball. Like every other kid in middle school, they were afraid of me.

Death was afraid of me.

"Listen to me. She doesn't control you. You control yourself. For a million years you managed your own destiny. Do it again. Leave Tyler out of it."

I could feel what we were doing, the blasphemy of it, deep inside me. My teeth couldn't stop grinding together and there was a cold sweat under my arms, around the back of my neck. I knew it was the eye of God watching us and I didn't care.

"Take a stand," I whispered, and I could see that I'd won.

Death nodded.

Maybe you shouldn't have dumped me, I thought, to the ex whose life I'd just saved.

When I woke up the next day, I was untethered. I laid in bed in my room and felt all the limitless possibilities of New York and America and the world outside. I called out sick from work and convinced Death to play hooky with me. We went to the Met and made a scavenger hunt to find all the racy art (which is when I, Sophie Collins, had the honor of explaining to Death how lesbian sex works, because they had no idea). Of all things Death liked the Asian art section the best; they lingered for a long time in front of a black stone carving of the god Shiva as conqueror of death. They stroked the small, carved fingers over and over, like a compulsion, until the guard came and yelled at them for destroying the precious artwork and unceremoniously booted us out.

After that we got pizza from the good place on 5th Avenue before wandering around the city. Death smiled and looked happy as they ate a deformed Spongebob popsicle, and I was so nervous it felt like I was going to shake apart. A part of me wanted to make sure that Death was with me when 2:09 hit, that I knew that they would follow through with their pact. A part of me wanted to hide from God, to take the subway underground all the way to Long Island and as far as I could go so she couldn't see me. A part of me wanted to climb on top of the fountain in Central Park and scream about what we were doing.

And then it was the afternoon, and Death was engrossed in some historical plaque, and I looked down at my watch and it was 2:09 on the dot. I said nothing, smoked my cigarette while people steered clear of Death with their pedophile-long hair, and at 2:10 I released all the breath in my lungs.

"You didn't trust me?" Death said, looking right at me.

"No," I replied, and Death smiled.

In retrospect it makes sense that we were at St. Patrick's Cathedral when I got the call. Death gave me a flat look when I wanted to go in, and I grinned back and dragged them by the hand inside. St. Patrick's is Catholic nonsense and Grandma would have a lot to say about these people with their idols up all over the place and the gaudiness of the stained glass, but I liked the majesty of it, the way that the cathedral soared over and around me without any input from anyone else. I especially liked watching Death, the way that they seemed calmer. Their eyes roved all over the space; not rapidly like someone seeing it for the first time, but slowly, carefully. Like they were seeking out their favorite parts, old stained glass windows and marble carvings, seeing if anything was different.

"Been here before?" I asked.

"Many times," they replied.

My phone went off, buzzing up a storm, causing glares from Death and a couple of Asian tourists. I pulled it out of my backpack and saw my mom's name flashing. The hairs on my neck stood up. I did not regularly talk with my mother.

"Uh, gimme a sec," I said. I ducked around the corner, next to the huge white statue by the altar. "Hi, Mom."

"Hi Soph," she said, with a sniffle in her voice. "Oh, hun, I don't want to be the one to tell you this."

"Tell me what?" I said, looking frantically at my watch. 3:16. Way past time.

"The home just called. Grandma...she was taking a nap and just...fell asleep. Apparently it was peaceful..." Her throat cracked, and my stomach dropped. *No.* "She just...I'm so sorry, I know you loved her, you can come home and say goodbye —"

I hung up, because I could see the guilt trip coming; the plea, even in one of the worst moments of my life, to come back home and take care of my mother in her pain. But my pain was also real, so real that I dropped into a pew, my knees buckling under me.

Death walked up. "What happened?"

"You mean you don't know?"

Death frowned. "Know what?"

I gaped, searching their face for signs of lying, because Death said that they had no idea about my grandmother's death, and if they didn't know then that meant —

In front of me, on the other side of the pew, God appeared.

I stared at her, mouth open and eyes wide, looking and feeling like a fish. "What?"

For the first time ever, God did not have an iPhone in her hands. They were clasped in front of her, in front of her sensible Ann Taylor blazer. "I'm sorry about your grandmother, Sophie. But it had to be done."

"What did you do?" Death said, sitting down beside me. God's face was still, lifeless, like the statue behind her.

"The two of you thought that you would scheme to ensure that Tyler Astin did not die today, as she was scheduled to. You offended the natural order of life, merely out of misplaced affection for a woman who left you. This behavior is unacceptable. You cannot dictate the flow of the world by abusing your relationship with Death. I had to step in."

"But that's against the contract," I said, dragging the words up. "When I moved in with Death. You would cure my grandmother's cancer. You broke the contract."

"I did no such thing," God said. "I cured your grandmother's cancer, as promised. She died of natural causes."

"You can't do that," I whispered, trying to stand up for myself even when all I wanted to do was fold to my knees and cry.

"You have no idea what I can do," God said, and a couple of people walking around her froze at the power in her voice. One man, engrossed in his phone, looked up and swerved away from her at the last second. *He almost bumped into God,* I thought hysterically.

"Keep that in mind the next time that you decide to rebel," she said, pulling out her iPhone again. "I am your God, Sophie Collins. You will respect me, or I will take all you hold dear and turn it to ash."

And just like that, she was gone.

I was left staring at the place she used to be, at the giant white marble statue. It showed a man and a woman, the man kneeling on the floor, slumped into the woman's arms, her face radiating static, frozen pain.

"Sophie, I'm sorry," Death said quietly. The rustle of conversation in the church was achingly loud. "I never thought that she would use her power on your family."

Grandma and I would never bake cookies again. I knew there were other revelations that would come later, but right now, this was the one stuck in my mind like a skipped disc. Grandma and I would never bake cookies again. She was the only one who'd ever bothered to make cookies with me. She was the only reason I'd ever go back to Ohio.

My eyes looked at the statue without really looking. The church slid in and out of focus. Tears welled up in my eyes, blurring the statue even more. I blinked them away, and finally recognized what the statue was supposed to be.

"Is that Jesus?"

Death nodded. "That is Jesus after he was taken down from the cross, lying in the lap of his mother."

"So he's dead there?"

"Yes."

"You killed him?"

Death blinked. "What?"

"Did you kill Jesus, or did God do it?"

One lady next to us overheard this conversation and turned to look at us. I fixed her with a glare and she backed away at the sight of my red eyes and tearstained cheeks and snarling mouth.

"I did it," Death said, with a heavy voice. "God did not want to kill her son, even though she was the one who said it was necessary. So I did the dirty work."

I relaxed back into the pew, just for a minute. My sadness started to ebb away, resolution calcifying in its place. Warmth filled me up, took roost in the marrow of my bones.

I might have found a reason to stay in New York.

"Okay, so you can kill a god," I said, stronger now, gathering speed. "You've done it before. You can do it again."

"*What?*"

"We're going after God," I said, and nothing had ever sounded so right. "You and I. We're going to take her down."

Death stared at me. I smiled, showing my canines.

They smiled back. Far, far above us, in the giant church spire, the great bell tolled across New York City.

*See Allison Brice's story "A Death in New York" online at
Metaphorosis.
If you liked it, leave a comment. Authors love that!
Remember to subscribe to our e-mail updates so you'll know when
new stories are posted.*

About the story

As a broke millennial living in an expensive city, I have had my fair share of roommates — some awesome, some awful. I have often used the phrase 'roommate from hell', and I thought that perhaps that could be literal. Living with Death as a roommate would certainly present some challenges. Would they clean up? How are their social skills? What music do they listen to? (No, non-existent, One Direction.) Obviously this would drive any normal person insane, so Death's roommate had to be just as much of a hot mess as they were. This created the character of Sophie, a crass, aimless, dirtbag lesbian who chain smokes and does not have her life together. Sophie, coincidentally, was named after my girlfriend's roommate's cat, who only occasionally allows me to pet her. New York is the city of possibilities, so that became my setting. I spent a lot of time there myself as a broke college student, so I remember some of my favorite haunts. The only thing missing was a wild card, someone to propel the story forward. Since the story already featured Death, why not add God? And while I was at it, why not make God a woman — a soccer mom, at that? Once those pieces were in place, I just ran with it to see where the story would go. Obviously, the answer was 'straight to Hell'.

A question for the author

Q: Do you write things other than speculative fiction?
A: Absolutely! I love the challenge of writing creative nonfiction; you have to write yourself as a character, with all the harshness and objectivity with which authors view their characters. I also have branched out into non-genre fiction, though in general if it's not at least a little fantastical I'm not interested. Also, I write critically acclaimed bathroom stall graffiti that has been published in multiple different languages.

About the author

Allison Brice was born in the deserts of Tucson, Arizona, but currently resides in Washington, DC. In her day job, she attempts to teach people United States history and mostly fails; at night she writes whatever comes to mind. She has never met a cow she did not like.
@_allisonbrice_

Tower of Mud and Straw III

Yaroslav Barsukov

III. The Tulips

This is part 3 of Yaroslav Barsukov's novella, *Tower of Mud and Straw*. Parts 1 and 2 ran in September and October 2020. What has gone before:

The 'tulips' are destroyed, and Brielle tells Shea they have three months before the tower crumbles. Shea starts drinking.

In an attempt to cheer him up, Lena, the duke's lover, takes him on a hunt. Something strange happens: the deer they chase disappears, but Shea discounts this as a drunken episode.

Lena and Shea sleep with each other. Shea confesses his actions have doomed the tower; Lena is happy the threat of the Mimic Tower no longer looms over the world and tells Shea she'll be leaving Owenbeg soon.

Aidan, a Dumian émigré whom Shea knows from his days at the court, arrives in the duchy. Together, they trick Patrick, who's been planning another attempt on Shea's life, and leave him stranded in Duma.

Aidan reveals he wishes to ally himself with Shea. Shea's 'exile' turns out to be a test: the queen is grooming a potential successor and wants to see how he would handle the local lords. However, with the tower's destruction imminent, Shea has failed his assignment.

1

In silence, as though overcome with modesty, the doctor hid his instruments and rolled them into a piece of black velvet. A brass syringe, a pristine-white probe-razor, a speculum oculi. Shea wanted to open his mouth, but his face was a rubber mask after all the morphine.

It was his sister who spoke out loud the question everybody in the room must've been thinking. "Will he become an idiot?"

And even before the doctor could answer, Mother broke into tears.

"Catherine, please," Father said, putting his hand—always sandpaper-rough, clay-rough—on Mother's shoulder.

Undaunted, Lena took a step forward. "Will he be the same?"

"Probably." The doctor drummed his fingers on the black roll. "He has a concussion, but nothing worse than that, it seems. Pupils are of equal size. It's a miracle, actually, given the tree's height. Of course, tomorrow we'll know more. He should rest—and give him water, but do not feed him or he may choke on his own vomit."

They filed out of the bedroom, Lena last, her face an oil painting rendered mysterious in the afternoon light.

The next time Shea opened his eyes, the curtains fluttered around a scattering of stars.

The door creaked, letting in blackness from the corridor and, with it, his sister carrying a tray that smelled of warmth and bakery.

"I think..." His head swam, but at least he was able to talk; that was good. "I think the doctor said not to give me food."

"Who cares?" She lowered the tray, then herself, on the bed next to him. "I bet you you won't choke. Anyone but my brother. Besides, Grandma made black truffle waffles."

"Smells great."

"Tastes, too. Here, open your mouth."

A few minutes passed in counterpoint to two twelve year-old jaws, chewing.

"I've been thinking," Lena said. "I've been thinking. You know what we'll do, you and I?"

"What?"

"Guess."

"Ask Grandma to make more waffles?"

"When we're old enough, I want a beautiful workshop," she said, and the wind breathed through the window, lifting, thread by thread, the shadow of her hair. "Chairs and tables like on those pictures from the capital. Maybe wardrobes, too."

"A carpenter princess."

Even in darkness, he could guess a hint of her smile. "Go on. Sneer all you want—I'm the one with the waffle tray." She paused, and he saw a reflection in her eyes—perhaps the moon, perhaps the starlight, perhaps the future. "I just don't want Ma to feel sad anymore when she buys new furniture. And I want it to be yours and mine, brother. I want that place to be yours and mine."

"This is not really a betrayal, is it?"

In the courtyard of the Owenbeg castle, a thin dash of white: a woman Shea didn't know, waiting—for something or someone.

He leaned against the window frame. "Sis, I need to talk to someone. I already know the answers *they'll* give me—Aidan, Brielle. So I'm going to pretend she..." He waved the bottom of an empty whiskey bottle at the woman. "...she is you. Tell me if what I want to do is forgivable."

His mind's eye spun figures under the golden lights, men and women coming together, coming apart.

"I want to be there. At the royal court, at the Red Hill. I've always wanted to. We both wished for things in our lives, haven't we? You understand. I had no idea my exile was a test, sis."

In his eight years at the Hill, had he ever seen anyone break the waltz? *Funny how, in dance, you take each step of your own volition*, Shea thought, *and yet all the while you're following a goal somebody set up for you.*

"Damn it, sis—I can be a successor to Daelyn, can you imagine that? If I only play my cards right, if I rescue the tower. If I revert what I did earlier. Listen, can we, can we do it in the following way—"

The woman turned and looked in his direction. He straightened—*had she heard him?*—and pulled lightly at the curtain.

"Let's do it like this," he whispered. "It's different, now that I'm here. I know the risks. I'll personally make sure everyone using the tulips is properly trained. There'll be no accidents, no chewed walls, no more blood. Can we do it, can we do it like this?"

Am I striking a deal with my own conscience?

A man strode into the courtyard below, ran up to the woman, and spun her around in his arms.

2

"I can get us new Drakiri devices." Shea turned to Brielle. "But I need you to promise you won't allow junior artisans to work unsupervised."

"I promise. I promise." She sat on the sofa, at the same place he'd found her two weeks ago with a half-finished bottle of wine. None of that old desperation remained, though, no mocking smile, no slouched posture. All straight shoulders now, straight back, full of hope. "What made you change your mind about them?"

Shea didn't answer, looking at Aidan—who, from the window, said, "You still haven't told us where you're planning to get the devices."

"Does it matter?"

"It matters to me."

From under the rosewood trapdoor, Shea almost answered. "From an abandoned workshop in Musk Valley."

"Musk Valley?" Aidan slid his gloved fingers between the curtains and peeked at something outside. "There's that city—what's its name?—Oakvale?"

"Oakville."

"How many devices are we talking?" Brielle asked.

"Thirty or thirty-five, I don't quite remember."

The black glove let go of the curtains. "Will this be enough?"

"Well, it's a fraction of what the duke has destroyed," she said, "but if we concentrate all of them at one place, at the top of the tower, I think we can create a sufficient upward pull that would stabilize the structure. I must do the calculations, of course."

"Wouldn't it be dangerous, putting all eggs so close to each other?" Aidan asked.

"Yes, but also easier to supervise. However, we'll still need to convince the duke."

"I have a few ideas there." Aidan shifted his eyes to Shea. "What's Oakville to you?"

"Am I under interrogation?"

"And what if you were?"

"In that case," Shea said, "I would choose not to cooperate."

"Listen, I'm trying to help," Aidan said. "We simply don't have the time. I'd like to understand if you're at risk of running into a Patrick Number Two in Oakvale."

"Why would there be a Patrick Number Two?"

"Because I feel there's more to it than you let on. This workshop, was it yours? Your family's? Why was it abandoned? Did something happen there?"

"What's Oakville to you, Shea?" echoed Brielle.

He studied them both.

"Oakville is home."

And that was all he told them.

Later, in another room in his quarters, he rolled across the sweaty sheets, the fat angel staring at him from the ceiling.

A hand touched his shoulder. "Thank you."

"For what?" he said, eyes on the painting.

"It was nice."

"This time it was different. You're different, Lena."

"Different how?"

"Gentler—no, wait, that's not it. Happier, I guess."

She rose on her elbow, making no effort to cover her chest.

"I am happy. I want to run out naked into the courtyard and laugh, laugh, laugh."

"Better not do that, though."

"I won't." She chuckled and traced his cheek with her fingertips. "I'll be fine now."

He turned to her. "I don't understand you. That book, from the settlement—it's just a legend. You can't seriously believe in the Mimic Tower."

How could he tell her? How could he tell her he was about to undo everything, to smash that happiness into pieces?

She paused, contemplating something. "Imagine living at the foot of a great volcano. You live there in a village, a town, a city—doesn't matter. It's all the world you know. And then, one day, you learn the volcano will erupt in five years. And all will be gone, the houses, the people, the trees, the brook where you used to swim as a kid."

"I would probably move somewhere else."

"You can't, that's the problem. The ash would cover the skies until the earth itself would grow cold."

"Then I would eat, drink, and make love as much as I can before the end comes."

"Trust me, you wouldn't. I've been living with that kind of knowledge for years, Shea. It breaks you. Makes you cry like a baby at sunset."

"But that's the point," he said. "It's not knowledge, Lena. It's some text and a couple of drawings. You don't even know if the copy you showed me stayed true to the original book."

"Do you remember what I've told you about my mother?"

"You said she was a famous landscape painter."

"She had a period, right after my father had died, when she couldn't paint—so she took on menial jobs to get us by. One of those jobs was restoration. She restored everything, from paintings to old books."

"So it was her." Shea studied her face, her black hair cascading unto the pillow. "She introduced you to that legend, didn't she?"

"The Mimic Tower is real, Shea. We've avoided an apocalypse by a hairsbreadth."

Something bitter rose in him and splashed in acid against the windpipe. "You're a child. A beautiful, proud, misguided child."

He immediately regretted his words, the clumsy attempt at hurting her. *You're trying to hurt yourself*, he thought, *you prick, for what you're planning to do.*

He opened his mouth to apologize—but she simply smiled at him, something maternal passing through her eyes.

"Have you ever entertained a thought," she said, "that the universe may be more complex than we're ready to admit?"

He remembered. There had been a day in his childhood, a last day of spring—he'd been seven, and his biology teacher strode into the classroom brandishing two daguerreotypes.

Here, kids, is an octopus—and what do you see now? Holding up a picture of an aquarium (and in it, something with more limbs than a living being was entitled to), switching the images with the practiced movement of a circus magician.

I see only rocks.

Look closely. This stone to the left, it's him. Mimicking his environment. Live matter is capable of wondrous things, kids.

Can rocks mimic life, too?

No. No, of course not.

But behind the classroom's window, the sunlight had filtered through the branches of an apple tree, a lattice which reminded Shea of the veins on the back of his grandmother's palms, and an idea had occurred to him then—vague and half-formed as it was in a seven year-old's head—which echoed what Lena had said just now: that maybe life carried more facets than even the scholars knew.

"It doesn't matter." Lena sat on the bed. "Everything's fine now. It'll be a while before anyone would attempt another construction on this scale."

How can I tell her? Do I have the right anymore to this intimacy?

He remembered thinking he was a cart on a track, with no option but to press forward—during his speech at the council chamber, when he'd told the duke to get rid of the Drakiri devices. Now he was retracing his own steps, following the pas in a golden dance.

"I want to leave Owenbeg," Lena said. "I want to travel the world, now that I have it. You could join me."

"Join you?"

"Yes. Why stay? You've said yourself the queen will blame the tower on you. Why wait for that? Let's run away together."

She studied him, eyes glowing, and the ballroom in his mind shook.

"It'll be wonderful, you'll see. We'll travel with a caravan to someplace near the ocean, live in a house at the beach, listen to gulls in the evening. Let's do it, Shea. Let's do it right now, let's run away tomorrow."

For a moment, the dance moves no longer made sense. He imagined breathing in the smell of her skin, looking at the stars through the strands of her hair. He saw her, in a light linen dress, ankle-deep in water. Sat with her, feet dangling, at the edge of a caravan's wagon, pine trees full of sunlight passing them by.

Then he glanced at the angel again, at the olive branch extended toward the hunter. *Paintings are a lie. They're frozen in time, but nothing can stand still, and all things are moving, drawn to some faraway goal.*

"I need to leave for a week," he said. "Let's talk again when I'm back."

3

He heard his sister before he saw her—or rather, he heard a crowd's rumble coming from the direction of Sun Plaza. He'd expected her in the morning, but something must've intervened. It was getting late. Squeezed between the roof tiles, the evening was a baked crust, the same gold and terracotta reflecting, Shea knew, off the grapes at home, at the vineyard.

He turned away from the street and dove back into the workshop's twilight. At this hour, the hall reminded him of a belly of some great ship, shadows accentuating all the wheels suspended under the ceiling and all the ropes stretched between them.

"Danny!"

The only man still working raised his head from a sand-yellow cabinet.

"She's coming. It's time."

Danny was a bit slow. Well-meaning, hard-working, but slow. A few seconds dragged by before he nodded, wiped his hands on his apron, and followed Shea outside.

The rumble: two streets away now, judging by the acoustics. One.

When a wooden cart rolled into the square and in front of the workshop, it pulled behind it a dozen onlookers: a flock of baby ducks in their mother's wake. Lena sat atop a pile of something big, dark, egg-shaped.

Beaming, she waved at Shea. "Look at this, brother!"

For a moment, for him, she became the girl with whom he used to play hide-and-seek at the vineyard, and he realized he was already smiling back. He took her hand and helped her to the ground.

"You're alone, sis?"

"So. Why?" She dusted her trousers.

"Show's over, guys," he said, picking out with his eyes the tallest person in the crowd, a woman in a linen coif. Then, to Lena, "I thought we've agreed you'd bring a Drakiri to help us."

"Are you afraid of a couple of flowers?"

"Flowers?"

People began to disperse—but slowly, like sleepwalkers.

"Tulips." Lena patted one of the dark things lying on the cart. "They *are* tulips, don't you find?"

"I'm not sure. Eggs, at most."

"Wait until they bloom."

"So you know how to operate them?"

"Of course," she said. "And anything I don't know, we can figure out together."

He paused, studying her, studying the devices. "Okay. Let's unload them, then. Danny, would you..."

"No need to." Lena turned and touched a valve on the tulip's surface.

With her other hand, she nudged a lever. Both motions appeared natural, light, as though she were weaving or playing a harp.

The dark egg hummed and rose into the air like a giant bumblebee, prompting a collective sigh from the people who still lingered in the square.

"And then you do... this." She reached around and slapped the hovering thing on the side, sending it gliding toward Shea. "Catch it, brother. Catch it, Danny! Catch it!"

Lena's laughter followed them as they ran—clumsily, in Danny's case—after the Drakiri device, headed for a back alley.

4

"It'll come," Shea said. "Two more hills, and we'll see it."

The place where the river meets the land, where the hillside scoops the sun's honey and the toy white boats ride the ripples.

He didn't know whom he was telling this—certainly not that calm silence which sat across the table from him.

Aidan fished a piece of meat from his plate, eyes on the airship's window. The black gloves stayed on even when he ate.

The dining lounge hosted one more passenger, an old lady with large, veiny hands. Although she held on to a fork, she didn't appear to be eating: each time Shea glanced at her, it was the same posture, same lowered head, as if she'd started the motion but didn't have the strength to finish it.

"Something seems to be bothering you," Aidan said. "May I ask what?"

His earlier words echoed in Shea's mind—'we must get rid of Patrick, I'm afraid'—as if Aidan had applied a knife to the sentence the way he'd been ready to apply it to Patrick's throat.

"Why are you asking?"

"Because we share a common goal, and I've no desire to see it compromised. And because I still know nothing about this workshop of yours."

Sunlit hills flowed below, trees at that distance turning into gilded fur.

"Musk Valley is my home," Shea said.

"Fine, don't talk." Aidan folded his napkin. "You seem intent on rejecting my help."

"What do you want me to say? Listen, when I convinced the duke to destroy the Drakiri devices, I believed in what I was saying. The stuff's dangerous. Heaven knows how many were maimed at the tower, perhaps even died—were there any deaths? Do you know?"

"I don't. Not that I care much, mind you."

The old lady twitched the way people twitch in their sleep. The fork clanked against her plate, and she finally started eating.

"What the hell am I even doing," Shea said, "bringing more devices to Owenbeg?"

"A chance at the crown means nothing to you, does it? Then consider this: if the tower doesn't get finished within the next two years, Duma will attempt an incursion."

Shea couldn't contain a hiss. "Come on, are you one of those idiots who believe Duma has the densest population of megalomaniacs in the world?"

"I don't *believe* anything." Aidan skewed his mouth, from the looks of it probing his teeth in search of a wayward piece of food. "I *know*. Duma is my motherland, I spent the first thirteen years of my life there; I know how they think, their opinion of other countries, of *you*."

"Well, it's not like we have a lot to do, so why don't you convince me that they're the furnace of the world's evil?"

"I'll tell you a story, Shea." Aidan slouched in his chair a bit, but one of the black gloves squeezed into a fist, crumpling the napkin. "It was my father who'd decided, single-handedly, that we needed to leave the country. He decided it when the crown prince, only fifteen then, only three years older than me, assumed command of the royal cavalry battalion.

"People went crazy. You know how it happens: everybody ecstatic, everybody talking of a new emerging leader. Father, he saw the writing on the wall. One morning at the end of summer I woke up and saw him through the window, in the sun, exchanging papers with a man I didn't recognize.

"They shook hands, and the man left. Father turned and walked, too. I couldn't see him past the window's edge, but I knew the front door would bang in a few seconds, and that moment was for me—I realize it sounds trite, but still—it was a loss of innocence. My sisters, Maria and Isabel..." He paused. "Maria and Isabel slept in another room. I remember a toy, a bear, perched on the table in mine.

"The door banged and he walked in, or rather, darted through the anteroom. I heard him say something to Mother in a loud voice —normally, he was all quiet in the mornings, afraid of disturbing our sleep.

"When I tiptoed over the ice-cold floor, into the living room, Mother was collecting things, some silly stuff—pictures from the walls, porcelain cats from the shelves. Father told her to stop, pack the clothes, and wake us up.

"The carriage already waited outside. Our cook flapped her apron at her face, and the stable-hand, Michael, ran after us, waving his hands. Michael had first put me on a horse and taught me to ride."

Aidan slid away his plate. "Past the city gates, I remember, Father relaxed. He even smiled at me. Isabel asked for her doll. That was when the bomb exploded."

He traced with his fingers a pattern on the table.

"Something hit me on the head, and I flew out through the carriage's door like a sack. I sat on the pavement, bawling, snot all over my face. My hearing was gone. And you know what the worst thing is? I don't even remember the corpses. I remember a wheel rolling past me, people running toward us, but not the corpses.

"Mother and Father survived—Isabel and Maria didn't. It was Michael who'd planted the bomb, of course. They'd found out Father wanted to leave the country, and they bribed our stable hand to blow us up."

"I'm sorry, Aidan," Shea said.

"You don't have to be. It was twenty-five years ago; I healed. Which brings me to another point..." He pinched the rim of his glove. "You're afraid that people at the tower will never learn to work with the Drakiri devices? Well, you can live with these things for your entire life."

In one motion, he pulled the glove off. The old lady at the neighboring table gasped, and her fork rang like a little bell.

Aidan's arm ended at the wrist; what came after branched off in metal and purple veins, glowed in sparks, roughly following the contours of a human hand—but only roughly. Knotted 'fingers' rolled in the air as though strumming a chord.

Carefully, Aidan put the glove back on and smiled at the old lady who sat there with huge, frozen eyes.

Shea exhaled. "Gosh. I never knew."

"Now you do. The bomb maimed me, and I had this thing fitted instead by a wandering Drakiri craftsman when I was twenty-one."

"You said you found out it was Michael who'd planted the bomb. What did you do to him?"

Aidan didn't say anything, but his smile sharpened while the eyes went to ice.

Isabel, Maria. Lena. Shea exhaled, struck by an analogy. *I could've been Aidan. If it were a* person *that had taken Lena from me, I quite possibly would've been him.*

And then they passed the next hill, and, sure enough, there were the ripples on water, and the white sails, and the valley's saddle onto which a palette knife had scrawled the contours of a city.

Somehow, the magic of it appeared dull; all he could think about was a boy looking at dead bodies, an image that held, in itself, a similar picture from his own past, like a Dumian stacking doll.

5

Upon entering the workshop, Shea ducked in a nick of time to avoid getting smashed against the wall by a gliding wardrobe.

"Sorry, brother!"

He scanned the room but couldn't understand where Lena's voice was coming from.

On the far side of the hall, Danny and another worker caught the wardrobe and stabilized it in the air. It hung there, spinning lazily, surreal in the purple light that oozed from the 'tulip' fastened to its back. Danny stared at it, mouth open. Other pieces of furniture floated across the workshop, too—a mahogany dining table, a padded sofa for four, an oak-and-leather chair: a scene from someone's dream.

"Grand, isn't it?" Lena descended to the floor, sitting with legs crossed atop a Drakiri device.

"This is dangerous, sis. You could fall."

"Why don't you give it a ride yourself?" She smiled, rose, and tapped the inky surface. "Come on."

"No thank you."

The moment the tulip had touched down, the purple light inside began to die.

"Look." She waved around the hall. "No more hauling things. No more accidents when something falls on someone. We can have twice as much space, we can get rid of all the workbenches—people will work on the furniture while it's suspended in the air. Hey, they can even work outside if they wish."

"Why didn't you wait for me, sis? I thought we wanted to try those things out together."

"I thought so, too." She thumped her fist playfully on his arm. "But today, you seemed more interested in that new maid—what's her name? Muriel? Did you take her out to the vineyards?"

Shea felt red rising to his cheeks. "No. Listen, I had a talk with that Drakiri, you know, the one who works in the town hall."

"Mmm?"

"He told me those things—tulips, eggs, whatever you call them—they're dangerous. So dangerous, in fact, that I asked him to come here and take a look at them, and he wouldn't even consider it."

"Brother."

"He said they're volatile and difficult to operate."

"There's a valve, and there's a lever. You saw how *I* operated them—did it seem difficult to you?"

"I saw *you* working with them, sis, yes. What about the others here?"

"I can turn the tulips on and off. Once they're in the air, you don't need to do anything else, just push them here and there. I can take care of everything."

"Perhaps," Shea said. "But what if you get sick? What if something happens at home, and you have to leave in the middle of the day?"

"Hopefully nothing happens at home."

"Yes, but what if...?"

"Then we'll deal with it when we get there. Oh, and by the way..." She turned and ran her fingers across the tulip's surface, now completely dark. "I've ordered another thirty devices from the Drakiri settlement in Owenbeg. They'll arrive in a few days."

"What? No! This is my workshop as well as yours, and I forbid it. Even those six..." He glanced at the people trying to get hold of the rotating mahogany table. "...they may've been a mistake."

Something sparkled in her eyes. "Let's make a bet."

"A bet?"

"A bet. Like we did when we were children. Give me till tomorrow evening, and I bet you I'll change your mind about the tulips."

Shea chuckled. "What do you...?"

She smiled dreamily. "I have an idea." Without warning, she stepped forward and squeezed him in an embrace. "Everything will be beautiful. You'll see, brother."

6

The carriage took them from the port's breeze into Oakville's narrow, sand-colored streets.

In no particular order: sunlight-watered shadows under the house bridges; a barber on the corner catching the clouds with his mirror; a bigger dog chasing a smaller one; a woman, her hand on her hip, talking to a man with bald temples.

Inconceivable how something could carry the sugary-powder flavor of childhood and, at the same time, a much more bitter, corroding taste.

"I never wanted to return," he said.

Aidan didn't respond.

Sun Plaza. Memory lane zigzagged around striped market stands, past doors the color of green bottle-glass. Summer always managed to prolong its stay here: yellow leaves on the cherry trees seemed simply an extension of daylight.

The driver half-turned to them. "Where to now?"

"Ashcr..." *Damn it.* Something made him swallow the word—whether it was the sun that stung his eyes, or all the things rising up his chest. "Ashcroft family workshop."

"What's that?"

"The furniture shop a few streets away."

"Oh." The man pursed his lips. "Oh. You mean Imogen's."

"I mean that street, right ahead. I'll show you the way from there."

What had he expected? After a decade—dead windows, still criss-crossed by wooden boards? Of course the place had a new owner, and he could only hope they hadn't discovered the rosewood trapdoor.

"You've mentioned the proprietor's name," he said.

"A gal called Imogen." The driver smacked his lips. "That shop, after what had happened, folks were afraid it was cursed or something. All those people who died—"

"What *did* happen there?" Aidan said.

The man shrugged. "People died. You know. Anyway, no one wanted to buy the place until Imogen came along and made it into a clothing store."

The carriage drove into a small square in front of a building which still reminded Shea—even though his young, romantic self had long faded—of a yacht: the dark wood of the first floor and the white sail of the second.

The sign read 'Flying Tulip Dresses.' Imogen hadn't simply bought the workshop—she'd bought its history, too.

Leaving the black gloves to meter out the coins, Shea hopped off the carriage.

"What do you have in mind?" Aidan called out to him.

"To talk."

The doorbell silver-chimed.

The main hall wasn't the way he remembered it: no more wheels under the ceiling—or ropes—no scent of resin and finished wood. No laughter; no clinking, somewhere in the corner, of beer mugs. People in white stood at equal distances from one another, each hunched over their own small table. Neat, clean, an invisible checkerboard.

A tall woman sailed up to him. "May I help you?"

"Good afternoon." Shea looked around, remembering. "I..."

"Are you here to order a dress?"

"No... Maybe. I would be interested in a guided tour."

"We don't offer tours, I'm afraid. But if you're looking to buy a dress, I can show you our fabrics."

"Sure," he said. "Thank you." *That door, across the hall. Still there. Here's hoping they hadn't tried to change the floorboards—*

"This is cotton with lozenges, and here's some striped linen. It's particularly beautiful with..."

There was zero chance they would get to the trapdoor with all those people around.

"When do you close?" Shea asked.

"...purple velvet. I beg your pardon?"

"When do you close the workshop?"

"At six. But it's still plenty of time to take your measurements if—"

"Listen, I've some money with me. I know it sounds very strange, but I assure you, there's no malicious intent involved."

"I don't understand."

"You just need to let me in after your close. I'll pay you whatever you ask."

"Let you in?"

Shea lowered his voice. "I won't take anything from the workshop. I'm not trying to rob you. I only require ten minutes ... I'll pay you, okay? I promise I won't get you into trouble."

She nodded slowly, staring at him. "Please give me a second."

A guy at one of the tables cursed loudly and puffed at his fingers—for a moment, that distracted Shea, and then the woman wasn't there anymore. When he caught sight of her again, she stood at the other side of the hall next to a bulky fellow with hands that, from the looks of them, could bend small trees.

Shea saw her say something and point at him.

Fuck.

The bell chimed again as he tumbled out into the street.

"Find out anything?" Aidan said.

"Found out we need to scramble, fast."

Rushing toward a back alley, déjà vu gripped him that he first couldn't place; then he remembered—*catch it, Danny, catch it.* The sudden influx of memory was so painful that he doubled over, palms on his knees.

Aidan interpreted this in his own way. "You should exercise more, my friend."

From the shadows, they watched the 'bouncer' step out through the front door, scan the street, disappear back into the shop.

Catch it, Danny.

"Let's forget the entire thing," Shea said. "Do you hear me, Aidan? Let's forget it and return to Owenbeg."

Aidan slowly turned his head and chuckled in disbelief. "What the hell is wrong with you?"

"Coming here was a mistake."

"Do you realize—damn it, I'm repeating myself—do you realize what's at stake? This is our future, combined. *And* the country's future—"

"No, this is your *belief.*" Shea pressed his back against the wall and slid down into a crouch. "Or Daelyn's belief. Against someone else's. You believe Duma would instigate a world war. The queen believes her legacy is a two thousand foot monstrosity. Drakiri believe that same monstrosity will bring about the apocalypse. One belief against the other."

"Except some beliefs have foundation in reality and some are pure superstition. What's the deal with the Drakiri, you said?"

"They're convinced…" Shea sighed. "They're *convinced* that once the tower is finished, another will materialize. They even have a name for it—the Mimic Tower. It's supposed to be a portal to hell."

"Surely you realize how crazy this sounds."

"Crazy, Aidan?" Shea glanced at him. "Same crazy as in 'devices we don't understand that can fly'?"

"That's different. That's technology, as opposed to superstition."

It was Shea's turn to chuckle.

"Look," Aidan said, "you have some weaknesses that would make it difficult for you to run the court, should all of this…" He raised his hands, palms up. "Should our plans work. You need to get rid of those weaknesses. Focus on the goal at hand."

Take the next step in the golden dance.

"I'm afraid we're out of options anyway—we can't get to the tulips," Shea said.

"Have you at least found out when they close?"

"At six."

"Then we're in luck, cause some of those bloody places stay open through midnight." Aidan turned around. "Let's meet here at ten."

"Where are you going?"

"You said thirty devices. We'll need help to transport them."

"How would we even get them?"

"Well, that one's pretty obvious," Aidan said. "We break in."

7

"Shea, wake up. Shea."

Hands shook him, disembodied hands, with no person behind them. He tried to free himself when things came into focus, arms appeared, then the face framed by strands of red hair.

Muriel.

"I had a nightmare," he said.

"Forget it. Look out the window."

"Let me just lie here for a few minutes."

"Wake up, something's wrong. I think something's happened in the city."

He sat on the bed, and a sickening feeling tapped on his abdomen. "Am I still sleeping?"

"What's the matter with you? Look out the window."

He did. It must've been seven or eight in the evening—he'd dozed for an hour, no more, and the void in his body left by the lovemaking had yet to close. In front of him, vineyards stretched down the hill's slope. A road snaked in the distance, and between it and the sunset orange of the river lay Oakville.

Against the darkening rim of the sky, a cone of purple light expanded from behind the roofs.

Give me time till tomorrow evening, she'd told him yesterday.

"What the hell is that?" said Muriel. "And what are you doing?"

He didn't answer, frantically trying to push his right foot into his pants.

The purple light boiled.

Heartbeat.

"I still think we should've simply smashed one of the windows," Aidan said. "Where did you learn to pick locks?"

"My sister taught me. She used to do it for fun when we were kids."

No questions followed: no *I didn't know you had a sister*, no *where is she now*. And anyway, in a few seconds, with a click, the front door opened into the transparent dark of 'Flying Tulips'.

"Shall we wait for your people, Aidan?"

"No, let's go in. They'll arrive in ten minutes or so."

Tables with fabrics heaped on them, clothing stretchers. A child's suit hanging from a coat hook. Shea had to remind himself why he wasn't a thief, why it was all warranted.

The door at the end of the hall drew closer, and with it, a vomit-inducing, ether-inhaling vertigo. There used to be a workbench here; Danny and himself had drunk beer over there. *You're fine, Danny, you're fine. Don't worry. You'll fit in.*

Voices in the street, Aidan's whisper: *Duck.*

Shea crouched behind a table, praying that the pile of cloth on it would be enough to conceal the top of his head. When the voices gained in force, he peeked over the linen waves.

A group of young people passed outside the windows. One of them, a girl, got close to the glass, either trying to look inside or examining her own reflection. A man laughed.

"Let's go..." Something loud and unintelligible. "Come on."

The girl leaned against the window with her palms. Darkness erased all features from her face, and moonlight went right through the hair. Shea imagined her lips moving.

The next moment, tiny purple garlands stretched among the shadows: Aidan pulled off one of his gloves.

More laughter. "...Let's go."

"Aidan," Shea whispered. "It's okay, they're leaving."

The girl pushed herself away from the window—but the garlands continued to shimmer until the voices outside became an echo.

Heartbeat.

The purple light boiled.

"Lena!"

In the square before the workshop—hands, more hands, tugging at his biceps, at the lapels of his suit.

"Get the fuck off of me." Shea slapped the palms and fingers away, shouldering his way through the crowd. "Lena! *Lena!*"

Of course she couldn't hear him. If she were even inside the workshop—he still clung to the hope that the mammoth vortex boiling purply toward the sky had nothing to do with her.

Maybe she'd gone to the vineyards. Maybe she'd gone for a drink.

The building loomed ahead, a shadow stretching over the centipede of the crowd.

He broke out into the free part of the square suddenly and unexpectedly, stumbling and almost falling. There was no transition, not a single onlooker left; ten feet before the front door, a dead zone started.

He noticed the details, the way the roof arched, as though crumpled by a giant hand, the way the windows curved inward.

Someone yelled, *Stop him*—and yet nobody did.

A second's hesitation was all he could afford. He raised his head. Somewhere above, invisible to him now, the purple cone swirled.

Shea stepped into the workshop.

Wheels and ropes, tangled into a nightmarish spiderweb. The wall opposite the entrance, grinning, and the wardrobe, no longer flying, squeezed into the hole.

It looked like something had tried to *suck the building in from the inside*, and from the ripples frozen into the ceiling, he gauged where this something was.

The epicenter lay behind the door at the other side of the hall.

Or rather, a door frame, a twisted and crippled one.

Heartbeat.

Aidan pushed on the doorknob.

It was a small room, twenty by twenty feet. Some shelves, brooms huddled together in thick shadow. Moonlight seeped in through the single window by the ceiling, reflecting off the lacquered floor.

"Okay, we're here, apparently." Aidan said. "So where are the devices?"

Shea tapped the floorboards with the tip of his boot. "We'll need a hammer and a crowbar."

"Or anything to tear apart wood. It doesn't have to be clean, you know. You go through those shelves, I'll look in the adjacent rooms."

Aidan's steps staccatoed through the main hall, and Shea swallowed the lump in his throat, wishing he could do the same with the fit of claustrophobia.

Forgive me, sis. I never wanted to return. But I need to see the dance to its end.

"I think this would do," Aidan said from the door frame, holding up an oil lamp and something that resembled a pair of goat's legs.

They worked in the jittering light like two coal miners, taking a pause each time Shea lost the grip or hit his finger—he could no longer feel his hands, heartbeat having occupied the entirety of his body.

One by one, the floorboards came off and the rosewood trapdoor emerged.

Aidan slid the crowbar between its edge and the floor.

"A hand here?" he said. "The damn thing's heavy."

Together, they lifted the door into an upright position. Underneath, a black rectangle gaped at them, all stale air and the reek of mildew. Shea put his foot on the first stair and thought, *help me, sis, help me save face, help me not to faint.*

"I can't see a thing." Aidan swung the lamp behind him.

"You will."

At this point, Shea didn't need light. He descended the staircase and took a few blind steps forward.

His hands found a lever and a valve.

Forgive me, Lena.

Then it occurred to him he no longer knew which Lena he was apologizing to.

The tulip hummed, rising into the air, painting the cellar in purple, rows upon rows of the Drakiri devices stacked on top of each other like wine barrels.

Aidan whistled. "Well, I'd be damned."

Heartbeat.

A twisted, crippled door frame. Past it, a small room, twenty by twenty feet. Good for keeping brooms in, good for indoor picnics.

The ceiling and the top of the walls had been torn off—a sculptor's mold of a closet, started, but not finished. At head height, a black egg hovered, wobbling and spewing purple light into the sky in a circular pattern.

Lower, soot covered the plaster where the two oil lamps had smashed into it.

Even lower lay the chairs with twisted legs—and the bodies.

Danny was dead, mouth agape in childlike wonder, skin on the right side of his face one big burn—he'd probably held a lamp when everything happened.

Lena's chest was still going up and down.

The only sound Shea could produce was a cawk. He fell on his knees, crawled up to her.

"Lena, Lena, Lena."

He stretched out his hand, then pulled it back, not knowing what to do with that broken flower of a body, whether to try and hold it.

She opened her left eye. "Shea. Danny... Where's... Where is he?"

"Sis, sis, lie still."

"Where's... Danny..."

"Danny's dead, Lena. Please, please." He touched her hair with his fingertips.

"Wanted... to teach him... show you how easy... that even he could use..." She coughed and spat blood.

Anyone but my brother, he remembered—and realized she could choke any moment. He gently wrapped his arm around her shoulders and pressed her face into his chest.

"You have to stop it," she mumbled. "Switch off... the device."

"Everything will be all right," Shea said. "We'll sit here for a while. For a little while. Everything will be okay."

"You have... to stop it."

"I have to, yes."

He never realized tears could flow uninterrupted, without beginning or end, the body simply fulfilling one of its biological functions.

"I love you, sis."

"Love you... too... brother."

With his boot, he pulled the remnants of the nearest chair under the tulip. Keeping balance atop that heap of wood proved difficult, but somehow he managed—maybe because he wasn't thinking anymore.

He screamed and fell when the black surface burned his hands. The device was red-hot.

"Damn you." He slammed his fist into the floor. "I don't have time for this. I don't have time for this."

When his palms lay on the lever and the valve again, he clenched his teeth and tried to forget about his skin melting away, turning and pulling through the pain's curtain, turning and pulling the way Lena did it.

The device shook one last time, spewed the last of its phlegm, and lowered itself onto the floor.

He smiled briefly. Chuckled. "I did it, sis. I did it."

There was no answer.

The people who found him—the ones who'd mustered enough courage to venture into the crippled building once the vortex had died—said he sat beside her body like a praying monk. He hadn't said a word, allowing himself to be brought to his feet, bandaged, and led out.

He didn't speak the next day either, or the day after. Only listened.

Heartbeat.

Heartbeat.

Silence.

8

Someone infantile had painted those trees and that morning light, someone who had just discovered whitewash and aerial perspective. In the same way, the sounds also lacked character: flat clicking of the horse's hooves, dry tapping of the three pairs of boots that flanked the cart loaded with dark eggs.

Aidan had hired some real goons.

He strode beside Shea, black gloves on, whistling something, visibly pleased with 'the catch'.

Pines squeezed the road on both sides. When a gap opened on the left, a trail behind a decrepit wooden gate, Shea said, "I need to take a detour."

"Pardon?" Aidan shot a sideways glance at him.

"The airship won't depart for another three hours. I'll meet you at the pier."

"As you wish—but try not to be late."

Shea hopped over the gate and followed the trail into the nascent day and along a cliff's edge. Beneath him, Musk Valley gained form, soaking up light like an orange sponge, white houses and mansions, tiny figures scurrying between rows of grapevine, preparing them for winter.

Morning sun always touched the Ashcroft estate last.

Between it and the vineyards lay something new, a small field of red flowers. Tulips.

He lowered himself onto the road. If he watched long enough and squinted hard enough, he thought, he would see a girl strolling among the flowers. He would wave to her, and she would wave back, inviting him in, telling him to come home.

When an airship crawled out of the clouds, still a distant and transparent contour, Shea got up and headed back for the main road.

9

Owenbeg greeted him with the same children slinging dust at each other, the same butcher in a stained apron, the same blind lattices of windows.

It felt like a different life—and maybe it was, everything alien, the castle, the battlements, even the tower. Events from a decade ago seemed more real than what had happened to him here.

In his quarters, he walked up to the glass-fronted cabinet. There were no golden lights in the reflection, no figures spinning in a grand waltz, only the desaturated monochrome of his own face.

Voices emerged from the courtyard: Brielle, talking to the people Aidan had hired.

Bring the devices to the tower, he mouthed what he couldn't discern. *Prop my tower up.*

As for him—he waited for Lena.

She came without a knock. She wore the same hunting suit as when they'd kissed for the first time, but she was even more beautiful, infinitely more beautiful now that he knew he was about to lose her.

He tried to imagine again riding with her in a caravan wagon, her standing in the ocean waves. Just a few seconds more in the world they never got, a few seconds before she speaks.

And she spoke.

"You piece of shit," she said. "What have you done?"

"I'm sorry." Shea held out his hands to her, then dropped them as he realized how pathetic he must have looked. "Forgive me, Lena."

"You've betrayed me. You little piece of... I'll tell the duke about our affair. I'll do it right away, and I really hope to see you hanging from the first tree they find for you."

"I had to do it," he said. "I love you, but I had to do it. If you believe nothing that I say, please, at least believe that."

"Love me? You think it matters to me, you think I cared for you? You think I care for you now? All those things I've told you about leaving Owenbeg with me—it was all a con. How could you be this delusional? I was using you, I didn't even like you, I was using you all along, as a collateral, as a backup plan in case the tower somehow survived.

"And now," Lena said, "I will destroy you."

The gulls went silent. The imaginary caravan wagon exploded just as Aidan's family carriage had.

A dark tongue licked the ocean waves away.

See Yaroslav Barsukov's story "Tower of Mud and Straw III: The Tulips" online at Metaphorosis.
If you liked it, leave a comment. Authors love that!
Remember to subscribe to our e-mail updates so you'll know when new stories are posted.

December

The Skin of Aquila Cadens

Chris Panatier

TRANSMISSION T+10968.0 Authenticate: M. Saenz, Research Barque *Lyrae*

Pod is down from the *Lyrae*, upright and undamaged. Aquila Cadens, population: one. Surface scans show polymorphs of calcium carbonate with intergrowths of dolomite and huntite, limestone. Visual identification of a large iron deposit near the water to the East. No apparent vegetation. No apparent life, unfortunately, but I have only surveyed megascopically. I will put soil samples under glass tomorrow, hopefully. I'll move on to the water after that. See what swims.

Maricella dispatched the message. It wouldn't reach home for twenty-five years. She'd be eighty-nine by then, having long since completed her mission and quit the planet. She leaned over to flip down a row of switches and caught a glimpse of herself in the pod's display screen. The woman that reflected back had been young when she'd set out from Earth almost eleven thousand days ago. She raised an eyebrow and sighed. Half of her life spent transecting the void.

She sealed her helmet and crawled from the pod to stand on the bleached and crumbling caliche-like surface. Aquila Cadens orbited on the outer edge of Vega's habitable zone, but the star was a big girl and could cook dirt just as well as the Sun over desert. The planet's tilt was to the black, meaning it was something like spring at the landing site. Near the end of the mission, going outside would be impossible with the heat, especially in an environment suit.

Maricella instructed the pod to deploy the habitat, though it was more lab than living quarters—a lab-itat. She scanned the horizon as the structure unfolded. The desolate setting aside, the planet had air, water, and the basic elements needed to build life, all facts she and her team had already gleaned through a few inches of glass from light-years away. But the distance muddied the answer to the larger question. For that, they had to see for themselves. The short scan she'd done on her deceleration burn and orbital period hadn't flagged anything. Now, standing on the surface, she was still strangely hopeful despite the subtrace odds.

The little bugs Maricella and her team had developed were an evolutionary grade of mostly free-living protozoans, genetically engineered to concentrate all of the best adaptive and proliferative characteristics. Designed to survive in a wide range of settings, a thousand varieties had been dispatched to potentially habitable planets in the hope that some might stick and jumpstart ecosystems. The Earth—the place it had become—wasn't going to give humankind the time, the decades upon decades, needed for probes to reach planets light-years distant and then beam back their findings. Out of necessity, they'd eschewed a systematic approach, opting instead to fire a shotgun, as it were.

In the runup to launch, her team had worked tirelessly to develop the tiny animals for their brutal charge. Maricella had been consumed by the task, eschewing relationships, pushing friends and family aside in her dogged effort to develop Earth's first world builders. *There'll be time for all that later*, she'd thought. But then came the opportunity to walk upon one of the planets she'd seeded. The trade was thirty years in transit—a no-brainer. She'd leapt at it. Her team had identified eight candidate planets and then drawn lots to decide who would go where. She had gotten Aquila Cadens, a tan-blue marble of desert and sea. It came with an option at the end of the mission to visit another planet orbiting Altair, a nearby main sequence star similar to the Sun.

Four years after sending the bugs on their way, Maricella had set sail.

The bugs were chiefly mixotrophs, able to derive energy both from the consumption of other organisms and found chemicals, or through the photosynthesis of sunlight. The largest group would perform so-called 'soft' terraforming tasks—soil building, water and air purification, consumption of bacteria or fungal pathogens toxic to human life. A smaller subset included those that would occupy native hosts and modify them.

The decision to dispatch bugs that had the potential to permanently alter life on remote planets hadn't come without its share of infighting. The plan was to find life and appropriate it—to enslave a microbial ecosystem in order to serve the purposes of humankind. At the very least, they would be eliminating the ability of native life to freely evolve. But if they were successful, if they actually created something *new*, it would mean they had eliminated what life *had been*—an outcome some of the scientists went so far as to term 'microgenocide'. They'd bickered at length over the ethical considerations, but at the end of the day, the goal was to save the human race. And if it's us versus them, well...

The whole endeavor was contingent on the panspermia hypothesis of life proliferation being correct—that life in the local area of the galaxy shared a common source. If alien genetics were governed by something other than DNA, their bugs would be impotent to carry out their charge, and any philosophical misgivings would remain academic.

The mission allowed just over one Earth-year for surveys and analysis before she had to be up and away. At that time she'd have a choice: aim for home or Altair. The *Lyrae* was fast, but making either destination was dependent on a lone slingshot opportunity with Vega that came in four hundred days' time. Miss that window and she'd be the first human to die on Aquila Cadens.

With the labitat expanded and filling with atmosphere, she grabbed a collection kit from an outer compartment and headed east to where a range of rippling dunes signaled the sea's boundary.

The distance to the shore—only about a thousand meters—felt double in her suit. She hoped it was more the gravity and heat and less the effects of age. In her head she was still thirty-four. At the foot of a large dune, she stopped to catch her breath and hydrate, then took the ascent deliberately, pacing herself to make it up in one steady go.

From north to south, the sea was red. Maricella coughed out a laugh, felt her eyes tearing at the sight. Ignoring her exhaustion, she strode down the face of the dune, falling onto her rear and sliding to the bottom. She dusted herself off and took account.

From orbit it had looked no different than the iron-rich dirt covering huge swaths of ground back home. But she'd been wrong. It was an algal bloom; a red tide. The result, no doubt, of the modified dinoflagellates they'd sent down years before. She trotted to where the gentle surf softened the ground. The bloom meant that the water was packed with phosphorus and nitrogen. So much so that the protists were overeating. Spread out before her was undeniable proof that Earth-based lifeforms could flourish in alien waters. That alone was groundbreaking; fodder for a hundred peer-reviewed papers.

But the floating burgundy cloud was also something else. A telltale sign that the sea was devoid of other DNA-based lifeforms. The algal protists were endosymbionts, programmed to enter the cells of a host plant or animal, graft on the code Maricella and her colleagues had selected, and replicate with the newly revised genome. All in order to incite species diversification and proliferation. The goal had been to create Earth-like analogs in both flora and fauna, riding on the backs of native species. Evolution fired out of a cannon. The fact their symbionts had coagulated into a giant flotilla of algae meant they'd found no hosts.

Maricella stepped into the water until it came to her knees. Viscous, it resisted her movements, so plentiful had her protists become. She couldn't help but smile. It wasn't just the satisfaction that they'd successfully seeded another planet. Their tiny bugs had survived a journey of twenty-five light-years and were thriving, robust. She felt a mother's pride.

She filled several columns with the fecund water and headed back to the labitat. Buoyed by the discovery of her flourishing creation, she floated over the dune and the scorched white caliche.

All night she analyzed the eukaryotes under the scope. It brought another discovery, that not just one species, but several dozen distinct classifications had survived and adapted to Aquila Cadens' brackish water and cloying air. She spoke her findings aloud just to hear a real human voice, lavishing encouragement and praise upon them as she catalogued, even going so far as to name the various subtypes. Desmarella, Rhoda, Aurelia, Gyro, Dino.

TRANSMISSION T+10968.37 Authenticate: M. Saenz, Research Barque *Lyrae*

Happy to report with congratulations to all involved that our little ones are thriving. To date I have counted seventy-nine classifications overall, sixty-one eukaryotes in the local water and eighteen prokaryotes/archaea in ground fissures. No native life identified thus far. All details and data in the upload. I'll be continuing my exploration and analysis moving forward, with periodic check-ins.

Over the coming weeks, Maricella explored tirelessly, consumed by the chance of discovery. Her compulsion, she supposed, wasn't so different from a gold prospector's impulse to keep shoveling. Each new turn of dirt, like each new sample, brought with it a rush of possibilities, the chance to cry *Eureka!*

Every morning she set out in a different direction, stretching the radius of her known world. To the East, the sea. To the North, South, and West, blanched ground veined with cracks that seemed mantle deep. She took samples at varying intervals and depths, plotting the locations so any patterns might later be sussed. Aquila's giant moon was a constant companion, moving ever so slowly through the sky, following along like a milky eyeball. The pod's drones flew sorties out over hundreds of kilometers without noting anything different from what Maricella had seen on foot. Aside from the life they'd sown, there was nothing.

The bugs, though, had done their jobs. Those meant for the soil, a category of archaic diazotrophs, had propagated at around one meter deep, fixing nitrogenous compounds into ammonia, erecting a tentative microbial ecosystem. The waters teemed, swollen and virile, prepared to build new life upon old. But Aquila Cadens was inviolably barren. The rush of discovery from her first day faded, only to be replaced by tooth-clenching frustration. Repeated findings showed the planet and its new denizens in stasis. A holding pattern. Purgatory, in evolutionary terms.

Halfway through the mission, the days became warmer, which meant less time in the field and more in the labitat. When not conducting new analyses or re-running old samples, Maricella allowed her mind to unfold on how life could explode if given but a nudge. The planet was loaded with the necessary elements: oxygen, carbon, hydrogen, nitrogen, and sulfur. Even a modest population of multicellular natives would have allowed her brood to work wonders. She could accept her lot—that a decades-long endeavor would ultimately be fruitless—that had been part of the risk. But her heart ached for the beings they'd created, set forth on winds of scientific optimism, only to end up languishing on the surface of an otherwise dead planet. So much potential wasted.

With the hot season setting in, she could only bear to be outside the labitat in the early mornings and at starset. One evening, as Vega fell in the East, Maricella suited up and headed to the shore where she paced the water's edge. She sang songs. Lullabies she might have sung to a child, perhaps, but now to an audience of countless members. Her red tide. The children of Aquila Cadens.

This became routine. A way to commune with the living that wasn't a recorded transmission twenty-five years stale. Some evenings she carried her melodies into the sea and drifted among the swimmers, gazing skyward as the stars kindled. Together, they devised their own constellations. Something they could share, unique to them and no one else. The Warbler, Saloon Dragon, Sea Fox, Dalmatian Cat... She spoke to them about her life and how, even knowing the outcome, she would do it all over again.

Back in the labitat, Maricella ad-libbed. She ran off-book experiments in the hope of triggering uplift changes in her dutiful spawn, but their fundamental natures were hardwired. The bugs were piggy backers. Absent something to latch onto, they weren't going to elevate. And that was that.

TRANSMISSION   T+10968.246   Authenticate: M.   Saenz, Research Barque *Lyrae*

One hundred and fifty-four days remaining and there is nothing more to be done. Findings are archived and uploaded. Everything we needed was here, except for the ladder. I will await sling shot and advise of my decision to return home or carry forward to Altair at that time.

Maricella speaks to the bugs, the different varietals. Sings to them. Feels they will understand if she chooses her words carefully, intones her voice sincerely. Carries them about the labitat so they may enjoy changing views and exposures. Her evening floats drag on for hours, so as to be closer to them for longer. She shares secrets. Confesses to them her regret. Whispers apologies. Arrives back at the labitat, her suit's oxygen supply further into the red each night.

One evening, she spills through the pod's hatch euphoric with hypoxia, gathers up the vials for Desmarella, Dino, and Aurelia. Drunkenly, she sways to a song with no name, no melody, rearranges colonies about the lab, perceives the tumble of glassware. Cuts her finger on a petri dish.

The next day, Maricella wakes. Oxygenated, rested. Notes that sobriety brings no relief from the anxiety of coming separation. Abandonment. She pushes up from the floor. On the lab bench is a small tree, red and glistening.

Her little dribble of blood, full of living things. Already co-opted by Desmarella, who has built a delicate bronchus trunk spiked with tiny bronchiole branches. Alveolar buds would surely be visible were Maricella to place a cutting between glass. Given so little to work with, the bugs flex their potential. *Let us show you,* they say. *Oh, what you could have become,* she answers.

Later, silent, she packs her scopes and labware. Places sample columns and vials into cryo for transport, heart crumbling for those she must leave.

In the days leading up to departure, she prepares the pod, clears dust and debris from intakes. The heat, a combination of seasonal change and proximity to the star, is almost unbearable in the suit. She retreats inside, stinking, sweat pooled in every fold, the fingertips of her gloves.

She brings the reactor on-line. Follows protocols. Checklists and calibrations. T-minus fourteen hours.

Night falls to cool relief. She calms, dresses for her swim. The red tide greets her, a bath of her progeny. It is the last evening—she has not concealed the truth. They understand, hold no grudge. And this makes the idea of leaving them unbearable. She wishes them capable of resentment. Hatred at her desertion. Instead, they speak of understanding. Maricella cries until her eyes run dry.

An oxygen alarm pings. She considers letting it go. Even now, the dune is a formidable obstacle for what air she has left. Dying there with her 'zoa, supported on a bed of their flagellae, their tiny hands...she could think of worse deaths. Still, the mission, the future of humankind. She sits upright on the foot of a shoal, her bottom half submerged. Looks to the dune, imagines the ship on the other side, the void, Altair and the Earth beyond that. It is time.

Dawn comes and Maricella is in the water again, murmuring apologies and lamentations. Her mind replays the ethical debates of decades before. Thoughts drift to the cellular phenomenon of apoptosis, where sick cells, such as those with cancerous changes, undergo programmed death so as not to pass on the mutation. And how tumors result when some cells, for whatever reason, refuse to die. She leaves the water and marches back to the pod.

For the first time in four hundred days, she assumes her seat at the controls, brings up the trajectory display. An image of the planet moves in an arc at the end of Vega's invisible tether and two paths emerge. One to a rock in the habitable zone of Altair, and another, to Earth. The countdown begins in her ears, quietly, like a secret. Less than a minute to go. She does not strap in.

As the seconds expire, she considers the blue veins snaking over the bones at the backs of her hands. *Forty seconds.* Their stark topographical relief reminds her that while her body is sixty-four, she's only really lived for just over thirty. *Twenty-five seconds.* She glances at her helmet, hanging nearby. *Ten seconds. Five seconds.* Some cells refuse to die. *One second.*

The panel lights up. Alarms sound. A switch beckons from beneath its plastic guard. Maricella gazes back to the screen and watches until the display re-renders the *Lyrae's* trajectory, and it swings wide of both Altair and Earth. Dotted lines flash from white to red. Apoptosis.

TRANSMISSION   T+10968.400   Authenticate: M.   Saenz, Research Barque *Lyrae*

I have chosen not to leave Aquila Cadens in order to pursue a new line of research here. This is my final transmission.

I made you. But I did not give you what you needed to do the thing I designed you to do, my children, my issue. You needed life, and so I give it to you. I give you everything. The future. I give you Aquila Cadens. Make of it what you will.

Maricella selects a panel of her most aggressive endosymbionts and places them into solutions containing her own skin cells, plasma, and cheek swabs. Bulk elements are introduced. Within hours, new structures are visible, stretching and retracting in response to stimuli, respiring. She carries two dishes from the pod, one for the sea, one for the ground.

Mother absorbs into child. She feels the bugs, her sons and daughters, her sexless archaea, drinking in the new information and carrying it into nuclei and organelles. Repurposing. She senses the sharp angle of evolutionary inflection, the moment of speciation, the refraction of static paths, now jagged and ever changing. Nature freed to run wild, each mitosis an exponential leap.

Purple veins crawl like roots through prokaryotic nurseries in caliche crevices. Decided by some combination of eukaryotic programming and terroir, saplings sprout without rain, fleshy pink with thick tufts of autotrophic leaves for capturing Vega's light. All-seeing catkins loll from branches. Elsewhere, bulbs burst skyward with petals that explode in clouds of pastel seed and spore that flow across the planet and take root wherever landed. Maricella, gloves off, reaches down. A threadlike root unspools from a crack and spirals around her fingertip. Communion. She feels the cool depths that the archaea enjoy.

Years pass. Maricella grows old within a failing pod that can no longer clean the air or recycle waste. Outside, she is surrounded by the nascent world her children make. She almost abandoned them once. She would not do it now. She prepares aliquots of Desmarella, Gyro, Dino, Aurelia, Rhoda, and others. Introduces them via nasal mist. Children absorb into mother.

Her body given over, they draft their plans upon her substrate. Endosymbionts take to her cells, slicing in and occupying, editing. They weave and sew filaments of neural tissue into harmony with their primitive structures. Sentience shared, their plans are heard, repeated and circular, aspiring upward. Rung by rung they ascend. Maricella's genome evolves even as she lives. Bound together with her offspring, they become the next thing.

Eureka.

Her mind expands into a network of square kilometers below the planet's surface, aware of all each stripling perceives. Helmetless and fluid, Maricella leaves the pod for good, and is absorbed into the living superstructure that crawls to the horizon. The air, once acrid, is sweet and honeysuckle.

Her children bow and stretch, actualize. They feel pleasure and fulfillment of purpose. She feels it with them. They are a consciousness, the implanted code of primordial lifeforms towering from the human scaffolding upon which they build. A new organism is set on a course of its own making, freelancing within the dictates of the planet's offerings. Maricella's body spills into the network her bugs have created, consumed as raw material; the individual gutters to equilibrium.

The red tide recedes.

See Chris Panatier's story "The Skin of Aquila Cadens" online at Metaphorosis.
If you liked it, leave a comment. Authors love that!
Remember to subscribe to our e-mail updates so you'll know when new stories are posted.

About the story

While I doubt humankind will ever send crewed missions beyond our solar system, I'm intrigued by the fantasy of it. My head is full of all sorts of world-building and terraforming ideas from things I've read. In most of these stories, the terraforming either succeeds or fails, or "succeeds" but with catastrophic consequences. I saw the opportunity to tell my own terraforming story with a different sort of outcome, that also addressed the ethical considerations of the decision to spread the human species in the first place.

A question for the author

Q: How often do you think about writing during the day?

A: Constantly. And it takes one of two forms: either as anxiety that I am not writing and should be, or more constructively, as brainstorming plots and problem solving. I do my best thinking while running or bike riding, and the biggest challenge there is remembering what I'd figured out on my jaunt long enough to write it down when I get home.

About the author

Chris lives in Dallas, Texas, with his wife, daughter, a herd of dogs, and possibly one goat. He does album art for metal bands and writes short fiction. His debut novel, *The Phlebotomist*, comes out on September 8, 2020, from Angry Robot Books. As a civil trial lawyer, he represents people who have been poisoned by negligent corporations.

www.chrispanatier.com, @chrisjpanatier

The Three Thousand

Elise Kim

The walls of the city shuddered under cannon fire and smoldered with flames. Its defenders, too weary to march, stumbled through the streets to barricade the crumbling gates. In a dark cellar, the weight of their footsteps sent soft rains of dust cascading down on the faces of a young man and woman who sat huddled there. Somewhere in the cellar was a candle whose wick had drowned in wax a long time ago.

It was in the ringing silence left in the wake of a cannon blast, when the city shivered and held its breath, that she told him, "I believe it now—the three thousand years."

The three thousand years? He had heard the folktale all his life, heard the bards spin stories of the long, slow turn of the wheel of rebirth. Believing it had always seemed to him like an act of desperation: it was the story beggars told themselves to pretend that someday they'd be reborn as kings. But now, at the last moment, his heart began to change. Three thousand years...he could wait longer than that to see her again.

Sound ebbed back into the city. Soldiers barked orders. The cellar shook as a dozen boys who had been convinced to die on the walls like men ran overhead. Waiting in the cellar, they had become numb to this, and the only things real to them now were the sound of their voices hovering in the dark and the awareness of their hands, sweaty and cold, intertwined in a grip tight enough to defy death. The enemy would take the city, post their ash-black flags to flutter in the howling wind, storm the houses and the halls and the cellars, and kill them both—but they would not let go.

She leaned her head against his in the dark and said, "I had a dream last night...three thousand years long."

"Then tell me what you saw," he said. It was a folktale for desperate people, and he had become desperate.

So she began to tell her dream to him, and in her voice he forgot the suffocating night of the cellar, the sharp pain of his wounded leg, the cries of the city as it died. They had been through a moment like this once before, he remembered, in the early years of the siege. Whispering to each other in the dark, she had told him of the places she had wandered in sleep, soaring citadels of glass and beasts that glided like shadows beneath the surface of frozen lakes. They were only dreams, yet when she told them, he had felt that if he waited enough lifetimes he might see them with his own eyes. So he listened to her now, and the dream of their future spread out before him like reality.

"After this life we're born as songbirds, but you live in a forest an ocean apart from mine. Every day you fly as far as you can from the tree in which you slept, driven to search, although you do not know for what. You might have known it if you'd seen it, but you don't: you never reach the shore. Far away, I nest in the hollow of a dead oak and stay there as winters come and go. Each day at dusk, the both of us whistle to the winds, but the winds are too weak to reach across the waters. We die on the same day after three years."

"That's all?"

"We have two thousand and nine hundred ninety-seven more to go. We're born as foxes next. You grow lean, your bones a hard frame for your skin, because the hunt almost always escapes you and you wander alone in the mud and snow. We live in the same wood, but it is vast and winter never leaves it. A hundred miles away, I grow gray and blind before I ever become old, and after five years I lay down for the last sleep. The tip of my tail touches a twig that you broke eight months ago, while you were wandering with a hunger and a yearning that food couldn't feed."

"In your dream," he asked, "do we meet again?"

"Almost," she said. "We go two hundred years without passing each other, until we are reborn as silver fish. One day you find a stray current and let it take you to shallow waters. You see a gray gleam not too far away. Just when you might have come close enough to see what that gleam was—just when you might have seen me, waiting among the bright reefs—a fisherman's harpoon comes for you and the water tastes of blood."

She fell silent, but he didn't know what she was thinking.

Her fingers felt cold, and so he wrapped her hand with both of his own to warm them. "Go on," he said.

"We live and die and live again for centuries and centuries. Once we are swans, and you are traveling through a land you think is empty when you fly across a lake echoing with ripples. You go on, knowing you can't stop searching. You do not realize that I have just landed by the shore. I do not realize that the fleeting shadow passing over the reeds is you. Then we are leviathans, for a time, and we spend decades drifting through the deeps of the ocean. In a black trench where no light comes, I wait and wait. Once you come down, and we glide past each other and our sightless heads nearly touch, but it is dark as black ink and we are only faint shadows to each other."

Her voice was almost too soft to hear as the walls of the city finally thundered to the ground, and the trumpets of the enemy called out, clear and cold. Heavy drumbeats pulsed through the air, announcing with a steady trembling that the city was at its end. This much had become clear to him: the lives they were to have after followed the pattern of the life they lived now.

He remembered how they had met by chance in the early days of the siege, years ago. He had gone with his brother to fight on the plains outside the city walls, and seen him fall to his knees with a black arrow in his heart. He had carried his brother home on his shoulders; then, when he had cremated him, carried him to the temple in his arms. It was in that hour that he had met her, the daughter of a priest. Something had made her sit on the steps outside the temple that day, and something had made a sparrow perch on the branch above her head and cry its bitter and sweet song, and they met with the sudden sense that she had been waiting for him, and he had been searching for her. For a brief moment, all had felt justified.

But the shadow of the siege had hung over them all this time, and every one of their memories from the first to the last had a red tint. Soon the city would be destroyed, and the world would justify what he had come to believe in his most fatalistic moments, that being happy was other peoples' duty, and his was to lie forgotten in the dust. That she would lie there with him only made it worse.

He didn't know how she could tell him these lifetimes slowly, patiently, as if the knowledge of them didn't hurt her. But she had always been like that. In the long-ago red dusk when they had whispered their dreams, she had smiled at the remembrance of the things she'd imagined and told him she wanted to see the wide world when she grew older. Yet in the next moment she said she knew that in this lifetime she would not grow old. Her smile had dimmed slightly then, but it had not disappeared. "We'll have to wait", she'd said, "just for a small while." Sometimes he thought she knew the way and winding of eternity itself. Time couldn't frighten her. But it frightened him.

Shouts and screams echoed down the street as the enemy marched through the fallen city.

"Tell me of the end," he said. "Tell me...after three thousand years, do we..."

"After three thousand, we are finally born as humans again," she said. In her voice he thought he could hear her smiling softly. His heart rose. "You are the son of a soldier, and when you come of age you wear his armor to war. I am the daughter of a farmer, and when she dies, I till the fields she left behind. One day you hear your captain say that there is a field of roses in the valley nearby. I hear news that an army is camped in the mountains above. When you try to fall asleep that night, you find you can't. You feel that you must do something, but you do not know what it is. I sit by my fireplace and sense that I am living in a moment that will not come again."

"And then?" he asked.

The door slammed open on the floor above.

"Tell me. I come down from the mountains, don't I? I meet you in the field—I must."

Their hands were twisted together so tightly they could feel each other's heartbeat, fast and insistent, against their palms.

"You fall asleep," she whispered, "and so do I. When I wake up in the morning, the coals in the fireplace have become cold ash, and you have already marched away."

"That can't be."

"Don't cry."

"But you are."

"I know," she said. "But there will be another three thousand years for us."

Footsteps drummed overhead. Doors slammed open. Hoarse voices shouted.

In the darkness he tried to hold on to the memory of her face, the way she'd been on the steps of the temple, in the moment time had been kind to them. He imagined that moment coming again. "Another three thousand...and then we must be done with waiting. We must find each other."

"No," she whispered. "There will be another three thousand. And another after that, and another and another until the world grows old. But we will come closer and closer each time—"

A blaze of light blinded them as an enemy soldier kicked open the cellar door.

"So you must wait for me—wait for the years to fly past us, wait for us to wander through an unfathomable number of almosts, wait for a time where you and I—"

One day, in two separate forests an ocean apart, two songbirds began to whistle to the wind.

See Elise Kim's story "The Three Thousand" online at Metaphorosis.
If you liked it, leave a comment. Authors love that!
Remember to subscribe to our e-mail updates so you'll know when
new stories are posted.

About the story

I was reading Herodotus' *Histories* one summer when I found the initial inspiration for "The Three Thousand". Herodotus is a great author to consult for ideas. I like to imagine him as an intrepid but easily distracted explorer, more focused on what would make a good story than what is actually factual history. He writes this of the religious beliefs of the ancient Egyptians: "[they are] the first who reported the doctrine that the soul of man is immortal, and that when the body dies, the soul enters into another creature which chances then to be coming to the birth, and when it has gone the round of all the creatures of land and sea and of the air, it enters again into a human body as it comes to the birth, and that it makes this round in a period of three thousand years." I'm skeptical if this is factually true, considering how many of his other historical details aren't, but I think it's a fascinating foundation for a story. For several months the idea floated around in my head, gradually taking shape as a myth-like tale of two humans who wait for eternity to meet each other again, coming closer, then farther, but never quite meeting, as three thousand years come and go and come again. Over a year later, the story finally took shape as "The Three Thousand".

A question for the author

Q: Have you ever wondered whether ideas are thought waves directed at you by an AI supercomputer located in the distant future?

A: I can't say that I have, although I know I'll be thinking about it at random moments for some time in the future. It's entirely plausible, considering our rate of technological progress, but I don't think it's likely. The ideas that lead to the stories I like to write, and the ideas that lie at the heart of the stories of the writers I admire most, likely aren't of interest to AI in the distant future. To me, much of what lies at the core of a good idea is emotional, and I have always seen AI as distinctly logical. I have a hard time believing that artificial intelligence can be programmed to think of ideas evoking wonder, emotional connection, and empathy in the same way a real human being living in this age and this moment can.

About the author

Elise lives in San Diego, California, where she spends most of her time ignoring the perfect weather to scribble down stories indoors. When she's not writing, she likes to cultivate her ever-growing collection of fancy wood-case pencils, mechanical typewriters, and crumbly old books.

Heritage

Andrei Pechalin

I used to think my mother had me by accident. Could anyone blame me? My earliest memory is her hunched over a desk, one hand raised to silence me, the other scribbling furiously; her head never once turned towards me. All the while, I shook with violent, wailing sobs, bruised after a bad fall. She left me there for Dad's healing embrace, his calming parental touch, to scoop me up, carry me away, so she could continue her work in peace. It was a template for most of our relationship, until the final days, until she disappeared.

Back then, when I was still little more than muddy palms and scratched knees, my only understanding of her work came from her rare descriptions and my imagination. The slightest change of pressure in the air, a feeling of unease, of something tugging, drawing, stretching, and a small black square would appear. For a moment, it would hang a few feet above ground, like a displaced window or doorway, but without any sense of volume or depth, a two-dimensional plane. It would be completely still, as if surveying its surroundings, then all of a sudden expand in four directions at once, grow with symmetrical precision, like someone was wedging it open and applying steady, even pressure. Sometimes it would grow no larger than a few spans, sometimes it would occlude the horizon, large enough to fit the tallest of the city buildings, but always it would leave an impression of absence—not merely of superimposing itself over familiar surroundings, but disappearing them altogether. They would be back when the square eventually shrank and disappeared, but for the time of its manifestation, looked at head on, it felt like these things were cut out from the world, temporarily transported elsewhere.

When I was six, they decided to call this the Shiftspace. Mum was a member of the first expedition inside. I remember the hours before she left. She was wrapped in furs, a rifle on her back and an axe hanging from her belt. She looked like she was heading into the polar regions, but the truth was that no one knew what to expect from the expedition. She remarked darkly that once they did learn something, this information would be immediately sold or classified. My father laughed and called her a collectivist—he knew that she carried the label with pride—but they were more tense than they dared admit. At six years old it did not occur to me that Mum might not return.

She did return, four weeks later, but she was changed. There were the superficial differences: she was away from home most of the time, at government committees, academic conferences, industrialists' evenings; and she was in the press seemingly every day—first as a hero who had led the rest of the expedition out of the Shiftspace when they became lost in its featureless, abysmal darkness; later as a veteran of Shiftscience, carrying her authority with a measured, erudite calm.

But something had also changed at the core of her, some tiny, barely perceptible thing that sent out ripples of disturbance, billowing every so often into waves of rage or hysteria, getting worse as the years passed. I would hear her locked in her study, crying, laughing, or screaming, clawing at the walls like a caged animal. And between, I would catch her brooding over notes from the expedition. She would run a hand over her arm, absently, but squeezing and pinching so hard it left marks, as if her skin were a glove that needed to be pulled back over the muscle. There was something so utterly inhuman about this motion, so wrong, that I would run to find Dad and climb into his lap, terrified and quivering. He would stroke my hair and whisper for me not to worry, that Mum was just under pressure from her newfound responsibilities.

Eventually Dad gave up trying to pretend that things were fine. I could not blame him; if anything, I was surprised he had managed to keep it going as long as he had. I saw Mum less than ever, and Dad grew tired of making up excuses for her absences. Ten years spent living in the shadow of her growing catalogue of achievements had fractured his life; stunted his own modest attempts at a career as a publicist; made him feel small, insignificant, a sideshow to her success. He turned bitter and resentful, paced the house with a kind of deliberate, withering cynicism. It became increasingly difficult to be around him. Mum stopped returning home altogether, and several months later I moved out as well.

I applied to study Shiftscience at the Free Institute of Arwall. What other choice could I make? By this time the idea of the Shiftspace was an engraving worked into my bone and sinew.

I was sixteen years old and the youngest student at the Institute. They had accepted me largely on the strength of Mum's reputation. My supervisor had been a member of her expedition, and made it very clear that he could not refuse her daughter. It did not endear me to the rest of the student body or the Faculty, and I kept largely to myself and my studies in a private dormitory at the top of one of the old Institute buildings. The view made up for it: on a clear day I could see Arwall in all its fetid, fuming splendour, stretching into the distance in a haze of smoke punctured by sooty chimneys.

I did not see Mum; I never received or sent letters or telegrams, and she no longer gave lectures at the Institute, confined to a laboratory she had outfitted in Morton, near the original entry point into the Shiftspace. But her presence was everywhere. Textbook citations, heliotypes, countless theories, laws, experiments—all carried her name. She had never spoken to me about the expedition, so it was a shock to find her findings discussed so actively here—supported, refuted, refined, expanded.

I learned the foundational principles of Shiftscience quickly, eager to discover what had kept Mum so often away from home.

The Shiftspace manifests in places where the boundary with our space is already thin—not an observable fact, but assumed because it always appears in the same half a dozen locations. It closes within a few minutes if no one enters it, but it remains open while someone is inside. There it begins as a formless black void, stretching on indefinitely without any sense of direction or limit. Over time it adopts some properties that are familiar to us. At first it is rapidly filled with breathable air and begins to exhibit something like gravitational pull, though it is impossible to determine its source. Much later, the Shiftspace starts to spawn a fog-like geometry—faintly visible, ghostly surfaces that hint at the partial outline of a tree, or a house, or simple furniture, and grow more defined and solid as time inside passes. It is possible to float amongst all this by exerting the barest effort, pushing through the air in any direction like a caricature swimmer. This ease of motion with little reference point is terrifying; one can become disoriented, thrown off-course as easily as a raft in open water. Mum's expedition had almost lost four people in this way the first time they had made camp, and the ten of them had then lashed themselves together and to their equipment to avoid getting separated.

The geography of the Shiftspace does not correspond to known geography. Mum's expedition had entered it near Morton; they were found four weeks later in Chaing, a journey that would have taken twice as long by the Trans-Imperial Express. Dad may have laughed at Mum's cynicism, but the possibility of commercialising the Shiftspace for travel was suggested and widely discussed almost the day after the expedition returned.

Mum's explanation for all this—a theory that remains Shiftscience orthodoxy to this day—began by asking why such a profoundly alien space should come to have features that are familiar to us. Her answer was that the Shiftspace wants to put us at ease by mimicking our ordinary habitat. The longer we remain in the Shiftspace, the longer it can maintain the entry to our space open, and thereby better learn to copy its properties; in turn, the less likely we are to want to leave. All of this implies that the Shiftspace in some sense wants to maintain the entry from our reality open indefinitely. Mum posited that it is somehow sustained by our presence within it, so it has a natural urge to keep the entry open, to attract new visitors.

I learned most of this in lectures, and it wasn't long before I began formulating my own theories. I read from a yellowing, largely forgotten first hardcopy report tucked far into the recesses of the Institute library that one of the members of Mum's expedition had been from Chaing and carried pictures of his hometown. At camp he would pass these around and tell the others stories from his childhood—a way to hold onto fraying sanity as their time in the void dragged on and they seemed no closer to finding an exit. Mum claimed that eventually the images of Chaing were so firm in her mind that she fancied she could see the town even when she wasn't thinking about it. Not long after, she noticed a point of bright white light amongst the darkness. She made towards it and found their exit.

Even though the report had been dismissed as mere correlation, I had the intuition that there was a causal relationship here: Mum had managed to create an exit from the Shiftspace into Chaing by imagining and holding it firmly in her mind. I formed a hypothesis: that it was possible to establish a permanent thoroughfare through the Shiftspace by having someone inside it focusing on an exit point. By extension, I supposed it was possible to establish multiple thoroughfares using multiple individuals. Combined with what we already knew about the geographical properties of the Shiftspace, a secondary hypothesis: that it was possible to establish permanent shortcuts between different locations in our space-time via the Shiftspace. Indeed, since it took some time for Mum to become familiar with Chaing through her colleague's stories, I supposed that the four-week shortcut between Morton and Chaing could be reduced even further.

I presented this to Professor Jacob Lukash, my supervisor. Even now I remember how he frowned, deep lines cutting into his face with a mixture of hesitation and unease. He looked up at me over the edge of the short essay I had handed to him.

"I understand where you are coming from with this,. I really do," he said, "It's interesting, potentially ground-breaking. But we won't be able to get funding for it."

"Why not?" I was twenty, naïve in the ways of research politics.

He smiled. It wasn't patronising, more a pained twitch at something that he did not enjoy explaining.

"I'll tell you something that I would ask you do not repeat outside this room."

He leaned forward in his armchair and fixed me with a hard look. I nodded.

"Shiftscience is of great interest to the Empire; it has been ever since your mother's first expedition. *Our* expedition," he corrected himself with a wince. "The state has been considering military applications for the Shiftspace for a decade: behind-enemy-lines reconnaissance and insertion, guerrilla warfare, that sort of thing. In all this time, your mother has worked very hard to keep the state an arm's length away from Shiftscience—to preserve our academic freedom. She has provided just enough information in some circles, just enough disinformation in others. It's like walking the edge of a knife: make one wrong move and you do not just fall, you are cut to pieces. I do not envy her position."

I remember he paused then and something flickered across his face that may have been 'you remind me too much of her', or maybe just another one of his regretful smiles.

"What this means," he sighed, "is that your mother is *de facto* entirely in control of funding decisions for Shiftscience. And she will not recommend this for funding. If you happen to prove it, to publish it, you risk bringing about total government control over our field."

The following morning I packed a small suitcase and took the first train to Morton. I had not seen Mum for nearly five years, and as the train counted the miles under the steady chug-chug of its wheels, I realised that I was increasingly nervous, frightened almost, as if I were heading for an audition.

I was distracted by a man and a woman opposite me. Their daughter used the wooden slats of the row of train seats like a ladder to climb towards the emergency brake lever. The woman grabbed her around the waist just before she was able to reach it, and she squealed with delight as she was first piloted towards the man and then tickled by both parents until she was exhausted.

I watched them, and perhaps for the first time I considered that my relationship with Mum had never had this familial warmth or simplicity. When I was a child, she had spent most of the time locked in her study, too consumed by her work to pay me much attention; when I was a teenager she was too famous to be at home; by the time I was a young woman she had disappeared altogether. And in spite of all this, my father's and my lives had been defined by her. She was not my role model—I don't remember ever looking up to her—but the shadow she cast was inescapably long.

Watching the young family in front of me, a quiet, simmering anger slowly took the place of my anxiety. I counted the years of our family to the rhythm of the train and found that most of them had been without Mum. She was not neglectful; neglect requires a failing of character—some malady or incompetence or evil to override reason. She was simply completely and utterly indifferent.

I arrived in Morton by late afternoon. Mum's house was a detached stone cottage on the outskirts of the town. It was large, but the living quarters were modest, most of the space occupied by a laboratory filled with measuring equipment and calculation engines. The first entry point into the Shiftspace, the one that Mum had used fifteen years earlier, was on the cottage grounds and she monitored it and processed new findings in the laboratory.

She was waiting for me as I stepped out of the motorised carriage I had taken from the train station. She must have heard the whir of the engine or the rustle of the wheels against the cobbled road. As I walked towards the door, raising my collar against the bracing cold, some of the fight I had built up on the train left me. Mum was always calm, even, just short of haughty, and this gave her a presence that far outweighed her slight build and modest height. It tugged me back into her orbit as steadily as if I were a small, barely observable satellite.

I slowed my pace and took a long look at her. Her hair had turned a brilliant white and she had let it grow long and tied it back into a tight ponytail. Her face was a little more lined than I remembered, the bags under her eyes heavier, but she had the same brilliant green gaze. She wore her usual long black skirt and a tightly fitting jacket, all in black, that pulled her back straight. When I was at school, before I really understood Mum's work, I imagined that she must be a headmistress, stern and upright.

She watched me without outward emotion, save for a small, tightly controlled smile.

"Jacob telegraphed," she said drily and let the words hang.

Mum was letting me know that she had been informed why I was here, that she was willing to discuss it, but had had time to consider it and her mind was largely, if not entirely, made up.

The first words she had said to me in five years and they were a carefully judged, timed, weighed attack. She greeted me like a junior colleague, subordinate to her control of Shiftscience, rather than like her daughter. I felt the anger from the train resurface. I made a point of not replying. She raised an eyebrow; her lips twitched.

"Come inside."

The cottage was clean, meticulously organised, utilitarian: sparse furniture, plain walls and carpet, nothing in the way of decoration. There were occasional piles of books on the floor, overspill from wall-length, ceiling-high shelves, but even these piles were carefully organised by subject and alphabet.

"I've brought my work," I said, reaching inside my coat for the notes that explained my hypotheses about the Shiftspace.

Mum reached out for them without turning around, skimmed them as we walked the length of the cottage and entered her study, a large room with a single desk, chair, lamp, and books along each wall. She sat down, leaving me standing. I could not say if it was another power play or she was too engrossed in her reading.

She reached inside a drawer, rummaged through it for a moment, pulled out several sheets of creased, yellowing paper held together with a paper clip and pushed them towards me across the desk.

"Read it," she nodded towards the bundle.

I picked it up, scanned the title: "How to Use the Shiftspace to Bridge Locations". I shot Mum an incredulous look; she watched me carefully.

"This paper," I found that I was reading the paper abstract out loud, my voice growing heavy with emotion, "reports experimental data that tests two hypotheses. Firstly, that it is possible to create an exit from the Shiftspace by visualising it in a particular way. Secondly, that, combined with the existing entrance into the Shiftspace, this can be used to form a bridge between two locations in our space-time. The data supports both hypotheses."

There was more, but I stopped reading. I felt fifteen again: inadequate, undermined, insignificant. I had not given myself account of it, but somewhere at the back of my mind an ugly thought had been festering: I had begun to nurture the idea that my theories would buy me recognition and fame enough not only to escape Mum's shadow, but to eclipse it with my own. Now I was looking at a paper dated fourteen years old that not only made the same claims, but tested and proved them.

"You didn't publish this," I whispered, unable to control my voice.

Mum shook her head.

"Why?"

She gestured at the paper again. "Just read it."

"The data supports both hypotheses," I read again, "However, the hypotheses also imply that someone must remain within the Shiftspace for the duration of the bridge, exerting sustained effort to visualise the exit. This effectively turns them into what we may call a Shiftslave, raising many of the ethical ramifications we typically attach to other forms of slavery. It also raises significant safety concerns: what happens to the Shiftslave or to those using a Shiftspace bridge if the exit is lost and cannot be re-established?"

I half-threw, half-dropped the paper towards Mum. I felt faint, steadied myself on the corner of her desk, then gave up and slowly sank to the floor, pressing my back against the wood of the desk hard enough for it to rake my spine.

I knew I was not thinking rationally, but it felt like she had anticipated my every move, had planned for it and closed it off years before I had even thought of making it. The anger I had kindled on my way here spilled over into tears of frustration, a sense of bitter futility. It seemed to me that no matter what I did, I could not untether myself from her dominance.

I sat on the floor, staring without recognition at a wall of books with Mum's name on them, my back to her.

"You and I can see this isn't just about the academic freedom of Shiftscience," she said. "If the Empire gets hold of this research, they will want to commercialise and militarise it no matter the risks or the human cost."

There was something about her choice of the conjunction 'you and I'—perhaps the pitiful concession of it, the morsel of credit she was willing to throw my way—that brought back all my venom in a sudden surge. I lost control of myself.

"Tell me something," I said, still sat on the floor staring ahead of me. "Do you cry and scream when you're alone, like you used to?"

It was a low and ugly move, but I had made it and I was determined to play it out.

"Do you try to tear your skin off and scratch the walls when no one is looking? Do you have anyone to cover it up for you, to make excuses and keep the place in order, like Dad used to do?"

She did not reply, so I got up, turned around to look at her. Her face was still, but pale as chalk. She gripped her chair with white-knuckled intensity, squeezing so hard I could hear her skin creak against the varnish.

"Do your colleagues know how unstable you are? That you haven't been right for fifteen years? That all of this," I waved a hand at the shelves around me, "Was dreamt up by a sick mind?"

After a long moment, our eyes locked but nothing passing between them, she drew one long, deep breath and relaxed her grip on the chair.

"I think we are done here," she said quietly.

After I returned from Morton I locked myself away in my dormitory in Arwall and did not attend any teaching for two months. A fortnight into my seclusion, Jacob came to visit to make sure I was alright. He found me dishevelled and sleep-deprived, surrounded by every available library text on Shiftscience, various diagrams, scribbled notes, and calculations pinned to my walls and laid out on the floor, one on top of the other in a collage of mad science. I briefly explained that I was working in a new direction suggested by my earlier hypotheses and a conversation with Mum. I appeared calm and focused, despite my exhaustion and dishevelment, and I was obviously entirely absorbed in study, so he left satisfied.

At the end of the two months I had written a paper. Maybe it was all that time with little food, sleep, and too much work, or perhaps I sensed the repercussions it would have, but I decided to forego the usual dry scientific titles in favour of something more lyrical: "A Bridge through the Void".

Based on supposition and extrapolation from existing theory and data, I proposed methods to create and hold open a bridge through the Shiftspace. My proposal still required someone to host the bridge—a Shiftslave, in Mum's terminology. It was a point of ethics that she had explored at length, but which I ignored entirely. Nor did I factor in the risks in the event that a host was unable to visualise, or to continue visualising, an exit.

Looking back, it pains me to admit that I simply did not care about these things. What mattered to me was the desire for recognition, the need to make my own mark on Shiftscience. The irony that my findings were identical to Mum's unpublished draft in almost every respect spurred me on rather than held me back. I told myself it mattered that I had developed my theories independently, without assistance or feedback. Nonetheless, the similarities frustrated me. It was all I could do to convince myself to focus on the immediate gains from publication, the platform it would give me for further study that would eventually render Mum's broader research programme obsolete.

I made a copy of the paper and placed it in an envelope addressed to the Scientific Oversight Office, the arm of the state's censorship. I had considered Jacob's and Mum's concerns about governmental interference in Shiftscience and rejected them. They seemed to me like short-sighted conservativism, a risk aversion that came with age rather than reason. I was desperate to collaborate with the Empire if it could launch my reputation as quickly as it had Mum's.

I remember very clearly my walk to the Office. The heavy Arwall air was cut through with the frosty breeze of an early spring morning. A haze hung over the streets, and through it the streetlights appeared like lighthouses, daisy-chained into the distance. I ignored the five-storey stone edifices around me and imagined I was crossing some vast archipelago, each island marked by its own flickering orange glow.

A motor-carriage rolled past, the wooden cabin swaying between two pairs of suspension rods like a bow-legged insect. Two policemen strolled in the opposite direction, their steel-capped boots echoing into the street. Despite what I was walking towards, I felt serene, almost weightless, giddy with excitement. Later, I would feel only the abrasive weight of guilt and regret.

The raid came three days after I had left the paper at the Scientific Oversight Office. I was in one of Jacob's lectures. The irregular tap-and-hiss of chalk against the large board and the steady baritone cadence as he narrated the progress of his calculations were suddenly interrupted by a rising murmur. I looked up from my notes. The other students were arguing in hushed, nervous voices and pointing outside. Through the tall windows of the lecture theatre, out on the green of the Institute grounds, I could see six groups of figures in long coats and dark berets spill out of black motor-carriages. One, a tall, heavy-set woman with short fair hair, got out last and separately from the others. She looked around, barked an inaudible order, and then joined the group headed towards our building. The others dispersed around the campus. Moments later I heard the muffled echo of their march through the corridors, growing louder and sharper until it seemed like the striking of a hammer.

I glanced over at Jacob and found his eyes on me. Something in my expression must have confirmed his suspicions, because he looked away in bitter disappointment. Suddenly he seemed composed, resigned even, and he began to wipe chalk from his hands and gather his notes. I wondered later how many years he had spent in fear of this kind of visit.

The double doors to the lecture theatre swung open with a clang and four figures filed in, led by the fair-haired woman. I and the others looked around nervously as two took position at the back of the theatre and two at the front. All were armed.

"Professor Lukash?" The woman addressed him. The weight of her voice matched her frame.

He nodded.

"Undergraduate Shiftscience?"

"Final year." His voice was small but steady.

"You and the students here are under arrest." She swept her gaze over the lecture theatre, took each of us in for just a moment. I could not say if she knew who I was.

"The order comes by emergency imperial edict, so I do not need to tell you the charges until you are brought into custody. Form a line and accompany me outside, where you will board a motor-carriage. I have the authority to shoot anyone who resists arrest or breaks file."

Jacob was silent for a few seconds, as if waiting for one of us to speak up.

"Student politics isn't what it used to be," he smiled. "May I see the papers?"

There is a rumour now that staff and students were shot during the raid. It is not true; there may have been violence—I saw some bloodied heads when they were transporting us—but no one was killed. The other five military groups raided the rest of the Shiftscience student body and staff at the same time. Every ongoing lecture and seminar was disrupted, and individuals were arrested in their offices and homes. Later I heard that similar operations were carried out simultaneously in Palaja and New Leven, the only other cities in the world with Shiftscience programmes. I told myself that it would not have been possible to effect this level of coordination in just three days. Given that Palaja and New Leven are outside imperial jurisdiction, I suspected that the plan for the raids had been worked out months in advance; it just needed a catalyst to be put into action. It was likely true, but it did not make me feel any better.

At the Scientific Oversight Office I had had the romantic notion that after I submitted my paper, I—I alone, an unrecognised genius of Shiftscience—would be approached to develop the bridge through the void promised in my paper. But the cold gunpoint reality of my situation and the misery I had inflicted on others had a sobering effect. I stared wide-eyed, shocked into passivity, as I was first jostled against the other students in one of the carriages, then spent two days in a holding cell, then finally was transferred to solitary confinement in what I later learned was Centre 17, a transit jail for political prisoners. I spent three months there without any account of the charges I was held under—a violation of imperial law, but I learned a common one: the prosecution needed time to gather evidence and find a charge to fit it.

Despite the uncertainty of my situation, I was relatively comfortable: I had a bed and a chair in a white-brick cell large enough for me to cross in three paces, with a wide slit for a window at the top of one wall. If I grabbed the edge and pulled myself up, I could see waves at the end of a long stretch of sand, cresting like a myriad folding hands, breaking against the mass of the sea before merging on the horizon into the blue-grey of the sky. At night the flicker of a distant lighthouse reminded me of my walk to the Scientific Oversight Office. It left a sour taste in my mouth.

I was not visited during this time and was given only trivial reading material. I could not complain; having something to occupy me, however basic, kept me sane. My meals—served three times a day—were delivered through a small flap in the centre of the cell door that locked from the outside and was also used to check that I was not attempting anything prohibited. I was not; the isolation and the relative comfort and idleness provided ample opportunity to reflect on the things I had done, to imagine the consequences, to try to come up with solutions, and this consumed me entirely.

On my best days, I fancied that the Empire had captured and held us to establish without interference a government monopoly on Shiftscience applications. If no one had access to Shiftscientists, then no one could affect imperial designs. I was convinced that once these designs were irrevocably in motion, we would all be released and allowed to carry on like nothing had happened. On my worst days I imagined that we were the test subjects for the theories I had developed in my paper, each of the Shiftscience scholars and students used as hosts for the Shiftspace bridges I had theorised—turned into Shiftslaves. All the time—on good and bad days—I was overcome with guilt. I was restless in that way one gets about things one has a responsibility for but no control over. The worry took its toll: despite the lack of exercise and the reasonable diet, I lost weight, my hair was streaked with premature grey, and new lines found their way into my skin like the imprints of a blunt knife pressed too hard and for too long.

Some time in my fourth month in Centre 17, I had my first and last visitor. It is difficult to express the emotions I felt when the cell door opened and I saw Mum in her usual black skirt and jacket, standing alone and with a slight smile curling her lips. An upswell of the guilt and remorse I had lived with for three months, but also relief, hope, the joy of seeing another human being, perhaps even something approximating a familial bond.

Mum watched me silently for a short while, then nodded to someone outside the cell, came in, closed the door, and sat across from my bed on the lone chair.

"How did you get away from the raids?" I asked. It was the first thing that came into my head and I said it without thinking.

Mum winced. "Is that really what you'd like to talk about?"

She paused. I said nothing.

"I had a notion of what you might do after our last meeting," she said. "I had no way to stop you, so I assumed the worst and prepared for it. You didn't disappoint."

"You didn't help it," I bristled.

"No," to my surprise she nodded, "I didn't."

We sat in silence for a few moments. Her admission weighed awkwardly between us. My eyes were fixed on the floor but I could feel Mum studying me, examining the damage three months in solitary confinement had done. As much as our last meeting felt like an audition, so this felt like a post-mortem. I shuddered.

"I need you to know that I came as quickly as I could," she said at last in a small, quiet voice. I was incredulous: was this the start of an apology?

"It took time to find where they were holding you and to negotiate terms," she continued. "I have friends in the major newspapers and in several government positions, which is how I am able to be here at all."

There was another pause. I looked up from the floor; Mum's eyes were glazed over and her jaw set tight, as if she were consciously clenching her teeth. It was too difficult to imagine that she was holding herself back from tears.

"I've negotiated your release," she added.

I was not sure how I felt. I brushed down the creases in my trousers to distract myself with the motion.

"You said 'terms'?"

"Yes," she sighed. A long pause. "I've agreed to run the imperial Shiftslavery programme."

I looked back at the floor, my eyes darting to find something in the uniform grey of the concrete that I could fixate on so I would not have to think about this. It went against everything Mum had planned for Shiftscience, against her entire career of keeping the government away from her discoveries and their misuse. I ran my hands over my trousers again.

"But this isn't something I can do alone," she added. "I need your help."

A circle appeared at my feet, painted a darker grey than the rest of the concrete floor. Then another, then two at once. I wiped at my cheeks and nodded.

I found out that Mum had begun relocating her laboratory as soon as I had left her cottage in Morton on my last visit. Her public profile and years of influence in government meant that no one had dared to interfere with her even as the rest of the Shiftscience programme had been arrested.

She moved to Symoni, in South Coral, about as far away from the Empire's influence as she could get without running out of friends or people who owed her favours. The Empire had a delicate relationship with Coral that it did not want to upset and, until Mum's arrival, Coral had no organised Shiftscience programme, so she was confident that we would be safer there than anywhere else.

Mum took us back to Arwall and we chartered a small steamboat to Symoni. She had negotiated my release as an explicit condition of her involvement in Shiftslavery, but the authorities refused to recognise this formally in her contract, so she preferred to keep a low profile during our travel. A private ship also left us at liberty to discuss Shiftscience without fear of being overheard.

The voyage took six weeks, largely through waters outside the Empire's jurisdiction. In the mornings, if it was sunny, I would sit out on the deck and read old newspapers that the captain—a well-meaning man in his sixties who, remarkably, did not seem to know who Mum was—had collected before the voyage. He did not care for the sensationalist fearmongering, as he called it, but they made good kindling for the furnaces that powered the ship's engine and he did not mind if I leafed through them before they were burned.

The rustle of the pages in the fresh breeze and the distant squawks of occasional sea birds put me at ease, but I was melancholy at the sight of the sea—it reminded me of the view from my cell window in Centre 17.

In the afternoons and evenings, I studied with Mum. From the beginning she made it clear that she had no intention of supporting Shiftslavery in the long-term, but that we had to put ourselves in a position of sufficient knowledge and trust to dismantle it. Awareness of this objective kept me focused and motivated, even if her lessons left me ambivalent. On one hand, they were a revelation; Mum moved through Shiftscience with a confidence and speed that Jacob could not hope to match, knew things he had only guessed at, and proposed and rejected theories with a confidence that was not weighed down by fear of peer review. For the first time in my life I could see for myself how she had earned her reputation. On the other hand, she seemed to be holding something back. Even when the lessons were ostensibly presented as freeform, I sensed an underlying structure. It was as if Mum had crafted a secret curriculum that was shaping me towards something other than what she was willing to discuss openly. I could not guess what it might be, but I did not confront her for fear of destabilising the relative semblance of family life that we now had. This sense of secrecy kept us at a distance from each other, despite everything we had been through.

We arrived in Symoni at the end of summer. With each day closer to Coral, the sun seemed to shine brighter and longer, until the heat was so strong that I could not tolerate my mornings on the deck and spent them instead in my cabin with the porthole open and the door left ajar to attract a draught. In Symoni's harbour—moored downwind of its famous fish markets and incense parlours—the heat was compounded by a stench that made me gag for an hour before I was able to acclimate to it.

Mum's new laboratory was in a three-storey townhouse at the end of a palm-shaded avenue in a quiet residential part of the city that did not see much traffic; it would help maintain a low profile. Apart from the bright yellow wallpaper and the extravagant glass light fixtures, the décor was similar to what I remembered of her cottage in Morton: frugal, minimalist, devoid of imagination. But after the unbearable brightness and heat outside, it felt like an oasis of darkness and cool.

"Welcome to your new home," Mum said. "Get settled and then meet me on the top floor. I need to show you something."

Her tone put me on edge. My suspicion that she had been working towards a secret agenda returned with tenfold intensity. I gave her the same long, appraising look I had given her in Morton. It was not comforting; she had aged terribly in the last few months, clearly under the weight of a large and unshifting burden.

She noticed that I was assessing her and tried to smile in reassurance, but it only made things worse. In all the time I had known her, Mum had never been one for polite comforts. "You make your choices and don't look back, or you don't make them at all," she used to say when I was little.

"What is it?" I said.

She sighed. "Well, you might as well come up now if you are going to ask."

We climbed two flights of stairs and Mum pushed open a wooden door to a space that filled the entirety of the attic. A pair of skylights cast uneven, trembling light shafts. Dust motes danced between two rows of chest-high wooden tables stacked with equipment. From what I could tell, most were measuring stations and calculation engines. Their dials glittered like cat eyes. Between the rows of tables, partially covered by a yellowing sheet, was something that looked like a metalwork arch or doorway, about a head taller than me and wide enough for one person. I don't know why, perhaps it was the fact that it was hidden, but looking at it put me ill at ease. I walked to the arch and removed the cover. With the whole contraption exposed, I could see that it was a long metal tube bent into a U-shape and inserted into two stands bolted to the floor. Countless cables, wires and antennae wound around the length of the tube like the vines of creeper plants. They trailed loosely from connectors dotted sporadically around the arch, across the floor and up to the tables and the equipment there. I looked at Mum. She had remained standing near the door.

"I call it a Shiftlens," she said. "It thins the boundary between our reality and the Shiftspace, which induces the Shiftspace to manifest within the span of the lens. The encasement also means I can monitor it precisely. If you want to put it crudely, it's a gate attached to a calculation engine."

Shiftscience orthodoxy was that no one could exert any control over the way the Shiftspace manifested; it did so when it wanted and as far as it wanted in a handful of known places. During our voyage, Mum had been explicit that I could enter any values for location and dimension I wanted in my calculations, which I had assumed was because they were unimportant to her lessons. Now I realised it was because she had been gradually steering me towards a new way of looking at the problem.

"Why didn't you just tell me about this?" I said wearily.

"A number of reasons," she shrugged. "It's easier to believe in something and to work with it when you already understand the theory. But mainly I didn't want you to know this too early in case anything happened to us during the voyage."

For a moment I felt a surge of the resentment I had felt in Morton—still untrusted and unworthy of Mum's most closely guarded work. But whether through the months of incarceration or the weeks aboard a ship together, I no longer had the energy to sustain that feeling.

"What else haven't you told me?"

She walked towards the Shiftlens, ran a hand over it absently, then looked up at me. For some reason it was the first time I realised that I was taller. She seemed suddenly and strangely vulnerable.

"Your paper is essentially correct," she said and I couldn't help the fleeting sense of self-satisfaction. "But you assume that the Shiftspace will admit of an indefinite number of hosts, all visualising their own exit points, all exchangeable for other hosts. That's understandable, given the state of mainstream Shiftscience, but it's not right."

Mainstream Shiftscience. Moments ago I would have balked at the term—hadn't Mum's work defined mainstream Shiftscience?—but the existence of the Shiftlens suggested that she had been working on her own agenda for some time.

"The Shiftspace is a kind of parasite," she continued. "I believe that fundamentally it's just a void that cannot be touched or entered or filled. It's a nothing in almost the literal sense of that word. But when it opens, it looks for a symbiont. To keep the symbiont within it, to keep them comfortable, the Shiftspace tries to mimic its natural habitat."

"This is textbook Shiftscience," I shrugged, "The Shiftspace wants to keep the entry from our reality open so it can better mimic our environment and attract additional hosts, which sustain it somehow."

"Not *hosts*—plural," she shook her head, "*host*—singular. It forms a bond with the first person through the entry, and, as far as I can tell, that bond is in place for life. I've always supposed that it feeds off organic matter—perhaps the brain waves we give off, or our pheromones, or something else—I don't know. The point is that the Shiftspace benefits from having as many of us inside as possible. But there is only ever one host. That's where your paper goes wrong. At best you can generate just one exit point from the Shiftspace, and you'd better make sure you never lose your host."

She let me think about that for a moment. In the silence I noticed one of her old mannerisms: she ran one arm over the other and pinched at her skin as she did so. It looked like she was trying to adjust a sleeve or peel away a carapace. It had terrified me when I was a child; now I only found it repulsive.

"Why do you do that?" It spoke to how much we had been through in the last few weeks that I felt able to ask the question.

She looked down in surprise. "Oh, that." She trailed off. "That first expedition, fifteen years ago: I was the first to enter the Shiftspace. And, well, I already said that it bonds with the first one through."

I stared in horror. "Are you saying that it's sentient? That it's some sort of organism bonded to you?"

"No, not in the way we usually understand sentient organisms anyway. It just has a certain basic degree of...*tropism*. Yes, I suppose that word will do here. It latches on to a host and mimics its habitat the way a flower knows to open towards the sun: it's a primal reflex, not sentient intent."

Her face caught somewhere between a smile and a shudder. After so many years of seeing her seemingly in control, it was difficult to come to terms with how much of it had been pretence.

"As for the bond between us," she continued, "It's less sinister than you might imagine. I feel the Shiftspace beside me every moment, even when it is closed, but it's not like someone watching or dictating my actions. It's more like a calling to return to it, a yearning to get back to an entry point, re-enter it, and never leave."

She looked back at me and her eyes suddenly refocused and held their usual calm, balanced detachment. I realised that it was a defence mechanism—for all these years not a mask of superiority or power, but a wall between whatever was inside her and the outside world.

I gazed at her wide-eyed in disbelief. Fifteen years paired with that nothingness, unable to extricate herself, bound to the science she had founded through more than just ambition or curiosity, unwilling to tell anyone in case...in case what?

"Why didn't you tell anyone? For all this time?"

"I did." She smiled. "I told your father as soon as I came back from that expedition and understood what had happened."

I doubt I could have expected a more surprising admission.

"Dad knew all this time?"

"He did," she nodded. "We agreed that the information was too dangerous to us to make public. We decided to keep it secret until I found the means to break the symbiosis."

We decided, *we* agreed, dangerous to *us*. There was something like a family there after all, once.

"But you never did." My voice was hoarse.

"No." Mum looked over at the Shiftlens. "The Shiftlens was my attempt. It was supposed to act as a substitute for a live host. Fifteen years of rebuilding and fine-tuning suggest I was wrong. It can open the Shiftspace, but it cannot replace me as a host. There is only one way out."

Mercifully, she left it unsaid. She had already explained that the symbiont needed to die to break the link with the Shiftspace. It did not bear repeating.

"I think your father came to terms with that years ago," she added bitterly, "he said farewell long before I could say it."

A silence settled between us. I stared dumbly at the Shiftlens, as if it held all the answers, or perhaps because in some abstract way it represented the Shiftspace and Mum's attempt at liberating herself from it. She had called it a gate, after all. Within a few minutes my knowledge of Shiftscience and my past had been rearranged into an entirely new worldview. It was humbling and it was overwhelming. Above all I tried to make sense of the new perspective I had on Mum and Dad as a family. It felt awkward somehow, unpractised, forced, like I was peering back at two people who did not know how to be with each other.

"Listen," Mum said eventually, "Why don't we pick this up tomorrow? We'll both feel better when we've had some sleep."

Sleep eluded me. The bed—in a small room on the ground floor—was too soft and the air too close. I got up, walked barefoot to the window and threw it open. A gentle breeze drifted in from a small garden planted thick with white flowers that glowed pale in the bright moonlight. Swarms of insects unknown to me darted amongst the stems and settled on the petals. The breeze covered my skin in goosebumps. I padded back to the bed and climbed under the thin sheet, took a deep breath of the cool night air.

I was exhausted, but my mind worked frantically to reassemble old information in light of new, and kept me awake. Assumptions, memories, long-held opinions were reworked like a song played on unfamiliar instruments: different timbre and pitch, new harmonies, but recognisably the same. I stared up with unblinking eyes. Images from my childhood, my Mum's face, Dad's, passed before me like a slideshow projected onto the ceiling. It was difficult to comprehend that instead of a decade of living distant and separate lives, my parents had followed a pact to protect each other. That despite Mum's mounting success and reputation in Shiftscience, her primary goal—to break her symbiosis with the Shiftspace—was a source of constant and repeated failure. I admired her resilience, but then I supposed that perseverance was easier when forfeit was not an option. I had better perspective on Dad's descent into bitterness and spite; he had waited ten years for Mum to unmake the choice she had made, to return to her family, even as that family withered away. They saw less and less of each other, I grew up, and what he waited for became with every year less important, more abstract, something he believed in by rote, something he believed he ought to believe.

After a while I became aware of a low humming sound and a vibration that seemed to penetrate the whole building. I got up again and leaned out of the window. The sound was almost inaudible now, but I could feel the vibration through my feet, which meant the source was likely inside the house. I wondered if Mum was still working in the laboratory, and I imagined the Shiftlens, thrumming with energy as it held a space of black emptiness within its span. It occurred to me, suddenly and unbidden, that Mum's symbiosis with the Shiftspace put a halt to any imperial plans for Shiftslavery. She had confirmed that the theory and method I had developed in "A Bridge through the Void" were in most respects correct, but until her existing link with the Shiftspace could be severed, the Empire would be unable to use another host. They would be unable to force that host to remain within the Shiftspace and demand that they hold a bridge open by visualising some exit point.

I had a sudden, awful feeling somewhere at the core of me, a premonition I could not ground in anything concrete Mum had done or said, but it arrived with dreadful certainty all the same. At once I thought I knew the reason for the low humming vibration through the building, what it signified.

I raced out of my room and up the stairs. My nightshirt and hair flailed around me and my bare feet slapped against the wooden floors. By the time I reached the bottom of the staircase to the lab the vibration and the humming had ceased, and I was running through a deathly quiet filled only with foreboding and the echo of my footfall.

I slammed open the door to the lab. A wave of heat buffeted me. The heat grew more intense as I walked towards the Shiftlens. I reached out and almost immediately jerked my hand back in pain. The Shiftlens's surface was hot enough to brand the skin. I could see parts of it glowing pink and turning a faint amber as it cooled.

I glanced around. The lab was empty. The moonlight streamed through the skylights and cast everything in silver outline like a heliotype negative. Nothing was out of place from earlier in the day, except that on one table there was a stack of paper with a single sheet next to it. Hesitantly, anxious, I picked up the stack and placed it under one of the skylights. In the moonlight I could just make out the title on the first page: "A Bridge through the Void". I recognised it as the copy I had left with the Scientific Oversight Office five months ago.

I should have guessed that the authorities would consult Mum after they received my paper. I wondered how much say she'd had in the political decisions they had taken. Either way, the fact that for months she could not find where I was imprisoned suggested that things had not gone according to her plans.

I looked over to the single sheet of paper. My lips were dry. I ran my tongue over them and found that I was struggling to breathe. I read the note.

"The basic principles of Shiftscience extend to the Shiftlens. It can create a new entrance into the Shiftspace, but the entrance will remain open only as long as there is a host inside.

"You are the legal owner of this building and you have the knowledge to use the equipment here. I also give you a list of people—the teachers and fellow students captured with you— whom I couldn't find. What you do with all this is up to you; I can finally give you that choice. Just remember: make it and don't look back, or don't make it at all. Love, Mum."

It read like a note to pick up the groceries, like it wasn't the first time Mum had told me she loved me, like it wasn't a farewell. I looked back at the silent, cooling metal of the Shiftlens, around at the empty lab.

She had left it unsaid because she knew that I would understand. She was gone. I did not need to see evidence or learn the grisly details of her passing to know it with certainty. Her connection to the Shiftspace and her grip on Shiftscience were broken. For the first time the Shiftspace was without a host, and Shiftscience without a patron and master. The choice of what to do with this knowledge was my inheritance. Strangely, there was no part of me that needed to deliberate what to do with it. In some way I had always known it—I was a satellite, finally freed from its orbit.

I took the note, but left my paper where it was. With a bit of effort I tore out two cables from a pair of calculation engines and rubbed the exposed ends together until they sparked. The paper caught fire—a small flame that somehow looked like an inferno in the dark room and cast wild shadows across the walls.

I hurried downstairs, dressed, collected the luggage I had not had a chance to unpack and stepped out into the street.

A stream of charcoal grey smoke and the occasional lick of flame poured from the attic and some of the second-storey windows. I could hear a few panicked shouts and the sound of running. A man dashed past me with a bucket but did not pay me any attention.

I looked towards the seafront. The ship that had brought me here from Arwall would still be moored in the harbour. I clutched the list of names Mum had left me and set off towards it, never looking back.

See Andrei Pechalin's story "Heritage" online at Metaphorosis.
If you liked it, leave a comment. Authors love that!
Remember to subscribe to our e-mail updates so you'll know when new stories are posted.

About the story

I grew up in a family with quite a few high achievers: actors, journalists, engineers, etc. That puts some pressure on you to be something – you want to be successful as quickly as possible, almost so you can tick that off and move on. It can lead to bad decision-making, and I made some mistakes in my late teens and early 20s (although none as drastic as the protagonist's, I hasten to add!). So I guess that's where the core idea – how do you choose to live your life in light of your heritage? – came from.

I've written a few stories that are perhaps too obsessed with world-building detail and that introduce too many characters, so I wanted to do something more stripped down and focused on what makes those characters work. That's how I ended up with just the protagonist and her mother. After a while I realised I didn't have to name them, which for me underscores that this is about them as people. It also shows, I hope, that it's possible to tell a story with strong female leads without ever mentioning their names.

The idea of the Shiftspace is really just the old trope of parallel dimensions, but I've given it some odd properties to make it weird and a bit dark. This works better with the overall mood of the story and the ending. I actually introduced the Shiftspace in an earlier story, 'Jurisdiction', where it's used for extraordinary rendition, but I had to expand the lore significantly here.

I also play a lot of video games and there have been an increasing number of stories focused on parent-child relationships (maybe the medium is maturing, or maybe game developers are just getting older). It's difficult to ignore *The Last of Us* and the last *God of War*, for example. I didn't consciously reference these, but perhaps they shaped some of the overall direction subconsciously.

A question for the author

Q: What is the scariest or most disturbing story you've ever read?

A: Bret Easton Ellis' *American Psycho*. It has the most horrifying and gratuitously extreme violence I've ever had to imagine, and makes the film look like a family blockbuster by comparison.

About the author

Andrei Pechalin has lived in England for over 20 years after emigrating from Russia. He studied law and analytic philosophy when he was younger and now works in higher education. He is convinced that video games have something interesting and important to contribute to narrative form, and will write one someday, right after that novel he keeps putting off.

www.pechalin.com, @APechalin

Tower of Mud and Straw IV

Yaroslav Barsukov

IV. The Tower

This is the final part of Yaroslav Barsukov's novella, *Tower of Mud and Straw*. Parts 1, 2, and 3 ran in September, October, and November 2020. What has gone before:

Faced with the prospect of greatness, Shea makes a deal with his own conscience: he knows a way to save the tower. He and Aidan travel to Shea's old home in Musk Valley to retrieve the 'tulips' buried there.

It is revealed that it was Shea's sister who coined the 'tulips' moniker. Together, they used to run a furniture workshop in Musk Valley, and she planned to use the Drakiri's anti-gravity devices to increase the production efficiency. The plan backfired horribly, killing Lena and another worker and destroying the workshop. Shea buried the 'tulips' she'd bought under the workshop's remains.

Shea and Aidan retrieve the 'tulips' and take them to Owenbeg. Lena, who's previously offered Shea to leave Owenbeg with her, perceives this as a betrayal. She's furious. She claims she's never really cared for Shea, and promises to confess their affair to the duke.

1

How many steps can a person take until the course of events becomes irreversible—fifty? A hundred? In his mind, Shea counted Lena's: now she rushed through the corridor, now she passed through the criss-cross shadows that had slipped from the window grates.

She'd said she would destroy him, but he was already a man caught under the rubble: one part of him would've given everything to run after her, the other paralyzed, repeating the same word. *Guilty*.

Guilty, but at least he would have power; if that would be worth the cost—at all.

What would he have told her, had he followed her? There was nothing he could tell her.

Outside, a chickadee let out a 'dee-dee-dee'. He remembered his and Lena's visit to the Drakiri settlement, the garlands, the roundabout spinning sunlight into black hair—and fatigue, gray, featureless, rolled over him.

"It's too late, little bird," he said. "One's dead, and I've betrayed the other one."

The sound of his own voice finally allowed him to move, and he stepped out into the corridor.

The courtyard stood deserted save for Aidan's men—creations of a sculptor too drunk to have been allowed anywhere near a chisel—and Brielle. She was still discussing something with them, waving her hand at the cart loaded with black egg-shaped things.

"I need to talk to you," Shea said.

She turned her whole body to him, beaming like a child on New Year's Day.

"Thirty-two devices, Shea. Thirty-two. You're a genius."

"Please. I want to talk."

He took her aside, under a creeper stretching its feelers across the wall.

"I understand it's awkward, but I've absolutely no one to turn to. It's about Lena."

"Okay, an interesting start. I didn't expect that, to be honest. What kind of *advice* are you looking for?"

"She's an acquaintance of yours, right?"

"Barely. I mean, we're both part of the duke's entourage, but we almost do not cross paths otherwise."

"She's going to confess our affair to the duke."

Brielle's eyes widened. "What the... What happened between you two?"

"This happened." He pointed at the cart. "She believes in an old Drakiri legend, another tower emerging when ours reaches a certain height. Something like that."

"*Emerging*?"

"Yes, from hell. Don't ask. She was happy when she learned the tower was about to crumble."

"What?" Brielle's face went one shade paler. "You told her? You've *told* her? We've agreed to keep it between ourselves—"

"It was like..." *The lovemaking, the angel, the olive branch.* "Listen, she wasn't going to tell anyone."

"Did you tell her I'd made a mistake in the calculations?"

"No, of course not. Why would I tell her that?"

"It's important to me, Shea. Did you tell her I'd made a mistake?"

"No! Besides, it's not relevant right now. Right now she's, let's say, extremely angry with me."

"Because you've brought in fresh devices."

"Because I've brought in the tulips."

"Why don't you talk to your friend from the capital?"

"Because he *worries me*, Brielle. He has certain tendencies... I don't trust him."

"Wow." She glanced back at Aidan's goons. "Oi! Don't touch those things, fellas! Sorry, Shea. I assume you've tried to reason with her?"

"*How* would I reason with her? You can't imagine what this legend means to her. *I* knew it and I didn't say anything to her, about going to Musk Valley and retrieving the tulips. Now she won't listen to me. I've betrayed her."

"Stop being melodramatic." Brielle chewed on her lip and looked up at the sky. "Listen, I need to take care of the devices before dark. Have you considered the fact she's got as much to lose as you do? Her relationship with the duke we all know nothing about and we all suspect exists?"

She's right. Of course she's right. You overreacting idiot.

"I don't think anything will happen, Shea. I think she's just mad at you. This'll blow over. I'm no expert on relationships, but I would wait a few days and try talking to her again. If she's still mad by then, I'll talk to her myself, I promise."

"Thank you," he said. "You know, I can't say we're friends in the strictest sense of the word..."

"I know." Brielle smiled. "More like battle comrades."

"Yeah, but I mean, I just want to say—thank you, Brielle."

"Before this gets awkward, I'll dash off and attend to those idiots—otherwise they'll blow themselves up. Stop worrying about things, you shoulder way too much blame."

He watched her figure sail up to the cart, then turned and went back into the castle.

2

Brielle turned out to be wrong.

They came for him during the night, and they weren't exactly courteous. The dream in which he'd been cutting a rotten grapevine collapsed as he spat out caked dust from the rags someone had shoved into his mouth. He blinked: a person—or persons—stood behind an oil lamp swinging in a blurred kaleidoscope. Darkness extended hands which yanked him out of bed. He tried to twist away, but they held him fast.

Shea kicked blindly, and a man cursed in a rich baritone, letting go of his right arm.

Free from the grip, his fist found something soft, probably the guy's guts. This prompted a grunt and another curse—but immediately, almost like the body's own sympathetic reaction, Shea's solar plexus flared up, and the world drowned in white sparks.

No more violence followed: they must've had orders not to leave any marks. They simply twisted his arms behind his back and dragged him out of his quarters.

From his new position, Shea could only see the floor tiles, but it was irrelevant: he had a hunch where they were headed.

Down, up, up, down, through a hallway.

A door threw open, and light bit into his eyes. The men who held his arms—he still wasn't sure, but there seemed to be three of them in total, two assailants and one who'd been responsible for the oil lamp—pushed him to his knees.

Legs swam into focus, stretching out of a night robe, sticks painted in varicose. Then came the rest, sitting on the edge of a grand four-poster bed, under a canopy filled with figures carrying swords and pitchforks.

"Ashcroft," the duke said. "Ashcroft."

He looked normal, even more controlled than usual: focused, spider-like eyes, hands gripping the knees as though calcified into them—but he didn't seem to be able to push out more than a single word.

"Ashcroft."

She was there, too, in her long black dress, staring out a window which couldn't have shown much apart from the torches down in the courtyard. Shea remembered the yellow room, how she'd seemed, in the same way, detached from whatever was happening around her.

"Lena," he said, and his solar plexus exploded again.

She didn't turn her head.

"Why don't you shut up for a change?" The duke's hand came alive and ran over his colorless lips. "You know, I did have a hunch something had happened between you two, Ashcroft. Still, I hoped common sense in you would prevail—forgetting how people always find ways of letting me down."

"Sorry to disappoint you."

Out of the corner of his eye, Shea saw the man on his right start a movement, but the duke made a dismissive grimace.

"Leave him be. It's a bit too late to feel sorry, Ashcroft, sincerely or otherwise."

"Hurt me, and you'll have a hell lot of explanation to do to Daelyn."

"Will I?" The duke smoothed down his hair as if preparing for a morning routine. "Remember, when you'd paraded in here, you didn't even know about the Drakiri devices—or the sabotage attempts. I tell my people to keep a lid on something—they do. They're loyal to me. That's what good leadership brings you."

Shea chuckled.

"Look at him," the duke said. "Look at him, Lena. Defiant to the end. I said *look at him!*"

She didn't move—in fact, she ceased all movement. She resembled a statue now.

"Anyway." The duke's palm touched his lips again, wiping the spit. "I've got a couple of ideas about you, Ashcroft. Both are marvelous, in their own way. One: we take you to the cellars and put your neck through a noose. Or two," he leaned forward, "these fine gentlemen here castrate you."

Shea felt blood rush away from his face. The walls came alive, bending around him, morphing into huge, cold fingers. The room shook.

"Your choice," the duke said.

"Lena." Shea tried to stand, but hands shoved him back into place. "Lena. Look at me."

Look at me. A small motion, barely noticeable: she dug her fingernails into her palms.

"So what will it be, Ashcroft?"

"Your Grace," the guy with the baritone said. "My boys and I are ready to do both."

The face above the night robe brightened, and for the first time since the yellow room, Shea saw an emotion other than anger or irritation pass through the duke's features.

"What a wonderful suggestion," he said. "Gosh. Absolutely splendid. Pull down his pants."

I've got a few seconds left. If I drop to the floor...

The entrance door creaked, and a voice called out, "Your Grace." The duke jerked in surprise. For a second, the pressure on Shea's shoulders weakened.

...I can sweep one of those bastards.

He threw himself on the stone tiles, rolled over, and drove his boot into the ankle of the guy to his left, who let out a short scream. In rapid succession, he glimpsed Aidan's face through the door, the canopy above the duke's bed, knuckles of a bear-shaped fist.

When the room stopped rocking, he and Aidan were on their knees next to each other.

"Exactly when we need a witness," the duke said. "What the hell are you doing here?"

"Your Grace, I just want to talk," said Aidan.

"What's the harm now?" The old man flexed his wrist as though considering shoving him between the ribs. "Let's hear it. What did you want to say?"

"Your Grace, before you do anything *irreversible*, you should know something about the Drakiri woman. That person isn't who you think she is."

"Meaning?"

"She's behind the sabotage attempts at the tower."

What is this nonsense?—but then Shea glanced at Lena. She no longer looked impartial, or distant, or trying to contain something. She took a step back from the window, eyes locked on Aidan.

"Very funny," the duke said. "Very, very funny. There were no sabotage attempts, my lord, Ashcroft himself proved it. Our workers couldn't handle the devices."

"Lord Ashcroft *theorized* unskilled labor was the problem. It was a good theory, too—however, only partially correct."

"Go on."

"She was using you, Your Grace, to get access to the tower. I have proof. My people have detained her fellow saboteurs."

His people—Colm? Or did he bribe more?

Lena shifted her gaze from Aidan to the duke, then to something behind Shea's back, then to Shea. And looking into her eyes, he was, again, a man split in two, one half sensing the tables reversed on the person who'd put him into this situation.

The other half though, a warmer and larger one, wished to cover her with his own body. The roundabout, the smile, the smell of strawberries. *I didn't lie*, he realized. What he felt here and now, on the floor of this hideous old man's room, was something beautiful.

"The witnesses are ready for your questioning, Your Grace," Aidan said.

"Aren't you going to say anything?" The duke half-turned to Lena. Having received no answer, he tsk'ed. "What's the motive?"

"That's what I didn't understand until recently, either," said Aidan. "It's no secret Drakiri aren't fond of the tower, but two days ago, Lord Ashcroft really opened my eyes. Apparently, they're prone to some kind of a doomsday superstition. How do you call it?" He pointed his chin at Lena. "The Mimic Tower?"

Still no answer, but she smiled—a sad, wise smile.

"So that's how it is." The duke lowered and shook his head. "Lena—I assume, by your silence, these allegations are at least partially justified?" The muscles in his jaw tightened. "All right, we'll consider the evidence."

At that moment, Shea saw with perfect clarity how the master's anger mirrored the servant's—the same detached rage Patrick had displayed against everything and everyone he considered an enemy, against the Dumians, against the 'capital types'.

"You want to punish someone—punish me, motherfucker," he said. "Leave her alone."

Aidan grabbed him by the arm. "Have you gone mad? Your Grace, he's simply—"

"Do whatever you've got to do. You wanted to punish me, so do it."

The duke collected himself.

Heavens, I've just doomed her. He'll get two for the price of one

—

"Let Ashcroft go," the duke said. "Let both bastards go. But if you get wind of them talking to someone about this... In the meantime—"

Lena looked Shea in the eye and, with the same smile, mouthed a single-syllable word. Then, in one move, she tore at the hem of her dress, leaving an ugly ragged edge. The wave of heavy fabric fell, no longer constraining her movements.

She hurled herself at the window.

He bolted to his feet and dashed to the black rectangle edged with broken glass. Below, at the courtyard, in a pool of moonlit shards, a figure stretched like a bird. *Lena. Lena.*

But it wasn't over. The limbs twitched, and the figure stumbled to its feet. A step, another, a lurch forward, a stride.

Improbably, as though he observed events unfolding in reverse, she raced for the gate.

"Fucking Drakiri," the baritone said from the other window with a shade of admiration.

"What's happening? What's happening?" The duke's voice, high-pitched. "Is she alive? Go after her."

Lena dove under the gate, legs flashing so fast they were butterfly's wings in the torchlight.

"If I may, Your Grace," said Aidan. "She's probably headed for the construction site. I've already taken the liberty of alerting the people there."

Over the battlements, the tower was a shape someone had cut out from the sky. *No, no, no*, Shea thought.

"Lena!" The only things listening to him were the horizon and the stones in the castle walls.

He took three long strides across the room, pushing aside one of the duke's men, and darted out into the corridor.

He didn't know how he'd gotten to the gate, how he'd crossed the first mile of the fields—he only came to his senses when a string of bleak yellow emerged from the darkness ahead.

Wives, he remembered. *Fiancées. Lanterns for the foremen who're staying for the night.*

The lights picked out a tall, thin figure slurring past them.

"Lena!" He stumbled, fell, tore at the grass, jerked to his feet, sprinted. "Turn back. It's a trap."

But she was too far away, and of course she was too fast for him—a smudge moving at an inhuman speed. When he passed the women in linen cloaks, she was already only a rough outline, shrinking. When he finally reached the tower, there was only him.

Night hid in every little shadow between the bricks, and portals up in the circular wall, like eyes, metered out a glow which could've been starlight. Shea bent over, hands on his knees.

"Lena," he cawed—then, straightening, loudly, "Lena!"

The wind came and rustled the grass.

He put his foot on the first step leading into the tower's mouth when something moved against the sky: something plummeted from the opening directly to the left and above him. But it wasn't like the earlier fall, a bird breaking through the glass—this time, it was like a sack being thrown out, a useless, inanimate thing.

He couldn't run anymore; he had to make an effort not to fall.

It took him minutes to find the body: the night didn't care for things the way daylight did, all dark malt and caked-together shapes.

His fingers touched a wet spot on her left breast.

And when he raised her from the ground, wrapping his hand around her shoulders to bring her face to his chest, déjà vu washed over him—only, unlike the other Lena from his past, this one didn't call him by the name, didn't ask anything, didn't say she loved him.

Didn't say anything.

The roundabout in his memory stopped; under the garlands, she stepped back onto the pavement, smiling at the sun that tickled her nose.

"Thank you," he remembered her saying, and how he'd kissed her hand, and how nothing much mattered anymore.

You told me once, sis, that you could read hands. We were both kids, and it was all hogwash, of course—but to a child, things like fate do exist. I recall you said I would meet a beautiful, extraordinary woman whom I would fall in love with, and we would live happily ever after.

Funny how stuff from deep childhood holds sway over you. Looking back, now, I think I've always been waiting for the thing you'd told me to come true.

And hey, maybe you could read hands—that one time. Because the first part happened; it's the 'ever after' you got wrong.

3

There were crows—crows straddling the tree branches and crows in coats. The Drakiri settlement didn't look as rainbowy as it had the last time he'd been here, colors washed out by the rain into small puddles across the pavement.

Coming to think of it, the pavement wasn't as flat as he remembered it, either.

At the gates, he'd caught a glimpse of Brielle leaving in a carriage—but other than that, no faces from the castle.

A compact graveyard, maybe a hundred tombstones, filigree gratings: a place of refined sorrow. Shea passed under the iron archway that depicted two trees fused at the top. In an oak's shadow, a row of graves protruded from the ground like a procession of small animals that had gone somewhere but never made it.

He stopped.

A crowd of mourners surrounded a dark object he was afraid to look at. A man—a Drakiri—was making a speech, the wind only carrying individual words: 'beautiful', 'talented', 'loss'.

I shouldn't be here. I'm just as guilty as the people who'd killed her.

He caught the gaze of a tall woman in the front row; there was something familiar about her, something sweet and painful at the same time. Shea leaned against the oak, watching the graves, the Drakiri, the graphite clouds consume each other.

He brought himself to glance at Lena the moment before the coffin disappeared into the ground.

When everything was said and done and the people dispersed, the woman remained. She stretched her hand toward the fresh strip of earth. Then she looked at Shea again.

He straightened as she strolled up to him.

"You're Lord Ashcroft?"

He recognized the voice. "Yes." The pain of loss broke through the surface and sprouted. "I'm... I'm sorry we meet for the first time under these circumstances."

Her face went through a rapid cycle of grief: twitched, dropped, hardened. "I'm sorry, too."

He offered her an elbow, and they wandered past the graves.

"Lena told me you were a famous painter."

"She told me about you, too. I wanted to thank you. I think she loved you." Her voice broke for a second. "It was difficult to tell with her; she always hated showing weakness, and love can be one. But I think you were the only bright thing about her life at the castle."

The roundabout made one final swirl, and, risking a fall, he squeezed his eyes shut.

"How did she die?" she asked. "They told me next to nothing."

"They... they killed her. The duke's people at the tower. I think she was trying to destroy it, and I was trying to warn her, but it was all too late."

They walked in silence for a while.

"*You* taught her that story, about the Mimic Tower?" Shea asked.

"It's not a story. It's something, something real and terrifying." She seemed to trail off in thought. "She was a unique child. So talented. I never lost hope she would take up painting seriously."

"She said she painted a bit."

"Oh." As though sunlight had brushed across the woman's face, and the pain made Shea shrink inside: at that moment, she was an older version of her daughter. "Oh. She was a beautiful painter. Please, you need to come by sometime—I'll show you her works. Lena herself..." She broke off and pursed her lips.

Suddenly, even for himself, like a criminal who'd been holding out on a confession, he said, "I loved her, too."

The woman didn't respond. She nodded, either to his words or her own thoughts. Then she stopped and reached into her pocket. "She asked me to give something to you. 'You'll know when'—I only understand now what she meant."

Shea took an ornamental key from her and turned it over in his fingers. "What does it open?"

"I don't... I think it's from her quarters in the castle."

"Thank you."

"I would be grateful," she said, "I would be grateful if you could bring me something of hers."

4

The key began as a pair of hands entwined in the shape of a heart; the place where they connected to the stem so thin that Shea paused before the lock, afraid of breaking something beautiful and fragile.

Then he realized he'd already done that.

The keyhole let out a click.

Drakiri don't let strangers in, he remembered. *We have no records of where we came from, only that we'd arrived from elsewhere, and letting someone under your roof feels like sharing this vulnerability.*

The windows were leaded glass with shapes of clouds and wheat ears, orange lozenges here and there letting in rays of light, autumn on autumn. Fluid cornices above the windows mirrored the pointed arches which rested on spiral columns, creating a kind of a vestibule. Past them, drapes, orange too, fluttered on the walls like wings of an invisible insect.

A thin-legged writing desk stood slashed open, as did a wine cabinet, drawers on the floor, half of them smashed into splinters—somebody had been here already, either the duke's men or Aidan's.

Had they taken what she'd wanted him to find? Shea squatted and picked up, one by one, things scattered across the floor: a brooch. A muff.

Papers.

The sentences, in a free, floating handwriting, weren't in Drakiri. He shuffled through a few sheets to find what was apparently the beginning: *This won't be in my mother tongue because it's a diary of a different life, a life among different people.*

The pages were numbered, and in the setting sun through the orange lozenges, he crawled around the floor on all fours, trying to piece together what remained of her thoughts.

The duke...

The tower...

Patrick, Brielle, and the others...

That festival I've loved since my childhood...

The tower.

Next to one of the paragraphs stood a doodle of a face—his own.

'We rode on that thing, a thing for children, and I felt happy for the first time in a long while. I felt like a little girl. I may need to use him (do I? Maybe the situation will resolve itself before that?), and I'm torn. He may be my sailor. I don't want to lose that—in life, we aren't given many chances.'

Shea froze. Then he folded the pages in two, slowly, accurately. Ran his finger across the edge, feeling the paper fluffs crumble. Put the diary into his pocket.

Something boiled down his lungs, knocked at his throat, looked for a release.

He picked up the nearest drawer and hurled it into the wall. Another. And another, each next one with greater force, finally sliding into a scream, trying, but unable, to reach for the part of himself he wanted to hurt and make stop hurting.

He leaned his hands on the table and doubled over in dry sobs. *A proud, misguided child*, he thought. *I called her a proud, misguided child.*

The senses came back after a while: the smell of chipped wood, the room, the wheat ears, the drapes. His head felt the way it does when one catches a cold.

That was it. Somehow, it was not the funeral but reading her innermost thoughts that made him realize—really realize—that he would never see her again.

"Was it the diary, Lena? Did you want me to find it?"

His gaze fell on the door into the neighboring room.

She must've used it—the bedroom—for art practice. In the corner, a drawing table squatted, blank sheets of paper and pencils in a fine mess. Sketches occupied every inch of the walls, sketches —

Wait a second, not sketches. A sketch. They're all the same.

Or rather, they were of the same place: the clearing on the forested hillside where he and Lena had hunted and lost a deer.

Had the deer really vanished? he thought. 'I saw something, in a flash. Different colors,' she'd said.

He tore off a drawing and stared at it.

5

Brielle's face appeared in the crack between the door and the jamb.

"What is it, Shea?"

"May I come in?"

"I've been at the top of the tower all day. Installing the devices."

"Can you let me in?"

"I'm preparing for sleep."

"It's important."

"What isn't?" she said, stepping aside. "All right. You'll need to excuse a certain degree of messiness, though."

He didn't mind the clothes over the couch's back and cup rings on the table—it was everything else, the normal things, that, after *her* quarters, seemed bland and alien. Linen curtains, cornices and moldings he'd seen a thousand times.

"Remember, two days ago, I told you about the Mimic Tower?" he asked.

"Yes, you said it was a Drakiri superstition or something."

"What if it isn't?"

"Hmm?"

"Technologically, they're centuries ahead of us."

Brielle took a cup from the table—tea or coffee. "Doesn't mean they aren't..." She broke off.

"They aren't what? Human? If you think they are, go outside and hire a drikshaw."

"Doesn't mean they can't be prone to the same fear of the irrational as we are."

"Yes, but my point is, we won't be able to tell. We're children playing on the beach. *We* won't be able to tell their fear of irrational from legitimate concern."

"So you believe in this Mimic thing now?" Brielle said.

"No. Maybe. I don't know." He walked up to the window and glanced outside, at the tower, the finger pushing a purple crown against the cold blue: the devices were already active, an upward pull to hold the giant together. "Listen, Lena and I were on a hunt, right after the duke decommissioned the tulips—"

"The Drakiri devices."

"Right after he'd decommissioned the tulips. We chased a deer across the hillside—you know, the hills to the west of the castle. There was a clearing. The deer vanished."

"What do you mean, vanished?"

"Disappeared. Dropped out of reality. No idea."

"Shea, I'm afraid to ask, but... Were you drunk when that happened?"

"Lena..." Shea swallowed. "Lena saw it, too."

"So she was also of the opinion the deer has *dropped out of reality*?" Brielle raised her hand, palm open, when he glanced at her. "Just trying to assess the facts."

"She said she saw *different colors*."

"Did you try to find out what happened? Maybe a hallucinogen in mushrooms or something, you stepped on them and—"

"She wrote it off as a hallucination too. The deer—we thought it simply ran away from under our noses."

"So..." Brielle took a sip. "I suspect now you've reconsidered."

"Now I've reconsidered."

"May I ask why?"

"Because of this." He took out from his pocket and unfolded the sketch. "There's at least a dozen more of those in, in *her* bedroom. All of the same place where we hunted."

Brielle took the drawing from him and studied it. "She had talent. And this proves what?"

"This *proves* nothing. But maybe, just maybe, there's a possibility..." He looked at the first stars dipped in the water-thin film of clouds. "Maybe a portal of sorts formed there. Is forming. A doorway."

"To the Mimic Tower?"

"Like I said, Brielle, would we be able to tell their superstition from knowledge?"

"Okay. Why are you telling *me* this?"

"Because I need you to go to that place with me."

She chuckled—but, after studying him, her brows came together. "Shea, you've been under a lot of stress lately. You sound... off."

"Perhaps I sound the way I should, for the first time in my life. I need you to go with me because I can't make the decision alone—you were right the other day, I can't shoulder any more blame. I can't betray you, as well. If the decision has to be made, we'll have to make it together."

"Which decision, Shea, what are you—"

"We may need to do something about the tower."

"Like hell we will." She slammed her cup onto the table, and the porcelain swirled in a small pirouette. "You already did something about it, twice—you removed the Drakiri devices, then brought them back. Make up your mind already."

"I—"

"Make up your goddamn mind!"

"I forgive you."

"What?"

"The mistake in the calculations you've made—I forgive you for it."

She frowned. "What the fuck, Shea?"

"I forgive you. It wasn't your fault. The duke's an asshole, he pushed you to the limit, you made a mistake. It's human. It's normal."

Her face twitched.

"I forgive you, do you hear me?" He strode up to her and squeezed her arms. "Do you hear me? I forgive you for your mistake."

Brielle inhaled sharply. "I only wanted to do my job. He'd changed the deadline—"

"It wasn't your fault."

"Others might disagree."

"Then to hell with them. You know? To hell with them."

She kept silent.

"Please. Come with me to the hillside tomorrow, and let's just see what's out there. I owe it to her. If there's even the slightest possibility of her being right, I need to... Otherwise, I won't forgive *me*."

6

The black mane, a cloud of breath embossed by the sunlight. Their horses trudged forward, and the hillside drew nearer, a slope passing from the unformed of the waking world into some semblance of order, into the forest's ragged outlines.

"Do you remember where that place of yours was?" Brielle said.

"A clearing. It was a clearing up the hill."

She snorted. "This is as generic a description as it goes."

"We followed this road." Shea waved at the wide trail between the trees. "Then, at some point, turned off."

"Where exactly?"

"Listen, it was a hunt."

Brielle mumbled something.

"Sorry—didn't hear you."

"I said, what the hell am I even doing here."

Shea didn't answer. He remembered *her*, standing in the stirrups, the smile, the laughter. *Guide me*, he thought. *Allow me to do at least some good.*

But nothing came back—the trail remained just a trail—until, on an impulse, he urged his horse into a gallop, mirroring his speed on that day.

They'd kissed.

They'd made love.

She'd been the smell of bonfire and the taste of strawberries.

"Hey, where do you think you're going?" Brielle called out.

Faster! In Shea's mind, Lena drove her heels into her horse's flanks, and he did the same. A hundred feet more, straight. Left, into the aspen grove, into the thinner path, between the two birches.

The trees ahead parted, and the tower stared at him through the morning haze, the memory and the present twin beads on an invisible umbilical cord.

"That's it. That's it!"

They darted into a clearing. He pulled on the reins and glanced around.

"Are we there? You sure?" Brielle said from behind.

He took out the sketch and held it out to her.

"Well." She shrugged. "Seems similar enough—but then again, it's just trees and a glade."

"Trust me, this is the place. It all happened when we dashed in here."

"I personally didn't experience any visions."

"We came through there, same as now." He pointed at the road behind them.

"Maybe..." she said. "And mind you, don't take this to mean I believe in a doorway to the other dimension or some such. But maybe you and I didn't pass through the right spot? After all, you said yourself the deer disappeared and neither you nor Lena did."

Even more painful to hear another say her name than to say it myself.

He shook his head to disperse the memories. "Worth a shot. Would you please hold my horse for me?"

The path led back into the forest, into the bush where the morning quiet held its sway, only the leaves moving, fawning over the wind. He stretched out his hand and walked toward the trees, waving his palm left and right like a blind man.

The first step, second, third—and then he had no fingers anymore.

An instinct yanked his elbow back.

Somewhere, a branch snapped and a small animal darted into the bushes.

Shit shit shit, his heart drummed out.

"Brielle!"

"What?"

"I think I've found it."

Slowly, he raised his arm again.

Void ate everything up to his wrist, and this time, he made an effort not to recoil. He moved his hand to the left, and the cutoff line across his skin bent: whatever was in front of him seemed to be spherical or cylindrical in shape. He circled the thing in the tiny steps of someone walking along a cliff's edge.

The doorway was probably wide enough to devour a horse, but not wider. One could easily miss it.

"Wait," Brielle said. "Wait, I'm coming."

But he had already taken a step forward, and forward-backward-to-the-side.

Direction didn't matter anymore, and—

The sky bled crimson and orange.

The air that wrapped around him tasted of salt and reeked of rotten eggs.

Something that *resembled* trees—multi-necked, multi-fingered foliage in *vertical* stripes, like someone had stripped the real tree trunks clean and glued brushes to them—pushed the clouds away from the ground's uniform burnt crust.

A bout of wind slapped him in the face, making him turn, and that was when he saw it.

Less of a tower, more of a giant centipede, standing upright and sprouting thorns instead of legs—if thorns could be the size of a house. Behind, a cloud formation—a tornado?—turned around lazily.

He backed away like a sleepwalker.

"What the..." Brielle appeared, breathing in a marathon runner tempo. "What the... Where are we?"

"I don't know," his lips answered.

"This is a hallucination. I'm dreaming, I'm dreaming, dreaming."

You are you are you are, his mind echoed.

"No," he said, "no. We've arrived."

Right there, twenty feet away from him, next to the tree line, lay the decomposing carcass of a deer.

Brielle took a few drunken sailor steps and probed the ground with the tip of her boot. "The soil is baked." She glanced up, and her face changed. "Oh my."

"Exactly."

"I can't believe it."

"The Mimic Tower," he said.

Brielle squinted, raising her hand to the sky, thumb and pinky outstretched, a trembling, but still a professional gesture. "A thousand feet, give or take. Same as ours. Gosh." She opened and closed her mouth. "Am I... Am I responsible for this?"

The thorns, like handles some inconceivable being might use on its climb to the skies. "Lena said it builds itself—but yes, as far as I understood, it's our tower that allows it... to manifest."

After a brief pause, Brielle chuckled. He glanced at her: *had she gone crazy?*

"Funny how the brain works," she said.

"The brain?"

"I've had a small revelation."

"What do you—"

"Funny." She chuckled again, running her palm through her hair. "If it's all true, then my mistake, Shea—it was actually something good, wasn't it? If she was right. If she was right all along."

She was.

Brielle extended her arm toward him. "There's a freedom in—"

A distant rumble rolled. Her face changed, and he looked where she looked, at the thing he'd taken for clouds.

After all, clouds do resemble people sometimes—*but*, he thought, *while they may look like people, they never move like ones.*

A naked figure, an overgrown baby, shifted against the sky. Only the top part of the body was visible, everything waist-down concealed by the trees so that it looked as though it waded through the forest.

Brielle gasped. "It's a human... a human... a fucking giant."

He felt the hair on his head move. "Not a human."

"Not *entirely* human—"

"The movements, Brielle, look at how it moves."

A fluid half-dance, part walking, part sailing...

"My gosh. Are you saying they're Drakiri—"

"That, or something related." *Heavens, it's huge. Did it see them? Was it able to* see *in the conventional sense of the word?*

Brielle whispered, "What is this place?"

...only that we'd arrived from elsewhere. The light's orange tint, the vertical foliage—like the drapes in Lena's quarters. Decorating your home in a bow to some vague ancestral memory.

Realization washed over him.

"This is where they came from. Their place of origin. She told me Pangania was a waystation, that they'd come from somewhere else—here."

"Gosh," Brielle said, "my gosh. Maybe a, a catastrophe happened here or—"

At that moment, the air moved. Something ruffled through the brush-like leaves, rising above the trees. The giant's head turned.

It *looked* at Shea—or rather, two stones rolled under the eyelids until the gaze weighed him down. For the longest second in his life, there were only those eyes, black, expressionless—or was it that he didn't *understand* the expression, that it was so vast he simply couldn't wrap his mind around it?

A palm rose from behind the trees, a steady, graceful ascent. Moved forward.

At first, he kept telling himself the giant was too far away to reach them.

Then Brielle screamed, and something crashed into his shoulder: she pushed him out of the way.

"No! Brielle, no!"

But the hand had already closed around her body.

As though on a picture, dashes of white came through: she hammered her fists on the fingers which could've belonged to some colossal monument.

The sight tore Shea free from his paralysis. "Let her go, you mound of shit!" He sprinted, uselessly, after the hand as it moved away at double the speed.

"Destroy it," Brielle screamed when he caught her gaze. "Destroy—"

His foot sank into a hollow in the ground. He lost his balance and fell, stretching out his hands—and as his forearms disappeared, he realized he'd run straight into the other side of the portal.

The next instant, he was back to the forested hillside.

He doubled over and threw up into the morning dew.

"Brielle! Brielle!"

Some sensation returned to his body—all that time, his heart hadn't stopped playing drums on his ribs.

He started, swaying, toward where the doorway was.

The wind changed its tune, and five *things* stretched out of nowhere in front of him—each one could've been a tree trunk. A palm reached into the world and, slowly, swung left to right, feeling for something—or someone, crumpling the bush. Then it retracted back into the portal.

Above, a chickadee sang.

"Brielle! Let her go, you piece of—"

He darted through the spot, but nothing happened—and, frantically, he waved his hands.

This time, his fingers remained his own. He glanced around, at the waking forest, the lazy sunlight. Perhaps the doorway only opened, for each person, only once. *Or perhaps something on the other side didn't want him to come through again.*

The chickadee clung to its bravado.

"Brielle."

He tried for a whole hour, but that was it. The doorway into the world Lena had told him about had closed.

7

Autumn leaves crumbled under his feet.

The horses, finally free, darted past.

Make up your goddamn mind already.

He tore off his jacket and hurled it into the bush. Ice crept under his shirt, but this was okay, this was fine: it was new air, entering his lungs.

Destroy it.

Such a simple idea, really, such a correct one, free from his own former indecisiveness.

Go to hell, Daelyn. I don't want the kingdom, the throne, the golden dance. You can take it all. Take everything. Take my title, my family name, my estate. I don't want any of this. I don't need it.

"You hear me?" he shouted. "Take everything!"

Brielle had been right—there *was* a freedom. In not having a choice anymore.

He descended the hill's slope. The distance clear of the morning's sediment, the tower gained form, its top leaking thick purple into the day.

Thirty-odd Drakiri devices, all in one place. He had to hope an implosion of that magnitude would be enough to bring the mammoth structure down—and with it, if he'd understood everything right, the doorway.

And this time, there would be no changing one's mind, no possibility for a flip-flop, no rosewood trapdoor to go back to.

Forgive me, Lena. I should've listened when you talked. I should've looked. Tulips will finally bloom—for you.

A week after his workshop's destruction, he'd talked to the Drakiri at the town hall, the one who'd warned him. *Five minutes*, the man told him; his sister and Danny had only had five minutes to live from the moment Danny had touched the valve.

Shea didn't know if five minutes would be enough to get out of the implosion radius—or what that radius would be. One tulip had chewed through a two-story building; he could only imagine how far three dozen would reach.

But it hardly mattered anymore.

He expected guards at the entrance; there were only the artisans, diving into the gate's gap-toothed mouth, diving out. The duke had found his saboteurs; Lena was dead; there was no need to waste resources on guards.

He'd found her body over there, in the grass.

Shea reached for his pocket, for her diary—realizing he'd discarded it together with his jacket. He turned around; for a moment, that was all that mattered.

Then he squeezed his fist and entered the tower.

Brielle's beast had beauty. It had perfect symmetry. The spiral staircase folded into a snail's shell above his head, and coals burned, scattered across cities on the steep climb. *Cities*—the impression from his first visit remained like a daguerreotype of a childhood love: settlements built out of pulleys, carts, and treadwheel cranes, shot through with harmonies of tools squeaking in the shadows.

For a moment, the idea of destroying all this—worlds hidden within a world—made the stone weight squeeze around him.

"Hey!" Shea flinched at his own voice ringing through the empty space. "Hey! Everybody leave, now!"

He didn't actually think this would work—but a sprung coil inside demanded release.

Two men approached him, wearing cream-colored aprons and worried faces.

"What's going on?" the taller one said.

"Don't you recognize me?"

The pair exchanged glances. "You're Lord Ashcroft."

"Yes. Lady Brielle asked everyone to vacate the construction site."

"We… we haven't heard anything to that effect."

"The Drakiri devices at the top are about to implode."

Worried faces went chalk-white. "We haven't heard—"

"Do you hear me *now*?" He grabbed the tall guy by the arm. "Hey. Do you? Or shall I spell it out for you louder?"

The man's face was two fears fighting: that of making an administrative mistake and another, a deeper one—for his life.

"What's your name?" Shea said. "All those people die, it's your fault."

That settled it. The artisan turned to his fellow. "Inform the crew. I'll spread the word up."

"No," Shea said. "I'll do it myself. You take care of your own guys. Stay organized, and we'll all get out of this alive."

He headed for the staircase, and through the pain of loss— the one which had happened and the one which was about to happen—euphoria kicked in.

"Vacate the site." He waved at another worker walking past him. "Others are already on their way out."

"Vacate the site."

Heavens, how easy. How laughably easy it was, bending the giant to his will. Same instructions, to anyone he encountered. Soon, it wasn't even needed: on the staircase's second whirl, he counted three men rising in wooden cages, probably to warn the workers at the upper levels, and in ten minutes he had to keep to the wall in order not to be pushed over the edge by the steady stream of people rushing downward.

A domino effect—you see others below, fleeing, your instincts kick in.

By the time he got to the top, he was walking through abandoned towns: a frozen pulley, an overturned bucket, somebody's shirt over a grinding wheel.

The top, however, was still alive, and it was a whole new world.

8

A massive flat platform, sanded to perfect white under the autumn sun, supported the tower's jawline.

He finally understood why his sister had called them 'tulips'. Those bumps in the unfinished wall weren't Drakiri devices—or 'egg-shaped things'—those were flowers, grown through the stone, ready to bloom. Those were gardeners, standing knee-deep in the purple rolling across the wooden planks.

Two people, peeking over the edge.

One of them turned and waved. "Lord Ashcroft. What's happening?" He ran—a clumsy half-walk, half-run, a parody of how Drakiri moved. "Why is everybody fleeing? We were told the devices are about to implode—"

"They are," said Shea.

"But they aren't!" The man stretched out his hands, palms cupped. "We've, we've checked every single one. They're operating as—"

"How long have you been working here?" Shea looked him in the eye, and the hands dropped.

"We—"

"You've made a mistake."

"My lord—"

"This isn't a debate. You don't want to take chances with those things."

Paranoia. I don't know about yours—but that's how our race survives, Lena. That's how we've always survived.

"We've checked every one of them." Practically a whisper now.

Shea pointed at the staircase. "Vacate the site."

"And you, my lord?"

"I'll try to prevent the catastrophe."

The man reminded him of the fellow with sad labrador eyes whom he'd forced to operate a device a month ago: same baggy trousers, same frightened gaze. Same willingness to follow orders, regardless of where they led.

When both workers disappeared down the staircase, he allowed himself to breathe.

Was it him, or had the purple thickened? *The tulips, are they opening for the sun?*

He walked up to the device closest to him. 'Here, let me show you,' she'd said and touched the dark surface, lightly as though weaving or playing a harp.

He put his hands on the valve. Took a second's hesitation he could still afford. And unscrewed the valve, all the way.

He thought he heard chickadees, but, of course, at this height it was impossible.

Something hummed through the tower's arteries. Something woke up within the stone, stirred, and squared its shoulders.

"Away from the device, now."

He turned around. *Four minutes forty seconds.*

In calm, measured steps, Aidan ascended the staircase and stepped onto the platform.

"Away from the device, Shea. Damn—I should've known. Any idiot could see you were too weak to handle power."

"The tower needs to be destroyed. I've been to—"

"Put it back. Whatever you just did, undo it."

"I can't. And I won't—not again."

"I should've known," Aidan said, pulling off his glove, "right there, at the beginning, at the capital. When you'd refused to gas that mob. The plebs. I would've done it without batting an eyelid."

He advanced, rolling the 'fingers' of the knotted contraption he had for a hand. "I need this tower."

"No."

Four minutes.

"I should've simply killed you and fulfilled the queen's mandate myself."

He made a wide swing, and Shea caught him by the wrist—immediately realizing how futile an attempt it was. It was like trying to stop a horse at full speed.

The Drakiri hand must've weighed at least three pounds, and Aidan knew how to use it. All Shea was able to do was deflect it an inch; for a few seconds, he felt his head existing separate from his body, a torn-off part of a rag doll. Next came the pain and the wall's stones, crashing into his forehead.

He slipped and steadied himself. "Fulfilled her mandate?" He spat blood at the white boards. "The duke would've disposed of you, same as he tried with me."

Aidan smiled. "I'm afraid the good old duke is unwell at the moment. Something in the food, I hear. He won't be bothering me any longer."

Three minutes.

Another swing—this time, Shea ducked, and Aidan's fist sent a cloud of crushed rock into the air.

"Think about your country!"

"You're blind in one eye because of your Duma hatred." Shea stabbed his finger at his own bloodied face. "Get it through your head: they aren't attacking us."

"And we won't be waiting for that, either." Aidan spun his arm as though preparing to shoot a sling. "From here, we'll stage a preemptive strike. We'll attack ourselves."

"You're fucking insane."

"Put it back, you idiot!"

"I won't."

Two minutes.

The blow landed on Shea's left biceps, pain spreading through the body like fire: a bone had broken inside.

A spasm made him double over, and at that moment a wave of heat licked his face. He froze. The tulip he'd rigged was opening; it swelled—as though it were a wart the wall tried to push out—and tore itself apart in the process. The heat came from the expanding crease, and he remembered the skin of his fingers melting against the surface of another device, in a different life.

He shifted his gaze to Aidan.

"Time's up," his adversary said, raising his fist. "You're walking away from something I should've had."

"I've never needed it, you fucker. You can have it."

This time, he didn't try to block. With his healthy hand, Shea grabbed Aidan's wrist and deflected the motion right into the purple crease.

The knuckles went in with a screech. Aidan grunted, trying to free himself, and that was when the tulip changed its song. It seemed bigger, a moment later smaller, alternating between two ends of an invisible compressed path.

The device spat Aidan's hand out. The arm bounced in a wide arc like a wooden toy.

Halfway through, the hand exploded.

With a wail, the wall began to bend, the mist at its base collecting itself into a funnel.

Aidan must've been dead the moment his body touched the platform.

Shea froze, staring at the disfigured lump—dreams, ambitions, and memories, under a film of blood and thin white cloth fluttering in the wind.

For a moment, he considered dragging Aidan to safety. Then he realized he had no more time.

The next tulip opened, pulled into the implosion radius of the first. And the next one: a chain reaction.

The beautiful garden his sister had wished for, coming to life.

Shea dashed toward the staircase, a ripple passing through the boards underneath his feet, and he almost made it—right to the first step, where he felt his body being hauled back.

Not like this. Not like this. Ignoring the white-hot pain in his left arm, he waved his hands like a bird and propelled himself forward.

Even in free fall, as the darkness sped up past him, he sensed the tremor which shook the mammoth structure: the collapse had begun.

I did it, Lena. I did it.

And, to his surprise, the abyss answered. *Come home*, it said.

The abyss responded in Lena's voice—only he didn't know which of the two anymore.

Does it matter? he thought, enjoying the numbness that comes with the air battering the body. He let the voice carry him and remembered the dog he'd seen on his penultimate day at the capital, the poor mongrel who'd tried to get at the lamp post. It staggered him how, back then, he'd failed to recognize that desire—to reach something huge, but utterly useless.

A gust of wind spun him around. A treadwheel, a whirl of the staircase. Purple glow from above, blooming for the last time.

It's a dance, it dawned on him. Not the one he'd wished for—an illusion, all lacquer, all empty hopes—but something real, something that rendered even his mistakes, his earlier indecision, insignificant.

"It's a dance!" he shouted, the wind immediately snatching his words.

And who knows, perhaps the final pas isn't the fall.

Perhaps the real dance takes you through the halls, farther and farther away, until you come across a room with flowers where a girl with hands made for weaving or playing a harp, a black wave of hair rolling down her shoulders, would raise her head and smile at you.

Welcome you home.

See Yaroslav Barsukov's story "Tower of Mud and Straw IV: The Tower" online at Metaphorosis.
If you liked it, leave a comment. Authors love that!
Remember to subscribe to our e-mail updates so you'll know when new stories are posted.

Copyright

Title information

Metaphorosis 2020
ISSN: 2573-136X (online)
ISBN: 978-1-64076-187-2 (e-book)
ISBN: 978-1-64076-188-9 (paperback)
ISBN: 978-1-64076-160-5 (hardcover)

Works of fiction

Publisher

Metaphorosis
a magazine of speculative fiction

Metaphorosis Magazine is an imprint of
Metaphorosis Publishing
Neskowin, OR, USA

www.metaphorosis.com

"Metaphorosis" is a registered trademark.

Discounts available

Substantial discounts are available for educational institutions, including writing workshops. Discounts are also available for quantity purchases. For details, contact Metaphorosis at metaphorosis.com/about

Metaphorosis Publishing

Metaphorosis offers beautifully written science fiction and fantasy. Our imprints include:

Metaphorosis Magazine

Plant Based Press

Verdage

Help keep Metaphorosis running at
Patreon.com/metaphorosis

See more about some of our books on the following pages.

Metaphorosis
a magazine of speculative fiction

Metaphorosis is an online speculative fiction magazine dedicated to quality writing. We publish an original story every week, along with author bios, interviews, and notes on story origins. Come and see us online at magazine.Metaphorosis.com

Keep Metaphorosis running! Support us at
Patreon.com/metaphorosis

You can also find us at:
Twitter: @MetaphorosisMag, @MetaphorosisRev, @Metaphorosis
Facebook: www.facebook.com/metaphorosis

We publish monthly print and e-book issues, as well as yearly Best of and Complete anthologies.

2020
Best of　　**Complete**

2019
Best of　　**Complete**

2018

Best of   **Complete**

2017

Best of   **Complete**

2016

Best of   **Complete**

Plant Based Press

plant
based
press

Vegan-friendly science fiction and fantasy, including an annual anthology of the year's best SFF stories.

Best Vegan SFF of 2020

The best vegan-friendly science fiction and fantasy stories of 2020!

Best Vegan SFF of 2019

The best vegan-friendly science fiction and fantasy stories of 2019!

Best Vegan SFF of 2018

The best vegan-friendly science fiction and fantasy stories of 2018!

Best Vegan SFF of 2017

The best vegan-friendly science fiction and fantasy stories of 2017!

Best Vegan SFF of 2016

The best vegan-friendly science fiction and fantasy stories of 2016!

 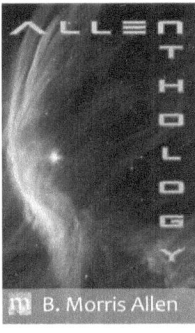

Susurrus

A darkly romantic story of magic, love, and suffering.

Allenthology: Volume I

A quarter century of SFF, including the full contents of the collections *Tocsin, Start with Stones,* and *Metaphorosis.*

Verdage

Science fiction and fantasy books for writers – full of great stories, but with an additional focus on the craft of speculative fiction writing.

Reading 5X5 x2

Duets

How do authors' voices change when they collaborate?

A round-robin of five talented science fiction and fantasy authors collaborating with each other and writing solo.

Including stories by Evan Marcroft, David Gallay, J. Tynan Burke, L'Erin Ogle, and Douglas Anstruther.

Score

an SFF symphony

What if stories were written like music? *Score* is an anthology of varied stories arranged to follow an emotional score from the heights of joy to the depths of despair – but always with a little hope shining through.

Reading 5X5

Five stories, five times

Twenty-five SFF authors, five base stories, five versions of each – see how different writers take on the same material, with stories in contemporary and high fantasy, soft and hard SF, and a mysterious 'other' category.

Reading 5X5

Writers' Edition

All the stories from the regular, readers' edition, plus two extra stories, the story seed, and authors' notes on writing. Over 100 pages of additional material specifically aimed at writers.